I0766455

The Steve Williams Series II

By

J.E. Taylor

J.E. TAYLOR
SUPERNATURAL SUSPENSE
& DARK FANTASY AUTHOR

The Steve Williams Series

Special Agent Steve Williams excels at his job, catching the most heinous of monsters walking the earth.

Serial killers.

When his job brings him face to face with a psychic, he struggles to accept her gifts in his neat little black and white world. Armed with her visions, along with his skills as an FBI agent, he hunts the worst of the worst, but will he catch the killer before they set their sights on him?

Unstoppable, breath stealing, and terrifying all at once.
Gripping, rich and magnificent!

The Steve Williams Series mixes compelling crime thrillers with supernatural forces that will grip the reader from page one. This six-book series takes you through some of Steve Williams' darkest cases in his FBI career.

The STEVE WILLIAMS SERIES II hard-cover edition includes Georgia Reign, Crystal Illusions, and Saving Face.

Georgia Reign
Chapter 1

FUNNY HOW THE TUNE from an adored childhood movie could strike such terror. Terror that makes the body tremble. Terror that locks screams in the throat. Terror that squeezes drops of piss from the bladder. And yet, like Pavlov's response, that's exactly what happened to all my patients.

"Whistle While You Work" echoed off the walls—the jovial melody streaming from my lips in stark contrast to the dread-filled moans pervading the room when the lights came up. Alex trotted ahead of me, his tail wagging, excited, expecting a treat. He looked back at me and then slipped into the brightly lit room.

She whined a pitiful "no" when I entered. Her battered and bruised body shaking while the stench of urine and feces hung in the air.

"Tsk, tsk, tsk. You've soiled your diaper." I swung my head back and forth, approaching the ten-year-old, and she went from whimpering to blubbering. Something deep inside me cringed, and I shut the door on that half, blocking him out of my mind. He didn't belong here. He would ruin everything.

Instead, I refocused on the insolent child on the table.

"I'm, I'm s-sorry, I'm s-so s-sorry, p-p-please d-don't hurt me again. P-p-please!"

I pulled the sheet away from the surgical instruments, running my gloved fingers over the steel, loving the cool sterile power they projected. I stopped when I reached the scalpel. My instrument of choice. Cool. Shiny. Sharp. Perfect.

"No, no, no," she repeated over and over and over, yanking at the straps holding her to the table, bucking her torso, arching, popping the stitches that already traversed her abdomen.

Blood oozed, but it wouldn't matter much longer. I turned to Alex. "You've been such a good dog. How about a special treat today?"

Alex responded with a swish of his tail followed by the thump, thump, thump of it hitting the floor, patiently waiting for his tasty snack. Panting, he licked his golden chops.

Flipping the pages in the medical book on the edge of the table, I stopped at the page outlining the human liver, memorizing the location and the best way to access the organ. I glanced at the table of instruments, reaching and moving the rib retractor close enough to grab once I had her spread open. I took one more glance at her tear-stained face and sighed. "Such a pity," I said, focusing on the task before me. I pressed down with the scalpel, slicing through tender flesh and muscle.

The girl's scream reverberated off the concrete walls, carrying through the caverns of my lab. She hit a peculiar high note, a wailing screech sounding more like a hawk dive-bombing its prey than a human.

The note failed, replaced by choking sobs that gave way to silence.

Georgia Reign
Chapter 2

STEVE WILLIAMS SAT ON the stairs of the dock, looking out over the lake. Gravel crunching under tires interrupted his fragmented thoughts, and he turned to see a Cadillac sedan pull to a stop behind his roadster. A small, mousy woman slid out of the car with an attaché case in her hand.

"Mr. Steven Williams?" she asked, pushing her glasses higher on the bridge of her nose as she approached the dock.

Steve nodded.

"Lynn Trueman. I'm Mr. Ryan's attorney," she began, extending her hand.

He shook her hand, pulling information from her thoughts. His brow creased. "Chris put me in his will?"

"Mr. Ryan came to see me at the beginning of last week to set up the trust fund for the victims of Kyle Winslow." She rummaged in her bag for the documents, pulling out an envelope and a couple of legal forms. "He said if anything should happen to him, you were to become the executor of that trust." Her lips spread in a ghost of a smile.

"But that wasn't all he requested, was it?"

"No, sir." Lynn handed the envelope to Steve. "He asked that I give you this."

He glanced between the document and the lawyer in front of him. Sliding his finger under the seal, he ripped open the envelope. The handwritten letter contained a check made out to Steven Williams in the same graceful long hand.

The amount leaped out at him, and he took a step back on rubbery legs. If he had been a cartoon character, his eyes would have shot out of his head with a grand AYEOOOGA, sound effects and all.

Somehow, he remained standing and shot his gaze back to hers. "Fifty million?"

She nodded. "Yes, that's your settlement from the trust."

Steve sat down hard on the lawn and stared at the letter. The script was wide and looping, slanting across the page. *Chris must have gotten straight A's in penmanship*, he thought.

Steve,

I'm assuming that you're probably sitting on your ass on the lawn just staring between the check and this letter right about now. I'm also assuming you believe you're responsible for my death. Get over it. You aren't. It was my time.

I knew it was coming, but I didn't know there would be a chance at redemption by saving your sorry ass. If I've done the job right, you're still breathing with a little extra juice you hadn't bargained for.

Now, for the favor. Keep an eye on my son. This whole thing is going to push him close to the edge, and I'm not sure Tommy can keep him from going over this time. He needs someone who can keep him in line. You've now got a significant piece of his father flowing through your veins, so he'll listen. Eventually.

As a side note, watch the temper. That's when you'll find the juice gets away from you. Otherwise, relax, it's your time in the sun, kid, enjoy it.

Best Regards,
Chris Ryan

He raised his eyes from the letter to Lynn. "Fifty million dollars?" he asked, glancing back at the check in his hand.

"Yes, Mr. Williams. There's another sixty million in the trust for distribution."

His eyes shot back up to hers. Kyle only had ten million dollars to his name. He blinked a few times as his thought process jump-started again. *Jesus, Chris put another hundred million of his own money into the trust.* He raised his eyebrows, his jaw slack.

"I need your signature on the trust document and the affidavit for receipt of funds." She smiled down at him and reached her hand out to help him off the ground.

Steve looked at her hand and took it after a moment's hesitation. Once on his feet, he led her into the barren cottage, rummaging through his office for a pen.

"There is one more matter that needs to be settled as well," she said, retrieving a document out of her case. "Under directive in his will, Mr. Ryan left the penthouse in New York to you." She handed him the deed now in his name.

He slowly sank into the chair behind the desk, staring at the paperwork in front of him. He leveled his eyes back at the petite lawyer. "You're shitting me, right?"

She shook her head. "No, sir, I'm not. Mr. Ryan was very specific in his requests, but there is one stipulation that you must adhere to."

Steve raised his eyebrows. "What's that?"

"That you keep this place."

"Why?"

"Mr. Ryan did not enlighten me as to the reason, but he insisted on the stipulation."

Steve blew a stream of air between his lips and nodded. The irony of the request struck him, especially since he and Jennifer had already discussed the cabin. Jennifer's idea was to sell, but he wasn't ready to ditch it just yet, despite all that happened. He knew signing the papers in front of him and agreeing to Chris's terms would put more of a strain on his already frayed marriage.

With the pen poised over the signature line, he traded a glance with Lynn. A thousand reasons to refuse came to mind, but only one reason surfaced that made him press the tip to the paper, signing his name and sealing his future.

Chris Ryan died because of him, regardless of what his letter said.

"This isn't a joke, is it?" he asked, handing the signed paperwork to Lynn.

"No. It isn't." Lynn peeled off Steve's copies, handing them back along with her business card. "Here's my card. Any instructions regarding the trust should go through my office and if you need a suitable banker, I can give you the name of the man who has handled Mr. Ryan's portfolio for the past fifteen years."

"That probably would be a good idea." He looked at the check and back to Lynn. "I'm not sure what to do with this," he said.

Lynn shrugged. "Enjoy." She reached into her briefcase and pulled out another business card. "That's Mr. Ryan's banker. I expect he will be at the funeral tomorrow." She passed the card to Steve. "Will you be attending?"

Steve nodded. "Yes."

"Then I'll see you there." She smiled and left Steve standing behind the desk in shock.

He sat down, listening as the car pulled out of the driveway and the noise faded into the distance. He had never seen so many zeros. The whistle he produced broke the silence, and he dropped the check back on the desk. Jennifer would be home from the store soon. He'd deal with it then.

Steve walked to the dock and resumed drinking the beer. The peaceful silence of the lake was broken by the shrill ring of the cell phone in his pocket, and he pulled it out, flipping it open. "Williams here."

"Where the hell have you been?" Assistant Director Ron Cleary demanded.

"At my house in New Hampshire. Where else would I be?" He sent over his report the day after

Chris died and hadn't bothered returning any calls.

"I need you in Atlanta."

"Sir, no disrespect, but I think I deserve a couple of weeks off right now," Steve said, closing his eyes. He wasn't ready to get back in the saddle again. Not after coming so close to killing that bastard. Not after having to explain to the two young boys that their father wasn't coming home ever again. And especially not after almost dying in the warehouse.

He needed time to figure out what he really wanted to do with his life. He needed time with Jennifer.

"We have another serial killer," Cleary said. "And you're the best I've got. I need you on this case, Williams."

Steve opened his eyes and sighed. "Look, I've got a funeral to attend tomorrow. In the meantime, send me the information and I'll take a look."

Cleary swore under his breath.

"Sir, I need some time. Jennifer just came out of the coma and in the past three weeks, I've lost everyone else I was close to. I need to get my shit together before I jump into the line of fire again." He could hear Cleary's train of thought and kept his mouth closed, waiting for the verbal reprimand on the line.

"I'm heading to Atlanta tomorrow and I'll give you until Sunday morning to get your ass down there. Otherwise, you can kiss your career goodbye. I'm sending the file now," Cleary snapped.

Steve closed his eyes. He wasn't ready to jump in again, but he also wasn't ready to walk away from the FBI. "Fine." He paused. "Sir, what's the protocol for will settlements?"

"As long as it's clear in the documentation, there should be no problem with inheritance."

"Thanks," he said, although Cleary was thinking about his parent's estate and not the possibility of a billionaire leaving him a windfall. Steve ignored the silent reference, opting not to bring up his most recent inheritance just yet. "I'll look today."

"I'm sending it now."

"Will do." Steve stood, flipped the phone closed, picked up the cooler of beer, and retreated to his office. He opened his laptop and typed the command to access the FBI email system, waiting for the file from his boss.

Steve picked up the letter from Chris. "I can't believe you still went to New York," he mumbled. If the tables were turned, *he* would have spent the rest of his days with his wife and kids instead of hunting down a killer with a hostile stranger.

The beep of his computer interrupted his thoughts, and he opened the email, reading the case file Cleary sent.

Steve leaned back after twenty minutes. Atlanta definitely had a serial killer stalking the streets, one who liked to chop his victims to pieces. Kids, he corrected, *he's chopping kids to pieces*. Steve stared at the screen, disgusted, intrigued, motivated.

He wanted to catch the bastard and watch him fry.

His eyes fell to the check on his desk, alternating between the computer and the fifty million dollars in his name.

He raised his gaze to the door. Jennifer leaned against the molding with her arms folded.

"What's up?" She offered a hint of a smile, but it didn't reach her eyes.

Steve took a deep breath. What to hit her with first, the fact they were filthy rich or the fact he was heading to Atlanta after the funeral. Opting for the good news first, he picked up the letter and check, holding them out to her.

Jennifer crossed the room and took the papers. She read the letter and raised her eyes to Steve. "He knew he was going to die?"

Steve nodded. "Look at the check." He pointed, and she sank into the chair on the other side of the desk. Her jaw drooped and her eyes bulged.

Steve chuckled.

Jennifer ripped her eyes from the check, meeting Steve's gaze. "For real?"

"Yep." He picked up the deed to the apartment in New York. "And he left us this."

Jennifer's hands shook as she took the second document, scanning it before she looked back at him. "We're millionaires with a penthouse in the city?"

"Ayup." Steve leaned back in the chair. "And there's another serial killer on the loose in Atlanta."

Jennifer's hands dropped to her lap and her mouth closed, the reminder of his job obviously not welcomed.

His eyes drifted to the computer screen and back to her hard features. Unhappiness radiated from her, and he stood, walking into the empty living room, crossing to the bay window.

Hunting and chopping up adults was one thing, but what this guy was doing to kids was beyond unacceptable. It was downright infuriating. He chewed the inside of his cheek, staring at the lake, refusing to look at the stud walls of the kitchen where his daughter died.

Steve glanced over his shoulder at the office. Jennifer hadn't followed him. She was still staring at the check, trying to figure out why Chris Ryan would do such a thing, and on the heels of that thought came the conviction that he should quit his job before someone else got hurt.

Turning, he sat on the window bench and waited. When she appeared in the doorway, he spoke. "What do you want me to do?" He already knew, but he wanted her to say it aloud.

"I want you to quit."

Steve inhaled sharply. If he hadn't taken the call from his boss, if he hadn't opened the file, if he hadn't seen the photos, he might have considered quitting, but not now. Those kids deserved justice, and he was more than ready to deliver it with an archangel's vengeance.

"But you already knew that." Jennifer crossed her arms.

He dipped his head, looking at the floor, and nodded. "I can't walk away from this case, Jen." He raised his eyes. "And I need to get that check in the bank." He stood and crossed the room, stopping at her side and meeting her gaze, reaching and running the back of his fingers on her arm. "You know I love you."

"But?"

The right side of his lips curled for an instant, revealing a crooked smile. "But this guy is killing kids. Kids, Jen. I can stop him."

"What? Like you stopped Kyle?"

The barb stung, and he stiffened, pulling his hand away from her. "This time I can stop the killer. I've got a distinct advantage now."

"What exactly does that mean? That you can read minds and put yourself between the blade of a knife and a victim? What good will *that* do against another madman like Kyle?"

In the few days since the warehouse incident, Steve hadn't disclosed the extent of what Chris left him, and with a tilt of his head, the picture window disintegrated, shattering into a thousand pieces.

"And if that's not enough." He closed his eyes, willing the window right again. The screech and creak of glass shifting, scraping, and reassembling filled the otherwise silent room. When he opened his eyes, the same slack-jawed look of shock she'd had in his office graced her face.

"Chris gave me more than just money and a penthouse, babe," Steve said, his voice clipped tight. He didn't like her train of thought, her doubts in him, in his ability, in their marriage, and he stepped away without looking.

When he returned to the living room with the check in his hand, he asked, "You coming?"

Jennifer tore her eyes away from the window. "What did he do to you?"

Steve shrugged. "Gave me a little more juice than I bargained for," he said, quoting Chris's note. "You coming?"

Jennifer looked at the window and back to her husband. Her mouth slightly parted as if to speak. *Who the hell is this man?* She locked eyes with him again and slowly shook her head. "I think I'll hang back." Her voice shook.

Steve nodded and turned, walked out of the house, and slammed the door behind him. Anger throbbed in his veins, making his skin tingle and itch for something to take aim at, something to release the coiled weapon inside him.

Georgia Reign
Chapter 3

JESSICA RYAN SAT AT the end of the dock on a lake not that far from Brooksfield. Her hand slowly glided along the soft fur of the shepherd's head in her lap. The kids argued over their video games inside the house, and she tuned them out, staring at the sun glinted water.

The lake house had been her grandfather's decades ago, and Chris bought it from the subsequent owners as a gift. Despite the last ten years of summer vacations on the lake, it still reminded her less of Chris than their Maine home, where every turn was a painful memory. Even so, the sunset on the water was like a shard of glass embedded in her heart and the dog let a huff of a breath escape that matched her sigh.

Empty, like a shriveled cornhusk at a fall festival, she shut the valve off and her tear tracks dried. Sam whined, and she looked down. "I know. I miss him, too."

The door banged on its hinges, and Sam's head shot up, looking toward the house. Jessica tilted her head at the soft patter of feet. When

Tommy sat next to her, she offered him her best reassuring *It's going to be okay* smile.

Tommy laced his fingers through his mother's hand and looked out at the sunset.

She knew he didn't need to be psychic to understand her pain; he felt the devastation, too. Like a lamb that wandered into wolf territory, he was lost and terrified. Losing his father had done more than just injure his heart; it put a wedge between him and CJ. The older twin ranted at how unfair it was that Tommy could see the ghost of their father and he couldn't.

He looked down at the beloved shepherd with its massive head in his mother's lap, her hand stroking in methodical, repetitive strokes.

Tommy still didn't understand why his father had to die. And for it to happen in that godforsaken warehouse where they all almost died five years before was just too much of a coincidence.

"It wasn't a coincidence," Jessica said, her voice hollow with grief as she met her son's gaze.

Tommy's chin quivered.

"None of us should have walked out of the warehouse that day." Horrific memories swirled, and she inhaled, turning away from Tommy's wide blue eyes—eyes reminiscent of his biological father and not Chris.

Honest, honorable eyes—eyes that saw between the folds of the universe.

"Your dad made a deal, Tommy. It was time to pay up." She squeezed his hand.

Tears cascaded in slow motion down his cheeks, and his sobs were quiet enough to produce only a whisper of an echo on the lake. She reached her arm around his shoulders and her heart cried for her innocent nine-year-old boy.

Her boy who could see ghosts.

Georgia Reign
Chapter 4

STEVE PULLED INTO THE strip mall housing his bank, and the phone buzzed. He pulled into a front parking lot and dug the cell phone out of his pocket, noting the New York exchange, and flipped it open, accepting the call. "Hey."

"Steve?" Her tentative voice came over the speaker.

"Hi, Sarah," he replied and bit back on responding to her jumbled and confused train of thought, letting silence fill the space instead of slapping her with sarcasm.

She sighed. "I rehearsed this a million times."

Steve leaned back in the seat, filtering through her private thoughts, all of which pointed to the fact he'd aided and abetted a known felon.

"I'm still trying to sort it all out."

"Which part? Me, or Chris Ryan?"

Another sigh.

"Are you coming up for the funeral?" Steve asked. The conversation she wanted to have was not one he wanted to broach on his cell. Phone calls could be recorded, and he didn't want an admission of guilt captured on tape.

"I don't know."

"Why don't you take a ride up here today? You can stay with us, and we'll go over in the morning together."

"That's fucking presumptuous of you."

Steve huffed. "Fine." He snapped the phone closed and got out of the car. *Oil and water,* he thought and crossed the parking lot.

Steve walked into the bank and stood in line, ignoring the phone vibrating in his pocket. He didn't want to talk to Sarah any more than he wanted to discuss staying with the FBI with his wife. He hadn't even broached the condition of keeping the cottage with Jennifer. That was going to catapult her over the edge.

When one of the tellers freed, he stepped to the counter, reading the woman's nameplate before he spoke. "Hello, Karen, I need to make a deposit." He pulled out the check, signed the back, and dropped it on the counter along with his checking deposit slip. His lips twitched into an amused smile at her reaction.

Her jaw dropped. "Fifty million?"

Her gaze shot to his face, and he nodded. "Yes. Fifty million dollars."

"Um, I need to speak with the manager."

Steve watched her trot away and huddle with the bank manager in the corner. Moments later, the manager approached him with the check in hand.

"Please, come with me," he said, leading Steve into the corner office and closing the door, motioning for him to sit in the seat across from his desk. "I just wanted to make you aware of our policy in depositing checks of such substantial size," he began. "You won't be able to draw from the balance until the check clears."

Steve nodded. "I naturally assumed that," he said. "How long does it usually take for a check to clear?"

"Usually five business days." The manager's eyes still hadn't deviated from the check in his hand.

Steve cleared his throat.

The manager offered a nervous laugh. "It's just that I've never seen a check this large." The bank manager's voice cracked, and he punched in the account number on the deposit slip. "Can you verify your social security number for me?"

"Yes." Steve rattled the numbers off.

"Your address?"

"My current address is 1658 Lake View Drive here in Brooksfield," he said when the manager raised his eyes from the computer screen.

The manager nodded and typed the amount into the computer, waiting for the deposit slip to print out. "Is there anything else I can help you with today? Perhaps a look at our investment options?" He smiled, thinking of all the ways he could siphon money out of Steve's account.

Steve let his lips curve into a smile and waited until the deposit slip was in his hand. He glanced at it, verifying the account numbers and the balance were as they should be. He leaned over and spoke very softly. "While there are at least a hundred ways to siphon money out of my account, I wouldn't try if I were you." He stood.

"I will know, and you *really* don't want to fuck with me."

"I... I... I wouldn't dream of doing something like that." The manager stuttered, his eyes blinking rapidly as his face flushed and hands trembled.

Steve turned to leave.

"Thank you for doing business with Brooksfield Savings Bank," the manager said in a weak, small voice, like that of a child whose hand was caught in the cookie jar.

Steve sent a quick glance over his shoulder and raised his hand for a moment, acknowledging the manager's salutation. He gave a shudder at the sudden need to take a shower to wash off the feeling of dealing with a slime ball.

Steve slipped into his car and the cell phone rang again. He glanced at the number and sighed, flipping it open. "Are you done being a bitch?"

Sarah was silent. "I'm sorry."

"So, are you heading up this way or not?" Steve turned on the car and let it idle in neutral while he waited for her to answer. The flurry of activity in her head assaulted him. "I'll answer every one of your questions, but only if we're face to face," Steve said.

Sarah let out a short laugh. "Yeah, so you can stonewall me again?"

"No. I'll answer your questions." Doubt clouded her mind. "Honest," he added. After what Sarah went through at the hands of that madman, she deserved to know how she got out alive.

"All right, Steve, I'll be up there tonight."

He closed the phone and leaned his head against the seat, exhaling and rubbing his face before dialing the cottage. Jennifer answered on the third ring. "Looks like we're having company tonight."

"Excuse me?" Jennifer said.

Steve closed his eyes, wishing he'd waited until he was home to have this conversation. When he opened his eyes, he gasped, his eyes widened, and he glanced at his barren living room and Jennifer's equally wide eyes.

The phone dropped from her hand, and she gawked at him.

Steve's eyes darted around the room and landed on Jennifer again. *Shit! This is freaky as hell.* He took a step toward her with his heart pounding in his throat. The floor under his boot was as solid as if he was actually there in person.

"What the fuck?" she whispered.

A shrill laugh escaped Steve, echoing his shot nerves. He crossed to her, curious as to his limitations in this transitional state. When he reached out and pulled her to him, her warm body pressed against him, and his lips crushed hers. With the taste of her cherry lip still on his lips, he knew.

He was physically in both places—another gift courtesy of Chris Ryan. He pulled away, perplexed.

Jennifer stared at him, her eyelids fluttering in a confused blink. Her fingers ran over her own lips before she found her voice. "Are you really here?"

This time his laugh was more natural. "I think so, but I'm also sitting in my car at the bank, probably just staring into space in a state of suspended animation."

The space between her eyes creased. *This is impossible.*

"There's a lot of shit that seems impossible, babe." He gazed into her shimmering emerald eyes.

"What the hell are you?" She pushed away from him.

Steve shrugged and felt the transition begin again, the pull of it dragging him through a tunnel, an elongated black wormhole, back into his car. He drew in his breath and opened his eyes to the hot asphalt of the bank parking lot. "God damn," he whispered into the phone.

The phone shuffled, and her breathless voice came through the line. "Steve?"

"I'll be home in a few." He disconnected the call, slipped the phone into his pocket, and put the car in gear. He had a ghost to confront.

Georgia Reign
Chapter 5

STEVE PULLED INTO THE driveway and slipped out of the car, crossed the lawn, and trampled over the wet leaves covering the path to Paradise Cove. When he stepped into the clearing onto the soft moss, he closed his eyes and hung his head, wondering if Jennifer would ever accept what he'd become.

The chuckle startled him.

Steve spun around. There, leaning against a tree, was the ghost of Chris Ryan—the edges of his pristine white wings peeking out from behind his shoulders. The bright sunlight behind him gave off an eerie glow and before he could stop it, the thought popped into his head.

Angel of death. Jesus.

"Angel of death. That always cracks me up," he said, straightening up.

"That's what you are, right?"

The sigh that followed caused the water to ripple. "No. I'm not the angel of death, even though the term tickles me to no end."

Steve raised his eyebrows. "Why am I not dead?"

Chris's musical laughter filled the clearing. He approached, stopping parallel to his friend, staring out at the water, his brow furrowing. "It isn't your time, and you know it." He sent a sideways glance.

Steve glanced out over the water. "Fifty million? What the hell am I supposed to do with fifty million dollars?"

"Anything you want." Chris's smile turned sly. "And you need to divvy up the remaining sixty million to the other survivors."

"Is that why you're here?"

Chris faced Steve, shaking his head. His expression turned serious. "No. I'm here because I was told to look after you. That's my penance." He rolled his eyes and shoved his hands into his pockets.

"You're my guardian angel?" The thought of it raised goose bumps on his exposed skin. *Ty Aris as my guardian angel? What the hell did I do to deserve that?*

Chris shrugged.

"Jesus. I am *so* screwed." Steve chuckled.

Chris smirked. "Have you figured out how to control the power yet?"

"I had the unsettling pleasure of astral projecting myself today. *That* is truly freaky."

"Surreal."

"Yeah, like this conversation." He glanced at Chris. "Are you going to pop up on me everywhere I go?"

"No. Well, at least not like this. This is the only place you can see me." He waved at the lush cove. "However, you'll be able to hear me any time I feel like intruding on your life."

Steve stared at the angel grinning at him. "What the hell does that mean?"

Chris just laughed and sent a wink in his direction.

Steve raised an eyebrow. It wasn't like he and Jennifer had been intimate in the past few days, any time he got near her. She flinched, her mind jumping back to Kyle and what he'd made her do. That alone was enough of a turnoff, and it enraged him, but the thought of Chris Ryan having an unlimited view of his private life burned him even more.

"So, help me God, Ty," Steve said between clenched teeth. "I swear, if you eavesdrop on me and Jennifer, I'll..." He bit down on the rest of the sentence. Any threat to him was long since over, but there was one thing he could use to control Chris. "I'll drag your wife into custody."

A subtle change occurred in Chris's expression. His eyes turned a shade darker, sending a hard, stony stare in Steve's direction. The muscles in his jaw worked, pulling the flushed skin taut over his cheekbones and thinning his lips to a white streak that matched his spreading wings. "You do not give *Me* ultimatums!" The wings beat, raising Chris off the ground.

Steve laughed, watching Chris rise, his own anger edging to the surface. He yanked mentally, and the laugh caught in his throat as the angel plummeted to the ground, hard.

On his hands and knees, Chris looked up at Steve, his blue eyes wide and full of surprise.

Steve leaned over, balancing his hands on his knees. "Apparently, I do. I want to know why? Now."

"Why what?" Chris asked, getting up and brushing himself off.

"Why me? Why the money, the powers? Why'd you make the trade?" The anger blew past the surface. "Why didn't you just let me die on that cross?" He was yelling now. "Everyone died because of me. Why did you save me?"

Chris stepped back, letting Steve fill with the anger and grief. There was no more denying the ability to feel. It was hitting Steve like a bulldozer.

"Why?" the question belted out, echoing off the lake.

"Self-preservation," Chris answered.

Steve's jaw went slack, his anger sputtering to a low simmer.

"Saving you got me into heaven."

"Why?" Steve whispered. "What makes me so special?"

Chris cocked his head to the side. "You just are." He shoved his hands in his pocket and studied the moss at their feet before returning his gaze to Steve's. "My time was up." He shrugged. "And my job before I died was to make sure you didn't kill Kyle." The inhale of breath filled the cove. "You didn't." He looked out over the water. "That's why."

Steve's eyes narrowed. "How did you know I wouldn't kill him?"

Chris smiled and raised his eyebrows. "I didn't. But I know deep down, even with all this other shit flying around, you're still a fucking boy scout."

Steve huffed and turned toward the water. His mind raced. "Why the hell am I so special?"

"Because I'm not here to watch over CJ."

Steve's gaze snapped to Chris's. "And that has to do with me how?"

"I need *you* to look after him. To keep him in line. Without me around, the burden falls on you."

A burst of laughter echoed on the water. "You have got to be kidding me!"

"I'm dead serious, Steve. As I said in the letter, you've got a big part of me flowing through you now, and he will listen to you. Jess is not capable of keeping him in line. She doesn't have the strength to match his."

"And I do?"

"No, but you've got the integrity."

A scoff came from behind them, and they both turned to see Jennifer standing at the entrance to the cove. Her eyes were glued to Chris and his white wings.

"What the hell did you do to him?" She pointed at Steve.

Chris turned his gaze to Steve, raising his eyebrows. "Boy, she's a pistol, ain't she?" He hooked his thumb toward Jennifer.

Steve stifled the laugh when Jennifer glared at him.

"There's darkness in him that wasn't there before." She glared at Chris with her hands resting on her hips.

Chris's expression changed, and he took a step closer to her, towering as he let his wings uncurl. "I had nothing to do with the changes in him. That happened when he lost his daughter and had to deal with a comatose wife for a year."

"Enough!" Steve stepped in front of Jennifer, blocking her from the angry angel.

"What did you do to my husband?" Jennifer yelled, her hands balled into tight fists.

"I gave him what he needs to look after my boy."

Jennifer's brow creased. "Who are you?"

"Does the name Ty Aris ring a bell?"

Steve glared in his direction, but it was too late. Jennifer recognized the name from a movie that came out a few years ago.

"That movie." She shot her gaze back to the angel. "<u>Survival Games</u>."

"One and the same." Chris bowed to her. "Actually, my God-given name was Ty Alexander Ryan, but *you* can call me Chris."

Jennifer's eyes went wide, and her hand shot to her mouth as her gaze darted between Steve and the angel. She stepped back, locking glances with Steve. "Did you know?" she asked from behind her hands.

Steve nodded.

"You knew he killed those people, and you didn't bring him in?"

Steve went to speak, but Jennifer turned, storming back to the cottage. He turned to Chris. "Thanks, thanks a lot."

"You're in the doghouse." Chris nodded toward the path.

"Yeah, well, it hasn't been a picnic since we got back. And things are going to get a little hairier when Sarah shows up."

Chris raised his eyebrows. "The hot cop is coming?"

Steve nodded. "She's got a lot of questions and she's coming with us to your funeral."

"Oh." Chris turned away and looked at the sky before glancing back at Steve. "Yeah, about that." He buried his hands in his pockets again.

Steve waited.

"I need you to bring CJ here after the funeral." He shot a glance at Steve and received a slight nod in return. "Without Jess." He shuffled his feet with his hands still buried in his pockets.

"How am I supposed to get your son here without your wife?" Steve asked.

Chris shrugged. "You'll figure something out, but I need to talk to him. I need to set him straight, or all this will have been in vain."

Steve let the quiet descend. "It was hard on her, you know." He glanced at Chris. "She had to be sedated."

When Chris looked in his direction, a single tear slid down Chris's cheek and when the sunlight kissed it, the tear sent prisms of light through the cove.

"You sure you don't want me to bring her?"

"Yes. She won't leave." He looked away. "And I'm not so sure I could let her go."

"Okay. I'll figure something out."

Georgia Reign
Chapter 6

CJ RYAN STOOD ON the porch, watching his mother and Tommy talking. He didn't need to hear what they were saying. Their thoughts swarmed, drowning out his own. His mother wanted death. She wanted to be with his father as much as she wanted to be with them.

Tommy just wanted things the way they had been. The way they were before Eric died and Steve Williams walked into their lives.

He stepped outside and crossed the lawn. "What time are we leaving?"

His mother turned, and the flash of pain in her eyes shot straight to his heart. She glanced at her watch. "In about an hour."

CJ gave a quick nod and turned away, unable to deal with being the source of her anguish. However misguided it was, it still hurt like hell. His jaw tightened, and he blinked the sudden onslaught of tears back until they stung his throat.

He wanted the same thing as his brother, but deep down, he knew.

He knew that if it hadn't been a bullet, it would have been something else that killed his father.

Just as he knew their time of darkness hadn't ended.

Georgia Reign
Chapter 7

JENNIFER SAT IN THE gazebo swing, the chain creaking as she kept up the slow arc, pushing off periodically with her feet. The silence of the lake once gave her a feeling of tranquility. Now it only brought a near crippling dread.

Steve once told her he wanted to tear the cottage down and rebuild. At the time she talked him out of it, saying it was charming, but now all she wanted was to burn it to the ground. She wanted it to become a pile of ash and soot. Maybe then the memories would fade.

With a sigh, her thoughts snapped back to Steve. What the hell was he doing partnering with a killer?

As if on cue, Steve slid next to her on the bench, looking out over the lake. "I made a promise."

Jennifer glanced in his direction. "That man killed people," she pointed toward the cove. "For fun."

Steve dipped his head in a nod. "Yep."

"That's all you can say?"

He finally turned toward her. "I made a promise." The words came out between his clenched teeth. "A fucking promise to a dying kid! You, of all people, should understand what that means." He stood up, undressed, discarded his clothes in a path from the gazebo to the end of the dock, and dived into the cool spring water in only his underwear.

Jennifer's eyes misted, and she blinked away the tears. She studied the wedding ring on her hand, her heart pounding with a fear she couldn't name while his graceful stride created consistent whooshes as he sliced through the water. She lifted her chin, watching him swim laps. *I don't know you anymore.*

Steve veered, heading back toward the dock, hopping up on the wooden deck moments later, staring at her. His eyes blazed with anger. His perfect, unblemished skin mocked her. It mocked their past, and Jennifer pressed her lips together.

"What do you want from me?"

"I want my husband back."

Steve raised his eyebrows and spread his arms out. "I'm right here, Jen."

Her chin quivered, and she shook her head. "You're not the man I married. The man *I* married would have never let someone like *that* walk free." She pointed toward the cove.

Frustration lined his handsome features, and he scooped up his clothing. "I had no choice, Jen. Not only did I make a promise to my partner, but I made a deal with Jessica. I'd forget everything I knew about them, if she would work her magic on you."

"Oh, so now you're blaming me for your lapse in judgment?"

"Jesus Christ!" He spun and stormed across the lawn into the cottage.

She sat in the swing, staring after him, barely containing her own anger. She stood and followed him inside the cottage, confronting him in the bedroom.

"What do you want, Jen?" he asked without turning, his voice low and on edge.

"I don't know. What do *you* want?"

"I want my wife back!" He spun facing her and running his hand through his wet hair. "You haven't even shown the slightest hint that you want to be here, that *you* want *me* here!" He slid into the rocking chair in the corner, his soaking underwear pooling water on the wooden seat as he rested his elbows on his knees and his head in his hands. "That you want me," he whispered, closing his eyes.

The slow scrape of the rocking chair filled the room.

Jennifer sat on the edge of the bed. "I can't do this."

The chair stopped rocking, and Steve slowly looked up at her. "You want to leave?"

Jennifer held his gaze. "You're not the same man I married."

Steve tilted his head. "Who exactly am I then?"

"You're that monster." She nodded toward the cove.

Steve shook his head and stood, crossing toward her. He stopped at the foot of the bed, letting his gaze slide over her. "No, Jenny. I'm not. I'm just a man who's lost everything he's ever cared about." He turned and walked out of the bedroom.

⊷ ⊷ ⊷

STEVE LEANED HIS HANDS against the front wall of the shower, letting the water stream down the back of his head and neck, his muscles taut under his skin as he fought to control the welling anger. When she walked into the bathroom, he made no indication he was aware of her presence. He stood and let the hot stream pelt his face before stepping back and flipping the water off. After stepping out and wrapping a towel around his waist, he met her gaze.

Jennifer lowered her eyes and started out of the room.

A burst of anger escaped Steve, and the bathroom door slammed before Jennifer could reach it. She spun with wide eyes, and he pushed her against the door in a silent command. Her shirt shredded, and Steve crossed the distance between them. He stood looking down at her, water dripping from his hair onto her upturned face, reminding both of them of the same situation a lifetime ago.

"Don't," she whispered, still held to the door by an invisible barrier.

Steve ignored her plea and pressed his lips to hers. His hands found the curve of her waist, and he pushed his wet body against her. Jennifer made a sound of protest, yet her lips parted, giving his tongue access. The kiss was slow, but insistent and he wrapped his arms around her waist, releasing the mental hold and pulling her against him.

"I need you," he said against her lips.

Her hands flattened on his chest, pushing him away. "I can't." Tears welled in her eyes, cresting and making slow tracks down her cheeks. "I can't do this. Not here." Her entire form shook, and he could smell the fear radiating off her.

"I need you," he whispered. Holding her in his arms still felt right despite her reservations. His eyes blurred from the wave of tears, turning her frightened features into that of a fun-house mirror. He blinked, feeling the heat of his tears trace down his face. "Do you..." He closed his mouth on the question. Asking her if she still loved him right now might produce the answer he was most afraid of.

Instead, he closed his eyes and hung his head, released her, and stepping back, giving her the space she needed. He cleared his throat and took a deep breath, focusing on her earlier thoughts. "You want to tear down the cottage and build a house here?"

Jennifer blinked and wiped her face. "I, uh..." She looked around and then back at him with a nod and a shrug. Her eyes lowered, lingering on his chest, and she swallowed. "His wife, she's the one who..." Jennifer waved at his scar-free chest.

Steve nodded. The last couple of days were a blur of doctor visits, validating that Jennifer was indeed okay. Between that and the reconciliation with her parents, they hadn't had time to talk about what happened in the warehouse, never mind the events leading up to Kyle's arrest.

"Do you want to leave me?" he asked, feeling vulnerable in only a towel. Her mind went into a flurry of activity, rendering his mind reading abilities useless. He held his breath, waiting for an answer, and when her eyes met his, he almost collapsed. All strength left him at her uncertain gaze.

"I don't know."

He stepped back and sat on the closed toilet seat. The pressure on his chest was almost unbearable as another piece of his heart shattered. "Then I guess Kyle won after all." Bitterness seeped into his voice.

Jennifer's head snapped back like an invisible hand slapped her and her expression changed, crumbling into a mask of absolute horror. Her uncertain gaze cleared through the layer of tears, and she shook her head. "He can't win, I just... I just can't get away from him here. And you, you're so different."

Instead of denying her statement, Steve looked down at his hands. "Jen, I had to live without you for a year. They told me you were brain dead and, after losing Samantha, I couldn't lose you, too, so I hung on. Chris was right—losing everything I cared about changed me. And not for the better, especially since the bastard was out there somewhere, still taunting me, and still killing."

The mere mention of Samantha's name brought a searing pain to Jennifer, palatable enough that Steve inhaled with almost a wince.

Fresh tears cascaded down her face and he closed his eyes. "It takes time."

"What takes time?"

"Mourning our daughter's death." He opened his eyes, meeting her teary gaze. He stood, tightening the towel around his waist before crossing and cupping her cheek with his hand and wiping away the tears with his thumb. "You're going to have good days and bad days, just like I did."

She nodded and nuzzled his hand for a moment before pulling away. "Where... where is she buried?"

"Brooksfield Cemetery."

The color drained from her cheeks and her chin trembled. Memories of their ordeal in the crypt clouded her mind.

"Her grave doesn't face the crypt, it faces the mountains. I'll take you there after I get dressed." He reached beyond her for the door, and she sidestepped to let him pass. "We'll have to make the bed in the guest room. Sarah's coming up tonight and going to the funeral with us in the morning," he said as he walked to the master bedroom and rummaged through the drawers for clothes, slipping them on before facing her. Her melancholy mood turned, and he didn't need to read minds to see the irritation lining her jaw. Before she spoke, he added, "She has as many questions as you do." He paused and plunged his hands in his pockets.

"But?"

"But she doesn't know who Chris really was. She has an idea, but it was never definitively confirmed."

"And you want me to lie?"

He bit his lip, debating on how to answer. A part of him wanted her to lie for him, but this wasn't an undercover case, and he couldn't ask her to do that. It wasn't right.

"No. I don't want you to cover for me."

The relief that flooded her features made him smile. "Let's go." He ran his hand through his wet hair, combing it into some semblance of order, and then grabbed his keys off the nightstand.

She followed him to the car.

He sat in the driver's seat, staring at the cottage. "When the funeral's over, do you want to move into the apartment in New York until we can rebuild here?"

Jennifer's eyebrows rose. "I, uh." She surveyed the cabin, lawn, and lake before glancing back at him. "I guess."

"That way you can audition for anything you want." Steve turned the key, and the car rumbled to life.

"Was there something between you two?"

"What two?" Steve asked, glancing her way as he pulled out of the driveway.

"You and Sarah."

Steve kept eye contact and sighed. He allowed a nod. "Not in the way you're thinking, but, yeah. You were clinically brain dead. Your parents filed an injunction to take you off life support." He focused back on the road. "Jessica's... whatever... hadn't started to work its magic."

"So, how long were you...?"

Shaking his head. "We weren't together, Jen," he clarified. "I lost it when I was told there was still no brain activity and she was there." He shrugged. "We kissed, but that's as far as it went."

Jennifer struggled with the information, her mind going back to his infidelity with Desiree in their efficiency apartment when he was undercover in New York.

Steve cocked his head. "It wasn't anything like Desiree, Jen, so don't go there." His eyes hardened a fraction, and he sent her a sideways glare. "It was only a kiss and considering a year of hanging on when everyone said I should give up, I'm amazed I had the strength to say no."

Her scoff set him off. "Look, the shit I dealt with for a year, from the doctors and your parents, wasn't easy. A year of being told I should pull the plug because, while your body was still running, you weren't there. That you were brain dead, and your organs could help someone else lead a happy, healthy life." He shook his head. "I prayed for a miracle every single day. And every day I was told there was no hope. If I had given in to Sarah, it felt like I was giving up my belief that a miracle was possible."

"I guess you got what you prayed for."

Steve let out a laugh. "Yeah, a miracle of epic proportion." His eyebrows furrowed. "I have no idea what my limitations are." He sighed. "The only hint I have is what I got from Eric's memories and even that only grazed the tip of what Chris was capable of."

Jennifer stiffened in the seat as they pulled into the cemetery.

"You want to know something even more frightening?" he asked, offering her something else to think about besides the crypt visible in the distance.

She nodded and met his questioning gaze.

"Chris's son, CJ, is a hundred times stronger than I am." He pulled into a parking space on the far side of the lot and glanced out the window. "And he's only nine."

"That's a hell of a lot of responsibility for such a young kid."

"No shit. Chris expects me to keep an eye on him."

"The angel of death wants you to watch over his son?"

Steve met her gaze. "Pretty much, and apparently Chris is *my* guardian angel."

A small smile broke through her stoic features. "Oh, Steve, you are *so* screwed."

Georgia Reign
Chapter 8

THE KNOCK ON THE door startled Steve, and he picked his head up off the desk. The case file sat open on his computer and a couple of empty beer bottles lay beyond the keyboard. He stood, and all the muscles in his back stiffened from his impromptu nap. Groaning, he shuffled to the front door.

The knocking continued.

"I'm coming," he muttered and swung the door open while wiping the sleep from his eyes.

"You look like shit," Sarah said.

"Well, hello to you too," he shot back, instantly irritated. He held the door open, and she carted her suitcase inside, dropping it at his feet. "I'm not your fucking concierge." He swung the door closed and stepped away from the suitcase, pointing across the cottage. "Guest room's over there."

"You really do look like shit, Steve," she said.

Steve glared at her and grabbed the suitcase, hauled it across the cottage, and tossed it into the room before he turned to her. "I fell asleep at my desk." He waved toward his office.

Sarah crossed the room, stopping inches from him, her hands on her hips. "So, you're going to answer all my questions?"

Steve clenched his jaw and met her gaze. "That's what I said." His hands slid into his pockets.

Sarah looked around and returned her brown eyes to his. "You still don't have furniture?"

Steve tilted his head. "Still? What do you mean, still?"

Sarah looked at her hands, but her thoughts betrayed her.

Steve stepped back, his eyebrows rising. "When the hell were you here?"

Sarah brought her gaze back to his. "I stopped here before I went to Jessica's house in Maine. Before..." She shifted her gaze beyond Steve.

"The furniture's being delivered tomorrow," Jennifer said from behind him.

Her thoughts, her sizing Sarah up, accosted him. Her observation of the similarity to Desiree sent his blood boiling, and he sent a glare in her direction. He was painfully aware of the likeness and the fact that when Sarah was in the room, the friction between them could ignite like an oil spill, obliterating everything around them like the explosion that rocked their cabin. He swung his gaze back to Sarah.

Sarah dug in her pocket and pulled out the badge and letter of instruction signed by none other than Assistant Director Ronald Cleary, handing both to Steve. "Your boss read your report and, for some reason, he thinks I'd make a good babysitter."

Steve stared at the orders in his hands. "You're my partner?"

"Yep, and before we go down south, you are going to tell me what the hell happened in that warehouse."

Steve handed the papers back to her and took a deep breath. He hadn't told Jennifer he was going to Georgia after the funeral, and Sarah's timing couldn't have been worse. The visit to the gravesite drained both of them, and Jennifer refused his empathy, pushing him away and retreating to the bedroom. Yet her thoughts had come through loud and clear, and they all shouted he was to blame.

That's when he dove into the Georgia case and the cooler full of beer until he couldn't keep his eyes open any longer. And now this.

"Chris left me fifty million dollars," he said, changing the subject.

Sarah took a step back, her eyebrows curving like McDonald's golden arches. "What?"

"Chris put me in his will." Steve met her shocked stare.

"Why?"

Steve shrugged.

"You didn't know him that long. Did you?"

Steve shook his head. "Just a couple of weeks."

"Why would he leave you fifty million dollars?"

"I don't know. Maybe he thought it was my fair share of the victim's fund."

"Victim's fund?"

Steve allowed a brief smile. "We siphoned all Kyle's money out of his accounts."

Sarah gawked. "Kyle had more than fifty million dollars?"

Steve chuckled. "No. Kyle only had ten million. Chris put another hundred million in the kitty with a directive that I get fifty and must divvy up the remaining money between the families of Kyle's victims." His lips slowly curved. "So, I guess I get to figure out how much of a cut you deserve." He pointed at her.

"I don't want his blood money," Sarah snapped.

Steve let out a laugh and crossed to the cooler by the door. "I need some air." He reached inside and grabbed a beer, flipping the top off on the cooler's bottle opener before disappearing outside, leaving both Jennifer and Sarah to stare at each other.

Georgia Reign
Chapter 9

"**W**HAT ARE YOU REALLY doing here?" Jennifer asked, the edge to her voice alerting Sarah that she was not welcome.

Sarah looked out the window at Steve sitting on the dock with mixed feelings. On one hand, she thought he was an arrogant, irritating shit, and on the other, she wanted to kiss him, to seduce him, to love him.

"He saved my life, and I don't know how." She brought her gaze back to Jennifer's. "I need to know what happened. I need to know exactly who Chris Ryan was."

Jennifer laughed. "Bullshit."

Sarah's jaw tensed, and her eyes narrowed. "Look..."

"Why are you here?"

"He's my new partner."

"You are so full of shit. Just like he is," Jennifer pointed out the window and then spun and marched into the bedroom, slamming the door on Sarah.

Sarah stared at the closed door and then turned, crossed to the cooler, and grabbed a beer before she headed outside. She took a seat next to him on the end of the dock.

"Fifty million? Why would he do that?"

"I don't know." Steve glanced in her direction. The gentle breeze blew her blonde hair around her face. "He left me more than just money." Steve took a swig of the beer.

"What else?"

"His penthouse."

"Holy shit!"

Steve laughed and shrugged. "No kidding. I'm a fucking millionaire."

Sarah turned his wrist so she could see it and ran her finger over his perfect skin before tipping the beer to her lips and taking a long swig. She witnessed the crucifixion. Kyle drilled screws through Steve's wrists and feet before raising the cross that he intended Steve to die on.

In her nightmares, he died on that wooden cross.

In her nightmares, when Kyle raked the knife across her throat, it cut through her flesh.

In her nightmares, blood flooded her mouth, choking her last breath.

But this time, reality was even stranger than the dream. Steve somehow stopped the blade from slicing her throat, even though he was nailed to a cross seven feet off the ground.

That was before Chris Ryan had shown up. Before Chris unleashed his brand of hell. Before a bullet ricocheted off Kyle's knife and blew out Chris's brain.

She stared at his perfect wrists and then turned her gaze to his. "Jesus, you're a regular freak show."

"A multi-million-dollar freak show." Steve tipped his beer in her direction and then raised it to his lips, draining it in one long pull. "With a badge."

"And now I'm your partner."

Steve scoffed and stared at the lake, refusing to look in her direction.

"Thanks for the vote of confidence," Sarah snapped.

"Look, you're a good cop, but I'm not sure why the hell Cleary brought you on board."

"I guess it was the rave review in your report."

Steve cocked his head and smiled. "I told him you came to the same conclusion I had about the Bondino connection."

He glanced in her direction, and the playful twinkle in his eyes brushed heat over her skin. She quickly took a gulp of the cold beer, chilling her libido from the raging boil to simmering.

His eyebrow rose. "You really need to keep those thoughts in check. Especially since we're partners."

Sarah's cheeks burned, and she looked away, blowing a stream of air out with her exhale. He was right. She couldn't think of him as her unwilling sex toy.

He sent an endearing, dimpled grin in her direction.

"So, are you going to tell me about what happened in New York?"

His grin disappeared, and his eyes darkened before they scanned the lake. "We should be dead right now."

"No shit, Sherlock."

He rolled his eyes and glanced at her, his expression telling her to shut up if she wanted the score, and she did. She nodded for him to continue.

"We owe our lives to the Ryan's." He paused, picking at the corner of the bottle label. "They're not your normal family."

"No shit," she answered.

"Don't be a smart ass!" Steve snapped and drew in a breath.

"Chris Ryan was actually Ty Aris, wasn't he?" Sarah asked.

"No."

He kept his gaze straight ahead, and she knew he was lying to her. "You want to start this partnership off by lying to me?"

"Sarah, he was never Ty Aris."

Sarah looked into her beer and back up at him, accepting the statement because this time, he returned her gaze. "Okay, he wasn't Ty Aris. So, tell me what he was, because he certainly wasn't your ordinary run-of-the-mill billionaire."

"You're right. The Ryan's are not your ordinary family. For one, you saw, Jessica can heal people. I asked her to bring Jennifer back from the dead and she did." He turned his gaze to Sarah. "And you saw what she did to me at the warehouse. Not a scar to be found." He showed her the same wrist she had traced earlier. "And we can't say a damn word to anyone. Understand?"

Sarah balked.

"No, I won't have their lives ruined because you couldn't keep your fucking mouth shut." His eyes were hard and unyielding. "Not a word. Understand?"

Sarah nodded.

"What about you?" Sarah asked. "You were the one who stopped Kyle from killing me."

His sigh filled the yard. "That was from my partner, Jessica's son. It came along with the mind reading abilities. I guess I can put myself between danger and people I care about."

The admission stunned her, and he looked away, leaving only silence to fill the space between them. "Is that it, or is there more?"

"There's more." Steve glanced her way. "I got whatever *gifts* Chris possessed when he died."

The crease between Sarah's eyes deepened. The memory of the warehouse came flooding back—the screws holding Steve to the cross exploding from the wood and embedding in the brick like deadly projectiles, the bonds that held her to the table evaporating, and the furniture moving like a tornado blew through its path. "And what might those be?"

Steve tossed the empty bottle toward the lake, and it stopped just shy of hitting the water. The bottle floated to his extended hand like a boomerang coming home, and only when his fingers clasped the glass did he turn and offer a smile. "I guess the correct term is telekinesis."

Sarah stared between the bottle and his grin of amusement. "Holy shit." Their weird conversation just catapulted into the land of the bizarre. Psychic abilities were not something in her repertoire of beliefs, and yet, what happened at the warehouse was not explainable any other way. "So now you're what, super human?"

"No. I'll still bleed if you cut me."

Sarah raised her eyes, meeting his gaze.

"I can still die, but it makes it much more difficult to get to me."

The smile that spread on his lips sent shivers down Sarah's spine. It was utterly captivating, and she exhaled. For an instant, she faltered, letting him sucker her in with his grin, and she blinked, clearing her mind. "I feel like I stepped into an episode of the *Twilight Zone*."

His laugh echoed off the lake, rich and full, the kind of laugh she could get used to.

He leaned close. "Seriously, I'm married. You need to stop thinking about me like your private sex toy."

"Stop reading my thoughts."

"Can't help it. They're as loud as you are."

"What the fuck does that mean?"

He raised an eyebrow in her direction, silently challenging her question.

"Okay, fine, but what the hell can I do?"

"Stop thinking in a linear fashion."

"What?"

"To create static, you need to think of more than one thing at a time. Try it."

Sarah nodded and closed her eyes, her thoughts tossing between the incident at the warehouse, seeing Kyle being handcuffed to the gurney, howling in pain, and the case in Atlanta.

"Not bad. All I caught was Atlanta, but you need to master creating static. It's really important because there are others out there.

Others who can get in your head easier than I can."

"Are you talking about Jessica?"

Steve nodded. "And Chris's son, CJ. I'm sure there are others out there too, but I haven't run across anyone with this level of psychic power." He laughed. "Hell, I didn't even believe in the realm of the supernatural until I met Jennifer."

Sarah absorbed this and drained her beer, watching the fish pop to the surface of the lake chasing moonbeams and skimming insects. "It's really beautiful here," she said.

Steve nodded. "Yes, it is, but I think we're moving to New York."

"Why?"

"Too many memories here and not all of them are good."

Sarah grunted. "And you think New York is any better?"

"Chris's apartment doesn't hold any bad memories for Jennifer. I think she'll love that place." He gave Sarah a sideways glance.

Sarah nodded. The place was stunning. "You're probably right." She glanced out at the water. "Did you read the Atlanta case file?"

"Yep." Steve dropped onto his back, staring at the stars before turning his gaze to Sarah. "Jen wants me to quit."

"I gather from the way you put that, you don't share her thoughts."

"No, I don't. Especially not with these extra advantages. Imagine the damage I can do now."

Sarah's laugh echoed across the lake. She couldn't imagine a criminal standing a ghost of a chance against him. Not with what she'd witnessed in the last week.

"You still have questions?"

Sarah bit the inside of her cheek while she formulated her thoughts. "You answered most of them, but I keep getting stuck on why neither you nor Chris Ryan killed that bastard."

Steve inhaled and stared at his beer bottle. "If Chris hadn't died, he *would* have killed Kyle." He paused and looked out at the lake. "I can't say I didn't want to kill him because I did. I wanted to tear him apart with my bare hands. I wanted him to suffer like he made me suffer. But in the end, I believe killing him was too easy. Sitting on death row in the state he's in is vengeance enough."

Sarah glanced at his tight jaw, wondering if he was right or not. If he hadn't stopped her, she would have killed Kyle. He swung his gaze in her direction, his blue eyes shimmering in the moonlight, revealing a hatred so strong she recoiled.

"I'll be there the day they inject him, and I'll make hell seem like a country club."

Georgia Reign
Chapter 10

CJ STARED AT THE smooth mahogany of the closed casket, running his hands on the edge, feeling with more than his fingers, trying to reach into the dead mind of his father, but only silence came from the coffin. No thoughts, no feelings, nothing, a sharp contrast to all the strangers filling the mortuary, paying their respects to his mother.

He scanned the room, gaze flitting from his grandparents to Uncle Danny, to Tommy. The absence of his older brother Eric was clear in the hollow eyes of both his mother and Uncle Danny. Sandy came running over, inappropriately exuberant and smiling, her bright hazel eyes catching his.

"Hi, CJ. I'm sorry 'bout yer dad." She bounced as she spoke, barely able to contain her energy, her blonde ponytail springing in time with her feet. Even at almost ten, she was as spastic as she had been at four, but she was pretty, and he didn't want to be rude.

CJ barely inclined his head in a nod.

Sandy reached out and ran her hand down his arm, stepping closer.

CJ followed her touch, and his eyes misted. The simple motion stirred something deep within him, and he raised his eyes to meet her stare. This time his nod was more pronounced, and he bit his lip to keep the tears from flowing. He hadn't cried and now, with the floodgates dangerously close to bursting, he closed his eyes, hung his head and concentrated on building up the levy he'd erected around his emotions when his father left for New York.

His concentration broke when her arms wrapped around him, pulling him to her chest. The sweet scent of strawberries filled his nostrils, and he wrapped his arms around her, burying his face in her shoulder. The tears broke through the barrier.

Sandy's soft voice whispered "Shhh," in his ear over and over, in time with the motion of her hand running through his thick hair. Her breath tickled the line of his neck and he sobbed, clinging to her refuge.

They held each other in the coffin's shadow, away from the crowd milling about. CJ pulled away, wiping the tears and snot off his face with the sleeve of his shirt. "Sorry," his hoarse voice cracked.

"It's all right," Sandy offered a smile and stood still, her hand resting on his arm.

CJ put his hand over hers and met her gaze, twitching his lips into a semblance of a smile, remembering Eric's funeral and the quiet hug they shared. Sandy cried that time, leaning on CJ at the loss of their half-brother less than a month ago. Eric had been a stable presence in both his and Sandy's lives, not showing favoritism between CJ, Tommy, and Sandy. In Eric's eyes, they were all tied together as family.

"How's your dad doing?"

Sandy glanced over her shoulder at her parents. They stood talking with his mother. She shrugged and looked back at CJ. "He's doing better than your mom."

CJ inhaled, his eyes drifting back to his mother. Losing Chris on the heels of losing her oldest son had taken its toll. "She isn't doing very well," he confessed.

"Can you blame her?"

CJ's gaze shot back to Sandy. "I guess not." He slid his hands into his pocket and dug the toe of his shoe into the carpet, torn between wanting Sandy to linger and wanting to be alone.

"Do you want me to hang out for a while, or did you want to be alone?"

CJ shrugged, not meeting her inquisitive gaze. Sandy leaned forward and pressed her lips to his cheek, creating a warm flutter in his stomach under the layer of despair.

She disappeared into the crowd and CJ turned back toward the coffin, his fingers touching the spot where her lips had been moments before. Curious, he stared at the slight pink sheen of her lip-gloss that glimmered on his fingertips.

A small smile formed on CJ's lips and, for a fleeting moment, he believed everything would be all right.

Georgia Reign
Chapter 11

THE RIDE TO YORK Beach was quiet, and Steve mulled over the conversation with Sarah the night before. He lied to her about who Chris was and that weighed on him, but the alternative was just as bad. If the roles were reversed, he wouldn't care how good a cop she was, or that she had saved his life. If she turned her cheek to someone like Ty Aris, he would throw her ass in jail.

Jennifer hadn't said more than two words to him since Sarah's arrival and now she sat with her arms folded across her chest, just staring out the window.

"Will you just cut me some slack?" Steve whispered, drawing her attention.

"Me?" She pointed at her chest and her glare dug under his skin.

"Yes, you." He glanced in her direction. "I didn't know Kyle was alive. If I had any clue, I never would have left you alone that day." There, he said it. He finally answered the main "why" question in Jennifer's mind.

"Why didn't you put down your gun like he asked?" Tears filled her eyes.

"Because if I had, you know damn well we all would have died."

"He's right," Sarah said from the back seat.

"Who asked you?" Jennifer snapped.

"Excuse me." Sarah put her hands up and leaned back in the seat.

"That was uncalled for." Steve sent a glare in Jennifer's direction. The tension in the car ratcheted up, thickening between the three of them. Logically, he knew Jennifer needed to go through the motions of grief before she came to terms with Samantha's death. Now that Kyle was behind bars, she focused all her anger and all her blame on him. He met Sarah's gaze in the rearview mirror.

It's all right. Sarah thought.

No, it isn't. She doesn't have any right to lash out at you. He sent the words back to her and watched her eyebrows rise.

Give her some slack, Steve.

Steve snorted and focused back on the road, turning up the radio to drown out their thoughts.

When Steve pulled into the Congregational Church in the center of the small coastal town, he uttered a sharp laugh, surprised to find the parking lot full. He opened the door for both Sarah and Jennifer, helping them out of the car.

They entered the church and took a seat in the back.

Tommy Ryan stood in the front pew and slid into the aisle, scanning the crowd with his bright blue eyes until they landed on Steve. He marched up the aisle with purpose, keeping eye contact.

"My mom wants you in the front," he said when he stopped at the edge of the pew they sat in. The boy reached, taking Steve's hand, and headed back toward the front of the church.

Steve grabbed Jennifer's hand, pulling her with him. He didn't want to be up front alone. He wanted her with him, even with the hostility raking her mind. He looked back when her hand slipped out of his.

"I don't feel right," she whispered.

"Please," he said, feeling all eyes and thoughts on him and Jennifer. When she nodded, he reached out, taking her hand in a vice grip she couldn't break if she wanted to. There was room in the pew behind Jessica and CJ, and Steve waved Jennifer in, taking the aisle seat as Tommy sat in the front pew next to CJ.

Jessica turned, her calico eyes meeting Steve's gaze. He offered what he hoped was an appropriate smile of support and not a grimace and reached out, placing his hand on her shoulder. No spoken words passed between them, but the sudden stiffness in her back and the full turn in his direction was enough.

"You've seen him?"

CJ turned, and his eyes hardened. A shiver struck the base of Steve's spine, and he clenched his jaw against it.

"He's seen him. Ain't that right, Agent Williams?" Even the tone of the voice mimicked Chris's, dripping with sarcasm and an undertone of something more dangerous. CJ's gaze traveled to Jennifer. The hardness in his eyes softened, transitioning back to that of a vulnerable child before he looked away.

Steve leaned into Jennifer, kissing her cheek. CJ frightened her more than Chris had, and her thoughts screamed that fear. He wrapped his arm around her, bringing her close, and her mind cleared. He couldn't blame her. CJ could toast everyone in the church without breaking a sweat, and that was a frightening prospect for a nine-year-old. Neither CJ nor Jessica gave anything away beyond static, but Tommy clearly mourned his father's passing and the rift it put between him and his brother.

The service was nice and when it was time for mourners to speak on behalf of the deceased, Jessica turned. "I think you should say something about my husband."

Steve's eyebrows rose. He wasn't prepared to speak to a church full of people about a man he was ambiguous about. He started to refuse, and CJ turned.

"It's the least you can do considering..."

Steve met the boy's stark stare and slowly stood and released Jennifer's hand. The walk to the pulpit was close to twenty feet, but it might as well have been two hundred miles. From the casual observer's view, he walked normally, but in his mind, everything slowed to a crawl. When he turned to the congregation, he didn't know what would come out of his mouth. What did surprised even him.

"I knew Chris Ryan for only a matter of weeks." Steve stopped, looking out at the crowd. "He saved my life and countless others, but in doing so, he paid the ultimate price."

Holy god, what a fucking cliché, can't you do any better? Chris's voice barreling in his head caught him off guard and he stumbled on words, going silent before he burst out laughing in front of the crowded church.

It took him a moment to get his focus back. "Chris could be a royal SOB too," he allowed a smile. "He certainly knew how to push my buttons. There were several times where I got to the point I could have just throttled him, but then he'd pull out that brittle sense of humor and I'd find myself laughing out loud instead of throwing the punch I had been gearing up for."

Really?

Steve ignored his guardian angel's question. "He was brilliant. I'm talking the kind of smarts that puts Einstein in the dust. What he could do with a computer was frightening, and I was humbled by his willingness to help track down the man who killed both our kids." Steve paused, waiting for another catcall from beyond the grave. When none came, he continued. "I have to admit, I'm glad he was on my side, because having him as an adversary would have been a real bitch."

Chuckles erupted in the church as well as from the great beyond. *Nice.*

"I don't know how many of you really know the Ryan's, but Chris and his family had a profound effect on me."

Yeah, if they only knew.

Again Steve faltered and had to bite back on the sideways response that wanted to slip out. *Just shut up while I do this, will ya?* He sent the silent thought and got a chuckle in return.

"They gave me hope when I didn't have much to cling to and opened their doors when I had lost everything. He even kicked my ass when I was wallowing in self-pity."

Another wave of chuckles erupted in the congregation, and he saw some heads nodding, deducing they must have been students of Chris's dojo when it was operational.

"Now, I'm a little younger than he was," More chuckles and Steve broke out in a grin. "And I like to think I'm in fairly decent shape, but my second-degree black belt didn't hold a candle to Chris. He was the fastest sparring partner I've ever had and knocked me on my ass quite a few times. He also knocked some sense into my thick skull, which, as my wife will tell you, is a really hard thing to do." He waved toward Jennifer and then hooked his thumbs in his pockets and walked to the front of the church, standing next to the casket. His smile faded, and he sighed.

"He offered to be my friend at a time when that was as good as signing his own death warrant." His gaze scanned over Jessica's ex-husband and then moved to Jessica herself. "Unfortunately, that's exactly what being associated with me turned out to be, and for that, I'm sorry." Steve turned away from the congregation.

I'm touched.

"If this was your idea of a joke," he whispered, staring at the casket, "I'm going to kick your ass when I get back to Brooksfield." Tears blurred his vision, and he blinked them away.

I'm truly touched. The soft chuckle that followed got a rise out of Steve.

"Fuck you, Ty." His uttered words were so low that they were almost imperceptible, and Steve turned, taking his seat again.

Jessica stared at him, her mouth agape, and when he met her gaze, he knew it was going to be impossible to keep her out of his head, especially since she heard her dead husband cajoling him while he gave his little speech. He offered a nod and looked away, aware that her eyes were boring into him, creating a hot spot on the flesh of his forehead right between his eyes.

She reached for him, and it was Jennifer who interceded, grabbing her hand.

The power transition from Jessica into his wife nearly sparked the air between them. Both women stared at each other, eyes wider than usual, and their grip broke. Jennifer stared at her hand, rubbing her thumb along her fingertips before she looked back at the woman in the front pew.

Steve saw it first, just as Jessica turned away. The aging process took over, along with her grief, and the lines in her face deepened. Crows-nests sprouted from the corners of her eyes and strands of silver threaded through her dark hair. It wasn't all at once, but it was noticeable to Steve. Jessica Ryan now looked every bit her fifty-seven years.

He turned away, focusing on what her ex-husband was saying about the body in the coffin a few feet away. The man who destroyed his marriage, who caused his daughter's death and yet, Dan Connor was talking about him with reverence, like he was a saint.

Steve had to stifle a laugh, a saint; not in his book, more appropriately an agent of death, and now the man was *his* guardian angel.

The succession of people who spoke surprised Steve. Chris Ryan had touched a lot of lives in the fifteen years since he changed identities, but to Steve, that still didn't make up for all the black years he stood by while his stepbrother ruined innocent lives, raping and murdering at will while Chris caught it all on film.

Once again, Steve wondered if Chris had lived, would he have kept his promise? Would he have left the family alone, or would he have put the man behind bars?

He studied his hands, mulling it over. The music brought him out of his thoughts, and he stood as they carried the coffin to the hearse.

Steve turned to a tap on his shoulder. CJ's expression held both anger and awe as he looked at Steve.

"You can still hear my dad?"

Steve bit the side of his lip, debating on how to answer the question, his eyes switching between CJ, Tommy, and Jessica. He returned his gaze to CJ and nodded. With that, he turned away and headed down the aisle, with Jennifer at his side, to meet Sarah in the back of the church.

Steve didn't say a word until they were in the car, and then he pounded his palm on the dashboard. "You're an asshole, you know that?" he cursed under his breath, looking at the roof of the car. A soft chuckle reached his ears. "You think this is funny?" No response came this time, and he glanced in the rearview mirror at Sarah's dumbfounded stare. He turned to Jennifer, her expression mimicking Sarah's.

Steve glared at her. "He was making side comments while I was trying to talk."

"Who?" Sarah asked from the backseat.

"Chris Ryan."

"You know he's dead, right?"

Steve turned in the front seat, staring Sarah down. "I know he's dead. But unfortunately, he's been assigned as my guardian angel, and now he can interrupt me any time he damn well feels like it."

"Okay..." Sarah said, pushing herself deeper in the back seat, looking at Steve like he just escaped from a mental hospital.

"Steve's not crazy. I saw him too."

"You saw him at the church?"

"No. Yesterday at Paradise cove."

"And you saw him at the church?" Sarah turned toward Steve.

Steve shot a glare in the mirror and followed the trail of cars to the cemetery. "No. I can't see him, but I can certainly hear his fucked-up commentary."

Sarah burst out laughing in the back seat.

"This isn't funny."

"Oh, yes it is," Jennifer sputtered, letting the first wave of laughter flow.

Steve bit back another derogatory response, annoyed at being laughed at. But, after a moment, the humor of the situation seeped in and he let a grin surface, glancing in Jennifer's direction. Her smile brightened this depressing day.

Steve pulled over in the cemetery. He sighed and scanned the landscape. Headstones mingled with stone mausoleums; reminding him of the cemetery in Brooksfield where their daughter was buried. A sobering spin hit their lighthearted laughter, and they stepped out of the car, approaching the crowded gravesite. He hung back, keeping his distance.

Jessica Ryan's sobs drifted over the crowd as they lowered the casket next to the graves of Eric and Emily Conner. The family plot. Steve shivered, looking out over the vast cemetery, expecting to see Chris in attendance, his white wings folded as tightly as his arms, but he was nowhere to be seen and unusually quiet.

At the house, Steve took the same post by the ocean he had for Eric's funeral less than a month earlier, but this time, he had company. Jennifer stood on one side and his new partner sat on the rock wall. "I need to figure out how to get CJ to the cabin." He glanced at Jennifer. "Without Jessica." His gaze drifted back to the ocean.

"Why?"

"Because Chris needs to have a word with his son, and I'm supposed to make it happen."

"Good luck with that." Sarah's skepticism with this whole situation bled through in her tone.

"Why don't you do what you did yesterday?" Jennifer asked.

"I've seen what suspended animation looks like and it's a lot like what you look like when you're having a vision. That's nothing I can hide in the wide open."

"So, find some place where you can," Jennifer said.

Steve tilted his head. It wasn't a bad idea. "I'm not sure I can pull someone through with me." He took a sip of the scotch in his hand. "But it's worth a shot."

"What the hell are you two talking about?" Sarah asked.

Jennifer sent an annoyed glance in her direction and turned toward Steve. "Go. I want to talk with Jessica, anyway."

Steve nodded and looked at Sarah. "I'll explain later."

Jennifer's annoyance turned south, boiling into a quiet anger that Steve didn't understand. Instead of questioning her, he turned, leaving the women alone.

It didn't take long to find CJ, primarily because he announced his intentions silently as he walked into the house.

CJ popped up from the couch, meeting his gaze, and then headed for his bedroom. Steve followed the boy upstairs and locked the door behind him. "Your dad wants to talk to you and I'm not sure I can do this, but it's my best bet of getting you to my place without your mother knowing."

"I've never projected myself." CJ fidgeted on the bed, and Steve took a seat next to him.

"Well, I've only done this once." He took the boy's hand and laced it in his, taking a deep breath.

"I thought you had to be on the phone with the person in order to transition—or be in front of a mirror." CJ said.

"I don't know how this really works, so I'm going to try something different and if it doesn't work, we're going for a ride." He traded a glance with CJ and then closed his eyes, letting CJ into his mind as he pictured the cove, the soft moss, and the water. He squeezed CJ's hand, wishing he was there, and felt the transition begin.

When CJ tightened his grip and gasped, Steve opened his eyes. Gradually descending before them was Chris, his white wings spread and fluttering softly as he touched the moss. The grand wings folded behind him, and he looked from Steve to his son.

Chris kneeled in front of CJ, wrapping his arms around the boy. CJ kept Steve's hand in his grip, wrapping his free arm around his winged father. When Chris pulled away, he glanced up at Steve. "Thank you."

"We're not really here," Steve said, compelled to share and unsure of whether or not he could let go of CJ's hand.

Chris nodded. "Maybe it's better that you hang on for now." He brought his gaze level with CJ and touched the boy's face, wiping the tears from his cheek. "You can't be mad at Steve. He was just doing his job."

CJ threw himself back into his father's arms. "Why'd you leave?"

Chris closed his eyes. "Because I had to. This was the only way to ensure I'll be with you and your mother forever."

"I want you here, now." CJ pulled away.

Chris hung his head. "I'm here," he raised his bright eyes. "I'll always be here if you need me. And you know what I gave Steve, right?"

CJ looked up at Steve. "You gave him what he wanted."

"No, CJ, he never wanted this, not in the way you're thinking. He didn't want me dead, and as far as the powers you and I have, he didn't understand what it meant to have this running through his veins." Chris glanced up at Steve. "He didn't understand the responsibility. But he does now." His eyes traveled back to his son's, and he pressed his index finger to CJ's chest. "I gave him the best piece of me, the piece you gave me in that warehouse. He'll keep it safe, and you can bet he'll use it to do good things. So, you can't be mad at him. This wasn't his fault."

CJ tried to pull his hand away, but Steve kept the grip.

"It was my fault, CJ. I made the choice to go. And yes, I knew I wasn't coming back. I was out of time, son, and I had a choice: help him find the man who killed Eric, or die in my bed at home. I chose to do something that ended up saving my soul. So, before you go stewing on about how Steve took me away and got me killed, you just think about that for a while." He stood, towering over CJ. "And so help me, CJ, if I ever catch you using your powers for anything bad..." His wings uncurled in all their majesty. "You'll have to answer to me. Understand?"

CJ nodded, silent, and awed, as his father beat his mighty wings, rising into the clouds and disappearing. He shifted his gaze to Steve.

Steve's upturned face tilted down to CJ, and the transition took hold. Steve blinked, and they were sitting on the bed in CJ's room, hands still clasped. Neither of them broke the bond at first, and then Steve relaxed his grip and CJ pulled his hand out.

"I'm sorry your father died."

"I know," CJ replied. He stood and walked to the door. "My mom wants to die now, too." CJ glanced over his shoulder at Steve, tears filling his eyes.

Steve inhaled and slowly let the air out of his lungs before he spoke. "When Jenny was first in the coma and they told me she'd never recover, I felt the same way your mother does. But she'll be okay. She has you and Tommy."

CJ smiled a bitter smirk, one that should never grace a nine-year-old's face. "I remind her of my dad." He turned and left Steve with that thought.

THE MOMENT STEVE STEPPED out of view, Jennifer sent a glare at Sarah and crossed the lawn, cornering Jessica alone. "What did you do to me in the church?" Voices of strangers rambled in her head and had been since she grabbed Jessica's hand after Steve's eulogy.

Jessica allowed a brief smile. "I guess I transferred my abilities to you like Chris and Eric did to Steve." She turned to leave, but Jennifer stopped her.

"What does that mean?"

"That means you can read minds and heal people."

Jennifer took a step back. "You.. I... huh?" She tilted her head, then shook it to silence the continuous drones. "How do you shut them up?"

An amused smile played on Jessica's lips, but it didn't reach her pain ridden eyes. "Concentrate on one person at a time. The easiest thing is to target someone creating static. That's when you find silence. Otherwise, it gets real loud, real quick."

She tried it, concentrating on Jessica and all the noise subsided, replaced by a light static buzz like that of an un-tuned television turned way down. No thoughts came through the channel, and Jennifer cocked her head.

"I can't hear anything from you."

"I know how to block people from my mind."

"Oh. And how do you do that?"

"Think of more than one thing at a time."

The answer was not something Jennifer understood. She wasn't sure it was possible and yet this woman had her tuned out. Instead of pushing the issue, Jennifer took a moment to study the memory download that occurred with the transfer. She bit her lip against the layers of emotions that came with each memory. "I got your memories..." Her vision distorted with tears. "I felt your pain."

Jessica took her hands. "We have more in common than you think. I saw your life, too, and despite what you're feeling right now, you are a strong woman, Jennifer. You'll get through this."

"I lost the only child I'll ever have. How do you get through that?"

Jessica's expression changed, and she looked down at their clasped hands. "Lean on your husband. Trust him. He's a good man."

The answer wasn't what Jennifer expected, and she looked toward the house. "I don't know if I can."

"Do you know what a soul mate is?"

Jennifer thought she knew. She once thought Steve was hers, but now she wasn't sure. Not with everything that had happened. She met Jessica's calico stare and shrugged.

"A soul mate is your other half. Without him, you are incomplete. Empty. Lost." Jessica paused and swallowed, blinking back a bright sheen of tears. "Steve is yours, just as surely as Chris was mine."

"We both know his name wasn't Chris." Despite the memory swap, Jennifer still had to ask. "Why? Why him?"

"Because, without him, I wasn't complete. I was restless and always looking for something missing in my life. The way we finally met was not the most conventional of ways, to say the least." Jessica surveyed the backyard. "But even then I knew, when I first saw him, the energy was there whether or not I wanted it to be." A blush crept into her cheeks and she sighed, refocusing on Jennifer. "If you throw away what you have with Steve, you will never find peace. It will haunt you to your grave, and Kyle will have won."

For the second time in as many days, that threat was laid at her feet, and she recoiled. "I don't know Steve anymore." The words seemed hollow and empty coming from her lips.

"That's an excuse. You got through what happened your senior year in college, you can overcome this too. Kyle only has power over you if you let him. Sure, he abused your body and messed with your mind, but the rest is up to you. Are you going to continue being his victim?"

This time Jennifer actually took a step backwards, away from the now angry eyes of Jessica. Her mind raced, flipping the pages of Jessica's memories back to the concrete prison. She wanted to ask a million questions, but all that came out was "How?"

"I made a decision and there were several times that I lost sight of that decision, but in the end, it's what helped me survive and get past what happened—what Frank did. Can you tell me what that decision was?"

Jennifer looked at her hands and nodded. "You decided they could do anything to your body, but they could never touch your spirit."

"Bingo."

"I'm not as strong as you are."

"Bullshit."

"I don't know…"

Jessica raised her hand. "I know. He made you do things you never wanted to in order to save your daughter and then killed her, anyway. It wasn't Steve that killed your daughter, it was Kyle. If Steve had put his gun down, none of you would have survived and Kyle would still be out there killing innocent people."

"He killed your husband."

Jessica's eyes misted over. "No. A ricocheted bullet killed Chris."

"But the stab wound."

Jessica raised her eyebrow, and her thought echoed in Jennifer's mind. *Have you seen what I can do?*

Jennifer laughed and nodded. "Yeah." *And I have to figure out what to do with it now that you gave it to me.*

"Don't let Kyle ruin your life. Don't let him have that kind of power over you."

With a nod, Jennifer blinked back her own tears. "What are you going to do now?"

Jessica shrugged, and sorrow traced lines through her face. "I have no idea."

On impulse, Jennifer stepped in and wrapped her arms around Jessica in a hug. "You'll be just fine. You have your boys to get you through this."

Jessica squeezed and then stepped back. "Thank you." She walked away.

STEVE STEPPED OUT IN the backyard, scanning the crowd for both Sarah and Jennifer. He caught Jennifer's gaze across the lawn and offered her a small smile. She nodded back and headed toward him.

His phone vibrated in his pocket, and he dug it out, checking the number before flipping it open.

"Williams?" Cleary asked.

"Yes, sir."

"I need you and Agent Connelly down here as soon as you can. We've got another missing child."

"Sarah and I will be there, sir. We're booked on a flight this evening." He closed the phone and focused on Jennifer, creating static in his mind because she now had Jessica's repertoire of powers, including the ability to read minds.

"Focus," he whispered in her ear and got a creased brow in response.

"Focus on one person at a time. That helps with the noise," he clarified and scanned the crowd for Sarah. He caught sight of her talking to Jessica and headed her way.

He approached Jessica and CJ by the rock wall, talking to Sarah.

"We need to go," he said to Sarah before turning to Jessica. He offered a slim smile and put his hand on CJ's head, messing up his hair. "If either of you need anything, don't hesitate to call." He reached into his pocket and pulled a couple of business cards out, handing one to Jessica and the other to CJ.

He crossed and offered a card to Tommy. "If you ever need to talk, or CJ misbehaves, call me, ok?"

Tommy looked at the card and up at Steve. "What about me? What if I start misbehaving?"

Steve scrunched down. "You already know the answer to that."

Tommy tried not to smile. "Yeah, I'd have to answer to Dad."

Steve did smile. "Yes, but you'll also have to answer to me."

Tommy rolled his eyes.

"I'm no picnic when I'm angry. And I'll be pissed if you decide to rebel. Got it?"

Tommy's smile faded, and he nodded. "And if CJ rebels?"

"Well, then I guess I'll have to come by and kick his ass. Won't I?"

That brought a smile to his face and in his mind, he was laughing because the kid knew his brother could crush Steve with a thought. Instead of answering the question, Tommy focused back on the game in his hand, the gesture dismissive, signaling the conversation was over.

Steve turned away, heading out the door with Sarah and Jennifer with one thought on his mind. He had another serial killer to nail, and this time, he would not let him get away.

Georgia Reign
Chapter 12

"YOU'RE KIDDING ME!" JENNIFER stood outside the bedroom door as Steve threw clothing into a carry on.

Steve straightened up. "No, I'm not kidding. Do you want to come with me?"

"To Atlanta?"

"Yes, Atlanta," he said, creating static in his mind and keeping the irritation out of his voice. Sarah had already left, but she started this spat by announcing she'd see him at the airport.

"The furniture's coming tomorrow," she said, and he knew it was an excuse. Anything not to be alone with him, to face her fears that they might never get back to that place where they once were. In love. Invincible.

Steve closed his eyes and counted to ten before he spoke. "We were never invincible, Jen."

"Please, stop snooping in my head."

"I'm not. Your thoughts are broadcasting like a bullhorn. I can't shut them out."

"You can't, or you won't."

Steve slammed the carry-on closed and yanked it off the bed. Her unwillingness to bend, to get through this together, grated on his nerves. "I'm not dignifying that with an answer."

"Fine." Her lips pressed together and the glare she sent in his direction almost pushed him over the edge.

He stopped the bitter retort from leaping from his lips, closing his mouth and turning his back on her. He stared out the picture window at the late day sunshine glazing the lake in a reflective frost. "Cancel the furniture order and come with me."

She tilted her head, looking down at the floor. Her hair slipped from behind her ears and obscured the side of her face closest to Steve. He turned, scanning her mind, her heart, and what he saw sent another fractured splinter through his.

Jennifer snapped her gaze to his. "I need time."

"Grieving alone isn't a good thing."

She sighed. "I don't want to go to Atlanta."

"You mean you don't want to go with me."

She didn't answer him, instead she walked into the barren living room, her thoughts transparent and centered on her conversation with Jessica. "I don't want him to win."

"Then come with me."

She turned, and the turmoil in her eyes cut straight to his soul. "I'm not ready yet. I can't stay here either, so I thought I'd go visit my parents while you're gone."

Ouch. That stung more than he wanted it to. Her father may have apologized to him, but there was no love lost between them, and Steve was sure the man would thrive on driving a bigger wedge between them.

"I won't let him."

Steve's eyebrows shot up.

"I won't let my dad influence my decision, and this doesn't mean I'm leaving you. I just need time."

"You reading my mind now?" He pointed at his chest.

She smiled, a blush crept into her cheeks, and he forgot to breathe for a moment—her beauty taking him by surprise yet again. He reined in his thoughts and sent a grin back her way. "Okay. I'll back off for now."

"I'm still going to cancel the furniture order. Okay?"

"The apartment in New York is furnished." He reached into his pocket and pulled the keys out, handing them to her. "Check it out if you want."

Curiosity etched her features, and she reached out, taking the keys from him. "I will."

Steve glanced at his watch and sighed. "I have to go." He turned and grabbed his suitcase from the bedroom before returning and setting it on the ground next to her. Without a word, he gave her a soft hug, and she returned it, wrapping her arms around his neck and holding on tight. Such a simple gesture, but it gave him a ray of hope that they could get through this.

"I love you," he said, pulling out of her grasp and running his palm along her cheek.

Jennifer leaned her face into his hand and tears bloomed.

She didn't speak the words he needed to hear, and he pulled his hand away, disappointed. "I've got a plane to catch." He walked out of the cottage for the last time.

Georgia Reign
Chapter 13

JENNIFER LEANED ON THE doorjamb as he drove away, wiping the tears off her cheeks and waving. She turned, looking at the empty cottage and out the front window, making a mental note to pack things she might want in New York City. Her gaze landed on the path to Paradise Cove, and she wondered if she now had the power to call on an angel.

With purpose, she crossed the lawn and traversed the overgrown path to Paradise Cove, taking a seat on the big flat rock; she slipped her shoes off and rolled up her jeans before she slid her feet into the cool water. Leaning back, she tilted her head to the sun-streaked sky and whispered, "Ty."

The air shifted, and ripples covered the sheer surface of the cove. Chris Ryan stood at the edge of the water, glaring at her.

"Only Jessica can call me that."

"But you have to come anytime that name is used, don't you?" She swung her legs back and forth in the water, creating small swells, her smile more dominant than friendly.

His face turned beet red, his eyes altering to a deep ocean blue instead of the normal shimmering topaz. "Are you testing me?"

"Perhaps I am." On the exterior she remained calm, but inside, her heart rumbled with adrenaline, leaving a slight metallic taste in her mouth.

Chris tilted his head, studying her a little closer, then his eyes went wide. "Jessie gave it to you?"

When she nodded, his eyebrows furrowed. "Why the hell would she do that?"

"I don't think she had a choice." Jennifer shifted on the rock, leaning her hands on the edge instead of behind her, still gently swishing her feet in the water, studying the patterns as they fanned out. She glanced up at him. "Is my little girl in heaven?"

Chris's eyes softened, shifting shades again, and he took a seat on the moss. "Yes."

"Have you seen her?" The shake of his head squeezed her heart and tremors started in her chin. She clenched her teeth against the quiver.

He lifted his hand. "Don't cry. It's just that I haven't seen much of heaven, that's all. But I'm told she's there and her grandparents are taking good care of her."

"When am I going to see her?" They had skirted death so many times; she couldn't help but ask the question.

"It won't be for a really long time."

The answer hurt more than Jennifer expected and tears slipped over her lashes like the beginning breach of a crack in a dam. She wanted to see her baby girl.

Chris sighed. "I know how you feel."

"No, you don't," Jennifer answered.

"Maybe I don't know exactly how you feel, but I've lost kids, and one of them was because *I* had to choose which one died. Try to live with that sacrifice."

"Still," Jennifer started, and her voice cracked with emotion. "Still, were they your only child? The only one you'd ever have?"

Chris offered a sad smile. "No."

"Then don't tell me you know how I feel." She wiped the tears off her face and stared at Chris. "I got your wife's memories," she said, moving the conversation away to something less painful.

"Really. Isn't that interesting?"

The sarcasm lacing his voice made her smile. "Extremely interesting. In her eyes, you're quite something."

"What about in your eyes?" His wings ruffled, and he leaned back on his palms.

Jennifer swayed her head back and forth, her eyes traveling the distance between his eyes and his toes and back. She exhaled and shrugged. The memories Jessica fed her contradicted everything she'd dug up about the man. Articles said he was a psychopath, a natural born killer, but that's not what Jessica had seen.

Jessica saw the man beneath the hard impenetrable exterior and because of that; she had lived through the ordeal with his stepbrother. She thought her past was bad, but the shit that woman went through in that hellhole was astounding. "I don't know what to think. Her memories paint you as a flawed saint, and I don't think you're anywhere near the realm of a saint."

His laughter echoed off the water. "You're right on the money there." He pointed in her direction. "I am not even in the vicinity of a saint, despite these pristine wings on my back." He flexed, spreading them wide, showing off, and then they folded neatly away. "Flawed saint. That really is funny."

"So, with you as a guardian angel, my husband is truly screwed." Her lips formed a genuine smile. Despite her misgivings, she was beginning to like this man.

A belly laugh was the best way to describe the sound coming from Chris as he nodded. "Pretty much." After the laughter wound down, he glanced at her and sighed. "You know, you're not half bad when you relax."

"And you're not such an asshole when you're not giving ultimatums."

"Touché." He hopped to his feet, his expression turning serious. "How was she today?" He dug his hands into his pockets, looking more like his boy, CJ, than an angel.

Jennifer stood and approached him. "It was very tough on her. She's trying to be strong for the boys, but she misses you." She pressed her lips together in a smile of support.

He nodded, lowering his head.

"She knows you love her." She reached out, touching his chest with her hand. He was surprisingly solid and warm.

Chris covered her hand with his. Just for a second, he felt the essence of his wife and he breathed a sigh that disturbed the silent reverie of the cove, bowing flowers and rustling the leaves.

When his eyes met hers, she felt the connection, the heat, the magnificent power surging through her veins and gasped, yanking her hand off his chest. The bond between Jennifer and Chris was severed, but the effects were hauntingly familiar. The only man who ever made her feel that way was Steve.

Without thinking, she stepped closer, placing her hand back on his chest, her gaze locked with his. His wings fluttered, and his lips formed a playful smile when the connection ignited.

"You are playing with fire, little girl." His hand ensnared her wrist, pulling it away from his skin.

Jennifer blinked and stepped back. His rebuff stinging in a way she couldn't explain.

"Look, you're a beautiful woman, but I haven't strayed from Jessica since the complex and I don't intend to start now." He raised an eyebrow. "You need to work out those feelings with your husband. Remember him?"

"Y-yes," she stuttered, still trying to get her arms around her behavior. It made no sense. Whenever Steve touched her, she cringed because the memory of Kyle clouded her mind. But here, with this dark angel, she had wanted to be taken—wanted to feel the moss on her back and his majestic form on top of her.

"Jessica said I had that effect on women," he laughed and took a step back.

The distance was like a slap of sanity, and Jennifer felt her cheeks heat.

"Maybe a change of scenery will tear down that mental block where Steve is concerned." Chris stepped back, uncurling his wings and taking flight.

Jennifer watched him flee, wondering just how long it would be before she would feel that same spark again with her husband.

Georgia Reign
Chapter 14

STEVE ARRIVED AT THE airport with his badge fully displayed and his gun case in the carry-on luggage. With travel permit papers in order, he slipped through security and met up with Sarah on the concourse.

"Do you have the file?"

Sarah pulled a folder out of her attaché case, handing it to Steve. "Son of a bitch is targeting kids."

Steve nodded. "They confirmed the age of the last victim." He shook his head. All the victims were under 12, and sex didn't seem to matter, but race was consistent. They were all white and all of them had signs of torture before death. Steve flipped the file closed and pushed the heels of his palms to his eyes. He wasn't ready to deal with this yet, but he had no choice, not if he wanted to remain in the FBI. He lowered his hands and glanced at Sarah. "We need to catch this bastard fast, before he hurts another child."

"I agree. But where do we start looking?"

Steve leaned back in the chair and sighed. There was no consistent pattern of where he grabbed the kids. The mall, an arcade, a bowling alley, a flea market. As he listed off the places in his mind, it strove for patterns, and one came through. They were all crowded places where a little chaos was overlooked.

He flipped the file open again and pulled up a map on his laptop, marking the addresses where the abductions took place with numbered red dots, and then he marked the addresses where the bodies were found with numbered white dots. Turning the computer toward Sarah, he said, "Not much of a consistent pattern. At least not much more than the police reports show. He's hitting in crowded areas where the abduction might not be noticed right away." He turned the screen back and stared at it. "There's definitely a pattern in here, but I just can't make it out yet." He bit his lower lip, reading the statements of the parents. "In all cases, the kid is out of view of the adult they were with." The vision of the girl he found in the woods in Brooksfield surfaced. "Damn it." He slammed the folder closed and handed the case file to Sarah.

"What's wrong?"

Steve just shook his head. "There's nothing that sets me off more than a monster going after children." He stood and walked to the window, staring out at the planes on the tarmac. His arms crossed, and his feet planted firmly, the anger biting at the underside of his skin itched to get loose. His gaze shifted to his reflection. Chris's words about watching his temper came creeping back, and he inhaled.

The boarding announcement came over the loudspeaker and he collected his things, heading toward the plane without saying a word to Sarah. The fuel in his veins was pumping, and he had to concentrate on securing the hatches, so it didn't escape.

The plane ride was quiet. Sarah studied the file while Steve closed his eyes, giving the impression of sleeping, but he actually used the time to scan her mind, absorbing her ideas, her strategies to crack the case. He sighed and opened his eyes. "You're not that far off. He's picking off easy targets, but I'm still wondering how he's getting them out of the buildings without notice. No one heard any screaming or saw anything out of the ordinary. They mentioned surveillance tapes, but again, nothing. We'll have to take a look at those when we get to the station." He glanced in her direction. "I'll tell you one thing, if this guy's thoughts are linear and I come across him, I've got him nailed."

Sarah just nodded, sending a glance sideways. "You were in my head that whole time?"

Hot skin flushed over his cheeks, and he smiled, offering a shrug. "Sorry."

Sarah chuckled. "Talk about violations of privacy."

Steve joined her, chuckling low and leaning back in the seat. "Better watch those thoughts, Agent Connelly. I'm a married man."

Georgia Reign
Chapter 15

THE PLANE TOUCHED DOWN and Steve and Sarah retrieved their bags, getting in the flashy car he rented.

"The bureau won't pay for this, you know," Sarah said, sliding into the passenger seat of the little red Jaguar.

"I don't give a shit," Steve replied. "I've got money to burn, and this is what I'm in the mood for." He hit the gas, shifting the gears and speeding out of the parking lot, leaving slack jaws in his wake.

The police station was no different. When he pulled in with the coup, all eyes turned, checking out the car and the two getting out. Shock registered when they saw the FBI badge hanging from Steve's pocket. Usually, the FBI showed up in a black SUV like the one the little red Jaguar slid next to. He flipped off his sunglasses, offering a curt nod, and stepped into the building.

A tall, intense looking man with sandy gray hair and his mouth turned into a scowl approached him. "What the hell are you doing?"

Assistant Director Cleary snapped, pulling Steve aside and pointing to the flashy car in the parking lot.

"Look, I can afford it; the bureau doesn't need to worry about the rental expense."

Arrogant little shit. Cleary's lips went white.

"And please, stop referring to me as arrogant," Steve said, slipping his sunglasses into his front pocket. "That is just irritating." He turned, leaving his shocked boss staring after him. Steve walked into the crowded police station, scanning with both his eyes and his mind.

Sarah already stood before the information board in the situation room, studying it. Victims' pictures lined the corkboard next to the map of Atlanta and the surrounding counties. They even mimicked what he had done on the computer, putting a connecting line from the abduction site to the place where the body was found, but this view left an interesting pattern that hadn't shown up on his computer screen. One that Steve recognized, and a chill slithered down his spine. *Why the hell did the pattern have to be a pentagram?*

He turned to the officer in charge of the investigation, his eyes dropping from the man's cherub-shaped face to the badge hanging out of his pocket. "Lieutenant Danforth, these dots," he said, pointing to the ones without lines. "They're all reports of missing kids?"

Lieutenant Danforth nodded. "Yes, and you are?"

"Special Agent Steve Williams." Handshakes were exchanged, and then they turned toward the map, shoulder to shoulder.

Cleary stepped next to Steve. "What do you think?"

Steve sighed, scanning the map. He tapped the missing group of photos that didn't have connecting lines. "We need to find out where these kids were last seen. This UNSUB targets specific locations, crowded and chaotic. But he gets the kids out with no struggle, so I'm thinking the person is dressed as someone these kids trust. A priest, a cop, a fireman, an EMT, a nurse, a security guard. Those are all people kids have been programmed to trust." He paused, looking at the victims. "Are they in the same school system?"

"No, different districts."

"Then a teacher wouldn't make sense." He chewed on his bottom lip and glanced at Lieutenant Danforth. "But I'm not telling you anything you haven't already thought of."

Lieutenant Danforth smiled and shrugged. "You actually threw out a couple of vocations I hadn't thought of. But we ran down the teacher lead and it's a dead end."

Steve returned his gaze to the board. "Do you have the surveillance videos I can look at?"

"Sure." Danforth led Steve into a small computer room and pointed to the discs and folders sitting beside the console. "Have at it."

Steve nodded and plopped the first disc in, scanning for the proper date and time scribbled on the CD holder. He rewound thirty minutes and leaned back to watch. Nothing unusual until a few minutes before the timestamp in the folder. Jody Reece pointed and pulled away from her mother, running down the aisle and out of view of the camera. That was the last time her mother saw her.

Smart bastard knows where the fucking cameras are and how to stay just out of range.

Steve paused the tape and rewound, zooming in on the girl's face. It lit up like a football stadium at night and she pointed, mouthing the words, *Mom look.*

"Huh." Steve grunted.

There were precious few things that could jump-start a kid like that. The first thing that came to mind was a clown, and on the heels of that, a Disney character, neither of which fit the bill. Especially since the parents reported nothing out of the ordinary and both those examples would have been deemed well out of the territory of ordinary in Atlanta.

Another thought popped into his head.

A dog.

"Shit." That was another sure thing that would excite a kid.

Steve scribbled on his notepad all three ideas and popped the disc. The next four victims reacted in the same manner, the excitement and then bolting away toward something. In all cases, the parents smiled at whatever was just out of camera range and moved on.

Steve sat back.

All the parents smiled.

What would a *parent* allow a kid to run toward?

What would *he* allow *his* kid to run toward?

He stopped and rewound the tape a little further, studying all glances in the direction the kids went. Everyone that glanced the way the children went looked either at eye level and then down or the exact opposite.

Steve thought about the first time he saw Chris Ryan with his guide dog. The difference in height between the shepherd and the man's face was almost the same as the difference in each glance.

That narrowed the field down to one thing and one thing only. A dog—and with the abduction locations, he could narrow it further—to a guide dog.

He raised an eyebrow and stood, crossing into the room where his boss sat. "I think I found something." The statement created a wake of silence and all the cops gathered around the desk.

"I believe the UNSUB is using a dog to lure the kids in." He let that hang in the air and from the thoughts radiating from the group, he wasn't telling them anything new.

The nearest officer smirked and glanced away.

"You've got something to say, Officer Gagnon?"

Gagnon shrugged. "No shit, it's noted in the file."

Steve glared at the officer and bit down the reaction to his thoughts, turning to Danforth instead. "Why wasn't that in the notes delivered to us?"

"It should have been," he said, glancing over Steve's shoulder at the officer.

"What else is missing?"

"I'll have to take a look at what was sent and get back to you," Danforth said.

Between his glare and the angry thoughts pervading his mind, Steve knew he was less than thrilled with his subordinates.

"Fine, in the meantime, I'd like to talk to each of the parent's again."

Gagnon exchanged a glance with Danforth and got a nod in return. "I'll take you."

Steve followed Gagnon out of the precinct, slipping into the front passenger seat of the squad car, covering a yawn.

"Y'all want coffee?" Gagnon's Georgian accent came across thicker than it had inside, accompanied by an unspoken hostility.

"Is there a reason you don't like me?"

Gagnon glanced in his direction with a tight jaw. "You feds are all alike—you waltz in and think you know more than us local cops. Like we don't know our ass from our elbow."

"I didn't mean to offend you."

"You didn't think we would ask questions? You figured we were so ass-backwards to not see the excitement in the kid's faces, or the fact that the parents walked away, trusting their kids to a stranger?"

"I'm sorry, but the file that was sent to us was missing some of the key points—like the dog," Steve said. "I'm here to help catch this bastard. I'm on the same team as you are."

Gagnon drew in a breath, exhaling and nodding. This time, when he glanced in Steve's direction, it didn't contain a glare. "I know. It's just... I knew Jody Reece and her family pretty well. Jody was their only child, and telling them their daughter was dead was the hardest thing I've ever done. I can't imagine losing either of my kids." He pulled into the parking lot of the local Starbucks. He wiped his face and sighed. "I know we're on the same team. I'm just frustrated as hell. The bastard seems to be a step ahead of us at every turn."

Steve snorted in agreement. "I've been there before. Hopefully, we can help catch him before the missing kids are killed." He opened the car door and stepped out. "You want something?" He asked, hooking his thumb over his shoulder at the building.

Gagnon hesitated, debating, and then he nodded. "Grande Black, if you don't mind."

Steve ran inside, ordering a double vanilla latte for himself and the Grande Black for Gagnon. He closed his eyes, letting the coffee scent mix with thoughts of strangers. Nothing. He opened his eyes just as the counter clerk handed him the coffee.

The Reece's were cordial and still displayed that southern charm Georgia was famous for, but Steve knew it was a struggle. He didn't have to rely on mind reading. Their eyes were ringed with hollow bruises from lack of sleep and their corneas were surrounded by a web of bright blood vessels signaling tears had recently been shed. Tired didn't truly describe it, more like the walking dead going through the motions of daily life, and he could relate. That's exactly how he had been the first few weeks after the explosion.

"I know this is hard, and I know you already went over this with Officer Gagnon, but I need you to go over it with me. Can you tell me exactly who your daughter ran to see?"

"There was an officer with a dog in training. She ran to see the dog." Mrs. Reece sniffled.

"German Shepherd?"

Mrs. Reece shook her head. "My heavens no, I would never let Jody run up to a German Shepherd. This was a Golden Retriever. I didn't think much of it. We see working dogs all the time."

Steve sat back in the chair and glanced at Gagnon.

"There's a canine training school in the area," Mr. Reece added.

"Can you tell me what the officer looked like?"

Mrs. Reece tilted her head. "I'd say he was about my husband's height. Thin but muscular, with dark hair. I didn't see his eyes because he had sunglasses on."

Steve nodded and stood. "Thank you for your time."

The other conversations were principally the same; a cop with a Golden Retriever in training. The description of the man's hair varied, but the clothing, height, and physique were the same. There was a cop out there, or someone posing as one, who was abducting, torturing, and killing kids.

Sitting in the car after the fifth family, Steve turned to Gagnon. "What's your take on this?"

Gagnon stared out the windshield. "I don't know if it's a cop or just someone pretending to be one. Either way, there are only a handful of us on the force who know this, and we didn't send it in the profile either."

Steve closed his eyes and pinched the bridge of his nose. "Have you started looking at the histories of the officers in the area?"

"Yes, especially those in the canine units, but honestly, there are over a thousand cops in the greater Atlanta area, and it's taking us way too much time."

"Time you don't have."

"Yes, and if it isn't a cop—we're wasting our resources." His sigh filled the car.

"What about the missing kids?"

"We've got a dozen reports, but only two fit the profile. The rest, well, they're more ambiguous, sad stories just the same, but they had nothing to do with our perp. I'm betting those are cases of estranged spouses grabbing the kid or a true runaway that will turn up eventually."

The odds were the two families with similar circumstances would end up with another dot and a line on the map, same signature, same horrific ending unless they could catch him in time. Steve stared at his notes as Gagnon headed back to the station and his skin burned with frustration.

Standing in front of the pictures in the precinct house, Steve whispered, "Talk to me." He slowly looked from one photo to the next. Reaching up, he removed the pictures of those families that didn't fit the profile. The two that Gagnon mentioned remained a nine-year-old boy and an eleven-year-old girl. He moved their photos next to the others and ran his fingertips over the images. André and Katie. He memorized their names, their faces, before turning around.

"How long between abduction and finding the bodies?"

"Usually a week," Danforth answered.

Steve closed his eyes, hanging his head. That gave him two days to save André and another day or two to find Katie. Not enough time, and he knew it.

Sarah stepped close and put her hand on his shoulder.

He turned his troubled gaze to her.

What good is everything Chris gave me if I can't stop the monsters?

Georgia Reign
Chapter 16

SARAH TAPPED HIS HOTEL room door with the back of her knuckles and waited. When he didn't come to the door, she glanced at her watch. It was 7:30, he should be out of bed by now, and she rapped harder.

The chain scraped and then he opened the door, his sleepy gaze meeting hers before he swung the door open and let her in. She watched his bare back and underwear clad ass cross the room toward the bathroom.

"God, how the hell did you sleep on that?" Sarah said, pointing at the mess on his bed. It looked like a hurricane hit with papers scattered over both beds, along with quite a few empty chip bags. Stacked on the nightstand were half a dozen empty soda cans to add to the clutter.

"I was up late." Steve disappeared into the bathroom.

"How late?"

"I don't know—maybe three or four." The answer came from behind the cracked bathroom door. "Give me a couple of minutes."

"What's the plan for today?" She cleared a place at the small table and put the coffee tray down, grabbing hers from the cardboard holder.

The shower went off and Steve stepped into the room wrapped in a towel and rummaged through his suitcase. The sight of his glistening chest brought the blood straight to her cheeks and between her legs, creating a dull throb of wanting. She crossed her legs and quickly glanced away until he pulled out a pair of jeans and a t-shirt.

Sarah raised her eyebrow at the contradiction between her deep-blue tailored suit, with matching high heels and his dungarees, sneakers, and onyx-blue t-shirt. The two-day stubble didn't help either, and she had to remind herself he was married.

Steve ran his hands through his wet hair before straightening up the piles of notes and papers, dropping them into his backpack, along with his wallet, badge, and gun. He slid his glasses on, approaching Sarah, smiling his famous smile, the one that made women do almost anything he asked. "Let's roll," he said, swiping the car keys and remaining coffee cup off the table.

Sarah stared at him, forcing herself to ignore that smile. Instead, she focused on his attire. "You're wearing that?"

Steve looked down at his clothing and back at her. "What's wrong with what I'm wearing?"

Sarah let out a laugh and stood, stepping toward the door. "You don't look like an FBI agent."

"That's the point." Steve slid by her and unlocked the car. "You, on the other hand, stick out like a sore thumb."

Doubt lined her skin, and she adjusted the skirt, smoothing the fabric before speaking. "I look like a federal agent," she said, and he rolled his eyes in her direction.

"Sometimes incognito is better."

"You don't like the suit?"

His glance skimmed her for a moment and then focused back on the road. "The suit is nice, but it screams fed. If you weren't packing, you might pull off corporate executive, but that bulge gives you away." He nodded to her concealed gun. The ride from the hotel was quick, and he pulled up in front of the station. "I'll be back in an hour or so."

Sarah settled back in the seat and turned toward Steve. "Where are we going?"

"*We* aren't going anywhere. I'm checking out the canine training school and I don't want to be made as a cop." He slid his sunglasses down his nose. "With you there, we'd be sunk."

His audacity prickled her skin, and she was tempted to push the issue, but the look in his eyes said otherwise. "We aren't undercover here," she said.

"People have a tendency to talk more if they aren't talking to an FBI agent. Now if you don't mind..." He waved at the door.

Sarah cursed under her breath and nodded. "Fine, but what do I tell Cleary?"

"Tell him I'm fishing around and tell him I'll buy lunch for the precinct when I get back." He flashed a grin and pushed his sunglasses back up, peeling out of the parking lot the moment the passenger door closed.

<hr>

STEVE PULLED INTO THE canine training center and slid out of his car. He surveyed the grounds, raising his eyebrows. There weren't just German Shepherds here, there were black and chocolate labs, Dobermans, Golden Retrievers and Rottweilers all being trained in different capacities. Steve let out a grunt. It wasn't going to be as much of a snap as he'd hoped.

He entered the reception area and slid off his glasses, flashing his Mother Teresa smile. "Hello. My name's Steve Winchester." He extended his hand to the cute receptionist, never missing a beat, even with the alias. "I just moved here from the northeast and I'm looking for some information about the training program. My dog is just a puppy at this point, but I'd like her to be trained to protect my son."

"This isn't an obedience school. We train guide dogs and police dogs," she said.

"I'm not looking for an obedience school, ma'am. I'm looking for the same type of training a police dog would have. My Sadie, she's a little too friendly, and I'd like her to be more vigilant around my son, especially when I'm working."

The receptionist looked up into his blue eyes and sighed. "What kind of dog do y'all have?"

"A Golden Retriever."

She smiled and nodded, picking up the phone. "Bob, I have someone out here who would like to enroll in the police training class."

104

She covered the receiver. "Are you a police officer?"

Steve shook his head.

"No, he isn't. But." She paused, glancing up at Steve. *But he's just so hot!* "But he seems...Okay. I'll tell him." Pouting, she hung up the phone. "Unfortunately, that training class is only open to the members of the force."

Steve let his shoulders slump a little. "I was told this place is the best around. You sure there isn't anything you can do for me?"

"I'm sorry, sir, but the owner is pretty strict about these things." *I tried, believe me, I tried.*

A deep sigh. "Okay, then, do you know of any training or obedience schools that offer a similar program?"

Another shake of her head. "I'm really sorry, sir."

Steve nodded. "I understand. Thank you for your time."

He slid into the car and drove back to the precinct. The information he now had confirmed his suspicions. It definitely was a cop or someone who once was a cop. "Shit."

Cleary grabbed his arm and yanked him into a room, closing the door before he exploded. "You are not an undercover agent anymore. What the hell do you think you're doing, dropping your partner here and taking off?" His voice was loud enough for the officers closest to the door to exchange glances.

"The killer's a cop," Steve whispered.

"You're out of your fucking mind."

Steve shook his head, and instead of speaking aloud, he laid it all out silently. *Look*

Ron, there are a handful of cops in this precinct who know the full details of the case. They suspect it's a cop and all the parents confirmed it was a man dressed as a cop with a dog in training. I just came back from the canine training school, and they only offer training to members of the force. Now, it could be a civilian posing as a cop, someone who stole the training school insignia. But my gut tells me otherwise. We only have a couple of days before the body of André Lucas will be dropped somewhere. I'd like to say I can find him before then, but I can't guarantee it. I can't even guarantee I'll be able to nail the bastard before the last victim is recovered. If I can't, I'm betting the son of a bitch will change his M.O. I don't want the cop-dog angle released to the press just yet. It will create a panic and the police will not be able to do their jobs. If the UNSUB changes M.O. then it is a cop with inside information.

Cleary sat down hard at the desk, his jaw askew and eyes wide. "Jack, uh, Jack never, uh, mentioned this to me."

"Jack never knew. This is a fairly new development, sir." Steve took a seat. "And it isn't foolproof." He looked down at his hands and shrugged.

Cleary was dumbfounded, his mind racing over all his thoughts about this kid since he pulled him out of the police cell in Torrington.

"Yes, I heard it all," Steve said, offering a crooked smile to his supervisor. "And yeah, I actually am an arrogant asshole most of the time."

Cleary raised his eyebrows and started chuckling.

"I was a good investigator before this," he waved at his head.

"According to Jack, you were brilliant."

Steve rolled his eyes. "Not really." He picked at the hangnail on his thumb. "I didn't figure out Kyle was alive until it was too late." He raised his gaze to his boss. "And if I'd had this..." he trailed off and shrugged.

Cleary leaned forward on the desk. "I don't think it would have made a hoot of difference. You still wouldn't have put that gun down."

Steve inhaled. "If I'd had this, I would have known he was there waiting for me, and I would have taken him out the second I walked in the door."

Cleary leaned back in the seat. "I have to say, I don't know if I could have done what you did in that warehouse. You did the right thing, and while I think you're arrogant, I also respect your integrity."

Steve felt his cheeks warming at Cleary's comment. Integrity. Jennifer would scoff at that. For a moment, his skin broke out in gooseflesh and a shiver itched the base of his spine, forewarning him that the dark days had just begun.

"So, when did you develop this, this?" Cleary waved at Steve. "This talent?"

"I don't know, sir. After the explosion," he said, glazing over the truth. "I don't know how or why, but it just happened. You know my wife's clairvoyant, right?" He changed the subject from his present talents, pushing the spotlight to her.

"Jack mentioned that." He didn't know what to make of his star agent, but he was damn glad to have him onboard.

"Do I have the latitude to act if I hear something?" Steve needed to know, because if they wanted to follow protocol to the tee, he'd have to get reasonable proof before taking any action.

Cleary was old school, but this case razzed him as much as seeing his oldest friend gutted in a hotel room. He slowly nodded. "Yes, but report to me before you do anything, so I can pave the way."

"Thanks." Steve stood. "Also, if I'm going to remain inconspicuous, Sarah has to stop dressing the way she is."

A smirk appeared on Cleary's lips, and he bit back an inappropriate comment. "I'll talk to her."

Steve smiled. His boss thought she looked damn fine in the suit. "Thanks." He stood and wandered into the pit, poking Sarah in the side from behind. "Hey there, sweet thang," he drawled in her ear in the perfect southern accent.

"I'm telling your wife." Sarah turned her head in his direction.

Steve's laughter shattered the low murmurs in the room. "Sorry I was late, guys. I had a small errand to run." He took a seat at the table and scanned the officers.

"Gagnon was just filling us in on yesterday's interviews. He said you didn't uncover anything beyond what we already knew," Danforth said. "And considering the latest abductions, I think we need to let the public know the perp may be using a dog to lure the kids away from their parents."

Steve traded a glance with Officer Gagnon. He hadn't informed his superior of the cop angle, and Steve wondered why. "Do you think that's wise?"

Lieutenant Danforth tilted his head. "Excuse me, but this is my case, and I think the public has a right to know."

The room was quiet, all eyes shifting from Steve to Lieutenant Danforth, waiting for the next card to be played.

"We are not sure that the dog owner *is* the UNSUB. If he is, releasing the information will force him to change tactics, and then we're back to square one." He folded his arms, glancing at Sarah.

"He has a point." Sarah backed him just as Cleary stepped into the room.

"What you could say is that right now we're looking at every avenue to find those kids, even canvassing witnesses for information that could lead us to the killer. We haven't been able to track down everyone, so if you have any information regarding a witness with a Golden Retriever working dog, or anyone who was at X between Y and Z, please contact us. That way, it isn't a red flag, per se," Steve said.

"I agree with Agent Williams. We shouldn't release the specific information just yet. We have a modus operandi for this bastard. I say we use it to our advantage," Cleary said.

Lieutenant Danforth inhaled. All eyes swung in his direction. "Okay," he agreed. "But so help me god, if another child is taken and we could have prevented it..." He pointed his index finger at Steve, the rest of his fingers curled so tight that his knuckles turned white.

"I want to catch the bastard before he finishes off those two kids." Steve pointed toward the pictures of André and Katie. He looked at the wall and knew he might already be too late.

Silence filled the room as he filtered through the thoughts of everyone present. Only a couple of the officers were unreadable, Danforth and Gagnon included. He needed to pull Gagnon aside and find out why he hadn't informed his superior of the complete set of facts. His gaze drifted over the timeline again, particularly the overlapping timelines.

"He's got to have a pretty sizeable area."

"What?"

Steve slid his chair out and walked to the timeline. "He's got two or three kids at a time." He pointed at the board. "So, the area he keeps them has to be pretty big and with what he's doing to them, it would have to be pretty remote. Those kids are screaming." His voice cracked. "And no one can hear them."

Georgia Reign
Chapter 17

STEVE STOOD AT THE entrance to the alley. His jaw clamped shut, his eyes scanning the carnage. His fists clenched and unclenched methodically as he attempted to rein in the anger.

Katie's remains had been scattered through the alley like a fisherman would throw chum to attract sharks. Her head had been propped on the dumpster with a mocking grin stitched in place.

André was still missing, which meant they just hadn't found him yet or the UNSUB was having more fun torturing him than this poor girl. The coroner's report said she likely died due to shock from the multiple dismemberments prior to having her head surgically removed.

Steve wanted to smash something. The fury built inside along with the power, shaking his frame. He turned and stormed away, leaving before the power escaped.

He had to stop this bastard.

His mind whirled, and he studied the blades of grass covering the pristine park in front of them. Suddenly, his head shot up.

He needed bait, and he had just the right boy in mind.

Don't you dare. The voice that had been silent since he left Maine piped in.

Steve ignored his guardian angel and flipped open his phone, making flight arrangements home, and then back with company. He turned as Sarah approached. "I've got to take a quick trip back home."

"Is everything all right?"

"Everything is fine." He looked around. "I've got an idea, and I need to go home to get the ball rolling." He leveled his gaze.

"What ball?" Sarah shifted, the dread at his next words visible in her gaze.

"Bait."

The line between Sarah's eyes deepened. "Steve, our UNSUB is going after kids."

He nodded, and a grin formed. "There's only one kid I'd put in harm's way and that's because he's more dangerous than this bastard."

It still didn't connect, and she tilted her head.

"CJ Ryan."

Sarah actually stepped back. Her eyebrows shot up and her mouth opened. "Nuh-uh." She shook her head. "No way."

"Look…"

"—No way, Steve. We can't use a kid to trap a killer. That isn't right."

No fucking way! Chris's voice echoed her sentiments.

"CJ won't get hurt. Trust me." Steve stepped toward his car and Sarah grabbed his arm.

"That's irresponsible," she hissed. "He's just a kid."

"He's a kid who has ten times the powers that I have. If this bastard grabs him, he's a dead man."

"You can't..."

"I can, and I'll bet he'll be more than willing to help me catch this guy."

"He might be, but I'm sure his mother won't let him."

"She won't have a choice." *I think it's a cop, Sarah, so you can't utter a word.* He leveled his gaze at her and stood with the car door open. *I'll be back tonight, with both CJ and Jennifer.*

"Jennifer?"

He cut her off. "Not a word." He slipped into the car, hightailing it to the airport. As he sat waiting for the plane to board, he flipped his phone open. "Jen, are you at your folks' house?"

"Yes, why?"

"Because I have an idea on how to catch this guy, and I need your help."

"I don't know..."

"Please Jen, this guy's carving up kids. I need to catch him before he kills another one."

"Why do you need me?"

"I need you to pose as CJ's mother."

Silence met his comment, and he waited. Her mind completely blanked.

"CJ?"

"CJ Ryan."

Her gasp came through the phone line and her thoughts bloomed, running in circles between he's a child and he's dangerous.

"If we're lucky, CJ can help me catch this son of a bitch." The call for boarding interrupted the conversation and Steve opened his eyes to the Atlanta airport. "I've got to go, the plane's boarding. I'll let you know where we're flying from when I land. Okay?"

"I don't know Steve."

"I'm going to see if Ted can fly us back tonight."

"Ted?"

"My friend from Yale. He owns a private charter company. He's the one who flew me to New York when I was looking for Kyle."

Her flinch at the mere mention of his name came through the line in a sharp inhale and she didn't speak. Her thoughts snapped to her father's words—that Steve used people to get what he wanted, and she would be better off without him.

"I'll call you when I land. Please consider it." He flipped the phone closed. Her last thought burned him, and the leather first-class seats didn't alleviate his aggravation.

Before they taxied out on the runway, he scrolled through his address book and found Ted Beaumont's phone number.

"Good morning, Beaumont Travel, Ted speaking."

"Just the man I was looking for."

"Steve?"

"A-yup. What are you doing this evening?"

"Having dinner with the family. Why?"

"I'd like to hire you to fly me and a couple of guests to Atlanta."

Ted laughed. "On your salary?"

"Dude, I could buy your entire business with cash to spare."

"You win the lottery or something?"

"Something like that. Are you available?"

Silence and shuffling paper filled the line, and Steve waited.

"Is this something like New York?"

"No, this is legit, and you'll get to meet the wife this time. She's coming down to visit while I'm on a job."

"The earliest I can take off is eight. Will that work?"

"Perfect. I'll meet you in Ellington, right?"

"Actually, can you meet me at Brainard—we've got a hangar there now. I'll text the address."

"Will do."

"Don't you want to know how much the different options cost?"

"Whatever option will get us there the fastest is what I want."

"I can get you there an hour from lift-off, but that's pricey."

"I'm not worried about the cost, Ted. Just text it along with the address, and I'll have a check for you when I get there."

"Damn, you really won the lottery, didn't you?"

Steve was quiet and sighed. "No. Inheritance."

The word hung in the air, and Steve could hear Ted's stammering thoughts. "Your parents?"

"Yeah. That and a victim's fund."

"Jesus."

"He had nothing to do with it."

More silence. "You can fill me in tonight."

"Will do. I'll see you at eight." He folded the phone closed and leaned back in the plush seat, wishing this leg of his trip would only be an hour. Unfortunately, commercial airlines didn't run as fast as a G6.

Georgia Reign
Chapter 18

STEVE PULLED UP TO the Ryan's house and stared at the touchpad, suppressing the urge to just press the buttons and let himself in. This wasn't his home, and he had no right to enter at will. Instead, he pressed the buzzer and waited.

"Hello?" Her voice sounded frail.

"Mrs. Ryan. This is Steve Williams. I need to talk to you."

The gate opened and before the car was in park, CJ flew out the door, sliding to a stop on the gravel near the front of the car with a duffel bag already slung over his shoulder.

"I'm going with you," he said, his breath taxed from his mini-sprint.

The passion in his gaze gave Steve pause, and he raised his eyebrows. "It's dangerous, CJ."

"I don't care. I can help."

"And what does your mother think?" Steve glanced up at Jessica standing in the doorway, her eyebrows creased, her expression questioning.

"I, uh..." CJ glanced over his shoulder. "I didn't tell her anything."

"I need to get your mother's permission."

"Permission for what?" Jessica asked.

"I need CJ to help me with a case in Atlanta."

"Excuse me?" Jessica stepped onto the front stoop.

CJ spun on his heels. "I can help the police, Mom."

"CJ, let me talk to your mother," Steve interrupted the pending argument. "Go play with your brother while I talk to her, okay?"

CJ met his gaze and nodded, running off to find Tommy in the backyard.

Steve crossed the walkway to the front door, where Jessica stood. White streaks in her hair now starkly contrasted the natural, deep brown strands. Deepened wrinkles framed her eyes and clear laugh lines now broke the perfect skin of her face. Her eyes, still vibrant calico, showed signs of exhaustion in the deep, dark craters surrounding them.

"Mrs. Ryan, I need CJ's help," he started, and she put up her hand, shaking her head.

"You said that. Explain exactly what you need him for."

Steve opened his mouth and closed it, framing what he wanted to say in his mind before he spoke. "I need CJ to draw out a suspect."

"He's nine."

"Yes." He let his answer hang in the air as Jessica studied him.

"How can a nine-year-old help you?"

Steve exhaled and looked up at the house before bringing his gaze back to her. "It's a long shot." He shifted. "CJ is the right demographic for our UNSUB."

"What exactly is your UNSUB doing?"

"Practicing surgery on kidnapped kids."

Jessica stepped back, her hands flying to her mouth and her eyes widening at the implications. "And you want to use my son as bait?" The horror in her expression bled into her words.

"Yes."

"Not on your life," she said, and stepped farther into the house, her face transforming into a mask of anger.

Before she could slam the door in his face, Steve stopped her with a mental wall, holding her in place until he'd said his peace. "I need him."

"Like you needed Chris?"

"No. I need him to stop this killer and we both know CJ can take care of himself. If this works, he's got the power to hold the UNSUB in place and act like a human GPS until I can get there. CJ is my best chance of catching this guy before another child dies."

Jessica's eyes glazed with tears, and she blinked them back, her face tight and unreadable as her mind.

"CJ will be just fine."

"No."

Steve didn't want to resort to this, but he stepped forward, crowding her, staring down into her stubborn features. "Yes," he said, his voice nothing more than a whisper, but the will behind it was as strong as an iron sledgehammer.

Jessica blinked, her eyes narrowing in suspicion as the word 'yes' escaped her lips.

You bastard. Chris's voice echoed in Steve's head, angry and righteous, and in concert with Jessica's single thought.

"If you take him, I'll have you arrested for kidnapping."

Her penetrating glare prickled his skin, bringing his own anger to the surface and his hands balled in response. He closed his eyes for a moment, reigning in the power. When he opened them, she flinched, and Steve stepped closer. "Do you really want to mess with me?"

She shook her head. "But I'm not letting my son step into the line of fire. Not after what happened with Chris."

"I'll be fine, Mom," CJ said from behind Steve, his voice brittle and on edge, breaking the battle of wills.

Steve stepped back, giving Jessica space and wondering what, if anything, CJ would do to him for trying to coerce his mother.

"I'm afraid something bad is going to happen," Jessica said, addressing CJ.

"Something bad is already happening, Mrs. Ryan. This guy carves the kids up, piece by piece. He kills them slowly, and we can stop him."

Jessica shook her head. "You're not invincible."

"I know that."

"Neither is CJ."

"He's less likely to get hurt than I am, and you know it." Steve inhaled. "We can stop this guy!"

Jessica didn't like it. She didn't like it one bit and the echoes of her thoughts penetrated Steve's like a fist pummeling a punching bag. There was only one thing to do that could turn the tide. He had to make a promise, and a promise for Steve was like the seven seals of God. If broken, all hell would break loose, and he wouldn't allow that. "I promise, nothing will happen to CJ, and you know I never break my promises."

She inhaled through tight lips. "You promise nothing will happen to my son?"

"I promise," Steve said.

She looked beyond Steve and then brought her gaze back. "Okay. Let me throw some things together."

Steve held his hand up. "No. I'm not bringing you and Tommy down there with us. I can't guarantee your safety."

Jessica balked. "Who's going to watch him?"

"Jennifer."

Jessica looked at the empty car in the driveway. "She's not in the car."

"No, I'm meeting her at Brainard Airport for an eight o'clock flight."

"What about school?"

"You can have the school email the lesson plans to me and I'll have Jennifer go over them with him."

"Mom, let me help," CJ said.

With all arguments exhausted, she looked at Steve and her son and gave a nod. "So help me, Steve, if anything happens to him, I'll skin you alive."

"I promise, nothing will happen to CJ." Steve repeated, and reached in his pocket and pulled out his card, scribbling a couple of numbers on the back. "I'm giving you Jennifer's cell as well as Sarah's, so you can get a hold of us at any time."

Jessica took the card and slid it into her pocket before she crossed to CJ and gave him a hug. "Are you sure?" Steve couldn't see her expression, but he could feel the worry filling the air.

"Yes, I'm sure." CJ traded a glance with Steve.

Tommy came running around the corner of the house and he stopped in the driveway, his eyes drifting between the three of them and falling on a spot behind Steve. The smile on his face faded. His gaze snapped to Steve. "Dad is pissed."

"Thomas Patrick!" Jessica said, releasing CJ from her arms and standing.

"Well, he is," Tommy said, his hand waving toward the ghost only he could see.

"I don't want to hear you using that kind of language again."

A blush crept into Tommy's cheeks, and he turned his attention to his brother. "You're going on a trip?"

"Yep," CJ grinned. He pulled the duffel bag back on his shoulder.

"Can I come?"

"No." Both Steve and Jessica said in unison.

"Not this time," Steve added after trading glances with CJ. "But I promise I'll take you someplace special when we get back. Okay?"

Tommy shifted his eyes back and forth between Steve and the empty space behind him, and then nodded. He walked to his brother and gave him a hug. "See you when I see you." He broke the grip, crossing to stand next to his mother.

Steve opened the trunk and took CJ's duffel bag. "You sure you have everything you need?"

"Yes."

"Toothbrush?"

"Yep, underwear, too, and I brought my DSI." He pulled the handheld game console out of his pocket.

"His bedtime is at nine," Jessica said from the lawn.

"He'll be in the hotel and tucked into bed tonight by nine-thirty." Steve opened the back door for CJ. "I've got a friend who's flying us by private charter," he said to her raised eyebrow.

"Ah," she said. She still wasn't a hundred percent on board. Her eyes drifted to her son in the back seat and sent him a reassuring smile. "Keep him safe, Agent Williams."

"I will." Steve slid into the driver's seat and spun the car around, heading for Connecticut and another woman who needed convincing.

Georgia Reign
Chapter 19

CJ WATCHED THE SCENERY pass, his stomach a jumble of nerve endings and, despite how hard he tried, he couldn't focus on the Pokémon game in his hands. Instead, he focused on Steve and his silent concentration in the front seat.

Steve sighed and glanced in the rearview mirror. "Maybe this wasn't such a good idea."

"I'll be okay, Agent Williams."

"Are you so sure it's going to be okay?"

CJ stared at Steve, opened his mouth to speak, and then closed it, shaking his head.

"Do you know what we are going after?"

"A monster," CJ said without hesitation.

"He's hurting kids around your age."

Yep, and you're bringing my son into the lion's den. His father's voice echoed in Steve's thoughts, driving the loss deeper in CJ. Tommy could see their father and Steve could hear him, but he couldn't do either, and that aggravated him.

"And your father isn't happy with me at all for bringing you with me."

"I know. Sucks to be you," CJ said.

Steve met his gaze, and wrinkles of humor formed around his eyes in the rearview mirror. A soft chuckle erupted from the front seat. "It certainly does."

THE KID DIDN'T KNOW the half of it. He not only had to deal with a pissed off angel, now he had to face Jennifer's father, which always provided for a good dose of tension and with his temper frayed by the situation in Georgia, he hoped like hell he would be able to keep it in check. Steve sighed and focused back on the road. "So, what are you doing in school these days?"

"Learning cursive, estimating math problems, and studying King Arthur. Cool stuff like that."

"You like school?"

"Yeah, but sometimes it's boring."

"What's your favorite subject?" Steve remembered his favorite subject in grade school was gym.

"I like science. Learning about the weather and the solar system is fun, and they let us play on the computer too."

Steve smiled. If CJ was anything like his father, he'd be a wiz with technology. "I assume you're getting straight A's in all your classes."

CJ nodded at him in the rearview mirror. "Tommy doesn't get all A's, though. He has a harder time in school than I do."

"Think you'll be a genius like your dad?"

"I dunno." CJ looked out the window.

Sadness shrouded his features and Steve felt a pang of guilt for bringing the subject up. "I'm sorry, CJ."

CJ brought his gaze back to meet Steve's. His eyes glimmered with tears.

Steve sent a small smile back to the boy. "I know how it feels. I lost my dad, too." All he got was a nod in response and static from the back seat. CJ had closed down on him for the time being.

He flipped on the radio and when they passed from Interstate 95 to Interstate 495; he took a quick glance in the mirror. CJ was sound asleep and slumped against the door.

Steve sang softly to the tunes as they shuffled on the radio and before he knew it, he was cruising over the Charter Oak Bridge, glancing at the Hartford skyline. A little over an hour later, he pulled off the Merritt parkway in New Canaan.

CJ hadn't stirred during the ride and now, with the slowing of the car, he uttered a moan from the backseat. "My leg!"

"We're almost there," Steve said, glancing at the boy's grimace in the rearview mirror. The sleepy whine continued, and CJ shifted in the seat, his discomfort palatable in the stale air of the car. "Your leg fell asleep?"

CJ nodded, rubbing the sleep from his eyes. "It hurts."

"Keep moving it. It'll get better." Steve focused back on the road. The whine in CJ's voice brought home the fact that he was walking a kid into the devil's lair. The closer he got, the more he questioned his plan, and he was sure Jennifer would be just as critical.

Pulling into his in-law's driveway, he braced himself for an unpleasant interrogation. With the keys in his pocket, he slid out of the car and held the back door for CJ. Steve shrugged at his questioning gaze. "My father-in-law doesn't like me," he said.

CJ had the wherewithal not to say a word, but a smirk appeared for a brief instant, and he fell in step behind Steve.

JENNIFER HEARD THE CAR followed by Steve's jumbled thoughts and she strode to the door, opening it before Steve's knuckles rapped the mahogany. The sight of CJ standing next to him caught her off guard and her gaze bounced from the boy back to Steve's bright blue eyes. "I really didn't think you'd go through with this." Her voice carried with it the disappointment etched into her bones.

"I wanted to come," CJ said.

Steve put his hand on CJ's head. "CJ, I appreciate the thought, but I'm already in the doghouse with my wife and you can't fix it. Now, let's go see what we can drum up for you to eat." He scooted around her, leading CJ through the house and into the kitchen.

Jennifer saw the tightness in his shoulders relax with the absence of her father's sarcastic wisecrack and Steve glanced over his shoulder at her.

"Where are your folks?"

"At the club. Dad had a tee-time and Mom has bridge. I told them I might not be here when they got back."

"Might?" Steve set his jaw in that arrogant 'might, my ass' fashion and pulled a couple of slices of bread from the bread drawer. "Peanut butter and jelly?" he asked CJ.

"Yes, please," CJ answered and took a seat at the table.

Jennifer observed the dynamics between her husband and CJ, seeing an undertone of respect layered between them. She waited until the sandwich and a glass of milk were set on the table before she pulled Steve aside. "I don't know, Steve," she said, not wanting to be party to this insanity.

"Jen, I need you there."

"You're still using people to get what you want."

Steve rolled his eyes and sent a glare in her direction.

Instant irritation stung her tongue, and she snapped. "Don't you even think about giving me the evil eye?"

He blinked, opening his mouth to deny it, but she caught the look and his cheeks bloomed blotchy red. He snapped his mouth closed and took a breath through his nose. "CJ knows the plan. He knows what I'm asking of him and while I agree, it's not the best idea I've ever had. It's the only one I can see resolving this case before the latest kidnapped child dies. If dangling him as a carrot leads us to this psycho…"

"—You are insane. What do you think his father is going to say?"

"He hates the idea. And since when are you concerned with what Chris Ryan has to say?"

"I talked to him after you left for Georgia."

Steve took a fraction of a step back. "Where?"

She hated to admit it, but the dark angel she spoke to wasn't what she expected. He neither oozed evil nor did he grow horns, and when she touched his chest, all that flowed through her was love and a visceral attraction. "The cove, and he's not half bad."

Steve's eyes hardened, and his lips pressed tight together. "I'm not sure I like you chatting it up with him, even if he is just a ghost."

Her eyebrows rose at the stubborn hint of jealousy radiating from him.

I'm not sure I like you taking my son to Georgia.

Chris Ryan's voice reverberated in Steve's head, broadcasting loud and clear, and Jennifer's gaze shot to CJ. The boy had his sandwich frozen halfway to his mouth and his wide blue eyes locked on Steve.

CJ's eyebrows shot up and he cocked his head, a smile gaining traction. "Sucks to be you." He went back to his sandwich before the chuckle erupted from Steve.

When Steve brought his gaze back to hers, her heart skipped at the underlying humor reflected in his bright blue eyes. It had been a while since she saw that twinkle and her skin flushed with the memory. She turned away before he caught the nuance in her eyes.

"So, are you coming?"

That was the question she'd tossed around ever since he called. She wasn't ready to step back into the marriage, not yet, not with the issues plaguing her.

"I'm not staying at the hotel with you. You'll be sharing a suite with CJ," Steve said, his voice going cold and flat, just like the spark in his eyes.

"Oh. I just assumed."

"You assumed wrong." Steve glanced at the clock and then back at her, his eyes now dark and stormy, like he knew exactly what she had been thinking.

His mind was unreadable. So was CJ's, and that irked her. *You know what I'm thinking and yet you won't let me into your head?*

Steve huffed and turned away. "I'm not playing games, Jen."

"Neither am I. You can pull sh..." Her gaze slid to CJ. "Stuff from my head, but you've got a mountain of a wall erected between us."

"CJ, why don't you go into the family room and watch a little television?" Steve took the empty plate from the table, depositing it into the dishwasher. He waited until the television was on and sounds of a cartoon filled the house before he turned back to Jennifer. "You're the one who built that wall, Jen. You're the one who doesn't want me around. Do you even love me anymore?"

Jennifer stepped back, distancing herself from his venom. Her mind scrambled for an answer. Yes, she loved him, but she couldn't stand anyone touching her. Not after what Kyle did, and she couldn't bring herself to speak the words, not to Steve. That would be akin to admitting Kyle won and she would rather die. Instead, she changed the subject. "What time's the flight?"

"Eight. We're meeting Ted at Brainard." He stared at her, waiting with the expression she knew too well.

She ran her hand through her hair and glanced toward the family room. "It's not you, Steve. I've got a lot of shit to deal with and I can't do this right now."

"I'm your husband. Please let me help. I know a thing or two about the effects of rape, so I understand your aversion to physical contact, and I saw the videos. I know what Kyle made you do. I know how different it was from what happened at Brooksfield U. I'm sure being at the cabin didn't help. And we don't have to go back until the new house is built. Okay?"

His words struck her like a slap upside the head, bringing stinging tears to her eyes and blurring her vision. He knew, and that's why this was so hard.

"But I need to know. I need to know if you still love me." His voice cracked, and his eyes shined with tears. "Do you?"

Her chin quivered, and she swore under her breath. She didn't want to break down in front of him, and the dam was threatening to burst at the vulnerability in his eyes, at the pleading she heard in his mind. With her voice locked in her chest, she nodded ascent and accepted his warm hug.

RELIEF FLOODED THROUGH HIM, and he pulled her into his arms as tears spilled over her wet lashes and he felt his own track down his cheeks. The walls he erected to safeguard his heart from breaking crumbled, and he kissed the top of her head.

"I'll be patient. I promise," he whispered.

She raised her tear-stained face from his chest and nodded. "Thank you."

"We'll get through this." He took a deep breath. "Now, about Atlanta."

"I'm still not sure it's a good idea, but if you need me there, I'll be there."

He smiled. "I'm not sure it's a good idea either, but I think CJ can hold his own. The tricky thing will be to get the UNSUB to take the bait. There's no way to guarantee that at all."

"You're that desperate?"

"Yes, I am." The admission burned his throat more than the tears. "I told CJ he just has to hold him until I can get there."

"And what if he can't? What if his only recourse is killing?"

Steve shook his head. "CJ can hold anything in place for as long as he wants." He glanced up at the doorway where CJ now stood. "Right?"

CJ nodded. "Yes. I know what I'm getting into, Mrs. Williams."

Jennifer turned toward the boy. "Please, call me Jennifer. Mrs. Williams makes me feel so old."

"Actually, you're going to have to get used to calling her mom in public. That's the cover."

Without missing a beat, CJ turned to Jennifer. "I'll be just fine, Mom." The tone screamed exasperation, with just the right mix of embarrassment, and he added an eye roll for good measure. He looked at Steve. "Like that?"

Amusement laced Steve's tongue, and he suppressed the chuckle that bubbled at the base of his throat. "Yeah, like that." He grinned and slid his glance sideways toward Jennifer. The same level of humor graced her expression and when their gaze met, she flashed a full-on smile in his direction, stealing his breath away.

Georgia Reign
Chapter 20

THEY PULLED INTO THE airport and parked in an assigned spot in the VIP lot. Steve glanced at Jennifer in the passenger seat and offered a strained smile. The light humor found earlier in the day had all but evaporated and in its place came angst on both their parts. She had never seen Steve so ambivalent about a course of action he put in effect, and it did nothing to settle her nerves.

Without further ado, he stepped out of the car and retrieved the bags from the trunk.

"This is an airport?" CJ asked, looking at the diminutive building.

"Yes. It's a private airport, so it's a lot smaller than the public ones like Logan Airport up in Boston."

"Oh." CJ glanced between Steve and Jennifer.

"I've never been on a private plane either," Jennifer said. All she could envision was a junky little twin prop with duct tape holding the wings together. She tried on a smile, but the nervous tick in her cheek gave away her discomfort.

Steve glanced in her direction, picking up her unrest. "Don't worry, hon, this isn't a little puddle jumper. It's a high-end corporate jet. You'll understand when we board."

The three of them walked into the terminal and approached the check-in counter. The receptionist smiled and before he could introduce himself, a voice echoed across the empty lounge area.

"Steve!"

Jennifer turned toward the voice in time to see a voluptuous red head crossing the lobby toward them. A smile lit up Steve's face and shock, along with a vein of jealousy, wound through her stomach like a serpent eyeing their quarry.

"Heather, I didn't know you were coming." He accepted the enthusiastic hug before introducing Jennifer and CJ. "This is my wife Jennifer and a friend of the family, CJ Ryan. Guys, this is Heather Beaumont."

Jennifer extended her hand. "Nice to meet you," she said, her voice layered with snark, especially with the complete adoration Heather shined on her husband.

Steve cast a quick glare in her direction.

Ease up. His voice echoed in her head, and she swallowed the green-eyed demon, taking a mental step back to study the dynamics.

Steve turned to Heather. "Is Ted gassing up?"

"Yes, I figured you wouldn't mind me tagging along. It's been way too long, and I didn't get to go the last time you two went on an adventure."

Jennifer cocked her head. *And when exactly was that?*

"New York," Steve answered her unspoken question. *Before Kyle attacked you.*

Heat drained from her cheeks at the mention of his name, and she gave a nod of acknowledgement. Another reminder of what that bastard did to her life, and she closed down, putting another layer of bricks around her heart, retreating farther into her shell.

CJ reached out and took her hand, offering her a small smile of support. She looked between their clasped hands and his bright blue eyes. Eyes that could see into her soul. Eyes just like his father's.

A lump formed in her throat, and she inhaled, smiling and blinking back the tears clouding her vision. The sweet gesture suspended her retreat for the moment.

"Should we head out?" Steve asked, shifting the duffel bag on his shoulder.

Heather nodded, and they followed her out on the tarmac where the sleek Gulfstream 650 sat.

Steve whistled at the sharp jet and Jennifer's first impression was one of awe. Her attention pulled away from the pristine plane toward a tall man clad in jeans and donning a Red Sox cap striding in their direction.

"I see you got a new toy," Steve said, sticking his hand out to the man. After a handshake and a pseudo hug, Steve turned to Jennifer. "Jen, this is Ted Beaumont. Ted, this is Jennifer."

Ted smiled and stuck his hand out. "Pleasure to finally meet you." His grip was warm and firm, much like the smile on his lips.

"Same here," Jennifer said.

"And this is CJ; he's a friend of the family."

"Hi, CJ. When we reach cruising altitude, would you like to sit with me in the cockpit?"

CJ's eyes widened, and Jennifer thought they'd just about pop out of his head, pulling a genuine smile from her heart. This man knew how to awe his audience, especially the younger set.

"Can I?" The question was aimed at Steve.

"Of course."

"Cool!" CJ broke the grip on Jennifer's hand and vaulted up the steps, disappearing into the fuselage.

Steve pulled out his wallet and handed Ted a check. "That should cover it."

Without a glance, Ted pocketed the money and waved toward the plane. "After you."

Jennifer climbed the steps, curious to see the inside, but when she stepped through the door, her breath was stolen away. Plush leather seats and shiny granite-like tables graced the interior. "Wow."

CJ had thrown himself on the couch and lay on his back staring at the ceiling, an awed smile plastered on his lips.

"Told you it wasn't a puddle jumper," Steve whispered in her ear and hauled the bags to the holding bay in the back.

"The refrigerator is stocked with both soda and beer if you'd like, and I've got a few snack type things in the cabinet." Ted closed and locked the outer door.

Heather scooted into the cockpit taking the co-pilot seat.

"Relax and enjoy the ride." Ted nodded and disappeared into the cockpit.

"CJ, come over here and put on a seatbelt until we're up in the air." Steve pointed to a chair in the group of seats where Jennifer sat. Steve took a seat on the opposite side, facing them.

"I could get used to this," Jennifer said. Her fingers traced the soft leather as the plane taxied onto the runway.

"I told Ted I'd call when we were ready to head back."

"Really?"

"Yep, especially now that my car is at Brainard." He grinned.

The smile warmed her heart, and the heat built in her cheeks. She looked away before he caught the blush, focusing on the diminishing ground as the plane accelerated, climbing higher into the sky.

As soon as they reached cruising speed, Heather came back into the main cabin. "If you'd like to go up in the cockpit, Ted said right now would be a good time." She smiled at CJ and his seatbelt was off and he disappeared within a blink.

Jennifer watched him go before bringing her gaze to Heather as the woman took the seat next to Steve and gave his knee a pat. The gesture struck her as overly friendly, and she cocked her head, sending a questioning glance in his direction.

STEVE CAUGHT THE LOOK in Jennifer's eyes and had to press his lips together against the smirk. Jealousy was written all over her face and he turned to Heather, ignoring Jennifer's quizzical expression. "So, how are the kids?"

Heather dug out a small wallet from her pocket and pulled out the latest Christmas photo, handing it to Steve. "They keep us on our toes."

"How old are they now?" Steve asked, studying the happy family of four before handing the picture to Jennifer. A twinge of sorrow bit at the edges of his heart, creating a dull ache in his chest. He should have had a family of four right now, but the gods had a different plan for him. He swallowed the bitter thought, forcing a smile to his lips for Heather.

"Jeremy is four, and Kiley's two. I'm trying to talk Ted into another one, but you know how he is."

"You've got a beautiful family." Jennifer handed the photo back to Heather.

Steve saw the same melancholy in her eyes that he felt. It caressed his nerve endings, lining the back of his throat with burning tears, and he had to look away. The clouds passed like giant cotton balls and after he was sure his eyes wouldn't betray his thoughts; he turned and met her gaze with a half-hearted smile.

Heather tucked the picture back into her wallet and slipped it in her pocket. "So, you're babysitting for a friend?" she asked, hooking her thumb toward the cockpit.

"Yeah, you could say that."

Heather raised an eyebrow and traded a glance with Jennifer before focusing back on Steve. "He's not part of your latest case, is he?"

Steve grinned and rolled his eyes. "No. If you hadn't noticed, he's just a kid."

Heather shrugged. "Yeah, well, I know you. You'll do almost anything to crack a case, and Ted said you're working."

Steve didn't answer. The comment wasn't meant as a dig, but it still didn't settle quite right under his skin. He unhooked his seatbelt. "On that note, I better check up on CJ."

"I didn't mean…"

"—Don't worry about it, Heather. I know you didn't mean anything by it." Steve stood and shuffled toward the cockpit, wondering if Jennifer would talk to Heather or just sulk in the chair, looking out at the clouds.

"I REALLY DIDN'T MEAN to offend him," Heather said.

"Yeah, well, you certainly called it right. He'll do anything to catch this one." Her discomfort with the situation resounded in her words and Heather's head cocked to the side.

"He isn't thinking about…"

"Using CJ?" Jennifer finished her sentence and shrugged. "I'm not entirely sure whether he really will, but CJ has certain gifts that could help with the case."

"Really?" Heather perked up, and Jennifer caught her sense of intrigue.

Jennifer nodded but didn't elaborate. "So, tell me a little about how you and Steve met?" The question brought a flurry of activity in Heather's mind, feeding Jennifer with details of her assault and Steve's heroic save.

"He was assigned to a case at Yale. At the time, I didn't know he was with the FBI. I thought he was just another arrogant law student who happened to be roommates with my boyfriend. I'm damn glad he turned out to be a cop and a smart one at that. Steve figured out who was attacking women on campus and caught him before he had a chance to rape me."

Jennifer nodded, wishing he had figured things out earlier with the Slasher case. If he had, Samantha would still be alive. The thought constricted her throat and unshed tears blurred her vision. She looked away, but not before catching the empathy in Heather's features that echoed in her thoughts.

The hand that slipped over hers caught her attention and she snapped her gaze back in Heather's direction.

"It's okay. I know a little of what happened to you and Steve, and I was so sorry to hear about your daughter."

The tears spilled over, and she nodded, pressing her lips together. For her, it had been only a week. A week of being awake and feeling the loss of their child like a dagger through her heart with every breath. Heather's kindness shattered the wall she'd built up in that brief span of time.

STEVE STIFFENED, TRADING A glance with CJ right before the sound of sobbing drifted into the cockpit.

Ted turned, leveling his gaze at Steve. "Everything all right?"

Steve raised an eyebrow. "I think so. She needs to let it out. She's held it together since she came out of the coma, so this is due."

CJ made a move to get up, and Steve shook his head. "Not now, CJ. Let her get it out otherwise, she'll put the brakes on, and the grief will just fester, eating her up from the inside."

"But..."

"—CJ, leave it," Steve said, sharper than he intended, and CJ's gaze clouded over, and his features hardened. He turned his attention back to the sky before him.

"My wife is real good with things like this. Us guys need to stick together up here and let the women work it out," Ted said, smoothing over the tension in the cockpit. He sent a *cut the shit* look in Steve's direction.

Steve got the message, not only did the look penetrate, but Ted's thoughts echoed the sentiment and he slid into the jump seat behind CJ. "So, what has Ted shown you up here?" he asked, refocusing the conversation on something more pleasant than the choking sobs behind him.

"He told me I could take the controls if you said it was okay."

"He did?"

CJ turned and smiled. "Yes, he did."

"Before I let you fly this plane, I want you to repeat what I told you about flying."

"I need to keep the plane level, using the altitude indicator as a guide." CJ tapped the correct instrument. "Just like on Wii Sky Crawlers and World War II Aces," he finished.

"A video game is different..."

"—Actually, it uses the same principals as a flight simulator," Ted said.

Steve wasn't sure it was the same, not after his near disaster at the controls of a plane. "I don't know, Ted."

"It's not like he's trying to *land* the plane," Ted said with a smirk. "I wouldn't let a novice try to land a plane."

Steve laughed. "Oh, yeah? You learned your lesson back in college?"

CJ looked between the two men and chuckled. "You almost crashed a plane?"

"Yes. Ted was trying to teach me to fly. I did fine up in the air, but landing wasn't as easy as I thought it was. He had to take the controls before we crashed his father's twin prop into a hangar."

"I bet I could do a better job landing than he can," CJ said, hooking his thumb in Steve's direction.

Ted laughed. "I'm sure you could, but I'm not going to chance a brand new bird to someone your age. I'll let you take the controls up here for a little while, okay?"

CJ nodded, and Ted pointed to the controls. CJ wrapped his small hands around the yoke and took over the job of flying the jet.

"Check it out. I'm flying a plane!"

Steve smiled at the exuberance in the boy's voice and the wide grin on his face, praying that this high would last because what waited on the ground in Atlanta was darker than he could ever imagine.

Georgia Reign
Chapter 21

FOR SUCH A MECCA, the Atlanta airport was quiet for nine in the evening. A few dozen people traversed the concourse and fewer people volleyed in the rental car lines.

Jennifer followed Steve to the Ritz Carlton on Peachtree Street. "I'm three and a half blocks north at the Days Inn on Baker Street. The police precinct is on the corner of Bell and Auburn, a few blocks southeast from here. There's a lot to do downtown and a bunch of parks on the outskirts," he said, carrying both Jennifer's and CJ's suitcase into the hotel. CJ trailed behind, looking around at the downtown lights. The streets weren't as busy as New York, but there was still a fair amount of traffic.

When they were settled in the hotel suite, Steve turned to CJ. "The man we're looking for is pretending to be a police officer. He's got a police dog, a Golden Retriever in training. If you see anyone like that, regardless of where you are, call me."

"Okay."

"I'm not talking about calling me on the phone."

"I know," CJ said. *I got it.*

Steve nodded. "All right. Now it's time for you to get some sleep." He pointed to the bedroom where he put CJ's bag.

Steve turned to Jennifer.

"What if something goes wrong?" she asked.

He didn't react at first. Instead, he walked to the window, shutting her out of his mind as he looked over the city, pondering the question. What if...

"Well?"

"Nothing can touch CJ." He glanced at her reflection. "Nothing." He turned in her direction. "He's untouchable, even by me."

Georgia Reign
Chapter 22

STEVE REACHED FOR THE ringing phone sitting on the nightstand. He could hear his boss even before he got the receiver to his ear.

"Where the hell were you yesterday?" Cleary's angry voice came barreling through the line.

"Road trip. I'm here now." He sat up. Cleary's mind was like an immediate info dump. "Where'd they find the body?"

"Centennial Olympic Park," Cleary snarled. "Get your ass over here now!"

Steve vaulted out of bed. "Give me ten minutes," he said. The phone slammed on the hook, and he was in the shower rinsing off the jet lag and out the door, fully dressed in his signature jeans and t-shirt, with his wallet and badge tucked into the back pocket of his jeans.

Sarah leaned against his car and when he stepped out, hand combing his hair in place, she straightened. "What time did you get in?"

"Sometime after ten. They're staying at the Ritz."

"Mrs. Ryan let you take her son?" She slid into the passenger seat with a raised eyebrow.

"Yes, she did. Jenny's with him and I told her to take him to the parks today." He glanced in her direction and slammed the car into gear. True to his word, he walked onto the crime scene ten minutes later, glad he hadn't had breakfast.

This time, the killer took artistic license with the kid. It wasn't just a dumping ground for the body; he positioned it in pieces to read FBI punctuated by a hand with the middle finger sticking up.

Steve met his boss's stare, containing the fury rippling over his skin by clenching both his jaw and fists. Beyond where Cleary stood, he caught a sight that caused him to physically step back. The boy's head sat on the ledge of a water fountain thirty feet away, the eyelids somehow tacked open, showing bloody dark eye sockets where his eyes had once been. Steve pointed, and Cleary nodded.

"Do we know how..." he trailed off, looking at the carnage. Of course, they didn't know how André died, not yet, but the brutality and message was obvious. A few of the officers had stepped away to empty their coffee and donuts away from the crime scene, and Steve had to turn to get his stomach under wraps.

Sarah stopped on the stairs, unable to take another step. She surveyed the carnage. She met Steve's gaze, and that's all it took. She spun, vomiting over the side of the railing into a small garden.

Steve glanced away, taking in the beautiful ornate fountain before he closed his eyes, concentrating on anything except the thoughts and feelings of those surrounding him. The sheer power raging through his veins reached the boiling point, burning his insides, leaving smoldering fury that got away from Steve. Steam hissed, and his eyes snapped open, his head turning toward the sound. The liquid in the fountain boiled, rolling and violent, sending steam into the air like thick plumes of smoke.

Steve's jaw went slack. The sight of boiling water reigned in the fury.

"Holy shit." He traded a glance with Sarah, her eyes wide as she wiped her mouth with a Kleenex, her gaze shifting between Steve and the steaming fountain. He let out a laugh, glad he hadn't flattened a building or blown someone up. The yelp of an officer investigating made its way to them. He obviously checked the water by sticking his fingers in because he came running toward the crime scene, clasping his reddened hand.

Steve glanced toward the fountain. "Cool," his voice a hissing whisper unheard over the rolling water. He closed his eyes and thought of ice. When he opened his eyes, the steam had subsided. Within the time it took to blink, the world spun under Steve's feet, and he took a shaky step backwards.

Sarah's hand on his arms righted the world, and he glanced at her.

"You look like shit," she said, her eyes searching his face, worried.

"Why, thank you," he said, finding the humor in the situation and getting his bearings back. He glanced at Cleary and edged around the body, walking toward the severed head alone. As he stood before André's eyeless skull, he sighed. "Sorry I wasn't able to save you." The smell of vomit and blood drifted from the open mouth of the child and Steve turned away.

This meant the bastard was on the hunt again. "Shit!" The swear came out louder than he anticipated, and Cleary turned. Steve left the crime scene and found a bench, taking a seat and studying his hands.

Cleary took a seat next to him a few minutes later.

"Was our presence announced to the public?" Steve asked, still staring at his hands and the cracks in the sidewalk beyond.

"No."

The media was all over this case, but they hadn't been privy to the inclusion of the FBI's behavior analysis unit yet. Steve turned his head. "It's a fucking cop."

Cleary leaned back on the bench, contemplating. "Where were you last night?"

"I flew back home to get something."

Cleary's eyes narrowed. "What did you get?"

"Bait," Steve said quietly. *That has to stay between me and you.* His eyes met Cleary's.

"What kind of bait?" Cleary shifted in his seat.

"The kind this bastard grabs."

Cleary's head tilted, and then his eyes slowly widened. He jumped to his feet, pointing at Steve. "No, no way in hell I'm setting up a child for this!" He waved toward the remains of André.

Steve pressed his lips together, glancing at the carnage and back to Cleary. "He's special, in the same ways I am."

Cleary shook his head. "I don't care if the kid is superman. I will not put a child in harm's way. Find another avenue." He took a step away. "And if you..."

Steve put his hand up and looked at his boss. "I know. If I step over the line on this one, I'll lose my badge."

Cleary nodded.

Steve sighed and watched Cleary storm away. He turned away from the scene, relieved at the direct order. He glanced at the park in front of him and took a deep breath. What he had done was impulsive, and he knew it, but no harm, no foul. He walked back to the crime scene, studying it as the coroner's office removed the body parts.

Georgia Reign
Chapter 23

JENNIFER SAT AT THE table with their breakfast spread out in front of her and CJ flipping through the channels on the television. He settled on "Tom and Jerry" and put the remote down, turning toward the stack of pancakes in front of him without looking away from the show.

"So, Steve tells me I need to walk through your lesson plans with you," she said, trying to drum up conversation and ease her discomfort.

CJ glanced in her direction and shrugged. "I guess."

"Did you bring your books?"

"No."

Jennifer sighed and approached CJ from a different point of view. "I met your dad."

That got his attention, and the television muted with a tilt of his head. He turned toward her. "I know."

"I'm not talking about at the warehouse. I saw him at the cove near our cabin the other day."

CJ's eyes turned a shade darker, just like Chris's had when he was angry. "So?"

"So, he misses you."

CJ's jaw tensed, and he looked away. "How come everyone can see him but me?"

Understanding dawned on her, and she reached across the table and took his hand. "Steve brought you there the day of your father's funeral. Didn't you see him then?"

"Yes, I saw him when I was with Steve. But I can't see him the way Tommy can or hear him the way Steve can and he's *my* father."

His eyes misted with unshed tears, and she squeezed his hand. "You can come to the cove and see him any time you want to," she said.

"Really?" He pulled his hand away and wiped his face.

"Yes, really, now let's..." Her phone rang before she could finish her sentence and she glanced at the unfamiliar number before flipping the phone open.

"Mrs. Williams?"

"Yes."

"This is Quint McCormick. I'm with the Concord District Attorney's office."

Jennifer pushed the chair back and excused herself from the table, crossing to her bedroom. "What can I do for you, Mr. McCormick?" She could hear his train of thought and took a seat on the edge of the bed, not trusting her legs to hold her.

"We would like to sit down with you and go over your statement."

"My statement?"

"Yes. Your statement regarding what happened at your house with Kyle Winslow, as well as what you witnessed at the warehouse."

"I, um, I'm not in New Hampshire right now."

"We would like to get your statement in order before we go in front of the grand jury next week. Can I set something up for Thursday?"

"No offense, but I'm in Atlanta, Georgia, and I'm not sure how long we're going to be here."

The click of the computer keys filled the line. "I can have the Atlanta county clerk take your statement on Thursday if that will work for you."

Jennifer looked toward the living area of the suite and CJ turned his gaze from the television in response. "I guess that would work." She didn't think the case would be wrapped up in a couple of days, but she'd have to figure out what to do with CJ while she was being interviewed. Being in the room with her wasn't an option, not with the questions swarming in the District's mind Attorney.

"I will be on the phone, and I'll have a court stenographer taking notes. You will be required to show identity and sign the affidavit once we are through."

"Okay."

"Thank you, Mrs. Williams."

Jennifer folded the phone and stared out the window. Her heart raced in her chest like Thumper's foot gone wild, and her mouth lost all saliva. The thought of reliving Kyle's attack yet again crippled her, and her lungs seized in a panic induced asthma attack. The more she tried to draw a breath in, the harder it became, and the phone slipped from her hand.

CJ DROPPED HIS FORK and bolted into the bedroom. Jennifer's panicked thoughts drowned the wheeze coming from her mouth. "What do I do?"

Can't breathe. Steam. I need steam. Help me to the bathroom and turn the shower on as hot as it can go.

He reacted, slinging his arm around her waist and helping her into the bathroom. She slid down the wall onto the floor, still wheezing, her face taking on a bluish tint from lack of oxygen, and he flipped the shower on, feeling the first tendrils of panic himself.

CJ closed his eyes and sent out the SOS

Georgia Reign
Chapter 24

STEVE SWERVED, THE VOLUME of CJ's voice in his head was almost blinding, and he pulled to the curb, throwing the car in park. "I'll be right back," he said, ignoring Sarah's gape. "Just hang tight for a few minutes."

He closed his eyes, focused on CJ, and felt the pull. When he opened his eyes, he stood outside the bathroom, the shower on full blast, and the door cracked. Under the noise of the water, he heard the telltale wheeze. "Shit."

He pushed through the door to find Jennifer struggling to draw a breath and CJ holding her hands, his face just as panicked as hers. He kneeled next to Jennifer and turned her face toward him, and their eyes locked. "Breathe," he said in that soft commanding tone he used before, but this time, it was more than just a calming tool. This time it had the will behind it, forcing her airway to unlock with the command.

She gasped, the air flowing in a great rush. After a few breaths, her cheeks flushed with renewed oxygen.

"What happened?" he asked when her breathing calmed to normal.

"The Concord District attorney called. I have to give a statement the day after tomorrow down here at the county clerk's office."

He wiped the hair out of her eyes and rubbed her cheek with the back of his hand. "I'll be there with you if you need me."

Jennifer nodded, and the tears came saturating her cheeks and he pulled her to his chest before meeting CJ's gaze.

"Thanks for calling me," Steve said.

"I didn't know what else to do," CJ said.

"You did good." Steve released Jennifer from his grasp. "I have to go before Sarah freaks out."

Jennifer wiped her face and stared at him. "You're not really here?"

He smiled and shook his head. "No, I pulled my car over when CJ called. Last thing I said to Sarah was hang tight, I'll be right back."

Jennifer broke out in a grin. "And you're just sitting in the car like a breathing corpse?"

"I guess."

A moment later, a low chuckle escaped from CJ, and Steve glanced in his direction, expecting to see his father instead of just a nine-year-old boy. "Oh, she's definitely freaking out," he said.

With a laugh of his own, he closed his eyes, and the transition took over, pulling him through the wormhole back to his car. The burning sting of a slap prickled his right cheek and his head rocked to the side. "What the hell?" he snapped, and his vision cleared enough to see Sarah's wide brown eyes in the passenger seat.

"Don't ever do that to me again!" Sarah punched his arm.

"I told you I'd be right back." Steve rubbed his cheek and glared at her.

"You went catatonic. You're lucky I didn't drag your ass out of the car and start CPR on the side of the road."

Steve choked the laughter down and put the car back in gear. "I'm fine."

"What was it? Some kind of seizure?"

"No. It's called astral projection. CJ called." He tapped his temple. "I told him to call if he ever needed help."

Sarah stared at him. "What the hell are you talking about?"

Steve pulled into the police station and sighed, shutting the car off before he answered her. "It's another one of those gifts I inherited from Chris Ryan. I can project myself to another place. In this case, to the hotel where CJ and Jennifer are staying."

"You can what?"

"I can be in two places at once," he said, breaking it down to the simplest form.

Sarah opened her mouth to speak, and nothing came out. Just a silent exhale and her expression and the thoughts in her head leaned toward a padded room for him.

"I'm not crazy, Sarah. Go inside and find a room where you are alone and can see me in the car in the parking lot. Call me and I'll prove it to you."

Sarah laughed and raised her eyebrows, looking at the police station and back at him. "You're serious."

"Yes, go." He shooed her out of the car and watched her climb the steps into the station. She disappeared, and a few minutes went by. He flipped open the phone when it rang and glanced at the second-floor window. "You're alone?"

"Yes."

He closed his eyes and felt the transition. "So now do you believe me?"

Sarah spun around and stared at him, her eyes wide, and her knuckles white as she clutched her cell phone. She glanced out the window at the car where he sat in suspended animation and back to his form in the room with her. "Holy shit."

Steve laughed and stepped toward her, and she reached out, placing her palm on his chest. "Yes, I'm solid." He took a quick look at the car and then back at her. "I better get my ass back before Cleary gets to my car." The transition took hold, and he opened his eyes to the inside of the car just as knuckles rapped on the window. He folded the phone and stepped out of the car, trading a glance with Sarah before turning to Cleary.

"I think we should alert the public before our UNSUB snatches another child."

Steve stopped and stared at the station. "If we do that, we'll never know if it's someone with inside knowledge." He swung his gaze toward Cleary. "We'll lose our edge."

"If we don't, we may lose another child."

Steve didn't want that either, and he nodded. "This is going to make it impossible for the Atlanta police to do their job."

"Not necessarily."

Steve laughed at Cleary. "You think just because we give specifics it won't impact the public? That's naïve. Every cop is going to be the suspect in their minds."

Cleary sent a glare in Steve's direction. "I've been doing this job for years. Watch and learn."

Steve leaned on the front of his car and watched Cleary approach the ranks of the press. His performance in front of the media was impressive. Calm, succinct and earnest, giving just enough detail to diffuse mass hysteria and still keep parents vigilant.

Georgia Reign
Chapter 25

THE RINGING PULLED HER out of the dream, and she reached for the cell phone, gazing toward the coffee table where CJ sat with his computer open and his pencil poised over his notebook.

He returned her stare for a moment and then went back to work.

Jennifer flipped open the phone without looking at the number. "Hello," she said, her voice hoarse with sleep.

"Hello?" the soft female voice on the other end replied.

Jennifer sat and cleared her throat. "Mrs. Ryan?"

"Yes. Jennifer?"

"Yeah, I'm sorry if I sound a little out of it. I guess I dozed off while CJ was doing his homework."

"Where are you two staying?"

"The Ritz Carlton. Why?"

"I'm in town."

Jennifer rubbed her eyes. "Huh?"

"Tommy and I flew down this morning."

CJ stopped writing and looked up. "My mom is here?"

Jennifer nodded and focused back on the phone call and not the imploring eyes of the child sitting with her. "We're staying in one of the penthouse suites. Room 1302."

Jessica relayed the hotel name to the cab driver. "I'll be there in a little while."

"Ok. We'll be here." Jennifer closed the phone and sent a smile in CJ's direction. "Your mom will be here in a little bit."

CJ didn't smile. He looked out the window, biting on his lower lip. "Tommy's with her?"

She nodded, and her smile faded at the worry lines appearing on CJ's face. "What's up?"

"Tommy shouldn't be here."

"Why do you say that?"

CJ turned his sharp blue eyes in her direction and the shock of his brazen glare made her push back in the couch. His gaze pierced right through her, beyond her, into the darkness shrouding their lives.

"Can't you feel it?"

She forced a swallow. Dread laced her mouth, drying the spit and she shook her head, lying because he was a child and she needed to protect him from the evil that existed within mankind.

His eyes narrowed, followed by the tightening of his lips as he pressed them together. He didn't have to say the words; they were clear on his face. He didn't believe her one bit. Instead of calling her out, he turned back to his notebook, his scribbles more pronounced, almost violent.

Jennifer studied him, his mind transmitting only static, that low-volume hum that she constantly got from Steve, and she stood, retreating to her bathroom and throwing a splash of cold water on her face. With a towel in hand, she stared at her reflection. Her fingers traveling to her perfect cheekbone—the one Kyle liked to backhand. Memories surfaced, and she closed her eyes, blocking them, but the shadow of each punch remained.

CJ SAT STARING AT the computer screen, attempting to ignore the morbid mini-slide show filtering through Jennifer's mind, but it was useless. Her memories assaulted his mind, and he stood, crossing to the bathroom door and knocking.

The flow stopped abruptly, and the door opened. Jennifer raised her eyebrows.

"Sorry, but I could see your memories."

Jennifer blinked, and the color drained from her cheeks. "Oh."

Awkward silence settled between them, and CJ turned, returning to the computer and his homework, glad for the sudden silence. He glanced at the screen and sighed. History bored him, just a litany of dates and events—a memory exercise and little more. Now science was another story, especially computer science. He'd take a programming problem over history any day.

Tommy's thoughts intruded on his studies even before the knock on the door resounded through the hotel room. Before Jennifer could cross to answer, he was up and running.

Excitement at having his brother there overshadowed the dread.

With the door open and Tommy grinning like a lunatic on the other side, CJ forgot about Jennifer and his mother and slung his arm around his brother, yanking him into the hotel room and the daily wrestling match began.

The door slammed, and his mother's voice pierced through the laughter. "Boys, stop it!"

CJ climbed to his feet with Tommy at his side and turned toward her. Guilt threaded through his stomach like a garter snake on the run, and he couldn't help but smile in response. He knew wrestling wasn't allowed, and heat stroked his cheeks. "Hi, Mom."

"Don't I get a hug?"

CJ crossed and wrapped his arms around his mother, squeezing once before letting go and stepping back. "Why'd you come down here?"

"I missed my boy." She ran her palm over the side of his cheek.

He raised an eyebrow and clamped down on the response. She didn't miss him half as much as she missed his father, and not having him around as a reminder left her empty.

That's why she came. Well, that and the murders in Atlanta went national.

Distancing himself before the anger surfaced, he took a step toward his computer. "I need to finish my homework." Even he heard the edge in his voice.

THE TENSION IN THE room increased, and Jennifer exchanged a glance with Jessica.

"Do you mind watching them? I need to let your husband know I'm in town," Jessica asked after dropping the bags on the floor.

"I can call him if you'd like?"

"I would like to speak with him in person."

Jennifer recognized the determined look in Jessica's eyes and although all she heard was static, she was certain Jessica Ryan was going to give her husband a piece of her mind. For a moment, she wished she could witness this confrontation, sure that either sparks, or more likely, a solid punch would fly.

Georgia Reign
Chapter 26

STEVE SAT IN THE war room, studying the files along with Sarah and Cleary, as well as a dozen local police officers. His concentration was shit with everyone's hostile thoughts. Guilt and anger pervaded the room. The "what if's" circled at a maddening pace, and he glanced toward Danforth and Gagnon, catching only static from that direction. Focusing on them controlled the din until both Danforth and Cleary's thoughts sang out the same word at the same time.

Damn.

He followed their hungry gazes and a zap equal to a mild taser rattled his frame.

What the hell is she doing here? Chris's voice echoed his sentiments.

"Mrs. Ryan," Steve said, standing and crossing to her.

"Can we talk in private?" The tight set of her jaw matched that of her icy stare.

"Sure." Steve scanned the offices lining the war room and zeroed in on an empty one escorting her that way. The minute he closed the door, her scathing voice pierced his ears.

"I saw the news. I saw, and I'm pissed that you want to put my son in that kind of a situation!"

Steve spun toward her; the anger at the entire situation wrapped around his heart and squeezed the humanity from it. "Your son is the only child in this city that I'm not worried about. Nothing can touch him, and you damn well know it."

"He isn't invincible."

"He's the closest thing to invincible that there is." He put his hand up to stop her protests. "Even so, I can't utilize CJ. My boss said under no uncertain terms can I put a child in harm's way. Not with this madman. So, you can take him home with you any time you'd like."

"I've got a flight scheduled for the three of us on Sunday."

"Three?"

"I've got Tommy with me."

Silence settled on the room, and Steve exhaled. The itch at the base of his spine bloomed, and he shifted, uncomfortable, but he didn't understand why. "I'm really not sure having him here is a good idea." His gaze bounced from her to the busy bullpen and back. "Maybe you should move your flight up."

Jessica raised her eyes. "You said..."

"—I said *CJ* can take care of himself. I'm not sure he can take care of you and Tommy. Not in Atlanta." *Especially not since the bastard will be trolling for victims again.*

"I made plans on Saturday with friends."

Steve clenched his jaw and nodded. "Fine, but if you insist on staying here, you'll have to avoid the UNSUB's target area." He turned and opened the door, leading her to the map and the accompanying crime photos. A small smile of satisfaction formed at the gasp behind him, and he turned, taking in her pale features before focusing back on the map. "These areas are reasonably safe to take your kids. He pointed to the outlying areas beyond the drawn perimeter lines. "As you can see, there are some nice parks to the east, although I'd seriously consider not letting them out of your sight and keeping a lookout for anyone with a Golden Retriever."

Jessica's gaze bounced between the photos and the areas that Steve outlined, and then she turned away with a nod.

Cleary crossed the room, stopping in front of Jessica, his eyes glued to her with intent interest. "Mrs. Connor?"

Jessica's head cocked to the side and her eyes narrowed, studying Cleary. Her brow scrunched in concentration. "It's Mrs. Ryan now," she said.

"I don't know if you remember me," he began and offered a strained smile, "but I was on the team that interviewed you after your ordeal in Albany."

She blinked, and Steve watched, curious at the expression etched in his boss's face. If he didn't know any better, he'd say his boss was smitten.

Jessica's brow smoothed, and she smiled. "Special Agent Cleary, wow, it's been almost fifteen years."

Cleary's smile eased, and he nodded, reaching his hand out in salutation. "I'm Assistant Director now."

"I understand you knew Eric." Jessica clasped his hand in a quick shake.

Cleary's smile faltered, and he nodded. "He was one of the best recruits we've had in the last decade. I'm sorry I wasn't able to attend his funeral." He shifted and glanced in Steve's direction. "I'm also sorry to hear about what happened to your husband. You have my deepest condolences." He reached out and gave her shoulder a little squeeze.

Jessica's eyes misted, and she forced a smile. "Thank you."

Is he using my death to flirt with my wife? Chris Ryan's voice barreled into Steve's mind, making him wince and suppress a grin at the same time. It certainly looked that way, and he wasn't the only one in the room taking notice of Jessica Ryan. Despite her age, she was still a hot ticket, and the thoughts of the men in the room echoed that sentiment. One of them was making his way across the room with the same hungry look present in Cleary's eyes.

"Well, hello, ma'am, I'm Lieutenant Danforth. To what do we owe the pleasure?" The southern accent rolled off his tongue with the smoothness of a snake charmer and even Steve suppressed a shiver of revulsion.

Jessica sent a half-hearted smile in his direction, accepting his handshake before returning her attention to Cleary. An obvious rebuff that echoed in Danforth's expression for an instant, then it was gone, erased by the layer of southern charm. But Steve caught the nuance.

"I'm afraid this is no place for a lady," he said, and clasped her arm. "Let me escort you to your car."

Jessica raised her eyebrows and dropped her gaze to his hand and back. "I'm perfectly capable of leaving without an escort."

Danforth's hand dropped from her arm and his smile turned sour. "Then by all means..." He waved toward the door.

"I'll walk you out," Cleary said.

Jessica sent a warning glare in his direction. "Thank you, but I'll be just fine." With that, she turned on her heels and sashayed out of the building, leaving the two men staring after her.

The chuckle from the afterlife filled the room, and Steve couldn't help but smirk.

"What are you looking at?" Cleary snapped.

"Nothing," Steve answered, putting his hands up in the air, and retreated to the table where the case files waited for the umpteenth review.

Danforth bowed out, disappearing into his office with a sour expression on his lips like he'd taken a sip of lemonade that was way too tart. Steve caught the look and sighed, diverting from the group to the Lieutenant's office. He knocked, and without waiting, he stepped inside.

Danforth turned from the window, frustration creasing his brow and casting a shadow over his eyes. "What do you want?"

Steve put a hand up. "You need to understand; Mrs. Ryan just lost her husband last week..."

"—and that's supposed to make me feel better about her obvious dismissal?"

"Maybe not, but she's going through a rough time. I'm sure she meant nothing by it. Everyone reacts to loss a bit differently."

Danforth uttered a bark of a laugh. "I know a little about grief, son, but that doesn't make it all right to be rude."

Steve knew he wasn't going to win this argument, so he switched gears, focusing on what Danforth just said. "What happened?" he asked. Danforth cocked his head to the side and before he could ask the question, Steve said, "You said you knew about grief. What happened?"

Danforth studied him, his mind a complete blank, broadcasting only static and, try as Steve might, he couldn't access Danforth's thoughts. Just when Steve believed he wasn't going to share anything beyond the hard glare, Danforth said, "My wife and kids were killed by a serial killer a couple of years ago."

The admission threw a curve ball into Steve's gut, and he sat down, blowing air from between his lips. He could relate. Not so long ago, he thought he'd lost everything to a serial killer, too. "Man, I'm sorry."

Danforth kept the glare in place. "I don't need your pity."

Steve stiffened. "I'm not offering pity. I'm offering my condolences. I lost my daughter a little over a year ago."

Danforth turned away from Steve, his gaze traveling to the window. With a nod, he acknowledged Steve's comment. "I guess I'm not used to being dismissed like that."

Steve studied his tense back and ventured a guess. "Was that the first time you've approached a woman since you lost your wife?"

A bark of a laugh escaped the Lieutenant, and he nodded, sending a glance over his shoulder at Steve. "Yeah. I guess I don't have it like I used to."

"Don't take it personally," he said. "Her wounds are still fresh, so..." He stood.

"Thanks." Danforth took a seat at his desk and raked his hands down his face. "What do you think our guy will do next?" he asked, pointing his chin toward the war room.

"I'm willing to bet he changes his M.O. now that we've outed him."

Danforth huffed. "I hope we catch this bastard before he grabs another kid." He stood and stalked out of the office.

Georgia Reign
Chapter 27

BLEACH ALWAYS REMINDS ME of starting fresh. I scrubbed down the tables, the floors and my utensils until they glistened—winking steel now ready for my next test subject. That cocky FBI agent gave me my new hunting grounds when he pointed out the safe zone to that woman.

That woman—the one both the lead FBI agent and the good lieutenant drooled over—taking one of her precious children would be a big middle finger to the force, not to mention putting the arrogant bitch in her place.

I dropped the soiled rags into a plastic bag and stripped out of my scrubs, shoving them into the bag as well. Alex whined and rubbed up against my leg, his warm fur tickling my skin, and I patted his head for a moment before resuming my cleaning spree.

I tossed the bag in the incinerator and pulled out a map, spreading it out on the table, studying the area Special Agent Williams had pointed to. My gaze fell to my location, and I sighed, measuring the distance between the two spots. A little too close to home for comfort, but the payoff would be worth it.

Her child will have all the answers to my questions.

Georgia Reign
Chapter 28

STEVE'S HEAD BOBBED ONTO the desk, and he jerked into a sitting position, blinking his eyes open. They had been at it all day and it was running into the wee hours of the night. Given his lack of sleep the last few days, the raw data on the screen in front of him acted like a hypnotist and he dozed.

"Looks like you might need this."

Steve looked up at Officer Gagnon and the Starbucks coffee in his hand. He smiled and took the offering. "Thanks." An undercurrent of antiseptic drifted from Gagnon's hands. "Been cleaning?"

Gagnon nodded. "Kids have the flu, so I scrubbed down the house. The last thing I need right now is the stomach bug."

"I hear you." Steve took a sip of coffee, scanning the nearly empty war room. Sarah and Cleary headed back to the hotel for some sleep a little before midnight, but he stayed on to analyze the data, looking for a missing link. "Anything new?"

"Nope. Just a load of nothing." Gagnon slid into the chair next to Steve with his own coffee in hand.

"I can't figure out this bastard's next move."

"He's going to grab another kid."

Steve sent a sideways glance at Gagnon and bit down on the *no shit* comment that popped into his head. "I'm hoping this guy is dumb enough to follow his same M.O."

Gagnon snorted. "Somehow I doubt that'll happen."

Cleary's statement had been played repeatedly on the news stations in Atlanta, and sound bites made it into every radio station in the area. The likelihood of a K9 officer being accosted by an angry mob was more probable than their UNSUB using the same modus operandi, and they both knew it.

"So now what?" Steve stretched and stared at the map across the room.

"I doubt anything will happen tonight. Kids in his demographic are fast asleep at this time of the night."

"Mhm," Steve agreed. He glanced at the clock—three in the morning—no wonder why he was so tired. "I've got to take my wife to the District Attorney's office first thing in the morning for a deposition."

Gagnon's eyebrows creased. "Your wife's in town?"

"Yes. She flew in yesterday." He scanned the room again, wondering if he should divulge the information to a member of the Atlanta Police force—to a possible suspect, no less.

"What's it for?"

"The New Hampshire state District Attorney needs her deposition in the case against the man who killed my daughter and nearly killed her."

"Jesus."

Steve's lips twitched into a sarcastic smile and he sent a sideways glance in Gagnon's direction. "He had nothing to do with it," he said, quoting one of Ty's favorite phrases.

"Then why's she testifying against him?"

His attempt at humor was lost on Gagnon and he took a deep breath, reminding himself that he *was* in the Bible belt after all. "Sorry—I meant Jesus had nothing to do with it."

Gagnon's face reddened, and he chuckled. "Good one. That flew right on by."

Steve nodded and climbed out of the chair, arching his stiff back to get rid of the kinks. "On that note, I'm going to call it a night. As you said, nothing's going to happen on this tonight."

"Catch you tomorrow," Gagnon said, raising his coffee cup in salutations.

"See ya." Steve left the building in a fog of sleep deprivation.

Georgia Reign
Chapter 29

JENNIFER PACED, HER SKIN tingling in agitation. Steve should have been there by now and his phone kept dumping to voicemail. She switched the television from the Disney Channel to the local station to catch the news and see if there was another abduction or a break in the case that would keep Steve from making it. With a glance at the clock, her heart rate increased, and her lungs tightened. Fifteen minutes. She needed to be there in fifteen minutes, and she had no clue how far the Atlanta District Attorney's office was in relation to the hotel.

Jessica paused at the door. "Do you want us to stay?"

"No, go to the park, let the boys get some energy out," Jennifer said, sending a strained smile in her direction. She really needed quiet to relax and having two nine-year-olds running around the hotel room was driving her batty.

"Okay. I'll see you later." Jessica closed the front door.

Silence descended, blessed silence, lifting the edge off Jennifer.

The knock at the door disturbed the quiet, and she crossed, opening it. Steve stood in the hallway, his hair still dripping wet, leaving water stains on the shoulders of his t-shirt.

"What'd you do? Jump out of the shower without drying off?"

He smiled. "Pretty much. I didn't get to sleep until after four and I slept through the alarm. At least I had the forethought to schedule a wake-up call."

Jennifer waved him inside and crossed to the bedroom, grabbing her purse off the nightstand before returning to the living area.

"You ready for this?" Steve asked.

"No." She sighed. "But I'm going to do it anyway."

He stepped closer and the clean scent of old spice drifted on the air, wrapping her in a warm sense of comfort she didn't expect. She met his concerned gaze and offered a semblance of a smile before turning away. "I'm not sure I want you in the room while I answer the district attorney's questions."

"Okay," Steve said after a beat of silence.

"And I don't want you in my head either."

His lips clamped down, and a shadow passed over his eyes and he stared her down. "I'm not sure I can do that," he finally said.

"You don't need the details, Steve." Jennifer met his glare and crossed her arms, cringing at the thought of relating the events within mind shot of Steve.

"I already have enough details between the videos and your nightmares. How much more is there?"

"Please."

Steve closed his eyes and hung his head, his mind as unreadable as his features.

"This is going to be hard enough and I'm not sure I can give them the details with you listening. I need to know you'll be there, but just not in the room."

"Fine." He turned, holding the door open for her. "We have to go."

"Thank you." She walked into the hall. Dread filled every pore and when they pulled into the parking lot of city hall, her mouth filled with that metallic taste of fear.

"You will be just fine, Jen. You can do this." Steve slid out of the car.

She stared at the building, frozen in place. The reality of what she had to do, to relive the nightmare with strangers in the room, caught her breath in her chest. When Steve opened the passenger door and squatted next to her, his gaze broke through her paralysis. He blurred in the sudden wave of tears that filled her eyes. She didn't want to do this alone, and she didn't want to burden him with the details.

"It's not a burden, babe."

"I'm afraid." She finally voiced the core of her issue.

"What are you afraid of?"

Usually, the soft-spoken voice he used was a calming influence, but right now it fanned the flames of fear, and she shook her head, erecting the walls again, safeguarding her heart from what she believed would happen if he was privy to the session. He'd be disgusted with the sight of her and that would be the last she ever saw of him.

His eyes misted, and he blinked back the sheen of tears, shaking his head. "I will not leave you, Jen."

"But..."

"But what?"

"But I had to pretend it was what I wanted," she whispered, shamed at the admission.

"Key word there is pretend. You were doing it to keep Samantha alive."

He helped her out of the car, and they climbed the stairs in silence, his hand clasping hers, and before he opened the door for her, he paused. "Do you want me in the room?"

Indecision framed her response. On one hand, she didn't want to recount the events with him in the room, but he was her rock. He gave her strength when she didn't think she had any, and this was going to be a very difficult morning. "Do you want to be there?"

For the first time, she saw his hesitation. His gaze traveled to the street and back, and he sighed. "I want to be there for you, if you want me to be."

"I still don't want you to be in the room."

He opened the door, and the Atlanta City Hall swallowed them up.

STEVE THOUGHT FOR A moment she was going to let him into the deposition with her, but the rebuff stung. Instead of making a production of it, he escorted her into the District Attorney's office and took a seat in the lobby outside of the conference room where a court stenographer waited with the New Hampshire DA on the telephone.

He leaned his head against the wall separating them and closed his eyes, focusing on the court reporter instead of Jennifer. She never said anything about eavesdropping this way. He smiled at his ingenuity until the facts started spilling forth.

Jennifer's recounting left nothing to the imagination, and Steve's hands balled into fists. His nails bit into the soft flesh of his palm as anger spread through his form like a rabid dog. He concentrated on breathing and controlling the fury filling his form. The last time he lost it, a fountain boiled, and he didn't know what would happen if this fireball in the pit of his stomach escaped.

Alarm filled the stenographer and Steve's eyes flew open. It wasn't Jennifer's asthma this time. No, the court reporter thought she was having a seizure of some sort, but Steve knew better.

Her vision accosted him, his vision clouded, and he was standing in the woods.

Steve was on his feet and in the room within seconds of the call for help. Her vision continued in his head like a bizarre picture in picture television, ending with the fade to black that signified the subject's blackout. He didn't know who had been snatched, but he knew another kid was now in danger.

Jennifer recovered from the vision, confused and disoriented.

"Can you get me a glass of water?" Steve asked the court stenographer.

"I think we should call for medical assistance," the frazzled stenographer said as she handed him a glass.

"I'm okay," Jennifer said. "I must have had another mini-seizure. They happen when I'm under a lot of stress."

Steve raised an eyebrow, and she shook her head. *Let her think that. We can talk about the vision after, okay?*

He nodded and took a seat next to her. "I think she's good to continue."

Jennifer sent an exasperated stare in his direction and turned back to the stenographer with a reassuring smile. "He's right, I'm okay now."

"Are you sure?" a voice on the phone chirped.

Jennifer took a sip of water and said, "Yes, sir, I'm good to go now."

"Okay, where were we?"

The stenographer recapped the last statement Jennifer made before the vision interrupted.

Jennifer glanced at Steve and then continued where she left off.

The questions the District Attorney drummed Jennifer with took their toll. Her eyes dulled with each answer, and her complexion drained of color when she described the assault in the cabin with grizzly detail. Details Steve could have done without. The more he heard, the more he wished he had killed Kyle with his bare hands when he had the chance.

Georgia Reign
Chapter 30

TOMMY TOSSED THE BALL to CJ in the park and CJ swung, connecting, sending the ball into the woods nearby. Tommy jogged through the brush, swallowed by the thick cypress, searching for the ball.

"Hurry up!" CJ yelled.

"Gimme a second!" Tommy shouted back.

There was the stinking ball at the edge of a muddy path and he bent to pick it up. The dog startled him, coming out of nowhere, and he straightened with the ball in his hand.

Its cool nose pressed into Tommy's hand, smelling the ball, and his golden tail wagged. He stepped back, panting, staring expectantly between the ball and Tommy's face.

A hand reached around, pressing a cloth to Tommy's mouth and nose. C... Tommy wasn't able to complete the thought before all went black.

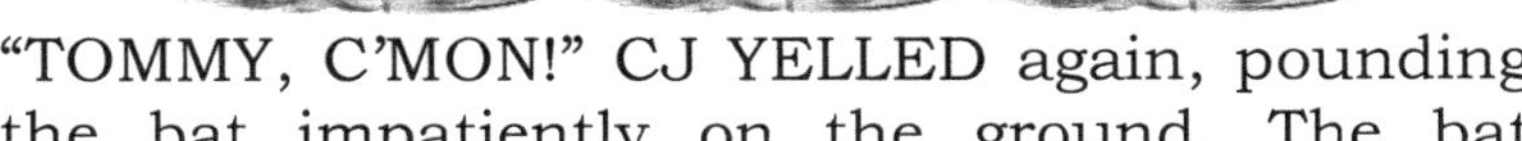

"TOMMY, C'MON!" CJ YELLED again, pounding the bat impatiently on the ground. The bat stopped mid-pound. A tingling sensation crawled over his skin and his head tilted. "Tommy?"

No answer. Something was wrong. Very wrong.

CJ shot a glance over his shoulder at his mother sitting on the bench a few feet away. She met his stare, following his gaze to the woods. Before she was on her feet, the bat fell from CJ's hand, and he sprinted.

"Tommy!" CJ screamed, taking the same path into the woods that his brother took minutes before.

Jessica followed, stopping short behind CJ.

CJ picked up the baseball, staring at it. He raised his eyes, scanning the woods, his mind reaching out for anything, any hint of his brother. Nothing. And he turned, meeting his mother's gaze. His mouth suddenly went dry, and his eyes stung with tears. He couldn't hear his brother anymore.

Tommy was gone.

Georgia Reign
Chapter 31

STEVE BOLTED STRAIGHT IN the chair as CJ's voice barreled in his brain. He winced and traded a glance with Jennifer. "I have to step out for a moment."

Without waiting, Steve left the conference room and flipped open his phone, pretending to take a call. "Where are you?" he asked and sent the thought back.

The answer came, and Steve closed his eyes, understanding why Jennifer had the vision. *Call 911. I'm on my way.*

He stepped into the room. "I have to leave. Will you be okay?" *It was Tommy in your vision.*

Jennifer's expression fell, and she blinked to cover the shock, her skin paling further. She sent a nod in his direction. "I'll be fine."

Liar. The thought leaped forth before he could catch it. He turned toward the conference phone on the table. "Sir, I need to leave, and considering Jennifer's episode, I'm not comfortable leaving her alone here. Can we finish this up at a later time?"

"Steve, I'll be fine," Jennifer said. *Go. The longer you hang here, the colder the trail will get.*

Steve met her gaze; the blood drew from his face in a fleeing rush toward his pounding heart. *Jesus, the bastard took Tommy.* With a nod, Steve headed out the door, leaving Jennifer to finish her deposition alone.

He slid into the front seat of the car, locking the doors, and closed his eyes, zeroing in on the panic in CJ's mind. When he opened his eyes, he was in a park. Steve walked straight to the pavilion and CJ turned before he stepped under the canopy.

"What happened?"

"We were just playin' ball." CJ pointed to the south part of the park beyond the tennis courts. "And I hit it long. He went into the woods down at the tip of the grass over there." CJ bit his lip to hold off the tears, but it was no use. "I shouldn't have let him out of my sight." Frantic eyes darted between the edge of the woods and Steve, glossed with tears. CJ could no longer hear his brother; the part of his mind constantly occupied by Tommy's thoughts now lay dormant. His twin brother was gone, and he was truly alone.

"This isn't your fault, CJ," Steve said. He turned, surveying the lay of the land. Woods surrounded the park, the southern end particularly thick, blocking the view of the abutting neighborhood. He turned back to the family. "Did you see anything, anything at all that I should know about?"

"An officer stopped us as we were crossing the road from the parking lot," Jessica said, swallowing. "He asked if we were the ones who owned the Chevy with South Carolina plates in the parking lot. He was in a police cruiser, and I didn't think twice about it." *And I didn't see a dog.* Her chin began to waiver. "Find my son." Tears tumbled down her cheeks. "Find my son, or so help me God, Steve, I'll rip your heart out with my bare hands."

He turned toward the parking lot, surveying the cars. Not one Chevy and no South Carolina plates. He turned back toward Jessica. "What'd the cop look like?"

Jessica shrugged. "I couldn't see much. He was in his car, and the shadow from his hat hid most of his face. He was white."

"Think, Jess." Steve said, crossing and putting his hands on her shoulders.

"His teeth were straight and white. That's all I can remember. The car windows were tinted. So, you couldn't really see what was in back."

Steve turned toward CJ. *You didn't pick up anything at all from him?*

CJ shook his head at the silent question.

"Okay. Sit tight, I'll be here as soon as I can," he said, and just before the transition took hold, Jessica's wide shocked eyes met his.

Back in the car, he turned the key, and the engine revved. He threw the car in gear, peeling out onto the streets of Atlanta, heading west toward Grant Park. He flipped open his phone, scrolling until Sarah's number was highlighted, and pressed the send button.

"Sarah," he said the moment the phone connected.

"What's up?"

"Tommy Ryan was just abducted."

Silence filled the line, and he heard the phones ringing in the background and the sudden chaos erupting around her. "Where?" she asked, her voice subdued.

"Grant Park."

"The call just came in. Cleary wants to know where the hell you are."

"I was at the District Attorney's office with Jennifer and now I'm heading out to the park."

"We'll meet you there."

Twenty minutes later, Steve slid into the gravel parking lot, taking the spot next to Jessica's rental car. Police were already combing the perimeter. The canine unit arrived at the same time as Cleary and Sarah, and a truckload of German Shepherds hopped onto the gravel. They made a beeline to the pavilion where the family was quarantined.

Steve stepped into the cool shade and traded a glance with CJ before turning to the officer in charge. "Show me the spot where they found the ball."

Gazes swiveled in his direction, and eyes narrowed.

Steve raised his eyebrows, waiting until the lead officer nodded and led him down into the woods, leaving Jessica and CJ in Sarah's capable hands.

"Did you find any tracks?" Steve asked when they were out of earshot.

"Not really," Officer Nathan Brown said. "How'd you know we found the ball?"

Steve turned his head toward the officer. "CJ called me and told me they were playing ball and he hit it into the woods. His brother either never found the ball or it dropped when he was grabbed."

"It was in the mud." Officer Brown pointed to the thick mud framing the small creek.

Steve stepped into the muck and yanked his sneaker out, watching as the hole filled up again. This bastard knew exactly what he was doing—the mud wiped all footprint traces away and gave them zero in the way of tracking. "Shit." He looked up and down the stream. "Does this lead to a road?"

Officer Brown nodded. "You can get to Loomis Drive from that direction." He pointed away from the small lake.

Steve followed the small stream to the point it fizzled out. A couple of muddy paw prints went up the embankment and then nothing. Steve looked through the woods out at the road within fifty yards of the stream. He walked the line with the officer trailing. Halfway to the road, he stopped. A partial footprint stared up from the dirt, and Steve flipped open his phone and took a picture of it. "This is where the bastard took him." He turned in a circle, surveying his surroundings. "Fuck," he said, snapping the phone closed and glaring at the officer. "Go back and get the forensics team. I'll wait here."

He watched the officer trot off and flipped open his phone. "I need to know who was on Loomis Drive at the time of the abduction," he said to Cleary. "And this is a different M.O."

"I'll get that info for you." And the line went dead.

Steve stayed planted in place until the forensic team arrived. They found another partial footprint closer to the road, along with a set of paw prints.

As soon as the forensic team finished, Steve went back to the pavilion. "We know where his car was parked," he said. A small consolation, he knew, but it was enough to give them some fragment of hope. "I'll find him." The words tumbled from his mouth, but he bit back the promise of alive and well.

He didn't know if that was possible.

Cleary stepped close to Steve. "We need to talk." He pulled Steve away from the scene and out of earshot of the officers. "We don't know if this was our UNSUB or if it's a bona fide kidnapping. If I recall correctly, Mrs. Ryan is worth quite a bit of money."

Steve bit down on the snide comment and took a deep breath to calm his irritation. "I know it's our UNSUB, Ron. Jennifer had a vision while we were in the deposition. And no, she didn't see our UNSUB. She only saw the Golden Retriever."

Cleary bit his lip, studying Steve, and after a moment he nodded ascent, although his features still formed a skeptical mask. "How do you know what she saw or didn't see?"

"I saw it too." Steve tapped his temple. "She transmits when she has a vision and now that I have this, I guess I'm a prime candidate to receive the transmissions."

"Ah," Cleary glanced toward the pavilion, his mind racing in a linear path, digesting the information with a grain of skepticism.

"Do we have a line on that police cruiser?" Steve asked, focusing Cleary on the case and not on his speculations.

"No, the closest cruiser was at least twenty minutes away."

Steve cocked his head. "Mrs. Ryan said a cop came by asking if she owned the Chevy in the parking lot."

Cleary pulled out his phone and punched a couple of keys before turning the display toward Steve. "If it was a cruiser, it's got to be a pretty old one because it isn't in the tracking system."

"We need a list of cops that were off-duty," Steve said.

"*You* were off-duty."

Steve snapped his gaze to Cleary's, the accusation clear in his tone and in the set of his jaw. Cleary's mind still whirled with the kidnapping angle, despite the course of the conversation.

"What exactly are you accusing me of?"

"I'm not accusing you of anything. If you're right about an inside job, then we need to be smart about this and not give our UNSUB a heads up."

"I agree. In the meantime, I'll take Mrs. Ryan and her son back to the hotel."

Cleary shot a glance at the pavilion and gave a nod. "Once they're settled in, let me know. I should have the list of off-duty officers by then."

"Will do." Steve headed toward Jessica and CJ. He handed Sarah his keys. "Can you bring my car back to the station?"

"Sure." Sarah took the keys, her eyes lighting up at the prospect of driving the sporty coupe.

"Mrs. Ryan, I'll take you and CJ back to the hotel." Steve took the keys to Jessica's rental and walked them to the car in silence. There was nothing he could say to calm their panic and the underlying fear encompassing their hearts, and he would not make a promise he couldn't keep.

When they entered the hotel room, Jennifer stood from her position on the couch, and he shook his head. *We didn't find him.* His silent admission stroked her features, turning them from the mask of concern to a portrait of sorrow, and she turned her attention to Jessica, crossing and hugging her without words.

CJ slumped on the couch and the television turned on. Channels buzzed by at his will until the selector stopped on some violent movie from the nineties.

"Turn that off, CJ," Jessica said, her tone harsh and the look he shot her made her hand fly to her mouth.

Steve caught the Fuck You attitude and turned his attention, along with his aggravation, toward the television and the liquid crystal display flared; going white and sending sparks from the components in the back of the box.

"What'd you do that for?" CJ jumped to his feet, glaring at Steve.

"You do not, under any circumstances, treat your mother like that, ever again." He crossed the distance and towered over the boy. "Do you understand?"

CJ faltered and swallowed and stepped back from Steve's invasion of his personal space. "She shouldn't have come, and she shouldn't have brought Tommy," he said, the spark of anger in his eyes rekindling to a razor-sharp flame.

Steve stepped forward, narrowing his eyes. "Are you blaming your mother for Tommy's disappearance?"

"Steve," Jennifer said, pulling his attention away from CJ for a moment, but it was enough for CJ's mental shove to catch him off balance and he stumbled backwards.

Christopher James! Chris's angry voice echoed in Steve's head, broadcasting loud enough for CJ to hear it without snooping in Steve's thoughts.

"I got this," Steve said over his shoulder in the direction the voice came from.

Bull. I'm going to throttle him if he continues to pull this shit on his mother.

"I'd like to see you try," CJ said to the disembodied voice.

Before the hostilities between the invisible angel and CJ could escalate, Steve's phone rang, breaking the tension. Steve stepped away and flipped the phone open. "Williams here."

"We got word that another abduction occurred about an hour before Tom Ryan was taken," Cleary said.

"Where?"

"Buena Vista Lake. A kid snatched on a field trip. The teacher's devastated, especially since she can't pinpoint the timing. They didn't discover her missing until lunch break when the groups came together, and a head count was done. Each chaperone assumed the child was in the other group, but we got lucky. One of the kids said she wandered off to help a dog. A Golden Retriever.”

“Did the kid see anyone with the dog?”

“No. He said the dog was alone at the edge of the woods and seemed to be limping.”

“Any evidence?”

“Forensics is working the scene right now. They found a torn scrap matching the shirt her parents said she wore and there’s a set of footprints and paw prints we’ll compare to those found at Grant Park.”

“Do you want me to head out there?”

“No. Stay with Mrs. Ryan and see if you can get her or her son to remember anything.”

“I’ll see what I can do here and then I’ll head down to the station. You’re still going to get that list, right?”

“I’m working on it.”

“Thanks.” Steve shut the phone and took a breath before returning his gaze to CJ. “Are you done with your little shit fit?”

“Steve!”

“What?” He turned to catch Jennifer’s incredulous expression.

“He’s just a kid.”

“I don’t have time for his poorly timed tantrum. Another child was snatched today and the description of the dog matches.” He crossed to Jessica. “Tell me every detail you can recall.”

“I already told you...”

“I know. You said it was a cop car. Describe the car.”

“Black and white with lights on top.”

“Was there wording on the car?”

Jessica blinked, and her eyebrows scrunched together. "I don't know," she said.

"What about the lights? Were they white, blue, red, a combination?"

"The lights were white... I think."

"What about the cop?"

"He had dark sunglasses and was wearing a gray shirt."

"Not blue?"

"No, it wasn't blue, it was gray, and it had short sleeves."

"What else?"

Jessica sighed. "He had the air cranked in the car and the window was only open halfway, enough for me to see his face and shoulder. I was more concerned about the boys running off, so I didn't pay close attention to the officer."

Steve nodded and ran his hand down his face. Even though the details she relayed were sparse, Jessica picked up more than most would have in the same circumstances. The gray shirt was the curve ball. They had been so focused on the UNSUB being a part of the local force—no one had broadened the potential list to include the Georgia State Police.

Georgia Reign
Chapter 32

TOMMY WOKE, CONFUSED AND confined. His arms and legs were restrained, and his back pressed against cool metal. He turned his head, his eyes adjusting to the darkness surrounding him. Twelve spirits congregated in the corner, whispering to each other, their eyes sad and their whispers hushed as they snuck glances at him.

"Where am I?" Tommy addressed the ghosts, and they froze in place, exchanging glances before looking back toward Tommy.

"You can see us?"

Tommy nodded, scanning each of the ghosts, and then he closed his eyes. It didn't take a genius to figure out where he was and who these kids were. He was still a little weary and when he opened his eyes again; he was alone. The ghosts had fled.

"CJ, where are you?" His weak voice broke the silence.

Tommy closed his eyes, concentrating on sending the silent message, when a small clicking noise caught his attention. His eyes snapped open again. Shuffling and the sound of chains reached his ears; he tilted his head, straining to hear.

Click, click, click, then soft panting.

Lights bloomed, blinding him. His hand stopped halfway to his face as he attempted to cover his eyes. Shuffling feet and panting got closer. Tommy squinted and made out the dog padding into the room.

The dog took a seat in the center, his soft brown eyes staring at Tommy, and his tongue lapped his drooling chops.

Somehow, the sight of the dog didn't ease Tommy's mind; when the whistling came closer with each shuffling step, Tommy fidgeted in the chains, yanking his arms as hard as he could, his bare biceps showing, more defined than most kids his age. He swung his gaze toward the door and a man in full surgical garb stepped into the room.

"You're in a shitload of trouble." The words escaped before Tommy had the sense to bite them back.

The man's laugh filled the room. "I think you've got that a bit backwards." He stepped to the table next to Tommy and pulled back the sheet, revealing all manner of surgical instruments.

Tommy's heart went from fast to racing the Indy 500, knocking on the walls of his ribs. He swallowed, trying to keep his fear at bay, but one look in the man's eyes told him he was right to be afraid, more afraid than when that woman held the knife to his throat when he was four.

He watched television. All those crime shows he wasn't supposed to see, but CJ taped them and snuck him downstairs after their parents went to bed. Every last one of them said if the victim can make the criminal see them as people; the bad guy had a harder time hurting them.

"My name's Tommy," his voice cracked. "What's yours?"

"I'm your new doctor," he said, looking at Tommy curiously from behind the surgical mask.

Tommy tried to smile, his eyes dropping to the dog and returning to the doctor. "Your dog is pretty." He wanted his mother in the worse way, but he refused to cry, and he couldn't pool his concentration to call CJ, not when he had to concentrate on making sure this man didn't touch him.

The doctor stepped toward the utility table, reaching for a scalpel.

Swallowing, he forced the lump of fear down to his stomach. "May I ask why?" He brought his gaze from the shiny scalpel to the doctor's brown eyes, eyes devoid of passion, devoid of mercy, eyes that scared the crap out of Tommy. *CJ, please, please help me. Please God, please.*

"Because I need to know, and because my dog is hungry."

The blade pierced the skin of his abdomen, digging through flesh and muscle. Tommy tilted his head back and clamped his mouth shut. He didn't scream, nor did he pass out, but a steady stream of tears flowed from the corner of his eyes. Pain like he never experienced before stole his voice and his ability to pull air into his lungs.

He prayed for darkness, prayed for anything to stop the sharp fire in his lower belly, but neither came. When the doctor pulled out his spleen, waving it in front of Tommy's eyes with a full explanation of what the particular organ did within the human body, Tommy knew he was in hell. With a flick of his wrist, the doctor tossed the spleen to the dog.

Tommy broke down, sobbing, his body shaking under the callous hands of the-would-be-surgeon until finally, mercifully, the darkness pulled him under.

Georgia Reign
Chapter 33

STEVE WALKED INTO THE hotel room at the Ritz at a little past midnight. Jennifer and Jessica turned from their positions on the couch; both their eyes and mouths open in surprise.

"I figured I'd stop in before I went to my hotel," he said, trailing off and looking at his feet.

He dropped onto the couch next to Jennifer and wiped his face, leaning back in the plush fabric. "We're sure the other child was taken by the same man who took Tommy. Her name is Annalee." He forced himself to meet Jessica's gaze.

"At least he's not alone." Her eyes were swollen and puffy and they asked the question her mouth didn't.

"I don't have any more information for you," he said. The weight in the pit of his stomach grew. They had combed through the list of off-duty cops, and nothing stood out. None of them fit the profile, and the sheer number of officers not on the clock or just starting or ending their shifts was disturbing. There wasn't enough manpower to check into each one without tipping their hand, and the list still didn't include the State police. Cleary was running down that avenue, but he was getting a wall of resistance.

Jessica lowered her eyes to her hands.

"How's CJ?" Steve asked.

Jessica shook her head. "He's inconsolable."

Steve hung his head. "I should never have brought him down here." He leaned over with his elbows on his knees, his hands covering his face. "I'm sorry, Mrs. Ryan."

"Just find my son before it's too late." Jessica stood and crossed to the bedroom she shared with CJ.

Steve closed his eyes and Jennifer's hand landed on his forearm. Her fingers gripped him, nails digging into his flesh, pain seared his arm, and he swung his gaze in her direction. The waxy pale face and film-covered eyes caught him off guard and he shot to his feet. The vision of the hotel room superimposed over the gruesome scene Jennifer was witness to.

"Jenny!" Steve yelled, attempting to peel her hand off his arm and break the connection, because he knew he wasn't the only one privy to the warped nightmare.

CJ screamed in the bedroom and Jennifer's eyes cleared.

In the thirty seconds of the vision, Steve saw enough to understand what was happening to the kidnapped children, and it was enough to cramp his stomach and boil his blood. Concrete and steel and a table full of surgical instruments. The fucker was pretending to be a doctor.

He turned to the window, looking out over the city, silently reviewing the vision. "When is this going to happen?"

"I don't know. The last time it happened instantaneously."

He spun and headed for the door.

"Where are you going?" Jennifer asked when he reached for the doorknob.

"I've got to follow up on something."

"He was..."

Steve's head snapped toward her and then the bedroom entrance, where CJ and Jessica now stood. He shook his head, silencing her. "He's alive and I need to follow up on something you saw." He stepped into the hall, closing the door tight and willing the hotel locks in place.

Georgia Reign
Chapter 34

TOMMY WOKE TO A dark room and screams coming from somewhere down the hall. High, shrill screams choked off by sobs. He let his eyes adjust to the dark and glanced around again. His wrists and ankles were still chained to the table, and he closed his eyes. "Daddy, I need you." The barest of whispers fell from his lips and the air in the room shifted. He opened his eyes.

The figure of his father stepped close.

Tommy's brow creased. "You're not my father."

The ghost of Tom Whitman nodded solemnly. "Yes, I am." His hand reached out and touched Tommy's arm.

Tommy shied away from the ghost. "I want my dad." his voice wavered.

The ghost pulled his hand away. "You have to call him by name." A bitter smile appeared, and he tilted his head. "I will be here any time you want to talk." With that, the apparition disappeared.

Tommy stared into the dark, digesting the small encounter. "Chris?" he whispered. Nothing. Hot tears slid down his throat. He closed his eyes and gathered all his mental strength. *Chris Ryan!* He opened his eyes, exhausted. The room was still empty and now silent. The screaming down the hall stopped.

Tommy held his breath, straining to hear anything. The soft click, click, click of toenails against concrete caused his stomach to bend into a knot of fear. The dog jumped up, his front paws sliding on the smooth metal until they dug into Tommy's side.

"Down," Tommy said with authority. He was used to having a dog around, although Sam was much smarter than this dog.

Instead of obeying, Alex swathed Tommy's face with his tongue.

"Get down," Tommy said again, turning his head away from the lapping dog.

The lights went on, blinding Tommy.

"You don't like Alex?" the doctor said from the doorway.

"I hate dog breath," Tommy shot back. He clenched his jaw, determined not to let this man see just how afraid he was. "But puppy breath is worse."

The doctor burst out laughing. "I'll give you that." He strolled into the room and regarded Tommy. "How old are you?"

"Nine. Why?"

He shook his head. "Too bad you won't see ten."

Tommy inhaled. "And why's that?" he asked, more to stall the inevitable, but also to steel himself for the next onslaught of pain.

The doctor picked up the scalpel. "Because none of my patients live."

Tommy met his gaze and swallowed. "But that doesn't have to be the case with me." His voice cracked, belying his fear before the uncontrollable shaking took over. His mind screamed in protest, screamed for his mother, his father, CJ, anything to keep the sharp blade from piercing his skin, but the conditioning he learned in Karate remained stubbornly rooted in the fiber of his being, keeping him from sobbing as effectively as the chains kept him from curling into a tight ball.

As the scalpel sliced into his flesh, the name his mother called his father when she thought no one could hear came barreling into his mind and hissed from his lips. "Ty."

The scalpel paused, and the doctor's brows creased together. "What did you say?"

Tommy's eyes widened. "N-n-nothing," he said, keeping eye contact with the angel now standing beyond the man.

Alex let out a yelp, pissed on the floor, and bolted from the room with his tail between his legs. The doctor turned his head, looking from the puddle to the door, his brow knit in puzzlement. He tossed the scalpel onto the utility table and took off, leaving an oozing gash in Tommy's stomach.

Tears tracked down his father's cheeks and he stepped forward, his wings ruffling with rage. He reached out and placed his hand over the cut in Tommy's abdomen, binding it together with a flash of light that filled the room.

"Daddy," Tommy whispered before his vision warbled with tears. "Help me."

Chris yanked the bindings that held Tommy in place but couldn't break them; instead, he leaned over and kissed his youngest son's forehead. "Help is on the way." His wings fluttered, and he ascended, fading into the backdrop of the concrete ceiling.

"Don't leave me!" Tommy screamed. His chest constricted with the sob he held in place. "Don't leave me." His chest rose and fell, air hissing into the clamped recesses of his lungs.

The doctor came back into view, dragging the dog with him. Alex whined as he dragged him across the threshold, his eyes darting from corner to corner. "Stay!" The doctor ordered, and when he let go of his collar, the dog backed into the far concrete wall, his ears back and his tail between his legs, his eyes still frantically scanned the room.

The doctor returned to Tommy's side, his eyes narrowing at the sight of the unscathed belly. When he picked up the scalpel, he stared at the blood-coated blade for a minute, and then his eyes switched to Tommy.

Tears pooled in Tommy's ears. His body shook uncontrollably. "I have to go to the bathroom," he said. He didn't know when the last time he went was, but the doctor had threatened him that if he messed the diaper he wore, the doctor would cut off his penis. "P-p-please." Even with the threat looming, Tommy would not be able to hold it much longer, especially if the bastard starting carving him up again.

The doctor slowly put down the scalpel and unclasped the dry diaper Tommy wore. He pulled out a metal bedpan and slid it underneath him.

Tommy closed his eyes and willed his body to relax. It took a few seconds, but then relief flooded both his bladder and his bowels, and they emptied into the metal container. "Thank you," Tommy muttered when he was done.

The doctor's eyebrows knit together, and he walked out of the room with the bedpan. When he returned, he had a cup in one hand and the clean bedpan in the other. He placed the bedpan on the far side of the table and brought the cup over to Tommy.

Tommy stared at the straw poking out from the foul aromatic liquid. He shook his head and forced a smile. "I'm not thirsty."

The doctor returned the smile. "I didn't ask you if you were thirsty."

Georgia Reign
Chapter 35

STEVE SAT BEHIND A computer scanning applications of the police personnel for Atlanta and the surrounding areas looking for anyone who had medical training. The flutter of wings brought his attention away from the screen. Despite the empty room, he felt the malevolent presence.

"Where is he, Chris?"

I don't know, but it's close. The angel's voice hitched. *The bastard's hurting my son.*

Steve closed his eyes and hung his head. "Why hasn't he tried to contact CJ?"

Because he's scared shitless and can't concentrate on formulating a coherent thought—what do you think?

Steve saw the room in the vision. He saw the table full of surgical instruments. He saw what the man was doing to Tommy, and he had to bridle the fury in his belly, because if it got loose, the ground would rumble under Atlanta until it broke open and swallowed everything and everyone in his path.

"Do you know who it is?" Steve asked.

No, but he's there now.

Steve's head snapped up, and his fingers flew across the keyboard. The printer whirled into action as Steve stared at the list of current off-duty police officers. "I got a list," he said, staring at the screen. He looked at the long list of names he scribbled in his search for those cops who had medical training or access to medical equipment, and every single one of them was on the off-duty list. "And I'm still looking through employment records."

He could feel the angel's impatience. "Go watch over him, will you?"

I'm your goddamn guardian angel. Remember? I can only leave you if he calls me.

Steve shook his head at the freakiness of the conversation and focused on the computer. "I can't concentrate with you tapping your foot or pacing or whatever you're doing," he said. "Just be quiet like you have for the last couple of days."

Silence, broken only by the click of the mouse, descended, and Steve sighed. "I know it's hard, Chris. I know, but I'll find him." He stopped short of promising anything because he wasn't sure that was in the cards anymore.

He ripped through the records of the two thousand officers in the Atlanta Police Department, cross-referencing them with the list of off-duty officers. The list of police staff with medical training in one vein or another and were off duty was still in the hundreds, and Steve leaned back, rubbing his face. He looked out the tiny window at the sunrise. Tommy didn't have the kind of time he needed to interrogate all of these men, and this list didn't include state police in the area. Even if he and Sarah and Cleary split up, they couldn't cover the ground quickly enough.

Steve focused back on the computer as the day shift arrived. He took his spreadsheet and dumped it into the FBI database and ran a query looking for cops' addresses that encompassed large or remote homes with facilities on the property. He turned when Cleary and Sarah came into the makeshift office.

"You look like shit," Sarah said.

"You need to think of something more original than that," Steve snapped at her.

"Have you been here all night?" Cleary asked.

Steve nodded. "Up all night and when this list comes back, I want you to get every one of them into a room." He pointed at the screen. "Our killer is one of these guys." He handed the list to Cleary.

Cleary flipped through the list and raised his eyebrows. "You're kidding, right?"

"No, I'm not." The computer beeped, and Steve hit the print button. He handed the list to his boss. "Get these guys in a room, and then come get me." He stood and headed out of the room.

"Where are you going?"

"To find a couch," Steve shot over his shoulder.

Georgia Reign
Chapter 36

CJ SAT IN THE living room, his arms wrapped around his legs, slowly rocking with his head on his knees. He could see Jennifer's visions as clearly as Steve and while the first one was bad, the second was much worse. The bastard had taken out one of his brother's kidneys and fed it to his dog. Tommy's punishment for vomiting on the good doctor.

If they found him alive, Tommy would never be the same.

"CJ, you need to eat." Jessica moved the plate of pancakes in front of CJ.

CJ tilted his head, and the plate flew across the room. "No."

"Damn it, CJ!"

He turned to his mother. "I saw, Mom, you didn't." His eyes bore into his mother. "And she can't fix him." He pointed at Jennifer sitting across the room, trying to bury herself in a book.

Jennifer raised her eyes from the book. "Steve will find him."

CJ's jaw tightened, and his lips pressed together. "How do you know?"

Jennifer kept eye contact. "Because that's what he does, and he is the very best the FBI has."

Her words stoked the fear in the pit of his stomach, and he clenched his teeth together. Despite his resolve not to cry, he could feel the quiver in his chin and his vision wavered against the sheen of tears. One escaped, tracing a fresh path down his cheek. "But can he find Tommy in time?" his voice cracked when he said his brother's name.

Jennifer took a deep breath, and even though the conviction wasn't there, she nodded. If anyone could do it, it was Steve.

Georgia Reign
Chapter 37

TOMMY WOKE IN THE dark, alone. He blinked a few times, letting his eyes get used to the blackness. No noise emanated from down the hall, no screams, no sobbing, no evil clicks of the dog's toenails and relief flooded through him. Hot tears formed, coating the back of his throat, but he clamped his lips together, refusing to let out the building moan of pain.

Silence was better.

Silence meant the whistling wouldn't start.

Silence meant the scalpel wouldn't cut.

Silence was better.

He closed his eyes.

CJ?

No answer. Tommy didn't have enough energy to scream in his head. He shifted to find a comfortable position, but that evaded him. His abdomen felt like someone dumped hot coals on his skin. Burning pain gripped him at the slight shift, and he felt the darkness beckoning.

He had to get a message to his brother. He had to!

Tears choked, and he blinked them away. The air shifted, and he tilted his head toward the corner. There they stood, staring at him, waiting for him to join the ranks of the dead.

"Can you help me?"

The boy in the front pointed at his chest, his eyes a little wider.

"Yes, you." Tommy closed his eyes for a moment, the effort to speak almost too great. When he opened his eyes, the ghost stood at his side. "What's your name?"

"André." The ghost looked around at the room. "I died in here."

Tommy guessed that much. "I need you to find someone for me." His voice was frail and shaky. "Can you do that?"

André brought his gaze back to Tommy and shrugged. "I don't know."

"Can you try?"

André glanced over his shoulder at the posse behind him, then back at Tommy. "Who?"

"Steve Williams. He's with the FBI. You have to lead him here."

André's eyebrows creased. "I'm not sure I can do that."

Tommy inhaled sharply. The word barreled from his chest. "Ty!"

The ghost's head snapped toward the sound of fluttering wings. His eyes widening at the sight of the angry angel transformed from thin air.

Chris Ryan stared at his son, his anger banished, replaced by pain, pain more excruciating than a knife to flesh. He stepped close, running his fingers along Tommy's cheek.

He turned his glance to the phantom next to him and then beyond at the crowd of curious spirits.

"Dad, take André to Steve." Tommy nodded toward the ghost at his side. "He's gonna try to help."

André shied away from Chris, his form fading.

"Please," Tommy whispered before the apparition disintegrated.

André turned, meeting his pleading stare. He glanced back at the winged angel, solidifying again, and he nodded.

Chris brought his gaze back to Tommy, his hands sliding down to the rough stitches in his abdomen. Tears glistened, sending prisms through the room as they rolled down the angel's face. "I'm sorry, son." He leaned down and placed a kiss on Tommy's forehead. Hot tears fell on the boy's face, drizzling light with them. "I'm sorry I couldn't stop him."

"Daddy, it's not your fault."

"If I was here..."

Tommy squeezed his eyes; tears fought their way out of the corners. "I'd still be that bastard's carving toy." When he opened his eyes, his father was gone, and so was André.

"Daddy!" The wail filled the room, and the air shifted. The ghosts in the corner faded and the man from earlier appeared, slipping his hand into Tommy's.

He squeezed the spirit's hand, keeping eye contact.

"If anyone can save you, it's your father." The ghost conceded, looking up at the ceiling and bringing his gaze back to Tommy with a wisp of a smile. "But I'll keep you company as long as I can."

Tommy's chin quivered. The darkness surrounded him, blanketed him, pulled him down farther into the abyss.

Georgia Reign
Chapter 38

"**S**TEVE!"

Steve sat upright, blinking, disoriented, the office unfamiliar and the voice in his head leaving a twang of an echo. He looked around and nearly stumbled off the couch, his back finding a wall to press against. His breath stopped, his heart clanged in his chest, and he stared at the bloodied spirit of the last victim. Recognition fired in his mind. "André?" Even his voice sounded like sandpaper, brittle and rough.

"Tommy sent me."

Steve wondered if he was dreaming. The only place he ever saw a ghost was in Paradise Cove.

"You're awake."

Chris's voice gave him a start, and he looked at the ceiling and back at André. "You brought him here." The statement didn't need an answer. "Why?"

André offered a smile. His teeth were grotesquely covered with a sheen of blood, but thankfully, his eyes were whole. Steve shivered, his teeth chattering at more than the frigid air conditioning. White plumes puffed from his mouth, the temperature plummeting as André stepped closer.

"I'm supposed to bring you to Tommy."

A knock interrupted, and Steve turned toward the door. When he brought his gaze back, André was no longer in the room. "Fuck!" He crossed and swung the door open, his gaze sharp and angry enough so that Sarah took a step back.

"What?"

"Everyone's here just like you asked," she said.

Steve scanned the room again. Empty, damn. He rubbed his eyes, locking the start of a yawn in his throat. He ran his hands through his hair and rolled his neck, shaking his head to clear out the last remaining cobwebs. "Did anyone come in particularly late?"

Sarah shook her head. "No, they all arrived around the same time, give or take five minutes."

Steve sighed and followed her down the hall into the small, packed auditorium. He walked to the front and scanned the crowd, opening his mind and letting the thoughts assault him. Nothing leaped out, nothing useful in this case, anyway. "As you know, we have two more missing kids." Heads nodded.

Anyone with a police scanner knew. Anyone with a radio knew. Anyone with a television knew. The media had latched onto this one like a mad dog, vicious and unrelenting, sensationalizing the snatching of Tommy Ryan, turning the entire case upside down. A billionaire's son at the hands of a killer was just too juicy.

Speculation that a ransom call would come hit the airways, but Steve knew better. He knew it was someone in this room. Someone in attendance had Tommy and was doing unimaginable things to the boy. He knew in the hot pit of his stomach that if they didn't find him in the next forty-eight hours, Tommy was dead.

He ran his sharp glare over the crowd, looking for anything, any twitch, any shift that would play out. Nothing. Shit. *Do I play my hand or not? Shit. Chris, is André still with you?*

No. He couldn't hold the connection.

God damn it! He could identify the son of a bitch!

Somehow I doubt that. I can't even identify him. Bastard was wearing hospital scrubs.

"We need all hands on this one. As you know, one of the victim's family is pretty powerful and has some serious connections." Nods. *Was there a logo on the scrubs?*

Silence met the question.

Chris, was there a fucking logo?

I don't know. I was concentrating on getting the fucker to move the scalpel away from Tommy.

Steve exhaled and nodded. "After speaking with the families of past victims, it has come to light that our UNSUB is pretending to be one of you. A cop with a police dog in training. A Golden Retriever. Every parent mentioned this and one kid saw a Golden Retriever when the girl was snatched." He let that sink in, doing another mind scan, but only fuzz and static met him this time, the exhaustion taking a toll to the point where he couldn't even get a read on Cleary.

"You're not telling us anything we don't already know." Officer Gagnon said.

"I know. I just wanted to reiterate what we are looking for and tell you that until this case is solved, there will be no days off." He knew he couldn't do that, but he wanted to see the reactions. Grumbles cascaded through the room, and he traded a glance with Cleary, getting a slight shake of his head in return. His eyes scanned the crowd, seeing quite a few lips pressing together in thin flat lines. If glares were daggers, he'd be bleeding plenty.

Lieutenant Danforth stood and crossed the distance. "Can I speak with you?"

Steve nodded and allowed Danforth to lead him out of the room.

"What the fuck was that?" Danforth asked, pointing toward the room.

Steve tilted his head. "We need all the available assets on this case, Lieutenant."

Danforth sent some silent blades of his own. "You don't have the authority."

Steve smiled and raised his eyebrows. "I beg to differ."

Cleary stepped into the hall, closing the door behind him. "We have the authority." He didn't exactly like what Steve did, but some reactions were more visceral than necessary and he took down names, narrowing the field to some twenty officers, including the good lieutenant standing before them.

"These men have families!"

"So do we," Cleary said. "You don't see me bitching about being here or bitching about the chance to nail this bastard to the wall." He stepped in to crowd the Lieutenant.

Danforth stepped back. "I don't want my men burning out. I need them sharp, and time off keeps them clear and focused."

Steve rubbed his temple, studying Danforth. Too much static. Unnatural static. His eyes narrowed. Dark hair, right height, right build. "Do you own a dog, Lieutenant?"

Danforth's head snapped in Steve's direction, his jaw unhinged at the veiled accusation. "No, I don't."

Indignant, the Lieutenant barely held it together. A red hue spread over his face and neck, his nostrils flared, and his lips thinned to nothing.

"Can you tell us your whereabouts yesterday afternoon?" Agent Cleary asked.

"I was at home."

"Can anyone confirm that?"

He shook his head. "I was alone." *As usual.*

Steve heard the thought, narrowing his eyes.

Cleary glanced at the Lieutenant's left hand and the gold band glinting in the light. Before Steve could stop him, Cleary asked, "Your wife wasn't home?"

The crimson tone vanished from his cheeks, his skin going very pale suddenly and he turned his gaze to Steve before swinging it back in Cleary's direction. "My wife died a couple of years ago." With that, the Lieutenant turned and stormed down the hall out of sight.

Cleary turned to Steve, pointing toward the room full of officers. "You pull another stunt like that and you're off the case. Go get some sleep, you look like shit." Cleary didn't wait for a rebuff; he walked back into the room and shut the door.

Steve was too tired to argue, he was too tired to drive. He found Sarah and handed her the keys. "I need to swing by and see Jennifer before we head back to the hotel. Do you mind driving?"

"Sure." She swiped the keys from his outstretched hand.

Georgia Reign
Chapter 39

THE RITZ CARLTON PARKING lot was a zoo, and it didn't get any better when Steve stepped out of the car. The media swarmed like a flock of pigeons going after a single crumb of bread, pecking and clacking, yelling questions and sticking microphones and cameras in his face, capturing his mumbling "No comment" over and over and over.

Steve sighed as the elevator closed on the clan, closing his eyes and leaning on the back wall, bracing himself on the banister. He cast a weary gaze in Sarah's direction.

"You look like a dung heap, Steve."

He snorted. He felt like it too, but at least she changed it up this time. Exhaustion crept into every cell of his being. And while he had pulled all-nighters in the past, this was different. This was beyond exhaustion, and he didn't know why.

It's the juice.

"Thank you very much for the commentary," he said with his eyes closed. It took almost all his strength to open his eyes when the elevator stopped. He stumbled into the hotel room and instead of sitting down and chatting with Jennifer, he headed to her bedroom, oblivious to the stares of Jessica, CJ, and Jennifer from the couches.

JENNIFER STARED AT SARAH, whose gaze bounced between the bedroom door and her.

"He's tired."

"Doesn't he have another hotel room?"

"Yeah, but it looks like he's crashing here." Sarah waved at the door. "He barely made it from the elevator."

Jennifer stood and slid into the bedroom, leaving Sarah with CJ and Jessica.

She crossed to the bed and put her hand on Steve's back, trying to read him, but she came up empty. Tired was an understatement. He didn't stir, not to the movement of the bed and not to her touch. He had hit the bed and passed out like he'd drunk a gallon of hard liquor. His chest rose and fell in the even rhythm of deep sleep.

She curled next to him, rubbing his back gently for what seemed like hours, her own eyelids getting heavier and heavier with passing time.

"I don't know if I can stop him."

Jennifer turned her head, staring at his glossy blue eyes.

"I don't know if I can stop him," he repeated. Tears brimmed, gathering at the corner of his eyes before he blinked, and they tracked down the bridge of his nose.

"You can," she said with conviction. The
slight curve of his lips belied his dark thoughts,
and Jennifer shivered. "You have to."

Georgia Reign
Chapter 40

A KNOCK ON THE hotel door woke Steve, and he stumbled out of the room, swinging the door open and rubbing the sleep from his eyes.

Cleary stepped inside. "A report of a third child came in after you left."

The bedroom door opened, and CJ stepped into the living room, shutting the door quietly behind him. It was dark out, but the knock on the door had woken him as well.

Steve glanced at the boy. "CJ Ryan, this is Special Agent Ron Cleary. My boss. Ron, this is the boy I mentioned. His brother was the one taken the other day."

Cleary raised his eyebrows at the sleepy nine-year-old. "Do you mind if I speak with Steve for a moment?"

Steve and CJ exchanged a look.

"He can hear what you're thinking anyway, Ron."

Cleary cocked his head. "Frankly, I don't care. What we need to discuss is not for his ears." *I need to know where you were this afternoon.*

CJ's eyes narrowed. "He was here."

Steve shot his gaze to CJ and then to Cleary. "You..." He trailed off, dumbfounded. Anger swelled and the vase on the table next to Cleary shattered. "I can't believe you would even ask." He spun, staring out at the lights over Atlanta, reigning in the anger. He glanced over his shoulder at his boss. "Where were you?"

Cleary inhaled sharply, staring at the shattered vase. "You know damn well where I was." He glanced at the boy and back to Steve, wondering which one had broken the ceramic piece.

"I did," Steve said, focusing on the reflection of Cleary.

Jesus.

Steve laughed and turned back. "He's got nothing to do with this." He turned his gaze to CJ and raised his hand, pointing toward the bedroom. "Go back to bed."

CJ argued, but Steve shook his head. "Bed, now!" The command sounded more like his father than Steve, and CJ nodded, retreating into the bedroom.

Steve's gaze snapped to Cleary once the door closed. "You had no fucking right to throw that accusation my way."

"Where'd the money come from, Steve?"

Steve tilted his head. "What?"

"Where did the fifty million come from, Steve?" Cleary stepped closer.

"A trust fund that Chris Ryan set up for Kyle's victims. Chris designated fifty million to me and named me successor trustee to distribute the rest."

Cleary's eyebrows rose.

"I can put you in touch with Chris's lawyer if you'd like." He reached into his back pocket and pulled out his wallet, fishing for Lynn Trueman's card and handing it to Cleary. "I asked you about will settlements and you said there was no problem."

"I was talking about your parent's estate, not Chris Ryan's."

"It's legal, Ron." He slid his wallet back into his pocket. "He also left me property."

"Why the fuck would he do that?" Cleary slid the card into his shirt pocket. He would follow up on the name when he got back to his hotel room.

"I don't know."

Tell him you reminded me of Eric. Chris's voice whispered.

"Maybe I reminded him of Eric. Maybe he just didn't have any close friends. Maybe he felt sorry for me because at that point I had nothing. Kyle had killed my daughter, my folks, Jack, and anyone I got close to. And Jenny, Jenny was in a coma." He took a breath. "How the hell should I know why?" He turned away, still asking himself those questions. He still didn't understand it, not in the least.

That's pretty much it in a nutshell, but you forgot to mention maybe it was a bribe. Chris's chuckle erupted in his ear.

"Just shut up."

"Excuse me?"

"Nothing." Steve stared out the window. "Kyle almost wiped my family off the map and frankly, I don't really care what Chris's reasoning was, it was damn charitable of him to put a hundred million of his own money into the victim's fund." He refocused on the image of Cleary. "Maybe he couldn't do enough for the victims that his brother killed, and it's his way of finding atonement for the family name." Turning back to his boss, he crossed his arms. "I don't know, but I'm not giving the money back."

Cleary tilted his head, studying Steve. He glanced at the vase and then back at Steve, crossing his arms. "You said the other day that this..." He nodded his chin toward Steve. "...this stuff happened after the explosion."

Steve's eyes shot to the vase and back, hearing the silent questions flurrying in his boss's mind. "I didn't use this to coerce Chris Ryan to put me in his will."

"Why don't I believe that?"

Steve sat on the couch and took a deep breath, waving at the chair across from him. "Because if I was in your shoes, I probably would think the same thing." He shook his head and studied his hands. "All of this is courtesy of the Ryan's."

Cleary moved to the chair Steve had indicated and took a seat. "Tell me what happened."

Steve leaned back against the soft cushions. "It started with Eric. Eric could read minds and one night when we were having an argument, he grabbed my wrist and something happened." Steve traced his right wrist and a small laugh escaped. "I'm not sure what happened really, just that in the matter of seconds, I had his entire history embedded in my brain and his ability to read minds. I'd always wondered what it would be like to hear what everyone was thinking." He shook his head and brought his gaze to meet Cleary's. "It was nothing like I imagined. Always having the drone of other's thoughts in your head can drive you crazy. It doesn't go away. Even when I was at the cabin with just Jen, it wasn't silent. I don't know what my range is, but anyone who comes within my radar, I hear their thoughts. Unless they don't think linearly, then I can't hear shit." He inhaled again. "That wasn't the only gift Eric passed to me, either."

Cleary pointed his thumb over his shoulder at the vase.

"No, that came later." Steve's hand ran over the spot on his chest where Kyle's knife had cut him instead of Jennifer. "I seem to be able to put myself between a knife and someone I care about, like a protective barrier, without physically being there."

Cleary leaned back a fraction, pursing his lips and crinkling his brow.

"Kyle was going to stab my wife." He shook his head. "And I was nailed to a cross seven feet off the ground."

"I don't understand."

Steve closed his eyes, concentrating on the picture, on the fraction of history of what happened in the warehouse, the crucifixion, Sarah's rape, Jennifer's miraculous recovery, and Kyle's subsequent attack on her. He bundled and transmitted everything about that day except the truth of who Chris Ryan really was. He opened his eyes when his boss hissed in disgust.

"Jesus!"

"He wasn't there that day, but Chris Ryan was, and he saved our lives."

Cleary's face blanched and his eyes shot to Steve's exposed wrists. Not a mark on the agent, nothing but smooth, perfect skin.

"When Chris died, I somehow got his unique gifts on top of what Eric gave me." Steve rubbed his face.

Cleary stared at him. "You have no scars."

Steve nodded. "I know. That's another benefit of the Ryans' collective powers." He chose not to divulge those details. Cleary was too good of a cop. Steve knew he still might put two and two together, but didn't want to point him toward who Chris Ryan really was. "I've got to keep a check on my temper now." He raised his eyes to Cleary. "I lost it the other day."

Cleary tilted his head. "The fountain?"

Steve nodded.

"What else can you do?"

Steve shrugged. "I don't know." He wasn't about to explain astral projection to Cleary or the latent ability to control others.

"And Jack?"

Steve shook his head. "Jack never knew about this. Kyle killed him before I was supercharged."

Cleary laughed at the description and then leaned forward, his elbows on his knees. "And you didn't use any of this to coerce the Ryan's?"

"No, he didn't."

Both Cleary and Steve swiveled toward the voice. Jessica Ryan stood leaning against the wall.

"How long..."

"CJ told me you gave Agent Cleary a glimpse of what happened in the warehouse. I've been listening ever since." *Thank you for not revealing the truth about Chris.*

Cleary's eyes narrowed as he studied Jessica Ryan. He had done his homework after her son was abducted and knew exactly who Chris Ryan was related to and where the billions had originated. He glanced back at Steve, noodling on the information he had just been given, and then turned back to Jessica. "Interesting that your husband did not know what his brother was doing, especially considering his, uh, gifts." His stare bore into Jessica.

Jessica's lips spread into a mocking smile. "What are you driving at, Agent Cleary?"

"Ron." Steve spoke, pulling his boss's attention from Jessica. When their eyes met, Steve continued, "Chris Ryan wasn't the original source of this."

Cleary tilted his head, his mind scrambling over the facts, and then his gaze shot to Jessica, his eyes widening. Her son Eric. Her son CJ. Her... "Jesus," he whispered, remembering the oddities in the video feed he saw of her escape from captivity. "Jesus Christ Almighty."

"She's the one who brought Jenny back."

Cleary's head snapped in her direction. *Holy Christ, what is she?*

"Jessica no longer has any of that power."

His head snapped toward Steve.

"Yeah, I have the power to kill and somehow the power to heal transferred over to Jennifer. However, none of this does me any good if I don't know who the hell has those kids. And yes, I can still die. A head shot would take me out just as effectively as the next guy." He flashed a sly smile. "But again, that's only if I didn't know it was coming."

"Uh, um," Cleary began and audibly swallowed.

"Need a drink?" Steve stood and crossed to the mini-bar, pulling out a couple of scotches. He dumped them in the glass and dropped a few ice cubes in before handing it to Cleary. "Try that."

Cleary downed it in one gulp and then stared at the ice in the bottom of the glass. "Is this shit for real?"

Steve tilted his head, and the glass lifted from Cleary's hands floated across the room and landed on the bar.

A new thought dawned on Cleary.

"Jennifer is a bona fide clairvoyant," Steve answered before Cleary could ask the question.

Cleary turned toward Jessica. "And your son, what's he?"

"He's a nine-year-old boy who misses his brother." She spun around and disappeared into her bedroom, closing the door on any further conversation.

Steve sighed. "CJ is a special boy, Ron. If the killer had taken him instead of Tommy, we would have him right now," he said.

"And Tommy, what can he do?"

"He sees ghosts."

Cleary glanced at the empty scotch glass.

"We could go down to the hotel bar if you want."

Cleary shook his head and reached into his pocket, pulling out a sheet of paper with twenty names written on it. He handed it to Steve. "These are the officers who had a more derogatory reaction to your little announcement."

Steve scanned the names. Both Lieutenant Danforth and Officer Gagnon were on the list. "I caught nothing from these guys."

"Those are the ones I want you to follow up on. You had a hunch when you pulled that stunt, and I watched their reactions." He leaned back in the seat. "I'm a kinetics specialist, Steve. I've got a doctorate in criminal psychology, and that's the only thing that made me buy all this shit you've been shoveling in my direction. Well, that and the little display with the glass." His lips spread into a smile. "But these guys..." He flicked the edge of the paper. "They're all hiding something." Cleary stood. "Find out what it is."

Steve watched Cleary leave and focused on the list. Twenty names. Twenty possibilities. He wiped his face and put the list on the table. He needed a couple of hours more sleep before he went at it again and wasn't sure whether Sarah took his rental.

He glanced at the bedroom and sighed. She hadn't told him to leave and the draw of lying next to her in the plush luxury of this hotel versus heading back to his own economy hotel bed won the battle. He crawled into bed with Jennifer; the sweet smell of her shampoo chased him into sleep.

Georgia Reign
Chapter 41

JESSICA CRACKED THE DOOR and crossed to the list lying on the coffee table. She picked it up, scanning the names and addresses before she gave a quick look toward the second bedroom. She snuck out, heading for the business center in the hotel and the copy machine.

With the sun just peeking over the horizon, Jessica dressed in her jogging clothes, pulled her hair back in a ponytail, and slid the folded list into her pocket along with the hotel key.

"Where are you going?" CJ rolled over, opening a sleepy eye.

"I'm going for a jog; I'll be back in a little while." She leaned over and gave CJ a kiss. "Get some more sleep."

CJ turned away and his breathing slowed to the rhythmic lull of sleep. Jessica scribbled a note for Jennifer and took off, grabbing a map in the lobby before she hit the street. Hailing a cab, she headed to the farthest house on the list.

She peeled off the cab fare, sliding the remaining cash in her pocket and slipped into the sidewalk outside the old southern mansion in Emory a half hour northeast of Atlanta. The cab disappeared from sight and she turned toward the estate. Her palms broke out in sweat, and she debated. *What if this is where Tommy is? What the hell will I do then?* She was kicking herself for not grabbing her cell phone, but that would have tipped off CJ, and she wanted this to be a stealth mission. She stared at the house and the surrounding woods.

Huge.

Secluded.

Just a stone's throw away from Chandler Lake and the VA hospital beyond.

Damn.

The police car sat under the portico, and Jessica took a step closer to the house. Her heart hammered in her chest, and she knew this was the right place. Ice prickled her bones, and she glanced around, spying for cameras of any sort. There weren't any readily recognizable, but the crawl of her skin told her she was being watched.

Georgia Reign
Chapter 42

TOMMY SHIVERED, UNSURE WHETHER his eyes were open or closed in the silent darkness. Not even a sniffle from the other rooms. He inhaled as deeply as his constricted chest would allow. "Hey!"

He strained, tilting his head toward where he thought the door was. Then he heard it, the slight scrape of a chain and a muffled moan.

"What's your name?" he yelled with the same force of volume.

"Annalee." the faint voice said.

Tommy closed his eyes for a second to gather the strength. "I'm Tommy."

A soft sob echoed down the hallway, along with the creak of a door. The familiar click of nails on concrete reached his ears and Tommy shook. Whistling followed, coming closer and closer. He squeezed his eyes shut, expecting the plume of light that came seconds later. The doctor stood in the doorway, regarding him with his cold brown eyes.

"My patients shouldn't talk to each other." He crossed the distance.

Tommy saw the gleam of anger in his eyes and his bladder let go. The surfacing of emotion was scarier than the void he had seen for the last couple of days. It transformed the doctor into a maniac, a bloodthirsty maniac and the only coherent thought that tumbled into Tommy's mind when the doctor shoved the retractor in his mouth and spread it wide was *Mommy*!

The forceps dug into his tongue, yanking it out between the sharp blades of the surgical scissors. The doctor pressed the blades quickly together, cutting Tommy's tongue in half. He tossed the amputated piece to Alex.

The scream barreling from Tommy's mouth rocked the walls before it drowned in the flood of blood filling the gaping cavity. Tommy coughed, swallowed, wailed and coughed some more. Nothing the doctor had done to that point prepared him for the onslaught of pain and despair flooding him faster than the blood filling his mouth.

The burning pain of the cauterization tool came next, searing the stump of his tongue and stopping the bleeding. The doctor removed the retractor and tossed it onto the table. "There, that ought to shut you up." He turned and stormed out of the room, turning the light off and leaving Tommy sobbing in the dark.

Tommy's stomach lurched, and he rolled as far to the side as he could, vomiting blood and bile over the side of the table. His chest hitched, the pain of the vomit on his ruined tongue akin to pouring acid on an open wound. He tried to spit but he couldn't, and the sob filled the dark space.

Down the hall, a scream as loud as his own shattered the air.

Georgia Reign
Chapter 43

JENNIFER SHOT OUT OF the bed, stumbling to the bathroom as the vomit catapulted out of her mouth. She reached the toilet just in time, her entire frame shaking and convulsing from the vision.

Steve kneeled by her side, wiping the hair away from her face when the retching stopped. "How long?"

Jennifer turned. "Minutes, hours, I don't know." Her tear-filled eyes found his.

The sound of shattering glass reached them, along with CJ's guttural scream, and Steve shot out of the bedroom, bolting across the living quarters, heedless of the shards of glass spearing his feet. He threw the bedroom door open, expecting to find CJ in Jessica's arms, but she was nowhere to be found. CJ sat in the center of his bed, wrapped in sheets, shaking in a pile of his own vomit, his eyes as wild as the scream filling the room.

Steve crossed, pulling him from the mess and leading him to the bathroom. "Where's your mother?"

CJ just sobbed, shaking his head. He let Steve undress him and place him in the tub.

Once the boy was clean, Steve wrapped him in a towel and closed his eyes. With a flurry of commands, the glass laden living area was swept clean, reinstated to its former glory. His feet ached from where the shards of glass pierced his skin and he took a seat on the toilet, fishing the tiny daggers out. Each plink in the garbage can accompanied by a suppressed wince.

CJ stopped crying and numbly watched Steve. "That bastard cut my brother's tongue out."

Steve nodded, pulling the last shard out and summoning Jennifer to fix his wounds. He wiped the blood off his foot with a towel and raised his gaze to CJ. "I know, I saw too," he said, attempting to keep the fear out of his voice. He had seen the vision in all its gory detail.

Without a tongue, Tommy couldn't plead for his life.

Without pleading, Tommy couldn't buy any more time.

Without time, Tommy was dead.

Georgia Reign
Chapter 44

JESSICA SLID AROUND THE side of the house, peering in the windows for some clue. She heard a noise and spun, ducking behind the large arborvitae. A tall, dark-haired man strode from the back building, muttering under his breath. His chest was bare, his feet clad in flip-flops, and his hair a mess of spikes.

Jessica ducked farther behind the tree until she heard the front door snap shut behind the man. She sprinted the distance between the house and the outer building, checking once behind her before she tried the door. It swung easily, and she stepped inside.

Her eyes took a moment to focus, and she slowly made her way across the expansive garage that housed an assortment of rare sports cars. Jaguar XKSS, Aston Martin, McLaren F1, a Miura Lamborghini, Testarossa Ferrari and a Maserati Birdcage. She stopped at the Corvette Stingray, running her fingers along the graceful lines and turning away suddenly as the pain flared in her heart. Chris would have loved these toys. Her eyes misted, and she blinked back tears, turning and surveying the walls, looking for signs of a stairwell or any entryway that led elsewhere.

At the far end of the garage was a small office. Remembering the elevator in Frank Aris's warehouse, hidden in his office closet, she jogged to it, testing the doorknob. It turned, and Jessica shook her head. These people were entirely too trustworthy. This garage should have been locked up like Fort Knox. The little office was just that, no closet, no hidden stairs in the wall, nothing. She stepped out of the room.

The door latched, but before she took a step away, the low growl permeated the garage. Jessica slowly turned, her heart pounded in her chest and her gaze landed on the massive Golden Retriever. His lips pulled back to reveal sharp canines, and the fur on his neck stood on end.

"Easy now," Jessica said, putting her hands up slowly, sliding her back against the wall. She moved inch by inch in the direction she came. For every step she took, the dog matched it. His growl was menacing, and she didn't dare take her eyes from his. She backed into something solid, her hands fluttered by her side and felt cool metal, one of the expansion posts she had seen on her way by, and she stopped. The dog stopped as well. If he was going to attack, he would have by now.

"Easy boy." She tore her eyes away, studying the lay of the garage again. "Where'd you come from?" She cocked her head, returning her gaze to the dog. He hadn't been visible when she stepped into the building. She studied the floor again, and that's when she saw it. A section of the floor dipped to a crevice—one like in a Jiffy Lube shop, so a mechanic could change the oil without raising the vehicle. She glanced at the dog, pointing toward the indentation. "Did you come from down there, boy?" Her voice was peppy and playful, the same tone she used playing catch with Sam.

The dog's tail swayed, and his fur-lined lips sank a fraction. His teeth were still bared, but the growl had ceased.

"Good boy!" She shuffled toward the opening. "You want a treat?"

The dog froze, his head cocked, and the tail swished.

"You want a treat?" Jessica asked again, and the dog jumped past her, diving in the hole and he turned toward her, his demeanor altered, his eyes glittering. He pranced in front of a thick door, his nails clicking on the concrete.

Jessica reached over his head, clasping the knob. This time it didn't give when she turned. The dog pawed at the door and a hatch opened; the dog bound through into the darkness beyond. "That's why I didn't see you before."

She crouched down and pushed through the flap, feeling the ground before her with her hands. As she moved forward, the ground dropped away, and she tumbled through the shoot and down the short stairwell, landing with a thud in the pitch black. The dog's cool nose touched her face, and she got to her hands and knees. The first thing that hit her was the smell.

Urine and feces, and a coppery undertone. Her breath hitched. Death, she smelled death.

"Oh, my god."

The dog left her, bounding down the hall toward an inhuman sound.

Jessica stood, running her hands along the wall, looking for a source of light, a source that would illuminate where she was. Panting as loud as the dog, she made her way toward the clicking noise, blinking madly, willing her eyes to adjust to the blackness surrounding her. Absolute blackness, surrounded by cool concrete. Jessica froze, suddenly aware of the fur rubbing against her leg. She reached down, feeling the dog's head, finding the spot behind his ears and rubbing.

"Light. I need light." She ran her hands along the concrete, to her right, covering the length of the unbroken solid wall. "Shit."

"O, peeee, o!" a voice called out between harsh sobs.

It was close, coming from her left, and she felt her way along the back wall, her fingers crawling along the joint in the wall, palms flat, searching until she found it.

A switch.

She rested her forehead against the cool concrete and closed her eyes, flipping the switch. Light filled the cavern, followed by frightened moans. She glanced at the dog dancing at her feet and her stomach rolled.

Her Tommy was in here, and so were others.

When she stepped into the first surgical bay, her hand shot to her mouth.

Georgia Reign
Chapter 45

TOMMY HEARD THE CLICK of the toenails, and his trembling body betrayed him. A low moan filled his throat, and he pressed his lips together, holding it in as long as he could. *No, please, no, please, no, please.* In his mind, the words formed correctly, but his mouth couldn't articulate anymore, not without a tongue.

The clicks of the toenails back and forth drove him nuts. And a hot stream of piss shot into the already soiled diaper. The moan escaped, repeating the horrid "O, peeee, o!"

The lights took longer than usual, and when he opened his eyes, his voice fell silent. For a moment, he wondered if he was dreaming, but the sudden appearance of Alex at his side and the cool swath of his tongue on Tommy's cheek told him otherwise. He blinked once, twice, and then the wail filled the room. "Momeeee!"

JESSICA LOWERED HER HAND and shot across the room. The dog danced around her feet and then sat expectantly.

"Oh, Tommy," she said, her hands fluttered over his battered body as her eyes surveyed the damage. "I don't have it anymore. I can't fix you." Tears poured out of her eyes, sliding down her cheeks. She yanked on the chains, staring at the shackles holding his wrists and ankles in place, so much like the ones in the hellhole she survived.

"Heee heee om." His eyes frantically jumped from her face to the door and back.

Jessica's eyes met his and lowered to his mouth. "What did he do to you?"

Tommy opened his mouth, tears blurring his vision at the look of horror on his mother's face.

Click.

Jessica froze with her hands on Tommy's cheek. She straightened, turning toward the door, staring down the barrel of a nine-millimeter. The dark eyes as familiar as the name on the sheet of paper and a rush of anger filled her.

"You bastard!" She launched herself at the man and the bullet tore a hole through her shoulder, twisting her body in an unnatural arch, knocking her back against the instrument table. Bone and blood splattered over the sheet and Jessica caught the edge for support, regaining her footing and spinning back in his direction, undeterred by the throb dulled by adrenaline. The deafening gun report in the small chamber left her ears ringing.

"You shouldn't have come, Mrs. Ryan."

The second bullet ripped through her knee, knocking her supporting leg out from under her. She crumpled on the floor, her hands wrapped around her ruined appendage, and a shrill scream launched from her lips. Pain flared white spots in front of her eyes. She wasn't the only one in the room screaming and her gaze switched to her mute boy.

Tommy strained against the chains. A guttural roar filled the room, replacing the echo of the gunshots. His eyes were now wild and filled with a hatred that went beyond anything she thought him capable. His roar was that of a bear and not a boy. The chords in his neck stood out, the muscles rippled in his arms as he yanked against his bindings, fighting to get loose. "Aaaayyyeee!"

Jessica's scream trailed off and her eyes widened. Standing behind the bastard was her dead husband with the most beautiful wings fluttering in anger, his face a mask of pain as his angelic eyes locked with hers. "Oh, God." Her focus switched to something coming down fast.

All went black.

Georgia Reign
Chapter 46

TOMMY BUCKED IN THE chains when his father's ghost disappeared. "OOOOOO!" he roared, kicking his legs and thrashing as the doctor dragged his mother from the room.

CJ, please god if you can hear me, please, please send help. He's got Mom.

Tears hot and burning filled his eyes and coated his throat, choking. His chest rose and fell rapidly, sucking air in frantically. And when the whistling started again, the sobs bled from his chest.

The doctor stepped back into his room, dropping his mother's clothes on the chair. Without a word, he pulled the cloth back and grabbed the bone saw and the cauterizer, retreating from the room with a smile and a wink.

Tommy stared at the pile, listening to the hum of the saw. When the hum quieted, the smell of burned flesh drifted into the room. Tommy closed his eyes, turning inside himself, retreating, running and finding a safe place at the core of his soul.

Georgia Reign
Chapter 47

JENNIFER SAT ON THE couch next to CJ, both drawing on the pads Steve had brought them. Silent and sullen after the last vision, she didn't want to broach the subject, and her eyes darted to the clock again. It was after ten. Steve had left for the office at a little after seven, and Jessica still wasn't back.

"What time did your mom leave?"

"It was still dark out," CJ said. He tossed the pad onto the table and turned, looking out the window, biting his lower lip. When his eyes returned to hers, they were full of unshed tears. "I don't think she's okay."

She didn't think so either. The knot in the pit of Jennifer's stomach tightened, and she reached for the phone.

He answered on the third ring. "Hey."

"She isn't back yet."

Silence on the other line. She could picture him holding the bridge of his nose as he formulated what to say. He had his guard up and she couldn't hear a sound other than distant static coming from his mind.

Steve was pinching the bridge of his nose, trying to grasp the ramifications of what Jennifer insinuated when the fluttering of wings caught his attention.

He has Jessie.

Steve felt like someone took a two by four to his gut. "Excuse me?"

"Jessica hasn't come back to the hotel."

He has Jessie!

Both Jennifer and Chris spoke at the same time and Steve closed his eyes, one hand dropping to his side as his head dipped. "Fuck!"

"What is it?" Jennifer, Cleary and Sarah said in unison.

"Where is she?"

"If I knew, I wouldn't be calling you," Jennifer said.

"Where's who?" Sarah and Cleary asked.

I don't know. But he has her right now! Chris hissed, drowning out the rest of the commentary.

"Right now?"

Yeah, right now.

"Jen, I gotta go. I'm on it, I'll find them." He flipped the phone closed and stepped out into the bullpen with the list in hand, crossing off names of those that were sitting at their desks. That left six people on his list. He turned to Cleary and Sarah.

"Anyone from your list missing?" She scanned the room and nodded.

Steve looked at Cleary. "You?"

He nodded and went back to the makeshift office. "Cross off the names of those already here and give me the remaining ones." They handed their edited lists to Steve, and he scanned the results. An even dozen and again, both Lieutenant Danforth and Officer Gagnon were on the list. He tapped his pen on the paper. "One of these guys has Tommy and Jessica." He raised his eyes to his boss.

"How do you know that?"

"Did Jennifer tell you that, or was it Chris?"

Cleary looked at Sarah and then back at Steve. "Chris? Chris who?"

Steve quietly glared at Sarah before swinging his gaze to Cleary. He shifted uncomfortably. "Um, Chris Ryan." He glanced back at the list.

"You realize he's dead, right?"

Steve nodded. "Yes, I'm aware of that." The feathers ruffled, causing the air in the room to ripple, and some papers on the desk took flight.

Do something!

"Cut the shit Chris, we've got twelve names. We'll catch him," he said to the ceiling and headed toward the door.

He shot Jessie.

Steve stopped mid-stride. The color drained from his face, and he glanced back at Sarah and then down at his list. "Did you see his face?"

Silence met the question.

"God damn it, Ty!" Steve yelled at the ceiling. "Least you could do is give me a fucking name!"

"Did you just say what I think you said?" Cleary eyed Steve.

Steve stiffened and looked down at the list in his hand before turning to Cleary. He inhaled. "We don't have time for this right now."

Cleary stared at Steve, his eyes narrowing into slits, and the blood vessel in his forehead visibly pounded with the fury etched in his gaze. "Are you kidding me?" The body of Ty Aris was never found, and things clicked into place in Cleary's mind.

Steve closed his eyes, listening to the pattern of his boss's thoughts. Piece by piece, he put the puzzle together. All the while, an underlying anger grew and when Steve opened his eyes, Cleary's face was beet red.

"You little shit. You didn't arrest that fucker when you figured out who he was. Instead, you blackmailed him."

Steve shook his head. "What are you talking about?"

Cleary stepped close. "You blackmailed them, didn't you? You traded your wife's health for their secret." The harsh words whistled from between his clenched teeth.

Cleary crowded him, and Steve stood his ground, meeting his angry glare. "Look Ron, we don't have time for this! You can have my badge once we catch this fucker, but right now, we need to move, and move fast. He shot Jessica Ryan, and we need to find him before he slaughters them all. Understand?"

Cleary's jaw set and he looked at the crumpled list in his hand. He pointed his finger at Steve's face. "This conversation isn't finished." Cleary and Sarah stepped out of the room.

Steve paused and looked up at the ceiling. *Can you give me any more than that?*

The guy has dark hair, but you already knew that, and he shot her with a nine-millimeter. Chris's voice shook, and Steve didn't know if it was from rage or fear.

Georgia Reign
Chapter 48

THE DARKNESS WORKS FOR me. It brings me back to the moment I crave, the moment of surrender in their faces, in their eyes. So, I study reactions, pain, and resiliency and feed my dog in the process.

Santana begged me. She begged me not to hurt the children, not to harm them, but I couldn't help it. I had to find out how far down in the dark the soul went before it gave up. I had to find out if the last moments of life brought peace.

Unfortunately, I didn't get answers that day despite the screams. Screams that still echoed off the walls of the mansion's basement, much like the lost souls here in my morgue.

The almost imperceptible sound of iron scraping metal reached my ears and pulled me from my reverie. This arrogant bitch will serve my purpose, my revenge for being forsaken.

JESSICA WOKE TO DARKNESS and pain. Her chest constricted with every breath, each rise and fall sending jolts of pain through her shoulder. The steel under her was cold against her skin and her left arm clasped the table above her head. Fear laced her mouth, dragging her back fifteen years to the concrete prison where she met Chris. The iron shackles clasped around her right ankle and left wrist stung with their chill, like they had been doused in ice. She assumed her right wrist and left ankle were clasped in the same manner, but they were numb, the bite of the cuffs lost with the pain.

"Bastard."

As if triggered by her voice, the lights went on.

He sat in the chair across the room, in full scrubs. His legs crossed and his wrists casually resting on his knee. The doctor stood and crossed to her, his dark eyes scanning her with contempt.

Jessica blinked, and her gaze landed on the dog in the center of the room. The dog gnawed on a limb and it took her a moment for the reality to sink in. The dog ripped a patch of skin and muscle, chomping and swallowing, taking a second to lick his chops before he continued. The dog was eating a human arm. A moan welled from her chest, and she lifted her head, staring at the stump where her right shoulder should have been.

The doctor laid his hand on her flat stomach, and she jerked, her eyes darting to him. His fingers ran suggestively lower, tangling in the small web of pubic hair and stopping. "Nice work," he said, nodding toward the perfect Brazilian cut. He ran his hand back to her belly button, studying her.

Jessica's eyes welled with tears, tears of fury. "You stood by consoling me, saying you were doing everything possible to find the bastard who took my son and all this time it was you?"

"My brother has a knack for compassion. I don't." The doctor's lips twitched into a smile, and he reached for the sheet covering the instrument table, drawing it back for her to see. "I try not to over feed Alex, but this puts me in a hell of a quandary."

A severely damaged lower leg sat on the table, the knee shattered from a bullet. Her knee. Her leg and she now understood the lack of feeling in her left ankle. Jessica clamped her eyes shut, counting to ten, and forcing her stomach to abide.

"My little patients rarely satisfy his appetite, but with this," He waved at the severed leg, "he'll be at it for the next few hours."

"They'll be looking for you."

His laugh was rich and deep. "Somehow, I doubt that. I plan on giving them something to keep them busy for a while."

His cavalier attitude mixed with his cold merciless eyes frightened Jessica more than Frank Aris had. "You're a sick fuck." The growl in her voice was enough to bring Alex's head up from his treat.

He chuckled, drawing a scalpel from behind his back and twirling it in his fingers. "Did you know the uterus is one of Alex's favorite delicacies?" He set the blade on her abdomen, and with a wink, he puckered his lips. Whistling, he drew the blade down her abdomen, slicing through flesh and muscle.

White hot pain gripped her, and Jessica screamed. In the distance, she heard Tommy's guttural roar. With each flick of his wrist, more agony gripped her lower abdomen, and she couldn't scream loud enough to voice her suffering. This was something she couldn't fix. This was something she couldn't walk away from. This was something she wouldn't escape.

Darkness would have been a blessing. Instead, she screamed until her vocal cords shattered and all she had left was a harsh whisper.

The site of her reproductive organ in his hand and the smile crinkles around his eyes filled her with rage, but the throbbing in her abdomen sucked what was left of her strength, each beat of her heart straining her chest and echoing in her lower belly. The copper smell of blood and feces filled the room.

Her screams faded, and darkness accompanied the pulls as he stitched her up, resuming the incessant whistling. Whistling that followed her to silence.

Georgia Reign
Chapter 49

CHRIS STOOD OVER JESSICA, tears spilling down his cheeks, his wings trembling as he looked at what that bastard had done to her. Her breath was raspy, hollow, shallow, and as sporadic as her heartbeat. She had lost so much blood, too much.

Screams erupted from the other room, but Chris didn't look away. He knew it wasn't Tommy. Not yet.

"Jess." He ran the back of his hand over her cheek. "Oh, Jess."

A long exhale wheezed from her lungs and Chris waited.

"Hold on, baby."

No inhale came, just a small stream of bright blood-tinged urine and then nothing. No flutter of the eyelids, no inhale, no heartbeat, nothing. Just death.

Chris stepped away, spinning on his heel and taking flight, bellowing his anger at the gods above.

Georgia Reign
Chapter 50

TOMMY SOBBED SOUNDLESSLY, HIS eyes squeezed shut, his heart pounded like a locomotive in his chest. His mother stopped screaming a while ago and Annalee had started. The air in the room shifted, a cold draft flowed over him, and he shivered, opening his eyes. Shock, anger, despair all volleyed for dominance as he looked into his mother's opaque face.

"I promise you'll walk out of here, Tommy." His mother leaned over, showering him with sparks of light, pressing her lips to his forehead. "I promise. Just hang in there. Help is on the way."

He blinked, and her image faded. "No!" The word formed perfectly, despite the absence of his tongue. He yanked at the chains, thrashing violently, screaming and slamming his head against the stainless steel.

Weak from his outburst, Tommy continued to sporadically thrash, the screams giving way to sobs, his body covered in a sheen of feverish sweat and the headache pounded in time with his heartbeat.

The whistling came again, and this time it got closer, but Tommy didn't care. He was beyond caring until he saw what was in the good doctor's hand.

The doctor set Jessica's head on the end of the table by his feet, facing him. The eyelids stitched open, her dead eyes forever gazing at Tommy. "I figured you might want your mother."

CJAAYYYYY!

The thought screamed in his head, threatening to burst through his skull and for a fraction of a second, he felt his twin, and then all went black.

Georgia Reign
Chapter 51

CJ SHOOK, HE COULDN'T help it. Even in Jennifer's comforting arms, he trembled, her vision still emblazoned in his mind. His sobs muted in her shoulder, but his eyes were wide open and staring out at the Atlanta skyline. He wasn't sure if he'd ever close them again.

"I'm so sorry, CJ," she repeated over and over and over, rocking slowly. Tears tracked down her cheeks at the violent memory of his mother being sliced at the hands of the madman.

CJ clung to her, clung to hope, and clung to what remained of his sanity.

Hope and sanity shattered when Tommy's voice barreled through CJ's mind, and he stiffened in Jennifer's grasp. His sob stopping in his throat at the vision accompanying the scream.

A low rumbling started, and everything in the room vibrated with it. Jennifer's wide-eyed gaze shot to CJ.

Despair transitioned to an uncontrollable fury, and he struggled to break free of her grasp.

"CJ, don't!" Jennifer held him tighter. "Please don't!"

The first thing to shatter was the table, and it exploded into a million tiny shards. The picture frames on the wall followed, and the drywall crumbled.

Jennifer, terrified at his swirling power, sent a silent cry to her husband, and held onto CJ, knowing he had heard the distress call, too.

Georgia Reign
Chapter 52

STEVE SLAMMED ON THE brakes, pulled to the side of the road, and closed his eyes, allowing the transition to take hold.

"CJ!" The command barreled from his throat, and he stared at Jennifer, holding onto the boy for dear life.

CJ's head turned, and Steve felt the mental shove, stumbling back a few steps. "Stop this now!"

"Mom is dead." His eyes narrowed, and the chunks of the ceiling peeled off the studs, falling around Steve.

"Ty, please help me here," Steve whispered.

The angry flutter of wings surrounded him. *You're on your own.*

Steve tensed, his jaw tight and his lips pressed together. He took a deep breath and focused on CJ. "You need to get control, CJ."

The picture window behind them cracked and a great spindly web permeated the glass.

Steve crossed the room, ripped CJ from Jennifer, and picked him up, holding him at eye level. "Stop this now." His eyes bore into CJ.

CJ's chin quivered, but his eyes still held fire and destruction in them.

"I'll find the bastard, but I can't if you're destroying the hotel."

The trembling stopped, and with it, the pressure in the air. Tears brimmed from CJ's eyes, streaking his already wet cheeks. "My mom..."

Steve nodded, understanding fully what CJ was experiencing. It coursed through his veins as well. "I know." He set the boy down and wrapped his arms around CJ, glancing at Jennifer. When he pulled away, he kneeled down, wiping CJ's face. "I promise I'll find him, CJ, but I need you to chill until I get back, okay?"

"Kill him," CJ growled.

He'd like nothing more than to do that, but he knew better. Steve shook his head. "Not unless I have to." *Or I lose control.*

CJ glared at Steve. "Kill him." This time he whispered the words, trying to impart his influence on Steve.

"You can't influence a spirit, CJ." Steve closed his eyes, feeling the transition take place and when he opened his eyes, he was back in the car, staring at the busy freeway.

Steve rubbed his face before glancing at the list. Two more homes left. He switched the car into gear and prayed they weren't chasing their tails.

He prayed it wasn't a state cop with a carving fetish.

Georgia Reign
Chapter 53

I WRAPPED WHAT WAS left of her mutilated body in cellophane and slipped the grotesque bundle in the hidden, plastic lined trunk of my cruiser.

"This ought to slow them down some," I said, chuckling at the irony as I slipped into the front seat, my uniform covered in a camouflage coverall stained with dry blood.

Whistling, I headed toward Grant Park.

It was still early, and the entry kiosk was empty. I pulled to the side and stared at the gate, debating whether I should enter a pass code into the keypad or jimmy the lock. I decided on the former and flipped open the roster, scanning the list until my eyes locked on the perfect patsy. I punched in his number and waited for the gate to open.

I backed the car right up to the gazebo and sculpted an art formation they wouldn't ever forget.

Georgia Reign
Chapter 54

STEVE PULLED INTO THE driveway and whistled. Lieutenant Danforth's estate was stunning with an expansive lawn, a gazebo that led to a pool right out of Architectural Digest, an oversized garage with four bays and what looked like a guest cottage on the fringe of a lake at the far side of his property.

Plenty secluded.

His feet touched the cobblestone driveway, and his cell phone rang, shattering the quiet call of the mourning doves.

"What's up?" he asked, scanning the yard.

"Grant Park," Cleary said. "Get your ass over here now."

Steve tilted his head, siphoning information from his boss's mind. "An adult?"

"Yep. Female."

Steve closed his eyes and hung his head, slipping behind the wheel again. "I'm at Danforth's house and still have one more stop after this."

"Who's on your list besides Danforth?"

"Gagnon."

"Danforth was the first to arrive onsite. Gagnon still hasn't arrived. I need you here. You can follow up on your hunches after."

"Okay, I'm on my way." Steve turned over the ignition and rolled out of the driveway.

Twenty minutes later, he stood over the gruesome statue. The well-manicured hand protruded from the neck, stitched in place of a head, and the hand formed the now famous bird. Taunting them.

A wedding band glinted in the late sunrise, a beam of light dancing off the diamond in a bizarre light and prism show. The naked torso propped on a single foot, and Steve wondered if it was surgically stitched in place or if there was a leg embedded inside the body. His objectivity fractured, and he had to turn away.

He inhaled and exhaled, counting each breath and praying he was wrong. He met Cleary's gaze and closed his eyes. "Where's her head?"

"It's not on the grounds here."

"He's mocking us," Steve said.

"I'd say so." Cleary jutted his chin toward the sculpture. "Anything there to identify the body?"

"The rings," Steve answered. "I believe hers was inscribed, if I recall correctly."

"If you recall? What the fuck does that mean?"

Steve met his gaze. *When I got this super-charged shit—I got their memories, too.*

Annoyance flashed in Cleary's expression, and he pressed his lips together in disgust.

"You asked." Steve waited for the forensic team to give the all clear. The moment they dispersed, Steve turned and held his breath, stripping the bands off her severed hand and turning the rings so he could read the inscription.

All my love always & forever, Ty.

Steve closed his fist around the rings and stared at the remaining pieces of Jessica Ryan. He took a few steps to another picnic table and took a seat, twirling the rings on the table to take his mind off the lump in his throat.

Jessica was the last vestige of friendship he had and seeing her carved into such a frightening display would give him nightmares for months to come. If he hadn't coerced her to let him bring CJ down here, none of this would have happened.

Cleary took a seat opposite Steve. "Jack gave me a little background on you before he died, and right now I can see exactly what he was talking about."

Steve shot his gaze at Cleary.

"He said you have a tendency to blame yourself when things go wrong."

Steve raised his eyebrows and waved toward the pavilion. "Well, this wouldn't have happened if I hadn't insisted on bringing CJ down here."

Cleary pressed his lips together and then nodded. He glanced at the butchery and back to Steve. "But you didn't do this. You're responsible for bringing them to Atlanta, but you had no control after that."

"I don't buy that."

Cleary's gaze dropped to the sparkling wedding band on the picnic bench. He picked it up and studied the inscription. When his gaze leveled with Steve's, his jaw tightened. "She married him?"

Steve nodded, and Cleary clenched his fist.

"When exactly did you figure this out?"

"I needed him Ron…"

"—Don't give me that shit. You took an oath."

"I know I did, but…"

Cleary held up his hand. "Right now, I don't want your excuses. I want you to find this bastard and nail his ass to the wall before we find her kid in the same circumstances." He waved toward the grisly scene. "Think you can do that?"

Steve remained silent and nodded. "Who was first on the scene?"

"Danforth."

Steve pressed his lips together, raising his gaze and letting it drift over the officers in attendance before they fell on Lieutenant Danforth. Considering the distance from where he lived, it made sense. "How'd he get in?"

"He used his code to open the gate, but it was opened earlier by none other than Officer Gagnon."

That comment snapped Steve awake, and he scanned the crowd. Gagnon wasn't there.

"There were two houses left on the list. Gagnon's and Danforth's. I think I should pay Officer Gagnon a visit."

Cleary nodded and leaned closer. "You pick anything up from the officers?"

"Not really. Everyone is stewing over this." Steve waved his hand toward the group of officers. "I can't get a read on a couple of them, but that's normal." He glanced back at the group and inhaled.

"Who can't you read?"

"Lieutenant Danforth, Officer Jaberry and Officer Hicks. They're just blanks at this moment." He turned toward the posed carnage. "She's the freshest kill they've found and doesn't fit the profile, so they're probably just mulling that over." He returned his gaze to Cleary, his own mind trying to wrap around it.

"How did she end up dead?" He leaned forward. "The last time *I* saw her, she was alive."

Steve stared at his boss, ignoring the unspoken accusation, and then his eyes widened. "Shit." He palmed his face. "I left the list on the table last night."

"So, she could have left in the middle of the night and not early this morning like her son thought."

Steve sighed and nodded.

"Go check on Gagnon. He wasn't on duty last night, either."

Steve pulled in front of the address on the paper and scanned the condo complex. This wasn't right, and he spiked the paper on the floor. Gagnon lived in a thousand square foot duplex. There was no privacy here, and Steve swore. If Gagnon was their man, the kids weren't here.

He approached the door and rang the bell.

Officer Gagnon opened the door in his pajama bottoms. His skin flushed with fever and his eyes were equally as red. He blinked at Steve, his expression turning ashen, and he checked his watch and closed his eyes, bringing his knuckles to his lips. "Sorry, man, I know they said we had no time off, but I've been sick all night." He spun, vaulting around the corner.

Steve followed, and when he rounded the corner, he heard the retching in the bathroom. Instead of leaving like his gut told him to do, he said, "We found another body."

Gagnon wiped his lips with tissue and closed the toilet. "I'm not sure you really want to be in here, Agent Williams. This flu is pretty damn nasty. All of us have it."

"Do you have anyone who can vouch for your whereabouts last night?"

Gagnon's face shed all color, and he took a staggering step backward, his jaw dropping and his mouth forming an indignant 'o'. "You think I'm responsible for these deaths?"

Steve shrugged. He was only getting sluggish thoughts from Gagnon, not enough to confirm his accusation or clear him. "You knew the first victim, and you withheld information from the FBI."

"Get out of my house!"

"Can you tell me where you were this morning at six-fifteen?"

"He was upstairs throwing up," a scratchy female voice replied.

Steve turned to see an equally sick woman standing at the base of the stairs in a ratty bathrobe. Her blonde hair formed a nest of knots, and she clutched the edges of the robe with one hand and the railing with the other.

"Are you sure?"

"Yes, because I was down here alternating using this bathroom with my daughter. I know exactly where everyone was at six-fifteen because the only healthy one in this house left to catch the bus for school."

Steve scanned her memories of this morning, and they validated her words. Gagnon was sick. Hell, all of them were sick throughout the night, and Steve wished he hadn't stepped inside this house of germs.

Gagnon wasn't responsible for Jessica's murder, or any other murder, for that matter.

He turned back to Gagnon. "Your access code was used to open the gate to Grant Park this morning. Can you tell me who has access to those codes?"

Gagnon was slowly putting two and two together, and a crease appeared between his eyes. "My access code?"

"Yes, that's why I'm here. Someone's doing a hell of a job pointing us in your direction."

He blinked, still unable to comprehend the idea of a fellow officer setting him up.

"Gagnon. Is there anyone who can retrieve those codes?"

"Besides Lieutenant Danforth?" He closed his mouth and inhaled. His thoughts swarmed through his exhale. "I don't know. Maybe Danforth's boss?"

"Tell me what happened to Danforth's family."

"He was too late to save them, and beyond losing his wife and kids, shooting his own brother messed him up good for a while."

"His brother killed his family?"

"Yeah. His twin turned out to be the Savannah serial killer."

Steve had seen a news story about that when he was in rehab, but the names hadn't clicked until now. The Savanna killer targeted entire families, and no one ever figured out why, because the cop leading the investigation shot him dead on the scene.

Jesus. Danforth shot his brother. Danforth.

Steve turned and sprinted to his car, tearing out of the parking lot and heading to the last address on the list.

Georgia Reign
Chapter 55

STEVE PULLED INTO THE looping driveway and Danforth's cruiser sat parked in front of the portico. Steve approached the glorious southern mansion, scanning with his mind. Just as he raised his hand to knock on the beautiful oak door, Lieutenant Danforth opened it.

"Agent Williams." Danforth's eyebrows rose, but his eyes belied his surprised expression.

Steve tilted his head, staring into the tired gaze of the Lieutenant. "Aren't you supposed to be at the crime scene?"

Danforth nodded. "I just swung home to change and grab a bite. You're welcome to join me." He swung the door wide, gesturing for Steve to enter.

All he heard was static from the Lieutenant and alarms went off in his head, but he forced a smile. "Sure." Steve stepped inside. The atrium was bathed in warm sunlight that sent prisms through the crystal chandelier, the tiny rainbows landing on the large staircase that split and elegantly wrapped to the second floor.

Steve whistled. "I didn't know the force paid so well in Georgia."

A bitter smile appeared on Danforth's lips, and he glanced around the foyer. "My wife. She inherited it from her family."

"Oh," Steve said, shifting his weight from one foot to the other and sliding his hands into his pockets. "She came from money?"

Danforth nodded. "Doctors. Every single one of them. They were a little disappointed that Santana married a cop." He shrugged and headed down the marble lined hallway toward the back of the house.

Steve followed. "What happened to her, if you don't mind me asking?"

Danforth stopped and sighed. "No offense, but I'd rather not talk about what happened to my family. Maybe after we catch this son-of-a-bitch, I'll take you out for a drink and we can compare notes." He waved Steve into the kitchen. His lips pressed together, and he turned away from Steve, crossing to the refrigerator and pulling out a plate piled with fried chicken. "Hope you brought your appetite."

Steve stared at Danforth, still receiving only static from the man's mind. His gaze dropped to the plate of chicken and his mouth watered. "I didn't think I was hungry until right this moment. Is that barbecue?"

"No, Cajun. My neighbor brings me food every so often and it's enough to feed an army. She's a damn fine cook, but she needs to learn a thing or two about portion control."

Steve chuckled and took a seat at the table, turning over the case, the profile they distributed. Danforth fit the profile like the last piece of a jigsaw puzzle. Steve glanced around the room again, looking for something very specific and when his gaze landed on the metal water bowl sitting on the floor by the door, he shot his glance back at the chicken on the table, praying his face showed no signs of his stepped-up suspicion.

Danforth turned, pulling two plates from the cabinet. "Lemonade?"

"Sure." He grabbed a chicken leg while the sound of metal clanking against glass filled the room. He sank his teeth into the chicken and was rewarded with the delectable taste of hot spices coating the crispy breading and the juicy dark meat below. His tongue tingled, and he smiled at Danforth. "This is out of this world." He held up the leg and got a nod in response.

"I told you she was an exceptional cook." Danforth slid a glass of lemonade to Steve before digging into the chicken. "I've heard stories about you." He grabbed the second drumstick.

Steve raised his eyebrows. "Really, like what?"

"That you're a hell of an investigator and if anyone can find those kids, it's you."

Steve shrugged and took a sip of the lemonade. His lips pursed at the sourness filling his mouth. He blinked, looking at the yellow liquid, the bitter tinge mingling with the Cajun spices in his mouth, creating an unpleasant taste.

"Not sweet enough?" Danforth asked.

"Nah, I'm just not a big lemonade fan." He slid the glass away. He took another bite of the chicken to mask the taste.

Danforth took a sip of his, and his lips curled in disgust. "Oh, man, this tastes like shit. I'm sorry about that. Looks like Dora forgot the sugar again." He set the cup on the table and crossed to the pantry, pulled out the sugar jar, and grabbed a spoon. "The lemonade is stellar once it's sweetened." He dumped four tablespoons of sugar in his glass and raised an eyebrow. "You want me to add some to yours, or are you good?"

Steve debated; the sourness still pinching his throat despite the second bite of chicken, along with Danforth's reaction, drove his decision and he nodded. Four tablespoons of sugar and Danforth sat stirring his own lemonade. He offered Steve the spoon and Steve followed his lead, taking a sip after the sugar granules disappeared. Now it was sweet with just a hint of a sour lemon bite.

"So, tell me something, Agent Williams. What brings you out here today?" Danforth asked after they devoured the chicken.

"I thought you might be able to help us figure out who had access to the department pass codes."

"Cleary said you were following up on the Gagnon angle."

"Yes, but Gagnon was nowhere near Grant Park this morning."

Danforth's forehead crinkled in confusion. "You sure?"

"Yes, he's got an airtight alibi. Any ideas who would have that kind of access?"

"Major Hammerstein, Deputy Chief Kendal and Chief Sexton, all have access to our codes."

"I assume you have access too?"

"Yes." Danforth stood and cleared the empty plates and glasses, setting them in the sink.

"Are they secure?"

"As far as I know, yes, but you know as well as I do if someone has the mindset to hack in and they have the knowhow, there's precious little you can do to stop it."

Steve's thoughts flew to Chris, and he nodded. "True."

"What kind of dog do you have?" Steve asked, waving toward the water bowl.

Danforth turned, staring at the bowl. He blinked and sighed. "I haven't had the heart to get rid of that yet. Not only did my family die, but so did my dog."

Steve glanced between the clean water and the Lieutenant. The sorrow in his eyes cut to the center of his being and he let it go. "You've got a pretty big piece of property here." Steve glanced out the window at the large building that sat to the right side of the house. "What's that?"

Danforth glanced at his watch and a subtle change occurred. One Steve couldn't put his finger on, but when Danforth lifted his gaze, it nearly pierced through him. "I think you'd have a fine appreciation for what I've got over there." A grin appeared. "Especially considering the sporty coupe you've got parked outside."

Curiosity scratched the surface, and Steve followed Danforth out of the house and across the lawn. When he walked into the oversized garage, he whistled in appreciation and shot a glance at Danforth. He crossed the floor, studying each vehicle. Jaguar XKSS, Aston Martin, McLaren F1, a Miura Lamborghini, Testarossa Ferrari, Maserati Birdcage and a vintage Corvette Stingray. He raised his gaze to Danforth. "How did you get these?"

Danforth grinned, his eyes shining with accomplishment. "It took me a few years to find each of these babies." He ran his fingers along the sides, like a lover returning home to his long-lost girl. "They're my pride and joy." He looked at Steve.

Steve glanced across the showroom floor, finding a break in the floor before he raised his eyes to Danforth. "You ever drive them?"

"Yes. There's a local antique chapter that has a show every couple of months. I bring one of these out each time."

Steve stepped toward the indent in the floor and stumbled. The world tilted, spinning like an out of control top, and he reached for the nearest car, missing the metal by inches. He landed on his knees and his last thought before all went black was *shit. I'm such a fucking idiot.*

Georgia Reign
Chapter 56

I STARED AT SPECIAL Agent Williams and spit the sickly sweet taste of lemonade on the floor, but it still clung to my mouth. The bastard fell for it; he bought the act. He thinks I'm my brother, the good lieutenant.

Fool.

I squatted and yanked the keys out of his pocket and slipped them into mine. Once I got him prepped for surgery, I'd have to move the car. I stopped. His car. I felt the smile form, and a low chuckle emitted from my chest. The perfect fall guy lay at my feet.

I grabbed a pair of surgical gloves out of my office and walked outside, popping his trunk and then my own. I opened the hidden compartment in my trunk and pulled the folded plastic out. I needed his fingerprints. Bringing the plastic inside, I pressed his hands and fingers over the plastic until I was sure there were at least three sets of valid prints before I stowed it in Special Agent Williams' trunk. With the evidence planted, I dragged Steve down the concrete stairs into the darkness, depositing him in the first room at the bottom of the stairs before flipping on the lights.

Neither of my wards woke to the bright splash, and I stripped and chained Agent Williams to the same table Mrs. Ryan had occupied in the wee hours of the morning.

Alex lay in the corner still working on the remains of Mrs. Ryan's leg and I turned, trotting upstairs and into the darkening day.

Georgia Reign
Chapter 57

CLEARY STOOD BEFORE THE hotel door with his head bowed, gathering his emotions into a tight ball, and shoving them into the pit of his stomach. He rapped his knuckles on the wood panel and waited. Steve's wife opened the door, her eyes bloodshot and puffy from crying. CJ Ryan stood beside her.

"Mrs. Williams, may I come in?" He shot his gaze down to the child and back to her as she swung the door open.

Cleary hesitated in the doorway, his eyes scanning the destruction before him. It looked like a hurricane had ripped through the hotel room, including the spiderweb of cracks in the great picture window and his head snapped toward CJ. *Holy shit. Did you do this?*

"Yes, sir." The child stared at the floor, his cheeks blooming red.

"You already know why I'm here?" His glance traversed between CJ and Jennifer.

"Yes. I had a vision this morning," Jennifer said. "And CJ got a message from his brother."

Surprise mingled with disbelief, tickling the base of his spine. "What kind of message?"

"A telepathic message," Jennifer said.

Cleary inhaled and squatted, taking CJ's hands. "I'm so sorry about your mother."

CJ raised his tear-filled blue eyes, biting the side of his lower lip. "Where's Steve?"

"He's checking out a lead." Cleary looked up at Jennifer and back, wondering what would happen now that both his parents were dead. CJ's eyes hardened, and Cleary mentally scolded himself for allowing that thought in his head while within range of this child.

"I'll be fine." CJ yanked his hands away and retreated to the couch, throwing himself on the cushions and grabbing his computer. Before he completely dismissed Cleary, he sent a glare and said, "My mother's head is on the end of the table that my brother's tied to. He's the one you should worry about."

Biting shock filled Cleary's skin, slithering over him and causing his arms to break out in bumps and a shiver to ripple down his spine, pulling his balls into his body for protection. The toneless voice coming from the boy sounded more like a cynical old man rather than a nine-year-old, and he looked at Jennifer.

"He's had a tough day." Jennifer studied the spackled covered carpet and let her gaze drift toward CJ before turning her attention to Cleary. "I tried to call Steve a little while ago and he didn't pick up." She brought her index finger to her mouth, chewing on the already ragged nail. "Have you heard from him?"

Cleary stared at Jennifer and shook his head. He flipped open his phone and dialed the familiar number. After four rings, it dumped to voicemail. "Check in when you get this." He ended the call. A quick glance at his watch told him Steve should have checked in by now. The last place he was headed was the same officer that hadn't shown up today at Grant Park. Their prime suspect-Gagnon. *Shit.*

A shadow passed over Jennifer's face, her tired eyes transitioning to worry.

Cleary lifted his hands. "Don't worry about your husband. He can take care of himself."

Jennifer shook her head. "Not if he can't hear who's coming after him. You know where he is?"

"I know where he went. Just sit tight and keep an eye on the kid." Cleary left the apartment. When all this case was wrapped up, he had a laundry list of things to talk to Agent Williams about and none more important than Ty Aris's son, CJ Ryan.

Georgia Reign
Chapter 58

AKE UP GOD DAMNIT!

Wings fluttered, and the breeze Chris created shifted the blanket covering the surgical instruments.

Alex cowered in the corner, shaking, the bone he had been gnawing on forgotten in the wake of the angry angel filling the room. He whined, pulling Chris's attention away from Steve for a fraction of a second.

"Wake up, Williams!" He reached out, attempting to shake Steve, but his fingers passed straight through his skin. The only time he seemed solid was when he stood in Paradise Cove. Frustration filled him, and he bellowed a guttural roar, swinging his open palm.

This time he connected, and Steve's head lolled away from the slap, his cheek reddening, showing the shape of a hand where Chris slapped him.

Steve stirred, letting out a small groan.

"Aeee?"

Tommy's voice filled the darkness and Chris turned away from Steve, torn. He looked at the door, biting his lip, his troubled gaze returning to Steve.

Steve had to wake up. Right now.

Another roar filled the room, and he balled his fist. "Wake your ass up, Williams!"

Steve's head turned toward the sound of his voice, and another groan escaped his lips. His hand started toward his face, stopping short because of the chains.

Chris gave him one last look before turning and answering his son's plea.

Georgia Reign
Chapter 59

CLEARY PULLED INTO THE condo complex and parked in front of Officer Gagnon's apartment, staring at the building with the same uncertainty Steve had earlier. It didn't fit the profile, and his casual scan of the lot didn't find Steve's car among the parked vehicles.

Still, he had to follow up. He had some questions for Officer Gagnon.

Gagnon opened the door wearing only a ratty robe and underwear. His eyes bloodshot and his face pale with a light sheen of sweat on his forehead and upper lip. His breath carried the stench of vomit and he glanced at Cleary, blinking his eyes in confusion. "Did Agent Williams find out who used my code?"

"I don't know. Did he say where he was heading after he stopped here?"

Gagnon shook his head. "I thought he was heading back to the station. I'm sorry about not making it to the scene today. I know you said we had to be at work until this case is wrapped up, but I've got a nasty case of the flu and I didn't think you'd want the entire Atlanta PD vomiting for the next twenty-four hours." He put the back of his hand to his mouth and spun, fleeing around the corner and down the hallway, leaving the door open, retching sounds drifted from the far hallway.

Cleary reached in and closed the door. Halfway to his car, the door opened. "Agent Williams might be talking to Lieutenant Danforth about who had access to all our codes."

"Thanks, I'll check in at the station." Cleary waved and slid behind the wheel. Instead of heading into the heart of Atlanta, he turned east, heading to the last stop on Steve's list.

Georgia Reign
Chapter 60

A GUTTURAL ROAR JERKED Tommy awake. Darkness shrouded him, but he knew that voice, he knew that roar. He had heard it in a warehouse a lifetime ago. "Aeee?" *Daddy?*

Nothing.

"Aeee?" Louder this time.

Chris Ryan stepped into the room, bathing Tommy in a soft glow. His white wings shivering as he crossed the floor, his eyes glued to the severed head sitting at the end of the metal table between Tommy's feet. Tears of sorrow and fury coursed down his cheeks, and he met Tommy's stare.

"Aeee, eh me ou a hee," he pleaded, his mouth unable to form the words without his tongue, so he repeated them in his mind. *Daddy, get me out of here!* Hot, choking tears burned the corners of his eyes and throat.

Chris stopped at the side of the table. "What did he do to you?"

Tommy opened his mouth like he had done with his mother and the horror reflected on Chris's face.

The angel tilted his head, bellowing with rage, his wings spreading, fluttering and lifting him off the ground. "Williams!"

Metal shook at the volume and velocity of the roar, the surgical instruments rattled like brass chimes, and then the lights went on. Fear shook his ragged form, squeezing hot drops of piss out of him, and Tommy started blubbering.

Georgia Reign
Chapter 61

HIS EYES OPENED, AND it was dark, pitch black. No light permeated the room at all. Steve blinked, confused at the cool metal meeting his back and he shifted; his movements were stopped by shackles around his wrists and ankles. He turned his head, and the world tilted, spinning. His stomach rolled. He clamped his mouth shut against the sudden stream of bile that lined his throat, swallowing. Closing his eyes and counting to ten before he opened them again.

The fucker drugged me.

The coherent thought brought his senses alive, and the stench hit him. The combination of urine, shit, and a bitter undertone made his mouth taste as if he chewed a wad of tinfoil. It was a smell he recognized. Blood. The cabin had smelled like this after the explosion.

Shit.

He concentrated on the restraints holding him in place. *Open!* The metal creaked and shattered, freeing him and he felt around, finding the edge of the table and he hopped to the cool ground.

A low growl permeated the darkness, and his head snapped to his right. He froze in place.

"Williams!" Chris's voice nearly split his head in half and Steve's hands flew to his ears, trying to block out the ringing pain accompanying the volume.

He had no clue where the light switches were, and he'd bet a year's salary that the owner of the growl was a big-ass Golden Retriever. "Lights." The command was simple, along with the force of will accompanying it and the entire maze of rooms lit up. Steve blinked, focusing on the beautiful dog bristling in the corner. "Sit." He pointed, and the dog sat, his growl cut off in his throat, forgotten in surprise.

A tacky liquid covered his back and legs and when he turned and glanced at the table, his gag reflex kicked in. He had been lying in blood and gore. Frantic, he grabbed the clothing on the chair and wiped his skin with his shirt, dropped it to the floor, and slid on his underwear and jeans before bringing his gaze back to the dog.

A few things registered, a partially eaten leg on the ground. The dog's blood-streaked fur surrounding his mouth. Steve shivered, his gaze falling back on the leg. The finely painted toenails triggered another thought. *Jessica, holy shit, that's Jessica's leg.* This time his stomach catapulted the partially digested chicken out of his mouth. He coughed and spit and then straightened to a new noise.

Sobbing.

Sobbing coming from the hallway and Steve sprinted, following the noise past two additional rooms, one empty and the other stopping him. A girl lay unconscious under the bright lights. Her abdomen lined with ugly black stitches and Steve stepped into the room, crossing to her and placing his fingers on her throat. A strong pulse throbbed against his fingertips, stronger than he expected, and he sighed with relief.

He glanced at the cuffs and, with a quick tilt of his head and a whispered command; the metal fell open, freeing her wrists and ankles before he headed toward the sobbing.

Steve entered the last room, and his heartbeat drowned his ragged breath as his gaze shot from the severed head propped at the foot of the table to Tommy. "Jesus," he whispered, and Tommy's bright blue eyes found his.

"Hep eee!" He thrashed on the table and Steve sent a small allowance of power out, shattering the binds that held Tommy.

He was halfway across the room when Tommy screamed, raising his finger toward the door.

Steve spun to a flurry of fur and teeth. The Golden Retriever hit him chest high, and he stumbled backwards, falling into the surgical supply table, knocking scalpels and retractors onto the floor. The dog's jaw snapped inches away from his face and Steve clasped his hand around the furry throat, pushing the sharp canines away. "I really don't want to hurt you," he said, but the dog kept coming and Steve let a burst of power escape, sending the dog across the room into the concrete wall with such force the breaking bones echoed through the room, louder than the dog's yelp.

Alex crashed to the ground and lay still.

Steve turned back to Tommy, helping him to his feet. "Can you stand?"

Tommy took a step and faltered, his eyes rolling back in his head, and he collapsed. Steve caught his tilting frame and laid him gently back on the table.

He stared at Jessica's dead eyes, the calico colors muted and the thread holding her eyelids open, straining, giving her eyes a double row of lashes. He shivered and focused back on Tommy and saw the same ragged stitching traversing his belly, like Annalee's, in the next room.

When Tommy's eyes blinked open, Steve offered his best smile under the circumstances. "I'm sorry I didn't find you faster, Tom." He reached out and helped the boy to his feet.

"Issh oa." Tommy stared at his mother's head and sucked in a shaky breath, clinging to the table for support, feeling the raw pain flaring inside from each brutal cut.

"No, Tommy, none of this is okay." Steve looked around the room for clothing beyond the hideous soiled diaper draped around the boy's waist. He ripped the cloth covering the surgical supplies and found a box of wipes besides the less than shiny utensils. "Think you can clean up by yourself?"

Tommy nodded, stripped the dirty diaper off, and tossed it away in disgust. He cleaned himself with the wipes, wincing but determined. When he finished, he balled up the soiled wipes, throwing them in the same direction as the diaper. He dropped the box when he was done, and Steve handed him a poncho he made from the fabric.

"That's the best I can do right now."

Tommy slid his head through the hole in the center and tied the gauze around his waist in a makeshift belt, covering his naked form. "Aaaee," he said, pointing toward the hall and meeting Steve's gaze, swallowing repeatedly.

Steve nodded and led him out of the room and into Annalee's.

Georgia Reign
Chapter 62

CLEARY SCANNED THE MANSION and the surrounding yard as he stepped out of the car. "I'm at Danforth's and Steve's not here. He still isn't answering his cell phone, so I have no clue where he is."

"His cell phone could have died," Sarah said. "I'll check the station and then I'll head out to Grant Park. He may be walking the grid."

He passed Danforth's cruiser and climbed the steps, rapping on the door with his knuckles. No answer. He rang the doorbell and waited. Still no answer and he turned, scanning the lay of the land. His gaze landed on the enormous building occupying the side yard. A curving driveway disappeared around to the side he couldn't see, but he imagined it was some sort of garage.

Just as he took a step toward the building, the front door opened. Lieutenant Danforth stood wrapped in a ratty terrycloth bathrobe, with his hair dripping wet.

"I thought I heard the doorbell."

"Sorry to bother you at home..."

Danforth waved off the comment. "I just swung in for a quick shower. What brings you out this way?"

"I'm looking for Agent Williams. Have you seen him today?"

"I saw him at Grant Park earlier. You want to come in for a minute?"

Sweat saturated Cleary's back, the oppressive Georgian heat squeezed every drop from his skin and the cool air filtering out from the house felt like heaven. "Sure."

"Can I get you some lemonade while you wait?"

Cleary considered the offer. He was thirsty and the idea of lemonade set his saliva glands on overdrive. "That would be mighty kind of you." He followed Danforth into the kitchen, waiting while he poured a cup from the glass carafe and spooned a healthy amount of sugar in, stirring and handing the glass to him.

"I'll be right down. Make yourself comfortable." Danforth left the room.

The minute Danforth was out of sight, Cleary did a quick pass at the downstairs level of the house, finding nothing out of the ordinary except the dog bowl in the kitchen's corner and a complete absence of dog hair on the carpets and wood floors.

Cleary gulped half of the lemonade and sat down at the table, facing the door to the living room. Moments later, Danforth stepped into the room in jeans and a polo shirt, his badge hanging out of his front pocket and his revolver strapped to his shoulder. A white blazer hung over his arm and when he slid it on, he reminded Cleary of Sunny Crocket from "Miami Vice", with one exception: the jet-black hair.

"So, you're missing an agent," he said.

"Yep," Cleary answered, taking a sip of the drink. "He's probably walking the grid over at Grant Park or expanding our search profile. Sometimes when he's digging into something, he blocks out the rest of the world."

"If one of my men didn't answer my call, I'd have his ass on a platter."

Cleary chuckled. "I hear you, but Agent Williams is special in his own way." He thought about his earlier display. Cleary wasn't sure what he was going to do with Steve when all this was over. He clearly broke the law where Chris Ryan was concerned, but so had Jessica Ryan, and he wasn't sure he wanted to drag her memory through the mud now that she was dead, and her kids orphaned. Pressing formal charges against Steve would do just that.

"Special how?" Danforth asked, pulling Cleary out of his thought process.

"He's the best damn investigator I've got, even though he *is* a bit unconventional."

"He thinks a cop is doing this, right?"

Cleary inhaled and nodded, his gaze falling on the dog dish before traveling back to the Lieutenant. "What kind of dog do you have?" He pointed his chin toward the bowl.

A shadow passed over Danforth's face, and he sighed. "I had a shepherd-husky mix."

"Had?"

"Yes. My brother killed my dog the day he attacked my family."

Cleary had read about the case prior to coming to Georgia and he read the psychiatric reports that released Danforth for duty. On paper, Danforth seemed much more prepared to step into the job than Steve had been after Kyle Winslow blew up Steve's daughter. However, looking at the clean water in the dog dish, Cleary had his doubts.

"I need to get to the station," Cleary said, hooking his thumb over his shoulder.

"Sure, sorry to hold you up." Danforth finished the refreshing lemonade and stood.

Halfway across the living room, Cleary's arms tingled, and he lifted his hand. The heavy limb came in and out of focus and his gaze traveled to Danforth. The smile on the Lieutenant's face caused his heart to throb, and he fumbled for his sidearm, but his hands no longer worked.

The last thing that registered in Cleary's brain was the floor coming quick and then all went black.

I STEPPED OUT OF the house with another stupid fed over my shoulder. This was going to be a royal pain in the ass. One missing FBI agent was easy to cover up, but two, two was more of a middle finger to all law enforcement arms. I saw the possibilities of making this a much more public display of what I thought about the FBI than that boy at Centennial Park.

Halfway across the lawn, the red light over the doorway to the garage started blinking and the low siren wailed.

I stopped short. My heart tripped to double time, and I dropped the unconscious Assistant

Director on the ground, charging toward the
building and the security breach within.

Georgia Reign
Chapter 63

STEVE STOOD NEXT TO Annalee, with Tommy right behind him. He gently patted her cheek. "Annalee?"

Her eyes fluttered open, and she shuffled back on the table, fear etched into her wide, dark-rimmed eyes.

"Iss oa," Tommy said, gaining her attention while Steve grabbed the sheet and made another poncho for her.

Annalee stared at Tommy, her eyes filling with tears. "I heard you scream and, and, and I cried because he wasn't cutting me."

Tommy nodded. Tears formed and slid down his cheeks. He looked at the floor.

The admission set off coils of fire in his stomach, and Steve clamped his teeth together at the fury riding up his back. The bastard was going to pay dearly for this, but in the meantime, he had to get them out of there now, before Danforth came back. "Annalee, I need to get you and Tommy to safety pretty damn quick." *Because I can't hear the bastard coming.*

Steve handed her the cloth and helped her off the table once she slid it over her head.

"Stay behind me," Steve ordered, and the two children fell in line. Tommy took a protective stance, grasping Annalee around her waist and helping her out of the room despite the pain etched on his face. Having someone else to protect gave Tommy strength, and Steve was thankful.

They entered the hallway, inching down the narrow path toward the closed door at the end of the hall. Steve stepped beyond the entrance to the room he was in and into the path of a red laser light. He paused, tilting his head, listening; he glanced back at the kids. "Stay here."

Tommy laughed. "Uh-uh. o ay." *No way.*

Steve sent a glare in his direction. "I'm serious, Tommy. Stay here." He reached for the knob and waved for them to get on the wall behind the door. "I'll come get you when it's safe. I promise."

Tommy's lips pressed together, and he pulled Annalee next to him against the wall, faking bravery.

But Steve knew. He felt the fear radiating from both kids and he stopped, meeting Tommy's gaze. "I promise," he said. "And I don't make promises I can't keep."

Tommy nodded, still shaking, but he understood, and Steve turned back toward the door, bracing himself for what lay on the other side. The heavy metal swung aside, and he stared up a dark stairwell. He gave a quick glance over his shoulder at Tommy and gave a reassuring nod. The siren was louder now that the door was open, and Steve closed his eyes. Taking a deep breath, swallowing the fear that rode along his spine, he took the first step and the second, climbing until he reached the top door.

Steve leaned his head against the wood, counting to three and then swung the door open. The blast tore through his shoulder, and he spun, slamming back first against the door, staring at Lieutenant Danforth. The pain from the bullet eclipsed the anger and Steve staggered, catching the handle to remain standing.

"Oo!" Tommy yelled from the bottom of the stairs and started to climb, but Steve raised his hand, stopping him.

"I don't know how you got loose, but that little stunt is going to end up being a very painful lesson," Danforth said.

Laughter, born of anger, leaped from Steve as Danforth aimed the gun, pulling the trigger. Steve erected an iron wall between the bullet and where he stood, and the deadly projectile stopped inches away from Steve's skin, dropping to the floor with a crisp 'tink', like the jackets expelled from the gun. Steve tilted his head, studying Danforth's wide eyes. Fury pounded against his skin, begging to let loose, but Steve kept it in check.

"Of all the people on the force, I would have never guessed *you* were the bastard killing these kids. You're a cop, for god's sake. What the hell happened to serve and protect?" Steve stepped forward and Danforth raised the gun, pulling the trigger. This time, nothing happened.

Danforth looked up from the defunct gun, glaring at Steve. "My brother was such a pussy. He cried and begged me not to kill Santana, but I had to know. I had to see if they found peace when the screaming stopped. And then the bastard shot me."

Steve stared at the man in the cheap 'Miami Vice' get up and his brow creased. "Lieutenant Danforth?"

"Hell, no! Although I can feel him screaming in my head, scratching at the bonds like he always does when I'm doing my research."

Steve's anger diffused a notch. "I want to talk to Lieutenant Danforth," Steve said, his voice calm and controlled, wondering if this was just an elaborate ploy to get an insanity plea. He still couldn't hear anything from Danforth's mind and a split personality or psychotic break would jumble thoughts beyond his mind reading capabilities.

"I don't think so." The gun leveled again.

"Why not?"

"Because he can't handle the truth!"

Steve almost burst out laughing at the audacity of the statement, especially when paired with the Jack Nicolson delivery. This bastard was playing with him; sick or not, this had to end here.

He took another step forward; the movement cascading pain through his shattered shoulder, and he focused on destroying those things that mattered to this heartless bastard controlling the Lieutenant. "Which one of these babies is your favorite?" He waved toward the cars surrounding them.

Danforth pressed the trigger again in frustration, but the gun jammed.

"The Aston Martin?" With a tilt of his head, the little silver car blew up, sending pieces of metal flying over their heads.

"You bastard!" Danforth flipped the safety off but, before he could get his finger around the trigger, the gun was yanked from his hand and was tossed clear across the floor, discharging as it hit the ground, and the bullet pierced the door of the Stingray.

"What do you care? These are your brother's cars."

"They're mine, you asshole! They were always mine!"

"What about the Maserati?" Another explosion followed a tilt of his head. The anger grew, along with satisfaction from the horror etched into Danforth's face, his mouth falling open, and his eyes staring at the destruction. He swung his gaze back toward Steve.

The fury took hold and Steve lost control. The ground rumbled, rippling with the power escaping from Steve. The surrounding building disintegrated behind the wall of power traveling out from Steve's center, attacking and bowing over everything that didn't have a heartbeat.

The gorgeous southern mansion that stood for nearly a hundred years crumbled as if a giant foot crashed down on a toy house, flattening it into the ground. A plume of dust and smoke filled the sky, blocking the stars from view.

"What are you?" Danforth asked, visibly shaking.

Steve's laugh echoed into the night, gloriously similar to that of Chris Ryan's. "I'm your worst fucking nightmare!" The power grew, filling his skin, threatening to strike out again and Steve clenched his fists, holding on, reining it in, keeping it in check.

Danforth's face molded into a mask of fury.

Kill him! CJ's voice echoed in Steve's mind and choked off the laugh. "Why should I let you live?" The question was almost lost in the sound of sirens nearing the destruction. He took another step, and it was Tommy's hand on his arm that held him back.

"You can't kill him."

The small voice came from behind him, and Steve turned. "Why not?"

You can't. Chris's voice echoed Tommy's thoughts.

The shuffle of feet caught his attention, and he turned in time to see a shard of metal flying through the air. He parried, and the edge stuck into his arm. Danforth charged and Steve thrust the heel of his hand into the Lieutenant's throat as hard as he could. Danforth's head snapped forward and his feet flew out from underneath him. The crack of his skull on the concrete floor echoed into the night. Steve yanked the blade out of his arm and grabbed Tommy's hand, leading both him and Annalee out of the ruined garage and into the flashing red and blue night.

Georgia Reign
Chapter 64

THE POLICE CAR SLID to a stop in the driveway and Sarah hopped out. The ground rumbled below her as she ran to the form lying face down on the edge of the path leading to the garage. Fear, thick and pungent as the burning metallic stench hanging on the air, assaulted her. Her heart knocked painfully on her rib cage and her breath caught in her lungs. *God, please don't be Steve.*

She slowed, scanning the body as she approached it and sighed, relief flooding her until she rolled the body over and looked at the bruised face of her boss. The mansion imploded, crumbling and creating a dust storm around her, surrounding the garage in thick smoke.

She pulled her gun and trained it on the side of the garage where the door had been moments ago, ignoring the sirens that pulled to a stop behind her.

A shrouded figure stepped out.

"Freeze!" Sarah commanded.

"Sarah, it's me. I've got the kids," Steve called, raising his hands in the air and stepping out of the fog. Tommy and Annalee followed, and Steve walked toward Sarah, his hands in full view of the swarming police force. "Lieutenant Danforth is unconscious inside. He's the one responsible for the murders."

"Bullshit!" Officer Clemmons growled, stepping into view with his gun trained on Steve. His face formed into a mask of hostility until his eyes landed on Annalee and Tommy. "Jesus," he whispered, lowering his gun with wide eyes. His gaze traveled to Steve, and he nodded his apology before bellowing, "I need an ambulance now!" Officer Clemmons holstered his gun and collected Tommy and Annalee, leading them toward the make-shift command center at the edge of the driveway.

STEVE CROUCHED NEXT TO Sarah and pressed his hand to Cleary's chest. The strong beat of Cleary's heart met the flesh of his palm, and he closed his eyes in relief. A wave of dizziness overtook him, and he sat on the ground, his shoulder screaming in protest at the jolt.

"What happened?" Sarah asked.

"Danforth snapped, psychotic break, split personality—call it what you will, but the bastard snapped."

"How are we going to explain this?" She waved at the destruction.

"I don't know, and frankly, I don't care. What I need right now is Jennifer." He closed his eyes, letting the fatigue take over.

Georgia Reign
Chapter 65

JENNIFER RAN INTO THE emergency room, her eyes frantically searching the officers for a face she recognized. Thoughts swarmed, and she couldn't concentrate until CJ took her hand.

"He's this way."

She nodded and let CJ lead her to the hall outside the operating rooms. Steve lay unconscious on a gurney, blood seeping through the fabric of his johnny and Jennifer shot to his side, pressed her lips to his, and pushed the healing power rattling through her body into Steve.

His eyes flew open, and a rush enveloped them. The sound like a rising storm penetrated, whirling around, looming, threatening, depleting.

Jennifer felt the vacuum draining the power from her.

Steve gasped and pulled away. Light danced over his skin, closing both the bullet wound in his shoulder and the gash in his arm. Then the power settled, transfixed, bonded to the darker influence he held inside.

The yin and yang, coupled in one being where it rightfully belonged.

"Holy shit." He sat up, his staring at her and his gaze traveled to CJ. He flexed his hands, gaining control of the surge before it transcended to something else. Something he couldn't control.

Holy shit is right! Chris's voice pierced the silence.

"What the hell was that?" Jennifer's green eyes widened. Residual traces of the power still sparkled on her skin, but she could no longer hear the constant din of thoughts or feel the surge in her veins.

HIS SHOULDERS ROSE AND fell, and he blinked, looking at his hands, flexing and straightening his fingers. The combined power raging in him was formidable, but he didn't know if it would be enough to put Tommy back together again.

"I have to get Tommy out of here, pull the car around to the emergency entrance, and I'll be out soon. While you're waiting, call Ted and tell him I'll pay him whatever it takes to get down here in an hour," he said, digging the phone out of his pocket and handing it to her. "Stay with her, CJ. It'll be easier to get him out on my own," he said, halting CJ's progress.

Steve left them in the hallway, heading toward the pre-op room where they had Tommy. Ignoring the scowls, he crossed the room to Tommy's bedside, his gaze locked on Tommy's frightened, pain-filled eyes. "How'd you like to go home?" he offered Tommy a smile.

Before Tommy could nod, the surgeon waiting for his release forms interrupted. "He needs medical attention. I can't release him until…"

Steve turned toward the voice, flipping his badge open. "I assure you, he will get the very best medicine has to offer; now if you don't mind, I'm taking him home."

"But, sir?"

Steve leveled his gaze and pushed his voice to a low, commanding growl. "Sign the release forms."

The doctor blinked and nodded, shuffling away to the counter and scribbling out a release form, signing Tommy over to the custody of Special Agent Steve Williams. He handed the paperwork over and focused his attention on the girl in the next bay.

Steve removed the IV tube and the oxygen mask and picked Tommy up, depositing him in a wheelchair before wrapping a blanket around him. "I can patch you up, but we have to wait until we're out of here. Okay?"

Tommy nodded, although his brow creased. *You have it now?*

"Aye-up," Steve said. "CJ's here, too, and he can't wait to see you," he added and pushed the wheelchair out into the heart of the emergency room. He got as far as the doors when an angry voice interrupted his progression.

"Where the hell do you think you're going?"

Steve turned and stared at his boss. "I'm taking the boys home. Jennifer's waiting outside for me." He waved toward the car idling outside the doors.

Cleary marched up to Steve. "He needs…"

"...to be fixed," Steve whispered.

Cleary raised an eyebrow. His gaze traveled to Steve's bloody, but perfect, arm. "We still need to talk."

"We can talk on the plane. I'll spring for a round trip if you need to be back here in the morning, but the boys need to be in a place where they feel safe," Steve said.

"And where's that?"

"I'm taking them to their grandparent's house in Connecticut. I'll get the address from my lawyer once we take off." Steve turned his gaze to Sarah when she stepped by Cleary's side. "Thanks," he directed to her.

"No problem, although I'd prefer to do without the mental phone call. Use the cell next time."

Steve shrugged. "Sorry, but Jennifer has my phone. Do you mind meeting us at hangar twelve at the Atlanta airport? I have a private plane booked to take off within the hour."

"Sure," Sarah agreed.

"Thanks." Steve traded a last look with Cleary before pushing Tommy out to the waiting car.

Cleary swore under his breath and followed, with Sarah close behind.

Georgia Reign
Chapter 66

THE DOOR TO THE hangar opened, and Steve stepped inside, carrying Tommy in his arms. He kept his mind focused on Tommy, making sure the kid didn't slip into shock before they boarded the private plane. CJ and Jennifer trailed, dragging the collection of suitcases and carry-on bags behind them.

Cleary and Sarah stood, trading glances with Steve.

"We stopped to grab their stuff." He set Tommy down on the couch, wrapping the blanket tighter around him. "You hanging in there?" Tommy nodded, but the rings around his eyes seemed deeper than before, and Steve knew time was running out.

He turned toward the counter, crossing the distance, but before he could ask about their flight, the outer door swung open.

"I got here as soon as I could," Ted said, striding toward Steve in his fancy flight suit reserved for the more elite clientele.

"Man, you are a sight for sore eyes," Steve said, the relief sweeping through him. "Where did I pull you from?"

"I was down in Boca Raton when I got your wife's call."

"I really appreciate it, Ted. I need to get those kids on board as soon as we can." Steve glanced over his shoulder at the group. Cleary approached with lines of irritation etched in his face.

"Jennifer said it was an emergency. Are they okay?"

"CJ is, but his brother is in rough shape. I'll fill you in when we're in the air. In the meantime, this is my boss, Assistant Director Ron Cleary. Ron, this is Ted Beaumont, a good friend of mine from Yale."

Handshakes were traded, and Ted glanced in Steve's direction. *You are in a shitload of trouble, aren't you?*

"Aye-up," Steve agreed to Ted's thought and winked at his friend. "We are about ready to go?"

"Yes. If you'll follow me, I'll get you settled in, and you can tell me what you need for the boy," he said, pointing his chin toward Tommy.

Steve carried Tommy on board and laid him on the soft couch.

"What do you need?" Ted asked, helping Jennifer with the bags.

"You wouldn't have a bathtub onboard?"

Ted laughed. "No, but we have an executive washroom through the galley on the right. It's small, but we're carrying enough water for you to fill the sink at least a dozen times. I've also got some cloth towels under the sink too, so you can clean up reasonably well." His gaze turned toward Tommy.

When Ted disappeared into the cockpit, Steve turned to Tommy. "I'm sorry I didn't do this at the hospital but..." he trailed off and shrugged.

"It would have been hard to explain," CJ finished the sentence for Steve and squeezed his brother's hand.

Ignoring the small crowd of eyes staring at him, Steve gathered the healing power until his entire body tingled with it. Harnessing the magic, he put his hand on Tommy and leaned forward, pressing his lips to the boy's feverish forehead. He willed enough juice into Tommy to erase his wounds.

Light leaped from Steve's hand, encompassing Tommy with the warm glow of sparks. Tommy cried out in pain and Steve closed his eyes, his heart breaking at the added torture he had to endure to heal. "I know it hurts, Tommy, but the pain only lasts a few minutes."

Tommy's cries turned to whimpers and Steve pulled his hand back, unfolded the blanket and watched the scars traversing Tommy's stomach fade away. He pressed his lips together, saying a silent prayer, one to return Tommy back to normal, for him to regenerate his lost tongue.

Tommy's eyes blinked open. The dark circles were gone, and his eyes were bright with a healthy glow.

"Feeling better?"

Tommy nodded. "Es," he said, and his expression fell, his eyes reflecting the horror present in his mind. Some things never grow back, and his missing tongue fell into that category. Devastation brought tears to his eyes.

"You're alive, Tommy." CJ slid next to his brother, wrapping his arms around him in a bear hug. Tommy returned the hug.

"Do you want to clean up and put on something from your suitcase?" Steve pointed toward the line of suitcases near the galley.

Tommy nodded and stood.

"Why don't you help him, CJ." Steve watched the two boys retreat to the washroom before standing and turning toward the audience of onlookers.

Cleary looked like his eyes were going to pop out of his head any second, his gaze traveling between the galley and Steve, his mind trying to reconcile what he just saw and misfiring.

"So, you want my badge?" Steve said.

Cleary blinked, focusing on Steve, his open mouth popping closed. "You broke the law, Steve."

"What are you talking about?" Sarah interjected.

"Aiding and abetting a known felon." Cleary sent a glare that silenced Sarah.

"He wanted to help track Kyle down, and knowing what I knew about the level of his gifts, you bet your ass I leveraged him. He was a fucking genius at computers, and he found Kyle in a matter of days. Days, Ron. We hunted that bastard for years and Chris pulled it off within a week."

"But what he did wasn't legal, was it?"

Steve inhaled and turned away for a second, his gaze landing on Jennifer. Her stark stare bore into him, willing him to come clean because their life would go nowhere if it was shrouded in lies. "No, he didn't exactly use legal means to track Kyle down."

"Do you know what that does to our case?"

Steve spun toward his boss. "The FBI didn't find Kyle. He kidnapped Jessica, Sarah and Jennifer and the only reason Kyle's in custody and facing a death sentence is because of Chris Ryan. I admit, the siphoning of Kyle's accounts was a little over the top, but if you'd like me to give the ten million dollars to the government as confiscated funds, I certainly can."

"How was Chris Ryan a felon?" Sarah asked, her mind racing to follow the conversation.

"Ty Aris," Both Steve and Cleary said at the same time.

Sarah's eyes narrowed at Steve. "You told me he wasn't Ty Aris."

"Technically, his proper name was Ty Alexander Ryan," CJ said from the galley.

All heads swiveled in his direction.

"CJ, this isn't your fight," Steve said.

"Folks, I hate to interrupt the love fest, but you all need to strap in," Ted said from the cockpit door. *Shitload of trouble is an understatement.*

Steve nodded. Ted witnessed the healing of Tommy and the rest of the ugly conversation, and his eyes now reflected doubt and unease. Ted was the only real friend left, and Steve kicked himself for putting that look in his eyes. "Did you want a co-pilot?"

Ted's gaze traveled to Steve's boss, and back, and he shrugged. "I'd love to have the kids up here once we get to cruising altitude."

Message clear. He had burned another bridge.

Georgia Reign
Epilogue

"**N**OW WHAT?" CJ ASKED, loosening his seatbelt.

Steve shook his head. "I don't know. I guess I've got to figure out what I'm going to do with my life now that I'm no longer an FBI Agent."

"I never said you were fired," Cleary said.

"I just assumed..."

"I'm not about to let you run around in the general public with whatever's burning inside you."

"But..."

Cleary held up his hand. "—I *should* take your badge, but I've been thinking about this since we found their mother. I don't want to drag her name through the mud, and now that I would classify you as a secret weapon, it would be irresponsible for me to cut you loose. Besides, Sarah will keep an eye on you."

"Excuse me?" Sarah's indignant voice chirped.

"You two work well together, and I figure you'll keep him in line."

"Yeah, right," Steve said, grinning. He glanced at the boys. "Ted said you two could hang in the cockpit now that we are up in the air."

Both sets of eyes sparkled at the prospect. As soon as they were seated in the cockpit, Steve escaped to the washroom and pulled out Lynn Trueman's card, dialing the home number she'd scribbled under her name.

"Ms. Trueman?"

"Yes?" Her voice was hesitant and laced with worry.

"It's Steve Williams. I'm sorry to call so late, but I wasn't sure who to contact. Mrs. Ryan was killed today."

Silence filled the line, followed by the release of a long breath. "Jessica Ryan?"

"Yes, ma'am, Jessica Ryan was murdered by a serial killer down in Atlanta and I'm not sure what to do with her boys. I know she has family in Connecticut."

Another sigh. "Chris Ryan was very specific in the event both he and his wife passed on." *Very specific and very adamant.*

"Can you give me the address for Jessica's folks? I'd like to bring the boys there and give them the news in person."

"I don't think you understand, Agent Williams. Chris Ryan made provisions in his will for this eventuality. CJ and Thomas will inherit the estate and he named you as their trustee and guardian."

Steve took a staggering step toward the closed commode. "Say again?"

"Chris Ryan named you as their guardian."

He slowly sank to the toilet seat. "Uh, um, is that legal?"

"Yes. It is legal. There are a whole host of provisions that I need to go over with you and, of course, there are papers to sign."

Steve was speechless, even with the small chuckle that erupted in his ear.

"Agent Williams?"

"I'm uh, I'm here."

"When will you be back in town?"

He pinched the bridge of his nose. "We're, um, we're flying now."

"I assume you're going back to Brooksfield?"

"No, Brainard, in Connecticut, and now I'm not sure whether to go to Maine or New York with the boys."

"Please let me know and I'll bring the paperwork to you, so we can discuss the provisions and conditions of Mr. Ryan's will."

"Okay."

"Good night, Agent Williams."

The dial tone followed, and Steve pocketed his phone. He stepped out into the galley and took the first seat he came to. Shock filtered through his system, and he looked up, meeting Jennifer's questioning stare.

"I just got off the phone with Lynn Trueman. She said Chris listed *me* as CJ's and Tommy's guardian."

"He did what?" The echo of all three voices filled the room and Steve looked from Jennifer to Sarah and then to Cleary.

"Chris Ryan named me as the guardian of his children."

The chuckle filled his ears, and he looked up at the ceiling of the flight cabin. "Why the hell would you do that?"

You are the only one capable of handling CJ.

"You've got Chris Ryan as a guardian angel, and you are responsible for his kids?" Jennifer said, his words finally sinking in.

"We, Jennifer, we are responsible for his kids," he corrected.

CJ leaned against the doorjamb of the cockpit with his arms crossed, just staring at Steve. "So, we're living with you now?"

Steve turned his attention back to Jennifer, raising his eyebrows before meeting CJ's gaze. "Based on your dad's will, I guess the answer is yes."

CJ smiled. "Sucks to be you."

Steve laughed and sighed. "I guess it does suck to be me."

The End

Continue The Steve Williams Series on the next page with CRYSTAL ILLUSIONS.

Crystal Illusions
Chapter 1

CAROLYN HASTINGS SAT ERECT and damp with sweat. Her heart played a staccato beat in her chest while the last note of her shriek tumbled into the darkness.

Outside, lightning flashed, creating shadows on her bedroom walls. Carolyn's gaze darted from one shaded spot to another, expecting the clawed beast from her nightmare to step out of the gloom.

Her hand flew toward the lamp on her nightstand, almost knocking it over. Mumbling a prayer, she switched it on and squinted from the light. She closed her eyes and trembled.

"Only a dream. It was only a dream."

She glanced around the room, still hesitant to believe it just yet. "Nobody is here," she reassured herself. Taking a deep breath, her heart slowed, and her sweating skin dried, leaving her shivering.

Carolyn hugged her legs, reviewing the dream with a shudder. She swallowed the metallic taste in her mouth and scanned the room again. It took a while, but she finally relaxed enough to lie down. It was only a matter of minutes before she drifted into a restless sleep.

The alarm went off at six, and Carolyn rolled, slamming her hand on the snooze button despite the busy day ahead. The shadows of her dream still haunted her, and her eyes opened to the stucco ceiling. With an uneasy sigh, she climbed out of bed and headed for the shower.

The warm water and regular routine did nothing to quell the nightmare. "Shit," she muttered and turned off the water. It had been years since she had a dream that vivid, and those memories were unwelcome.

She headed back to her room and picked out a cornflower blue suit with a pale pink silk shirt. Soft. She wanted to appear soft today, and as vulnerable as the state's client. Thoughts of the case erased any remnant of the nightmare, and she closed her eyes, pushing her emotions into a box and tying a sash securely around it. Angel needed her to be on her game, and if those emotions got loose, she'd blow the case.

Peering into the mirror, she adjusted her belt and tamed the few flyaway hairs that fell across her line of sight. Carolyn turned and headed to the kitchenette, stopping to grab the newspaper left on her doorstep. Tossing the paper on the table, she poured herself a glass of orange juice before settling in to read the headlines. She turned the paper over and inhaled the juice, the burn forcing her to sputter and cough.

The headline screamed:

TWENTY-THREE-YEAR-OLD　　　　BRUTALLY MURDERED

But it wasn't the title that caused her to inhale her juice; it was the photo of the woman. The woman killed in her dream.

God, it was real.

Deep down she knew it had been more than just her overactive imagination, but it took seeing the victim's face splashed across the front page for the reality of her vision to sink in. With it came both shame for not doing anything, and fear that there was some sort of connection—just like the last time. She shivered. Carolyn dropped the paper as if the beast from her nightmare would leap from the text and slice her to death.

"Boo!" a voice called from the kitchen doorway.

Carolyn let out a quick yelp and spun. "Damn it, Olivia!"

Olivia chuckled, crossing the kitchen with a lithe, sultry stride that screamed catwalk—tall and thin and in high demand with perfect chocolate skin Carolyn secretly envied.

"Sorry, I didn't mean to scare you," Olivia said, but the twinkle in her eyes belied her words.

Carolyn knew better. She sent Olivia the 'yeah, right' expression she'd practiced on several juries over the years—one Olivia was familiar with ad nauseam. Olivia was the queen of practical jokes, and she enjoyed scaring the bejesus out of her. "Besides, it wasn't you that spooked me. It was that." She pointed at the paper.

Olivia gave a quick, uninterested glance at the headline and turned her attention to preparing her breakfast. "You and Randy had some time last night! You woke me up. You were so loud!"

"Randy wasn't here last night. I had a nightmare."

Olivia turned toward Carolyn with raised brows.

"You mean to tell me you don't know the difference between a scream and the throes of passion?"

Olivia laughed. "With you, I'm never sure."

Heat colored Carolyn's cheeks. "What are you doing today?"

"I'm modeling for a new artist. My agent said he's superb, but we'll see. Is today the day your client takes the stand?"

Carolyn sighed. "Yes, and I hope we nail the bastard to the wall."

"I hope you do, too. That scumbag shouldn't be allowed to walk free after what he's done to that girl."

"Agreed, but today is going to be a tough one. I hate putting kids on the stand, but I need the jury to have zero doubts. With the smoke screens the defense is throwing at every shred of proof I've delivered, I don't think I have a choice."

"Well, good luck today." Olivia said, turning her attention to her breakfast.

"You, too, and be careful out there. We've got another wacko on the loose." Carolyn pointed to the paper as she walked from the kitchen and out of the apartment. She headed to catch the subway downtown.

Carolyn stood on the crowded subway, glancing around at the people surrounding her. The overweight suit clutching his briefcase by the door. Poor bastard's wife left him last week, now he's thinking about suicide. Her glance passed over a couple of boys who were not quite in high school yet. They were trying to get into a gang, but the gang wanted them to pull off a robbery. One was gung-ho, but the other has doubts. Too bad they'll both end up across from me in court. The old woman with the carriage full of cans and other garbage was dying.

Carolyn closed her eyes against the silent assault of information. She hated the occasional flood of facts she encountered, and had no idea when or why they triggered, but most of all, once they started, she didn't have a clue of how to shut them off. Today, of all days, she didn't need to be tuned into the psychic world; she needed silence, concentration, not the world's din.

"Sweet Jesus, will you just shut up?" she whispered, gaining a strange glance from the man standing beside her.

She got off at Park Place and headed up Broadway to City Hall, where the District Attorney's office was located. She needed to review the facts and the science of DNA testing, so she had her biggest guns in order, and she couldn't focus with the extra noise.

She slammed her door and shook her head to clear her thoughts. She needed to focus on her case. If all else failed, she'd put Angel on the stand. Glancing at her watch, she took a deep breath and gathered the papers on her desk, shoving them into her briefcase. She hurried downstairs and across the street to the courthouse, entering the courtroom early and setting up her space.

The doors opened, and child services escorted Angel, a ten-year-old Asian girl, to the prosecution table; giving a nod to Carolyn before leaving the girl at her side. Carolyn offered a smile, even though a little part of her heart broke every time she saw Angel. The girl's fear raked across her skin.

Since her mother died two years before, Angel's stepfather had subjected Angel to every abuse imaginable, repeatedly taking her at his whim, like a slave concubine.

"Good morning, Miss Hastings," Angel whispered.

"Good morning, Angel. Are you ready for today?"

Angel nodded, taking a deep, shaky breath.

Carolyn put her hand on the girl's shoulder. "I promise; he will never hurt you again."

Her oval brown eyes glazed with tears, and she took the seat next to Carolyn, folding her hands neatly in her lap. When the door at the side of the courtroom opened, Angel's hands clench until her knuckles blanched of all color.

Guards escorted Mitusi Yamakura into the courtroom. He was wearing the signature orange jumpsuit of the city lockup. He glared at Carolyn and Angel.

Anger laced Carolyn's mouth with a sweetness that made her want to spit. Instead, she took a deep breath and boarded up the emotions, saving them for the right moment.

"All rise. The Honorable Judge Burke presiding," the court bailiff announced.

Judge Burke settled into his seat and looked at Carolyn. "Miss Hastings?"

Carolyn looked down at her docket. "I wish to call Dr. Rutherford to the stand," she announced to the court.

A petite woman in her fifties navigated the aisle and found her way to the witness chair.

"Do you swear to tell the truth, the whole truth, and nothing but the truth, so help you, God?"

"I do." Dr. Rutherford sat in the witness chair.

"Please state your name and occupation." Carolyn approached the stand.

"Dr. Anna Rutherford. Forensic specialist."

"Please explain your specialty for the court," Carolyn directed.

"My specific area of expertise is in acid phosphate testing and DNA profiling."

"Can you tell the court what acid phosphate testing is?"

"Acid phosphate is an enzyme secreted by the prostate gland and is present in large amounts in seminal fluid. Finding significantly elevated acid phosphate levels is consistent with the presence of semen and is the basis for testing sexual assault victims. It also aids in DNA testing."

"And why is this important in this case?"

"Because a significant level of acid phosphate was found on Miss Yamakura's sheets."

"Was that the only test you conducted?"

"No. The semen was subjected to DNA testing, and we found the sequencing matches Mr. Yamakura's DNA."

Murmurs spread through the courtroom and Carolyn let the statement hang on the air as she looked at the jury.

"Thank you. No further questions, your honor." Carolyn crossed to the prosecutor's bench and sat down, satisfied with how today's witness had performed.

The defense attorney was looking through his notes. He stood. "How long have you been doing forensic studies of rape victims?" He addressed the doctor.

"Close to ten years," she answered.

"Have you ever been wrong?"

"Yes," the doctor began, "But..."

"Now, I understand acid phosphate testing is not always indicative of sexual contact. Is that correct?"

"With the levels..."

"Please answer with a simple yes or no."

"Well, yes, but..."

"The stains you found were on the sheets. Is it possible that Mr. Yamakura had sexual relations on those particular sheets with someone other than Angel?"

Dr. Rutherford blinked and looked in Carolyn's direction, her mouth slightly askew.

"Answer the question, Doctor."

"I guess that's possible."

"Thank you. That's all I have, your honor."

Carolyn scanned the jury and saw doubt in both their expressions and their minds.

Shit. She didn't want any doubt about what a sleazeball this guy was. She needed Angel on the stand. The bastard was careful not to leave any DNA inside Angel, so this was going to be a case of her word against his, but she was betting on Angel's innocence.

"Miss Hastings?"

"No further questions, your honor."

"You may step down," the judge instructed.

Dr. Rutherford climbed out of the witness stand and exited the courtroom.

"The prosecution would like to call Angel Yamakura to the stand." Carolyn stepped around the desk into the center of the courtroom.

Angel stood and approached the bench where she was sworn in by the bailiff.

Carolyn inhaled, calming the building frustration in her chest. "Angel, your mother died when you were eight, correct?"

"Yes, ma'am."

"Was your stepfather granted custody by this court after your mother died?"

"Yes, ma'am."

"How did you feel about that?"

"I was happy. Mitusi was good to my mother. He was a good father when she was alive." Angel studied her clutched hands.

"Do you still think he's a good father?" Carolyn asked.

Angel shook her head. Her fearful gaze shot to her stepfather and back to Carolyn.

"Please answer yes or no for the record," Carolyn said.

Angel leaned forward into the microphone. "No."

"What changed?" Carolyn asked.

"He started hurting me."

"How?"

Angel bit her lip and looked down at her hands again before speaking. "At first he hit me."

"Do you mean he spanked you?"

"No, he slapped me across the face in the beginning and then later he began using his fists when he wasn't happy with me."

"Can you give us an example of when he wasn't happy with you?"

Angel bit her lip and nodded. "When I emptied the dishwasher, if the silverware wasn't lined up in the drawer, he would hit me and send me to my room without dinner."

"Was that all he did?" Carolyn asked, her voice gentle and prodding.

"At first."

"What else did he do, Angel?" Carolyn asked again.

"When he came to apologize for hitting me, he'd touch me." Angel cleared her throat and shifted in the chair. "He'd touch me down there." She nodded toward her lap.

"Did he touch you with your clothes on or off?"

"Um, on, my clothes were on when he slapped me, but when he started hitting me with his fists, he would make me take my pajamas off before he said he was sorry."

Carolyn risked a glance at the jury, and what she saw made her want to raise her arms in victory, but she still sensed some waffling. So she pressed on. "How exactly did he say he was sorry?"

Even though they had practiced this line of questioning over and over, Angel still pressed her lips together and fidgeted in the seat, swiping the tears away from her cheeks and unable to raise her gaze from the spot on the floor in front of Carolyn.

"He w-would push his fingers in me and make me touch him."

"Touch him where?"

"His, his..." Angel swallowed. "His penis."

"Did you ever tell him you didn't want to?"

Angel nodded. "Yes."

"And what did he do?"

"He would punch me in the stomach until I did as he said."

"He punched you, fondled you, and made you fondle him..."

"Objection, leading the witness."

"I'll rephrase." Carolyn held up her hand at the judge and turned back toward Angel. "Was there anything else that your stepfather asked you to do?"

Angel nodded.

"You need to say yes or no for the court."

"Yes."

"What else, Angel?"

"He used to put his, his thing in my mouth and make me swallow afterwards so there'd be no mess."

"Beyond what you have already described, did your stepfather do anything else to you?"

Angel stared at her hands. "Yes."

"Can you tell us what else he did?"

"He put his," she paused and took a deep breath. "He put his penis in the same place he put his fingers." Her chin trembled, and tears spilled over. "It hurt, but he hit me when I cried."

Fury enveloped Carolyn and her jaw clamped tight, her teeth ground together at the injustice. She took a deep breath through her nose and refocused. "How often did he do this to you?"

Angel raised her eyes, meeting Carolyn's gaze, and shrugged. "A lot."

"What does 'a lot' mean? Every month? Every week? Every day?"

"He said he was sorry every day," Angel answered. Fresh tears stained her cheeks. "Every day until they took me away from him." She pointed toward the woman from child services.

"No further questions." Carolyn offered Angel a smile and a nod, conveying that she did a good job.

The defense attorney stood and approached Angel. "Miss Yamakura, did you and your stepfather get along when your mother was alive?"

"Most of the time," Angel replied.

"But not all the time, correct?"

Angel nodded. "Not all the time."

"And you were happy when they granted Mr. Yamakura custody?"

"Yes."

"Isn't it true that you got jealous when Mr. Yamakura started dating?"

"No, that isn't true."

"Isn't it true that after watching Memoirs of a Geisha, you decided your stepfather should marry a geisha and not the woman he was dating at the time?"

"Yes, but a geisha is an honorable woman, and the woman he was dating was mean and rude."

"Did you want to become a geisha?"

"Yes."

"So…you wanted to marry your stepfather?"

Angel recoiled in the chair, her face painted in horror, and she shook her head. "No!"

"Are you sure? Are you sure you're not making this up because your stepfather refused your advances?"

"No!" Angel cried.

"Then tell me why there was no semen found inside you, Angel? Tell me why it's only on sheets that could be used on either of your beds?"

Angel's eyes darted from the defense attorney to Carolyn. Wild desperation painted them darker than normal, and the tears came.

"Objection, defense is badgering the witness." Carolyn popped up from her seat.

"Objection sustained. I will not have you badgering this child in my courtroom," Judge Burke snapped at the young defense attorney. "Do you have any questions that are not argumentative?"

The defense attorney walked over to the defendant's desk and turned back toward Angel. "No further questions." He sat down.

Carolyn stood. "Angel, did you understand defense council's question?"

Angel's chin quivered, and she nodded. "Yes."

"Can you explain to the court why we only found evidence on your sheets?"

"He never, um, you know, inside me. He would, um, do it on my stomach or in my face and make me clean it up after."

"And you wiped up with the sheets?"

"Sometimes."

"Sometimes?"

"Sometimes he would make me eat it."

Revulsion snaked over Carolyn's skin, and she tried not to visibly shiver.

"That's all, your honor."

"You may step down now," Judge Burke addressed Angel.

The woman from child services escorted her out of the courtroom.

"Counselor?" Judge Burke addressed Carolyn.

"The prosecution rests," she announced.

Judge Burke addressed the members of the jury, giving them instructions as to their duty, and Carolyn surveyed each member, trying not to smile at the verdict she saw in each of their minds. The jurors filed out and court called recess.

Carolyn headed to her office across from the courthouse, waiting for the verdict to come in. She slid into the chair and leaned back, rubbing her face. Angel's fate was in her hands and while she was convinced when she left the courtroom the verdict would be guilty, she pondered the entire case, looking for weakness and reasonable doubt, anything that could derail her last impression.

She swung her chair around and glanced out the window. The view of the city was suddenly replaced by a damp, moldy place with undertones of grease, and a woman with dark hair and bright, frightened blue eyes stared back at her.

"No, no, no, no," Carolyn whispered as the claw from her nightmare rose in the air.

The blade ripped through the woman's neck, slicing straight to the spinal cord, sending a torrent of blood toward Carolyn.

Carolyn shot to her feet, pushing the chair back, and almost fell over. Her breath came in ragged pulls as she scanned the office. "Jesus!" She looked out at the bright sunshine against the tall buildings of the city.

She jumped at the rap on the door.

"The verdict is in." One of the office paralegals poked her head into the office.

Carolyn blinked and smoothed her skirt, regrouping and forcing her breath to come in even beats, quieting her racing heart. She pasted a fake smile on her lips and nodded. "Okay, let's do this."

The vision lingered, even as the jury read the verdict.

Guilty on all counts.

Carolyn smiled at her client, giving Angel a hug before relinquishing her to child services. She prayed Angel would be placed in a loving home. Foster care was such a crap shoot these days.

Packing up her briefcase, she focused back on the vision and shivered.

"Are you all right?" A voice whispered in her ear.

Carolyn snapped her head toward the voice, meeting the gaze of district attorney Jim Britt. She sent a nod his way.

Jim was a regal man in his early fifties. He had aspirations of entering the political arena but hadn't taken the plunge because of his unhealthy addiction to putting criminals behind bars. "You did very well, Carolyn."

Carolyn returned his beaming smile. "It certainly feels good to know he can't hurt Angel anymore," she replied, and her smile faded.

"What's eating you?" Jim asked, escorting her out of the thinning courtroom.

"I didn't sleep well last night," she lied. The visions of both her dream last night and the assault in her office this afternoon weighed on her. Someone else just died and there wasn't a damn thing she could do about it.

"You sure that's all?"

"Even though we won today, Angel still lost. She lost her mother and now she's going into the foster care system, which can be almost as brutal as what she went through in court."

Jim nodded. "Yes, it can, but at least we know she's safe now. I'll make a few calls to make sure she's placed in a good home and gets the help she needs." He escorted her out of the courthouse. "There's another case I'd like you to look at," he said as they descended the stairs.

"I've got a pretty heavy case load, Jim."

"I know, but this one is right up your alley." Translation, it was a sensitive subject involving a child.

Carolyn stopped. "I'm not sure I can take another case like Angel's."

"It's an eight-year-old boy."

That's all Jim had to say. They crossed the street in silence. Saving children had become her life's work and every new case that crossed her desk brought with it the horrors of the real world.

Carolyn didn't speak until they entered the offices, and she sighed. "Send me the file." She turned and strode to her office, closed the door, leaned on it, and bracing herself for another tough case.

Crystal Illusions
Chapter 2

CAROLYN SAT AT HER desk, staring at the case file, attempting to concentrate and push the visions from her head. She re-read the same paragraph three times before she gave up. The images were persistent, and she exhaled, swinging the chair around to glance at the Manhattan skyline.

Shuddering, she let her mind drift back to the deaths burned into her brain. The woman today looked like the girl from her dream last night. Dark hair, blue eyes and scared shitless.

A soft knock at the door interrupted her analysis.

"Come in," she called, swinging her chair around to face the door.

Trent Kaplan waltzed into her office, dropping the case file into her in basket. "Jim said you'd take this one."

He reminded her of a used car salesman—greasy, underhanded and just plain creepy. Being in the same room with him always made her want to drape a blanket around herself to hide from his obvious leer. She nodded and grabbed the file, opening it as he lingered. *Ah fuck, he's going to try to pick me up again.*

"What do you say we go out for a drink after work?" Trent smiled, leaning his hip on her desk.

Carolyn slowly raised her eyes. "I have a boyfriend," she said, trying to keep her temper in check. Trent was relentless.

"You don't know what you're missing." He walked out of her office.

Carolyn shivered. He repulsed her. She left the opened file on her desk and stood, walking to the window. Closing her eyes, she leaned her forehead on the glass and returned to the vision.

Claw? It can't be a claw.

Has to be some sort of blade bowed like a claw, which could mean several items from a sickle, which is unlikely based on the arc of the swing, but it could be a long knife or short-handled axe of some sort.

Ok, I've narrowed down the range of weapons. Now, where was the murder?

Alley last night.

Today's wasn't an alley. Where?

Carolyn closed her eyes again. The damp, moldy, greasy smell invaded her nostrils.

Greasy, like oil? Yeah, like oil.

Her eyelids slowly opened. "She was killed in a garage."

Carolyn took a seat at her desk and stared at the file without seeing the words. The phone rang, and she was so engrossed in her thoughts that the shrill buzz didn't penetrate the cloud of thoughts.

The rap on the door returned her to the present.

Jason poked his head in the room. "Got a minute?"

Carolyn focused on her paralegal. "You're late."

"I know. I had something come up this morning." Jason schlepped across the room and slid into the chair across from her.

"You should have called," she admonished. "We won, by the way."

Jason hitched his thumb over his shoulder. "So I heard." He shifted in the chair, trying to find a comfortable position.

"Is everything all right?" she asked. Jason wasn't his usual upbeat self.

He shrugged. "Not perfect. I just got sidetracked and had to take care of an issue."

Jason was hiding something, but she couldn't see into his thoughts to discern what it was. He was one of the few people she couldn't get a handle on, like he had an impenetrable steel wall blocking her abilities to see into his soul.

"I'm sorry," Jason said, fidgeting under her intense stare.

"I didn't say anything," Carolyn replied. She glanced down at the case in front of her. "I've got a new case." She folded the file and handed it to Jason. "I need you to write up a summary before the end of the day. I'm going to lunch." She left him sitting, holding the file.

Crystal Illusions
Chapter 3

CAROLYN LOUNGED ON THE couch with the television tuned to the local news and the evening paper spread out before her. The headline painted the death as a crime of passion, not connecting it with the death in the alley even though the signature was the same. What they didn't mention in either case was the killer planted a red lipstick stain on the victim's forehead.

Carolyn folded the paper and exhaled, rubbing her tired eyelids with fingers that felt like icicles.

The front door swung open, banging into the wall as Olivia made the routine grand entrance into the apartment.

"One of these days, that door is going to put a hole in the wall when you come in," Carolyn commented.

Olivia laughed. "You know I can't go anywhere without making an entrance."

"Humph," Carolyn grunted, returning her attention to the television.

"What's up your ass?" Olivia strode across the room.

Carolyn pointed to the paper on the coffee table. "Another murder."

Olivia snatched the paper and scanned the newsprint. "It doesn't say they're connected." She handed the paper back, dismissing Carolyn. "My day was exhausting." She slumped into the comfy chair on the other side of the table. "But the new guy is good. He's pretty fine and I think he had a hot date because he disappeared for a while and when he came back, he was all flushed and looking damn sexy."

Carolyn broke into a smile. "I'm sure Cameron would have an issue with that."

"Fuck Cameron, he hasn't called at all this week."

"It's only Tuesday."

"Yeah, well, he hasn't been all that attentive lately," Olivia pouted.

"Poor baby."

Olivia stood and left the living room in a huff.

Carolyn returned her gaze at the paper. "Son of a bitch is going to do it again," she mumbled. They always did, and again she wondered what connected her to the killer.

Why am I seeing these deaths?

Olivia came back into the living room, wearing comfortable flannel pajama bottoms and a skimpy camisole that showed off her perfect chocolate cleavage.

"We won the case today," Carolyn said once her roommate settled into the chair.

"That's fantastic!"

Carolyn shrugged. She didn't feel like celebrating this win. "She's now in the state's care, and that can be just as bad."

"When did you become so cynical?" Olivia sat up, studying her roommate.

"It's just been a long, draining case, and after everything that girl has been through, the thought of her landing in another abusive home makes my skin burn." *Besides, seeing these murders is a bitch.*

A knock at the door interrupted her thoughts, and she climbed off the couch, crossing to the door with as much enthusiasm as a snail crossing the road. She swung the door open, and Randy's gray-eyed gaze looked back. Randy Kincaid. Smooth talking Wall Street stockbroker with his hand on the pulse of the city. She wasn't in the mood for him tonight, but she stepped aside, allowing him to enter anyway. "Hi," she said.

"Hey, babe." He leaned in and planted a kiss on her cheek.

Carolyn gave him a grunt and shuffled back to the couch, throwing herself down onto the plush fabric.

"Heard you won the case." He plopped himself next to her.

Carolyn creased her brow. "Where did you hear that?" She didn't see the verdict in the evening edition.

"I saw Jason. He was downtown this evening, throwing back a few."

Carolyn nodded. He had handed off the file summary and skedaddled out of the office like a plague was ready to sprout. "Where did you go last night?"

"I had some business to attend to."

"Ah, eat and run. You know this isn't a fast-food joint, right?" Carolyn said, raising her eyebrows. The fact she had taken the time to cook a decent dinner after a long day at the office, coupled with his hasty retreat, irked her. And his nonchalant answer just fueled the fire.

Randy glanced at Olivia and received a shrug in return. "What's wrong?" he asked, concern creeping into his voice.

If he was that clueless, it wasn't worth explaining. Carolyn shook her head. "I'm not feeling well," she said, derailing the conversation.

Randy put his arm around her and pulled her close.

Not the right move. Not even in the vicinity of the right move. Carolyn leveled a glare in his direction and pushed him away. "I don't need to be coddled," she snapped and stormed out of the living room.

Carolyn stared at the ceiling, slowly counting to cool her shot temper. The door opened, and Randy stepped inside.

"What is wrong?" he asked and sat on the side of the bed next to her.

Carolyn continued to count the speckles in the ceiling, formulating the words. "What's wrong is such a loaded question."

"Why?"

She sighed and glanced in his direction.

"I'm still upset that you took off last night."

Randy cocked his head to the side, his eyes rolling. "You have nothing to worry about..."

"Did I say I was worried? I just said I was upset. Here I went to all that trouble to cook you a nice dinner, with my insane schedule, and you didn't even give me a proper thank you."

"Well, can I give you that thank you right now?" Randy's eyes sparkled with insinuation.

Carolyn stared at him, sending her *don't even think about it* look in his direction.

"You're really pissed at me."

"Ya think?"

"I told you I had a meeting."

"I know," she said under her breath.

"That's not the only thing rubbing you wrong, is it?"

He certainly could read her better than she wanted him to. "You'll never believe me." She returned her gaze up, studying the spackle job.

"Try me." Randy stretched out next to her and placed his hand on her stomach.

Carolyn took a deep breath. "I saw both murders."

Randy removed his hand from her stomach. "What murders?"

"The girl in the alley last night and the woman in the garage today. I saw them."

Randy slipped off the bed. "What do you mean you saw them?"

"Last night I had a dream and today I had a vision when I was in my office."

His eyes narrowed. "What exactly did you see?"

"In both cases, I saw their throats slashed open by something that looked like a claw," she said.

Randy bit his lip. "You didn't see who did it?"

"No. I'm seeing through the killer's eyes." She looked at her hands before returning her gaze to Randy, wondering if she'd gone too far, trusting him too much with such a crazy concept. "And what he is striking with looks like a claw to me."

Randy sat back on the edge of the bed. "You're not kidding, are you?"

"No." Carolyn met his gaze. "And he's going to kill again."

Randy tilted his head. "You're saying they're connected?"

Carolyn nodded.

"Why?"

It was Carolyn's turn to wrinkle her brow. "I don't know," she answered. "Why are you so quick to believe me?"

Randy smiled. "You have successfully repeated my exact thoughts more than a handful of times since the day we met. This isn't that far of a leap from reading minds."

Carolyn laughed. "I can't read minds."

"You may not realize it, but that's what you do every day."

She bit her lower lip. She hadn't divulged her abilities to Randy, and yet he nailed it. Her gaze found his, and she tried to read beyond the haze. His mind was a complete blank. "I can't read minds," she asserted.

Randy smiled and shrugged. "If you say so." He stretched out on the bed next to her again, running his hand gently over her stomach, pulling the shirt up to reveal her alabaster skin.

"I'm really not in the mood," Carolyn replied with a sigh.

"See. You can read minds." He smiled, continuing his exploration under her shirt, undaunted by her comment.

"Randy!"

He grinned. "What?"

"I'm serious."

"Fine," he snapped, his aggravation etched into the tiny lines at the corners of his mouth. He rolled off the bed and headed for the door. "I'll see you tomorrow," he said over his shoulder just before he slammed the door shut.

Carolyn returned her gaze to the ceiling. The bang of the front door elicited a twitch in her shoulders. Something akin to disappointment burrowed into the lining of her stomach, creating a small ache, and she closed her eyes, shaking her head from side to side in denial. "What the hell am I doing?"

Crystal Illusions
Chapter 4

CAROLYN SAT UP IN bed and her hand clasped her throat as the remnants of another nightmare flashed across her vision. She squinted at the bright overhead light that she had never turned off last night. The clock blinked a little after five in the morning.

Another day, another dead body.

With a sigh, she rubbed her face and swung her legs over the side of the bed. A stretch pulled her the rest of the way out of the covers, and she wandered into the bathroom. After stripping and leaving her clothes in a haphazard bundle on the floor, she stepped into the warm shower, but the water did nothing to wash away the vision.

After getting dressed, Carolyn walked into the kitchen, her mood much fouler than the prior evening. She shoved two pieces of bread in the toaster and slammed the button on the coffee machine, watching impatiently as the black liquid fell into the open pot.

She crossed to the front door, ripped it open, and swept the newspaper off the floor before returning to the kitchen and her burning toast.

Bitterness swathed her tongue, and she pulled the coffee cup from her lips in disgust. She needed Starbucks, not this crap.

"Good morning!" Olivia announced as she entered the kitchen.

Carolyn muttered and sailed past her, picking up her briefcase in the living room.

"Carolyn?" Olivia called from the kitchen.

"What?" She spun, glaring at her roommate.

Olivia put her hand on her hip. "I ain't your maid," she said, hooking her thumb over her shoulder.

"I'll clean up when I get home," Carolyn snapped and headed for the door.

"You need to get laid, girl!" Olivia called after her.

"Yeah, right," Carolyn mumbled and took the stairs to the exit. An icy drizzle fell from the heavens, further darkening her mood. She didn't have her umbrella and instead of going back to retrieve it, she forged on, making it to the subway in time to watch the train pull out.

"Shit!"

It would be another ten minutes before the next subway came by. She scanned the thin crowd and the mad narrative in her head began. "Stop it," she whispered.

The man next to her raised an eyebrow.

She offered a thin smile and a shrug.

Carolyn sighed, letting the assault of the surrounding stranger's lives overtake her. This one wants to beat his girlfriend, that one wanted to still be home sleeping. It was all so surreal. Yet she couldn't read Randy's mind when she tried. She shook her head, knocking the fleeting thoughts away as the subway pulled to a stop.

She steered clear of the Starbucks, opting for the silence of her office instead. Carolyn leaned back in her chair and took a deep breath before she delved into the stack of case files on her desk, dividing the cases into ones she was willing to take on and those that would end up on the junior district attorney's desk.

The summary Jason had written caught her eye. She glanced over the case. The boy's uncle sexually assaulted him multiple times, even violating a restraining order to get to the boy. Jim was right. It was exactly the kind of case she prided herself on winning.

Carolyn looked at the stack of files and back at the case before her. She closed her eyes and sighed. *Too many lost children.*

A knock on the door interrupted her reverie, and she opened her eyes. "Come in."

Jim popped his head in. "Morning, Carolyn. You're here awfully early."

Carolyn nodded. "I couldn't sleep."

Jim slipped into her office and took a seat in front of the desk. "What's eating you?"

Carolyn waved at the case files on her desk.

"Are you burning out on me?"

Carolyn laughed. "No."

"Then what is it?"

"Did you read about those two murders?" Carolyn asked, knowing her boss religiously perused the newspapers.

Jim creased his eyebrows. There were several murders in the paper over the last couple of days.

"The two women with their throats cut."

The light sparked in his eyes and Jim nodded.

"They're connected," Carolyn stated.

His eyebrows rose. "What makes you say that?"

Carolyn sighed. "Just a feeling, I guess." She closed the case file in front of her. "He's going to strike again, mark my words." She crossed to the window, appraising the way he was studying her in the reflection.

"You think?"

Carolyn glanced over her shoulder at him. "Yes." She brought her gaze back to the morning rush in the streets below. Her hand drifted to her mouth to cover a yawn. "I need caffeine," she said.

"I'll spring for coffee this morning." Jim stood, and Carolyn joined him on the other side of the desk. "And you can tell me what you think about the case." He pointed at the file on her desk.

"I haven't finished reading the summary Jason pulled together." They walked out, slipped into the elevator, and descended in silence.

Jim brought the coffee to the corner table Carolyn confiscated, sliding next to her. He handed her a hot cappuccino and unwrapped the muffin he bought. "So, tell me what you want to do with that case."

"Shoot the bastard." Carolyn sipped her drink. Jim's laughter was musical in Carolyn's ears amidst the thoughts of strangers. "He belongs behind bars," she said as her boss wound down.

"Can you win?"

Carolyn smiled. "Have I ever lost a case, Jim?"

Jim shook his head. "No, you never have, and that simple fact always amazes me. But there's always a first."

It was Carolyn's turn to laugh.

"You certainly are a piece of work." Jim glanced at her fondly.

"Don't worry; I'm not gunning for your job, counselor."

Jim shrugged. "It may open up sooner rather than later, and you are the natural candidate to take my place."

Carolyn rolled her eyes. Five years before, Jim confessed he had greater aspirations than being District Attorney and since then, they had this same conversation at least once a week. "Then get off your ass and run for office."

"Maybe I will." He leaned back in the seat, his expression turning serious as he picked at the muffin.

"Do you know we have had this same conversation every week for the past five years?"

Jim nodded. "I'm aware. This is my little pep talk." He smiled. "And maybe someday I will get off my ass and throw my hat in the ring."

Carolyn returned his smile. "Jim, what really is stopping you?"

Jim offered a shrug. "Skeletons in the closet."

"What skeletons?" She tilted her head and glanced at her boss, trying to dig into his secret thoughts. Instead, all she got was just a big fat blank page.

Jim chuckled and raised his eyebrows. "Wouldn't you like to know?" And with that comment, he stood and collected his coffee, signaling the end of their coffee date.

Carolyn followed his lead and slipped through the crowded sidewalk back to their offices in City Hall. She slid behind her desk and looked at her caseload again. Today, she had a few cases that weren't nearly as heartbreaking as Angel's. The first case was a repeat offender whose latest transgression was armed robbery. Caught with the gun and the cash from the register two blocks from the crime made for an easy open and shut case. The second of the day was another cut-and-dried case; physical abuse and neglect, and she was sure the defense attorney would enter a plea bargain.

Jason interrupted her train of thought when he entered and dropped the paper on her desk. "Looks like we have a serial killer." He pointed to the front page.

The headline jumped off the page.

SCARLET PSYCHOPATH STRIKES AGAIN

Carolyn picked up the paper, glancing at the copy. A third victim was found in the early hours of the morning with the telltale scarlet lipstick mark on her forehead and her throat slashed wide open.

Carolyn took a deep breath. "So, I was right," she said, tossing the paper onto the desk and looking at Jason as she bit her lower lip.

"They didn't release the lipstick mark information to the press until this morning." Jason slid into the seat across the desk. "He's targeting a specific profile."

"White, between twenty-five and thirty-five, brown hair, blue eyes, average height," Carolyn said as she kept eye contact with Jason.

Jason tilted his head. "You have an inside track with the police?"

Carolyn smiled and made no comment. She looked at the paper and continued reading. The pictures of the women were on the next page and the resemblance of all the victims side by side was startling.

"They all look like you," Jason said.

"And?"

"Watch your back." Jason stood and left Carolyn staring after him with shivers traversing her spine.

Crystal Illusions
Chapter 5

CAROLYN RETURNED TO HER office after a day in court and slid her shoes off, crinkling her toes in the plush carpet. She sat down in her chair and stretched. The dull ache in her calves reminded her she needed to wear more sensible shoes when pacing in front of a jury.

The phone rang, interrupting the lazy stretch, and she hit the speaker button. "Hello?"

"Hey, babe. Feeling better today?" The baritone voice filled her office.

Carolyn took a deep breath. "Yes." She let a smile form. "I'm sorry for being such a bitch last night."

"No need to apologize. I wasn't exactly Prince Charming, either. Can I take you to dinner tonight to make up for being such an ass?" Randy asked.

"I'd like that." Carolyn resumed the lazy stretch, flexing her feet. "Where?"

"How about the Seaport?"

"Mmmm." Carolyn murmured. "I don't know."

"Where would you suggest?"

"Harry's?"

"Uptown?"

"Yes, I'm in the mood for a killer steak," Carolyn answered.

"All right. I'll be up in a few."

Carolyn disconnected the call and sighed. Rummaging through her desk drawer, she found the box of band-aids, pulled a strip from the box, and stretched it over the angry blister on her heel. She slipped her tired feet into the cramped high heels and cringed. At least Randy didn't ask to go dancing. She snorted at the thought and flipped her computer on, glancing at the ominous buildup of emails. Randy would have to wait while she waded through the forty odd new messages and offered some level of response.

The soft knock came twenty minutes later.

"Come in!" Carolyn called out. She didn't bother looking up when the door opened. "I'll be a few more minutes." She had cut the email build up by a third and was hell bent on finishing.

"Sure thing, sweet cheeks."

Carolyn's gaze shot up along with her irritation level. If she hadn't been so focused on cleaning out her email, she would have heard him coming by way of his lewd thoughts. "Trent, get out!" She returned her attention to the task at hand, praying Randy would walk in and save her from the lecherous idiot.

"Come on, Carolyn." Trent parked himself on the edge of her desk.

Carolyn brought her gaze back to him. "I'm working. Please get out of my office." She was in no mood for this today.

Trent's lips pursed. "What crawled up your ass?" He stood, looking down his aristocratic nose at her.

Carolyn took a deep breath to keep her temper in check. "I need to finish this before Randy gets here. So, if you wouldn't mind," she said, a fraction softer.

"Fine." Trent snipped and sauntered out of the room. "But you don't know what you're missing." He threw over his shoulder.

"I'm sure it's not a whole hell of a lot," Randy interjected as he appeared in the doorway.

Trent shuffled off quickly without another word.

Randy leaned on the doorjamb, smiling at Carolyn.

"Thank God." She returned his smile.

Randy laughed and stepped into the office, closing the door behind him.

"I have to finish these emails," she said as he approached.

Randy raised his eyebrow. "Really?"

Carolyn chuckled and nodded. "Save that for later," she said, pointing toward the chairs. "Have a seat. It won't take long."

Randy sat in the chair, slinging his arm over the back as he watched Carolyn with a wisp of a smile on his lips.

Carolyn glanced up at him. "Stop!" Heat crept into her cheeks. His thoughts were quite graphic.

Randy's smile widened. "See, you can read minds."

Carolyn shifted in her chair, the blush now burning, and she dropped her gaze back to the computer screen. "No," she said, refocusing on her emails, but his train of thought kept dragging her away. "Do I have to send you out of my office, too?"

He grinned.

"Come on, Randy. I have to get through these," she pleaded and plucked the newspaper out of the garbage, handing it to him.

"Okay." Randy took the paper and flipped it open, scanning the old morning news between glances over the edge of the paper.

Carolyn caught each glance and decided against wading through the emails, at least not at the depth she wanted to. Instead, she tagged the ones that needed thoughtful follow up and shot off the quick hits. Twenty minutes later, she clicked the button to shut down her computer. "Thank you." She rounded the desk and planted a kiss on his cheek.

Randy dropped the paper on her desk. "That's what you were talking about?" He pointed to the headline.

Carolyn nodded. "Yes." Her mood altering. She caught herself before she let the dark frame of mind overtake her. "But I'd rather not talk about it right now." She hooked her arm in the crook of his.

"You got it." He escorted her out of the building, hailed a cab, and gave address instructions to the driver.

"How was your day?" Carolyn asked, melting into the seat next to him.

"Pretty good." He glanced out the window with a non-committal air.

Carolyn's brow wrinkled. "Really?"

He turned and smiled. "Yes. I had a couple of fruitful client meetings."

That was the extent of the information he offered, but she knew there was more to it. She just couldn't tap into what it was.

"What about you?"

"Plea bargains galore." She leaned her head against him, and he wrapped his arm around her shoulders. The heat radiating from him felt wonderful; like a warm soft blanket and she sighed, wishing they were headed home instead of to dinner. "My feet are killing me."

He glanced at her shoes and offered a small laugh. "Regretting your impulse buy already?"

"You would think I'd learn by now," Carolyn said.

"One would think."

She glanced up at him. "You should have stopped me from buying these."

Randy broke out in a grin. "When you get something in your head, there's no stopping you." The taxi pulled up to the restaurant, and he peeled off the fare before helping Carolyn from the car.

The smell of cooked beef drifted over the underlying smell of hot tar and garbage. Carolyn's mouth watered. "I'm starving," she said as they stepped inside the crowded restaurant.

They were seated at a cozy table in the back corner. Carolyn already knew what she wanted and tapped her foot while Randy perused the menu. When the waitress came, she rattled off her order, "Petite fillet mignon with bearnaise sauce, steamed vegetables, and a side salad with raspberry vinaigrette accompanied by a glass of Shiraz."

Randy wasn't quite settled on his order. "I think I'll have the same, no wait, instead of the fillet, I'll have the T-bone and instead of Shiraz, I'll have a scotch neat. Everything else is the same."

After the waitress left, he took a sip of water and leaned back in his chair. "Plea bargains, eh?"

Carolyn nodded. "I only have one more case on my desk that will be an absolute joy to prosecute. Looks like it could be as bad as Angel's case." She watched as the drinks were set on the table. "I need to take a look at the DNA evidence and make sure it will stand up. I'm not interested in plea bargaining that one." She lifted the wine to her lips and let the sweet taste fill her mouth.

Randy smiled. "Are you ready to celebrate Angel's win?"

Carolyn shrugged and nodded. "It's bittersweet," she said. "I'm glad her stepfather was put away, but she has no one. She's in foster care." Carolyn swirled the wine in her glass.

"You can't save them all," Randy said.

"I can try."

"That's why I love you."

Carolyn raised her eyebrows, unsure of the unsettled brew those words produced in her stomach. "You love me?"

Randy cocked his head to the side. "What do you think we've been doing for the past year and a half?"

Carolyn shrugged. "Dating?"

"Exclusively."

Carolyn nodded.

Randy leaned forward. "I'm going to let you in on a little secret. I never dated exclusively until I met you." He took another sip of his scotch. "I want you to move in with me," he added.

The shock of his words forced the wine down the wrong pipe, and she coughed, spraying the table with the dark liquid. She covered her mouth with the napkin and wheezed and sputtered the remainder of the stinging wine from her lungs. "What?" she asked when she got her voice back, wiping her watery eyes with the napkin.

Randy stared into his drink with his lips pressed together in his sure sign of irritation. "Not exactly the reaction I was hoping for."

"I'm sorry. It's just that..."

"What do you want out of this, Carolyn?"

"I don't know. I guess I never thought about it, not seriously." She tried to soften the blow. "My career is just getting off the ground and that's where my focus has been." She paused as the waitress set their salads in front of them.

"So, I'm just a good fuck?" Randy asked after the waitress was out of range.

"I didn't say that," Carolyn shot back. "I said it never occurred to me." She took a bite.

Randy wolfed down the salad without saying a word. He set the fork down and looked across the table. "Will you move in with me?" he asked again.

Carolyn glanced down at her plate, weighing her answer. When she raised her eyes again, his jaw clenched with aggravation. "Give me some time to think about it," she stalled.

Randy downed the remainder of his scotch and raised his hand, flagging down the waitress for another drink. He stared at Carolyn in silence.

Carolyn sighed. "I'll think about it," she said again.

He continued the silent treatment.

"I will not make a decision like that off the cuff." She sat back in the seat.

Randy nodded as their main dishes arrived. "When will you have an answer?"

"You'll be the first to know when I've decided." She glanced up at him. "I signed a one-year lease a couple of months ago. I can't just up and leave."

Randy took a deep breath followed by a large pull on the scotch. Indecision radiated off him.

She wasn't sure how she felt about him. Randy was fun and downright sexy, but she never considered him long term, yet there was no one else she'd rather be with. "I know you're pissed off, but just give me some time." She raised her eyes and offered him a small smile. "Okay?"

"Okay," Randy agreed, ending his silence.

Carolyn finished her meal. She lifted the half empty wine glass, finishing it in one gulp. "Are you staying tonight?"

Randy shook his head. "I don't think so." Coolness brushed his tone.

Carolyn raised her eyebrows in a challenge. "Will you at least come up?"

Randy cracked a smile for the first time since he blurted out the invitation to move in together. "Why?" He swirled the scotch, letting the ice clink against the side of the glass before he took another sip.

"Because I need a good fuck," she whispered.

He chuckled at her brazen response, the mischievous light returning to his eyes overtaking the raw irritation reflected in his gray-blue irises.

Crystal Illusions
Chapter 6

CAROLYN AND RANDY STUMBLED into the apartment an hour and a few too many drinks later. He was already groping her before the door shut behind them.

"Do you mind?" Olivia shot from the couch.

Randy didn't mind at all. Hell bent on making Carolyn realize the mistake she was making. He continued his exploration of her neck with his lips. Her scent drove him wild, a mixture of clean ivory and the spicy musk of her sweat was enough to stimulate every nerve ending in his body, driving his blood south.

Carolyn smiled in her direction, pushing Randy off for the moment.

He followed and shut the bedroom door against the increased volume of the television. The buzz of alcohol and burning irritation at her avoiding any commitment pounded in his chest, and both were as intoxicating as her scent. He spun her around and pressed her against the door.

Sweet Shiraz still lingered on her lips and bloomed in his mouth as her tongue circled his with the same level of heat and passion flowing through his veins.

God, how I want her, and not in this back and forth, part-time fashion.

He wanted every morning and every night. He wanted forever with her, but she just wanted this.

Randy tugged her suit jacket off, tossed it aside, and returned his hands to the silky fabric of her shirt. His fingers flew through the habit of unlatching each button, and seconds later, he peeled the shirt off. Her bare torso caressed his palms, just as silky as her shirt had been, and he gave in to the lust wracking his body, reveling in the need.

With a flurry of discarded clothing, he navigated her toward the bed, kissing, nipping, and stroking her body with every step. They tumbled onto the mattress; her chuckle muffled under his lips. Randy maneuvered his way down her body, alternating, running his tongue on her hot skin and blowing on the wetness, smiling as she broke out in goose bumps. He continued teasing her with his mouth and his hands, almost bringing her to climax and backing off, watching her cool down a fraction before he resumed.

The sheen of sweat covering her body, along with the escalation of her breathless pleas for him to keep going, gave him a certain satisfaction. His quest to drive her mad was working.

Her body trembled, and he pulled away again, diffusing her oncoming orgasm.

Carolyn let out a frustrated moan. "Don't stop."

"Move in with me." He flicked her with his tongue. He waited for an answer.

"Please, don't stop."

"That's not the answer I'm looking for."

"Damn it, Randy!" Irritation crossed her delicate features, and she went to sit up.

Randy pushed her back down, tempering his lust. This time he didn't stop when she trembled under the caress of his tongue, taking her to where she demanded.

His reward? A rush of wetness and a moan with his name on it.

Not exactly what he was looking for at all, but her husky voice drew his lust back into domination and he kissed his way up her body, lingering on her breasts before he moved back to her lips.

His entire being burned for her, and the first thrust into her wet canal brought him as close to heaven as he thought he'd ever get. Wet, slick and hot, and she cried out his name, bringing her hips to his in the same frantic, almost violent beat.

Panting and covered in sweat, they rode the next wave in together and Randy collapsed on her until his last shudder subsided.

With effort, he rolled off her onto his back and stared at the ceiling, and suppressed the chill that ran down his overheated body. No matter what he did, she still hadn't agreed to move in with him.

"Damn," she breathed and turned her head toward him. "That was so incredible, and so very unfair."

Randy allowed a slow, sarcastic smile to form. "But I still didn't get the answer I wanted." Bitterness edged into his voice, and he cursed himself for allowing her to get the best of him. He glanced in her direction. "Now did I?"

Carolyn sighed and shook her head.

Is she holding out for a ring?

Her gaze changed in response to his thought, becoming guarded and distant. Aggravation came back in full force, burning a hole in the lining of his stomach, his dinner souring in the mass of alcohol and acid.

Randy sat up and gathered his clothing, pulling them on hastily. He had to get out of there before he said something he couldn't take back. He glanced over his shoulder at Carolyn as he pulled on his shirt, and the thoughtful crease between her eyes gave him a spark of hope.

"What are you thinking about?" He took a seat on the edge of the bed and her eyes found his. He braced himself for the disappointment he knew was coming.

"I need a couple of days."

"Even after tonight?"

Carolyn offered him a smile and a slow nod.

It wasn't much of a consolation and despite the attempt to brace himself, her nonchalant attitude toward his offer burned him. "I'm sorry I brought it up." He stood and headed toward the door.

"Randy," Carolyn said, as his hand fell on the doorknob.

The question in her voice gave him pause, and he looked in her direction.

"What if I say no?"

Randy clenched his jaw against the raw hurt her question inflicted. "Then it's over." He slipped out, restraining himself from slamming the door.

Crystal Illusions
Chapter 7

CAROLYN SAT UP. BILE rose in her throat. She threw her legs off the side of the bed and bolted into her bathroom, barely making it to the toilet as the evening's overindulgence spewed into the commode.

She shivered on the cool tile and sat back, flushing the toilet. The vision persisted, and Carolyn spit a few more times, then stood on shaky legs, crossing to the sink. After brushing the acid from her mouth, she grabbed a bathrobe and her cell phone, dialing nine-one-one as she crossed to her bed.

"Nine-one-one. Operator thirty-three. What is the nature of your emergency?"

"I believe there was just a murder in Central Park," she said breathlessly. "In one of the tunnels."

"What's your name and location?"

Carolyn opened her mouth to answer and stopped. All the possible outcomes for answering that question flooded her mind, and she disconnected the call. She closed her eyes and swiped her face with her palm.

"What was I thinking?"

She knew well enough that they now had her phone number, and it was only a matter of time before someone followed up. She wondered what Jim would say. She trembled on the bed at the vision and flipped open her phone again.

Carolyn dialed the familiar number as she glanced at the clock. Her brow furrowed. It was three in the morning and Randy wasn't answering. She hung up and placed the cell phone on her nightstand. Her mouth still carried a hint of acid and she wandered into the kitchen, grabbing a glass of juice to wash away the bitter taste. She stood in the darkened room, looking out at the empty night. An eerie quiet settled over the city and she shuddered, thinking of the dead girl discarded in the park.

She turned, draining the glass and setting it on the table before she headed back to bed. Sleep didn't come, only the repetitive visions of the last four deaths.

"Why am I seeing this?" she asked the dark.

No answer came.

Crystal Illusions
Chapter 8

THE CLOCK STRUCK FIVE and Carolyn rolled out of bed, heading for the shower. She got ready for the day without enthusiasm. A soft rapping on the door interrupted her breakfast routine. She crossed the room, looked through the peephole, and stepped back, blinking. She looked again before swinging the door open.

"Jesus, Randy, it's the crack of dawn," she said.

Randy nodded, and she scanned his rumpled attire, the same clothes he wore last night.

"You look like shit."

Dimples made a brief appearance along with a shrug. "I've been thinking about what I said when I left last night." He stepped across the threshold.

"You've been out all night?" she asked, closing the door. He smelled like a distillery and his bloodshot eyes were encircled by dark crescents, evidence of his lack of sleep.

"Yes." He peeled off his trench coat. "Can I throw this in your washing machine? Some jackass spilled their bloody Mary all over it."

Carolyn blinked and nodded, pointing toward the small laundry area they had in the back. Randy stumbled down the hall and struggled with the folding door that led to the washer. She let out an amused laugh and came to his rescue, easily pushing the panels aside.

When she reached to take his dirty coat from him, Randy glanced sideways at her and pulled the coat away. "I got it." His voice clipped short, and he flipped the machine open, shoving the jacket inside.

Carolyn reached for the detergent, and Randy swiped her hand aside. "I said I got it," he snapped. He poured a capful into the machine and turned it on, closing the lid and turning full toward Carolyn.

His mouth opened and then snapped shut like a Venus-flytrap. Randy turned and headed back toward the living room where he flopped into the overstuffed chair and rubbed his face.

"I tried to call around three." Carolyn took the seat across from him, concentrating on his emotions, trying to gauge what his mood really was, but all she drew from him was a big blank.

Randy caught her gaze and shifted in the seat. "I'm sorry," he finally said.

Carolyn sat back, surprised. "For what?"

"For putting you on the spot." His gaze lowered to the coffee table and remained focused on the pile of magazines instead of her.

"Randy, I care a great deal for you," Carolyn began, soliciting his eyes to lock in on hers. "But I'm not sure I'm ready to move in with you," she added, watching his face harden.

"You don't love me," he stated.

Carolyn closed her eyes and threw her head back on the couch. "I don't know." She sighed and opened her lids to stare at the ceiling, analyzing her feelings. "You're always the first one I want to talk to when I have a good day or a bad day," she offered, bringing her gaze to his. "You're the one I called last night when I had another nightmare."

Randy raised his eyebrows. "Another nightmare?"

Carolyn nodded. "I couldn't get back to sleep, either."

Randy's expression softened, and he sighed. "But?" He returned them to the original conversation thread.

"But I need time," Carolyn stressed.

He closed his eyes and the muscles in his jaw worked. "You have said that a half dozen times since last night. Why?"

Carolyn flicked her fingernails together, studying her manicure. "Because I need to make sure it's right. I don't trust men. My father died of an overdose when I was very young. My Uncle took us in, and he was a tyrant of epic proportion and a mean drunk." She sighed. "So, all the male role models I had in my life were pretty shitty."

Randy waited. "I don't get it," he said when she didn't continue further.

"I wouldn't expect you to." Carolyn stood up, retreating to the kitchen. She poured another cup of coffee for herself and a fresh mug for Randy, adding the creamer and sugar the way he liked it. She returned and handed him the cup. "My dad abandoned me in favor of drugs and died, and my uncle had a mean backhand." She took a seat opposite him.

Randy's eyebrows went up. "So, you have abandonment issues?"

Carolyn laughed. "And trust issues."

"I'd never hit you, Carolyn, and the thought that someone did pisses me off."

His bloodshot gray-blue eyes bore into her, announcing his anger like a bullhorn, and she shifted in the chair. "I know you wouldn't. But I need time to make sure I understand what I'm feeling, okay?"

Randy took a sip of the coffee and leaned forward. "Okay." He set the cup on the coffee table and leaned back, rubbing his face with his eyes closed. "I'm going to have a rough day."

Carolyn couldn't help the laugh that escaped. "Yeah, you are."

He opened a single eye and his lips curved into a smile. "Want to start it out on the right foot?"

Carolyn glanced at her watch. "I can't. I have some prep to do this morning."

Randy groaned and peeled himself off the couch. "In that case, I should go home and clean up." He wandered to the door. "I'll pick up my overcoat tonight." He glanced back at her before he disappeared.

Carolyn cleaned up the kitchen, wiped her hands on the floral towel hanging from the stove, and collected her briefcase.

The subway ride to the office was again filled with aimless-thought assaults of the strangers surrounding her, but this time, her own thoughts of Randy and their relationship kept the assault down to a dull roar. Carolyn opted for the Brooklyn Bridge stop and a longer walk, hoping the din would quiet and she could concentrate.

It paid off, and she was able to ignore the thought streams of the strangers that passed.

Bits and pieces of the prior evening snapped off in her mind like a slide show. Randy's reactions to her every move, his smile, his kiss, and everything in between. When the snapshot of his pain-filled eyes flew in and out of her stream of consciousness, her heart plunged.

Before she analyzed her reaction, a strange voice overrode her thoughts.

What the hell? barreled through her mind at a volume that drowned out everything.

Carolyn shot her gaze around at the crowded streets, scanning back and forth, trying to find the owner of the exclamation. Nothing, no recognition, no source, just a cold and dirty chill grazing her skin like an unwanted lover.

Crystal Illusions
Chapter 9

CAROLYN TILTED HER HEAD, concentrating, but nothing else penetrated her thoughts. She stepped into the crosswalk, crossed the street, and turned the corner. Her thoughts returned to Randy.

Do I love him?

The question prompted her to utter a laugh. She had no answer to that either and took a detour into the Starbucks to get her morning cappuccino.

She sighed as she stepped inside City Hall and crossed to the elevators. When she reached her office, she dropped her briefcase inside and went in search of the District Attorney. She knocked on his closed door.

"Come in." Jim yelled. He folded the paper as Carolyn entered his office. She took a seat on the couch across the room, studying her hands instead of meeting his gaze.

"Something bothering you?" He got up from behind the desk and took the seat next to her.

"Randy asked me to move in with him."

"Ah." Jim stared. "I guess you were looking for something more permanent?"

Carolyn laughed. "No, quite the opposite," she answered, and his eyebrows shot up in surprise. "I guess I never considered he would get serious. He's a playboy, or at least that's what I know of his reputation." She met Jim's gaze and leaned forward. "How did you know?"

"How'd I know what?" Jim asked, crinkling his brow.

"How did you know it was right between you and Linda?"

Jim leaned back in the seat. "I knew the moment I saw her," he admitted. "I felt like I had been launched from a rocket."

"I'm serious, Jim. How'd you know?"

"I am being serious. It was instant for both of us." He gave her a shrug. "I guess I was a terminal romantic, but after that initial jolt, I wasn't about to walk away from that kind of connection." He sighed. "But then again, I was young and foolish."

Carolyn smiled, wishing it were that simple.

"Do you love him?"

"I don't know," Carolyn said. "I'm not sure what love is." Her boss's reaction manifested itself in his narrow-eyed scrutiny.

"Let me ask you a different question." He leaned forward in the seat. "Can you see your life without him in it?"

That was a more tangible question, and Carolyn thought about it. "No," she finally answered. She could not imagine life without him.

"That's a start." Jim leaned back with a smile, but she sensed an underlying disappointment.

"What do you mean?"

"It's somewhat simple, Carolyn. For most, love isn't the lightning bolt kicking your ass like it was for me. It's a realization that you can't live without the person in your life."

Carolyn's brow furrowed. "I'm not dependent on anyone."

Jim laughed. "That's not what I meant, per se. It is a dependency in some fashion, but not in the way you're looking at it. Let me rephrase. You've already stated that you can't see your life without him as a part of it. That, in itself, is the beginning. It's a mutual respect and caring that runs deep," he said. "Do you trust him?"

Carolyn thought before she answered. It was hard for her to trust anyone, but Randy had never given her a reason not to trust him. "I guess so."

"Do you think he can make you happy?"

"I'm in charge of my own happiness."

Jim shook his head and threw his hands in the air. "God, woman, can you be any more self-sufficient?"

Carolyn smiled. She had been this way all of her adult life, rarely letting anyone inside, holding everyone at arm's length, even Jim, whom she considered one of her closest friends. "I don't want to rely on anyone."

His gaze hardened. "Randy isn't your father or your uncle."

Carolyn's eyebrows rose, and her jaw went slack for a moment. She popped her mouth closed and sat back, blinking. She had never once mentioned her childhood in all the years they worked together. "You know about that?"

Jim cocked his head. "I'm the district attorney for the City of New York. You don't think I do background checks on the prospects I'm going to hire?"

"Let me rephrase. How did you know about my uncle?"

"I was a new associate in this office at the time, and I wrote the summary for the DA."

"You never said anything."

Jim laughed again. "It was never pertinent to the conversation."

That struck Carolyn as funny, and she burst out laughing. "Not pertinent? What about all those cases of abused children you sent my way?"

Jim shrugged. "You are motivated to put those animals behind bars."

Derogatory comments filled her mind and Carolyn thought twice before she let the curses leave her lips. Instead, she stood and marched toward the door.

Jim caught her before she reached for the door handle. "Carolyn." He put his hand on the mahogany panels, holding it closed as she reached for the knob. "We've been friends a long time. I figured if you wanted to talk about it, you would have."

She glared at him. "What makes today so different?" she asked from between clenched teeth.

"You are measuring Randy in the same light as your father and your uncle," Jim said.

Carolyn stepped back as if she were facing a cobra, the horror of his words snaking up her spine and drawing her lips into a frown. "I, uh, I don't think so."

"You are. *That's* your hesitation."

"You're not my shrink." She regained her voice and stepped toward the door, reaching for the knob, despite Jim's hand still firmly pressing the door closed.

"No, but I am your boss," he challenged. "And your friend," he added, when she sent him her best cross expression. He kept her blatant stare without wavering. "I like to think I've been able to show you we aren't *all* assholes." He cracked a smile.

Carolyn burst out laughing; she took a step back, relinquishing control of the conversation.

Jim relaxed, dropping his arm from the door and crossed the room, returning to his spot behind the desk. Before he sat, he said, "Seriously, Carolyn, don't let your past fuck up your future."

Crystal Illusions
Chapter 10

CAROLYN PICKED UP THE paper on the way into her office and sat down. The headline didn't surprise her, nor did the picture of the girl. She sighed, tossing the paper onto her desk. Closing her eyes, she leaned back in the seat, trying to block out images of the dead.

The creak of the door interrupted her thoughts, and she opened her eyes to Jason, crossing the distance with a fresh cappuccino in his hand. Usually, the offering of morning coffee cheered her mood, but not today. Today, it just irritated Carolyn. "You really should knock."

"Since when?" Jason handed her the steaming cup. "You know Thursdays are my day to buy the coffee."

"Holy cow. It's already Thursday?" She ran her hand down her face, blinking the cobwebs away before she took the cup from Jason, setting it down next to her already empty cup.

"Wow, you must have had a really rough night," Jason teased and broke out in a perky grin.

"You have no idea," Carolyn said. "Why are you so happy today?"

"I've got plans for the weekend."

Carolyn raised her eyebrow and leaned forward. "Do tell."

"I'm not jinxing it. Let's just say plans for now and I'll tell you all about it next week." He winked at her and practically skipped out of the office, making Carolyn chuckle.

Carolyn turned to her schedule, sighing. Her calendar displayed a free morning, and she nearly laughed at the deception. The number of email responses stacking up in her queue would take twice as long as the block of free time she had, and that was only if by some miracle everyone left her alone.

THE COUCH IN HER apartment never looked so good and Carolyn stretched on the plush fabric, exhausted. She turned on the news, flipping from channel to channel, trying to escape the continuous news loop about the Scarlet Psychopath.

"Who the hell came up with such a lame ass name for a serial killer?" she asked the television. "I would have chosen something more appropriate, like sick fucking bastard," she mumbled.

Her mind drifted to the conversation this morning with Randy. She stood and wandered down to the laundry area, pulling out the damp clean trench coat and inspecting it for any signs of the stain. It was gone, and she threw the garment into the dryer.

Settling back on the couch, she tuned out the drone of the television, closing her eyes and shutting out all outside noise. A peaceful silence descended, and she turned her thoughts to Randy.

Was Jim right? Am I projecting my insecurities onto my relationship?

The door banged open, interrupting Carolyn's peaceful meditation.

"Hi, darling!" Olivia announced.

Carolyn smiled at her roommate. "Hello. How was your day?"

"Fabulous! Damon is amazing." She was positively beaming. She hopped into the chair, slipped her shoes off, and rested her feet on the coffee table. "Once he gets his focus, he's an animal with the camera. He says he paints as well, and wants to capture me on canvas."

"I'll bet." She rolled her head back to look at her roommate. "Clothing optional?" she teased.

Olivia uttered a light laugh. "He is one hot man and yes, clothing is optional." She winked. "I'm posing for him on Saturday."

Carolyn sat up, her light mood changing to a more serious note. "Randy asked me to move in with him."

Olivia's smile faded, and her gaze became guarded, as if preparing for the worst. "And?"

Carolyn shrugged.

Olivia raised her eyebrows, waiting. "Are you?"

"I don't know." Carolyn leveled with her. "I'm not sure what I want."

Olivia blinked, the sweep of her complex feelings draped over Carolyn. Relief, followed by confusion which transitioned to irritation. "Damn girl. Randy is one fine man. What are you doing?"

Carolyn smiled. "It's not that simple."

"Sure it is. He treats you right, and you're willing to let him slip through your fingers?"

"He's being an ass lately." Carolyn stood, retreating into the kitchen. She opened the freezer and then the refrigerator in search of something to strike her fancy. Nothing did. "You feel like grabbing a bite to eat?" She called over her shoulder.

"Sure, but I'd rather have delivery." Olivia called back. "How 'bout Chinese?"

Carolyn tossed the idea around for a moment, deciding something a little spicy did indeed tickle her fancy. "You mind calling in the order?"

"No problem. What do you want?"

"I'll take Szechwan Shrimp and fried rice, thanks." She headed toward her bedroom to change into more comfortable clothing for a night lounging on the couch. She slipped into a well-worn pair of jeans and an old, oversized sweater and returned to the living room and their prior conversation.

"I told him I'd think about it," she said, answering Olivia's hanging question.

"What's to think about?" Olivia stretched like a cat on the couch.

Carolyn shrugged. "We just signed the lease to this apartment for another year."

Olivia cocked her head to one side and sat up. "Seriously?"

Carolyn nodded.

Olivia sighed. "Girl, don't you worry about the lease. I can afford this place on my own. Besides, doesn't he live in one of those posh apartments downtown?"

"Yes. It looks out over the Hudson. You can see the Statue of Liberty from his balcony."

"That's about a ten-minute walk to work for you, isn't it?"

"If that." Carolyn answered. "But I like Brooklyn." She looked around their apartment. "I like this place."

The doorbell rang, and Olivia retrieved their Chinese food from the delivery boy.

"You're insane," she said, carrying the bags to the kitchen table where Carolyn set out plates and glasses.

"I'm just glad tomorrow's Friday, even though the monthly song and dance with the Mayor and his staff is likely to be a nightmare with that killer on the loose." Carolyn sighed. "What do you have going on tomorrow?" She opened the Szechwan shrimp and fried rice boxes, spilling a quarter of each onto her plate.

"I don't have a thing tomorrow, but I have that sitting on Saturday. Do you want to come hang with me at the studio?" Olivia asked as she shoveled shrimp lo mein onto her plate.

"If Randy has nothing planned, that sounds like it would be fun. I can always swing by Macy's if I get bored."

"Oh, honey, you won't get bored with Damon!"

Carolyn rolled her eyes. "We'll see."

The rapping of knuckles on the front door interrupted their conversation. Carolyn crossed to the door and peered through the peephole, her heart jumping as it always did at the sight of him. She opened the door and smiled. "Hi, Randy."

His bleary eyes scanned her as he stepped inside, and he licked his lips. "I am so tired," he said just before planting a kiss on her lips.

"Why didn't you just go home?" Carolyn asked.

"Because I need my coat tomorrow." His lips curved into an adorable smile. "And I wanted to see you."

Carolyn rolled her eyes and closed the door. "Want some Chinese?"

Randy shook his head and slid his shoes off before lounging on the couch. "Had a big client lunch today," he mumbled, closing his eyes.

"You're going to wrinkle your suit," Carolyn said.

"I couldn't care less about my suit."

"Mind if I finish my dinner?"

Randy opened his bloodshot eyes. "Not if you don't mind me taking a quick nap."

"Sweet dreams." Carolyn planted a kiss on his forehead.

Olivia stifled a laugh when Carolyn took her seat, digging into the rest of her meal. She smiled as Randy's snores became louder and more pervasive.

"If you moved in with him, he wouldn't have had to come all the way to Brooklyn for his coat." Olivia whispered.

Carolyn chuckled. "And you wouldn't have to listen to that." She pointed her chopsticks toward the living room.

Olivia nodded. Her smile faded. "I'll miss having you for a roommate," she admitted, staring down at her plate.

"Who said I'm going anywhere?"

Olivia nodded her head toward the living room. "You're gonna go."

Carolyn turned her attention to Randy. He looked like a little boy all curled up on the couch. Both of his hands fit snug under his cheek and his mouth hung ajar, producing the baritone snore she had gotten used to over the past year and a half. She smiled at the endearing view and glanced back at her roommate. "Maybe," she conceded.

After cleaning up the kitchen, Carolyn took a seat on the edge of the couch, gently running her hand over his shoulder.

Randy's eyes fluttered open, and he glanced sideways at her.

"Hey, why don't you go sleep in my room?" Carolyn said, running her fingers through the hair at his temple.

Randy shifted and pulled her down onto him. "Only if you join me," he mumbled, placed a kiss on her cheek, and wrapped his arms around her waist.

"I'm not tired."

Randy allowed a brief smile to play on his lips before he spoke. "Maybe I'm not all that tired anymore either," he whispered, running his hands down her back and squeezing her ass. His eyes sparkled and the laugh lines at the edges formed with his smile.

Carolyn giggled like a schoolgirl, which was something only Randy could reduce her to. He stopped her giggles with an insistent kiss.

"Aw, come on!" Olivia said, interrupting them.

Carolyn pulled away from Randy's welcoming lips. "Go give Cameron a call," she said.

"Fuck Cameron. He hasn't called at all this week." Olivia stretched on the opposite couch and picked up the remote, settling on America's Top Model.

Randy rolled his eyes, sat up, let go of Carolyn, and rubbed his face. He let his glance travel the length of her body before returning his gaze to hers. Raising an eyebrow, he moved his head toward the hallway, silently asking if she wanted to head to her bedroom.

Carolyn bit her lip and glanced at her roommate, taking in Olivia's stiff form and the glare aimed at the television. Her mood had changed yet again, and Carolyn knew it had to do with the mention of Cameron.

Shit.

She turned to Randy. "Why don't I get your coat?" She stood, retreating down the hallway to the laundry machine. When she turned, he was blocking her way, his gray eyes gazing at her like he was trying to read what was in her soul.

"You're not going to move in with me, are you?" It wasn't a question.

"Randy, I don't know," she said, more unsure now than she was when he first asked. Instead of meeting his gaze, she turned to close the retracting doors.

He grabbed her arm and swung her toward him. "I'm in love with you, Carolyn." He pushed her against the doors and kissed her, pulling the air out of her lungs with the passion behind his lips. He took the coat from her, turned and left without another word.

"Shit," Carolyn muttered and squashed the urge to go after him and apologize. His mood swings lit her irritation and fueled her stubbornness. Instead, she leaned against the laundry room doors, banging her head lightly against the pliable fabric. She muttered under her breath and headed into the living room, taking the couch opposite Olivia.

"Trouble in paradise?"

Carolyn shot a warning glance in Olivia's direction. "Don't go there, Liv."

"Cut the drama and just move in with the man," she snapped. Olivia threw the remote on the table and stormed out of the room.

Olivia rarely snapped like that, and Carolyn watched her hasty retreat with shock shuffling the contents of her stomach. She wasn't sure who Olivia was more irritated with, Cameron or her. She stood and followed her, ignoring the underlying meaning of the closed door. Without hesitation, she barged into Olivia's bedroom, stopping just inside the doorway. "What's really eating you, Olivia?"

Olivia turned and sighed. "Can't you see he loves you?"

"So, he says," Carolyn said with a shrug.

"He does, Carolyn. It's in his eyes every time he looks at you. You don't have any idea how lucky you really are. You could have someone like Cameron who only comes around just for a good fuck." Olivia sat on the side of the bed, crossing her arms and her eyes welled. "You're lucky." Tears spilled over, sliding down her beautiful cheeks.

"Ah, Livi." She crossed to her roommate, giving Olivia a much-needed hug. "Cameron cares about you."

Olivia shook her head as she pulled away. "I think he's just going out with me for the publicity. I make him look good, that's all."

"For Pete's sake, Olivia." Carolyn stepped back. "He's probably holed up somewhere going over re-election strategy. Last time he had the sympathy vote, this time is different. The economy tanked, and he's up against a virtual saint. Southerland can do no wrong in the eyes of the public and they are crucifying Cameron based on his voting record. Give him the benefit of the doubt."

"And maybe he's breaking it off because of the election," Olivia said. Their relationship was very public, a supermodel and a state representative made for juicy news pieces.

"Cameron wouldn't do that," Carolyn said, but even as she spoke the words, she heard the distinct ring of a lie. Cameron Unger was an ambitious politician with grand goals and a supermodel girlfriend might just thwart those aspirations.

Olivia sighed and tilted her head, wiping her cheeks. "Yes, he would."

"Oh, Livi."

"I'm just a little jealous."

"Don't be," Carolyn replied.

Olivia laughed. "Easy for you to say." She gave Carolyn a quick hug and headed into the bathroom.

Carolyn returned to the living room and settled onto the couch to watch some mindless television. The soft rap on the door interrupted the drone of a sit-com.

After a quick peek through the peephole, Carolyn swung open the door. "We were just talking about you," she said, gazing at the infamous Cameron Unger and his six-three frame. His smooth chocolate skin broke into a couple of laugh lines around his shy smile. The bags under his eyes made them seem much darker than normal.

"Is Olivia pissed?" he asked in a timid voice, which struck Carolyn as odd and out of character from his usual commanding baritone.

"That's an understatement. You could have at least called, you know."

"I haven't had a moment to breathe, let alone call Olivia." He shoved his hands into the pockets of his finely tailored suit and stepped inside the apartment. "Besides, my former chief of staff didn't think it was good for my career to associate with Olivia."

"Former?" Carolyn closed the door and got a sideways look.

"I fired him when he insisted I cool the relationship until after the election. I didn't agree. I will date whom I want, when I want, regardless of whether it's an election year." He straightened himself up and nodded his head down the hall. "Is she in her room?"

Carolyn smiled; the man had just secured her vote. "Yes, she is." She watched Cameron shuffle down the hall and disappear into Olivia's bedroom. And she flipped the lock on the front door, settling back on the couch, and returned her attention to another mindless television show.

Crystal Illusions
Chapter 11

THE DOOR SWUNG OPEN, and all she saw was a shape in the doorway.

"Jesus," she gasped and fumbled for the light, her gaze never leaving the shadow while her heart pulsed in her raw throat.

"Are you okay?" Olivia's voice cut through Carolyn's terror and the shape stepped into the room.

Carolyn let out a hysterical laugh. She found the lamp switch and flipped it on, filling the room with light. Her eyes darted around the room and fell back on her roommate. She nodded. "Another nightmare," she whispered. The bed shook from her trembling body.

"You scared the crap out of me," Olivia said.

"Sorry." Carolyn glanced at the clock. The digital display blinked four-fifteen, and she closed her eyes, mourning the loss of another victim.

"Are you sure you're all right?" Olivia asked. "Because you look a little pale."

Carolyn nodded. "It was just a nightmare." Although her stomach still rolled in slow flips at the vision of the most recent murder. "Thanks for checking on me." This time, her smile felt more genuine, and Olivia took the cue, disappearing from the doorway.

Carolyn dropped onto her back and stared at the ceiling, knowing how impossible sleep would be with the violent scene on perpetual replay in her mind. She opted for a shower and an early start to her day.

The subway was virtually empty at six in the morning and Carolyn thanked the Lord for the relative silence. Only a thought or two bled into her consciousness and even at that, they were benign thoughts, like white background noise, and she tuned them out.

In her office, she stared at the computer, not registering the words in the email on the screen. Since the vision insisted on looping again and again, Carolyn analyzed it, turning the scene over and over and over, trying to get a bead on where the murder occurred. The murder could have been in any of the boroughs, in any dark alley with a fence barricade.

"Damn it, that's five," she whispered.

"Five what?"

Carolyn jumped and swung toward the door. Her boss leaned against the doorjamb. "Jim."

"Sorry, didn't mean to scare you. I didn't expect you to be in quite this early."

With a laugh, Carolyn nodded. "I didn't expect to be here this early either, but there's been another murder."

Jim's brow furrowed. "I didn't read anything in the morning paper."

"It happened around four. That's too late to hit the front page," she said.

Jim stepped inside and closed the door behind him. "You have an inside track with the police?"

"No."

A deep crease appeared between Jim's narrowed and clearly confused eyes. "A reporter?"

Carolyn shook her head.

Jim took a seat, studying her before he spoke. "How do you know?" He leaned forward, his eyes sharp and intense.

Carolyn sighed and rubbed her eyes. "God, how do I explain this to you?" She opened her eyes and folded her hands on the desk, squashing the urge to fidget in the chair. Finally, when the butterflies in her stomach settled, she met his gaze.

Jim spread his hands out. "Carolyn, nothing you can say will surprise me, so just say it." He leaned back, trying to emulate calm, but the muscles in his face and neck jumped with tension as he surveyed her.

"I'm seeing the murders in my dreams." Heat filled her cheeks at the admission.

His eyebrows went up. "Excuse me?" He shifted in the chair.

Carolyn laughed at the surprised expression on her boss's face. "I thought nothing could surprise you?"

"Did you say you saw the murder?" he asked, ignoring her comment.

"Not just one, Jim. I've seen all of them," she said, keeping eye contact.

Jim leaned forward to speak and then leaned back again, with his jaw askew. He blinked, his mind an open book as he struggled to process her statement.

Carolyn waited patiently until his mind snapped closed, and he spoke.

"Wha..." His voice cracked. He stopped and cleared his throat. "What do you mean?"

"I have seen each death." She leaned back in her seat, crossing her arms against his bizarre thought process. "Each and every one," she said, annoyed at his conclusion. "And I'm not crazy, I'm not overworked, and I don't need a vacation."

Jim blinked, raised his eyebrows and shifted in the chair under Carolyn's gaze. "I never said you were."

"No, but you thought it."

Jim's lips pressed into a thin slit, his eyes narrowing as well. "Can you identify the killer?"

"No. I'm seeing the murders through his eyes, or some manifestation of his psyche."

Jim cocked his head to the side like a cocker spaniel. "His?"

"I'm assuming it's a man just by the extent of the damage. I don't see a human hand with a weapon. I see a manifestation of a claw. But based on the news reports, it sounds like a single sharp object and not something an actual claw would produce. I'm also assuming the weapon is a bowed blade of some sort based on the arc of the strikes and the damage left behind."

Jim stared at her, silent.

"The only time I saw the killer leave a lipstick mark was the victim in the park," she added after the silence filled the room.

Jim's eyes narrowed. "Who knows about this?"

His tone and demeanor struck a chord, and she hesitated before answering. "No one," she said, leaving the conversation with Randy off the record.

Jim chewed on his lower lip. "Keep it that way." He stood. "Otherwise, you'll be the prime suspect in the case."

Carolyn hadn't considered that. The stupidity of her lack of insight struck her silent for a moment. On the heels of that, the late night nine-one-one call came to mind. "I, uh, I called the police about the murder in the park," she said. "But I hung up after I realized how ludicrous it sounded."

Jim pointed a stiff finger in her direction. "If the press gets wind of this, it will be the end of your career." He crossed to the door and paused. "Do you have an alibi?" he asked over his shoulder, but wouldn't turn to look at her.

"You don't think I had anything to do with the murders, do you?" The question came out as a gasp.

"Do you have an alibi?" He turned toward her this time, meeting her shocked gaze.

"I was at home or here."

"Did anyone see you at the time of death?"

Carolyn thought about the timings of the murders, and she nodded but didn't expand. She silently shuffled through the facts.

Jim nodded and walked out of her office.

Carolyn picked apart each memory and circumstances lining them up against where she was; compiling the case against her like Jim would do. Her alibis were concrete enough to create reasonable doubt if she was ever hauled in.

The conversation rattled her, and she picked up the phone, dialing the familiar number.

"Hello?" His groggy voice answered.

"Randy?"

"You okay?" Randy asked more coherently.

"Not entirely," Carolyn said. "I had another nightmare last night and made the mistake of telling Jim about the visions." She stared at the closed office door before swiveling her chair toward the windows. "He said this could end my career."

"Bullshit, Carolyn. You're the only one on staff who has a perfect record."

"He said if the press got wind of this, I could end up being the prime suspect."

Randy laughed.

"He was serious, Randy, and he was pissed."

"Give me a half hour and I'll meet you at Starbucks on the corner of Broadway and Fulton and we can talk over a coffee, okay?"

"Okay." A second later, the dial tone invaded her ear. She hung up and swiveled back to her computer, wiping the thoughts out of her mind, focusing on answering her outstanding emails for the moment. After twenty minutes, she locked the computer and headed out into the warm sunshine.

She took a seat in the deserted corner near the window where she could people watch, and the din of thoughts wasn't so overwhelming. When Randy approached, she sighed. He really was a handsome man, especially in the finely tailored suit he was wearing today. Randy sent a nod in her direction when he walked through the door and headed directly to the counter. He ordered coffee for both of them. With drinks in hand, he crossed to the table, setting her latte in front of her. The scent of vanilla and hazelnut drifted from his cup, and he placed a gentle kiss on her cheek before taking the chair on the opposite side of the table.

"Feeling a little better?"

Carolyn shrugged, glancing into his gray eyes, questioning yet again why she hadn't agreed to move in with him.

"C'mon, your favorite latte with your favorite man?" He spread his hands out and offered her a grin.

She couldn't resist that smile and bit the inside of her lip, thwarting the smile that wanted to sneak onto her lips. She tilted her head and rolled her eyes instead.

"I'm not your favorite man?" Randy asked, dejected, his eyes resembling that of a puppy, begging for a morsel of food.

"This isn't my favorite latte."

His slow, easy grin was infectious. The smile faded as he watched the folks scurrying on the street outside. "I'm sorry I left the way I did last night." He glanced sideways at her. "I was exhausted, and that didn't help."

Carolyn took a sip of her hot drink and nodded. "I don't know why you put up with me sometimes," she replied with a sigh.

"You know why."

"I still don't have an answer."

Randy nodded. He twirled the cup slowly in the holder without speaking, his expression somber and distant. "Tell me about the dream." He switched the subject before it crawled under his skin and festered.

"This time the girl saw him coming and tried to mace him, but he cut off her hand before slitting her throat."

Randy let a quick breath out of his nose and glanced at Carolyn. "Where?"

Carolyn shrugged. "In some alley where a locked fence cut off her path."

"What time?"

"Around four."

Randy studied his hands again. "And what exactly did Jim say?"

"He said, and I quote, that if anyone found out about this, it could mean the end of my career." She locked eyes with Randy. "He also asked if I had an alibi."

Randy raised his eyebrows. "What for?"

"Think about it, Randy. I've got in depth knowledge of the crimes. If the cops find out, I could end up as their number one suspect."

Randy considered the information and took another swig of the coffee. "Still, that's ludicrous."

"Yeah, well, he has a point. I have inside knowledge of each of the crime scenes, down to what the women were wearing and exactly how each of them died. I suspect the killer must be wearing something to protect his clothing, otherwise it would be fairly obvious to the casual observer that he was covered in blood." She sighed. "The only killing so far during the day was the second one, the woman in her garage, and for all we know, he could have gone inside and showered before leaving. All the others were at night."

Randy sighed. "Do you know why he's killing?"

Carolyn shook her head. "And I don't have any forewarning. It happens at the moment I'm watching." She took a sip of her latte and set the cup down. "And he has a specific profile that he's targeting."

Randy nodded. "They all look like you."

Carolyn shot her gaze from the window to Randy. "There are hundreds of women in this city who have dark hair and blue eyes," she snapped.

Randy leaned forward. "But they all don't have a striking resemblance to you," he said, and his gaze pierced her. "Move in with me so I can keep you safe."

"Don't be ridiculous," she scoffed.

"I would hate to see anything happen to you." He reached out and took both her hands. "Please Carolyn, move in with me."

"Who's to say anything will happen to me?"

"You fit the profile, Carolyn, and I haven't had a good night's sleep since I put that nugget together."

"Is that why you asked me to move in with you?"

He pulled away, sat back in the chair, and folded his arms. His cheeks flushed, and she couldn't tell if he was reacting to her accusation or if he was truly angry.

"Do you love me, Carolyn?"

She sighed and reached for him, but he scooted the chair out of reach. "I can't see my life without you in it," she said, pulling her hand back and giving him more than she ever had emotionally.

Randy matched her sigh. "Then I'll stay at your place until they catch the killer."

Carolyn blinked and stammered, "I'm not sure…"

"You're not sure of what?" His gaze overpowered her with its intensity.

"I'm not sure I want you there all the time," she admitted.

His face went crimson. "Carolyn Hastings, you are infuriating," he growled, finding his feet. He left her at the table alone. He didn't cast a backwards glance when he stepped out of the restaurant and crossed the street. He disappeared into the thickening morning rush.

Carolyn sat with her latte watching the spot he disappeared, reflecting on the sudden emptiness in the middle of her abdomen. She glanced around the restaurant before collecting her things and heading back to the office and catching an empty elevator.

Jim stood staring out the window in her office. "Are you ready for the inquisition?" he asked when she stepped into her office.

"I'm ready. Are you?"

Jim was always ready, but today he hesitated with a tenseness she had never seen before. He took a deep breath and nodded.

"You're still upset about this morning?" Carolyn crossed to her desk, skirting by him and sliding into her seat.

He turned toward her, leveling an icy gaze. "You realize that will be the topic of conversation today?"

"Yes."

"And you know that the meeting is televised."

"What are you driving at?"

"You are to stay quiet today, even if there is something you can lend to the case. Understand?"

Carolyn studied the pink hue of Jim's cheeks. *He's still stewing.* Her assessment drove hot anger through her, and she leaned back, crossing her arms in defiance. "Are you advising me as my lawyer? Because that certainly sounded like it."

Jim Britt leaned over, grasped the arms of her chair, and stared at her. "I'm advising you as the chief prosecutor for the state of New York. When they catch the son of a bitch, I will get the case. You are reasonable doubt," he said. His voice carried enough malice to keep her quiet. "And I don't like that at all. It gives the defense a loophole if it ever finds its way to the public record. So, you just keep your goddamn mouth shut," he growled and stormed out of the room, slamming the door behind him.

Carolyn had never been on the receiving end of his infamous temper before. She had seen him rip apart seemingly solid witnesses and go toe-to-toe with some of the country's most talented defense attorneys, but she never dreamed she would be the subject of his venom.

She slumped in her chair, aware that she was
now in his line of fire, and it was a very
uncomfortable place to be.

Crystal Illusions
Chapter 12

THE INQUISITION, AS JIM liked to call it, was a zoo. The council fired question after question at the chief of police, demanding answers.

"Hold on!" Jim yelled over the commotion.

The room quieted down at his uncharacteristic interruption.

"The police are doing their best to find this serial killer. What are you doing to keep the city safe?" Jim bellowed at the council.

Silence descended on the room, then the shift occurred, and everyone swung their inquisitive gaze to the council.

Chief Bromley's relief swept over Carolyn. Beads of sweat clung to his forehead, and he mopped it with a handkerchief. He let the council squirm for a moment before he cleared his throat. "We don't have very many leads, but the ones we have we are following up on."

Jim shot a glance in Carolyn's direction, his eyes flashing a clear warning before returning his attention to the front of the room and the ruffled council members.

Chief Bromley cleared his throat again. "We've also engaged the FBI's Behavioral Analysis Unit to help us with this case," he said, summing up the lack of information they had on the Scarlet Psychopath. "We need to issue a specific warning for women between the ages of twenty-five and thirty-five with dark hair. We think this is a wise avenue to take."

The council erupted in unison. "We don't want to create a panic in the city," the chairman said. "Besides, they've had warning by way of the news."

Chief Bromley bristled. "If we give a direct warning, it will limit the accessibility of the victims. If the women in the demographic travel in groups, it will save lives."

While the chief believed what he was saying, Carolyn was skeptical. Something was driving this killer, and she didn't think a buddy system would stop the animal.

Slow him down, maybe, but stop him, not a chance.

Crystal Illusions
Chapter 13

RANDY STROLLED INTO HER empty office at seven thirty. Her computer still hummed, but she was nowhere in sight, so he sat on the couch in the corner behind the door and waited.

The District Attorney didn't see Randy when he stepped into her office; he stared at her empty seat and exhaled. Crossing to the desk, Jim picked up the picture of Carolyn and Randy taken over the summer, and he traced her features with his index finger.

Randy's eyes narrowed at the obvious affection in his profile.

Is he the reason Carolyn won't commit?

Jim set the picture down, and with a sigh, he turned and left the room.

Crystal Illusions
Chapter 14

CAROLYN ENTERED HER OFFICE at a little before eight, and nearly jumped out of her skin when the door closed behind her. She spun to find Randy glaring at her.

"Jesus, Randy!"

"Are you screwing your boss?"

The accusation made her laugh. The thought of romantic entanglement with Jim Britt sent her into a giggling fit. "Jim? No. Why?"

Randy put his hands on his waist and waited until she stopped laughing. "Your boss has a thing for you and if you can't see it, you are blind."

All the humor of his previous statement fizzled at his angry stare. She was batting a thousand today with the men in her life. "Jim is happily married."

"Are you really that naïve?"

"What the hell are you talking about?"

"I've been in here a while waiting for you. He didn't see me sitting on the couch and he picked up our picture and traced your face with his finger. It was creepy as hell."

Surprise nestled under her skin like a nasty rash, and she glanced at her desk and back. "Are you sure it was Jim and not Trent?"

"I know the difference between your boss and that letch, Carolyn. Is Jim the reason you won't make a commitment to me?"

The question caught Carolyn like a prizefighter's knockout punch. She blinked and stared at Randy, recognizing both jealousy and insecurity in his questions. It wasn't his fault. She'd led them to this point, and she needed to rectify her mistake.

"No, Randy." She crossed to him, putting her hand to his cheek. The muscles underneath contracted as he ground his teeth. "There's no one else." Tilting her head, she tiptoed and kissed him, relishing the hint of peppermint on his lips. "I know you want to blame it on someone, or something else, but it's my beast to contend with, and I'll get over it eventually."

"I might not be here when you finally do." His eyes were as hard as his comeback.

"I hope you are, because you're the only one I've ever remotely considered anything serious with."

Another concession. His eyes softened, and he nodded.

Carolyn turned and grabbed her coat and headed out of City Hall on Randy's arm. As they crossed the road, Carolyn stopped. "Shit, I left my pocketbook in my office. I'll be right back." She left Randy standing on the corner and trotted up the steps.

With her purse on her shoulder, she opened the front doors and stepped into the night.

Floodlights shined on the steps of City Hall. The world tilted, changing to a street view, and she stared at herself through someone else's eyes. A wave of hostility overtook her, and her breath caught in her throat.

Blinking, the view shifted back with a wave of dizziness, and she reached for the railing, steadying herself before she tumbled down the stairs. When the spin stopped, she scanned the busy street below. Randy was the only one blatantly staring at her. A bus rolled by, blocking her view. No one else's gaze caught her attention and Carolyn bit her lip.

Could that have been Randy?

The thought was ludicrous, yet it was there, screaming inside her as Randy crossed the road and trotted up the steps.

"Are you okay?" He reached out to steady her. "You went deathly pale there for a second."

Carolyn stared at him, and then her gaze traversed the thinning crowd. Someone out there hated her and when she brought her gaze back to Randy, a small noise escaped.

Was it Randy?

"Are you okay?" he asked again, concern flooding into his eyes as he reached down and picked up her pocketbook that had fallen out of her grasp, handing it to her as he straightened.

Crystal Illusions
Chapter 15

THE SHOCK WAS LIKE a lightning bolt sent from Zeus.

There she stood, alive and intact, her hand miraculously attached and the tender flesh of her throat unbroken.

I wanted to scream.

I wanted to rush the steps.

I wanted to hack her into a million pieces so she couldn't come back, but there were too many people around.

I swallowed the scream, and a burning ball scalded the path to my stomach.

"Why, in God's name, won't you just die?" The words were barely a whisper, drowned by the rattling sigh of the bus as it passed, blocking my view.

Crystal Illusions
Chapter 16

"CAROLYN?" RANDY RAISED HIS voice. Carolyn jerked and clutched the purse he'd handed her. His gray eyes sparkled in the spotlights, taking on a malicious glint as doubt filled her.

"Are you okay?" he asked, this time softer, with more concern. The shadow created by the lights lifted, revealing nothing close to malice in his intense gaze.

"Yeah, I'm okay." But she wasn't. She was terrified, second guessing the man standing before her as the catalog of deaths swam in her head. She trotted down the stairs without further prompting.

His coat. The thought stopped her short.

She had washed his trench coat. Her gaze darted to Randy. *What did he say was all over it? Bloody Mary?* She shivered.

It isn't Randy! The tiny voice in her head, the one she followed religiously, spoke up. But this time, she wasn't so sure her instincts were right.

She felt like a puppet, stiff and unsteady as she walked beside him, letting him lead her down a busy Fulton Street, dodging construction and groups of people heading to catch the subway home to their families. The hot stench of the subway lines filtered up through the grates, creating small bursts of steamy air that billowed her coat behind her.

Taxis honked in frustration as the last-minute pedestrians shot into the road trying to make it across before the signs turned solid red. Downtown was still alive and pulsing, and would be for another couple of hours before it rolled up and went to sleep, a sharp contrast to mid-town Manhattan where the action never slowed.

When they settled into their table at the Harbor Lights Restaurant, overlooking the Brooklyn Bridge, Carolyn closed her eyes and took a deep breath, analyzing the facts again. She opened her eyes when Randy's hand gently settled over her own.

"Are you okay?"

"Yes, just had a moment there."

"What happened?"

Carolyn studied his expression. The worry crease between his soft eyes and the slightly pursed lips, all signs of concern, all signs that the eyes she looked through couldn't be his. "I saw through the killer's eyes again."

Randy pulled his hand away, sitting back in the chair. "What did you see this time?"

"Me, on the steps of City Hall."

The flesh of his exposed arms broke out in a rash of goose bumps. "You?" His voice went hoarse, and he glanced around the restaurant, guarded and tense, before he met her gaze.

Carolyn nodded.

Randy scanned the room again. "I won't let anything happen to you." A fierceness akin to earlier this evening reflected in his eyes when they locked on hers. "No way, no how."

She inhaled, tried a smile, and took a sip of her water. The words on the menu blended together, and she bit her lip, trying to concentrate on her dinner choice. Instead, the visions dangled in front of her field of view, distracting her and completely obliterating her appetite. She folded the menu and closed her eyes, exhaling. *If it is Randy...*

"Do you want to just go to my place, and I'll whip us up something for dinner?"

Carolyn nodded, opening her eyes. "Yeah. It's been a long day."

Randy made excuses to the waitress and escorted her out to catch a cab. They rode in silence to his apartment on the opposite shore of the downtown peninsula. When he closed the apartment door, he flipped the lock and turned toward Carolyn.

"I'm not really hungry."

"How about something light, then?" Randy asked as he took her coat, hanging it up in the closet. "I could make grilled cheese with some soup."

"That actually sounds good." Carolyn pulled out her phone. "I'm going to call Livi, so she doesn't worry."

He nodded and headed into the kitchen.

Carolyn dialed. "Hey Olivia, I'm at Randy's and I think I'm going to just stay here tonight, but I'll be home in the morning before nine. If you need me home earlier, let me know." She disconnected the call and closed her phone.

"You don't want to sleep in tomorrow?" Randy asked from the kitchen entry.

"I promised Olivia that I'd go with her to the studio tomorrow."

"Oh." Randy turned and headed into the small kitchenette.

His exit was immediately followed by the clanging of pans and Carolyn propped herself against the kitchen doorjamb, watching him prepare dinner. The muscles in his neck and shoulders knotted under his shirt, revealing the extent of his tension, and he banged the fry pan onto the stove.

"Did you have something planned for us tomorrow?"

Randy glanced over his shoulder and took a deep breath. "No, nothing specific. I just thought..." He let the sentence go unfinished, but the disappointment radiated from him as loudly as the ringing of the pans had. He dumped a can of clam chowder into the pot, turning the stove on. "I'll be right back." He slipped past her and disappeared. A few minutes later, he stepped back in the living room wearing an old pair of jeans, the cuffs frayed, and the fabric faded and soft. The light blue V-neck sweater brought out the natural blue flecks in his gray eyes.

Carolyn scanned him as he walked by. The jeans and sweater accentuated his muscular six-foot frame. His dark, slightly askew hair made her smile. He must have messed it up when he pulled the sweater over his head and hadn't bothered to put it back in order. She audibly sighed. Randy looked hotter than hell in the tattered jeans, and her appetite kicked into high gear. Food was the farthest thing from her mind.

Randy shot her his boyish grin.

"You've got that look." He turned toward her, flipping the grilled cheese over in the pan.

"What look is that?" She allowed a slow grin to form.

Randy laughed and turned off the burners, sliding the sandwiches onto a plate. "The kind of look that makes me want to carry you into the bedroom and forget about dinner."

"Hmmm. Maybe you're the one that can read minds," Carolyn said, taking a seat at the dinner table.

Randy hesitated with the soup pan in his hand, the ladle poised above the hot steam. He glanced between the pan and her, the debate clear in his gaze, but his growling stomach seemed to make the choice for him. He dipped the ladle, filling both bowls with the hot soup, and took a seat opposite her.

Carolyn chuckled, taking one sandwich and tearing off a piece. She dipped it in the soup and took a bite as he dug in. Her smile faded as she studied him.

Could he really be capable of the type of violence I suspect him of?

He caught her stare. "What's on your mind?"

"You."

The edge of his lips curved into a smile. "Why so serious?"

"Just thinking."

Before he could speak, his cell phone rang, interrupting their dinner. Randy looked at the number and closed his eyes. "I gotta take this." He stepped out of the kitchen.

Thunder rumbled in the distance, drowning out the conversation, but she heard the last thing he said before she heard the phone snap closed.

"Yeah, I'll be there in a little bit." His muttering curses filtered from the living room, and he stuck his head into the kitchen. "I have to go out for a little while." Randy disappeared again.

When he came back in the kitchen, he had a pair of socks and his sneakers in his hands. He sat at the table, slipping them on with his lips pressed together in disgust. "I'm sorry, Carolyn. I have to take care of something. I should be back in an hour or so."

Carolyn nodded, watching as he pulled a football slicker out of the closet and pulled it over his head. He didn't meet her gaze and after the door closed, the flip of the lock echoed in the empty apartment. She looked down at her bowl of soup and slowly finished her meal with his half empty bowl as her only company.

His complete lack of an explanation irked her. She glanced at her surroundings. The dark themes of his apartment screamed bachelor, but the adornments in the kitchen, including a rack of hanging pans, shattered the bachelor pad illusion. She looked at the door again and sighed, resolved to a night alone in his abode.

Clearing the dishes, she set them in the sink and reached for the pan. The room shifted, disappearing, replaced by the dark, wet city street.

I APPROACHED HER IN the empty alley, my claw dangling by my side, and got within a few paces when she glanced over her shoulder.

Her dark hair swung in wet strings, dripping with rain, obstructing her view. When the strands fell away, her eyes widened. Shock transitioned into something I hadn't encountered yet—anger—and it took me by surprise.

She swung around, and her pocketbook hit me on the side of the face, making me stumble a step, but it wasn't enough to save her sorry ass.

My blade shot through the air, slicing through her vocal cords, shutting the beginning of a scream off before it could begin. I swung the edge back, leaving only the bones in her spine, holding her head on her shoulders. I relished the spray of blood covering everything in sight, including me.

"Hey!" a voice interrupted.

I froze with the blade ready for another strike, and my heart thundered in my chest. In the span of a heartbeat, I spun and took flight down the same path I came, away from the voice and the footfalls. The footsteps faded long before the sirens began.

THE RINGING OF THE pan hitting the hard tile brought Carolyn back.

Her hand flew to her mouth, and she took a shaky step forward. She spun, vomiting her dinner in the sink; the stench of curdled clam chowder made her heave again. She turned on the disposal and splashed water on her face, rinsing the vile taste from her mouth.

Shivers took hold, starting at the nape of her neck and encompassing every cell until her entire body shook with fear.

Crystal Illusions
Chapter 17

CAROLYN KNEELED ON THE floor with the paper towels, swiping up the spilled soup. Her breath rasped out of her mouth as she struggled to control her stomach. When she finished, she dug her phone out of her pocket, flipped it open, and collapsed onto the couch.

"Randy, where are you?" she asked after his breathless greeting.

"I'll be home in a little while."

Carolyn stared at the phone as the dial tone bled through the line. Her lip trembled, and tears blurred her vision. Doubt crowded her mind, and it blew sky high when he walked in twenty minutes later, soaking wet and carrying shoes that looked like they'd been doused in blood.

Randy muttered under his breath and crossed to the slider, hanging the coat over the railing. He dropped his sneakers on the wet concrete and when he turned, Carolyn gasped. The black eye and split lip stood out against his wet skin.

Without a word, he stormed into the bedroom and the shower turned on.

Carolyn followed, staring at his stained jeans, her stomach knotted into a tight ball. "Where did you go?" she asked, pulling the shower curtain back.

RANDY TURNED HIS HEAD in her direction. The hot shower had done nothing to quell his aggravation, and he carefully examined his response.

How do I explain a black eye and the blood on my clothing to the assistant DA?

It was almost laughable, but the earlier events had dampened his mood. The truth would land him in a shitload of trouble, but he couldn't brush it off either. "I went to meet a client and got mugged on the way back."

Carolyn's eyes grew hard as she took a step back. "I had another vision." She took another step toward the bathroom door.

Randy's eyebrows drew together at the question in her eyes.

A vision?

Shit.

She thinks I'm responsible?

The sudden realization of her thought process burned through him like a ravaged wildfire. "You think I..."

Carolyn bolted out of the room.

"Fuck!" Randy cursed and grabbed a towel, sliding on the tile floor as he made a bid to catch her. Her hands shook as she tried to navigate the dead bolt on the front door, and he grabbed her arm before she figured out how to unlatch it.

He had to stop her, to convince her it wasn't him, and he spun her toward him. "I didn't kill anyone."

"But you weren't mugged, either!"

Randy's shoulders slumped, and his gaze traveled to the balcony and the bloody shoes. "No, I wasn't mugged. But I'm not a serial killer, either." He brought his gaze back to hers.

"You were covered with blood when you came in. What the hell am I supposed to think?" She yanked her arm from his grasp. "And your face, that's where she hit him with her purse." Carolyn's voice trembled as she pressed her back to the door.

The fear in her eyes churned his desperation into a raging fury.

She believed he was capable of murder, of killing innocent women—women who looked like her.

"Go ahead, test the blood." Randy pointed at the balcony, his anger bleeding from between his clenched teeth. "It's beef and pork blood, from my family's meat packing plant." He turned and stormed back into the bathroom, slamming the door behind him.

He drew on a pair of jeans and returned to the living room. "How the hell can you think I'm capable of that?" Anger radiated in waves, creating an uncomfortable heat across every inch of his skin.

Tears brimmed and slid down her cheeks. "Your trench coat, now this..."

"Jesus, Carolyn." Randy ran his hand through his wet hair, her accusation stewing, stirring his anger into a tizzy.

"I couldn't reach you the other night after the nightmare, and tonight you weren't here. Do you have an alibi for the other murders?"

Randy couldn't believe her audacity, her ability to believe he was capable of such things. "If it happened at night, I was here. During the day, I'm working."

"Can anyone vouch for you?"

Randy's jaw tightened, his teeth aching from the pressure. "I don't know."

Her head dropped to her chest, and her lips pressed together. "I have to go."

Of course she's going to run. That's what she does when things get tough.

"I'll take you home." He turned before she could argue, coming back moments later fully dressed. He grabbed his trench coat and ripped open the front door.

"Randy." The glare he sent her stopped her in her tracks.

"You think I'm a murderer? What else can I say?" he snapped. "This..." He pointed between the two of them. "Is over." He stabbed the down button and waited for the elevator.

HIS WORDS HIT HER with the same impact a physical blow would have, and her breath hitched.

Carolyn slumped against the wall. Randy had never spoken about his family, and she assumed he no longer had any around. She never put two and two together. Kincaid Packing was a large privately held company that owned several meat-packing plants in Manhattan.

Her intuition acted up again, telling her he wasn't the one, but she didn't trust that voice. It was too wrapped up in emotion; it was her heart talking, not her common sense. Tears stung her throat, and she blinked them back. "Please."

He turned toward her. "Please, what?" He spread his hands. "What Carolyn? What could you possibly say to me?" His eyes were hard, masking the hurt behind them.

"The evidence..."

"I don't give a damn about the evidence. If you loved me, you would believe me."

Carolyn laughed as her own anger sparked. "I've prosecuted for less! And don't you give me that line." She pointed her finger at him, jabbing it into his chest. "My loving you doesn't matter. What matters is reasonable doubt and right now, that's a pretty far stretch."

DID SHE JUST...

Randy stepped back, staring at her. It was the first time she admitted to loving him, albeit in a sideways slant, but it diffused some of his anger, enough for him to realize he didn't want her to go. Not yet, not with this wedged between them.

"Did you just say you loved me?" He stepped closer, towering over her.

She blinked and tilted her heart-shaped face up to meet his gaze. He didn't wait for an answer, instead he slammed her into the wall and crushed his mouth to hers, ignoring the twinge of pain from his split lip.

Carolyn didn't resist, instead she melted into him, stoking the intense heat building in his pants. Passion ignited, and Randy wrapped his arms around her, maneuvering them back into his apartment without breaking the kiss. The moment the front door closed behind them, the trail of clothing followed to the bedroom.

He took her with a combination of anger and desperation mixed with a desire so strong it unraveled his defenses. She met his frantic pace, rolling him over and riding him into release, and then she collapsed on him, with her hair fanned out over his chest.

Randy held her close, stroking her silky hair. He inhaled, taking in the exotic scent of her that reminded him of coconut suntan lotion and the warm sandy beaches of the Caribbean. He closed his eyes and put himself in her shoes, going over the accusations she made. He couldn't blame her; it wasn't a far stretch, especially with the absence of an alibi, but it still stung. When she raised her head off his chest, he met her gaze.

"I thought it was over." She cracked a smile.

"If you hadn't slipped, we wouldn't be in bed right now," Randy said. "I would have taken you home and written you off." He sighed and looked at the ceiling. "At least until I had some time to think about it."

CAROLYN STUDIED HIS FACE and sighed. Intuition won out. Randy Kincaid was not capable of cold-blooded murder. "Tell me about your family."

Randy rolled her off him and stood, dressing in silence. "I hadn't spoken to my family in years." He sat on the edge of the bed with his back to her, but his emotions played out across her nerve endings, more so than his closed thoughts. Raw, like an open wound doused with alcohol.

She waited.

He shifted, turning toward her. "One of my clients has wanted to buy the business for years and my family was never willing to discuss the possibility." He bit his lip. "I ended up buying my sister's shares this summer. I kind of coerced her into it, so I'd have fifty percent of the company." He studied his hands, picking a stray hangnail. "Last month, I sold the shares to my client in a private sale at a hell of a profit. He already owned some shares and the combination of mine and his gave him control of the company." Bringing his gaze back to Carolyn's. "Needless to say, my family is pissed."

Her mind was reeling. The words private sale, corporate takeover and huge profit only pointed to one thing. "Insider information?"

"It's not a publicly held company, so insider information doesn't apply." He shrugged. "Was it illegal? No. But buying my sister's shares *was* in the realm of unethical." He closed his eyes. "I knew my client was looking to take the business over when I bought her out and yeah, I had every intention of selling them if the price was right."

"Was it worth it?" Carolyn sat up, pulling the sheet around her.

Randy looked out the window. "Financially, I'm set, especially with my knack for investing, so if I didn't want to work, I wouldn't have to."

"But your family?"

"The business was killing my family and I couldn't stand to see another one of them die." He shifted, propping himself up in the bed. "If my office finds out, they'll fire me." He glanced down at her. "I've been formally disowned..."

"What'd you expect?" she asked, avoiding his eyes.

"I don't know. Maybe my father could relax and enjoy life instead of working himself to death." He raised and lowered his shoulders and kissed the top of her head in a manner that played with her heartstrings.

Carolyn reached out, grazing the black and blue skin under his eye.

Randy smiled. "My brother has a hell of a right hook. I met him in the warehouse, and he beat the shit out of me." He touched the tender skin surrounding his eye. "This one knocked me into the scrap trough and that's why I was covered in blood. I walked home hoping the rain would clean most of it off." He hung his head. "And my banner of a night ended with you accusing me of being the Scarlet Psychopath."

Standing, he crossed to the window, looking down at the Statue of Liberty in the harbor below. "I can't say I blame you, either. Looking at it from your point of view is pretty damning." He glanced back at her. "I'm not a killer and the accusation hurts like a bitch."

Crystal Illusions
Chapter 18

CAROLYN STEPPED INTO HER apartment a little before nine, her body aching with exhaustion. She and Randy talked most of the night, hammering out their frustrations, and the fatigue was just beginning to set in.

Their conversation helped mend the frayed bond between them, but she wondered if it would hold, especially since she wasn't ready to enter the type of commitment he wanted. The subway ride and the crisp morning air gave her the distance she needed to assess their relationship. She finally admitted to herself that she loved the man, but was that enough?

She sighed, knowing the answers weren't going to surface this morning, not without a hot shower and an entire carafe of coffee. She opted for the shower before coffee.

Clean and refreshed, Carolyn headed for the kitchen by way of the living room. Olivia stretched on the couch with a wide yawn. "How'd your night go?"

"It was long and grueling. We had a bit of a disagreement," she said without going into the details.

"Did you make up?"

Carolyn nodded. "For the most part."

"Was the boy pressuring you?"

"Just let it go, for now. I'm not in any condition to rehash the issues. Maybe after I've had some caffeine. Besides, I'd rather focus on something happier. Tell me more about your artist friend. What's his name again?"

"Damon." Olivia looked at her watch and stood. "I need to get ready; he's expecting me at noon." She disappeared, leaving Carolyn alone in the living room with the newspaper spread out on the coffee table.

The headline caught Carolyn's attention. It was a police artist's sketch of the Scarlet Psychopath. The ominous hooded coat, much like the football slicker Randy left the apartment wearing, was outlined on the front page alongside a picture of the latest victim.

Carolyn sat down hard, biting her lip. Doubt crept in like a cat on the prowl, slinking just under the surface of her skin.

Was he their city's deadly stalker?

No answer came to her in the light of day, no little voice denying the possibility, and Carolyn shivered, wrapping the throw blanket over her shoulders tightly.

Crystal Illusions
Chapter 19

DAMON ANDROPOLIS OPENED THE door, raising an eyebrow at her presence next to Olivia. "You brought a friend?" He flashed a set of neon white teeth that contrasted with the deep tones of his Greek heritage. His haunting green eyes followed Carolyn as he swung the door open, waving them inside.

Olivia was right; Damon was a feast for the eyes, from the thick curls of his unruly hair down to the obviously manicured toenails of his bare feet. Muscles rippled under his skintight jeans, and the unbuttoned dress shirt casually hanging off his shoulders revealed a chiseled smooth chest. His hands, poking out from rolled-up sleeves, revealed the signs of an artist, a conglomeration of bright and dark paint splattered against the lines of his fingers. Carolyn smiled as she stepped inside behind Olivia.

Damon studied Carolyn before swiveling his eyes to Olivia. "I will have to set up time to paint your friend here." He took Olivia's elbow, leading her into the studio. He posed Olivia, standing, holding onto a false balcony with a fan gently billowing her silk dress behind her, creating interesting ripples in the fabric. Adjusting the lighting to give the illusion of sunset, he tilted her head and stepped back. "There." He nodded and headed to the camera next to the easel. He snapped a shot before he stepped behind the canvas and began his creation.

Carolyn sat quietly on the bench near the door, staring at him as he painted. Every now and then she glanced at Olivia, who, amazingly, in three hours did not move a muscle.

Damon glanced at his watch when Carolyn shifted on the bench. "It's time for a break," he announced, setting the brushes down on the table. Stepping back, he scanned what he had on the canvas and nodded, turning away as Olivia stretched, relaxing her muscles.

"Can I get you two a bite to eat?" His gaze lingered on Carolyn before traveling back to Olivia.

"I'd love something." Olivia announced.

Carolyn shrugged. "Sure." She followed him out of the studio into a little efficiency apartment. He pulled a platter of cheese and fruit out of the refrigerator and laid out a tray of crackers next to it before cracking open a chilled bottle of white wine. She looked at the spread and then between Olivia and Damon. "I feel like I'm intruding."

"Nonsense!" Damon poured the two glasses of wine, handing one to Olivia and one to Carolyn. "I am pleased Olivia brought another beautiful woman with her."

Carolyn detected a hint of an accent. "How long have you been in the states?"

"Most of my life. I have dual citizenship. My mother was American, and my father is Greek." He spread his arms out. "And here I am."

"How long have you been in New York City?"

Damon poured another glass and took a sip. "Just a couple of weeks. I came from Paris and before that, Milan, running the fashion circuit." He waved at the cameras lined up along the bookshelves. "It was time to take a break and get back to my first love, painting. I haven't been in the city in years and thought it was the perfect inspiration."

Carolyn's eyebrows creased. "I thought you were here doing a photo shoot."

The laugh that came from his throat made her smile. "Ah, yes, I wouldn't have met Olivia if it weren't for that photo shoot." He ran the back of his finger down Olivia's arm. "And I wouldn't have had the pleasure of meeting you." He turned his gaze toward Carolyn. "I must paint you." He lifted her chin, turning her head this way and that as he studied her.

His touch sparked both heat and unease in Carolyn.

"What do you do, love?" he asked, running his fingers along the angle of her jaw before pulling his hand away.

"I'm an assistant district attorney for the city."

His eyebrows curved upwards. "Beautiful and smart. What a powerful aphrodisiac."

Olivia cleared her throat, gaining his attention.

"Are you ready to get back to work?"

"Yes." Olivia said, shooting Carolyn a questionable look.

"I'm going to get out of your hair," Carolyn said.

Damon reached into his pocket, producing his card. "Please call to set up an appointment. I'd love to capture you on canvas."

Carolyn took the card tentatively and turned to leave, feeling his eyes blazing a trail from her shoulder blades down to her ass. The sensation dragged across her skin, engulfing Carolyn, and she hurried out the door.

Crystal Illusions
Chapter 20

CAROLYN RAN HER HAND along the wooden door and hesitated before rapping lightly with her knuckles.

The door swung open. "I thought you were with Olivia today?"

"I was, but watching someone paint a portrait is as exciting as watching golf on television." She stepped into Randy's apartment. "So, it was either here or the office."

Randy closed the door behind her. "You skipped Macy's?"

Carolyn rolled her eyes and smiled. "Yes."

Randy took a seat on the couch and muted the college ball game he was watching. "I won out over the office." He raised an eyebrow.

Carolyn peeled off her coat and took a seat next to him, folding her leg under her so she could face him. She spoke and stopped, looking at her hands.

"If you've got something to say, just say it."

"Randy, did you kill those women?"

His face turned beet red. "No." He kept eye contact with Carolyn.

Carolyn nodded. This time, she believed him. "I want to move in with you."

Randy moved back in the chair, trying to catch up with her train of thought.

"I know, I'm coming at you from different angles, and you're confused, but I had to ask, had to see you answer the question."

"How did you get from asking me if I'm a murderer to agreeing to move in with me?" His color returned to normal, but the confusion in his eyes persisted.

"I can tell on direct questioning whether someone is lying."

His eyebrows rose. "And last night?"

"I've been turning things over in my head all morning and I never asked you last night. I asked where you were, and everything in between, but I never outright asked you. I needed to know without a shadow of a doubt."

"This isn't a court of law, Carolyn." Randy stood and grabbed his empty beer off the table, disappearing into the kitchen. He grabbed another beer and stood in the doorway with his thumb hooked into the front pocket of his jeans as he took a long pull on the beer. "I don't appreciate being treated like a defendant." He took another swig of his beer.

Open hostility radiated off Randy, taking Carolyn by surprise and turning the coffee in her stomach into a lead sludge ball. Her temper woke from within, and she stood, slamming her arms into her coat sleeves like they were the path to a punching bag. "You know, I don't need this." She crossed to the door and laid her hand on the knob, glancing over her shoulder at him.

He raised the beer, his jaw line tight and lips pressed together. The fire in his eyes gave her pause. To her surprise, her vision blurred with tears, and she swung the door open.

"If you walk out that door, don't bother ever calling me again."

Carolyn stood, crippled by indecision. Her pride demanded she walk out. Good riddance. She deserved so much better, but she could not take that first step. Not with Jim's question echoing in her ears. *Can you see your life without him?* She hung her head, still holding the door open when his hand landed on her shoulder.

Carolyn turned, meeting his still-angry gaze, but at least he was by her side. Slowly, she closed the door.

"I don't think it's such a good idea for you to move in right now."

"Why?"

Randy's lips curved into a small, tight smile. "I'm pissed at you. That's why."

She looked at his bare feet, unsure of what to do next. In past relationships, she never got to this point. The first argument was usually the last and even though she and Randy had been occasionally bitchy with each other over the last year and a half, they had never truly argued until this week. "So, what do we do?" She met his hard gaze.

Randy shrugged, and his intention of building up the barrier around his heart, putting emotional distance between them so next time it wouldn't hurt quite so much, came through more in his stance than his thinly guarded thoughts. "I don't know."

"I might as well leave if you plan on shutting me out." She turned toward the door again.

"God damn it!" The beer went flying across the room, shattering on the far wall. He turned back, crowding her against the door. "I didn't shut you out! You're the one that's kept me at arm's length this whole time and you have the audacity to give *ME* that shit?"

"We've been dating for a year and a half and last night was the first time you ever mentioned your family. What the hell is that?"

"I didn't know you were abused as a kid." He shot back with equal venom, crouching down to her height. So they were eye to eye. "Or that you had trust issues."

The little quotation marks he made with his fingers when he said trust issues set her off. "You are one to talk!" She stepped forward, meeting him toe to toe. "You're running around selling out your family. Did you ever think that if you trusted me enough to talk to me about that, I might have saved you from making a huge mistake?"

Randy straightened up and stepped back. "I don't consider that a mistake. The business is killing my father, and he's too pig-headed to sell."

"How is it killing him?"

"He has cancer! The same cancer that killed my mother. The same type of cancer my brother will eventually get if he doesn't get his ass out of the business!"

A dousing of gasoline would have been a more pleasant shock and Carolyn's jaw fell open. The implications behind his words calmed her anger, and she looked at him in a new light.

"The warehouse is killing them. I heard what the doctors told my parents when they diagnosed my mom with lung cancer; they pegged it on asbestos exposure. Before she died, I promised her I wouldn't go into the family business, no matter what my father said or did." Randy stopped yelling and turned away. "I'm not the heartless bastard you think I am."

Silence filled the room, and she reached for him.

"I don't need your pity." Randy shook her hand off.

"I never thought you were a heartless bastard. Opportunistic, maybe, but never heartless."

Randy glanced back at her. "Opportunistic?" He raised his eyebrows.

Carolyn nodded. "You are."

The edge of humor glimmered in his eyes, and he turned his attention to the shattered glass crossing the room to clean up the shards. Carolyn crouched next to him, helping clean up the mess he made. As he soaked up the beer in a towel, he glanced at her. "You really want to move in with me?"

After all that transpired, she hesitated before meeting his gaze. "Yes, I do, but only if you want me here."

"I want you here." Randy flipped the towel and pressed it into the carpet. "I'm sorry for being such an asshole. I'm just a little on edge."

Crystal Illusions
Chapter 21

RANDY REACHED FOR ANOTHER piece of pizza, waiting for Carolyn to finish packing some of her clothing. She insisted on being home when Olivia arrived, so she could let her know about the change in living arrangements.

He took a bite, and the door swung open. Olivia and her grand entrances amused him, and he nodded hello instead of greeting her with a mouthful of pizza.

"What happened to you?" She pointed at his right eye.

"Carolyn slugged me," he offered with a barely concealed smirk.

Olivia's mouth dropped open and her eyes widened. "She did not!"

Randy chuckled at her expression. "Ask her yourself," he said, pointing toward the bedroom and perpetuating the joke.

"Carolyn, darling, did you beat your boyfriend?" Olivia yelled toward the bedrooms.

Carolyn's head popped out into the hallway. "What?"

"Did you punch Randy?"

"No." She sent him her quizzical look, complete with the scrunched eyebrows he adored.

Olivia shot a glare in Randy's direction, her hands landing on her hips with authority. "That was bad."

"I had you going there for a second," he said before he took another bite of pizza and waved toward the pie in a silent offer to Olivia.

Her lips quivered in the attempt to suppress the smile, but they lost the battle and a hint of white teeth flashed in his direction. "Yes, you did. What's Carolyn up to?"

"Packing," Randy said around a mouthful of pizza.

Olivia took a seat opposite Randy and helped herself to a piece of pizza. "She finally said yes?"

Randy nodded. "It took some convincing, but yes, she finally agreed."

"So, when's the wedding?" Olivia asked with a wink.

Randy laughed and glanced down the hall to make sure Carolyn wasn't within earshot. "Like she'd ever agree to that."

"Have you asked?"

Instead of answering the direct question, Randy diverted the conversation. "How'd the painting thing go today?"

Olivia brightened up. "Fabulous! Damon wants to paint Carolyn, too. He told me he would showcase my painting at his art show if I could get her to sit for him."

"Really?" Randy raised his eyebrow, contemplating the idea and finding he liked it. Carolyn came in and dropped her bag by the door. "Olivia tells me the painter wants to do a portrait of you. I've got an empty wall in my office, and I think that would be the perfect Christmas gift."

"Wow, real subtle hint." She took a seat next to him, digging into the pizza.

"Damon said if I could convince you, he'd showcase my painting at his art show."

Carolyn's brow furrowed. "You're kidding."

"I think he wants to do a nude portrait of you," Olivia announced.

"Over my dead body." Randy wiped his lips with a napkin, trading glances between Olivia and Carolyn. "What? I don't want anyone else seeing my girlfriend naked. Sue me." He stood, taking his plate into the kitchen.

"Wow, he's got a jealous streak," Olivia laughed.

"Yeah, I've noticed." Carolyn nodded. "I'll give Damon a call on Monday," she whispered to Olivia.

"I heard that," Randy said from the kitchen doorway.

Carolyn smiled. "I promise not to take *all* my clothes off."

With a smirk, Randy asked, "You about ready to go?"

Carolyn nodded and turned to Olivia. "I told Randy that I'd move in with him."

"So, he told me," Olivia grinned, exchanging a quick glance with Randy.

Randy approached Carolyn and put his hands on her shoulders. "She asked what you were doing, so I told her."

"Ah." Carolyn sighed, looking between Olivia and Randy, her mouth opening to speak, but closing after a second or two.

"I told you before, it's not a big deal," Olivia said, standing and offering Carolyn a hug. "You're doing the right thing. This guy's a keeper."

"Thanks, Olivia." Carolyn pulled away and glanced at the furnishings, her brow scrunching into worry lines. "I have no idea what I'm going to do with all my stuff."

"It's ok, there's no rush, we'll figure out where everything goes later," Randy whispered in her ear and kissed her cheek before ushering her out the door.

Crystal Illusions
Chapter 22

CAROLYN SAT IN HER office reviewing her case files, refreshed from a nightmare free weekend and a leisurely stroll from Randy's apartment. Randy deposited her at the door to City Hall with a kiss before he disappeared toward Wall Street, leaving her in a jubilant mood despite the files before her.

Jim poked his head in the door, and Carolyn shot him a genuine smile. "I haven't seen you smile like that in ages. What's up?" He took a seat on the edge of her desk.

"I moved in with Randy."

Jim's smile faltered. It returned to full form in a blink of her long eyelashes. "That's great. What changed your mind?"

Carolyn bit her lower lip and tilted her head. "Actually, you did," she said as she rocked back in her chair.

"Moi?" Jim laughed.

"Yes, you. Are we going for coffee this morning?" Carolyn went to stand, but Jim shook his head.

"No, I've got some more information on that case." He slid off the desk and took a seat in the chair across from her. He studied Carolyn and took a deep breath. "Are you ready to try a murder case?"

Murder? Carolyn's eyebrows shot up and her gaze snapped to the case file in front of her, concentrating on Jim and his train of thought. "He killed his uncle?"

"Apparently."

Carolyn met his blatant stare. "You want me to try the child for murder?"

Jim nodded.

She stood, turning toward the window. Any hint of the morning jubilation evaporated with his affirmation. The contents of the file ran through her mind like a violent winter storm, raging and blowing facts around in a swirl of white noise. "What happened?"

"He attacked his uncle while the man slept, chopped him up with a meat cleaver."

This was the one time Carolyn wished Jim sugar coated things. She turned, waving at the case file. "There are extenuating circumstances with this case."

"It was premeditated, and the aunt wants the boy put away."

Carolyn shook her head. "I'm not interested in prosecuting this one. If you want to, be my guest, but I want nothing to do with it." She closed the file and extended the documents to him.

Jim ripped the file out of her hand and crossed to the door. He paused. "You work for me, Carolyn. If I assign the case to you, you will prosecute to the full extent of the law, understand?"

Carolyn crossed her arms and met his glare.

Jim turned, facing her with a hard and unyielding gaze. "Understand?"

"If you put me on this case, I'll hand in my resignation."

Jim's face transitioned to the color of beets, and he spun, storming out of her office with the file in his hand.

Carolyn sat, staring at the spot her boss had just occupied. He didn't want to try the case either, but he was getting pressure from the Mayor and Carolyn couldn't glean why. She sighed and headed out, grabbing two coffees from the Starbucks across the street.

On the sidewalk, her focus tilted, and she froze. A blink and her vision filled with her image, pale and gripping coffee cups outside the green, white, and black Starbucks sign. Another blink and the world swarmed into the view of the busy morning crowd hustling on the street in front of her.

The killer was here. Now.

A chill ran the length of her spine, and she scanned the crowd. A few pairs of eyes focused in her direction, but none of them resonated as a killer in disguise.

Crystal Illusions
Chapter 23

CAROLYN RACED BACK TO City Hall, determined not to spill the coffee she carried in her shaking hands. With her head down, concentrating on every step, she nearly mowed over Trent as she took the turn, heading up the steps. Startled, one of the coffee cups slipped from her grip, splashing all over her sandal. Sudden scalding pain encompassed her foot and her breath hitched. She squeezed the second cup so hard the top popped, and the hot liquid jumped out onto her hand. Reflex took over and the second cup followed the path of the first— but this time, Carolyn jumped out of the way before the coffee splashed her other foot.

Trent skidded out of the way of the hot liquid. "Jesus! Carolyn, are you okay?"

Carolyn clenched her lips together, willing herself to breathe through the pain. The skin on her right foot turned an angry red, equaling the throbbing agony gripping her. She gave a nod and glanced at the mess at the foot of the stairs. Her morning coffee littered the pavement.

"At least let me buy you a new coffee," Trent said.

Carolyn met his concerned gaze. "Don't worry about it," she said with a raspy voice no louder than a whisper, and hobbled up the stairs, each step reminding her how hot Starbucks coffee really was.

"Seriously, what were you drinking?"

With the way the morning was turning out, Carolyn could use a coffee, and she paused, half turning toward Trent. "Mocha latte," she said, "and can you get me a bag of ice, please?"

Trent glanced at her foot and nodded, taking the corner she had popped out from moments before.

Carolyn hobbled to her office and peeled the sandal off her foot. A throat cleared behind her, setting her heart into overdrive, and she jumped, spinning toward the sitting area. Lounging on her couch was a sharp-eyed federal agent. He stood and approached Carolyn, extending his hand, appraising her in a way that made her shift under his stare.

"Special Agent Steve Williams," he said with a firm, one pump handshake.

Heat rose in Carolyn's cheeks. "Carolyn Hastings, Assistant District Attorney," she introduced herself out of habit and offered a strained smile. His face seemed familiar, and then the rush of facts flooded into her memory. She had seen his face in relation to the Slasher case, and more recently, associated with a serial killer case in Georgia that gained national attention.

"Burned your foot pretty good there." Agent Williams pointed to the angry crimson tone of her skin.

Carolyn glanced at her foot and back at his frank expression. She tried scanning his mind, but all that returned was a static wave, like when a radio station fades out, instead of the usual silence she encountered from time to time. Narrowing her eyes, she studied him further. "How do you figure that?"

Agent Williams flashed a smile that under normal circumstances would have made her knees weak, but she was too tense to fall for his good looks and charming smile. "Educated guess," he said.

"Good to know your observation skills haven't gone soft over the years." She smiled at his raised eyebrows. "The Slasher case. You did a brilliant job bagging Kyle Winslow, and an even more exceptional job shutting down our extradition requests."

A slight tint of pink entered his cheeks and dimples appeared for a moment. "New York no longer has a death penalty. New Hampshire does, and Kyle Winslow deserves to be on death row." A shadow passed over his face and any hint of a smile faded. The darkness in his gaze sent a chill through her like the winter wind whipping down Broadway in the middle of January.

"I assume you're here regarding our newest menace?"

He sat down, steepled his fingers, and nodded.

"I can show you to Jim Britt's office. He..."

"I'm not here to see the district attorney. I'm here to see you."

The phone call. Shit.

His eyes narrowed like he heard her thoughts. He used the silence as an uncomfortable weapon, and she couldn't help but shift in her chair under his intense gaze. Unnerved, sweat lined her palms, and she pressed them to her thighs, pretending to smooth the creases in her skirt. "Excuse me, but is there a purpose for this visit?" She uncrossed her legs and sat straight in the chair.

"As a matter of fact..." He glanced at the door, putting his index finger in the air to halt the conversation. As if on cue, Trent walked in with her new mocha latte.

"I'm sorry; I didn't know you had someone in your office." Trent handed her the coffee, giving the FBI agent the once over, sizing him up. "Trent Kaplan." He extended his hand.

"Special Agent Williams." He accepted the cordial gesture with a quick shake.

"FBI?"

Agent Williams nodded.

Trent shifted, his eyes darting between Carolyn and the agent.

When he showed no signs of gracefully exiting the room, Carolyn interceded. "Thank you for getting me this. You didn't have to."

Trent blushed, his gaze landing on her chest for a fraction of an instant before returning to her face. "I didn't mind. Is your foot all right?" He pointed to the scalded skin.

"Yes, thanks for asking. Can we catch up later?" She offered her most embarrassed smile.

Trent nodded and, with another quick glance at the FBI agent, he started toward the door.

"And can you close the door behind you?"

Trent slunk out of the room and cast a worried glance over his shoulder just before the door latched.

Carolyn turned toward Agent Williams, thankful that Trent's interruption gave her time to regain her composure. "Now, back to the purpose of your visit," she said.

Agent Williams stood, crossing to the window overlooking the street. "I'm here because of the phone call you made to nine-one-one the other night."

Carolyn stiffened in the chair. *How?* She couldn't voice the words. They stuck in her throat.

"An unlisted cell number is still traceable. The only ones that are a bitch to nail down are prepaid phones." He turned, the hint of a smile toyed with her as he leaned against the windowsill, crossing his arms. "Can you tell me exactly what you were doing in Central Park in the middle of the night?"

"I, uh, I wasn't in the park."

Agent Williams' eyebrows arched, and his arms uncrossed. "Really." His voice dripped with sarcasm. "Then how did you know about the murder?"

Carolyn shifted in her seat, glancing at her now tightly clenched hands. *How in the world am I going to explain this?* She raised her eyes to his bright blue ones and sighed. "I know this sounds crazy, but I dreamed about it. I thought maybe..."

The muscles in Steve's face loosened, softening both his supple lips and his hard eyes. "You thought you could stop it." He finished her sentence and crossed to the seat, falling in the chair. Spinning the wedding ring on his finger, his brow creased, and he glanced back at her, offering a welcoming smile. "My wife has similar... gifts."

Is he toying with me?

"No. I'm not."

"You're not what?" she asked, ignoring the caution flags waving in her brain. There was something about his manner, his probing eyes, like he could see inside her soul plucking out her deepest secrets.

"I'm not toying with you."

Mind reader?

Ayup. His voice echoed in her mind loud enough for her to wince. He not only could read minds, he obviously could broadcast his thoughts. This new development stoked her nerves as much as his telling smile, and her thoughts drifted to Randy and the blood-soaked slicker.

The smile on his face disappeared. "Tell me about that night."

Carolyn knew he wasn't talking about her dream, but she wasn't ready to put Randy in the line of this unique federal agent. "I had a dream..."

"No, about the night your boyfriend came home covered in blood."

Carolyn's jaw fell, floundering, she started, "Wha..." She cleared her throat, trying to calm her racing pulse and wondered just how deep this man could go into her psyche. "What?" she asked, stalling any response as her mind shuffled through the events and situations leading to this bizarre conversation.

The air shifted imperceptibly around Agent Williams, intimidating, equaling his manner. His eyes narrowed to thin slits as he challenged her with silence.

"I'm sorry, but I don't know what you're talking about." Carolyn stood.

"Sit down."

His command was undeniable, and her body folded back into the chair.

"You are going to tell me everything."

Again a command, and again she could not refuse. The words tumbled from her mouth with lightning speed, even as her mind screamed for her to shut up.

What is this man sitting across from me? An FBI agent or some sort of demi-god?

Both heat and a chilling cold hit her at once and she shook, the words still coming, her doubts, her accusations and finally her conclusion. "He didn't do it."

Steve straightened up with a nod. "Why do you say that?"

"Because, I know." Tears of fear and betrayal clouded her vision, and she blinked them back, refusing to allow herself to crumble in front of this man. Instead, she let her irritation take control over her emotions. "What are you doing to me? Is this some form of hypnosis?"

"Let's just say I'm special." He leaned back in the chair, crossing his arms. "Just like you are."

Carolyn raised an eyebrow.

"Psychic."

Carolyn laughed in response. "Bullshit."

He shrugged. "Believe what you want, but you're actually a bit like my wife. She's clairvoyant, has visions, dreams that come true."

Carolyn's brow creased. This conversation was taking an unwanted turn into the surreal. "I'm not psychic."

Agent Williams flashed a grin that both annoyed and turned her on in succession. "Yes, you are. You have low-level mind reading abilities and have visions as well. How far in advance do you see the murders?"

Carolyn stared at him, dumbfounded, and blinked rapidly.

"How far in advance do you see the murders?" Agent Williams asked, enunciating each word slowly, like he knew her mind was misfiring as it attempted to wrap around the conversation.

"Um," Carolyn started, and her voice cracked, and she tried again, "I, ah, I assume I'm seeing them when they're happening based on the coroner's reports."

He sucked in his breath and exhaled, nodding in acknowledgement. "What can you tell me about the killer?"

"In my dreams, he's a beast with a bowed claw."

Agent Williams leaned forward, his elbows on his knees. "What else?"

Carolyn looked at her hands. "I see through his eyes. At first it was only at the time of the murders, but a couple of times, I've seen myself."

His brow furrowed, creases breaking the perfect smooth skin of his forehead. "You saw yourself where?"

"Here. Well, outside, on the steps and this morning I saw myself in front of Starbucks. He was watching me." The shiver culminated in her shoulders, and she stood up, crossing to the window to squash it.

"Is that what happened?" He pointed toward her foot.

She turned and nodded. "Yes, it threw me enough that I dropped my coffee."

He leaned back in the chair, tapping his index finger against his lips for a couple of beats. "When did they start?"

"The visions or the seeing myself through the eyes of the killer?"

"Both."

"It started with the first murder. I swear, I thought it was just a nightmare until I saw the front page of the paper the next morning." She let out a shrill laugh, exposing her jumbled nerves. "I should have known better, but you know how easy it is to deny your abilities, to talk yourself into believing it's only a nightmare."

He nodded, and she didn't know if it was an agreement or signal for her to continue.

"As far as seeing myself, the first time *that* happened was yesterday."

"Did you recognize anyone in the crowd?"

Randy, Trent, Jim, all flashed through her mind, and she met Agent Williams' stare. "Yes, but not the same person both times."

Agent Williams rubbed his chin, studying her again. "You keep referring to the killer as a male. Why?"

Carolyn turned. "I guess I figure only a man would have the strength to sever a head clean off. And he's targeting women." She bit her lip, pressing them together in a thin line as she shrugged. "Why?"

"No reason. I just wanted to hear your take."

Carolyn tilted her head. "You don't think it's a man?"

"Historically, serial killers are men, but I know from experience not to rule anything out. I'm not discounting anything at this point." He smiled and stood. "I've taken enough of your time."

"Am I a suspect?" Carolyn asked as he reached the door.

Agent Williams turned, his hand resting on the doorknob. "You were, but after this conversation, I can cross you off the list."

"Why?"

"I've been in your head and seen what you've seen. I know where you were for each vision and who to interview to validate your whereabouts."

His explanation was not what she expected, nor was it something she could fully grasp. "What do you mean in my head?"

"I'm more than a human lie detector, Ms. Hastings. And to be honest, your mind is open to anyone who has this ability." He tapped his temple. "You haven't mastered the art of static, which is a good thing at this moment, because if I couldn't read you, you *would* be my number one suspect. You're an open book, unlike most psychopaths out there, and when this is all wrapped up, I'll have to teach you to veil your thoughts."

Carolyn digested his explanation, biting on her lower lip. "What's so different about psychopaths?"

His hand dropped off the doorknob. "True psychopaths naturally generate static or worse—silence. Nothing. No thoughts filter through and I've learned to take notice of the complete absence of thought. It's unnatural."

She turned over his explanation in her head. "If I'm not a suspect anymore, who is?"

He reached for the door.

"Is it Randy?" The question was barely a whisper.

Agent Williams said nothing, just turned, and left, leaving her gawking after him.

"Shit." Carolyn tumbled into the seat behind her desk, staring at the open door as his echoing footfalls faded.

Crystal Illusions
Chapter 24

STEVE WAITED UNTIL HE was halfway through the park across the street from City Hall before he dialed the familiar number.

"The assistant DA was the one who made that call, but she isn't involved. She's got the same type of abilities as Jen, but she doesn't have any padding on time between the visions and deaths."

"Did you get anything from her?" Assistant Director Ronald Cleary asked.

"Nothing as far as the killer goes. In her visions, she's seeing a monster with a claw, and she's convinced it's a man."

"Why?"

"She believes only a man has the strength to decapitate another human with one swing."

"Do you agree?"

"No. I'm not convinced either way. This is a personal vendetta, and our unsub is using an extremely sharp weapon. It isn't as much a matter of strength as it is the speed and angle of the swing, so in my mind, unless we get evidence otherwise, it could go either way."

"What else?"

"I think Carolyn Hastings might be the actual target. There's a connection beyond the fact she fits the victim's profile. At least that's how Jennifer's visions work."

"You're making an assumption?"

"Assumption, educated guess, whatever. In the meantime, I'm going to keep an eye on Ms. Hastings and see if she can lead us to the killer."

"Anything else?"

"Yes, her boyfriend. She said he came home covered in blood the other night. Gave her a song and dance about a fight, but she isn't one hundred percent sure. I'm going to check it out right now."

"Don't do anything that would compromise the case."

Steve closed his eyes and bit his tongue, staunching the snide remark that almost leaped out. "I won't," he said.

"Good. Let me know what you find."

"Will do." Steve pocketed the phone and scanned the building in front of him until he stopped at her form in the window. He lifted his hand in a wave and turned, heading to the subway and his next lead.

Crystal Illusions
Chapter 25

THE DOOR SLAMMED OPEN, pulling Carolyn out of the case she was reviewing. She caught the glare in Jim Britt's eyes as he marched into her office and towered over her desk. "Trent tells me the FBI was here this morning."

Carolyn leaned back, pursing her lips, nodding. "Yes."

"Why?"

"My midnight nine-one-one call."

Jim's chest deflated, and he took a seat in the chair opposite her. "And?"

"And what?"

"What did you tell him?" His voice carried the weight of his thoughts, and they weren't centered on Carolyn's wellbeing.

Tapping her pencil eraser to the increased beat of her pulse, she met his questioning stare, swallowing the anger that threatened. "The truth."

He shot from the chair. "Jesus, Carolyn! Why the hell didn't you call me?"

"And what would you have done? Come to my defense or cover your ass?" She leaned forward on the desk, her words laced with venom.

Jim's face, already pale pink with aggravation, turned crimson, almost glowing. He glowered at her, clenching his teeth and his fists. He opened his mouth. "You should have had a lawyer present."

"Why? I can take care of myself."

"Considering all this, I think you should resign your post."

She shot to her feet, tossing the pencil into the middle of the collection of papers. "You want me to resign?"

"I think that would be best."

"For whom, you or me?"

"For you."

"Bullshit!" Her finger shot in his direction. "This is all about you and what this could do to your career. What about my career? What happened to innocent until proven guilty?"

"This could undermine the integrity of the district attorney's office."

"That is such crap. And you know it. I'm not handing in my resignation and if you think you can coerce me by making my life here unbearable until I give in and resign, think again because I'll slap a harassment lawsuit against you so fast your head will spin." Her eyes blurred with rage. "What would that do to your career?" She tilted her head in a silent challenge.

They glared at each other over the desk, anger sparking the air between them, thickening to the point of an electrical current. Neither spoke, nor did they break eye contact. The friendship they'd cultivated for the past five years torched to nothing but ashes in that split second.

"You're fired." Jim straightened his back, his eyes dark and wary.

Carolyn laughed. "Excuse me?"

"You just threatened me. Pack your things and get out." He pointed toward the door. "Now."

Carolyn's jaw dropped. "You can't fire me."

Jim nodded. "Yes, I can."

"For what?"

"Insubordination."

Carolyn sat down hard in the chair, staring at him. "You aren't kidding, are you?"

"No. I'm not. No one talks to me the way you just did, not even my wife. Now pack your personal items and make sure you drop off your ID badge at the door. You're finished here."

She stabbed the speaker on her phone. "Jason, please bring me a box. I need some help packing my things." She hung up and glared at Jim.

"If you make waves, Carolyn, you can kiss your career goodbye." He turned as the door opened. Jim stormed by a flustered Jason as he left the office.

Carolyn caught Jason's gaze and glanced at the mementos on her desk. Her mind triggered with adrenaline, anger overtook all her senses, and she had to ball her hands into fists and count to ten before she swept the contents of her desk across the room. Calmer, she unclenched her fists and took a deep breath. "I need a box."

Jason raised the empty paper box. "Is this okay?"

"That's perfect," she said, and the reality of the situation hit like Armageddon.

She no longer had a job. Her anger dissolved into a river of threatening tears that burned her nose and throat. She blinked them back, steeling herself to be strong until she was alone at home.

Packing the contents of her desk didn't take long. Pictures, knickknacks, brushes, make-up, a sewing kit, and first aid kit all fit neatly into the box. The only folder from within the desk that meant anything to her contained thank-you letters from her clients, and she pulled it out, scanning the contents before she dropped the folder into the box. The rest of the folders contained case files, reminders of her perfect record.

The last folder on her desk was the case Jim tried to pass off on her. A thought formed, bringing a bitter smile to her lips. She held the file, weighed her options, and she met Jason's inquisitive stare. "Can you get me copies of this while I pack my law books?"

Jason looked between the wall of books and the file in Carolyn's hand. After a moment, he nodded and took the file, leaving her with another paper box to house her books. With each manual packed, she became more determined in her quest. The boy had a lousy public defender, and he'd need much better to take on Jim Britt.

Jason came back, handing her the copies, and she slid them between her books with a smile. Standing opposite Jim in a court of law would be very interesting.

Her perfect record against his bravado.

"What are you going to do?" Jason asked, pulling her from her thought process.

"It's time I started my own law firm."

Jason's eyebrows rose in surprise. "Do you need an assistant?"

With a sigh, she glanced at her collection of boxes and then the empty shelves, before she returned her gaze to his. "I'm not sure I can afford you."

He laughed. "You know I'm an intern, right?"

"So?"

"This isn't a paid internship, so I think anything you can afford is better than what I'm getting paid now."

"You have a point, but aren't you graduating soon?"

"Yes."

"Won't leaving this office impact your internship grade?"

Justin shrugged. "I don't know."

"You need to find out, because if it does, I don't want to be the one to screw up your graduation."

Jason looked at the floor and shifted his weight, looking more like a lost puppy to Carolyn than a law student.

"Think you can help me with these boxes?"

He perked up. "Sure, I'll help." Jason picked up the box of law books. "How far are you going?"

"I moved in with Randy, so it's just a few blocks downtown. I can grab a taxi."

"I'll take the ride with you and help you bring this up. Okay?"

"Thank you." Carolyn smiled, dumped her badge on the desk, and scanned the room one last time before taking her walk of shame through the office. Her heart thundered with each step, and she stared ahead, marching with her head held high and not meeting anyone's inquisitive gaze.

In the elevator's safety, she pushed the button and waited, praying that she and Jason would be the only passengers. The doors closed, but a hand interrupted the path, and they popped back open. Trent stepped inside, looking between the boxes and Carolyn, his brow creased with a hundred questions.

"I'm sorry. I never would have said anything about that FBI agent if I had known," Trent said.

"If you had known what?" Carolyn asked and received the memory of the conversation Trent had with Jim. She clenched her teeth, waiting for Trent to sum it up in a sentence or two, but it still burned.

"Jim said he let you go because of your involvement in the Scarlet Psychopath case."

"I'm not involved in the case."

"He said you were a suspect."

Carolyn sent a glare in Trent's direction. "Jim's full of shit. I'm not a suspect. I just happened to look like the victims," she said, throwing a different slant on the conversation. She could tell by the way Trent cocked his head to the side that she just added a layer of complexity to his already confused brain.

Jason sat in the cab with the box on his lap, staring at the passing scenery. Carolyn couldn't ignore the tension any longer. "I'm not involved," she said, answering some questions fluttering in his head.

"I didn't say you were," Jason said, swinging his gaze to hers. "But you do look like all the victims." Worry pinched the skin between his eyes.

"Don't give me those worried puppy dog eyes. I already get that from Randy."

"Good. I'm glad he's looking out for you."

Carolyn rolled her eyes, and the cab pulled to the curb. After peeling off the fare and tip, she trudged into the apartment building and up to Randy's apartment with Jason in tow.

Jason put the box on the coffee table and glanced around the apartment before meeting her gaze. "I was serious about working for you, Ms. Hastings."

"I know. If it won't screw up your internship, I'd love to have you on my team," Carolyn said, leading him to the door.

"If I find anything else in your office, I'll bring it by." Jason stepped into the hallway with a wave.

"Thanks." Carolyn closed the door, waiting, holding her breath, listening for the ding of the elevator. When it came, and she was sure Jason was no longer within earshot, she let out a loud scream of frustration, which morphed into a string of curses that would make a sailor blush.

Once she stopped shaking and got control of her anger, she crossed to the kitchen and fished the six-pack from the refrigerator. Carolyn cracked open the first beer and stared at the boxes on the table. With the bitter taste of beer coating her throat, she crossed and pulled out the copy of the file she had Jason make, spreading the contents on the table. She'd like nothing more than to annihilate Jim in court on this one.

Sighing, Carolyn flipped the file closed. If she was going to take this case, she needed to contact her friend over at child services and get them to request her instead of the public defender, and that could be tricky. Anton was a minor, so he couldn't make the request and she couldn't approach him on the matter without bringing down a shitstorm.

She rubbed her eyes and scanned the boxes again, wondering just how pissed Randy was going to be when she unloaded the circumstances of her termination. Instead of worrying over what Randy would do, Carolyn opted for action and reached for the phone.

She dialed the familiar number. "Diane McKay, please," she said when the operator picked up.

"Diane McKay speaking."

"Hi, Diane, it's Carolyn Hastings. I'm calling about the Anton Harlon case."

Silence, followed by a sigh. "I understand the district attorney is taking this case on himself."

"That's what I hear as well. I'm wondering if Anton has the right defense lined up."

More silence and Carolyn imagined the confused expression gracing Diane's face.

"Someone's been assigned from the public defender's office."

"I'm aware of that. What I'm trying to say is, do you think he'd be better off with someone like me representing him?"

Coughing filled the line and Carolyn had to staunch a laugh. Poor Diane must have swallowed her ever present diet Coke wrong, and Carolyn wondered if she sprayed a mouthful all over the cluster of photos on her desk.

"Did you say you want to represent Anton?" Diane's raspy voice filled the line.

"If Sean thinks it's too much for him to handle, yes, I'd be willing to represent Anton."

"Really?"

"Yes." While Carolyn would have loved to jump on the gossip train, she left the subject alone.

"And you want to break yourself in on your first case opposite Jim?"

"I can't think of anything better right now. Besides, he's looking to try this kid as an adult. I don't agree with him on that, and I think this child needs someone on his side. Don't you?"

Silence.

"Diane, you know my record. You know I've never lost a case."

"Yes, but you've never been on a defense team."

"No, but I've got enough ammunition on paper to create reasonable doubt and prove Anton's actions fall under temporary insanity. Do you know how Sean is planning to handle the case?"

"I'm not sure. Let me talk with Sean and I'll get back to you."

"Thanks Diane." Carolyn closed the cell phone. She settled back on the couch and waited for Diane to make a decision.

Crystal Illusions
Chapter 26

HER CELL RANG, SHATTERING the silence, and Carolyn glanced at the number. She expected more time to pass before a decision was made, but it had been less than an hour and she didn't know what to make of that. She flipped the phone open. "What's the verdict?" she asked.

"Sean said he's already overloaded and if you want the case, it's yours."

Carolyn smiled. "Yes, I want it. When can I meet with Anton?"

"I can set something up for first thing in the morning for you."

"Perfect. I'll see you then." Carolyn hung up. She peeled off her suit jacket and headed toward the refrigerator, grabbing another beer, this time in celebration of her new calling.

Defense attorney.

This case would be a challenge. There was no doubt Anton killed his uncle, but the circumstances leading up to the murder were enough to make any sane adult snap. Never mind a child, and she hoped the jury would see what she saw. With a smile, she stretched out on the couch to catch a nap before Randy arrived, and she'd have to deal with that unpleasant confrontation.

The shrill ring of her cell phone brushed the start of a pleasant dream away like a cobweb snagged in the wind. She blinked and dug into her pocketbook, flipping the phone open before she was completely awake.

"What the fuck do you think you're doing?" Jim Britt's voice hissed through the receiver, snapping her eyes open and bringing her fully around.

"What do you care? You fired me," she said.

"I'll have your license revoked. You stepped over a line."

"How exactly did I cross a line?"

"You solicited an already represented client."

"I did not. I simply asked if Sean was still buried under a pile of cases and if he was, I'd be more than willing to take this one on."

"You coerced him."

"No, I didn't. Besides, this is really none of your business." She closed her eyes and reined in her anger before she spoke again. "I'll see you in court." She folded the phone, cutting off the mad ranting of the district attorney filtering through the line.

Just as she settled back on the couch, a soft knock interrupted her less than peaceful afternoon. She crossed and glanced through the peephole. Surprise swept over her, sending a tingle down her spine, and she swung the door open. "Agent Williams, what are you doing here?"

His eyebrows arched at Carolyn before taking a quick glance around the apartment. "I thought I'd pay a visit," he said when his gaze landed back on Carolyn. "You're out awfully early."

"Yeah, well, my boss didn't like the implications of impropriety your visit garnered, so he let me go." Carolyn turned and headed into the kitchen, dropping her empty bottle in the garbage and replenishing her drinking hand with a cold beer. She grabbed a second one and held it up as a peace offering.

Agent Williams looked at the golden Corona Carolyn held up and licked his lips before shaking his head. "I'm on duty."

"Pft." Carolyn scoffed and popped the caps off both beers, bringing it to him despite his verbal decline. "Here's to my new career." She tinked the bottle she shoved into his hand and took a seat, stretching her legs onto the coffee table. "Take a load off. Randy should be home any time."

Why not ruin my entire life?

Agent Williams stood by the open door looking at the cool beer in his hand, undecided whether to be pissed by her flippant tone or to be sympathetic. "I'm not here to ruin your life, Ms. Hastings. I'm here to do my job and follow a lead. A lead you gave me." He pointed the neck of the beer in her direction before bringing it to his lips. He closed the door and crossed to the adjoining couch. "Can you find me those sneakers?"

Carolyn pointed to the balcony where the red stained sneakers still sat. They stunk to high heaven when Randy brought them in yesterday, so he put them back on the balcony until he had a chance to wash them. Well, he hadn't gotten to it yet, so it would prove to be a blessing or a curse, but Carolyn didn't quite care right at the moment. The anger of being fired reared its ugly head. "You got me fired." She shot at him as he crossed to the sliders.

Agent Williams turned. "You sure about that?" He opened the sliders and crouched down, scratching a pocketknife to the dried gunk caked on the sneaker and putting the bits into a small vial. He filled a couple of vials with samples from the different surfaces of the sneakers, slipping them into his inner coat pocket before returning to the couch.

Carolyn hadn't answered his question.

"You think I was the one who got you fired?"

"Yes, I do, Agent Williams. If you hadn't come to my office, I'd still be assistant district attorney."

Agent Williams tilted his head and raised his beer with a shrug. "Sorry, just doing my job." He took a sip.

"Your job sucks."

The beer shot out of his mouth in a spray of laughter. Agent Williams mopped the beer off his chin with the sleeve of his jacket. "My wife thinks so, too," he said when the beer cleared his windpipe.

Carolyn picked at the corner of the label on her bottle, uneasy about having an FBI agent in the apartment with her—especially one who looked like Agent Williams. She glanced in his direction and shifted under his piercing stare.

STEVE STUDIED CAROLYN, WONDERING exactly when in her life the connection to the killer took place. The past, the present, or was this like his wife's dreams, forecasting a violent future? "So, tell me, do you have any enemies that would want to hurt you?"

Her eyebrows arched in surprise at the turn in the conversation. He knew his presence made her uncomfortable, but he wanted a face to face with her boyfriend to gauge his reaction. The amount of blood covering the sneakers on the porch bothered him enough to forgo her discomfort.

"What do you think?"

He leaned forward. "I think you are at the center of this case."

She recoiled in the seat, her grip on the beer tightening until her fingers turned white. "I thought I wasn't a suspect."

"Relax. I'm just trying to figure out your connection to the killer."

The fissure between her eyes deepened. "Why do you think we're connected?"

"Any psychic I've ever met had a link to their visions. It isn't just a random glimpse of the future, like most people think it is. Nothing is random."

"Don't tell me you believe in fate, Agent Williams."

Fate. In his book, fate should be another four-letter word. Steve leaned back in his seat, formulating an answer that wasn't snide or sarcastic. Yeah, he believed in fate, and he hated that bitch with a passion. Fate turned his life into a virtual freak show and saddled him with an unfathomable responsibility. Instead of answering her verbally, he stood and retreated to the glass doors and stared at the view beyond.

"Sore subject?"

"You might say that," he said, glancing over his shoulder at her. "However, *my* life isn't the one that's in danger right now, so let's get back to my question. Can you think of anyone who would want to hurt you?"

Carolyn laughed. "I worked for the district attorney's office and I've got a perfect record, so I'd imagine there are quite a few people out there who would like to see me strung up...but I highly doubt they'd mistake someone else for me."

"Are you willing to bet your life on that?"

Her face paled, and she shook her head.

"Then please make a list for me," he said, pointing toward the legal pad on the table.

She picked up the pad and rummaged a pen out of the carton on the table and started scribbling names down. He turned back to the view of the Statue of Liberty. "Nice view," he said.

The jangle of keys interrupted her scribbling, and Steve turned as the door swung open. The man on the other side of the door paused, looking between Carolyn and Steve before he stepped into the apartment. The insecure thoughts that swarmed made Steve want to laugh aloud, but he stifled the chuckle and gave a nod in his direction. Steve sized him up. Six foot, two hundred thirty solid pounds, and a jealous streak a mile wide.

Carolyn stood with the pad still in her hand and she waved it in Steve's direction. "Randy, this is Special Agent Williams of the FBI. Agent Williams, this is Randy Kincaid."

Randy's eyebrows rose. "FBI?" He swung the door closed and glanced toward the bloody shoes on the porch just beyond Steve, and then his gaze met Steve's.

"They traced that phone call I made the other night."

Randy's expression hardened, and his thoughts closed down like an iron door to a vault. "Carolyn has nothing to do with the murders."

With his curiosity piqued, Steve baited the conversation. "I beg to differ. She has everything to do with the murders." He shot a glance in Carolyn's direction before returning his gaze to Randy.

"She didn't kill those women," Randy said, his voice carrying the distinct hint of a growl.

"I never said she did," Steve said.

Confusion colored Randy's expression. His gaze was guarded and the crease between his eyes matched that of Carolyn's, except her face sported the red hue of anger.

HE'S GOADING HIM, CAROLYN thought, her anger rising from the center of her being, pooling in hot bursts in her cheeks. "Randy has nothing to do with the murders," she said, hoping her voice didn't carry her building fury.

Agent Williams glanced at Randy and then back in her direction. All she was getting from him was that annoying static she heard earlier.

She ground her teeth together in frustration. *He's blocking me.*

The hint of a smile that appeared on his lips struck a chord. *You're in my head?*

With a nod, he headed toward the door, pausing by her side. "Do you have that list?"

She ripped the papers from the pad and handed it to him, silently conveying her disdain of how he handled the situation.

He folded the piece of paper, glancing at Randy again and stashed the list in his pocket. Something in his expression prickled her skin, like he suspected Randy of wrongdoing, and when his gaze slid back to hers, she got the flash of a confirmation.

"I'll be in touch." He stepped out of the apartment, leaving her with Randy and a boatload of questions.

Randy closed the front door, turning toward the boxes still sitting on the table in front of Carolyn. Law books peeked out of one. Scattered knick-knacks littered the coffee table, and more were still tumbled in the other box. He crossed, plucking the picture of him and Carolyn off the top of the pile, holding it with a questioning gaze in her direction.

"Jim fired me."

"Why?"

Carolyn waved toward the door.

Randy turned, looking at the closed door and then back at Carolyn. "They think you killed those women?" His brow crinkled. "That's ludicrous!"

Carolyn shook her head and stood. "That's not the reason. Jim just didn't like the fact I'm involved at all—he's pissed because I provide 'reasonable doubt'" Carolyn made quotes with her fingers when she said reasonable doubt. "And he doesn't want the stigma on his bid for re-election," she added, rolling her eyes.

"I thought he was your friend."

"I guess when you're in politics, you have no real friends, only assets and liabilities, and I became a liability." Carolyn drained the beer in her hand and stood, heading for a refill. "You want one?" She glanced back at him, catching a nod.

When she returned and handed him the last beer, he wrapped his arm around her waist, planting a kiss on her lips.

"I wouldn't get all lovey-dovey with me right now," Carolyn said, and he pulled away. She took a deep breath. "I mentioned the other night to Agent Williams."

Randy tilted his head. The crease deepened for a second and then his skin smoothed and he straightened, hardening, his jaw tightening. "The blood."

Carolyn nodded, keeping eye contact. "I didn't mean to. It just spilled out along with everything else that's happened since I started having nightmares. I told him you didn't do it."

Randy flopped onto the couch and ran his hands over his face. "God damn it, Carolyn, that's all I need, the fucking FBI accusing me of something I didn't do!"

"He took samples off your shoes." She pointed toward the balcony.

Randy glared at her. "You let him in here to get samples to use against me?"

Carolyn nodded. "I let him get samples because I know it's only cattle blood."

Randy tilted the beer to his lips, taking a large sip while glaring over the bottle at Carolyn. "And what if there's a trace of human blood on those shoes? What then, Carolyn?"

She stepped back, shocked.

"My nose bled that night, all over the fucking place, all over my shirt, and I'm betting some dripped onto my shoes." He took another swig, his knuckles white from his tight grip on the bottle. "What if my blood type matches any of the women killed?"

"But your DNA is different."

"Can they extract my DNA if the blood is mixed with animal blood?"

"They should be able to, but I'm not one hundred percent sure."

"Why the hell did you say something? Do you still have doubts?" The anger sparked in his eyes. "You still have doubts?" He worked himself up into a fury.

"No. I don't have doubts. But Agent Williams pushed." There was no easy way to explain Agent Williams' ability to coerce, to command her to explain, and her inability to turn off the automatic response.

He finished the bottle and slammed it on the table. "So, you threw me under the bus."

"No, I didn't, he just... he just, arg!" She stood crossing to the sliders. "He's not your average FBI agent."

Randy came up behind her, spinning her around. "What the hell do you mean by that?"

"He can read minds. He heard my thoughts and made me clarify them."

"Oh great. Another telepathic freak. That's all I need." He rolled his eyes.

Carolyn's gaze shot to his and she pushed him back. "I'm not a freak!"

He grabbed her wrist, yanking her to him. "Yes, Carolyn, you are. Mind reading, dreams about killings, that's freakish."

"You just called me a freak." She tried to yank her arm out of his grasp, but he pulled her against him.

"Yes, I did. And you accused me of murder."

Fear replaced the anger, and she tried to weasel out of his grip, but he held tight. "Is this your way of telling me you did it?"

Randy's jaw tightened, and he squeezed his eyes closed, taking a deep breath and loosening his grip on her before he spoke. "You know I didn't kill anyone," he said, his voice calmer now and his gaze steady. "Look, being under the FBI's microscope doesn't please me and your explanation isn't much of a consolation."

Hot tears of aggravation blurred her vision, and she blinked them back. "For what it's worth, I didn't want to tell him anything that would put you in his line of fire, either."

"Ah." Randy studied Carolyn with a heavy sigh. Troubled and unsure of his next move, he headed into the bedroom to change.

Carolyn followed, leaning on the doorjamb as he peeled the finely tailored suit off his well-built frame. "What's on your mind?"

Randy spun toward her. "On *MY* mind?" He laughed. "You want to know what I'm thinking?

Jesus, if you don't know the answer to that..." He stopped, shaking his head. "You've implicated me for the murders. The FBI is combing through my private life as we speak. The DA is ripping mad at you and you're living with me, so by association, that doesn't bode well if they decide there's enough circumstantial evidence to charge me with murder. And to top it off, there's a psycho out there targeting women who look exactly like you. You've got some bizarre connection to him and eventually he's going to find you, Carolyn, and that," he paused, pointing at her. "That scares the shit out of me." He stripped off his shirt, flinging it onto the chair in the corner where a growing pile of dirty clothes was balled up.

"Well, if they charge you, at least you have the best lawyer in the state."

"I'm serious. The thought of that psycho getting his hands on you..." His hands propped on his hips, and he looked at the floor, his chest rippling with the angry flex of his muscles.

"Don't worry."

He laughed, not the musical, rich laughter she was used to, but a sharp bark of a laugh tight in his throat, menacing. He lumbered across the room until he towered over her. His fiery gray-blue eyes glared down at her. "Don't worry? Are you FUCKING kidding me?"

Alarmed by his barreling voice, Carolyn took a step back. Her mouth opened and closed like a guppy's, popping each time it clamped closed, with no words leaving her lips. Finally, a pathetically weak, "I'm sorry," hissed out of her chest.

Randy inhaled, raising his gaze to the ceiling. As he exhaled, he locked his gaze on hers. With a nod, he spun around, crossing to his dresser and rummaging for a short-sleeved blue-knit pullover. Jeans quickly replaced the dress slacks, and he turned back to Carolyn. "Do you want to go out to dinner or just order in?"

"I'm not in the mood for a crowd."

Randy gave her a curt nod and slipped by.

The rough banging of pots in the kitchen signaled the prevailing mood of the evening and Carolyn's head dropped, her chin touching her chest as she listened to the muttered rumblings. A combination of frustration and guilt ripped through her, springing a fresh layer of tears.

Could this day get any worse?

BAM. BAM. BAM. She jumped as a fist slammed repeatedly against the front door.

"Carolyn, open the goddamned door!"

Randy slammed a pan down and stormed to the door, ripping it open. Jim Britt stood in the hall, his fist poised for another bang and his face the color of a traditional crimson poinsettia. Carolyn couldn't remember seeing him this angry, and she bit her lip to keep the smug smile from surfacing.

"Where's Carolyn?"

"She's a little busy right now," Randy said without even a glance in her direction, and she slid to the side, out of range of Jim's glaring scan of the apartment.

Jim stepped forward, trying to crowd Randy, to intimidate him, trying to overpower the six-foot bulk blocking the door, but Randy just shifted his stance and crossed his arms, blocking Jim's path.

"Carolyn!" Jim called from behind the human shield.

"I suggest you turn your ass around and hightail it out of here before I call the police. This is my apartment, and you are not welcome here." Randy's voice was calm and rational, but his glare was anything but, and Jim stepped back, visibly debating his next move.

"Tell Carolyn I'm going to decimate her in court."

"I highly doubt that." He slammed the door in Jim's face and waited before turning to Carolyn. When he finally did turn, his lips pressed together in thought. "What the hell was that all about?"

"I changed sides. I'm defending a minor that he's prosecuting, and he isn't too happy about it."

"That's an understatement," he said, and a smile gained traction on his lips. "Baby, you've got the biggest pair of brass balls of anyone I know," he added and broke out in laughter. This time, it was the laugh she fell in love with. Musical, full and inviting, and she crossed to him, wrapping her arms around his waist in a warm hug, refreshed by the humor he found in the situation.

Crystal Illusions
Chapter 27

STEVE APPROACHED THE APARTMENT building on the north side of Central Park for the first time since Chris Ryan passed away. He paused, looked up at the high rise and sighed, then refocused on the entry and the smiling doorman.

"Good afternoon, Agent Williams," the friendly attendant said with a tip of his hat.

Steve searched for the man's name, and after a heartbeat, he smiled back. "Good afternoon, Fred." He offered his hand, and the doorman stared at it for a moment and then gripped it in a firm shake.

"Are you in the city for business?"

Steve's smile faltered, and he nodded. "Unfortunately, I am."

"Nasty business, those killings. Especially having one so close to home." He waved toward the park across the street and brought his gaze back to Steve.

Steve paused and glanced at the park before turning back to Fred. "Why do you assume I'm here because of the killings?"

Fred looked over the rim of his glasses with a raised eyebrow. "You are still an FBI agent, correct?"

"Yes, I am."

"From what I've read, you seem to be their go to man when there's a serial killer in the mix."

"You've been keeping tabs on me?"

A smile played on Fred's lips. "We like to know who our new tenants are."

"Fair enough," Steve said. *Especially with how I acquired the place.* He took a moment to scan Fred, coming back with nothing that could help with this case. Fred wasn't on duty the night of the murder. "Have a good evening, Fred." He offered a quick smile and a nod of acknowledgement before turning toward the lobby elevator bank.

"You, too, Agent Williams," Fred replied.

The elevator doors opened before Steve pushed the button and he stepped aside for the occupants, waiting for it to clear before he entered. Inside, he leaned against the back of the elevator and pulled out the sheet of paper Carolyn Hastings had given him, glancing at the dozen names on the sheet. The elevator bell sounded, and the doors slid open to the penthouse floor. Steve stepped out into the familiar foyer and dug into his pocket for the keys.

Steve stood outside the apartment door with the keys in his hand. Memories of the last time he stood inside the apartment flooded his thoughts and he clenched his teeth, willing them back into his dreaded memory box. Ignoring the chuckle of his guardian angel, he slid the key in the door and stepped inside. The minute the mahogany door closed and latched, he muttered under his breath, "Just shut up."

The laugh flooded his senses, and he shut his eyes. "Come on, Chris. Let it be. Okay?" The laughter stopped along with the flutter of wings and silence filled the void. Steve sighed, relaxing at the sudden shift in the air. His guardian angel had fled, leaving him to his own devices for now.

While the computer booted, Steve went to the kitchen and opened the refrigerator. He stared at the partial six-pack of Corona still sitting on the top shelf, like it had been the last time. "Jen's testifying this week," he said to the empty apartment.

I know.

Steve grabbed a beer and headed back to the computer. When the sign-on screen popped up, he looked at the ceiling. "What's the code?"

Jessica77

Steve nodded, ignoring the twinge of guilt, and typed the password before taking a sip of beer. "Thanks."

No comment came from the rustle of feathers and the light breeze produced by the invisible angel's wings.

He glanced at his watch and flipped open his cell phone, dialing the now familiar number in York, Maine.

"Hey, when are you coming home?" Jennifer asked, the strain in her voice saying more than her words could.

"Are the kids acting up?"

Silence met his question, and he closed his eyes, making the jump from New York to their newly acquired residence. One look at his wife's expression, the puffy eyes, and tear-stained cheeks and he turned, striding through the house with purpose.

The family room looked like a herd of elephants had traipsed through it and in the middle of the mêlée, CJ and Tommy were wrestling each other on the ground. Tommy's incoherent yells matched the string of curses coming from CJ, and Steve stopped at the base of the stairs, harnessing the anger buzzing in his head. "Stop right now." The words tumbled from his lips in a growl, sounding more like Chris Ryan than himself.

Both kids froze, their gaze swiveling toward the stairs. Their matching blue eyes wide with shock at the sight of their legal guardian. After the initial shock wore off, they jumped to their feet and pointed at each other.

"He started it," CJ said while Tommy sounded the same words without the articulation, the lack of a full tongue stinting his clarity, but Steve heard the words in his head, just as clear as CJ's.

"I don't care who started this. Stop now and you better have this place cleaned up before Jennifer comes downstairs."

"Or what?" CJ said, straightening his back in defiance.

Even at ten, CJ was a force to be reckoned with and Steve knew if he let up on him, the kid would be out of control in a matter of days. "Or you're grounded when I get back."

"Who says you'll come back?"

CJ crossed his arms, his face an angry blank slate, but brewing underneath was a level of insecurity and fear that was understandable under the circumstances. Steve's anger dissolved, and he crossed the room, putting his hand on CJ's shoulder. "I promise I'll come back," he said, looking between CJ and Tommy. "And I don't kid around with promises, do I?"

Both heads shook back and forth, but their eyes still held hesitation. He knew only time and keeping his promises like he had the last six months would reinstate trust in the boys. He didn't need this type of fiasco while he was on a case. "Look, I need you two to behave. Jenny's a little overwhelmed here and having you behave like animals isn't helping. Give her a break, okay?"

Tommy was the first to look down and nod. "Whe a oo comi home?"

"As soon as I help catch this killer."

"Be cafu," Tommy said, and his gaze shifted.

"I will. Will you be good for Jennifer?"

Tommy sheepishly nodded, and Steve turned to CJ. "Will you?"

CJ kept his gaze but refused to agree to his request; instead, he stepped back and jutted his chin in the air, tightening his crossed arms.

"If I'm constantly jumping back here to address your antics, it will take longer for me to solve this case. Is that what you want?" Steve asked, putting his hands on his hips, exasperated.

"Maybe I don't want you to come home." The remark came loaded with a mental shove.

Steve stepped back against the invisible pressure, catching his balance and sending a disapproving glare at CJ. He didn't have the right words to diffuse this boy's anger. Not today. "CJ, I don't have time for this little tantrum. I'm trying to stop a killer before someone else gets hurt."

"Like you stopped the killer in Georgia?"

The dig hurt. He hadn't figured out who was responsible in time to save their mother and it still weighed on him, but he did find Tommy before the maniac killed him. *I've got less to work with this time and a city of over eight million people...* Steve squashed the remainder of the thought and answered, "Yes, now will you give Jenny a break?"

Tommy nudged CJ, and CJ nodded, keeping his gaze glued to the floor.

"Thank you. Now clean up this room, will ya?" With that request, Steve let the transition take control of pulling his spirit back to New York and he opened his eyes to the apartment. Jennifer's breathing still filled his ear through the phone. "They should behave now. If they don't, call and if I can, I'll pop in."

"Thank you. And, Steve?"

"Yeah?"

"Be careful. CJ may not want you back home, but I do."

"I will." Steve disconnected the call and sighed. This was his first case since Georgia and the complications of a strained marriage and taking care of two very special kids didn't help his state of mind. Sweeping away the guilt building in his stomach, he sat down at the

computer and started researching the names
Carolyn gave him.

Crystal Illusions
Chapter 28

CAROLYN SAT UP IN the bed. Her scream filled the bedroom.

Randy switched on the light, his sleepy eyes full of concern. "You okay?"

Carolyn trembled, but nodded anyway. "Just a nightmare," she said. It was a collage of nightmares, each girl dying in succession, one brutal murder after the other. Not a vision, but memories burned into the fabric of her mind like the path of flame in a house fire.

"You sure?" Randy ran his hand gently over the silky nightgown covering her back.

"Yes. I'm sure." She met his questioning stare. "Go back to sleep." She forced a smile and settled into his arms after he shut the light off. The hideous instant replay continued every time she closed her eyes, looping and re-looping in her head.

Sleep was slow, but when it came, it was deep, and she didn't even stir when Randy's alarm went off. However, when he sat on the edge of the bed and pushed the hair away from her face, her eyes opened, unfocused until she blinked the sleep out of them.

"I have to go to work." He leaned down, planting a kiss on her forehead. "I'll plan on being home early and we can go out to eat, okay?"

Carolyn nodded, nuzzled into the palm on her cheek and closed her eyes again. She only had one place to go today, and no inclination to get out of the warm bed.

A buzzing sound broke through Carolyn's sleepy brain, and she opened one eye to the brightly lit room. The time on the clock caused her to shoot from the bed with a start. It was almost ten. "Holy shit." It only seemed like minutes ago that Randy kissed her goodbye. She grabbed the vibrating cell phone off the nightstand and flipped it open. "Hey," her scratchy voice enunciated.

"Are you still in bed?" The baritone voice asked.

"Yeah, what time did you leave this morning?"

"Seven." Randy answered.

"Why so early?"

"Kevin scheduled a meeting."

"Oh." Something about his tone shook the cobwebs from her head. "What's wrong?"

"My brother called the firm and filed a complaint."

"What does that mean?"

"It means I should have told my boss about the private securities transaction. He was pissed. The good news is I still have a job. I guess being the leading producer in the firm has its benefits. The bad news is he's watching me like a hawk." Randy didn't elaborate, but that would mean extra scrutiny on all his recommendations and an internal audit on his accounts. He had nothing to hide, so it was no more than a pain in the ass for him. "But if anything happens with your friend there, then the likelihood is I'll get my walking papers."

Carolyn sighed. Randy loved his job, and he was extremely good at finding the next hot investment and getting his people out before disaster struck. He had a sixth sense about the market that was rare. "Do you need a lawyer?"

His rich laugh filled the line. "No, besides, you don't specialize in securities law, babe. Now, get your ass out of bed and enjoy this beautiful day!"

"Yes, sir," Carolyn said. "I've got a case to prepare for, anyway."

"Good. I'll catch you tonight."

"Bye."

An hour later, she stepped outside in the warm sunshine. Her phone buzzed again, and she flipped it open without looking at the display. "Hello?"

"Damon was asking when you're going to call him," Olivia said.

"How about a how are you?" Carolyn asked.

"How are you?" Olivia played along.

"I was fired yesterday."

Silence. "Did you just say you were fired?"

"Yep."

"Why?"

"Jim and I didn't see eye to eye on a sensitive issue, and he decided it was important enough to let me go."

"You've got to be kidding me?"

"Nope, not kidding at all." Carolyn said. "But I've already got my first defense case." She jogged across the road and up the walkway traversing the construction of the Freedom Towers. "I'm heading over to the public defender's office to get the notes on the case. It was one that Jim wanted me to prosecute, and I said no."

"Holy shit."

Carolyn laughed. "Yeah, yesterday was a terrible day. I'll give Damon a buzz after I'm done."

"Good, because he was raving to me about how he wanted to paint you. Although I'm not sure Randy will like the idea."

"Do tell."

"He wants you nude, but with a red satin sash draped over your privates. It sounds delicious, and I think Damon is a little smitten with you."

"Oh, really?" Damon definitely had an attractive vibe, sensual, dangerous, mysterious, all the things she didn't need right now.

"Yeah, his eyes light up like the devil's dancing in them when he talks about you." Olivia sighed.

"Come on, he's got to be like that with all his prospective models."

Olivia laughed. "He is a devilish flirt, yes, but the gleam in his eyes is different when he's talking about you as opposed to the others on his list. And he does talk about his photo sessions and other paintings while I'm posing, but there's definitely a difference when he says your name."

Carolyn chewed her bottom lip as she approached the intersection of Fulton and Broadway. "Maybe I shouldn't call."

"Please, I really want to be the premier of his show on the 17th, even if I have to share the spotlight with you."

Carolyn sighed. "Okay, I guess I can call him." Randy won't like it at all, but maybe once he saw the final product, he'd get over himself.

"I have to run. I need to catch lunch and be back at the studio at 2."

"We'll have to hook up for dinner sometime this week."

"Sure thing, call me."

Carolyn hung up and approached the steps of City Hall, stopping and staring at the building. At least the public defender's offices were not on the same floor as the district attorney's. She climbed the stairs, holding her breath and praying she wouldn't run into anyone from the office. She almost made it to her destination.

"Carolyn."

She spun toward the angry voice. "Jim." The temperature in the lobby dropped a few notches as Jim approached her.

"You're out of your league here." His hand clenched tightly, but the index finger protruded in her direction like a metal barrel, loaded and ready to pump her full of lead.

Carolyn shrugged. "I don't think so. I think you're the one who's on the wrong side of the table this time, Jim, and you know it. Hell, you know my talent for playing to a jury."

Jim's lips pressed into a thin line, his face going a peculiar shade of red that Carolyn had never seen, almost purple in contrast to the stark white of his lips. The snort that came from his nose was enough to make Carolyn break out in a tight chuckle.

"Why, Jim, I don't think I've ever seen you like this." She tilted her head, toying with her ex-boss, knowing it would infuriate him even more.

The glare he sent in her direction was akin to dousing her with gasoline and lighting a match. The thoughts behind it were in the same vein.

"Now, Jim, you don't really mean those vile thoughts, do you?" Dramatically, she put her hands over her heart and widened her eyes in that sad look he abhorred, feigning hurt.

He stormed away without another word. Carolyn watched him march. Each footfall echoed louder than normal in the marble atrium, sounding more like a rushing crowd than just one man.

She chuckled. *I just reduced Jim Britt to an angry little boy!* Amused and feeling a bit more in control of her destiny, she turned and entered the Public Defender's office. Pulling the signed contract for representation out of her attaché case, she handed it to the receptionist. "I'd like everything you have on this case." She smiled and waited.

With the file in hand, she headed down the steps and into the park across the street from City Hall. The world tilted.

Crap, there she was, walking away from the building. She spun, and her vision righted. But this time, there wasn't a familiar face in the crowd. At least not one she could see, but that didn't prevent someone from ducking behind any of the trees or subway kiosks.

A chill gripped her. He had been far enough away to almost lose her in the crowd, but close enough for the hairs on the back of her neck to rise. She fumbled in her purse for her phone, standing perfectly still as people rushed by. The card was still stuck in the front pocket, and she yanked it out, stabbing the numbers frantically as her eyes continued their back-and-forth scan of the park.

"Agent Williams?"

"Where are you, Carolyn?" Agent Williams said.

She didn't stop to question how he knew it was her. "I'm in the park across from City Hall and he's here somewhere."

"Stay put. I'm just around the corner."

She folded the phone and moved to the nearest bench, standing next to it, and shaking. Who the hell is it? Her eyes jumped from face to face, gleaning thoughts in quick succession, none of which were ominous or even showed recognition of her. She kept up the frantic scan until her eyes landed on the baby blues of Agent Williams.

"Where were you when you switched views?"

Carolyn crossed to the exact spot. "I was walking toward downtown, and he was probably at least a hundred feet behind me." She turned. "At least."

"Okay. I'll stand here, and you go back until you have the right view."

Carolyn hesitated, scanning the trees.

"He's never attacked in broad daylight in a crowd. I don't think you have anything to worry about. Go." He waved her off.

Carolyn walked in the direction he shooed her in, stopping intermittently to look back until she found the spot, not because of the view, but because she stepped into a hot spot, a heat zone left by his aura that made her breath stop in her chest and her skin break out in goose bumps.

"Here." The word escaped, a rasp scratching her throat as she locked eyes with Agent Williams. Right here, I feel it.

The nod he gave clinched it. He heard her plainly as if she was next to him and that knowledge overwhelmed Carolyn.

He came to her quickly and took her elbow, leading her back toward the apartment without any words. His touch was reassuring, while his eyes scanned the crowd like a hawk zeroing in on its prey. When they were safely in the apartment, he spoke. "We weren't followed."

Carolyn nodded and tossed her attaché case onto the table. Anger and fear bristled, leaving her in an emotional turmoil. "Why? Why do I have this connection with the killer?"

Agent Williams led her to the couch. "I don't know. It could be your paths intersected before, or it could be your paths are destined to intersect."

Neither explanation helped, and Carolyn covered her face in frustration. She hated being scared, and today this bastard scared the shit out of her.

Agent Williams stood, his hand on her shoulder in support, but she could tell he was uncomfortable just by his slight shift from foot to foot. "I'll catch him."

Carolyn looked up. "Before or after he kills me?"

Agent Williams allowed a rueful smile and took the seat next to her. "I'm going to teach you a little something that may save your life if you remember how to use it."

Carolyn kept eye contact, skeptical he had any wisdom to impart that would actually keep her from the sights of this madman. "What, some sort of Zen master move?"

His smile gained traction at the attempt at humor. "Something like that." A beat of silence and then he continued. "You know how to read minds, but do you know how to project your thoughts to others?"

Her eyebrows shot up, and she shook her head.

"All right. Let's try this out." *I'd actually prefer it if you called me Steve instead of Agent Williams.*

Carolyn winced. His voice was louder than standing next to someone with one of those bull horns, but he hadn't spoken aloud. "You don't have to yell, Steve." She made a point of using his name.

Agent Williams smiled. "Now you try. You know my name. In order to project a thought, push it out of your head. You can actually feel it go."

Carolyn chuckled. "This really *is* like a Zen master move."

He rolled his eyes and nodded. "If you want to look at it that way, fine, but I'm serious. If you can do it here, you can call me from anywhere."

Carolyn stopped laughing, narrowing her eyes for a second before what he was telling her sank in. "So, I can call you from anywhere, but how the hell can that save my life?"

"If I hear you, I can get to you."

"What good would that do if I'm in a dark alley with an armed killer?"

Agent Williams allowed a smile. "I told you in your office that I'm special. Even the FBI doesn't know the extent of what I can do." *If they did, I'd be a lab rat in some hidden maximum-security research facility.*

Carolyn pushed into the back of the couch, away from him. His silent admission frightened her.

"Of course, that's if they figured out a way to keep me locked up."

"What exactly can you do?" The question came out in a squeak, and he chuckled in response.

"More than you can imagine, and it still freaks the hell out of me at times, too. Now, if we can get back to the Zen master thing..."

His nonchalant admission took her by surprise, as well as his attempt at humor, and she nodded. "By all means," she said, waving her hand and giving him the floor. "You still haven't told me how calling you can save my life, especially if presented with a situation like my visions."

"You call, I show up. It's that simple."

She still didn't get it. "Like today?"

"No—you call me in your head, and I can follow the psychic path right to where you are."

"What are you, Superman?"

Steve's dimples appeared, and a full laugh escaped. The smile reached his eyes and for a moment, she forgot he was a married federal agent. All she could think of was how good he must be in the bedroom. A jolt of shock followed, and she blinked, surprised at the effect he had on her. His laughter wound down and the color in his cheeks bloomed. *Oh crap, he must have heard me.*

"I get that reaction a lot." He glanced away.

"What, Superman, or the fact your smile could deflower the most devout of nuns?"

"Um, the latter," he said, and the red hue spread to encompass his entire face. The dimples persisted, and he stood, crossing to the window. "Back to my point. If you can call me, I can save you from being slaughtered."

"How?"

"I can be in two places at once. It's quite handy if I'm called at the right time."

Carolyn couldn't wrap her head around the concept. *Two places at once. Does he think I'm daft enough to fall for this hocus pocus?*

He turned. "I'm not bullshitting you, Carolyn."

"Okay..." She still didn't buy it.

"Look, let's just see if you can project. If you can, then I'll show you what I mean. Does that work for you?"

Carolyn sighed. "Sure," she said, to humor him. This was too farfetched to be real and, for the first time, she wondered if she was losing it.

"You're not losing it. Now focus the thought using my name as the target."

This is absolutely insane. The thought popped into her head, and she pushed it, imagining the words as a swinging saloon door in the Wild West. This certainly felt like something just as bizarre as waking up in the 1800s. Agent Williams' eyes widened a fraction, and he rubbed his ear. "Did I do it?"

He nodded. "Not as loud as some others who have done it in the past, but I still got an earache, so I know it was in my head instead of just being in yours. And yes, it is absolutely insane." His blue eyes sparkled, the smile showing hints of lines around his eyes. "Now the key is doing that when you're in trouble. I only need one word and I need you to scream it as loud as you can—not just a little shove like you just did. The louder and stronger the connection, the quicker I can get there. You don't have to know where you are, either; I'll just follow the psychic trail you leave behind."

Psychic trail, what the hell is a psychic trail?

"Here, let me show you." He stood and left the apartment, closing the door. The deadbolt clicked into place behind him.

Go somewhere else but the living room and try it. His voice rang in her ears, from the inside, and she now understood the earache comment. She rubbed her right ear to silence the throbbing and went into the bedroom, finding a spot with a clear view of the living room. "Here goes nothing," she said. *Okay, here I am!* The thought leaped out like a pouncing tiger, producing a dull throb in the center of her forehead.

A throat cleared behind her and she spun around to Agent Williams leaning on her dresser, his arms crossed in front of him, and his head cocked to the side.

"Go look in the hall." He pointed toward the living room and curiosity got the best of her. She nearly ran to the front door, ripped it open and stopped, staring at the frozen corpse in the hallway.

She shot a glance over her shoulder at the man standing in the bedroom doorway, disbelief melting away at the dual visions. He gave her a shrug and disappeared.

Her gaze shot back to the hallway. His pale corpse reanimated, like a ghost settling back into the human form. He blinked and met her gaze with a sheepish smile and an 'I told you so' raise of his eyebrow.

"Astral projection."

"What happens if you do that while you're driving?"

"I would imagine I'd get into trouble."

This is bizarre. "Does your..." She waved toward the bedroom. "Image, for lack of a better word, have the same abilities that you do?"

He smiled, nodding. "Yes, and I'm solid in both places. It is bizarre," he said, responding to her thoughts. "But it's come in handy a time or two."

"Were you born with this?" *How the hell are you not locked up in a government facility?*

"I told you, the government has no idea what I'm capable of, and as far as your question, no, this was bestowed on me a few years back, around the time the Slasher attacked my family."

"Bestowed, what the hell do you mean by bestowed?" She couldn't fathom what that meant. Every path her mind went down was of the unreal persuasion and she shook the thoughts from her head.

"It was basically something like a transfer on death." He shrugged. "But my wife was born with her talent, just like you."

Carolyn glanced toward the bedroom again. "I get you can suddenly appear when called, but how exactly can you save my life?"

"Go grab a knife and I'll show you."

Carolyn shrugged, now completely enthralled by the man. She headed toward the kitchen and froze, unable to move a muscle, held in place by invisible hands. Agent Williams walked into her field of view, his chin tilted toward his chest and his eye. Holy shit, the blue in his eyes seemed to swirl like a massive aqua waterspout. He smiled and released the mental hold, his eyes settling into that piercing blue.

"How much does the FBI know?"

Agent Williams pulled a deep breath, his gaze level with hers. "My boss knows a few things, but not everything. I'm not sure what he's told his superiors, but considering I'm still free to come and go as I please, I'd imagine he's kept it pretty close to the vest."

"Why confide in me?"

A crease appeared between his eyes, and he bit the side of his lip, studying her. "Are you planning on calling a press conference?"

"Expose Superman?" she asked.

The dimples appeared again, followed by a flash of teeth and a chuckle. "Not likely."

She smiled. "I have to say, I'm glad you're on the right side of the law."

"As opposed to the left?"

"Are you always such a smart ass?"

"Ay-up."

"Well, it seems you've got that down to a science."

Chuckling, he said, "I guess." He offered a shrug and his smile faded. "I understand the DA isn't too happy with your new vocation."

Carolyn raised her eyebrows.

"Defense attorney."

"Yes, but how did you know?"

He tapped his temple and pointed at her, indicating the thoughts swarming in her head. She sighed, wondering if there was anything she could keep from this gifted agent.

"Nope, not a thing." Steve grabbed his discarded jacket, slipping it on before he spoke. "In the meantime, just holler if you need anything." He gave a nod and slipped out the door, leaving Carolyn staring after him.

She caught her reflection in the glass of the curio cabinet and popped her mouth closed, keeping eye contact with her image. "That was just bizarre." If Randy thought she was a freak... a laugh escaped, not her normal full-bodied laugh, but a tight, nervous cackle that caused the hair on her arms to bristle.

Before she could crack open her attaché case and look over the contents, the ringing of the phone interrupted her. Recognizing the number, she picked up the handset. "Hi, Diane."

"Good morning, Carolyn," Diane said, but something in her tone set Carolyn's nerves on edge.

"When do I get to talk with my client?"

"About that," she paused, and the shuffle of papers filled the line. "The District Attorney's office offered a deal and we're going to take it, so Anton won't need your services."

"I didn't see any paperwork in the file regarding a deal."

"I hadn't signed the forms yet, Carolyn, so technically Sean was still Anton's attorney and he made the deal."

"What did Jim offer?"

"Juvenile detention until Anton is sixteen and then parole until he graduates from high school, at which time the records will be sealed."

"What's the charge on his record?"

"Involuntary manslaughter."

Jim certainly did an about face on this case. "I could have gotten him off, Diane. No jail time, no record, nothing."

Paper shuffled again. "I couldn't bet on that. The offer was good, considering the circumstances."

"Didn't you question the reason for the change?"

Another pause. This time, Diane's discomfort bled through the phone line. "I've already signed the deal, so whether or not I questioned the reasoning, it's a moot point."

A whirlwind of responses swirled in Carolyn's mind, none of which were appropriate and none of which escaped the confines of her tight lips. "Fine," she finally uttered and hung up before she said something more derisive.

Carolyn glanced at the file on the coffee table and stood, crossing to the balcony, curses falling from her lips with each step. *Jim Britt is going to rue the day he crossed me.*

With nothing left to do today, she turned and grabbed her pocketbook, rummaging until she found the card. Flicking it between her fingers, she weighed the options. How upset would Randy get? "To hell with it..." She picked up the phone and dialed.

"Hello?"

The accented greeting melted a fraction of her anger. "Hello, Damon? This is Carolyn Hastings, Olivia's friend."

"Ma Bella, I have been waiting for your call. When can I paint you?"

"Are you free tomorrow afternoon?"

"I will clear my calendar for you. Did Livi tell you what I had in mind?"

"Yes, yes, she did."

"Ah, good. What time should I expect you?"

Carolyn glanced at her watch and thought about her day tomorrow. With nothing on her calendar, she considered a morning appointment and ruled it out. She wanted to catch up on some sleep. "Is one okay?"

"That's perfect, my dear."

Crystal Illusions
Chapter 29

COOL AIR CARESSED HER naked skin, and yet her palms continued to sweat. The only place to wipe them was on the skimpy satin robe hanging on the door hook, and Carolyn opted to pass on marring the red sheen. Nerves danced, pricking her skin, and she slid the robe over her shoulders, covering what she could with the swatch of fabric.

With one last glance in the dressing mirror, Carolyn surveyed her flushed features. "Relax, it's not like you're going to sleep with the guy." Somehow, talking to herself only made it worse and she turned away from her image in disgust.

If Livi can do this, so can I... she thought and opened the door.

She entered his painting studio and stopped. In the center of the room was a gothic four-poster bed, deep mahogany, a contrast to the rumpled white satin sheets. Damon fluffed a pillow and moved a couple of the fabric waves he created just so. He stepped back to look at the masterpiece he was creating, unaware of Carolyn's presence. She cleared her throat.

He turned, his smile broadening. "Come, come." He waved her over to the bed, his gaze impatient as she stood next to him, making no move to remove the robe. He raised his eyebrows, waving his hand at her. "The robe?"

Heat filled her face and Carolyn imagined her cheeks now matched the red satin robe she wore. She forced her lips into a smile that felt more awkward than sincere and allowed the robe to drop from her shoulders. With the satin fabric now in her hands, she took a deep breath and handed the skimpy garment to him.

He glanced between her and the bed, tapping his lip with his index finger, debating, his train of thought focused on how he wanted to pose her. His waffling mind bounced between options and ultimately ended back at his first vision. With a nod, he met her gaze before he turned and traded the robe for a long, rich satin sash. He draped it over her shoulder, wrapping it around her in one graceful twist, and then he pointed to the bed. "I would like you in the center of the bed on your side, facing the easel. Don't worry about the sash, I'll adjust it once I get you positioned," he said in a manner that reminded her of a short-order cook, to the point and absent of the dripping charm he used to get her in the door. All business, which helped her relax enough to climb on the bed, although it did nothing to quell her discomfort at being naked in front of a stranger.

Carolyn lay on her side with her head propped on her hand. She didn't know what to do with her other hand and kept moving it, trying to obtain the look of casual comfort, but from Damon's expression, she missed it by a mile.

"That won't do." He climbed on the side of the bed, kneeling, towering over her as he considered what pose he best wanted to capture. "Roll on your back."

Carolyn rolled on her back. His proximity, his magnetism, his sexiness, radiated in waves despite the calculated thoughts on pose and lighting and overall vision. The blood vessels in her skin reacted, creating a hot tingling sensation.

"Relax for me," he said, his voice returning to that low, smooth timber, like a rich dark chocolate dessert, decadent and sinful but so worth the taste. When he touched her, positioning her arm over her head, in a graceful arch that left her fingers grazing her temple, she understood Olivia's infatuation. He positioned her other arm, so it rested on her abdomen, tilting her head slightly toward the easel. He pulled her right leg toward the easel, bending it and resting her foot on her outstretched leg, creating a graceful arch in her side. Offering her a smile as their eyes met, he reached for the sash, scanning her as he considered how he wanted to use the rich red fabric to contrast the bland whiteness of the bedspread and her winter-faded tan. He spread the fabric over her, swirling it in a zig-zag that covered her chest, rolled over to her back and curled around her legs, creating a vision of sensuality he strived for.

Carolyn breathed through her mouth, her eyes never leaving his intense face, and trying not to move a muscle as his hands grazed her most private areas to smooth out the red satin sash. Rapture. The word popped into her head so loud and clear, she almost flinched. That was what he called it in his head as he stepped away, fixing the bedspread.

Rapture.

That was the title for this piece.

"Don't move a muscle, especially in your face. That is the expression I want." He trotted across the room and pulled out his camera, taking a few shots at the same angle of his easel.

She knew those pictures would be used for completing the painting, but when he paused, looking over the lens directly at her, there was something else. Something she couldn't quite read. Then it was gone as the camera came back up, blocking his eyes.

He stepped behind the easel, bringing the brush to the paper. The soft sounds of the bristles filled the room as he sketched, outlining, formulating the portrait, his eyes bouncing between the bed and his rendition of her on paper. A hint of a smile formed on his lips as the brush stroked the canvas.

Carolyn lay perfectly still, perfectly posed. His eyes shimmered each time they raised to meet hers, and the connection created heat that sizzled over her skin. His dark Mediterranean skin, curly black hair, and eyes like the green Mediterranean itself, all as mesmerizing as the sounds of the brush swiping the canvas. *Oh, Livi, I so understand what you were talking about now.* She didn't know a man could make love to a woman with his eyes, but that was exactly what Damon was doing, and it was intoxicating.

I'm not sure Randy will understand this.

Her eyebrows knit together at the thought.

Damon stopped, glancing around the easel at her, a frown wiping away his smile. "Is everything okay?"

Carolyn offered a smile in response. "Yes, I'm just getting a little stiff."

Damon glanced at his watch and then at the easel before returning his gaze to her. "Would you like a drink?"

Carolyn nodded. "That would be wonderful." Her thoughts drifted to the sweet tea he offered her and Olivia the last time they were there, and her mouth reacted, salivating.

When he returned, he had a tray with a pitcher of the sweet iced tea along with sliced cheese and crackers. Carolyn sat up, wrapping the sash around her, hiding her privates from view. He set the tray on the table and poured two glasses, handing her one and taking a sip from the second.

"I thought you might enjoy a snack as well."

"That's very kind of you," she said, taking one of the cheese slices and a couple of crackers before she drank the cool tea.

Damon sat on the edge of the bed, his brow knit, and his lips pressed together in thought. Carolyn received some swirl of thought centered on the exhibit, but then his mind seemed to switch off, like someone unplugged her ability to read minds.

"I have a proposal for you," he said, turning his intense gaze in her direction.

She flushed, feeling the heat from her cheeks to her ankles and the cool air stroking her skin in a manner that made her wish for her clothing. "What kind of proposal?" she asked and pulled the sash tighter.

"Olivia is my main masterpiece. However, I would like you to be one of my highlights as well."

"Oh," Carolyn blinked, and her muscles relaxed from the initial tension his question originally prompted. "I don't mind you using the portrait at your show."

He smiled and shifted. "I don't think you understand the question. I want to paint you." He waved his hand over the length of her body. "I paint live models as well as canvas and I'd like you in my show."

She stared at him, not quite understanding. "Paint me?"

"Yes." Damon stood and crossed the room. He picked up a photo album and brought it to her. "It's a unique experience to include live art with two-dimensional art."

Carolyn flipped through the album, looking at the painted models, and her jaw dropped at the stunning beauty he created on their skin. "You paint on their skin?"

"No, no, I have my models wear a full nude color body suit to protect their skin. It takes me a few hours to paint each model. I also use some of the more promising students in the art classes I teach to help with the live models. But you, you and Olivia will be my masterpieces."

"I don't know..."

"Please Bella, you are perfect for my vision of original sin."

"Excuse me?"

He took the photo album from her and flipped to the last two pages. Two glorious angels were sketched on the paper. One in flowing white, the other sitting on a tree limb in flowing scarlet with wings that looked like flames and an apple sitting in her hand. He tapped the portrait in red. "This is my vision for you."

Carolyn stared at the rendition. "You can do that in a couple of hours?"

"Finishing touches are done the day of the show. I have the base details already painted on the body suits." He stood and crossed, bringing her the bathrobe. "Come, I'll show you."

Curiosity got the best of her, and she slid the bathrobe on, following Damon out of the small studio room into a larger room decorated with a dozen mannequins dressed in various stages of painted outfits.

"You're a size three, correct?"

"Yes," she whispered. Awe tingled up her spine, blooming through her as she walked among the art. The back of each outfit held a zipper, allowing the models to easily slip on the suits before they were completed. She stopped in front of the red angel outfit and her breath drew in at the intricate details. "It's beautiful."

"Will you wear it for me?"

"I don't know, Damon. I'm not a professional model."

"I'm aware of that. However, this exhibit requires the model to be seated. I would never

516

dream of putting an amateur in a standing position for the duration of the art show."

"How long are you talking about?" Carolyn asked without taking her eyes off the outfit.

"The exhibit lasts a couple of hours, and then we release the models from their positions so they can mingle with the guests for the remainder of the evening."

"Mingle with the outfits on?"

"Of course."

The entire idea intrigued Carolyn, and she turned, meeting Damon's gaze. "What happened to the original model?"

Damon studied her and then shifted his gaze to the outfit. "She died recently."

Carolyn bit her lip at the roughness in his tone. Pain filtered into his eyes when he glanced her way, and he offered a shrug that left her feeling like she missed something significant. "You cared about her?"

"Yes." He turned, leaving Carolyn alone in the mannequin filled room. She surveyed the exquisite designs once more and followed him back to the cozy studio, shutting the door behind her.

"Are you ready to continue?" he asked, pointing toward the bed.

Carolyn looked at her wrist and then rubbed the empty space where her watch had been. She offered a short laugh and looked at the bed and then out the window beyond Damon. Twilight had long since settled over the city and she gulped, swallowing the shards of shock before glancing at Damon. "What time is it?"

He glanced quickly at his watch. "Six-thirty."

"Oh, shit!" Her heart lurched in her chest, and she turned and bolted into the changing room, dressing in record time. When she pulled the door open, Damon was poised on the other side, his knuckles ready to rap on the wood.

"Are you okay?" he asked, pulling his hand away.

"Yes, no, well, I'm late and my boyfriend is going to blow a gasket."

Damon glanced at the easel and back to her. "Can you come back in the morning so we can finish?"

"Um..." Carolyn mentally scanned her calendar and offered a nod. "What time?"

"Nine?"

"Sure."

"And you'll have an answer for me regarding the show?"

His eyebrows lifted in a hopeful question which made him all the more enticing, and Carolyn couldn't help but smile. "Yes, I'll have an answer for you, then."

A smile appeared, along with a nod. "Let me catch you a cab," he said, stepping out onto the busy sidewalk with her.

"You don't have to do that."

"With everything going on in the city lately, yes, I do." His eyes glimmered again, and the smile revealed white perfect teeth that now took on a predatory look. Not the heat-seeking missile they had been when she first walked into the studio this afternoon.

Carolyn started to say no, but nodded instead, squashing the ridiculous urge to flee.

Crystal Illusions
Chapter 30

RANDY PACED WITH THE phone to his ear and his chest, a pounding jumble of nerves. The door squeaked, and he spun toward the noise. His heart skipped a beat at the sight of Carolyn and relief poured into his flesh, making his muscles relinquish their tight knots all at once, and he closed the phone. The rush was short-lived, and anger filled the void. "Where the hell have you been? I've been trying to get you on your cell phone for the past hour."

"My phone died." Carolyn opened her purse and pulled out her cell phone, holding the black screen in his direction before dropping the useless technology on the table. "I'm sorry I'm late."

Calm settled, brushing the tingling anger from his skin. *At least she's safe.* "Where were you?" he asked. A blush crept in her cheeks, and she planted a coy smile on her lips, the kind that usually drove him wild, but it only fanned the coals in his belly, leaving an unsettling taste in his mouth.

"Posing for your painting."

He was not prepared for that answer, and he raised his eyebrows with a mixture of intrigue and underlying unease. "Really?" The painting conversation flooded his memory. "And exactly what will you be wearing in my painting?" He allowed a smile to play on his lips, not entirely sure of what his reaction should be, but not expecting either the sudden fear that played under his skin or the absolute knowledge that it wasn't much.

"A red sash."

Randy kept his poker face, but under the neutral expression, a dangerous cocktail brewed. Jealousy and fear. He couldn't pinpoint what he was afraid of, so he focused on the jealousy. "You were naked in an artist's studio?"

Carolyn's reaction didn't help. She shrugged it off like it was an everyday occurrence. "I had a sash covering me where it counted." She was trying to be coy. He got that, but it still burned him that she voluntarily took her clothes off in the presence of a... a what? "Who's the artist?"

"Damon Andropolis."

In the presence of a man. There's my fucking answer. She was naked and alone with another man. Now he was pissed. Randy spun around and headed into the kitchen without another word, the jealousy transitioning nicely into anger.

"Randy?"

He turned toward her questioning voice, finding her lovely blue eyes begging for him to let it go, but he couldn't. "Were you in charge of placing the sash?"

Her mouth popped open in what looked like a rebuttal, then snapped closed and she shook her head. "No, he adjusted it the way he wanted it on the canvas."

There was no explaining the burning in the pit of his stomach, like she was extremely lucky to be standing in their apartment right now, like she narrowly missed being carved into little pieces, a certainty which left him physically shaking. Jealousy didn't cover this, this was something different.

Her expression changed, her eyebrows knit together, and she stepped toward him, reaching for him. "What are you afraid of?"

She was reading him again, and he swatted her hand away. "Don't. Not right now, Carolyn. Just don't." His hands were up in the air in front of him, fingers spread wide, pushing against the air yet holding her at bay. He shot past her into the bedroom, ripped his tie off, and tossed it on the floor. He sat on the edge of the bed, staring out at the breathtaking view of the harbor, blinded by the glimmering lights playing off the water.

THE FIRST TIME HE met her was at the bar over at the seaport, her laugh carried across the crowd, gaining his attention. Randy had left his group and crossed to her table, interrupting what looked like a date.

"I couldn't help but notice you," he said, ignoring the blatant glare of the man across the table from her.

The smile she flashed at him clinched it. He knew she was the woman he was meant to be with for the rest of his life. The. One. Overwhelmed by the sudden wave of certainty, he almost lost his nerve. Instead, he swallowed hard and went for it. "Go to dinner with me tonight."

She looked down at the plate in front of her, the full meal spread out on the table and then over at her date before returning his gaze...

HER HAND TOUCHED HIS shoulder, bringing him back to the present. He turned to the woman who took him up on that wildly inappropriate offer, wondering if he was the one who was going to get shafted this time.

"Randy?" Carolyn sat on the bed next to him.

He looked back at the harbor. "What am I afraid of? God damn good question." He turned toward her, taking her in and choosing his words carefully. "I'm afraid I'm going to be the one to ID your body. And I'm pissed you were naked and alone with another man. Even if it was for artistic purposes."

"The painting is for you."

He met her gaze. "Why? A consolation prize for after you bail on me?" He looked away. "A constant reminder of what I had? No thanks. I'd much rather have the real thing next to me in bed every night."

"And I want to be next to you every night."

The softness of her voice brought his gaze back to hers and when she reached out, her palm touching his cheek, he let it remain there, warm and steady against his five o'clock shadow. He raised his hand, covering hers and sighed, pulling her hand away and clasping his fingers in hers.

"Nothing's going to happen to me."

Randy laughed, throwing himself back on the bed and staring at the ceiling before lowering his gaze to hers. "You don't know that."

"I've got a guardian angel now." She stretched next to him, propping herself up on her elbow. "So, you don't have to worry anymore."

Her hand ran up his chest, reaching for the top button of his shirt and unlatching it. He watched as she repeated the quick flip of thumb and forefinger until all the buttons on his fine silk dress shirt were unlatched. Then he grabbed her wrist and glared at her. "I'm not playing games, Carolyn." He sat up, peeled his shirt off, and walked to the window in his undershirt.

Her breath hitched, and Randy glanced over his shoulder at her. A chill settled over his soul like someone just walked on his grave. Carolyn's eyes were almost lavender and glazed, and her cheeks carried the pale pallor of death. "Holy Jesus!" He ran to her side. "Carolyn?"

She wasn't breathing either, not that he could tell, but her heart raced, throbbing against the hand he placed on her chest. "Carolyn!"

Crystal Illusions
Chapter 31

CAROLYN INHALED, SHOOTING TO a sitting position and knocking her forehead on Randy's hard enough for her to see stars. Her chest, constricted by the vision, began to loosen and allow large pulls of air in. Her hand covered the knot on her forehead, and she stared back at Randy, who kneeled by the bed, holding the same spot on his forehead.

"Carolyn?" he asked, his voice shaking like he'd seen a ghost or two in the fraction of a second she'd been out.

"He heard you yell my name," she whispered, and the world slowly collapsed into a tiny pinpoint of light and then total blackness engulfed her. Cold settled on half her face and her eyes snapped open. She struggled to sit up, but a hand on her shoulder kept her prone on the bed.

"Stay still for a minute," Randy said.

She lifted her hand to the cold compress on her head. "What's this?"

"It's a bag of frozen peas. Now lay still for a couple of minutes. You've got quite a knot on your forehead."

"I need to make a phone call," she said, pushing her way into a sitting position. A storm of dizziness hit, and she slumped back, blinking at the spinning ceiling. *What did he say to do?* Carolyn closed her eyes and concentrated, focusing the energy in the center of her mind, and then she shot the thought out like a rocket launcher. A single name, just like he instructed.

Steve.

The effort drained her, and she blinked her heavy eyelids open at the clearing of a throat. She turned to the bedroom doorway to see Special Agent Steve Williams in jeans and a t-shirt, a far cry from the crisp tailored suit he wore earlier.

"You called?"

Randy shot up from the bed, his expression scrunched in shock. "How the hell did you get in here?"

Steve met Carolyn's stare and shrugged. "She called," he said, pointing toward Carolyn.

Carolyn struggled to sit up. "Randy, I told you he was special."

"That still doesn't explain how he got into the apartment," Randy said.

Steve crossed his arms, glancing between Carolyn and Randy. "There isn't a reasonable explanation, Mr. Kincaid. I'm here because your girlfriend called me with her mind." He turned his gaze to her, meeting her stare. "Are you going to tell me what this is about or what?"

"I had another vision." She swung her legs over the side of the bed and stood on wobbly legs. Randy stepped to her side, steadying her with an arm around her waist. She looked up at him. "I know you're having a tough time understanding right now, but I need to talk to Agent Williams, and I'll try to explain all this after, okay?"

Randy nodded and helped her into the living room, where she settled into the couch opposite Steve.

"Tell me about the vision," he said.

"He killed again." Her eyes filled up with tears. "But this time, he didn't stop slashing. He chopped her into pieces." She fidgeted in the seat. "He heard Randy call my name."

Steve's eyebrows lowered into a thoughtful pose, and he studied his hands. But she couldn't read his thoughts.

"What does that mean?" Randy asked when both Carolyn and Steve remained quiet.

"It means he may now be aware of the psychic connection; add the brutality of this murder, which differs from the past killings, and I am concerned. Something triggered this and I'm wondering if it had to do with yesterday."

Randy shot his gaze to Carolyn. "What happened yesterday?"

"He was somewhere outside city hall and saw me."

"How the hell do you know that?"

"Because I saw through his eyes." Carolyn studied her hands. "It's happened a few times. Remember when I dropped my pocketbook on the steps?" She waited until he nodded. "I saw out of his eyes then, too."

Randy sat back in the seat, pressing farther into the plush pillows behind him. Repulsed by the thought the killer was anywhere near Carolyn. He shot his gaze to Steve. "What are you doing to protect her?"

"Everything possible." Steve exchanged a glance with Carolyn. "Including calling me if she's in trouble."

"What about hiring a bodyguard?" Randy asked.

"I'm not sure a bodyguard is necessary. I'm a lot deadlier than any bodyguard the FBI has, whether I'm physically standing beside her."

Randy's jaw tightened, and Carolyn heard his mental argument before the words slipped out of his mouth.

"You don't even carry a gun." Venom and sarcasm intertwined in his statement. He leaned forward in a silent challenge. "What good are you without a gun?"

The sharp inhale that followed alarmed Carolyn. Randy's hands flew to his throat and his face transitioned from a light rose blush of frustration to a burgundy red. His eyes bulged, and his fingers clawed at his throat, leaving red welts on the skin.

"Stop!" Carolyn yelled, and Steve turned his gaze to her.

"He asked," he said.

"But you don't have to choke him."

Steve shrugged while Randy gasped for breath next to her, leaning over with his elbows on his knees.

"What the fuck are you?" Randy asked when he got his voice back.

"A criminal's worst fucking nightmare." A smile played on his lips, and he turned toward Carolyn. "I'll check to see if there have been any reports, and I'll call you." He sent a nod in her direction and disappeared.

Randy stared at the place Steve had occupied and then turned his gaze to Carolyn. His jaw hung slack, and his eyes were saucers of disbelief. Blotchy red spots on his cheeks gave as much away as his broken thoughts.

"You're freaked out."

Randy closed his mouth and nodded. "Yes."

"I'm sorry."

"I have no idea what to say to you right now." He waved at the empty seat. "That trumps all the freakish things you can do, and it's the stuff nightmares are made of." Running his hand through his hair, he continued. "I can't digest what happened here, so..." he trailed off and glanced toward the sliders and the deck beyond. "I need some fresh air and a little perspective." He stood abruptly and grabbed a jacket from the closet. "Are you coming?"

Carolyn thought for a moment too long.

"Fine, I'll be back in a little while." And with that, the door slammed behind him.

Crystal Illusions
Chapter 32

CAROLYN SAT AT THE KITCHEN table with a hot cup of tea, trying not to think about where Randy had gone. He didn't answer his cell, and the absence of contact had her on edge. Steve hadn't called with news either. It was like they both dropped off the face of the earth.

Her head ached. A dull throb centered in the knot on her forehead, and she grazed her fingertips over the lump and winced. This would not go over well with Damon tomorrow. And she closed her eyes, sighing. She picked up her phone and dialed Randy again. After three rings, it dumped her into his voicemail again. "Randy, where are you?"

She flipped the phone closed and glanced at the clock. *Two hours. He's been gone for over two hours. What the hell is he doing?*

Her cell buzzed, and she flipped it open. "Ms. Hastings?"

"Yes?"

"It's Steve, and we found the victim, but it looks like a fresh kill, which means there was a lag between your vision and the murder."

"But he heard Randy calling my name..."

Silence pervaded the connection, and then a sigh. "I don't have an answer for you on that, but I know the time of death was about an hour ago."

"Where?"

"An alley off of Gold Street on the lower east side."

Carolyn turned toward the balcony. Gold Street wasn't that far from where they were. A chill bit her skin, forming bumps and raising the hairs on her arms and neck. "That's..."

"Too close for comfort," he said, finishing her sentence.

"Is Randy there with you?"

"No, he isn't," she said.

More silence. "When did he leave?" Steve asked, his voice carrying a hint of suspicion.

"A little after you did."

STEVE TURNED, SURVEYING THE carnage, reading the doubts deep in Carolyn's mind. "Do you think your boyfriend might have a dual personality?"

He could tell from the stuttering response she hadn't considered it at all and at the mere mention her brain created a flurry of memories, some consistent, some not so much, and then she found her voice. "Randy couldn't do this, Steve. He's a good man."

"Are you positive about that?"

"Yes."

No doubts followed the answer and Steve turned away from the forensic team and walked into the open street with the phone to his ear.

He could feel the tendrils from her mind trying to unlock the wall securing his thoughts. "Stop trying to read my mind."

"Then tell me why you think Randy could be the killer."

Steve sighed and took a seat on an empty bus bench. "He has holes in his alibis and the blood on his shoes was a mixture of cattle blood and human blood. It didn't match to any of the victims, but there still is something he's hiding—besides just being insecure."

"There is something he confided in me, something he did recently that put him at odds with his family and wasn't exactly ethical."

"You mean the issue of coercing his family into selling the business?"

Silence filtered through the phone line. "You know about that?"

"I'm not an idiot, Carolyn. I followed up on his alibis. I spoke with his family and got their side of the story. The good thing is it jived with what he told you, but there are still some unanswered questions and with the killer hearing him..." He stopped talking and glanced back at the chaos in the alley.

"He's on the top of your list?"

"Yes. He's my top suspect at the moment."

"I'm telling you, it isn't Randy," Carolyn said. "What about Jim Britt?"

"The district attorney?"

"Yes, he turned on me like that."

He heard the snap of her fingers in the background.

"I'm still looking at your case history and everyone you've had contact with in the last month, but for the moment, Randy Kincaid is my top suspect."

"What's his motive?"

"I think jealousy may trigger it."

"You're out of your mind."

"I'm trying to keep an open mind here. I've been burned by not looking at everyone around me and I don't want you to get burned because you're blinded by your feelings. Just watch your back and call if he gets rough with you."

"He won't. Stop wasting your time with Randy and find the real killer."

Steve ended the call and hailed a cab.

When he settled into the cab, he pressed the speed dial on his phone and waited for an answer.

"You better have some news for me," Assistant Director Cleary said.

"I got a bunch of nothing."

"Do you need Sarah down there with you?"

Steve considered his spirited partner and shook his head. "No. Jenny's going to need someone with her."

"And you think Sarah's the right person?"

"She's better at this than I am, Ron. Granted, she's not necessarily the most ideal support system we've got in place, but it's better than Jenny going through her testimony alone."

"Okay, but if you have nothing by the end of the week, I'm sending her down to give you a fresh pair of eyes."

"Thanks. By the way, do you know of any skeletons in the DA's closet?"

"Jim Britt? No, but his wife has been in and out of institutions for years."

"For what?"

"From what I understand, she's got a drinking problem, among other things."

"What other things?"

"Why?"

"Because I'm not ruling anyone out."

"You are not going after the district attorney of New York or his wife."

"Okay..." Steve muttered, and his intuition prickled. *I need more information.*

"I'm serious. Leave the man alone."

"He's on my radar, Ron. I'm not dismissing anything. We did that in Georgia and look what happened."

Cleary huffed on the line, silently conceding Steve's point. "Fine, but tread lightly and try not to burn too many bridges this time."

"Don't worry—I won't," he answered and rolled his eyes.

CAROLYN PACED ACROSS THE apartment. Her gaze snapped to the clock again while she gnawed on a hangnail. He still wasn't home, and worry ate at her stomach, creating a sour taste in her mouth.

She reached for her phone again, and the jangle of keys caught her attention. She froze on the spot and stared at the turning lock. When the door opened, the sweet scent of Chinese takeout preceded Randy. Her emotions ran the same gambit as his had earlier in the day—relief followed by aggravation. It took a minute, but what he was wearing registered. Sweats and no coat. He had left in jeans and a leather bomber jacket, not sweats. Doubt as thick as a jar of honey coated her throat, and she cocked her head. "Where have you been?"

"I went to the gym and while I was working out, my clothes were stolen," he said, walking past her with the food. "It's a damn good thing I always bring my wallet and keys with me, otherwise I would have frozen my ass off in my shorts and t-shirt on the walk back." He glanced at her as he took a couple of plates from the cabinet.

"The vision I saw took place while you were gone."

Randy paused with his back to her, and the muscles in his shoulders stiffened. He lowered the plates to the counter and pushed them aside before turning in her direction. "And?" he asked through clenched teeth. His glare was enough to make her step back.

"And nothing." All the saliva in her mouth dried.

"You think I..."

She couldn't answer him. The anger in his features silenced her as effectively as a gag would.

He turned, sweeping the plates and the takeout bag off the counter with a guttural roar and when he turned on her, she stumbled backwards with the raw, tinny taste of fear lining her mouth.

He pointed toward the door. "Get out."

"I'll go pack." She turned and bolted toward the bedroom, closing the door behind her and grabbing her suitcase. Steve crossed her mind. *Should I?* but before she could formulate the thought, Randy slammed the bedroom door open.

"Do you honestly think I could hack a woman to pieces, Carolyn?"

She stopped throwing clothing into the suitcase and stared at him.

He crossed, towering over her, crowding her with his intense gaze, creating a whirlwind of fear inside her. "Do you?"

"Back off, Romeo," the voice came from behind Randy and when he turned, she got a glimpse of Steve Williams.

"Well, there's my fucking answer." He stepped away from her, lifting his hands in the air. "I give up." He stormed past Steve.

FURY LAYERED OVER HIS skin, and Randy clenched his fists, controlling the urge to break everything in his path. He stopped in front of the sliding glass doors, staring out at the Statue of Liberty in the bay, taking deep breaths to calm his fury.

"Where were you this evening?"

Randy looked at the reflection of the room behind him, zeroing in on Agent Williams. "Why are you here?"

"I thought we should have a little chat."

"Carolyn didn't call you?" he asked, turning to face the FBI agent.

"No. I followed you upstairs and thought twice about knocking when I heard the start of the argument."

"So, you just thought you'd eavesdrop and enter my house without a warrant?"

"I have probable cause. You scared the shit out of your girlfriend, and I've been assigned to protect her at all costs."

Randy refocused on the bay. Steve's answer calmed him a notch.

"Now, back to my question. Where you were between eight and nine this evening?"

"I was at the gym."

"Which gym?"

"Equinox down on Wall Street." Randy pulled out his wallet and took out the key card, tossing it to Steve. "You can check the times I swiped in and out. I'm sure they'll remember me, especially since my clothes were stolen tonight."

"Don't mind if I do." Steve tucked the card into his pocket. "Why don't you take a seat, and we can have a talk while Carolyn packs."

Randy glanced at the hallway and the bedroom beyond, and his heart plummeted into his stomach. Despite the anger throbbing in his temple, he really didn't want her to leave.

"You scared her. What'd you expect?" Steve said, taking a seat.

Randy sent a glare his way. "Look, I tolerate her reading my mind, but you've got no right."

Steve leaned forward and met his glare with a stark, penetrating stare. "Sit down."

Much to Randy's surprise, his body responded to the command, crossing and taking a seat in the overstuffed chair opposite the federal agent.

"Tell me what you are hiding."

Again, Randy had no control over his voice or the words that spilled out. "I helped my mother kill herself." The admission rolled out as if he was talking about the next prudent stock purchase to an investor. "The cancer was eating away at her, and she was in horrific pain, and she didn't want my father to stand by and watch her waste away to nothing. She didn't want her last days to be like that, and she asked me to help her with the morphine machine. She begged, and I couldn't say no." A noise in the hallway pulled his attention away from Steve and he looked into Carolyn's shocked stare. "I killed my mother," he whispered.

"Are you the Scarlet Psychopath?"

Randy's gaze shot to Steve. "No, I'm not, and I resent the question." He felt the influence release, and he glanced at Carolyn. "And I hate the fact that you still have doubts about me." He blinked and glared at Steve. "What the hell did you just do?"

"I'm just doing my job."

"Bull-fucking-shit. That felt like a hefty dose of truth serum, so you could dig out my darkest secret just for shits and giggles." Randy stood and turned away from both Steve and Carolyn. He shoved his hands into his pockets and returned to the spot in front of the window. "I didn't kill those women, and you didn't have to dissect my past to figure that out."

"Yes. I did. And I will still follow up on your alibi because it's my job." Steve stood. "I'll be in touch."

Randy waited until the door closed, and then he turned to Carolyn. "Are you happy now that you know my dirty little secret?" Venom laced his voice, and he ground his teeth, waiting for her to meet his glare. When she finally raised her gaze, the sight of her tear-filled eyes diffused his anger.

Carolyn shook her head. "No, I'm not happy right now. Do you really want me to leave?"

Randy scanned her from head to toe and back, taking her in, committing her to memory, and then he sighed and said, "I'm not sure I can deal with this. I thought I could but..." He trailed off and glanced at the clock on the curio shelf. "But it's too late for you to go wandering the streets with a suitcase."

"I can take care of myself." Carolyn headed toward the door.

He moved faster than she did and blocked the door. "No. Look, I can't let you go tonight, not with the killer in the area. If anything happened..."

"Then you wouldn't have to deal with this anymore," she said with more than just a hint of sarcasm.

Randy ran his hand through his hair in frustration. "Stop it. I have every right to be pissed at you."

Her suitcase clanged on the ground. "Can't you see it from my point of view?"

"No, I can't see this from your point of view. I don't understand how you can say you love me and are still so quick to think the worst."

"I saw the worst of humanity for the past ten years and I saw people blinded by their love for these monsters. I don't want to be one of those pathetic women who stands by killers and rapists and child beaters."

"Fuck you, Carolyn." Randy walked by her and into the bedroom, slamming the door behind him.

He stripped and headed for a shower to clean off the sweat and anger from his skin. The warm water pummeled his back, loosening the tenseness building in his muscles and he reflected on the disaster of an evening. In the steam-filled bathroom, he considered her viewpoint and while her lack of faith still burned him; she had cause for questions. But this time, he would not be the one to crawl back with an apology.

CAROLYN SAT ON THE COUCH, listening to the patter of the shower and Randy's thoughts, contemplating whether to stay or go. Randy's anger, while upsetting, was justified.

What if he had accused me? How the hell would I react to that?

"Not very well," she said to the empty living room. With a sigh, she stood and crossed the apartment. Entering the bathroom, she ignored his black thoughts. She stared at his bare back, the muscles glistening with streams of water, the trim lines of his back and the curve of his ass all made for quite the scenery.

Heat stirred within her, painting her skin with a flush, and she stripped her clothing and opened the shower door, stepping into the oversized marble enclosure. The only sign that he knew she had entered was the tightening of the muscles in his shoulders.

"What do you want?" he asked without turning.

"I wanted to say I'm sorry."

He glanced over his shoulder with a glare that gave warning of the emotional storm brewing inside him. "Sorry isn't enough this time."

She reached her hand out and he flinched away as if her touch was a deadly poison, and his reaction sparked the seed of her own anger. "What exactly do you want from me, Randy?"

His eyes blazed with aggravation, and he turned, cornering her against the sweating tile. "I want a fucking partner who believes in me and doesn't throw me to the wolves any time she damn well pleases."

"I did not throw you to the wolves." The muscles in her jaw stiffened in defense.

"Then why the hell was Agent Williams following me?"

She blinked and looked away from his intense stare and without thinking, she crossed her arms, distancing herself in the small, confined space he allotted her.

"Look at me." The request came out in a growl and her gaze snapped to his.

"Don't you take that tone with me," she began, and he stepped closer, crowding her even more with his towering mass.

"I'll take whatever tone I damn well please."

She uncrossed her arms and put her hands flat on his chest to hold him at bay, but all that did was aggravate the situation. His jaw clenched, and his glare became threatening.

"You'd better step out of this shower before I do something stupid," he said, the growl in his voice transitioning to a feral quality that promised pain.

"What are you going to do, Randy? Spank me?" Carolyn asked, goading him with a ghost of a smile, baiting him with something out of left field meant to diffuse his anger.

His eyebrows arched at the playful quality of her response, and he stepped back. His features transitioned, softened from the untamed fury displayed moments before to an ambiguous anger she could work with.

"Did you just..."

"I asked you if you were going to spank me."

"You can be so fucking infuriating..." he ran his hand through his wet hair, still staring at her, but now a smile edged his lips.

"Enough to spank?"

"No... well, maybe... but that's something to consider for later. Right now, you were in the middle of trying to show me just how sorry you were for questioning my innocence."

"I'm..."

"Words will not cut it, honey." This time he crossed his arms and stood tall in the shower spray and the things flitting through his mind made heat rush to her cheeks. He noticed and smiled. "There are much more gratifying things you can do with that mouth..."

Crystal Illusions
Chapter 33

RANDY OPENED HIS EYES and glanced at Carolyn draped over his chest in the warm bed. He ran his fingers through her hair, feeling the silky dampness of each strand, and wondered if they'd really make it through this.

She lifted her head and met his gaze. "Still having doubts?"

"Yeah."

"I'm sorry."

"I know you are, but I'm not sure I can deal with the constant distrust."

"You mean you can deal with the visions and me reading your mind?"

He smiled down at her and planted a kiss on her forehead. "I can deal with your visions, but I'm not so sure I like you in my head all the time. But I'll get over that. You not believing in me, well that's a whole other story."

She sat up, pulling the covers with her and leaving the cool air to brush his bare chest. "I believe in you."

He laughed at the absurdity of her words. "No, you don't. If you believed in me, you wouldn't *have* any doubts."

"Look, I..."

He put his hand up to stop her. "We will not agree on this, at least not tonight, so let's give it a rest. Okay?" His stomach piped in with a grumble that nearly shook the bed. "I don't know about you, but I'm starving." The covers shifted as he sat up in bed and reached for his clothes, sliding them on in silence. She followed him out to the kitchen and stood beside him in the entry, surveying the broken glass and spilled Chinese takeout. "I'm not sure this is salvageable."

"The food or our relationship?"

Randy met her glance and waved toward the mess. "The food." He wasn't in any mood to discuss a future right now.

"What about us?"

"Honestly, I'm still pissed." A subtle change traveled over her features. Her lips pressed together and the question in her eyes disappeared. "But you already knew that."

"Randy..."

"Don't tell me you can't read what's going on in my mind right now."

She looked down at her hands and nodded. "I can hear you."

"So, what is it you're hearing?"

"That you're not ready to shut the door on us just yet, even though you're still angry and disappointed."

"Right, so stop asking me and just let it be for a while." He turned and crossed to the closet, grabbing the broom and dustpan. "After we clean up that mess, we can go grab something to eat."

"Do you think Red will still be open?"

Randy glanced at the clock and shook his head. "They close at nine. I was thinking more like Harry's."

"Steak?"

"Yep—fury and sex really upped my appetite." He flashed a grin in her direction.

"Okay, steak it is," she agreed.

"I THOUGHT YOU HAD to have reservations to get seated here," Carolyn said after they were seated.

"Normally, you do, but they get their beef from Kincaid packing, so..." he trailed off and gave her a shrug. "There are some perks I've taken advantage of over the years, and this is one of them." He opened the menu and concentrated on what he wanted to eat.

Carolyn glanced around the crowded restaurant and sighed, a million questions flitting through her mind about Randy and his family, especially those revealed in the earlier conversation with Steve Williams. "Do you want to talk about what happened with your mother?" she asked and took a sip of water.

He glanced up and dropped the menu on the table while irritation settled into his gaze. "No." Shaking his head, he scanned the restaurant and then brought his attention back to her. "What the fuck are you trying to do to me?" Pushing his chair out, he threw the napkin on the table and headed toward the restrooms, leaving her staring after him.

His anger brushed off him in waves, even from the confines of the bathroom, and she blinked back the mist that covered her eyes. When he returned to the table, his jaw was still clenched, and his gaze was more of a glare than it had been before.

He took control, ordering steak and salads for both of them along with a scotch on the rocks for himself. When he had downed the alcohol, he closed his eyes and let it seep into his muscles, calming the angry lion within. When he opened his eyes again, he tried on a smile, but to her it looked forced. "So, what are you doing tomorrow?"

Carolyn shifted in her seat, knowing her answer was going to ruffle his feathers more than they already were. "I was going to stop and see Jim because I want my job back, then I'm going back to the studio so Damon can finish your painting."

Randy's face slowly transitioned to red, and he nodded, without speaking, but his eyes lanced into her like sharp daggers, piercing her skin with prickling pain. "You don't say."

"You're more than welcome to come with me if you'd like," she offered, hoping it would diffuse the volcano below the surface.

"What time is your appointment?" he asked, but the low timbre of his voice raked her skin, creating tiny bumps of remorse.

"I, um, I told him I'd be there at nine."

He pulled out his phone and checked his calendar; he looked up at her and nodded. "My morning is clear. I'd love to come."

"Good. You can meet me at City Hall at eight thirty and head over to Damon's from there. I think you'll be very pleased with the painting," she said, keeping up the pretense of civility in the public venue, but she knew the moment they were behind closed doors, he was going to have her head. "I didn't have the opportunity to mention this to you because of everything else, but Damon wants me to pose live at his art show."

Randy's brow creased in confusion. "What do you mean, *pose*?"

"Live art. Olivia is one of the models, too," she said, and didn't need to read his mind to know he didn't get it. "Damon starts with body suits he paints as the base for his creations and on the day of the show, we put them on, and he finishes painting us. The models pose for half of the art show and during the other half we get to mingle with the guests. It sounds kind of fun, don't you think?"

"You'd be on display?"

"If I agree to do it, yes."

"As what?"

"An angel representing original sin."

He stared at her and then cut into his steak without further comment, but his mind was full of snark and underlying bits of intrigue. Silence prevailed for the remainder of the meal and continued on the walk back to the apartment.

Once the door closed, he headed toward the bedroom, stripping his clothes, climbing under the covers and rolling on his side with his back to her.

"Is this the way it's going to be?"

He rolled to face her. "I'm tired and I don't feel like getting into another argument, so yes, this is the way it's going to be tonight."

"So, you're not going to rant and rave about me taking my clothes off for a painting again?"

"No, I'm not, because it won't do any good. You'll just go off and do whatever the hell you want, regardless of how I feel about it."

"Were you serious about coming with me tomorrow?"

"If you're serious about going, yes."

"Promise you won't make a scene?"

He laughed at her. "Regretting the invite already?"

Hell yes, she thought, but just sent a smile in his direction and headed toward the bathroom and her before bed rituals.

Crystal Illusions
Chapter 34

THE ALARM BLARED, AND Carolyn sat up, blinking the sleep from her eyes and glancing at the clock. Six o'clock in the morning came much faster than she would have liked, and she shook Randy's shoulder. "Time to get up," she muttered and reached over him, slamming her palm on the snooze button.

Without waiting for him to stir, she headed into the bathroom and jumped in a hot shower to wash away the sleep. When the air in the stall shifted, she glanced over her shoulder at his sleepy smile.

He wrapped his arms around her waist and kissed her shoulder.

She kissed his cheek and stepped out of the shower, refreshed and ready to take on Jim Britt. Randy stepped out of the shower just as she put on the finishing touches of her make-up. She smoothed her power suit and turned toward him.

"How do I look?"

"Like you're ready for a court battle."

"Good."

"Why is that good?"

"I've thought about it, and I want my job back. The idea of defending someone who could be guilty just doesn't sit well with me."

"You've gone from being gung-ho on defense to wanting back in the prosecutor's office in a matter of two days?"

"Pretty much."

"Look, Carolyn, he was livid the other night. Wait a few days before you spring this on him."

"He settled the case instead of taking a chance in court with me."

"Man, that's pretty arrogant thinking on your part. What if he took a closer look at the case and decided it was the right thing to do?"

"Jim never backs down unless he's sure he's going to lose. That's when he offers deals."

"Do you think he'll take you back?"

"He enjoys having a winning record." She shrugged. "So, you'll meet me at City Hall at 8:30?"

Randy grinned. "You sure you want me to tag along?"

"No, but I think it'll make you feel better about the whole painting and art show deal."

"I don't know about that, but I am curious. If you wait a couple of minutes, I'll walk you to City Hall." He grabbed his razor and started to shave.

"Sure." She left him to finish his morning routine.

CAROLYN GAVE RANDY A peck on the cheek and climbed the steps to City Hall. She paused at the top and sent a wave in his direction before turning and entering the building. She walked with purpose, steeling herself for a battle.

In the middle of the atrium, her vision wobbled, altering into another view that looked down at her. Her heart tripped in her chest. She locked gazes with herself, her eyes wide and an odd, luminescent blue. Fear laced her mouth, along with an underlying hatred that was as palatable as the metallic taste in her mouth.

She blinked and her vision righted, but there was no one looking down at her on any of the landing balconies.

He's here. Oh Shit. What the hell do I do now?

Carolyn's heart banged against her rib cage in a beat that fueled her fear. She took a heavy step backwards towards the door and paused again. Running outside wasn't the brightest of ideas. *The fucker wouldn't dare kill me in the middle of City Hall at this time of the morning—would he?*

She stepped toward the stairs, her brain trying to wrap around the actions of her body, screaming to run, to get out, but stubbornness directed her toward Jim's office, toward her original purpose. This was her battleground, and she would not back down. With each step, her mind categorized all personnel she had ever seen in the office so early and less than a dozen names floated to mind, but none of them jibed with the profile of a killer.

Carolyn scanned the halls and the few people she passed, none of them screamed murderer. Quite the opposite, in fact. Most had mundane thoughts, cataloging their to-do lists for the day.

Each stride closer to her destination brought both triumph and trepidation. Each corner presented a hesitation, a fear of the claw coming from nowhere and severing her head. Each door a traipse into hell, and when she arrived at Jim's office, dread sank into her stomach; turning her morning toast into a rocket ready to launch. Yet she pushed the doors open and stepped inside to an icy glare and a greeting in the form of a grunt.

"What the hell are you doing here?"

She closed the door and took a moment to compose herself before addressing his question. "Don't you think you've taken this far enough?"

"Get out before I call security."

"Why'd you choose to settle instead of facing me in court?" She crossed the room and took a seat opposite him, ignoring his directive.

"You know why."

"No, Jim, I don't. Why don't you spell it out for me?"

"Because it's not in my best interest to try a case like that."

"Afraid of losing?"

"It doesn't bode well for my record to lose."

"So, are you going to do this every time you find yourself across the aisle from me?"

He crossed his arms and glared at her. "What do you think?"

"I think you should just swallow your pride and hire me back on the team so I can continue to make you look good."

"Are you still under the watchful eye of the FBI?"

"I have a bodyguard of sorts."

His eyebrows arched, and he leaned forward. "Why is that?"

"Because the FBI suspects I may be the actual target."

Color drained from Jim's face, and he glanced out the window before returning his attention to her. His thoughts jumbled, confused and unclear, mingled with a low-grade static that irked her.

"Why wasn't I told?" he asked, his voice softening from the harsh rasp.

"Because it's a new development and I'm working with the FBI in the hopes we catch this maniac before someone else dies." She cleared her throat. "I also think the killer is in this building right now, or he was a few minutes ago."

Jim picked up the phone and pushed the zero on the phone. "Security please."

"What are you doing?"

"Getting a log of who entered the building today," he answered. "Can you give me a description?"

"No, I didn't actually see him, per se."

The phone slid back into the cradle and Jim stared at her. "Explain."

"It's one of those phenomena, like my visions. I can't really explain it." *Nor do I want to.*

Jim rubbed his face and then studied Carolyn. "How do you know you're the target?"

"Have you seen the victims?"

"Yes, but that still doesn't explain how you know *you* are the target?

"Agent Williams seems to think there's a connection somewhere along the lines and he thinks I'm the one the killer's gunning for."

"And he knows this how?"

"He's a specialist in psychic events."

"Oh, and does he also have a crystal ball?" Sarcasm filled the room.

"No, I don't."

Carolyn turned to see Agent Williams leaning on the doorframe. He stepped inside the room and closed the door.

"You really shouldn't have fired her because of my visit."

"Steve, I didn't ask you to come to my defense here."

His blue-eyed gaze turned in her direction, silencing her, and he turned back to Jim. "So, are you going to reinstate her or what?"

"For the record, I fired her because of insubordination, not your visit."

"Oh, come on, you concocted that story just to cover your ass."

"Stop helping me, Agent Williams," Carolyn said after the shock of his blatant comment wore off.

"You need her on your team."

"I don't need the headaches this will cause," Jim countered. "Visions aren't something that is considered the normal course of business around here, and I can't have that staining the record of the district attorney's office."

"Now you're discriminating against Carolyn? Interesting." Steve turned toward her. "I think perhaps a press conference is in order, don't you?"

She couldn't believe the brazen attitude, nor could she condone it aimed at Jim. "Look, Jim isn't like that..."

"Oh yes, he is. He's a political animal and they all go the CYA route as opposed to standing up for what's right. He'd rather lose his best attorney and spare the office some embarrassment over your natural gifts than take a leap of faith in you."

"That is not true. I have all the faith in the world in her abilities as a lawyer."

"Then why isn't she still on staff?"

Jim opened his mouth to speak, then popped it closed, his gaze traveling between Steve and her.

Steve leaned forward. "Tell me why she is no longer on staff."

"Because I'm in love with her and she doesn't feel the same way."

Silence fell over the room and Carolyn stared at Jim, digesting the words and the implications behind it. "What?" The sharp edge of accusation in her voice made his head snap in her direction.

"The weird visions just gave me an excuse."

"You son of a bitch."

Steve straightened and stepped back, the thickness in the air evaporated, and Jim glared at him.

"What did you just do?"

"It doesn't matter what he did, that you fired me without cause gives me enough ammunition to sue you. How will that look on your squeaky-clean record?"

"You wouldn't."

"Try me Jim, just try me." She turned, marching toward the door.

"Carolyn, stop."

She stood with her hand on the doorknob and anger brewing in the pit of her stomach. The battle got uglier than she ever thought and the fact that she'd had no clue how he felt about her also rubbed her wrong. *How could I not know this?*

"He projects a great deal of static, so you wouldn't have known."

Carolyn met Steve's gaze and then dropped her hand and turned toward Jim. "What about your wife?"

Jim looked down at his desk blotter and then out the window. "I've been sleeping in the guest quarters for the last few months."

"Jesus Jim, why didn't you tell me?"

He brought his gaze to hers and shrugged. "Would it have made a difference?"

She shook her head. Jim Britt was too much like a father to her for her to consider anything beyond friendship. Besides, Randy had swept in and taken over her thoughts on the romantic front. "We were friends, damn it."

Jim laughed. "Things aren't always what they seem."

"So, because of your puppy dog crush, I have to give up a job I love? That's insane."

"Better that you're out of the public eye than murdered by some psychopath," he retorted.

"Oh, now you're feigning being protective? That's just great." She threw her arms up in the air and turned her back on both Jim and Steve. "It doesn't matter what any of you do, the killer will eventually find me." She glanced over her shoulder at Jim, leveling a glare that could melt ice. "In the meantime, I'd like to still work and make a difference here, if you don't mind."

For a moment, she thought he was going to say no, then he nodded and picked up a case file, holding it out to her. "You can act as co-counsel on this with me."

"I'm glad we got that straightened out, now if you will be so kind as to finish that call to the security office to get a list of people in the building in the last hour, that would be even better," Steve said.

"Why?"

"Because she saw the killer, or rather saw through the killer's eyes just before she barged in here, and I want to know who was in the building."

Crystal Illusions
Chapter 35

RANDY TROTTED UP THE steps of City Hall and entered the lobby, scanning the crowd until his gaze landed on Carolyn and Agent Williams sitting on one of the benches, looking at a piece of paper. The presence of the FBI agent unnerved him, and they looked up as he approached.

"Everything okay?"

"Mostly," Carolyn answered and stood, giving him a peck on the cheek. "I got my job back."

"That's great." Randy traded a glance with Steve. "Why's he here?"

"I think the killer was here this morning," she said.

"And I was already downtown when you left the apartment building," Steve added.

"Were you following me?"

"I was until I got a bad vibe and doubled back to make sure she was okay."

Randy didn't know whether to slug him or thank him, so he turned his attention to Carolyn. "Why do you think the killer was here?"

"I had the same experience I had on the steps."

"You saw through his eyes?"

Carolyn nodded, and a stab of fear tightened his stomach. He glanced at the staircase in the great hall and the multiple levels lining the atrium.

"We're looking at the list of folks who entered the building using their key cards." Carolyn pointed at the piece of paper in Steve's hands.

"I've never had to use a card to get in here." Randy traded glances with Steve.

"It's a place to start," Steve said. "We've got some camera footage to look at, too." He pointed to the cameras covering the entryway.

"I guess I ought to thank you for keeping her safe." He shifted his weight, irked that he wasn't the one there for her when she needed protection. He glanced at his watch and raised his gaze to Carolyn. "Don't you need to be at that artist's studio at nine?"

"Yes." She popped up from the seat. "Can I meet you back here after lunch?"

"I have some leads to follow up on today. I'll bring the footage to your apartment this evening along with Chinese, okay?"

Carolyn nodded, and Randy offered his hand to Agent Williams. After a quick handshake, they headed toward the subway lines.

"Why didn't you call me?" Randy asked as they waited for the uptown train.

"I just wanted to get somewhere fast, and I didn't think I was in danger in the middle of City Hall."

"What if you were wrong?" Randy spoke even though he knew she heard his disturbing what if scenarios passing through his mind.

"You need to relax a little, honey," she said as they stepped onto the crowded subway heading for Bleecker Street and Damon's brownstone on the outskirts of Greenwich Village.

Relax, yeah right, I won't relax until this bastard is safely behind bars. Randy glanced at the crowd surrounding him, wondering if the killer was in their midst. He put his arm around Carolyn's waist and pulled her against him in a protective move that she didn't fight off.

They approached Damon's apartment at just shy of nine, and Randy glanced at Carolyn's profile. The bump from the previous night had turned a pale purple under the makeup and he pushed a stray hair out of her face while she rang the doorbell.

"Are you sure..." he started to say, but the scraping of a chain interrupted.

When the door opened, Damon's sleep tousled hair and bare chest greeted them. His gaze jumped from Carolyn to Randy and back, and the confusion manifested itself in a crease between his eyes and a slightly opened mouth. He glanced at his bare wrist and then over his shoulder before putting a smile on his face. "I seemed to have overslept." He waved them inside.

Randy didn't know what to make of the man in the doorway. He wasn't the stereotypical starving artist he envisioned. This man was closer to a Greek Adonis, and the fact he answered the door shirtless didn't sit well with him.

He rubbed his eyes and studied her for a moment, and then his eyes went wide. "What happened to your forehead?" His hand reached out, tracing the bump, and she winced, pulling away from him.

"We bumped heads last night." She waved to Randy. "Damon, this is Randy Kincaid."

Damon smiled and extended his hand. "It's a pleasure meeting you."

"The painting is for him, and I thought he'd like to see the outfit I'm going to wear in your art show."

"You've decided." He beamed at the answer.

"Yes."

"What exactly will this entail for Carolyn?" Randy asked, crossing his arms.

"I will show you once I get something more suitable on." Damon disappeared from the sitting room.

Randy turned to Carolyn. "I don't like this at all."

"I admit he's a little different, but..."

"That's the thing, he isn't different, and I'd bet a month's salary that he planned this, this, I don't know what to call it except seduction."

"He overslept."

"Bullshit."

"Randy, he's a professional."

"If he was a professional, he would have been up and had everything ready."

"Come with me." She grabbed his hand, pulling him through the apartment into the studio, stopping at the entrance.

Randy stared at the exquisite painting of Carolyn, and his breath caught in his chest. Both awe and irritation brushed his skin, and he exhaled. "I thought you said he hadn't finished yet."

"He wasn't nearly this far when I left yesterday."

"I spent most of the night on your painting," Damon said, and Randy turned, glaring at him. "I know she's busy, and I had the snapshot..." He pointed to the Polaroid clipped to the easel frame.

"Right." Randy attempted to keep his temperature in check.

"Do you need me to, uh, change?" Carolyn asked, still staring at the painting.

"No, Bella, I don't need you to change today." Damon gave Randy a nervous smile. "I probably should have canceled, but I was eager to hear your decision on the art show."

Randy crossed his arms, balling his hands into tight fists of aggravation.

Damon grabbed his elbow, pulling him forward. "Come, let me show you the concept of live art."

Randy let Damon lead him into the back room, which turned out to be the size of a warehouse. Randy looked around from the floor to the rafters. "You gutted a brownstone?"

"Yes," Damon smiled. "It gives me more flexibility for photo shoots and studio space for these shows." He waved toward the dozen painted mannequins.

"So, tell me how this works," Randy said, wandering through the maze, stopping and studying each work of art, along with the clipped photo of the final product.

"I'm almost finished with all the base outfits, so on the day of the show, the models come here, and we put on the final touches. I have both Olivia's and Carolyn's pieces, and the remaining models are divvied up to the most talented students in my art classes."

Randy stopped in front of the mannequin tagged as Original Sin. He whistled tunelessly at the drawing clipped to the palate next to the bodice. "Wow." He glanced at Damon. "Okay, I'm officially impressed."

"You see why your girlfriend is the perfect model for this, yes?"

Randy nodded. "I get it and while I know this is Olivia's gig, I have a feeling Carolyn's going to be the one to steal the show."

"Yes, well, I'll have to do something creative with her forehead if that purple bruise doesn't fade by Saturday."

"The show's this weekend?"

"Yes."

"Are you okay with this?" Carolyn asked.

Her voice echoed in the vast room, and he glanced over his shoulder at her standing in the entryway and offered her a smile before turning his attention to Damon once again. "How do you get these models in position at the gallery?"

Damon walked to a curtain and pulled it aside, revealing glass display cases holding various scenes.

The apple tree with a swing was easy to spot among the mobile sets and Randy crossed to it, studying the setup, the details of the set design right down to the tree roots, and painted apples littering the ground under the swing. He reached out and ran his fingers down the chains and cool metal met his touch. While it looked like a real apple tree, he was surprised to find the rough edging of bark under his hands, and he looked up at the chains anchored in the branch covering the ceiling of the case. "Is that real or are these anchored into the casing?"

"Both. The setup is engineered to take up to two hundred and fifty pounds. I don't think that will be an issue in Carolyn's case."

Randy laughed. "Yeah, she doesn't even weigh one-twenty soaking wet." He turned and smiled at her, feeling more at ease with the situation than he had when he stepped into the house.

"You are a lucky man." Damon offered his hand.

"I know." Randy shook Damon's hand, and they headed back into the small studio.

"I'll have the painting delivered to your home after the show," Damon directed toward Carolyn. "I'll just need the address."

Carolyn took out a pad and scribbled their address, handing it to Damon. "What time do you need me here on Saturday?"

"Nine, at the latest. We have a great deal of work to do to get everyone ready and then transported to the gallery."

"Do you need a hand?" Randy asked.

"I don't allow anyone but the artists here that day, but..." Damon raised a finger and then disappeared for a moment. When he returned, he had a VIP ticket for the event in his hand. "This will allow you into the gallery early."

"Thank you." Randy slid the ticket into his coat pocket before he and Carolyn headed for the nearest subway station.

"YOU'RE REALLY OKAY WITH all this now?" Carolyn asked. His behavior at Damon's impressed her, and she couldn't tell if it was just for her benefit or if he really warmed up to the artist.

"I'm okay with the live art concept."

"But?"

"But you being alone and naked with him yesterday still doesn't sit well."

"Are you really that insecure?"

Randy raised his eyebrows and hooked his thumb over his shoulder. "Come on, he looks like he stepped out of the pages of Greek Mythology. If I wasn't straighter than an arrow, *I* might be inclined to sleep with the man."

Carolyn couldn't help it; she burst out laughing at the thought. "I guess he is eye candy, but honey, have you looked in the mirror lately?"

Pink hues dotted his cheeks, and he glanced in her direction, offering a crooked smile that shot straight to her heart. "Are you going back to City Hall?"

"Yes, I've got some forms to fill out with Jim and he's got some case files he wants me to look at."

Randy walked her into City Hall, kissing her in the atrium before he walked out the door. Carolyn sighed and headed back to Jim's office.

This time, she knocked and waited for his invitation.

"Come in."

She opened the door and stepped inside. "Do I still have an office?"

Jim looked up from his desk and shook his head. "No, and I'm not sure this is such a good idea."

"We've worked together for years, Jim. I can do this if you can."

He leaned back in his seat and studied her. "It was easier to ignore how I felt when Linda and I still had some semblance of a marriage," he said.

"Well, you need to get over it, because it just isn't going to happen. Don't get me wrong, I care about you. You've been my best friend and confidant for a long time, but I can't see it going beyond that."

He inhaled, his chest puffing with the intake and then exhaled, nodding. "You've always been honest with me, and I appreciate that." He stood, handing her a stack of paper. "Reinstatement forms for you to sign. It will take a couple of days to get you back online, and I need to do some shuffling around to get you office space."

"Who's got my office now?"

"Bev Sinclaire."

"Who?"

"One of the attorneys I brought in a month or so ago."

"How come I don't know her?"

"I'm not sure. She did a great deal of legwork for Trent, so maybe he was hoarding her."

"Could be. So, what's her specialty?"

"White collar crime, but she was willing to step into the juvenile arena if necessary."

"Ah, I take it from your tone you didn't think she was ready for that."

Jim smiled. "She doesn't have your flare or your compassion."

"So, where do you want me to sit until you can finagle an office for me?"

"I'll have everything all set for you on Monday. In the meantime, enjoy the rest of today and tomorrow."

Carolyn didn't want to sit idle for the next couple of days. "You said you had a couple of files for me to look at?"

"You sure you don't want to relax before I throw you into some tough cases?"

"Thanks for the thought, but I've had a couple of days to rest already. I'm good to go."

"I'll tell you what. I'll send Jason over with the files after lunch. How's that sound?"

"Sounds good to me."

"In the meantime, let me introduce you to Bev." He crossed to the door, waiting for her to follow.

Carolyn's old office was still barren except for a couple of pads on the desk and the unmanned computer monitor propped to the side. No personality had been incorporated by the new occupant, and a chill played on Carolyn's spine as she glanced at the bare bookshelves. She traded a glance with Jim as they stood in the empty office.

"I thought I saw her this morning," Jim said, glancing at the sitting area behind the door.

"She sure hasn't done a lot with the place." Carolyn turned to leave the office. She stepped back at the sight of the Amazon in the doorway. At close to six feet tall, Bev Sinclaire towered over Carolyn. Her black hair was pulled into a tight bun, giving her a severe and unfeminine look. Her dark eyes squinted at Carolyn and her lips pressed into a thin slit before her gaze traveled to Jim. "What can I do for you, sir?" Even her voice was deep and disturbingly masculine.

"Bev, I'd like you to meet Carolyn Hastings. She's returning to work on Monday."

Carolyn tried to smile, but the absence of any thoughts or static coming from Bev unnerved her as much as the lack of personality did.

"Does this mean I should move my things out of this office?" she asked, dismissing Carolyn all together.

"I haven't looked at the office arrangements yet, but it may mean some shifting around. I'll have that ironed out by tomorrow."

Bev turned her attention to Carolyn and offered a tight smile. "It's nice to meet you." She extended her hand, and it engulfed Carolyn's in a hard squeeze meant to inflict pain.

Carolyn had to clamp her teeth together to keep from wincing. "Nice to meet you, too," she said after their hands disengaged. She forced herself not to rub her hand until she was safely in Jim's office and the door closed behind her.

"I don't think I've ever met someone with such a lack of personality before."

Jim raised an eyebrow. "She does impeccable research."

"I'm sure she does," Carolyn conceded and let it go. "Jason knows where I live, so..."

"I'll send him over with the files." Jim scooted behind his desk, putting distance between them.

"Thank you." Carolyn waited until he met her gaze before turning and heading home.

CAROLYN SAT AT THE kitchen table with her soup and sandwich spread out before her. Before she could take a bite, a knock on the door interrupted her. She folded her napkin and crossed the living room, taking a peek out the peephole.

Jason stood staring up at the ceiling, waiting for her to answer.

Carolyn smiled and opened the door, waving him inside. "That was fast."

Jason nodded. "I hear you're coming back," he said, handing Carolyn a couple of legal folders.

"That's the consensus, although I'm not sure where Jim will put me."

"It hasn't been the same without you."

"I've only been gone a couple of days."

"Yes, but you really added something to the office..." he trailed off. "I know I'm not supposed to say anything, but that woman who took your office is no more than a computer with human skin. She has no personality, and she honestly creeps the hell out of me."

"I understand she's good at research," Carolyn said. She wasn't one for office gossip, and while she shared Jason's opinion of Bev Sinclaire, she wasn't about to voice it.

Jason laughed and nodded. "I'll give her that."

Carolyn held up the files. "Have you looked at these?"

"Yes, and one is really sensitive. I'm not sure why Mr. Britt gave it to you, considering your connections with Cameron Unger."

Carolyn blanched and flipped open the case file. "Shit." She took a seat, waving to the couch next to her for Jason to sit. "This isn't good."

"I didn't think so either."

"It says here that his sister didn't know what was happening. That each count of abuse occurred while she was at work."

"Yeah, but isn't that what they all say?"

Carolyn met his gaze and nodded. "If she knew her husband was abusing her daughter and didn't speak up, it could screw up Cameron's bid for office." She shook her head and dropped the file on the coffee table. "Jesus, that makes this one so much messier."

Jason offered a slight smile. "I'm sure you can handle it. My notes are in the files, and if you need me, give me a yell."

Carolyn nodded. "Thanks for delivering the case file."

Jason gave her a nod and paused by the door. "They found another victim." He shot a glance over his shoulder.

"I know, I'm working with the FBI, so I've got the inside scoop," she said, and Jason hesitated, his mouth popping open, but no words came out.

He seemed to reconsider and gave her a wave before he shut the door behind him.

Carolyn sat staring at the file in front of her, wondering how Olivia was going to take her going after Cameron's family. With a sigh, she started culling through the different pieces of information, categorizing what they had put together. After a while, she sat back on the couch, her palms pressing into her tired eyes.

RANDY WALKED INTO THE apartment at a little after 4:30, stopping in the doorway to stifle a laugh. Papers were all over the glass table, the couches, and the floor and Carolyn was sitting in the middle of them, scribbling notes madly on the yellow steno pad in her hands. She didn't even look up when he cleared his throat; she only raised her index finger and continued writing.

He closed the door and disappeared to change out of his suit and returned, moving some papers aside to take a seat on the couch until she was done with her case notes. He had seen that look before when he picked her up at the office, and there was little he could do to dissuade her when she was in the zone. Sometimes it frustrated him, but tonight, as he watched her intensity, it moved him.

Carolyn raised her eyes, meeting Randy's gaze. "Really? This turns you on?" She waved at the calamity of paper surrounding her.

Randy slowly smiled. The color that surfaced in Carolyn's cheeks put him in motion, and by the time he reached her, she had tossed the pad aside. He kissed her, pushed her back on the plush carpet and slid his hand up her tight sweater. Her skin, warm and soft, set him on fire

and he stripped the cashmere off her, freeing her
flesh for exploration.

Crystal Illusions
Chapter 36

STEVE STOOD OUTSIDE THE apartment door with his knuckles poised to knock on the wood and he hesitated, feeling the heat rise in his cheeks at the dirty thoughts transmitting through the door. He thought twice about interrupting them and then looked at the zip drive in his hand. Finding this killer was more important than Carolyn's sex life, so he rapped on the door.

He stifled a chuckle at the sudden rustling behind the door, remembering those impulsive days with Jennifer before everything turned upside down. For a moment, he wished he could go back and change the course of their lives, starting with their first trip to Maine. If he could do it all over again, he would have kept Jennifer away from Brooksfield until after hazing week.

That still wouldn't have changed your fate. The voice accompanied by the shuffle of wings interrupted his thought process.

"Shut up," he whispered to his less than silent guardian angel.

He received a chuckle in response just as the door opened in front of him. Carolyn's wide eyes greeted him and then scanned the hallway before landing back on him. "Who are you talking to?"

"No one." He raised the flash drive. "I hope you have a computer here." He stepped into the apartment and glanced at the papers spread out over the living room table and couch. "Looks like the paper fairy vomited all over your living room."

Randy snorted a chuckle and threaded the last button of his shirt, trying to straighten it without being obvious. "And we have a computer in the office." He hooked his thumb over his shoulder toward the hallway.

Steve raised the large plastic bag dangling from his hand. "Food first?"

Carolyn licked her lips and nodded.

Pocketing the zip drive, Steve headed toward the kitchen with the takeout bag. "I wasn't sure what everyone liked, so I got a little of everything." He took out box after box, lining them up on the counter.

"Jesus, that must have cost a fortune," Randy said at the more than two dozen boxes.

Steve shrugged. "It wasn't that bad."

"The FBI pays that well?"

"No. But I don't need the paycheck these days." He offered a smile and rubbed his hands together. "Dig in," he said to the two of them, waving toward the containers.

Randy grabbed three plates, serving spoons and silverware, and then let Carolyn serve herself first. After they all piled food on their plates, they took a seat at the kitchen table.

"So, any breaks in the case?" Randy asked before shoveling a forkful into his mouth.

Steve debated and picked up a fork instead of the chopsticks. *Jesus, do you not remember how to use those things?*

Carolyn cocked her head, staring at him with her food halfway to her mouth. She put her fork down. "Are you hearing that?"

Steve sighed and nodded, digging into his food without further comment.

"Hearing what?"

"I think someone's talking to Agent Williams. Are you wearing a wire?"

Steve closed his eyes for a moment, and then opened them, meeting her gaze. "No, I'm not wearing a wire."

"Then who am I hearing?"

"I have a very opinionated, somewhat of a pain in the ass guardian angel."

Both Randy and Carolyn stared at him. Their thoughts swarmed with doubt, followed by suspicion. Finally, Carolyn spoke. "Can I see your badge again?"

The laugh from beyond irritated him, but he forced a smile and pulled out his badge. "If you want to call the local FBI office, they can confirm I'm an agent. You can even ask to speak to the assistant director Ronald Cleary. I report directly to him."

Carolyn studied the badge and then Steve before nodding and leaving the room.

"I guess she isn't that trusting," Steve said to Randy.

Randy sat rigid, his gaze hard and unreadable, but his thoughts betrayed him. The idea that Steve may be the killer swirled in his head and his hand clasped the knife in a death grip.

"I'm not the Scarlet Psychopath, Randy," he said, exploiting the fact that he could easily read the man's mind. "Enjoy your food. Carolyn's checking my credentials, and if she gets hold of my boss, he'll ease her mind."

"You can hear your guardian angel?"

"I call him my guardian angel for lack of a better description. Does the name Chris Ryan ring a bell?"

Randy nearly choked on his dinner, and after a couple of hearty coughs, he nodded. His firm handled the Ryan estate. He remembered seeing the transfer requests come in after their deaths and the name of the new trustee. "Steve Williams. Holy shit. You're *that* Steve Williams?"

"The one and only." He grinned and took a forkful of Szechwan chicken.

"You're worth billions."

"No, Chris's kids are worth billions. I'm only worth a few million."

Randy sat back in the seat. "I've done some work on your accounts with the partner at the firm."

"I know. I looked into it after your name came up in this case."

"Why didn't you say anything?"

"I've been a little busy tracking down a killer. Besides, until I ruled you out as a suspect, I didn't think a personal conversation regarding my finances was in order."

Carolyn stepped back into the kitchen and quietly handed the badge back to Steve, and took a seat.

Randy's mind wrapped around the conversation, and his eyes narrowed. "So, you're hearing Chris Ryan?"

"Ayup."

"But isn't he dead?"

"As a doornail."

"So, you're a ghost whisperer, too?"

Steve laughed. "No, I wouldn't say that. I guess Chris just latched onto me considering he died saving my ass. Now he thinks it's his job to continue being my vigilant guardian."

It is.

"And your girlfriend can hear his commentary as if he's talking out loud here in the room," Steve said, pointing his fork in her direction before returning his attention to the feast on his plate. "Eat up before this gets cold."

CAROLYN STARED AT AGENT Williams. While she could accept most of his extra sensory gifts, this just crossed a line she wasn't able to leap even though she heard the distinct voice. Even his boss said Steve was different, gifted with more than just an innate ability to ferret out killers. Different. His picture should be under the definition in the dictionary.

His gaze swiveled to hers and a gleam of humor reflected in his eyes, but he didn't comment on her train of thought.

Instead of dissecting more of this man, she focused on Randy and his thoughts while she ate, and she paused again when the billionaire's name flitted through his mind. Chris Ryan. She remembered the man and the inquisition looking into the death of the reporter who held his family hostage. It was one of her first cases in the district attorney's office and after looking at the depositions; they dropped all charges, categorizing it as a justifiable homicide.

"You know his office handles the Ryan estate?" Steve said, pointing toward Randy.

"I got that much from his thought process."

"Will you two stop digging in my brain?" Randy said.

Carolyn traded a glance with Steve and nodded. "Sorry, honey." She planted a kiss on Randy's cheek.

When the last of the plates were picked clean, Steve pulled out the zip drive. "We have the list of names that used key cards to enter City Hall today, but now we need to go through the videos of people entering the building this morning prior to when you arrived. I pulled the video feeds from five in the morning until you arrived at seven."

"How many cameras?" Carolyn asked.

"Three."

"So, there's six hours of footage?"

"Yes, but I set up a motion algorithm so the video will automatically fast forward when there is no activity, so it shouldn't take that long to go through this."

"You two go ahead. I'll clean up in here," Randy said.

Carolyn stood and led Steve to the office where he inserted the drive into their computer and started the feed. At six, the first person entered the building.

"That's Jim," Carolyn said, and Steve added the name to the list. "He shouldn't be a suspect."

Steve looked up at her. "Everyone who entered this building today is a suspect."

"Even the district attorney?"

"Yes, even the DA."

"Okay." She focused on the screen. "That's Trent Kaplan and my assistant Jason, damn he got there earlier than normal."

"Jason who?"

"Jason Anderson. He's an intern."

"What time does he usually get in?"

"When he worked for me, he'd usually roll in around nine."

Steve scribbled the information and then pressed the play button again.

"Pause the tape." Carolyn sat down.

"Who's that?" Steve tapped the screen.

"That's Linda Britt. Jim's wife." Carolyn wondered why she had gone to City Hall and, more importantly, why Jim didn't mention it.

Steve turned his gaze back to her and lifted an eyebrow.

"Keep rolling."

The next woman to stroll in carrying a tray with two coffee cups in it sent a frigid chill down Carolyn's neck and she shuddered. "Bev Sinclaire."

"You don't like her, do you?"

"Not one bit. Cold and no personality. I couldn't read anything from her."

Steve grunted and wrote the name down.

The clock on the display clicked to seven and two dark figures entered City Hall.

"Who are they?"

"Cameron Unger and Olivia Montenegra."

"They came in a few minutes before you did."

"I didn't see them, but then again, they'd be headed for the legislative end of the building and not our section."

Steve still wrote their names.

After cross-referencing with the names on the keycard list from the subway entry point, they ended up with twenty-one names. "Well, the good news is that Randy isn't on the videos, and his alibi last night proved to be solid." Steve folded the list, depositing it into his pocket. "I've got some work to do. In the meantime, try to relax and let me know if you have any more visions."

Carolyn walked him to the door. "How long before you know something?"

"I'm hoping our answer is on this list and we can nail the bastard before someone else gets killed."

Crystal Illusions
Chapter 37

CAROLYN SAT UP IN the dark, her breath locked in her chest and her hands shaking too much to turn on the light. This time the killer not only decapitated the woman, he cut off arms and legs and disemboweled the torso, spilling her entrails all over the alley. The last thing she saw before she woke was her head tumbling into the opening of a garbage bag and she swore she smelled Chinese food.

She reached for Randy and found an empty bed instead of his warm body. Thunder shook the windowpanes and sheets of rain pelted the glass with the force of a raging river, matching the nasty weather in her vision.

"Randy?"

No answer came, and she fumbled for the light, this time successfully illuminating the room. The jeans he had draped over the chair were no longer there and she slid out of bed on legs that felt boneless. Her stomach decided the food she ate earlier would be better elsewhere, and she lunged for the bathroom, flipping the lid and vomiting.

After brushing her teeth and rinsing her mouth, she tightened her bathrobe and headed into the living room, switching the lights on as she went. Randy wasn't in the apartment.

She rummaged in her pocketbook and dug out her phone, dialing his number with fingers that still shook. She listened to the ringing...once...twice...

"Hello," his breathless voice came over the line.

"Where the hell are you?"

"I had to get something for my head." He followed with a string of wet sneezes.

"Oh." Carolyn stood in the empty apartment, scanning the neat piles of paper and the empty wine glasses still sitting on the coffee table. "You ventured out in the storm to get aspirin?"

"No, my allergies went into overdrive, and I didn't have any more Benadryl in the house."

Carolyn headed to the bathroom and opened the cabinet. There were no antihistamines on the shelves, so she closed the medicine cabinet. "So, how far did you have to go?"

"The nearest 24 hour Duane Reade is on Broadway near City Hall. I should be home in about five minutes," he said, and another bout of sneezing took over.

"You should have woken me before you left."

"You were sound asleep, and I didn't have the heart to."

"Well, it sucked waking up and not having you there."

"Nightmare?"

"No, another vision."

Quiet only broken by the occasional wheeze filtered through the line. When he spoke, his voice carried a chill more severe than sub-zero. "And you think…"

"No, not this time," she interrupted, wishing she could shake the small nugget of doubt in her stomach.

"What makes this time different?"

"For one, the killer didn't sound like Rudolph with a mud-covered nose, and he wasn't sneezing up a storm either."

"I sound like Rudolph?"

"You sound awful."

"Yeah, well, wait until you get a look at me." The howl of the wind on his phone shut off. "I'm downstairs. I'll be up in a minute."

"Okay." She folded her phone and went to the living room to wait for him. At the sound of jangling keys, she opened the door. She hardly recognized the puffy-eyed, red and runny nosed, soaking wet man in front of her. He offered a smile before he sneezed into his wet sleeve.

"God, you look worse than you sound." She pulled him into the apartment, helping him strip out of the rain slicker. "Let's get you in a hot shower and to bed."

"I need to take a couple of these first." Randy dug a package of Benadryl out of his pocket, and she took it from him, leading him to the bathroom where he stripped out of his wet clothes, took the medicine, and stepped into the hot shower she started.

"I need to call Agent Williams." She closed the shower door, leaving him to the steamy heat of the water. She retreated to the living room and pulled out her phone, opting for the traditional means of contact rather than the mind connection.

He answered on the fourth ring. "Hello?"

"Agent Williams, this is Carolyn Hastings. I had another vision."

"Give me a second."

She heard the shuffle of fabric and then water running on the other end of the line.

"Tell me about the vision," a voice said from behind her.

When she turned, she took in a tousled FBI agent donning a t-shirt and jeans. Something about the disheveled, sleepy gaze lit a flame in her and she shook the improper thoughts out of her head with a glance toward the bedroom and the sounds of Randy's shower still in progress.

"This time he not only cut off her head, but her arms and legs too. I think he had garbage bags for each..." She couldn't bring herself to verbalize the remainder of the sentence.

"So, we're just going to find a torso in the alley this time?"

"A disemboweled torso."

"Lovely." Steve took a seat, rubbing his face. "Anything else you can tell me?"

"I thought I smelled Chinese food."

"All right, I'll catch you in the morning."

She blinked at the now empty space he occupied. *How the hell does he do that?* She thought and put the phone to her ear. Only the dial tone came through, and she disconnected the call. With one more glance around the living room, she turned out the lights and headed back to the bedroom.

Randy stepped out of the bathroom with his pajama bottoms on and slid into the bed next to her. "Are you okay?"

She nodded. "Did the shower help at all?"

"A little. I still feel like crap, though."

"Well, you look a lot better."

He kissed her forehead, and she turned, letting him spoon her in his strong grasp. "Sweet dreams," he whispered in her ear, and she hoped to God those words rang true.

Crystal Illusions
Chapter 38

THE ALARM CLOCK BUZZED, shocking Carolyn out of a sound sleep. Randy just stirred, and she reached over him, hitting the snooze button and silencing the harsh sound for another ten minutes.

Her eyes shut, and the alarm's piercing siren woke her again. "Randy, turn that damn thing off."

He grunted and slammed his hand on the clock, silencing the sharp alarm.

"Hey, Rudolph, you need to get up." She pushed his leg with her foot.

Randy opened a bloodshot eye. "Rudolph?" he asked with a scratchy, stuffed-up voice.

"Yeah, you," she grinned at his single-eyed stare.

"I'm not going in this morning," he grumbled and turned his head, rolling away from her.

"Don't you have meetings?"

"Not until after lunch," his pillow-muffled voice answered.

She ran her hand over his bare back. "Still feeling crappy?"

"U-huh."

His labored breathing evened out to the rhythm of sleep, and she rolled out of bed, cleaning up and taking a cup of coffee to the living room and her case files. After reading through the case involving Cameron's sister, she closed the file and tossed her notes on the table. "Damn it all to hell." She ran her hands down her face.

"Who are you talking to?"

She jumped at his voice and turned toward the bedroom. Randy stood in the hallway, his hair in complete disorder and his nose and eyes still red, but not as bad as they had been last night.

She pointed toward the file on the table. "This case is going to hit very close to home and I'm afraid I may lose my closest friend when all is said and done."

Randy crossed the room and took a seat on the couch next to her. "How so?"

"The mother of the victim is Cameron's sister."

"She was abusing her child?"

"No, her husband was, but she should have known. There are too many inconsistencies in her story and instead of stopping it; she turned a blind eye, ignoring the signs."

"So, what are you going to do?"

"I'm going after her, too."

Randy whistled and sat back in the seat. "That's going to put a dent in Cameron's bid for re-election."

"No shit, and I'm sure Olivia is going to be pissed at me for being the cause."

"Olivia should understand that you're just doing your job and considering the circumstances..." He offered a shrug.

"She's friends with Cameron's sister."

Randy's eyebrows rose, and he sighed. "Are you going to give her a heads up?"

"I can't. It's an active case and I shouldn't even be discussing it with you."

"I promise, it won't go farther than this room."

"Thanks." Carolyn rubbed his knee. "Are you feeling any better?"

He smiled and shook his head. "Not really, but I'll live. I'm hoping a shower helps to clear my head a little." He squeezed her hand before retreating to the bedroom.

Carolyn glanced at the clock and sighed, reached for the phone, and dialed her old apartment number. She hoped Olivia was up by now, but on some days, Olivia considered calls at ten in the morning obnoxious.

"Hello, darling!" Olivia's bright voice filled the line. "Damon tells me you're modeling in the show with us tomorrow."

"After Damon showed me the concept and the painted body suit, I figured, why not?"

"I have to warn you, it's an exhausting day, so make sure you eat a nutritious breakfast!" Olivia said.

"Thanks, I'll make sure I have a decent meal before I head over there tomorrow. But that's not the reason I'm calling. I understand you and Cameron were over at City Hall yesterday morning..." Carolyn paused, leaving the question hanging.

Silence filled the line for a moment. "I, uh… how did you know we were there?"

"I stopped in and had a heart to heart with Jim."

More silence filled the line. "Then you know."

"Know what?" Carolyn said, and her pulse throbbed in her throat. She couldn't read Olivia over the phone, but the silence followed by the deadpan tone chilled her.

"You know about Cameron's sister."

A measure of relief flooded Carolyn and the throbbing in her throat subsided. For a moment, she thought Olivia might have been the owner of the pair of eyes she'd been seeing through. "Yes, I'm aware of the situation."

"Can you help her? They took her daughter away, and she's devastated."

"Olivia, I got my job back yesterday."

"Oh. What does that mean?"

"I'm the prosecuting attorney on this case."

"I thought the DA fired you?"

"He did, but after our talk, he gave me my job back and this case is now on my plate. As such, I can't discuss this with you or Cameron or anyone involved until I'm officially back on staff."

"Okay… then why did you ask about City Hall yesterday?"

"It's a long story. I'll fill you in when I see you tomorrow, but it has to do with some weird things that have happened lately in relation to The Scarlet Psychopath."

"You're still having those nightmares?"

"Yes, and they're getting worse."

"Well, make sure you take a sleeping pill tonight. You're going to need your rest for tomorrow."

Carolyn smiled and closed her eyes, grateful that Olivia hadn't pushed the situation with Cameron's family. "I'll do that. See you in the morning."

"I can't wait!"

Carolyn hung up the phone and straightened her notes before heading into the kitchen with her empty cup. She brewed a new pot of coffee and waited for Randy to emerge from the shower.

Crystal Illusions
Chapter 39

STEVE STOOD IN THE sitting room of the Britt home waiting for Linda Britt. He scanned the bookshelves, noting where the District Attorney's legal textbooks transitioned to Mrs. Britt's trashy romance novels. An occasional photo of the couple graced the shelves, along with several knick-knacks.

"May I help you?"

Steve turned to the soft, feminine voice. Mrs. Britt stood in the doorway, her platinum blonde hair cut in an attractive bob framing her heart-shaped face. Gray-green eyes met his and crinkled in a smile as they traveled down his frame. Her blatant study of him unnerving to the point he wanted to hide in a trench coat. This woman may be a prominent staple in the political cog of New York City, but she radiated silence and her eyes held a base animalistic tendency that triggered the seed of suspicion.

"Hello, Mrs. Britt, I'm Special Agent Williams from the FBI." He opened his badge so she could see his credentials.

Her demeanor chilled instantly, and her smile faltered. "What can I do for you?"

"I'm here regarding your visit to City Hall yesterday."

She blinked a few times and her expression shut down like a steel trap. "I was visiting my husband. Why do you ask?"

Steve allowed a smile to form on his lips. "Did you see him?"

"No, he wasn't in his office when I arrived."

"Did anyone see you?"

"No. What is this about?"

"When was the last time you saw Carolyn Hastings?"

Linda's face flushed red. "That little hussy ruined my marriage." As soon as the words were spoken, her eyes widened, and her hand flew to her mouth. She sat on the couch and took a deep breath. "I'm sorry about that little outburst. My husband's infidelity still stings a bit."

Steve took a seat next to Linda, formulating his words carefully, as if he wasn't privy to the truth. "Are you insinuating that your husband had an affair with Ms. Hastings?"

"I could never prove it, but..."

"Then why were you visiting him at City Hall?"

"I wanted to see if he really *had* fired her like he said he did." She looked out the window. "That turned out to be a farce as well." Her eyes filled with tears. "Why would he do that? Why would he lie to me when he vowed to work on our marriage? Why?"

Steve raised his eyebrows. "I'm sorry. I don't have any answers for you on that front, but I have another question, if you don't mind."

She nodded and sniffled, wiping the stray tear from her cheek.

"Did you see anyone while you were at City Hall?"

"I told you, no one saw me."

"That's not what I asked..."

Her manner transitioned from the teary-eyed wife to the same hardness that overcame her when he introduced himself. "No, I didn't see anyone I knew, either." She answered and glanced at her watch. "Now, if you don't mind, I'm late for an appointment."

"Just one more question, Mrs. Britt." He paused and waited until her gaze locked with his. "Where were you between the hours of one and three in the morning today?"

"I was sleeping."

"Can anyone confirm that?"

Her jaw tightened, and she stood. "I think it's time for you to leave."

Steve nodded and offered his hand. She stared at it and then turned, walking out of the room in a darker mood than when she had entered. He took the cue and left, closing the door behind him.

Out on the sidewalk, he opened the list and put an asterisk next to Linda's name. The prospects of obtaining a court order to search the district attorney's house with the flimsy information he had were slim, and that did not sit well with him, especially after the brief and bizarre conversation. He'd have to follow up with the District Attorney regarding her whereabouts over the last few weeks. He stuffed the list back into his pocket and hailed a cab.

"City Hall." He leaned back in the seat.

His phone beeped, and he scanned the message that came in from his boss. "Shit," he muttered and swiped to the next text. "Change in plans. Can you take me to Central Park West and 110th Street instead?"

The cab turned around on 42nd Street and looped back up Fifth Avenue and around Central Park, dropping Steve off at the corner of 110th and Central Park West. He paid and headed toward the apartment building, steeling himself for the next confrontation.

She turned, her platinum blonde hair flowing in an attractive arc, followed by that captivating, brown-eyed gaze that met his with all the hostility of a Brooklyn mobster.

"Hey, Sarah."

"Don't give me that shit. You left me to babysit your wife in court."

He gave the doorman an awkward smile before he grabbed Sarah's arm and lead her to the elevator. "Do you always have to make a scene?" he asked when the elevator doors shut and the cabin began its ascent to the penthouse.

"I do when you're such a dick."

"I was needed here."

"You were needed at home," she countered, staring him down. "Do you know how hard it was for her to sit in that courtroom and go through the testimony without you?"

Guilt bit at him, prickling and itching under his skin, and he shifted with discomfort. He knew it was going to be hell on her, but if he heard her recount each horrifying assault in person, he would turn his anger on Kyle Winslow, finishing the job that Chris Ryan started. "I know."

"Then why the hell..."

"Let it go, Sarah," he snapped, sending a warning glance in her direction.

She stepped closer, the set of her jaw matching her offensive thoughts.

Steve's teeth clenched, and he willed his hands from following suit. "If I was in that courtroom listening to what she went through, hearing her voice shake and seeing the tears in her eyes... I. Would. Have. Killed. Him."

Sarah's eyes narrowed. "You don't think I wanted to shoot the bastard?"

He met her angry gaze. "You didn't have a loaded gun in the courtroom, did you?"

She bit her lip and stepped back just before the elevator doors slid open.

He crossed into the hallway and opened the apartment door with a thought, walked into the living room, and stared out at the panoramic view of the city.

"I haven't seen you lose your temper since the night we met," Sarah said

"Yeah, well, put me in a room with Kyle Winslow and..."

"You already had the chance to kill him, and you chose not to. Hell, if you hadn't stepped in, I would have killed him, so what's different between then and now?"

Steve ran his hand through his hair, frustrated with this line of questioning from his partner. Sarah always put him on the defensive and this time he had to head it off before he lost his temper. "Look, did you come here to work on the case with me, or did you just fly down to ride my ass?"

"As much as I'd like to ride you..." The rest of the sentence fell into silence.

He turned at the imaginary porn flick snapping off in her mind. "You're doing that just to piss me off, aren't you?"

She raised an eyebrow and her lips formed that come-hither smile that, if he hadn't been married, would have sent his libido into overdrive. Now, it only irritated him further.

"Stop it." He crossed to the desk, picked up the file, and handed it to her. "They've narrowed down the weapon to a collector's axe. You want to make yourself useful and start matching sales records with these names?"

"What are you going to do?"

"I'm going to City Hall to have a chat with half the names on that list. I'll be back." He headed toward the door.

"You can't just pawn off the case research on me."

Steve sent a smile in her direction. "Sure I can." He closed the door on her loud curses.

CITY HALL AT NOONTIME was a mass of people and Steve stood at the entrance for a moment, soaking in the thoughts of strangers. He turned and marched up the stairs and into the District Attorney's office with authority.

Jim Britt looked up from his computer and his expression hardened. "I don't appreciate you harassing my wife this morning."

"I really don't give a damn. I'm trying to stop a serial killer and if that makes you uncomfortable, so be it. You and your wife each have a motive to target Ms. Hastings, as do a handful of others in this office."

Jim's eyes narrowed, and his lips thinned into white lines. "You think I killed those girls?"

Steve flipped his notebook open to the page, listing the dates and times of the attacks. "At this point, I'm not ruling anyone out. Eight women are dead and I'm trying to make sure there isn't a ninth." He raised his gaze, meeting the now red-faced glare of Jim Britt.

Jim's thoughts turned into a flurry of information, none of which settled Steve's suspicions. He sent a curt nod in Steve's direction.

"What can I do to help?" he finally asked.

"I need to rule people out and I'd like to start with you," Steve said, toning his confrontational stance down a notch. He sat across from Jim and slid the notebook in his direction. "Can you tell me where you were during the hours of the murders on this list?"

Jim scanned the dates and times. "I was in the office last Monday morning. The rest of these times I was at home either working in my study or sleeping."

"And your wife?"

"I don't know where she was last Monday, but she was sleeping the other times."

"Are you sure about that?"

Jim scanned the times again. "Actually, I'm not sure what time she arrived home on Wednesday. She had a rotary club meeting and those sometimes run long. As you know, we haven't been sleeping in the same room for a while."

"So, the only concrete alibi you have is during the second murder?"

Jim looked at the list and sighed. "Looks that way."

"And your wife?"

"Look, my wife couldn't have done this. Despite how angry she is with me, she wouldn't go after Carolyn." He stared at the dates for a moment and then met Steve's gaze.

Steve noodled on his response for a moment and switched gears. "Do you collect weapons featured in gaming or fantasy and science fiction films?"

Jim's eyebrows rose, and his gaze jumped to the decorative sword mounted over the couch. And he waved his hand in the same direction. "I own an extensive collection of swords, axes and sabers that date back to the fifteenth century. Why?"

"Because we believe the weapon is a collector's axe." Steve waited for a reaction and all he got was a blink and the resounding clutter of static. "I'd like to take a look at the collection, if you don't mind."

That received more of a reaction. Jim Britt shut down, his eyes narrowing a fraction and his back stiffening. "Do you have a warrant?"

"I was hoping you would grant me permission."

The laugh that escaped from Jim took him by surprise and he focused, gathering his power of influence and directing it at the District Attorney. "Are you responsible for the murders of those girls?"

Jim shook his head. "No."

"Is your wife?"

This time, Jim's reaction was a lot less certain. "No..."

"So why don't you want me searching your house?"

His lips tightened, but he couldn't keep the truth from spilling out. "Because I've got a certain fetish that I'd rather not become a matter of public record."

Curiosity got the best of Steve and he raised an eyebrow. "And what exactly would that be?"

His face reddened. "I'm into light S&M."

The answer threw Steve, and he actually laughed. "Whips and chains?" he couldn't help the comment, it just slipped out and the glare the DA gave him was enough to stifle the chuckle. "Well, now that the cat's out of the bag, you shouldn't have an issue with me looking around."

Without Steve's influence over him, he stood and headed for the door, holding it open for Steve to exit. "I do have an issue with you rifling through my personal effects. Now, if you wouldn't mind, I'm late for court."

Steve took the blatant hint and stopped next to Jim. "I'll be back with a court order."

"Good luck with that." Jim turned, walking out of the office with purpose.

Steve watched him leave and turned to the stunned secretary in the outer office. "Where can I find Jason Anderson?"

"I believe he is in Beverly Sinclaire's office." She pointed toward Carolyn's old office.

Steve nodded and headed in that direction. He'd hit up Judge Henderson for search warrants when he was through with the next three interviews and hopefully by that point, Sarah would have sales records to give him probable cause.

His phone buzzed, and he glanced at the caller, diverting his path to a quiet corner. "What do you have for me?"

"I haven't gotten very far on the sales leads, but the backgrounds you requested came back," Sarah began, and he could hear paper shuffling. "Jason Anderson has a hell of a motive. Carolyn Hastings put his father away. The man was a teacher, and she convicted him for molesting little girls in his elementary class. Jason changed his name and dropped off the radar after his father was killed in prison," she said.

"What else can you tell me about him?"

"He's in his second year of law school. Says here he also has a black belt in karate and has competed in weapons tournaments, so be careful."

"I'm on it." Steve hung up. With a deep breath, he crossed the office and knocked on the door to Carolyn's old office.

"Come in."

Steve expected to see a man on the other side of the door—instead, he saw a woman who could only be categorized as an Amazonian mutant or a badly dressed drag queen. "I'm sorry. I was told Jason Anderson was in here."

"I sent him to pick up lunch." Beverly Sinclaire said.

Everything about her screamed man, except the eyeful of cleavage accented by the low-cut shirt. The most concerning thing about this woman was the lack of thoughts or static that people usually transmit. Steve's intuition prickled, and he stepped into the office, pulling his badge out of his pocket and flashing it in her direction. "I'm Special Agent Williams and I'm here regarding the Scarlet Psychopath case. Do you mind if I ask you some questions?"

"What can I do for you, Agent Williams?"

"How long have you worked at the district attorney's office?"

"A couple of months. Why do you ask?"

"Did you work with Carolyn Hastings at all?"

"No, but I believe this was her office. Has something happened that I should know about?"

Steve skirted the question and asked, "What can you tell me about Jason Anderson?" Still fishing for something of a thought in the woman's head, but he received nothing. Either this woman had peculiar thought patterns, or she was a killer in disguise.

"He's a bright law student. Why?"

Steve sent a smile her way. "I'm asking the questions, if you don't mind."

Her head cocked to the side, and her eyes narrowed. "What exactly are you fishing for, Agent Williams?"

Before Steve could answer, the door behind him opened and a man in his early twenties, close to Steve's height and build, walked in with a takeout bag. His gaze landed on Steve, and his gait faltered. He stopped in place and glanced between Steve and Beverly, his eyebrows raised in question.

"Jason, I presume?" Steve asked, flipping his badge open.

The blood ran out of Jason's face, leaving it pale. His brown eyes widened. "Did something happen to Carolyn? I mean Ms. Hastings?"

"Is there somewhere we can talk in private?" Steve asked.

"Yeah, sure." Jason handed the bag to Beverly without as much as a glance in her direction. He led Steve to an empty office overlooking the park and closed the door before turning to Steve. "Please, tell me Ms. Hastings is okay."

Steve studied him for a moment, hearing broken thoughts that bordered on panic, but not in the realm of being caught, more like panic relating to Carolyn. "She's fine, but I have some questions for you."

Jason closed his eyes and sat on the nearest chair. The relief in his features said far more to Steve than anything else. When Jason looked back at Steve, he waved toward the chair next to him. "What can I do for you?"

"Tell me about your father."

Jason blinked several times and his mouth opened in a shocked O and after a moment, he promptly shut it and the concern lacing his face transitioned to a hard stare. He shifted in the chair and an iron blanket draped over his thoughts, blocking Steve from obtaining any more information beyond the hint of feelings he received when they first entered the room.

"How did you find out?" he finally asked when he regained composure.

"I'm with the FBI. We have a way of uncovering the damndest details when we set our minds to it." He sat back in the seat and crossed his arms.

"Should I have a lawyer present?"

"Do you need one?"

"I'm not sure I like what you're insinuating."

Steve leaned forward with his elbows on his knees. "I don't give a rat's ass whether you like it. Does Carolyn know who you are?"

Jason shifted and studied his hands, his thoughts debating on whether he should have a lawyer present. "No, she doesn't know who I am," Jason said after a full minute of silence. "And I'd prefer to keep it that way."

"Why's that?"

"Because if she knew who I was, she might not want me in the same office."

"Why?"

Jason raised his gaze. "You already know why, so stop playing games with me."

Steve sat up and laughed. "You think I'm playing games?"

"I think you're trying to pin something on me when you should be out looking for the real culprit."

"What exactly am I trying to pin on you, Jason?" He cocked his head to the side and waited for the inevitable answer.

"You think I'm responsible..."

"For?" Steve asked.

Jason's mind went blank again, his features hardening and his arms crossing in defiance. "I think I'd like a lawyer present before we continue this line of questioning."

Steve stared him down and gave a nod. If he was in Jason's shoes, he'd lawyer up too, especially with the damning motive he had in his pocket. "Go ahead."

"Right now?" Jason's eyes widened.

"Yes. Call your lawyer and have him meet us at the Federal Building. I think it's time we have a long chat." Steve stood and took Jason by the arm, helping him to his feet.

"Are you arresting me?"

"No."

"What if I refuse?"

Steve leveled a serious gaze in his direction. "Then we'll have a real problem."

Jason yanked his arm from Steve's grasp and took a step back. "I don't need you carting me out of here like a common criminal."

"Are you refusing to come with me?"

"No, I just don't want to make a scene. You yanking me out of here by the arm will create a swirl and I'd rather keep under the radar, if you don't mind."

"I'm not sure that's possible anymore," Steve said. "But I'll let you walk with me if you promise to behave."

"I'm not a fucking child, so stop treating me like one," Jason muttered.

"Do I have to slap on a pair of cuffs?"

Jason's head snapped in his direction, and his eyes widened in a silent plea. "No, I'll come with you."

"That a boy." Steve opened the door, preparing himself for Jason to flee once they hit the streets.

Crystal Illusions
Chapter 40

CAROLYN LOOKED AT THE unfamiliar number, and her brow creased. "Hello?"

"Um, Carolyn?" Jason's worried voice crossed the line.

"Jason?"

"Yeah, I kind of think I need a lawyer."

Shock skittered over her skin and she closed her eyes. "Where are you?"

"At the Federal Building in a holding room."

Her eyes snapped open, and she stood from the couch. "You're in FBI custody?"

"Yeah."

A million different thoughts fluttered through her head, all landing on one reaction, and she sighed. "I'm on my way." She hung up and slipped on shoes, grabbing her coat before heading out the door.

Twenty minutes later, she stepped out of the elevator on the twenty-third floor of the Federal building and crossed to the front desk.

"May I help you?" the perky receptionist asked.

"Yes, I represent Jason Anderson." She waited while the receptionist picked up the phone.

"Mr. Anderson's attorney is here. Okay, I'll tell her." She hung up and smiled at Carolyn. "The special agent in charge of Mr. Anderson's case will be out in a few minutes. Please take a seat." She waved toward the waiting area.

Carolyn crossed to the waiting area and was just about to sit when the door opened, and Steve strolled out. When his gaze landed on her, his mouth popped open and his eyebrows shot up, the surprise embedded in his expression enough to make her chuckle.

"Jason called you?"

"Yes, he did and I'm telling you, you're barking up the wrong tree."

Steve pressed his lips together and nodded toward the hallway. "There are a few things you need to know before you come to that conclusion."

She followed him to the observation room where she could clearly see Jason sitting at the table, fidgeting, and she turned toward Steve. "I already know about Jason's past. I'm not an idiot and neither is Jim. Jason shows a tremendous amount of promise, and we didn't want to hold his father's sins against him when he applied for the internship."

"I think he had ulterior motives."

"Stop right there," Carolyn said, raising her hand. "He isn't the killer."

"He fits the profile, Carolyn."

"Your profile is wrong. I know he came to the district attorney's office based on what happened, but you are not in possession of all the facts of the state's case against his father, and I'm going to leave it at that until I've talked with my client." She turned and entered the holding room without further comment.

Jason stood, meeting her gaze before he looked down at the table, shifting his weight from one foot to the other.

"Sit down, Jason," Carolyn said, and he obliged, avoiding eye contact.

"Did they tell you why I'm here?"

"Yes. Did you hurt those women?" She had to ask, had to see his reaction.

Jason flinched and sat back in his seat. "No! God, no." His eyes pleaded with her not to believe the accusation.

She could feel the truth of his statement as clearly as she could see the dread in his heart with the next bit of truth he had to share with her. "I believe you and I know why they think you'd want to target me, or women who look like me." She paused, waiting for the information to sink in. When he blinked and cocked his head, she continued, "I've always known who you were. Jim and I had a long conversation when your background check came in and we both agreed that you deserved a future."

"You knew?"

"The day you came in for the interview, I knew. I remembered you, Justin. How could I forget what your father did to both you and your mother? It had been almost ten years, but, as you'll find out soon, you never forget a child's face. Ever."

He studied his hands and then looked up, tears tracking wet rivets down his cheeks. "I haven't been called Justin since then."

"I know." Carolyn reached across the table and took his hand.

"You know he's dead, right?"

She nodded.

STEVE LISTENED TO THE conversation, more aggravated than he had been at City Hall. He had Sarah pull strings to get a warrant to search Jason's apartment with the local forensics team and, all the while, Carolyn knew about this kid's past and didn't feel the need to enlighten him. That pissed him off, and he stepped into the room, his gaze bouncing between the two of them. "You knew about his history, and you didn't think it was pertinent to this case?"

Carolyn pulled her hand away and leaned back in the seat. "It has nothing to do with this case. Jason isn't the Scarlet Psychopath."

"Well, I haven't made that determination. Right now, we've got a forensics team searching his place for evidence."

"You have a warrant?" Carolyn asked.

"Ayup," Steve answered, *thanks to Sarah*, he thought and received a sideways glance from Carolyn. "My partner used to be a cop here, and she's still got some close ties high in the judicial system."

"You're wasting your time," Jason said, oblivious to the silent communications occurring around him.

"You have collector's axes for your karate tournaments, correct?"

"Yes, I do, but you won't find anything on them except traces of fabric from my tournaments."

"Now that you have a lawyer in attendance, let's get down to business. Can you tell me where you were during each of the murders?" He slid the list across the table to Jason and he picked it up, scanning the dates.

"I was with my new girlfriend the first weekend and I dropped her off back at school on Monday." He glanced at Carolyn. "That's why I was so late to the office."

"I figured it was something like that," Carolyn said.

"Would she be willing to testify under oath?" Steve asked, still not completely discounting this kid from the list, but the more the conversation continued, the more his mind opened up.

Jason put the paper down and stared at Steve. "She'll confirm I was with her the last two weekends," Jason said.

"But?"

"But I'm willing to bet after you question her, she won't be my girlfriend anymore."

"Well, if you really have nothing to hide, then she shouldn't hold it against you, but if you are responsible, then I hope she runs away from you as fast as she possibly can."

"You're really a prick, you know that?"

Steve raised an eyebrow. "What I am isn't up for discussion. I'm more interested in what you are. Now, what about the other dates and times?" Steve tapped the paper.

Jason turned red.

"Was that really necessary?" Carolyn asked, interrupting the flow.

"Yes, now if *your client* would answer the question…"

"I was at my apartment," Jason said, heading off a building argument.

"Can anyone vouch for that?"

"I was alone," Jason said under his breath.

"So, you don't have an alibi for most of the dates on the list."

"No."

"What about cameras in the apartment building?" Carolyn asked, and Jason rolled his eyes at her.

"In Brooklyn? Are you serious?"

Steve glanced at the address and nodded. He knew the place. It was right around the corner from where he and Jennifer had a flat a few years back when he was still undercover, and they didn't have cameras in that neighborhood.

His phone buzzed, and he excused himself, stepping into the observation room and taking the call. "Hi, Sarah, please tell me you have something."

"Nope, not a trace of blood on any of the weapons. Besides, none of them match the forensic reports, anyway. The kid's apartment is clean."

"Shit," he said.

"You getting anywhere with the questions?"

"No, I'm thinking this was a mistake and it could cost us."

"You make a mistake?"

"It happens," he said, opting to admit to it rather than argue with her over the timing of her sarcasm.

Silence met his response. "Wow, you must be a bit rattled. Normally, you would have jumped down my throat for a comment like that."

"Yeah, well, the remaining suspects on the list are going to be tricky to get answers from. I was kind of hoping for a slam dunk this time around."

Sarah laughed. "It doesn't always work out that way. So, who's next on your list?"

"You will not like it," he said.

"Spill."

"I have nothing on this one, but Beverly Sinclair rubbed me wrong on so many levels that I'd like to check into where she came from and if there is anything in her past that would show this kind of violence."

"I'll check her out, but a hunch isn't going to get us a warrant."

"I'm aware of that."

"You have anyone else?"

"Yes. I have an itch regarding the district attorney and his wife."

"With what probable cause?"

"In some respect, they both blame Carolyn for screwing up their marriage."

"That's not enough of a compelling argument to get a search warrant. What else have you got?"

"Jim Britt only has an alibi for one of the murders and I still have to validate it, the rest are his word and that of his wife—but they don't sleep together anymore, so that's a hole and he admitted as much."

"That's a little more compelling, but we have to have some serious shit on the man in order for a judge to issue a search warrant."

"Jim Britt collects fantasy and gaming weapons along with antique swords. Plus, he seems to have a small S&M fetish."

"Jesus, this just gets better and better."

Steve chuckled at her reaction. "While he's got some issues that I'm sure he doesn't want the public to know, I don't think it's him. However, I'm a little more concerned about his wife. Her emotions swung the pendulum when I was there, and I understand she's been in and out of rehab for drinking and prescription drug issues. I think the separation is impacting her stability and the rest of the stuff just lines up right."

"I think I can go to a judge with this information. If he won't issue a warrant, we can pay them a visit tomorrow and see if we can talk them into cooperating with us."

"He didn't seem all that cooperative when I talked to him earlier."

"Well, Jim and I have a bit of history. I think I can influence his decision."

"What kind of history?"

She laughed. "Not what you're thinking. I'll catch you later."

Steve pocketed his phone, turning his attention back to his current charge. With a sigh, he entered the room and took a seat at the head of the table, folding his hands on the smooth wood.

"Well?" Carolyn asked.

"Well, that was my partner." He glanced at Jason. "Your apartment is clean. You're free to go."

Jason's eyebrows arched. "That's it?"

"Yes, that's it. With the new information that Ms. Hastings provided and the lack of any sign of evidence saying otherwise, it doesn't make sense to keep you under observation."

They both stood.

"Ms. Hastings, I'd like you to stay for a few minutes."

"Oh, okay." She sat and gave Jason a reassuring smile.

"I'll see you at the art show tomorrow." Jason stepped out the side door that Steve pointed to.

Steve waited a minute before turning his heated gaze in her direction. "You should have told me about this." He waved at the table and leaned back in the chair. "I just wasted the remaining daylight hunting down a judge, getting a warrant and sending a team of specialists to his place, all because I didn't have all the information. Is there anything else you've conveniently left out?"

Carolyn bit her lip and shifted in the chair. "I know why Cameron Unger was at City Hall yesterday with my old roommate."

Steve leaned forward, aggravation leaving him itching to let a dose of his dark side loose. "I already know why he was there. Tell me something I don't know, like why Beverly Sinclair dislikes you so much."

"I have no idea. I've only seen her a few times."

Steve had enough, and he took a deep breath, closing his eyes and forcing his way into her mind. He ignored the gasp along with the whimper that followed. He shuffled through memories, thoughts, and facts, pulling what he needed within the passage of a couple of minutes. The release was more abrupt than he expected, and with it came a dizzy spell that made him grasp the edges of the table.

When his vision cleared, her pale, wide-eyed stare met his.

CAROLYN WATCHED AS THE swirl in his eyes settled, stunned at the mental invasion. "What the hell did you just do?" *And more importantly, what the hell did I just see?*

Steve flashed an uneasy smile. "I guess the geek term for it would be something akin to a Vulcan mind meld."

"What?"

"I siphoned through your memories."

The mere thought caused a chill to run through her, leaving her body cold to the core. Her gaze dropped to his unscarred wrists, but the image imprinted in her mind was Steve nailed to a cross. "And you left some in the process."

"Unfortunately, that *is* a byproduct of..." He trailed off.

"A byproduct of what?"

"I have no idea what to call it," Steve said. "I'm sorry, but I had to be sure. I thought you might be hiding something more, but there's nothing else there that I don't already know."

"So, what exactly is the disturbing image you left me with?"

"Which disturbing image from my past are you referring to?"

She could tell by the set of his jaw and the cock of his head, he was playing dumb, but for the life of her, she didn't know why. "I only got one impression and it sure as hell couldn't be real."

"Having nails hammered through your wrists is excruciating, but having a half inch spike pounded through both feet is infinitely worse. They say crucifixion is an extremely painful way to die, and they weren't kidding." He leaned back, crossing his arms.

"You're joking."

"Afraid not, but this isn't the time or place to discuss my unfortunate past. I suggest you go home while I concentrate on the here and now and catch this bastard before he kills again."

Crystal Illusions
Chapter 41

CAROLYN LAY IN BED with Randy snoring on the pillow beside her. Every time she closed her eyes, that morbid vision of Steve hanging from the cross haunted her and she cursed under her breath. She needed sleep, but it eluded her like a child playing hide and seek in a mansion.

Another hour passed, and Carolyn tossed the covers back, retreating to the living room and grabbing the remote. She surfed the late-night shows, found nothing of interest and turned the television off in disgust. Wide-awake, she wandered into the office and flipped on the computer, deciding to do a little research of her own on Special Agent Williams.

The news articles surrounding Steve gave her both chills and a calm sense of reassurance. While horrifying circumstances and violent death outlined his caseload, his ability to ferret out the killer was renowned, and in every case, he displayed the valor and honor of a true hero.

"A real live Superman," she whispered at the screen.

"What are you doing?"

She spun toward the voice and saw Randy standing in the entry rubbing his eye. His sleepy, questioning gaze made her smile. "I couldn't sleep."

"And you're surfing the net?"

"There was nothing on television, so I figured I'd see what I could find on Special Agent Williams."

His eyebrows arched, and he stepped into the room, taking a closer look at the computer screen. "What'd you find?"

"More than I wanted to." She stood, offering him the chair and the news links, outlining the cases that garnished public attention.

He scanned the article in front of him and sighed, looking up at Carolyn. "If someone hurt you the way this psycho hurt his wife, I'd kill them." He waved at the news copy outlining The Slasher case.

"It's a good thing you're not a cop," she said, reaching over him and turning off the monitor. "Now I really need to get some sleep." She yawned and stretched her back before leading him to the bedroom. This time when he pulled her into the spooning position, she snuggled, and sleep settled over her and held tight.

STEVE THREW THE FILE on the table and leaned back in the seat, rubbing his face and stifling a yawn. "There's nothing in these files that leads us to the kid."

"I thought you had already ruled him out?" Sarah said from the couch.

"Yeah, well, I had, but since you couldn't deliver on the search warrants, I thought I'd take another look at the data."

"Oh, that's good. Blame your lack of progress on me."

He picked up the last three files. "The answer's got to be in here."

"Look, you haven't slept more than a handful of hours in the last few days. Why don't you catch some sleep and I'll look at what you've got." She stood and stretched, arching her back and sweeping her blonde locks into a makeshift bun, making her way to the desk.

"I don't have time to sleep..."

She raised her hand, stopping his protest. "Fresh eyes..."

"Yeah, yeah," he muttered. Fatigue pounded at his muscles, leaving him little more than an aching pile of bones. He could use a couple of solid hours of sleep, so he gave her a nod, relinquishing the seat. He headed toward the bedroom. "Wake me if something happens."

"I will."

Hitting the pillow didn't even register, but his dreams were filled with Carolyn Hastings's nightmares.

Crystal Illusions
Chapter 42

EIGHT O'CLOCK ROLLED AROUND much faster than Carolyn expected, and the shrill ring of the alarm cut through her stupor like a shark fin through the water, setting her heart into overdrive. "Shit!" The numbers on her clock mocked her, and she ignored the buzzing, leaving it to Randy as she bolted into the bathroom and hopped into a lukewarm shower.

Randy followed her into the bathroom, and they traded spots in the shower. "Don't worry, we'll get there in time," he said when she stepped out of the shower.

"We?"

"Yes, I'm making sure you get there, okay?" He sent a smile in her direction and instead of arguing with him, she nodded and dried off.

JUST SHY OF NINE, Carolyn and Randy walked up to Damon's door. Carolyn hesitated with her hand poised to knock.

"What's wrong?"

"I'm nervous." She dropped her hand, turning to Randy. "What if I screw this up?"

He smiled down at her. "Listen, you'll do just fine. I'll be there, and Olivia will be there, too." He kissed her cheek. Randy had all the confidence in the world in her; besides, having her detained in the art world for the next fifteen hours eased his mind. At least he knew she was safe, that she would not be prematurely yanked out of his life by a madman today.

Carolyn took a deep breath and knocked.

When Damon answered the door, he sent a quizzical look in Randy's direction.

"Don't worry, I'm just making sure she arrived safely." Randy watched as Carolyn was swallowed by the swirl inside.

Damon nodded. "She's in good hands. We will see you at the studio this evening." He closed the door.

Randy sighed and headed toward the subway, oblivious of the shadow tailing him.

"ARE YOU SURE YOU want me following this guy?" Sarah whispered into the phone.

"Yes," Steve said, scanning the paper in his hand.

"Why am I tailing her boyfriend?"

"Because he's on my list and I've got tails on everyone today."

"Well, at least mine is easy on the eyes."

He chuckled. "I'm glad you're happy with the assignment."

"I never said I was happy—just that the view is pretty fine. All things considered, I'd rather be on the hunt with you."

"I don't need an ex-cop with a chip on her shoulder with me while I'm talking to the next two suspects. As it is, I'm going to alienate them enough."

"You mean you're still not putting those public relations classes to use?"

Steve stopped in his tracks, scanning the crowd in front of him before he responded. "I see you and Jennifer have been talking about me." Her laugh confirmed it. "That's just great."

"What can I say? She finally warmed up to me."

Regret scratched at his skin. Maybe he shouldn't have asked Sarah to stay with Jennifer while she testified. Having both of them on the same team was going to be like dealing with a hungry lion in the middle of a wildfire. Then again, perhaps it would calm Jennifer's insecurities.

"Steve?"

"Hmmm?" he said into the receiver.

"You weren't listening, were you?"

"Sorry, what did you ask?"

"What's the plan for later, after you talk to the two co-workers?"

"If nothing comes of either conversation, we can meet up and head over to Jim Britt's home."

"Steve, I know Jim. There's no way he's doing this."

"He's the only one who has an extensive collection of swords and axes, and according to the sales records, a few of them match the specs of the murder weapon."

"Someone could be setting him up."

"Possibly, but I don't think so, at least not on a conscious level. The cases where Carolyn switched into the killer's head, I didn't get any clarity outside of an irrational hostility bleeding through and there are only two people I've encountered with that level of animosity toward Carolyn. Anyway, I'm at Trent Kaplan's place. I'll catch you later." He folded the phone and glanced at the townhouse. Queens was farther than most of the staff and based on the location, he doubted Trent was his man, but he had to check it out.

Trent opened the door in a ratty robe and a coffee in his hand. In an instant, any hint of sleepiness disappeared from his gaze. "Special Agent Williams, what, ah, what are you doing here?"

Steve noted the confusion in Trent's mind and then the snap of a thought rang clear. "I've got some questions for you relating to Carolyn Hastings."

"Is she okay?"

Raw concern laced his tone, and Steve nodded. "Yes, she's fine, but we're following up on all the folks that were at City Hall Thursday morning and, according to the records, you arrived a little before seven."

Trent waved Steve into his home and pointed him toward the living room. "Can I get you a coffee?"

Steve did a quick scan of his mind, looking for any hint of malice. He'd been burned in the past by accepting drinks from killers, and he wasn't in the mood to fall prey to it again. When he found out Trent was just offering him coffee, he nodded. Instead of waiting for it to be delivered, he followed Trent into the kitchen and watched him pour fresh coffee from the pot.

"I can go from here if you point me to the sugar and creamer," Steve said, reaching for the cup.

"Sugar's on the table. I've only got vanilla flavored creamer. Is that okay, or would you prefer milk?"

"That's fine." Steve took a seat at the table.

Trent brought both the creamer and the pot over to the table, topping off his cup and setting it aside. "What can I do for you today?"

Steve took a sip of coffee and then settled back in the chair. "Are you usually at the office that early?"

"No, usually I come in around eight, but one of my cases was the first on the morning docket and I wanted to go over my strategy with Beverly and Jason and get their feedback on the way I wanted to take the case."

"Is that normal?"

Trent sighed. "I used to talk with Carolyn when I was nervous about a case. She had a way of..." he trailed off and stared into his coffee.

"A way of what?"

Trent's face reddened. "A way of distracting me from my nerves."

"Really?" Steve leaned forward, setting the cup on the table and resting on his forearms, pulling the arsenal of Carolyn's memories. This man made her uncomfortable and, until recently, she avoided him at all costs.

Trent raised his gaze. "Yeah."

"So, you what? Went into her office to mentally undress her in order to calm your nerves?"

He nearly dropped his coffee. "Did Carolyn say something?"

Steve laughed. "She didn't need to. I'm a pretty observant guy. Did the fact she didn't reciprocate make you angry?"

"No."

"Come on. It must have irked you at some level?"

"Well, maybe a little, but she has a boyfriend."

"Were you angry enough to want to hurt her?"

Trent blinked and sat back in the chair. "Are you cross-examining me?"

"Just answer the question."

"I'd never hurt Carolyn."

"What about someone that looks like her?"

"I'd never hurt anyone," Trent said. "And I understand why you have to question me, but I really don't like your tone, especially since I willingly let you into my home." He picked up his coffee, sulking as he sipped.

His pouty response took Steve by surprise, and he fully understood Carolyn's aversion to this man. "So why the leering?"

Trent looked up. "You've seen Carolyn. She's stunning and I can't help it," he said. "She even called me out on it, too."

"How'd that make you feel?"

"Damned uncomfortable. I didn't realize it was so... noticeable."

Steve pulled the list of dates out of his pocket and slid it across the table. "Can you tell me where you were for each of those days and times?"

"I was asleep for most of these, but I've had some really long hours at the office the last couple of weeks. I've been in by seven and haven't left until after nine at night. I use the subway entrance, so my access card would show the times I entered the building and my Metrocard account should have all the times I've left."

"That accounts for a couple of the times, but what about the others? Can anyone vouch for you?"

Trent shook his head. "As you can see, I live alone."

"Do you have a computer so we can look up your Metrocard activity?"

"Sure." Trent stood. "Let me get my laptop for you."

After Trent left the room, Steve took a couple of sips of coffee. He folded the list and tucked it back in his pocket. He didn't believe Trent was the killer. The man was just too transparent. Even his thoughts were easily read, like they were tattooed on his forehead. But after the last case, Steve didn't trust the transparency. He wanted definitive proof before he crossed the name off the list. So, he waited for the laptop and the confirmation of Metrocard usage times.

"SIT STILL, BELLA," DAMON cooed, and Carolyn wanted to scream. The paste they slathered on her to prevent chafing and irritation had long since hardened, creating a buffer between the heavy, wet, painted suit and her skin. But it didn't stop the rogue itch here and there and right now, her right shoulder blade burned with a fierce itch.

"Can someone scratch my back?"

Damon raised his gaze, giving her a look reminiscent of her mother's when she was young and asking for something impossible. "Close your eyes for a moment."

Carolyn complied and felt a tap on her back, almost at the point of the itch.

"A little more to the right."

Another tap found the spot.

"Yes, right there."

Pressure replaced the tap, and she alternated tightening her muscle and relaxing it, satisfying the insanity.

"Better?" his voice whispered in her ear, and she shivered at the heat his timber caused.

"Yes." She opened her eyes. Shock filtered through her. Damon still sat in front of her, with her foot in his hand and his thumb pressing a pressure point. He released and smiled up at her, resuming creating his masterpiece.

"Acupressure," he said after a few strokes.

"You're just full of talent, aren't you?"

His eyebrows arched, and he chuckled, meeting her gaze. "Well, when you indulge in live art, you have to know how to satisfy your model's itch." He winked and continued painting.

Carolyn glanced to her right, and Olivia sent a strained smile in her direction. Damon had finished the major details in her outfit before he had Carolyn dress, and now Olivia was surrounded by a bunch of student artists, putting the minor finishing touches on her.

Her stomach growled in protest, and her gaze bounced to Damon. He raised a hand and signaled one of the interns, and she came running over like a happy little puppy.

"Yes, sir?"

"Mix up another batch of the protein shakes. Please, we don't want these models to faint from lack of food now that presentation time is nearing."

"Yes, sir!" she said, running off to do his bidding.

"Thank you."

He glanced up at her. "It will help steady you for the show." He stood, stepping back from the display case where she sat on the swing, one wrist secured to the chain with a clear plastic strip and her legs now crossed at the ankles and secured together to keep the pose in place.

He gave a nod, dropped the paintbrushes on the mobile palate and clapped his hands, gaining the attention of everyone in the room. "It's time."

The reaction was nothing short of chaos and Carolyn watched as the team brought out a dozen black cloths, enough to cover each of the displays. Just before they draped one over her case, the little puppy girl was back with a straw bearing glass that she held to Carolyn's lips. The thick chocolate liquid quenched the rumble in her stomach and left her with a pleasant chocolate aftertaste. After a pat of a napkin on her lips, the curtain fell over the opening and the case jostled, rolling toward the distinct sound of metal doors retracting.

A hot flash gripped Carolyn, and she tried to cry out, but no sound came from her mouth, just a tight wheeze. When the case stopped moving and another door closed, the small space filled with paint fumes, creating a buzzing in her ears.

"Carolyn?"

"Livi?"

"Yes."

"Where are we?" Carolyn asked, and even in her ears, her voice carried the pitch of panic.

"Relax, we're in the moving van. It's not that long of a ride."

"I've got to admit, I'm a little freaked out at the moment."

"This is the toughest part, so hang in there," Olivia said.

"Thanks." Carolyn concentrated on her breathing, relaxing the tension in her neck. She knew this would not be easy, much like a summation in front of a skeptical jury, but being basically tied to a swing in the dark wasn't making it any easier. "Are you always tied to the set?"

"Yes, especially for the transport. It's safer this way."

Carolyn laughed. "Safer, like in seatbelt safe?"

Olivia's laugh joined in. "Well, no, I guess not. More like safer in the 'I've fallen and can't get up' kind of safe."

The truck stopped and started several times before the distinct beep of reverse gear filled the cabin. Soon after the engine cut; the rattle of the doors resonated along with voices. The pressure on Carolyn's chest eased along with the tightness in her shoulders, and by the time they rolled her into the gallery, she was relaxed.

"She goes here." Damon's voice reached through the fabric and her case moved. "She is my centerpiece. The others should be set up in a half moon around her."

When her case stopped, Damon lifted the corner of the tarp and sent a smile her way. "The gallery opens in less than a half hour and I'll be introducing the live pieces at eight. Is there anything you need in the meantime?"

"What time is it now?"

"A little after six-thirty."

"I think I'm good." Carolyn prayed she'd be able to stay still for the next few hours.

He winked at her. "You only have two and a half hours before I let you out of the set. If you need anything, call out and my assistant will get it for you."

"Thank you."

The curtain dropped. "Anna." He clapped his hands.

"Yes, sir?"

Carolyn recognized the puppy-dog voice and smirked in the dark.

"Stay here. It's your job to make sure my girls are happy until showtime."

"Yes, sir," the chipper voice answered, and the sound of Damon's footsteps echoed, followed by a slamming door.

Crystal Illusions
Chapter 43

"DAMN IT. I GOT nothing," Steve said into his phone and headed toward the subway. "Anything on your end?"

"Nothing here. Her boyfriend is just hanging out at a bar down the street from an art gallery that has a show tonight. He's checked in at the door twice already."

"Makes sense. Yesterday, when I was grilling him, Jason said he'd see Carolyn at an art show."

"Where to now?"

"Over to Greenwich Village. I need to have a chat with the Britts."

"Can we grab something to eat before we intrude upon the DA?"

"Just grab something on your way. I'm all set."

"Fine, I'll be there in a few."

RANDY PEELED ENOUGH BILS off to cover his tab along with a decent tip and headed back to the gallery. This time when he flashed his pass, they opened the door and let him inside. Damon crossed the nearly empty hall and stuck his hand out, shaking Randy's.

"Carolyn has done well today."

"Can I see her?"

"Not yet, not until the big reveal. In the meantime, look around."

Randy scanned the people rushing around and then strolled through the gallery, studying each exquisite piece until he stood at the center, in front of the portrait of Carolyn.

His painting.

His girl.

His future.

"You like this one?"

Randy turned to the feminine voice and smiled. "Damon did a great job capturing her here, but wait until you see her as original sin in the live show."

The blonde next to him raised her eyebrows and scanned the clipboard in her hands. "That model is here?"

"I haven't had a chance to see her yet. Damon's keeping the live art room closed until he's ready for the unveiling." He rolled his eyes.

She pulled the pencil out of her hair and marked the clipboard, flashed a smile, and wandered off.

Randy glanced at the painting and sighed before heading back to the entry and the gathering crowd. He scanned the people outside the door and his gaze fell on a few familiar faces. Jason stood outside with a petite red head and next to him stood a tall woman he had seen in the halls at Carolyn's office. He couldn't remember her name, but the face was familiar.

In line, a couple of folks back from Jason, stood Cameron. He sent a nod in Randy's direction when their eyes met, and Randy returned the silent salutation.

JIM BRITT OPENED THE door and stared at Steve before his attention turned to Sarah. "Officer Connelly?"

"It's actually Special Agent Connelly, now." Sarah flipped open her badge. "S.A. Williams here is my partner." She nodded her head toward Steve. "Can we come in?"

Jim's gaze flicked to Steve and his jaw tightened a moment before he nodded and swung the door open.

"Is your wife home?" Steve asked, scanning the entry with both his eyes and his mind.

"No, she's helping with the coordination of an art exhibit tonight down in Chelsea."

His gaze snapped to the district attorney while a gnawing started in the pit of his stomach. He went to speak, and Sarah touched his arm, silencing him with her thoughts.

Let me handle this.

"Jim, I've been looking at the weapons profile for the murders along with purchase records of all the people on the list Steve gave me, and it seems you've had a few sales over the years that would fall into that profile. Is there any way we could see your collection so I can definitively rule you out as a suspect?" Sarah asked, and Steve did a double take at the saccharin tone and the sweet smile that accompanied it.

This wasn't the abrasive partner he was used to. This was much more like the subdued

632

woman he almost had an affair with long before The Slasher got hold of her. Charm oozed from her and, despite their history, a heated flash flickered in a region much lower than his stomach. *Did she just bat her eyes?*

Jim Britt reacted much in the same way Steve did, blushing at the subtle flirt. He glanced at the elegant stairwell and sighed before bringing his gaze back to her. Hunger blazed in his eyes, and he licked his lips before putting on a smile. "You always were direct and to the point."

Sarah smiled and blushed, sweeping one foot on the floor in an 'aw shucks' move that almost made Steve laugh. She was playing the district attorney, and he was falling right into her trap, making him wonder exactly what kind of history they had together.

"Well, I know you couldn't possibly be the killer, but I have to prove it to my partner here." She hooked her thumb toward Steve and cocked her head, flashing a winning smile. "So, what do you say?"

Jim nodded and led them up the stairway to his office. When they stepped inside, Steve couldn't help but whistle. His vast collection had axes, swords, lances, and daggers that dated back to the Middle Ages. It was enough to leave most medieval fanatics drooling and his gaze landed on the centerpiece over the desk. A more modern, short-handled, double-edged axe was mounted on a wooden plaque. The signature of the weapon matched the drawing their specialists had sent over, and he glanced at Sarah.

She was also staring at the focal point in the room and pulled a spray can of BlueStar out of her purse. "Do you mind?" She asked Jim.

He nodded, and Steve tapped into his thoughts. Jim Britt received the authentic Serenity Long-Bearded Axe right after the series Firefly went off the air. When this piece went up for auction, it was an easy purchase for Jim and fueled his interest in sci-fi, fantasy, and gaming.

Sarah pulled the chair next to the wall and climbed up. She sent a smile over her shoulder and then sprayed the blade. Silence settled over the room as dark streaked patterns appeared on the metal and the handle.

Shock filtered through Steve, and he felt the same slam through the district attorney. Jim stumbled backwards and sat hard on the couch. His gaze locked on the blood splatter pattern on his prized weapon. Questions filled his head, every one of them falling on his wife, and the lack of answers he got from her earlier as to where she had been the last few weeks or where the pair of soaking work boots, he found in the basement came from.

"There are boots in the basement?" Steve blurted.

Jim's gaze peeled away from the axe to Steve, and he nodded.

"Sarah, go spray those boots."

Sarah hopped off the chair and left the room. She came back a few minutes later with a pair of boots spattered with dark marks where she sprayed them. She dropped them on the table, her gaze now hard and unyielding, more like the partner Steve was used to. "These things stink, and they were covered in blood at one time. You want to start talking?"

"Those are Linda's." He glanced up at the wall. "Jesus, it can't be her." His voice lacked the conviction of the words and he put his head in his hands.

Steve crouched down in front of him. "When exactly did you tell her you were in love with Carolyn?"

"I don't see why the timing of that makes any difference. She had moved into the guest quarters at least a month before she pushed the point."

"When was that?" Sarah asked.

He looked up at her and said, "Two weeks ago."

Steve stood. "That must have been the trigger."

"She's at an art show tonight?" Sarah asked.

Jim nodded.

"Steve, Carolyn's *in* an art show tonight."

Both Jim and Steve's gaze snapped in Sarah's direction and then they scanned the walls. "Is anything missing?" she asked, waving at the wall of weapons.

Jim stood and scanned the walls. "No, but..."

"But what?"

"But she owns a handgun and carries it with her when she goes out."

Steve and Sarah exchanged a glance before gazing at the axe. Steve moved first. "Get a forensics team in here now." He started for the door.

Jim shot to his feet. "I'm going with you."

Steve paused. "I'm not sure that's such a good idea. If your wife has a gun and the propensity to use it, she might turn on you, too."

"She hasn't turned on me yet," he argued.

"Look, you aren't out of the woods, either..."

"I know my rights and yet I am allowing you to bring a team into my home without a warrant."

"Jim," Sarah started.

"No. If my wife is the one, then she is seriously disturbed, and you'll need someone who can talk her off a ledge."

"And you're the right person to do that?"

He shrugged and looked at the axe on the wall. "If she isn't the one, then we're being framed, and she's in as much danger as Carolyn is."

Crystal Illusions
Chapter 44

CAROLYN DOZED AND EACH time her chin dropped to her chest. She jerked awake. Light music piped into the room, making the dark a little less intimidating. "Um, hello?" she called, and the shuffle of feet approached.

When the curtain pulled back, the chipper little intern smiled at her. "What can I get you?"

"Can I have an energy drink or coffee or something that will keep me awake?"

"Sure, I'll be right back."

The curtain fell again, obstructing her view. When the door opened, the sounds of the crowd filtered in, creating a small jolt of adrenaline that woke her up. The door closed on the din and silence settled under the soft crooning of Josh Groban. Carolyn sighed and shifted her weight. Her muscles protested, sending a cramp through her back. A few deep, soothing breaths eased the pain.

A moment later, the door opened and closed, and shoes clicked across the floor. The curtain moved and a little canister with a plastic straw appeared in the sliver of light. "You're one lucky lady; this is the last energy drink available." Anna smiled in the dark room, her chipper whisper making Carolyn more relaxed, and she wrapped her lips around the straw and sucked the sweet berry syrup into her mouth.

"Thank you," she said after she drained the container. "How much longer?"

"We're almost ready. I'd say another fifteen minutes."

The coverlet dropped.

"Does anyone else need anything?"

A chorus of "no" echoed in the room.

"Okay. It's almost show time, so I'm going to leave you lovely ladies here while I go help Damon get ready." Anna's shoes clicked away, and Carolyn heard the plink of the container hitting the bottom of a metal garbage can and she sighed, letting both the adrenaline and the contents of the energy drink erase the fatigue from both her mind and body.

RANDY SAW THE INTERN slip out of the live art room and headed in that direction. With a quick look over his shoulder, he slipped into the room unnoticed. He needed to see her, to make sure she was there.

His eyes took a moment to adjust to the dim lighting, and he scanned the covered cases, focusing on the one in the center. His footfalls echoed no matter how softly he tread, and when he pulled the edge of the tarp away, she squinted and then broke out in a smile.

"Hi, babe," he whispered.

"What are you doing in here?" she asked, but he could tell by the sparkle in her eyes that she was glad to see him.

"I'm just..." The click of a door interrupted him, and he turned. "I better get out of here before I get caught by the little Nazi intern."

Carolyn chuckled. "I understand Anna can be fierce."

"Yeah—she was pretty much like a bulldog guarding a bone."

"Go, before we both get in trouble."

He dropped the curtain and headed toward the entry, navigating through the seating area as quietly as he could. Movement caught the corner of his eye, and he turned in time to see a small two by four coming in his direction. Randy had no time to react before the board hit him. The last thing that registered before all went black was blonde hair.

STEVE AND SARAH HOPPED out of the cab in front of the gallery and Jim scrambled to catch up. With their badges displayed, they circumvented the doormen and skidded into the main gallery where a waiting crowd blocked the live display room entrance.

"RANDY, ARE YOU OKAY?" Carolyn called out after the clatter settled.

The curtain peeled back, and the world tilted.

Carolyn stared at her startled face, painted in scarlet like the rest of her form, and she knew the killer was here, now, and there was nothing she could do. Fear as strong as the paint fumes paralyzed her, and she blinked, willing herself back into her own body.

When the world righted, the form in front of her made no sense. This couldn't be the killer. It was a woman. A woman she knew.

"This time you won't escape death."

"What the hell are you doing?"

Linda Britt sprayed Carolyn with a can of turpentine like it was lighter fluid and she was just a wooden set. The moment the liquid hit her, it seemed to trigger the curtains and lights, like this horrific event was a planned part of the show.

Fumes choked her, and Carolyn coughed. Her eyes darted around the room looking for Randy, looking for anyone to help. She struggled to pull her wrist and ankles free from the bindings, but to no avail and panic swallowed her sensibilities.

The door swung open, and people started shuffling in.

Linda glanced over her shoulder and dropped the can, trading it for a book of matches, lighting them with a brass lighter. With a toss of her wrist, the flaming pack touched the turpentine-soaked surface and it ignited.

Fire. With it came sudden overwhelming heat and Carolyn renewed her struggle against the bonds, her lungs opening from the adrenaline rushing through her and a scream peeled out. Her feet were no longer numb. They were burning, and she couldn't get away from the flames. They jumped at her, dancing on the paint covering her, igniting, climbing toward the top of the glass case. Pain gripped her, fueling the power behind her screams. Flames spread over her skin, fast and furious, eating away, scorching, burning, and leaving only a blackened, smoldering path behind.

"Oh my God!" someone in the crowd screamed.

THE SCREAMS PULLED HIM from the darkness and Randy rolled on his side, staring at the flaming set. *Carolyn, Jesus, that's Carolyn!*

He was on his feet, running toward her before the thought finished.

Out of the corner of his eye, he saw the crowd part and Agent Williams barreling into the room, but that didn't stop his course to save Carolyn.

Randy launched through the air, ignoring the searing heat, and he wrapped his arms around her waist, yanking her with him. The glass plate acting as the backdrop shattered before he hit it and he tumbled to the ground with Carolyn's burning body in his arms.

He rolled, trying to douse the flames with his body, the heat and burning paint searing them together. Chaos filled his world. Screams of terror and pain echoed through the amphitheater.

With the flames doused, he lifted his head toward the display case and another shock ripped through him. The case no longer existed, only a shower of dust and a blonde woman with a deranged smile aimed a gun in their direction.

Jim Britt stepped into view, yelling, "Linda, no!"

The woman reacted as if an electric shock hit her, jumping at the sound of his voice and turning the gun in his direction.

A roar filled the room and Jim Britt spun around, falling into the line of people behind him with a red stain spreading over the back of his shirt.

He went down amid screams of terror.

Randy turned his attention to the whimpers under him. "Come on, baby, hang in there," Randy said, holding her smoldering form to him, ignoring the burn on his chest. Her blue eyes held infinite pain, and the shallow draw of her breath crushed him. He had enough experience with industrial accidents to know Carolyn had little hope of survival, but still he clung to the thought of a miracle.

"What are you doing, Bella?" Damon's voice pulled his attention away from Carolyn and he watched the drama unfold.

Linda turned toward Damon, her face scrunched in an angry, petulant expression. "I couldn't let you leave me for that bitch." Linda cocked her head toward Randy and Carolyn.

"Put the gun down," another FBI agent said, her gun trained on Linda.

Linda jerked toward the voice, and another blast echoed from her gun. This time Steve took a step backward, and blood spread from his right shoulder. "Drop it," Steve said, his voice a growl, and the gun tumbled from her hands.

Steve turned his intense gaze toward Randy and stumbled in their direction. In the distance, sirens wailed, and Randy turned back to Carolyn. "Help is on the way. Just hang on."

Steve kneeled down next to them, pulling his attention away from her. The blood spreading on his shirt drew a sharp inhale from Randy, dampening his outlook. If someone like Steve Williams could get hurt, what hope did he have?

"More than you think." Steve leaned forward, pressing his lips to Carolyn's forehead, and little rivers of light danced along her charred skin.

"What did you just do?" Randy asked just before Steve planted a kiss on his forehead. A surge of energy filled him, and every fiber of his being tingled, turning the pain into an excruciating white light.

LIGHT-HEADED, STEVE SAT AND stared at the surrounding chaos. His ears rang, and he gave Sarah a weak smile as she handed Linda Britt over to the New York City police. Everything moved in slow motion, and he was drenched in blood with the charred stench of burned flesh filling his senses. He shook the memory clear just as the paramedics lifted Jim Britt onto a gurney and rushed him out the door. Steve wondered if the man would survive and then the mending pain in his shoulder brought down a curtain of black.

Crystal Illusions
Chapter 45

"I'M FINE." CAROLYN INSISTED, although she did not know how. Her last coherent memory was Randy telling her to hang on, but even that was drowned by the pain that gripped every fiber of her being. She had been roasted alive, and when she came to in the emergency room, she heard the doctors discussing her prognosis.

The initial assessment was third and fourth degree burns covering over eighty percent of her body. They believed the paint acted as an accelerant and needed to remove it to understand the extent of the damage. But when the doctors peeled away a section of the hard-shell surface, they found her epidermal layer intact, albeit pink, like a slight sunburn.

"I've been running this burn unit for close to thirty years and I've never seen anything like this. It's a miracle."

Randy sat in the chair in the corner staring out the window, still playing back the day's events, stunned, bordering on shock, and Carolyn knew the feeling.

"I'd like you to stay overnight for observation," the doctor stressed.

"Dr. Benton," Carolyn started, reading his nametag as she swung her legs over the side of the bed. "I'd like to go home." She met his level gaze. "It's been a hell of a day and I'd like to sleep in my bed."

Dr. Benton flipped the chart closed and gave a curt nod, leaving the room just as Steve and a blonde woman walked in. Her gaze jumped from his face to the red stain on the front shoulder of his shirt. "You got shot?"

He smiled and shrugged. "It just grazed the skin," he said.

"How are you feeling?" the blonde asked.

"Who are you?"

"This is my partner. Special Agent Sarah Connolly, meet Carolyn Hastings and Randy Kinkaid."

They exchanged handshakes, and Randy's confused glance landed on Steve. "You were bleeding a hell of a lot more than just a graze."

Steve turned to him. "Look, I'll explain everything when we get you two back to your apartment. Okay?" He handed both Carolyn and Randy scrubs. "It's all I could find."

Carolyn took the items and disappeared into the bathroom. She stared at her reflection, marveling. It looked like she'd just had too much sun, and the debilitating pain was a distant memory.

The car ride was silent as questions swirled in Carolyn's head. The burns she sustained were catastrophic; by all accounts, she should be dead right now. She sent a questioning glare in Steve's direction.

"I will explain at the apartment," he said again and the static emitting from his mind shut off any further discussion.

The minute the apartment door closed, both Carolyn and Randy turned toward Steve.

"This defies reason," Randy said. "I've seen enough industrial accidents to know Carolyn was a goner, and I wasn't far behind."

"Did you do this?" Carolyn waved a hand down her body like a magician announcing TaDa!

Steve nodded and traded a glance with Sarah.

"He has a very special healing ability," Sarah explained.

"And they don't need to know any more than that," he interceded, cutting off Sarah's impending recount of what he did for her when they were at the mercy of The Slasher.

Carolyn picked up parts of Sarah's thoughts, which included the same vision of Steve nailed to a cross that she had seen after their mind meld. She brought her gaze back to Steve and offered a smile. "Well, thank you."

"Anytime." Steve returned her smile.

"So, what the hell happened?" Randy asked.

"It seems Linda Britt snapped," Sarah said.

"Ya think?"

"Randy, let them finish before you get sarcastic." Carolyn placed her hand on his arm and waved toward the couch. "I think I need to sit down for this."

Randy nodded, stepped into the kitchen and came back with four beers, handing them out. "I think this requires a drink."

"Go on," Carolyn said.

"Jim's marriage was more in the shitter than even he knew. It seems Linda had a brief affair with Damon and after he broke it off, Linda had the conversation with Jim regarding you. Both things in such close succession set her off. Damon's girlfriend was the first victim, and she looked a hell of a lot like you."

"We've got her fingerprints on the weapons and traces of blood, no alibis to speak of and the scene last night just clinches it. The kicker is Linda Britt thinks you're immortal. In her twisted mind, it's been you she's killing over and over. She's now at Bellevue and at this point, they are planning on playing the insanity card."

"How's Jim taking this?"

Steve and Sarah traded glances. "Jim's in the hospital. Unfortunately, the bullet shattered his spinal cord and he'll be in a wheelchair for the rest of his life."

"Jesus." A chill crawled into Carolyn's spine, and she shook her head.

"Hell, it could have been worse...," Sarah paused.

"How?" Both Randy and Carolyn said at the same time.

"She could have killed all of you," Sarah said.

Silence descended on the room.

All four of them reached for the beers and tapped bottlenecks in the center of the table.

"Here's to being alive."

Crystal Illusions
Chapter 46

MY ARRIGNMENT WAS FIRST thing Monday morning, and I sat at the defense table in the nasty orange jump suit with my hands and feet chained together like a common criminal, but I was at peace. I wasn't the only one who saw her burn and there was no way she survived that. I would have been happier seeing her turned to dust, but the charred unconscious form wheeled out of the gallery was enough.

"All rise," the bailiff announced. "The honorable Judge Matthews presiding."

The judge took the bench and opened the folder in front of him just as the courtroom doors swung open. All eyes swung toward the click of high heels singing off the floor.

I turned and nearly fell out of my chair.

I had set her on fire, smelled her flesh burning, heard her screams of pain. Yet, here she stood unscathed, not a goddamn mark on her body except for the healthy pink hue of her skin and the shorter crop of her hair.

She had the nerve to smile at me as she took a seat.

I lunged for her, but the chains stopped my progress and the bitch's smile never faltered.

My deranged screams echoed off the courtroom walls as they dragged me away.

The End

Continue The Steve Williams Series on the next page with SAVING FACE.

Saving Face
Chapter 1

THE TREES SWAYED IN the breeze. Dry leaves rustled, and the stars disappeared behind a bank of clouds, drawing out the already dark shadows. Shadows he hid within, watching, waiting, frozen in place by his obsession, his bloodlust.

Testing the air with a sniff, he tried detecting a trace of her perfume but came away with only the distinct scent of fall. Crisp. Clean. Carnal.

His edgy hands begged for action, and he clenched them, dropping his arms to his sides. Tilting his head, he caught a rhythmic pulse, like that of his heart, but accented with crunching leaves. She was coming. His hand shot to the worn handle of his hunting knife.

Patience.

His fingers stroked the soft wood like a lover, and he stared at the jogger-beaten path. The bounce of her headlamp filtered through the thick brush. He blew a slow stream of air through his lips, calming his pounding heart.

Patience, he told himself again. He didn't want to give her enough time to react, to bolt in the opposite direction. Instead, he counted her steps, watching as the light approached, bouncing with each of her long-legged strides.

It wasn't her lithe frame he was after. It was her face, her scalp. She had passed by him at the store, catching his fancy and fueling his desire. A fine specimen. An excellent addition to his collection; with fragile features stretched into a scream—forever captured in his art.

He crept closer to the path, crouching and ready to pounce the moment she crossed. The light drew closer and now he could smell the mixture of Poison and sweat, a sweet concoction that aroused his hunger and almost uncoiled his predatory posture. He inhaled deeply, relishing the scent. Her footfalls brought her close enough to make out her dark form behind the bright light.

He waited, and when the twig he placed in the middle of the path snapped, he sprang. In one leap, he caught her, wrapping his arms around her as he tackled. The yelp of surprise brought a smile to his face, and he unsheathed the knife, plunging it into her chest before she could regain enough oxygen to produce a blood-curdling scream.

Her eyes widened, blinking at him in the light of her fallen headlamp.

The thrill of the hunt, of the capture, fueled his blood; pumping it frantically through his veins, throbbing in his temple, producing little spots of red at the edges of his eyesight. Ripping flesh accompanied each of his thrusts, along with muffled cries of pain that gave way to an airy wheeze.

He grabbed her hair, pulled her head forward, and sliced the base of her hairline with surgical precision. Sliding his fingers under the gaping wound, he peeled the scalp from the back to the front, separating her skin from the bone.

She did scream then, a high gurgling wail that died moments later, when his knife separated the mass of skin and hair and lips that he peeled from her bones, severing her carotid artery. With the prize pelt in his hands, he stood, sheathed the knife, and took off toward the river.

Saving Face
Chapter 2

*E*IGHT HOURS EARLIER...

"You are ruining my life!" CJ Ryan bellowed.

Steve Williams crossed his arms and stood his ground. "I don't care. You snuck out of the house after I said you couldn't go to that party. You knew damn well I'd find out, and now both you and your brother are grounded until graduation." His gaze traveled to CJ's mute brother, Tom. "And you, what were you thinking stealing that car?"

Tom thrust his hands in his pockets and stared at the ground.

Steve clenched his teeth together and glanced out the observation window at the Brooksfield police department pit.

"You can't ground me. You're not my father."

His gaze snapped back to CJ, and he tilted his head, narrowing his eyes. "I may not be your biological father, but never doubt my authority here."

"It's your fault my parents are dead."

The mental shove made Steve stumble back a step, and he caught himself. In two strides, he stood toe to toe with CJ. His gaze blazed into the azure blue of the seventeen-year-old's equally furious eyes.

"You really want to play that game with me?" he asked, his voice low, almost a growl, but the kid struck a chord. His father had been caught in the crossfire of one of his FBI investigations and his mother, his mother, was a completely different story. He had led her right into the belly of the beast.

CJ dropped his gaze, his eyes traveling to Tom's, before he shook his head.

"Why'd you let him steal a car?"

CJ sighed and shrugged. All the hellfire burned out of him for the moment.

"Why?" Steve asked and stepped back, addressing Tom.

I wanted to see my dad. Tom thought, meeting his questioning stare.

"Bullshit." Steve snapped. *You see him all the time. You probably can see him pacing the room behind me. Can't you?*

Tom's gaze moved from Steve's to the angry angel pacing the room behind him. Wings fluttered, and a wealth of curses dropped from his lips, his iridescent blue eyes glaring at the two boys. Tom nodded. *I wanted to talk with him.*

"You could have asked me to bring you here." Steve softened. It had been a couple of months since they visited Paradise Cove. The magical portal where their father could speak to them, to see them, and where Tom had a ghost tongue along with the miraculous recovery of speech. It was the only place on earth that he could articulate his thoughts since the psycho in Georgia had cut his tongue out.

But neither boy had the same mental bond Steve had with their father. Their father was now his guardian angel, a constant presence intruding on his every thought. Steve could hear Ty Ryan any time of day or night, even times when he'd rather not have the voice of reason on his shoulder. Sometimes he wished for the blessed silence he knew before he met the Ryan family. The absolute cluelessness to the surrounding thoughts, to the ghost haunting his every waking minute, and to the powers he inherited when Ty died. Reading minds came in handy as an FBI agent, but the constant din in his head was maddening.

"You've been too wrapped up in *that* case to take us," CJ answered.

That case. He almost laughed at the venom in CJ's voice. That case shrouded his life, leaving time for nothing else, and he missed more football games and nights of homework and family time his wife set aside, because of *that* stinking case.

Another killer was loose. The Windwalker eluded the police, eluded the FBI, and eluded him like he was made of smoke. They had gotten to the last victim minutes after she died. With her body still warm, they scoured the woods for clues, but the tracks disappeared at the bank of the river, just like every other dead, skinned body they found. Stealth, like fog rolling from the snow during strawberry spring, in and out quickly before the victim really knew what happened, and it burned him. Becoming a mission. An obsession.

CJ knew how frustrated he was, and to bring it up here was just his attempt to get a rise out of him, to skirt the real issue.

He ignored the dig. "So, you sneak out of the house, crash that party, have a few beers and decide it would be a great idea to steal a car?" Exasperated, he traded glances with the boys. "You crossed state lines. Do you have any idea how serious this is?"

CJ started to speak, then closed his mouth. He sank into the chair, fidgeting with his parent's wedding bands, which he wore on the chain around his neck. Tom followed suit, taking the seat next to his brother.

I'm sorry. It was my idea, not CJ's.

"Grand theft auto is serious and you two are close enough to eighteen for the courts to look at this as an opportunity to teach a hard lesson." He slid into the chair on the other side of the table and leaned forward. "I had to pull a lot of strings to make this disappear, but this is the last time I will bail you out. You hear me?" He pounded his index finger on the table, punctuating his words. "The last time!"

THE MAGNIFICENT WINGS FLUTTERED, and a chill tingled down Tom's spine. The incarnation of his father stood before him on the leaf covered moss of Paradise Cove. CJ's mirror image with grand white wings implanted in his back—a dark angel saddled with the responsibility of keeping Steve Williams safe for the rest of his natural life.

"I can't believe you would do something like that!" the voice bellowed, shimmering off the water and sending ripples through the surface of the cove. Trees shook under the booming tenor, bowing away from the power of it. "I could just wring your neck."

He took a step back, right into the solid mass of Steve, blocking the only entrance to this sacred ground. His escape thwarted, and anger sparked under the layer of fear.

The angel crossed, towering over him, extending his wings to their intimidating breadth. "You *stole* a car!"

"That's right. I did." Tom spoke, standing a little straighter and jutting his chin. His voice was unmarred by the absence of a tongue. Smooth and perfect, like it should have been.

"I never thought you would be the one to rebel. What the hell happened?"

"I don't know, 'Dad'." Sarcasm laced his musical tone. Nightmares still plagued him. Night after night, he relived the days locked in the basement in Georgia. All the snippets of torture, all the grotesque dreams, all the horror, culminated in the reigning fury throbbing in his veins and the dam finally burst. Tom's eyes narrowed into a glare. "Perhaps it was my mother's severed head sitting next to me while that bastard carved me up. And you...you didn't stop him."

Ty's wings trembled, retracting a fraction. "I couldn't stop him, Tommy." His eyes misted a bright sheen over the unearthly blue. One slipped down his cheek, creating prisms of light like a diamond as it traced his skin and fell to the ground. "I tried, but all I could do was scare his damn dog."

"Are you telling me, with all your powers, with all your insight, you couldn't figure out who had taken me any faster than Steve?"

Silence blanketed the cove.

Tom glared at the image of his father and the pained tears streaking his cheeks, guilt and sorrow etching his features. It was enough to make his stomach clench.

Ty swiped his face and shook his head, the self-loathing look replaced with indignation. "Look, what happened, happened. That does not give you the right to steal a car."

"Pft," Tom scoffed.

"Your mother would be so disappointed."

Those six words deflated him, and a lump formed in his throat. Disappointing her was not on his to-do list, and he slid his glance to CJ. It was a low blow and they both knew it. The kettle top holding his frustration rocked under the steam and the slow simmer over the last eight years finally boiled over.

"What gives you the right to tell me what I can and can't do?" Tom shoved his hands into the angel's chest, pushing with all his strength. "You aren't even my real father."

"I am your real father. I'm the one who raised you to know what's right and what's wrong; and what you did today is wrong!"

"Ha! You teach right from wrong? You're kidding, right?"

"That's enough." Wings fluttered again, agitated.

"What, Dad? You didn't think we'd ever find out what you did in that prison of yours?" He took a step closer to the angel. "You killed for sport. You are no better than the psycho in Georgia. No better than the murderer in Maine right now."

"*I* did not kill for sport."

"But you sure as shit stood by and watched."

The angel's blue eyes traveled to CJ's and then dropped to the ground, and he yielded, stepping back. "What I did close to thirty years ago is not under discussion. We're talking about *you* breaking the law today." He raised his gaze again. "I did a lot of things I'm not proud of. Things that should have landed me down under, but for some reason..." He shook his head. "No, because of *your mother,* I landed on the sunny side of heaven. Don't you *dare* use the mistakes I made as some sort of excuse for pulling this shit!"

He turned to Steve. "Thanks for bailing them out. Now get 'em out of here." He turned, his wings extending, taking him swiftly up beyond the treetops.

Saving Face
Chapter 3

STEVE OPENED THE GARAGE door, holding it for both of the boys, and then followed them into the kitchen. "Upstairs." Steve pointed toward the stairwell. They trudged upstairs.

He exhaled and turned toward his wife sitting on the couch with a script in her lap. "I don't know what else to do with them."

"We've done all we can." Jennifer Williams closed the script. "They're almost eighteen, and they've been rebelling ever since Jessica died."

"Can you blame them?" Steve met her sincere eyes.

He hadn't been prepared to raise a stranger's children, never mind two teenage boys with baggage that rivaled disaster victims, but after what had happened in Georgia, Steve couldn't just leave the children in the care of their aging grandparents. They weren't equipped to deal with the aftereffects of Georgia any more than Steve and Jennifer were, and they certainly weren't prepared for the responsibility of CJ Ryan; the prodigal son, the offspring of Ty and

Jessica, and the only human being capable of destroying the earth on a whim.

"No, but it still feels like I'm failing miserably at being a parent." He sat next to her. "They're constantly in trouble. Shoplifting, underage drinking, DUIs, and now this. Where the hell did we go wrong?"

"You didn't do anything wrong, Uncle Steve. We screwed up." CJ stepped into view on the stairs.

Steve met CJ's gaze. "I can't keep bailing you out."

CJ nodded. "I know and I'm sorry." He disappeared from view.

Steve glanced at the script on Jennifer's lap. Another B rated horror flick. "Is that any good?"

Jennifer shook her head. "My character is killed off pretty quick."

"I don't know why you don't just go back to the theater or that soap that keeps calling."

Jennifer pressed her lips together and looked at the ceiling. "I don't know if that's such a good idea. I think they need me around." She slid her gaze back to Steve. "Especially Tom. He gets angrier and angrier as each year passes."

A hand banged on the railing and they both jumped. Tom glared at them and then signed a frantic comeback. *I don't need you here. I don't need anybody.*

Steve heard the words even before his hands finished signing.

"Tom." Jennifer stood, and he put his hand out like he was stopping traffic.

Don't! Don't look at me like I'm some freak. I don't need your pity. I just need to be left the hell alone. So, go to New York, or wherever your jobs call you, and stay the hell out of my life.

CJ appeared on the stairs. "Don't talk to her like that."

Tom turned, glaring at him. He raised his middle finger and turned, hopped to the landing, and stalked toward the front door. CJ reached him before Steve could intervene and the minute CJ's hand landed on Tom's shoulder, Tom spun, sweeping CJ's feet from under him. CJ reacted just as quickly, yanking Tom with him as he fell, and sending Tom crashing to the floor. Both boys held black belts in various martial arts disciplines and were equals in height, weight and talent, so when they fought, things tended to break. But this time, when they got to their feet, CJ tilted his head and Tom crashed into the wall, held in place by an invisible hand.

Let me go! Tom's thought barreled with a strength that had grown over the years, and CJ winced but shook his head.

"No." His chest heaved. "You can't leave."

Tom's laugh filled the room.

"CJ, put him down." Steve crossed the distance, righting the table they knocked over. "He isn't going anywhere." He turned to Tom. "Isn't that right?"

Tom glared at both of them and kept quiet, neither nodding nor shaking his head. He was protecting his thoughts from both of them. When his eyes landed on Steve, his teeth snapped together and his eyes narrowed.

Steve caught the tail end of Tom's thought process, something akin to wanting to kick his ass. "CJ, I want you and Jen to go upstairs right now." Steve pointed to the stairs, without breaking eye contact with Tom. "Now!" the command filled the room, shocking both CJ and Jennifer into motion. They scurried up the stairs, and Steve waited and listened. No wings fluttered, and he sent a silent warning to his ever-present ghost to stay put before returning his full focus on Tom. The fury in the kid's eyes worried him enough to take drastic action.

"We're going for a ride." He grabbed Tom's arm and hauled him to the car, shoving him in the passenger seat. He flew out of the gate and navigated the roads like an Indy 500 driver, slamming on the brakes in front of the deserted beach.

"Out!" He yanked Tom out of the car and practically dragged him onto the wet sand. "You want to kick my ass?" He stretched his arms out. "Here's your chance, boy."

Tom didn't hesitate; he threw a punch that Steve parried, sidestepping away.

Tom's emotions swamped Steve, saturating his mind and movements. Anger prevailed, but there was something underneath, something darker, something that if he followed, it would lead him down a path to despair. He let him swing, and kick and go through the motions of forms, knocking each and every tag out of range until Tom sat on the sand and put his face in his hands, sobbing in frustration.

Taking a seat next to him, Steve threw his arm around his shoulder, offering him support without words. He stared at the ocean and sighed.

"O u me." He shook Steve's arm from his shoulder.

Steve put his arm back despite Tom's plea not to touch him. "What happened? What's going on?"

"O-ee." Tom knocked Steve's arm away again.

"Bullshit. This isn't normal behavior for you and we both know that."

Tom turned his head, his blue eyes shimmered with tears. "E oke u wi me."

He sighed and threw his arm around his shoulder again. "It happens."

You don't understand. She broke up with me because I couldn't kiss her like the other guys.

Bitterness accompanied the thought, and Steve didn't know what to say.

I just want to be normal. I want to be able to talk, to...to kiss.

Steve pressed his lips together and looked out at the ocean. "I did what I could, Tom. Things just don't grow back."

Your eye did.

Steve shook his head. "My eye was never removed. Deflated, yeah, gross as hell, but I didn't want it taken out." He turned to Tom. "So it was there when your mother did her magic. But the things he took from you..."

They're gone.

Steve nodded. "I'm sorry."

Tom rested his head on his folded arms.

Steve closed his eyes and gently rubbed Tom's back, letting the kid wallow for a few minutes. Until today, Tom seemed to have adjusted just fine to his handicap. His grades were top-notch. He was a star running back on the high school football team and he had his share of girls lining up to talk to him on facebook every night. Sure, now and then he'd get frustrated, but not like this, not this complete anguish.

Tanya, his latest girlfriend, was a beauty, a cheerleader with the body of a goddess and the face of an angel.

"You really liked this one."

He nodded without raising his head.

"I swear someday you'll find the right girl and your issues won't matter at all."

Tom tilted his head, raising his eyebrows. *Issues? I'm a f-ing freak!*

"No, you're not. You're a good kid who was dealt a raw hand. As I understand it, you're a lot like your biological father. Your dad had a very high opinion of him, you know."

Tom nodded. He knew. His folks made sure he knew what his father had sacrificed for them.

"You've got a good heart, and that's a rare thing these days. So what, if you've got this handicap, screw 'em if they can't accept you for who you are."

That's easy for you to say...

"Yes, it is, but here's the thing. You bring a lot to the table and if Tanya can't see that, she's blind. So what if you can't stick your tongue down her throat."

He laughed, shaking his head. *Just shut up now. You don't know what it's like to be me. You don't know what it's like not to be able to do those things. Yeah, I can drive her crazy with my hands. I can even screw the daylights out of her, but she wants more, and I can't give her what she wants.*

Steve raised his eyebrows. "You're sleeping with her?"

Tom's eyes widened, and he looked away, his cheeks turning a rosy pink from more than the cool air. He turned back. *Don't give me that shocked look. I am almost eighteen. How old were you?*

Steve cleared his throat and looked out at the water, stumped. He was seventeen when he lost his virginity, so he understood more about teenage hormones than he wanted to give away. "We're not talking about me. Tell me you're at least being smart about it?" He returned his gaze to Tom.

He rolled his eyes and nodded. *Yeah, I am.* It was his turn to look out at the water. *I want to bring her to Paradise Cove.*

Steve stiffened. "Why?"

So she can hear my voice and I can kiss her the way she wants me to.

"And introduce her to your father?"

Tom raised his eyebrows and shook his head. *No way. I'd ask him to be scarce.*

"Did you ever think it might be *his* presence that gives you the ability to speak?"

Tom's face went ashen, and he shook his head.

"And I think he'd have an issue with you sucking face with a girl in front of him."

Tom snorted. *I thought he liked to watch?*

Steve couldn't help it. He burst out laughing. "That's sick, Tom."

A grin surfaced and some of the good humor
he possessed made its way into his eyes.

Yeah, well, ok, maybe you're right.

"Oh, you know I'm right." He glanced at Tom
and slapped him on the back. "Let's get home
before Jen has the local police scouring the town
for us." He stood and started brushing the sand
off his backside.

Uncle Steve?

"Yeah?"

Thanks.

"Anytime."

Saving Face
Chapter 4

JENNIFER SHOT UP IN the bed, her hand over her mouth, stifling the scream. She reached out, knocking the lamp, but it never hit the ground. Stopping mid-fall, it teetered and righted itself on the nightstand, its light encompassing the room, and Jennifer turned to Steve.

His sleep-encrusted eyes met hers. "Another nightmare?"

She nodded, and he wrapped his arms around her, pulling her next to him on the plush bed. "Another murder," she said, her voice scratchy with exhaustion and fear.

His eyes closed, and a long exhale cut through the darkness. "Shit." He squeezed her tighter and kissed the back of her head, taking a moment to extract the memory. Another gift from the Ryan's—reaching into another's mind and extracting information, like he was the one who had the nightmare, the thought, the secret.

The details were as vivid as if the memory was on screen in front of him, and it spared her from having to relive the vision, to describe the crime scene in her dream. Extracting memories was as handy as mind reading, along with the power to control matter and, on a limited basis, control those around him, but it was also just as disturbing and unnatural.

She shivered in his grasp. "I hate it when you do that," she whispered.

"I know, but it's easier than drilling you for details."

"Yeah. Okay. If you say so."

He chuckled at her lack of enthusiasm and then turned his focus to her nightmare. Again, she took the perspective of the killer, a viewpoint she hated with a passion. Being in their heads, their twisted minds disturbed her more than the actual killings she witnessed. This one made him release her and jump to his feet. His eyes traveled to the door, and he bolted down the hall without a word, swinging Tom's door open to make sure.

The room was empty.

"Shit," Steve cursed under his breath as both anger and worry built in his stomach, leaving it a molten rock of acid. He turned and crossed the hall, opening the door to CJ's room.

CJ snored in response, and he closed the door, returning to his bedroom. He stared at Jen. "When?"

"I don't know. You saw it, you tell me?"

He shook his head, glancing at the clock and grabbing his jeans. Four in the morning. No one runs this early, but in her dream, it was dark enough for the victim to need a light. "I have to stop this one."

"Why?"

He focused on her instead of the buttons on his shirt. "Tanya. Tanya's the girl in your vision."

Jennifer's eyes widened, and he could tell she hadn't made the connection.

"And Tom's not home. Damn it." He stood and walked back to CJ's room, sitting down on the edge of the bed. "CJ, wake up." He shook him.

CJ's eyes fluttered open. "What?"

"When was the last time you saw Tanya?"

A shadow passed over his face and he blinked, cocking his head to the side. "What?" The skin between his eyebrows creased.

"Tanya, when was the last time you saw her?"

"Tom took her home after practice."

"Is that when he told you they broke up?"

CJ nodded.

Steve wiped his face, the unease ratcheted up a notch, squeezing his abdomen like a belt pulled too tight. "Damn it," he whispered under his breath. He stood and took a step away. CJ's grip on his wrist stopped him and he looked back.

"What's going on?"

"Nothing you need to worry about right now," Steve said. "Go back to sleep."

Saving Face
Chapter 5

STEVE'S EARLIER RACE TO the beach was like a Sunday drive compared to his supersonic jump to Tanya's house and the car screeched to a stop in the driveway. It was now almost five, and he pounded on the front door, waking the poor folks inside the house.

Carl Angelo opened the door wearing a ratty bathrobe, and a rumpled expression. "Agent Williams, is everything all right?"

"I'm sorry to wake you, but I was hoping to speak with Tanya," he said, knowing just how strange the request sounded, but with every passing second, the sky lightened, and his heart pumped out a warning to hurry before it was too late.

"Can I ask why?"

Steve knew the truth wouldn't settle well, so he threw up a smokescreen. "Tom didn't come home last night and I'm a little worried," he said.

Carl's face smoothed over, and he nodded, waving Steve inside before he disappeared upstairs. A few minutes later, he descended to the ground floor. "She already left for her morning run, but I'm sure she'll be back in a little while. I can make a pot of coffee if you'd like."

Steve glanced at his watch and the fading darkness. "Does she jog over on the river path?"

"Yes, why?"

"I think I'll try to catch her at the park entrance." He smiled, heading for the door. "If she comes back before I talk to her, have her give the house a call."

"Will do. I'm sure Tom is just fine," Carl said.

Steve gave him a wave and jogged to the car. Dread filled every pore as the horizon lightened in the distance. *Shit, I'm running out of time.*

He pushed a button on his car phone and the ringing filled the car, followed by a sleepy baritone. "Detective O'Keefe."

"I need some manpower," Steve said.

After a beat of silence, "Agent Williams?"

"Yes. River Trail. He's going to hit again on the River Trail."

Another beat. "You got it."

"Let them know I'll be out there, too." Steve hung up.

Where the hell was Tom?

He didn't have time to worry about Tom and shook the thought out of his head. He pushed harder on the gas pedal, spinning to a stop in the first of many parking lots lining the jogging trail. Tanya's car sat in the parking spot closest to the path and he parked next to it, closing his eyes and scanning the area for any indication of thought.

Nothing.

Empty.

Silent...and his heart plummeted. He swallowed the acid lining his throat and stepped out of his car.

Maybe she was out of range; he pulled his gun out and checked the clip before snapping it back in. He flipped the safety off, crossed to the path, and followed the footpath to the cover of the trees where the ground only appeared briefly here and there through the thick coating of leaves lining the path. Jennifer's dream came back, and he took a deep breath, scanning the trees, looking for the spot. With each step, dread crept further and further under his skin.

His gaze swept from side to side, no sound, no thoughts, and his heart pounded in his chest, throbbing in his temples. The sky was too light, and a sense of futility took control.

A half-mile down the path, a voice yelled from around the bend, "Freeze!"

Steve moved swiftly. He flipped the safety on his gun before holstering it. He slowed, feeling hostility and satisfaction radiating from the spot just out of view, and he swung around the foliage toward the voice.

He froze, staring at the scene in front of him.

Tom kneeled with his hands in the air and Tanya's dead body draped across his lap, half in and half out of an inlet stream, his clothing wet and blood soaked, and his horrified gaze locked on the scalped body on the ground.

Swallowing the bile lining his throat, Steve pulled out his badge and held it out for the officers on the scene. "FBI," he announced, calling their attention, along with their gun barrels, away from Tom for a moment.

"Special Agent Williams?" the closest officer asked.

Steve nodded and scanned the muddy area where the jogging path traversed the stream, trying to reconcile Tom with the morbid scene.

"Looks like we finally caught up to you," Officer Callaway said from behind Tom and clasped a handcuff on Tom's wrist. Twisting his arm behind his back, he secured the other wrist.

"I ia o i," Tom said, his cheeks lined with a steady stream of tears. *I didn't do this, Uncle Steve.*

"You've got the wrong man, that's my son." Steve scanned the ground for evidence that would exonerate Tom on the spot, but the stream kept the exit path of the killer a secret, like most of the prior murders.

"We found him covered in her blood," the officer replied, not moving to un-cuff Tom.

"Did you find the murder weapon and the scalp?" Steve asked, raising his eyebrow in a silent question.

"No, sir. But he could have ditched it before we got here," Callaway said.

Steve met Tom's gaze. "How long have you been here?" Steve signed, trying not to let his irritation show. Tom had compromised the crime scene and Steve glanced toward the river a few hundred feet away, knowing any trail they found would end at the water's edge, but this time, he was sure the local cops wouldn't look any farther than the boy covered with his ex-girlfriend's blood.

"Coup miues," Tom said. *A couple of minutes ago. I wanted to talk, to convince her to come back and when I jogged by, I saw her in the stream. I didn't know it was her until I saw the bracelet and then I tried to get her out of the water and slipped, and that's when the police showed up. Did you see what that bastard did to her?*

He knew. He had seen half a dozen victims over the last year in the same condition, all left in remote areas, and all with water access. He crouched and took Tanya's wrist, checking for a pulse he knew wasn't there. Even if she had a pulse, his power to heal wouldn't bring her face back. A limitation he learned from Tom. *If it's gone, it won't grow back* no matter how much mojo Steve pumped into the person. And he certainly couldn't resurrect the dead.

Tom bit his lip and blinked, sending another trail of tears down his smudged cheeks while the cops read him his rights. *I used to run with her on this trail and if we hadn't broken up...*

You would have been with her, Steve finished the thought and took a deep breath, keeping the anger and worry at bay. Everyone was itching to solve the Windwalker case, and Tom just handed them an easy scapegoat.

Did you see anything? Steve asked, sending the thought, and the ball of stress tightened at Tom's shake of his head.

Steve stood, meeting Officer Callaway's gaze. "He isn't the killer."

Tom took another glance at the body and visibly shuddered.

"Until we find evidence to the contrary, we'll be keeping him in custody." Callaway pulled Tom away from the scene.

Steve nodded and snapped his gaze to Tom. "say nothing until I get there, Tom."

Officer Callaway glared at Steve for a moment and then continued on his way down the path, leaving the other officer to secure the scene.

Steve turned away, following the stream, looking for signs of evidence to exonerate Tom, but the muck on either side of the waterway along with the turning tide eradicated any signs of evidence. At the mouth of the river, he scanned the water with both his eyes and his mind, and nothing stirred but an eerie silence.

Anger danced over his skin, seeping into his bones. "You bastard! I swear I'll find you. You hear me?" he bellowed, and the echo reached the far side of the river and beyond.

Saving Face
Chapter 6

"EVERYTHING YOU HAVE IS circumstantial," Steve said outside the interrogation room.

"I know he's your son, but he was found at the scene covered in her blood and he has a motive," Detective O'Keefe said.

"Where's the murder weapon?" Steve asked, frustrated with the inability of the police force to hear reason.

"He could have ditched it in the river before we arrived."

Steve wiped his face, resisting the urge to make the detective do what he wanted. The only time he allowed himself to use the ability to influence was in an emergency where life and death was a factor. And while this was worrisome, it didn't qualify under the strict guidelines he imposed on himself for utilizing his powers. Instead, he counted to ten and then met the Detective's gaze. "You can't question him without a legal guardian present or without legal representation."

Detective O'Keefe waved his hand toward the room. "You're welcome to sit in, and while we're on the topic, do you want me to get you a public defender?"

Steve huffed and narrowed his eyes, digging into the Detective's private thoughts, pulling out his assessment of the case and Steve bristled. "Your charges will never stick." He turned away from the detective and paused with his hand on the doorknob. "And you'd better get that warrant to search my house, because I'm not feeling all that cooperative right now." He stepped inside the room and closed the door, meeting Tom's gaze.

You're in a shitload of trouble right now. Steve signed and took a seat next to him. He inhaled and ran his palm down his face before he added, *it's time for us to lawyer up.*

Tom's eyes widened. *They think I killed her?*

Steve nodded, and a fresh set of tear tracks flowed down Tom's cheeks before he folded his arms on the table, burying his face in the crook of his blood-smeared arms. His sobs filled the room and Steve put his hand on Tom's back and closed his eyes, buffering his soul from Tom's sorrow and fear.

The door opened, and Tom raised his head. Steve pulled his hand away from Tom's back and folded his arms across his chest, staring down Detective O'Keefe. "You could have at least let him clean up."

"We gave him a fresh uniform," he said, waving toward the standard issue jumpsuit. "Besides, he didn't seem to mind the blood when he slit her throat." The detective threw the case file on the table and took a seat on the opposite side of the table.

"I..." Tom started, but Steve raised his hand, silencing him.

"I'm advising my son not to answer any questions."

Detective O'Keefe's lips pressed together, and his eyes narrowed in disgust at the trump card Steve just played. "When can he answer questions?"

"After his lawyer arrives. When is his arraignment?"

"Monday morning," he said with a smug smile. "Is this why you haven't been able to crack this case as quickly as the others?" He waved his hand toward Tom.

Steve balled his hands into fists, glaring at the Detective. "I'm going to pretend you didn't say that." He tried to keep his voice even, but his words bristled with the snarl of anger. "I trust until I can post bail, he will be kept away from the adult population?"

"Yes," Detective O'Keefe said. His answer was clipped and his glare just as telling as Steve's.

"Wha?" Tom said, his gaze bouncing from the detective to Steve and back.

"You're going to have to stay in here until Monday."

Tom's eyes flashed over with fear. "Why?"

Reading more than just Detective O'Keefe's mind, Steve said, "They think you're the Windwalker."

Saving Face
Chapter 7

STEVE WALKED INTO THE house and threw his keys on the table in disgust.

"The school called. Tom never showed up this morning. Do you know where he is?" Jennifer asked from the stairway.

Steve met her gaze. "He's in jail."

Her eyes went wide and before Steve could answer, the buzzer sounded, and he pressed the button to open the driveway gate.

"They have a search warrant," Steve said, nodding to the approaching squad cars before turning away from the wide-eyed shock on her face. "Neither of us got there in time."

"Tom was there?"

"Yes. He took off early to talk to her. She was already dead when he found her, and I was about five minutes too late. The cops found him first."

"You mean the Windwalker could have been close enough to kill Tom?"

Steve hadn't considered that, and the hair on the back of his neck bristled at the thought. The Windwalker didn't discriminate between men and women, the only common thread was all his victims were exceptionally good looking, and Tom certainly fit the bill.

"Probably." He crossed to the door when Jennifer didn't move from the spot on the stairs.

Detective O'Keefe stood on the front step with Officer Callaway slapping a folded warrant in his palm. He handed it to Steve with an expression bordering on hostile. Steve opened the paper and waved the officers inside. "Just don't make a mess," Steve said as they stepped into the living room.

"We'll do our best," Officer Callaway said with a nod.

Steve headed out to the backyard, ignoring the chill in the air, and slipped his phone out. He scrolled down the list of names until he found the one he wanted. It was time to call in some favors.

"District Attorney Kincaid's office. How may I help you?"

"Is Mrs. Kincaid in the office?"

"Who may I say is on the line?"

"Tell her it's Special Agent Williams," Steve answered. Hold music replaced the chipper receptionist's voice.

"Steve?" Carolyn Kincaid's familiar voice filled the line.

"Hey, Carolyn. I'm calling to ask a favor."

"What do you need?"

"I need the best criminal defense lawyer in Maine. Tom's been arrested."

Silence filled the line, and papers shuffled in the background. "Why?"

"Have you been following the Windwalker case in the news at all?"

Another pause. "They can't possibly think that sweet boy is the Windwalker?"

"That sweet boy is seventeen, and yes, that's exactly what they think. They are going to try him as an adult."

"I've got a name for you. Sheldon Kryminski. He's out of Portland and he's supposed to be the best in New England." She rattled off the phone number.

"Thanks, Carolyn."

"Let me know if there's anything else I can do."

"I will, and the next time we're in New York, we'll have to catch up." Steve ended the call and walked to the stone wall, ignoring the slide of the door behind him. He stood watching the flow of boats in and out of the harbor and when Jennifer stepped next to him and sat on the stone ledge, he met her gaze.

"What happened?"

Steve sighed. "Tom wasn't in his room this morning when I checked." He scanned the water. "And while I know he's not the Windwalker, I'm thinking back to every murder and trying to place where he was at the time. The bitch of it is, I can't." He paused and met her gaze. "I'm hoping you and CJ can vouch for his whereabouts, because Tanya certainly can't."

Invisible wings fluttered. "You know..."

"Ty, not now," Steve snapped, dismissing the invisible angel.

"Fine, but it's your funeral," Ty Ryan said.

Steve paused and cocked his head, turning toward the house. "What are you talking about?"

"If they search the attic, they might find a few things of mine."

A chill skittered down Steve's spine and he clenched his jaw, trading a glance at Jennifer. "Like what?"

A flash of annoyance crossed Jennifer's features, and she crossed her arms. Steve knew she hated it when he had half conversations with his guardian angel.

"Like DVDs."

Steve raised an eyebrow.

"From the complex."

"Shit, Ty," Steve spun and stared out at the bay. "Is there anything in there that implicated Chris?"

Silence met the question.

"That's just fucking wonderful."

"What?" Jennifer asked, her voice clipped with sarcasm.

"He says there are DVDs in the attic that incriminate Chris. This day just gets better and better."

Jennifer's brow creased for a moment and then the wrinkle smoothed, and her face transitioned into a hard glare. "He kept DVDs?"

"Apparently." Steve closed his eyes and mentally scanned the house, zeroing in on Detective O'Keefe's train of thought. His eyes snapped open, and he spun, nearly sprinting to the house, with Jennifer following.

Steve bounded up the stairs and swung Tom's bedroom door open. His gaze landed on the mutilated photographs the detectives found under Tom's bed. He stared at the number of slashes scored into each picture and his stomach tightened, sending cramps through his abdomen, but he stood fast.

"Tell me about these?" Detective O'Keefe asked.

"Tanya broke up with him recently," Steve answered. "He wasn't taking it very well."

The detective's eyebrows rose. "Considering what he did, I'd call that an understatement."

"Tommy didn't kill anyone," Jennifer said from behind Steve before sliding in front of him. "He was upset and hurt and angry, but that doesn't mean he killed her."

"Then what was he doing this morning?"

"They jogged together every day, and that was one of their favorite paths. He was going to talk to her." Steve looked at the pictures in the detective's hands. "He wanted to patch things up."

The detective fanned out the pictures so Steve could see them. "These don't look like they're from someone who wants to patch things up."

Steve couldn't argue with the detective's deduction, because if the tables were turned, he would think the same way. "I believe my son, detective."

"Jeffrey Dahmer's parents believed in him, too."

"You did not just compare my son to that monster," Jennifer snapped, her green eyes flashed with the anger etched in her features.

"Sir?" Officer Callaway said, holding up a hunting knife. The sprayed edge revealed traces of blood.

Shock filled every fiber of Steve's body, tingling his skin, but he kept his features neutral, like having a hunting knife in the bedroom was the most natural thing for a teenage boy. *Don't react,* he sent the thought to Jennifer, but it was too late.

"So, he has a hunting knife," she said. "He also has a fishing pole in the garage and a fish cleaning station, too."

Steve put his hand on her shoulder to stop the beginning of a full out angry rant and she shook it off, sending a glare in his direction. Despite his recent antics, Tom and Jennifer had become very close over the years and she was in mother bear mode right now, protecting him at all costs.

After a moment, he cleared his throat. "Jen, we should let them do their job."

"What? So they can fabricate evidence against our son? I don't think so," she snapped, leveling her famous glare toward Detective O'Keefe.

"They have a warrant, and we have nothing to hide," Steve said through clenched teeth. He wrapped his hand around her arm and pulled her away from Tom's bedroom, but not before he saw the knife drop into an evidence bag.

He didn't stop until he was in the backyard, out of hearing range. "What the hell were you trying to do back there?"

"I am trying to protect Tom," she snarled. "What are you doing to protect him?"

"I'm not obstructing justice." Steve closed his eyes and took a deep breath. "I'm also getting the best defense lawyer in the state for Tom, and while you and I know he didn't do it, we will need to sit down and figure out where he was for every murder once the police leave. Understand?" Steve opened his eyes and met her gaze.

"CJ's going to flip."

"I know." He wiped his hand over his face and glanced over his shoulder at the house. "I hope they're out of here before he gets home from school." *And I hope like hell they don't find those DVDs because that would bring on a shit storm of epic proportion.*

Saving Face
Chapter 8

TOM SAT IN THE jail cell staring at the floor and shivering. Every time he closed his eyes, he saw what remained of her once beautiful face and his stomach rolled. He decided the stained gray floor was a better alternative. His gaze traveled to his arms and the streaks still marring them and his fists balled against the urge to scrub until his skin was as raw as hers had been.

Tears burned the back of his throat, and he blinked back the sudden blur, tightening his jaw against the unwanted tears. He was damned if he'd let them see him cry again.

"Boy, when we get a hold of you, we'll give you something to cry about," the prisoner in the next cell said.

Tom had had enough of the threats from the surrounding inmates and shifted his gaze to the adjoining cell. He raised his middle finger and flashed a smug smile.

"You're a dead man, Windwalker," the man hissed.

Tom shrugged off the threat and looked out the tiny window at the afternoon sky. Monday was a long way away, and he sighed, wondering if Uncle Steve would be able to pull some strings and get him out early.

The door on his cell rattled open, pulling his attention away from the window. Shock skittered down his spine at the hulking mass in the doorway and he stood, backing up against the concrete wall behind him. His gaze darted to the officer standing next to the man with the sadistic grin.

The officer sent a glare in Tom's direction and pushed the large man into the cell, closing the door behind him. "Enjoy," he laughed as he walked away.

Tom's heart pounded in his chest with the rush of adrenaline, and he blinked, his gaze bouncing between the danger in front of him and the cackling man in the adjoining cell, egging the man on. He thought about sending an SOS to CJ or Steve or calling on Ty for help, but he didn't have time.

The man lurched forward, bringing a knife from his pocket. "I'm going to make you squeal, boy," he growled.

Anger bubbled to the surface, wiping out any fear or sorrow left in Tom's heart. Years of martial arts training kicked in, and Tom parried, grabbed the wrist of the hand holding the knife, and twisted while pulling the giant closer and rolled him over his hip and into a flip that threw the man into the back wall. Instead of going in for the kill, Tom stepped into the center of the cell, waiting for the attacker to regain his faculties.

Stunned silence settled on the adjoining cells, and Tom kept his focus on the man with the sharp blade. He didn't need to be a mind reader like CJ to understand what this bastard wanted to do to him. He'd had enough of being the victim, and was damned if he'd let this thug get the best of him.

"I see you want to dance a little before we get down to business," the man said, getting to his feet. He approached Tom more cautiously this time, switching the knife from hand to hand. The men in the adjoining cells were at the bars now, cheering their fighter on.

Tom kept his eyes on the knife as the man circled him in the small space. Every time the man sliced toward him, Tom sidestepped out of reach. He didn't follow through with a defensive blow, instead; he danced away, enjoying the anger and frustration in his attacker's face. It wasn't until he brushed up against the bars of the adjoining cell that he understood his mistake.

Hands grabbed him, pulling him against the bars and a voice whispered in his ear, "We've got you now, boy." A hand tugged his head back and feet collided with the back of his knees, dropping him to the concrete floor.

Tom struggled to free his arms, but the men in the adjoining cell held fast, pulling them through the bars to his elbows and a hand gripped a healthy handful of his hair, yanking his head back against the metal hard enough to daze him.

When his vision cleared, the point of the knife hovered less than an inch from his eye. Fear tightened his throat, and he turned his gaze up to the man's grinning face. The sound of a zipper sent shockwaves through Tom and panic overrode his senses, dulling the pain in his hyper-extended shoulders.

He closed his eyes and silently shouted Steve's name, the thought barreling like a freight train in his head, just like Steve had taught him.

Saving Face
Chapter 9

STEVE SAT AT THE dinner table, going over the appointment calendar that usually graced the kitchen wall, cross-referencing dates with those of the killings. Not one offered a concrete alibi, and he clenched his jaw, running his hand through his hair in frustration.

"Damn it all," he cursed and traded a worried look with Jennifer. Not only had the police taken the pictures and the knife, they also found a stash of unmarked DVDs hidden in a secret hideaway in the attic floor. "What else could go wrong?"

Tom's panicked call reverberated in his brain, answering his question and he closed his eyes, grabbing hold of the telepathic signature and transported his consciousness into Tom's cell. One glance sent hot irons of fury through his fingers and his hands balled into fists, controlling the fiery rage from escaping. Instead, he threw a punch into the side of the bastard's head, knocking him out cold before he could pull his dick out of his pants.

"I suggest you let go of my son," he said, shaking the sting from his knuckles. His voice wavered with building fury. Hands released Tom, and the men scuttled away like he was a demon incarnate.

He turned his attention to Tom, helping him up before turning to the beastly pig on the floor. "How did he get in here?"

One of the officers let him in. Tom signed in answer.

"Damn it." Steve reached into his back pocket. The handcuffs from this morning were still in his jeans and he yanked them out, kneeling over the man and securing his wrists behind his back before turning back to Tom. "Stay put, I'll be back in a few."

The transition started, and Steve opened his eyes, back in his kitchen, and met Jennifer's worried gaze before getting up from the table. "Those assholes put him in the adult section of the jail," he said.

"What?"

"I don't have time to explain right now." He turned and headed for the garage. "You need to stay and deal with CJ," he shot over his shoulder and closed the door on her imploring gaze.

A few minutes later, he stormed into the York police department holding area, his gaze landing on one of the cockier officers that continually rubbed him wrong. He crossed and towered over the desk, scanning his mind and confirming this was the dirt bag that let that monster into Tom's cell.

"Hathaway, why did you put that jerk off in the cell with my son?" he said, loud enough to call the attention of the entire room, O'Keefe included.

"The drunk tank was full and there was an extra bed in that cell." Hathaway sat back in his seat with his arms crossed.

"Bullshit." Steve balled his hands into fists and shot a glare in O'Keefe's direction. "You were supposed to segregate him from the adults. He's a minor, for god's sake."

"He's being charged as an adult," O'Keefe stepped closer, verbally defending Hathaway's actions, but Steve saw into his thoughts and the man was pissed, too.

Steve stared at O'Keefe. "Do you have any idea what they were trying to do to Tom a few minutes ago?"

Hathaway started typing and Steve glanced at his hands, willing them to freeze over the keyboard. Steve reached out, turning the monitor in O'Keefe's direction. "Too bad Hathaway isn't as accomplished at erasing videos as he thinks he is." He glanced at Hathaway. "Rewind the video."

Hathaway's wide, horrified gaze watched as he typed the proper commands, and the screen went blank for a moment before coming back at the point he opened Tom's cell and pushed the large man into it. The audio captured his mocking words as the cell door latched closed.

O'Keefe's jaw clenched at the following scene and when Steve stepped into the frame and cold cocked the man, he turned his gaze to Steve. "How did you get in there?"

Steve held up a set of keys to the lockup area that he'd had for years now. "I came to make sure you were true to your word. Guess it was a good thing I showed up when I did, otherwise that animal would have made Tom his bitch."

The comment settled on the room, and Steve released control of Hathaway's hands. Hathaway pushed back from the desk, his features filled with trepidation, and Steve sent a warning glare in his direction.

"I am taking Tom home. Now."

"His arraignment..." O'Keefe started and trailed off at the silencing glare Steve sent in his direction.

"I'll keep him under house arrest in a safe environment," Steve said. "And once he's in my custody, I'll give you the keys to un-cuff the unconscious pig in his cell."

"I suggest you do what Special Agent Williams is requesting," a baritone voice came from the doorway.

Steve turned to see Director Ron Cleary standing in the entry with a slip of paper in his hand. He crossed, dropping it on the desk, giving Steve a sideways glance.

"I went over your head," he said to Detective O'Keefe. "Tom's not a flight risk and the terms of his house arrest include school and home until a court date can be worked out. In other words, Special Agent Williams has custody until a verdict is returned."

As soon as O'Keefe left the room, Steve turned to Cleary. "Thanks." He stuck out his hand.

He returned the handshake and pulled out another paper from his coat. "You've got bail to settle up." He handed the bill to Steve.

Steve glanced at the slip of paper and raised an eyebrow. "They set bail at a million?" Cleary nodded, and Steve understood the hoops he jumped through to get this deal and the seriousness of the prosecutor in trying this case. "He didn't do it, Ron."

"Are you sure?"

Steve nodded. "Yes. I'd stake my reputation on it."

"You've been fooled before," Cleary said.

"Once and that's because I didn't know the signs. Tom's an open book. He doesn't know how to hide a secret from me, not something like this."

Cleary nodded toward the holding cell entrance and Steve turned to see Detective O'Keefe escorting him across the station.

"Sit here," Detective O'Keefe pointed to a chair next to his desk. Tom sat, rubbing his wrists, and Detective O'Keefe sent a glare in Steve's direction before he disappeared.

Steve turned back to Cleary. "Could you stay with him while I settle this up?"

Cleary nodded, and Steve headed off to the bail bond office. When he came back, Tom was sitting with his arms crossed and a decidedly sour expression on his face, and Detective O'Keefe was squatting, fitting the tracking device around Tom's ankle.

Steve met his gaze and crossed the station just as Detective O'Keefe stood.

What the hell is this? Tom signed and pointed at his ankle.

"It's part of the stipulation of your home arrest. You can go to and from school and that's it. If you violate those terms, they'll put you back in jail."

What about my job? He signed.

"You'll have to take a leave of absence," Steve said.

"Why?" Tom asked.

"Because it's across state lines," he said. "Home and school. That's it until we can clear you of all charges."

Tom lowered his gaze to the ankle bracelet and nodded, but Steve knew he was not happy with the current situation.

"Are we good?" Steve asked Detective O'Keefe.

Detective O'Keefe entered a few commands on his computer and a red light on his ankle bracelet went on. The printer whirled into action, and he turned, grabbing the piece of paper that had spit out. "I've mapped out the route to school for you." He handed Tom the paper. "If you deviate from this route, your ankle bracelet will blink red. That means you've violated the terms of your house arrest. Tonight, when you get home, that will turn green. I've given you twenty minutes to get home before the alarm goes off. If he isn't home within twenty minutes, he is in violation of his house arrest. Understand?"

Tom stared at the paper and then handed it to Steve. He met Detective O'Keefe's gaze and gave a nod. "Ye." He signed yes along with his verbal confirmation.

Steve gave a nod as well and grabbed Tom's arm. "Come on, we've got to get moving." He led Tom outside, knowing he didn't have time to fool around. "At least it isn't summer," he said when they slid into the car. "Otherwise, we'd be screwed."

Tom nodded. Without traffic, it took a good fifteen minutes to get from their house to the police station, provided you kept to the speed limit, but in the summer, Long Sands Road was wall-to-wall traffic, and it could easily take twice as long to drive the same distance.

I can't take the bus.

"I know." Steve had seen the direct route along with the timeframe allowed for the commute. It didn't allow any leeway at all, and he sighed. "I'll drive you in and I'll see if Jen can pick you up."

I can drive.

Steve sent a glare in his direction. "No, you can't." He pulled the paperwork out of his pocket and handed it to Tom. "Regardless of the stipulations, it's better than sitting in jail until this gets straightened out."

Tom scanned the paper, raising an eyebrow in Steve's direction, when his gaze landed on the amount of bail required for the arrangement. He blew out a stream of air and continued reading, each word bringing with it a deeper despair, and by the time they pulled into the security gate and his ankle bracelet blinked green, his eyes filled with tears.

"When we get inside, we need to map out exactly where you were for each of the murders. We need a couple of concrete alibis."

They really think I'm the Windwalker?

"Yes, and they found the mutilated pictures in your room."

Tom put his hand over his eyes and hung his head.

"They are going to try to nail you for Tanya's murder, regardless of whether they can pin the rest on you."

I didn't kill her! Tom signed as well as projected the thought.

"I know you didn't kill her, but there isn't any evidence to refute it, so the cops are doing exactly what I would have done in their shoes." He glanced at Tom. "Minus what happened in the jail earlier. That's unacceptable and I'll be filing a complaint as soon as we get inside. Having internal affairs on their ass won't help their case either, and the lawyer I've hired will have a field day with that transgression."

Steve turned the car off and closed the garage door. "The stunt you pulled the other night isn't going to help your case, either." He rubbed his face and opened the car door. "With all the trouble you and CJ have gotten into over the past year, it just makes it harder to prove what we already know. You're a good kid, even though on paper it looks like you're a rebel who has no regard for the law."

I'm sorry, Uncle Steve. Tom thought and met Steve's gaze over the roof of the car.

"I'm sorry about Tanya," Steve said, and Tom's calm demeanor crumbled. Tears sprang into the corners of his eyes like someone turned a faucet on and Steve rounded the car to give his adopted son a much-needed hug. Tom sobbed on his shoulder like an inconsolable toddler.

Saving Face
Chapter 10

EACH SOB THAT RIPPED from his chest burned, and Tom couldn't get control over the flow of tears or the pain hammering his muscles. Steve's awkward pats on his back did nothing to help quell the hurricane, and all he wanted to do was curl up and die.

Steve gripped his shoulders and Tom pushed him away, giving him a glare that sparked a layer of anger under his skin. He hated it when either Steve or CJ read his mind, and he ripped himself out of Steve's grip. Disgust roiled in his stomach, and he stormed into the house, wiping his nose on the sleeve of the hideous police-issue jumpsuit he still wore.

CJ stood up from the couch and turned in his direction as he crossed the living room, but he ignored the concern painted on his brother's face. He took the stairs two at a time and ripped at the fabric covering his skin, leaving the jumpsuit crumpled at the bathroom door. With his heart pounding in his throat, he reached into the shower and turned the water on. The scorching spray bit at his skin, dulling the pain in the center of his chest and he focused all his energy into scrubbing every inch of his skin, removing all traces of Tanya's blood.

When his skin was raw enough to burn under the water flow, he stopped and turned off the shower. He ran his hands through his dripping hair, pushing it from his face, and leaned against the wall, waiting until his breath slowed to normal before he wrapped a towel around his waist.

Tom opened the bathroom door and stared at the hallway, thankful someone else had gotten rid of the orange jumpsuit. He stopped in the doorway of his room and met CJ's gaze before he continued to his dresser and slipped on a pair of clean clothing. Tom didn't want to talk about what he witnessed, or the near disaster at the jail, and he recognized the itch of CJ's mind scan. After he pulled his jeans on, he turned to CJ.

"Stop," he signed, and the release of CJ's silent interrogation left him dizzy and unsteady. He reached for his bureau and blinked the swoon away. CJ stared at the floor with that guilty expression Tom was used to seeing, and he had to bite the derogatory comment to keep it from spilling into his mind or out of his mouth. He clenched his fists in response and slipped a t-shirt over his head before sitting on the edge of the bed next to his brother.

It sucked, he thought.

"I'm sorry." CJ put his arm around Tom's shoulder.

Tom blinked the sudden sheen of tears away and nodded, allowing his brother to offer him comfort in his own way. He could tell CJ wanted to say more, but he kept quiet, and the sting of tears coated his throat. CJ understood, just like he always did, and while that silent knowledge sometimes angered him, this time he was thankful for not having to explain any of the emotions crushing his chest.

CJ pointed to the ankle bracelet. "Do you want me to remove that for you?"

Tom wiped his face and shook his head. *No,* he signed. *I don't want to go back to jail.*

"Those assholes really believe you're the Windwalker?" CJ asked with a voice filled with disbelief and disgust.

Tom nodded.

"Stupid hicks," CJ muttered.

"He has to play by the rules on this, CJ," Steve said from the doorway and met Tom's gaze. "You about ready to go over those dates and times now?"

Tom nodded and stood. *Thanks,* he signed to CJ before he followed Steve downstairs.

Papers covered the table along with the calendar from the kitchen that had work and sports schedules scrawled all over the pages, and Tom slid onto the seat that Steve pointed to.

Steve turned the calendar back a month and pointed to the date circled in red. "He strikes on the new moon, when it's the darkest in those woods." He flipped the calendar backwards, showing Tom the clear predicament they faced. Not one of the dates had work hours or sports events that coincided with the killings. "He likes to strike just after sundown or just before sunrise, and the tide always works to his advantage."

Tom bit his lip and took the calendar from Steve, flipping back over the last year. A ball of fire erupted in his stomach, burning his esophagus as he swallowed it. The last few morning deaths were easy to explain. He was either sleeping or jogging with Tanya. Neither of which provided him with any concrete alibi.

He couldn't remember what he had done on the three evening dates on the calendar and sighed. It didn't help that the Windwalker killings started around the same time he asked Tanya out. If they had happened before they became a couple, he'd have at least a half dozen different alibis lined up because most of his nights when he wasn't working were spent with whatever girl was free.

He raised his gaze to Steve. But since they started dating, most nights, he took Tanya home after football and cheerleading practice. Again, a dead end as far as an alibi was concerned, and he covered his face. He doubted her folks would offer any help, especially if they believed he killed her.

"There's nothing?" Steve asked, leaning back in his seat. "No dinner dates or anything you can think of?"

Tom just shook his head, devastation increasing a notch in his bones. He lowered his hands and stared at the array of paper before raising his gaze. *Doesn't the Windwalker take the scalps?*

"Yes, and nothing beyond the mutilated pictures and your fishing knife was found here."

Steve inhaled. "Will they find anything other than fish blood on that blade?"

Tom shook his head, but his mind drifted back a couple of months when Tanya had gotten a splinter in her foot in their canoe. He used the blade to catch the end of the sliver and when that sucker came out, her foot bled enough for him to wrap it up in his t-shirt and take her home.

"Tanya's blood is on the knife?"

I don't know; he signed and shrugged. He wasn't sure if he washed the knife since then or not. *But her parents took her to get a tetanus shot.*

Steve's expression remained guarded. "That means there are traces of blood in the canoe, too, right?"

Tom nodded

STEVE STARED AT THE array of papers on the table, digesting this new fact. None of it boded well for Tom except for the tetanus shot. If he could get the details on that, he'd have a reasonable explanation for the blood on the knife and in the canoe. The absence of the scalp was another item that could provide reasonable doubt; however, if the signature of the knife matched the murder weapon, then he was back at square one.

He raised his gaze and took in Tom's pleading eyes.

"I know you didn't do it, but this doesn't look good on paper." He waved at the table. "There's nothing concrete we can offer to exonerate you. Are you sure you didn't catch dinner at Tanya's on any of these days?" Steve asked, knowing he was reaching for any alibi at this point, but he had to be sure.

Tom glanced at the dates again, a crease between his eyes hammering home his level of concentration to remember details that just blended together in a teenager's mind. And then the crease smoothed, and he tapped a date two months back. "Maybe," he said, meeting Steve's gaze.

"What did you have for dinner?"

Tom's eyebrows arched, and he shrugged.

"Come on. You need to do better than that. What did you eat that night?" Steve waited while Tom clicked off the meals he had at Tanya's for the past two months and then shook his head.

It was either lasagna or spaghetti or chicken parmesan. He signed. *Wednesdays are Italian night and I always tried to get an invitation if I could manage it.* He offered a shrug. *It beat trying to choke down Jennifer's cooking.*

Steve suppressed a grin. His wife had issues in the kitchen and most of his evenings had been taken up with the case, so he wasn't around to save the kids from her cooking. "Why didn't you say that to begin with?"

Because sometimes it didn't work out.

"Are you sure you had dinner with her family on this particular night?" Steve asked, praying the answer was a solid yes. Instead, doubt painted Tom's face.

I'm sorry, Uncle Steve, he signed, and his thoughts echoed the same sentiment.

"That's okay. I'll talk with Tanya's parents and see if I can get them to confirm you were there on that date."

Tom's gaze dropped to the table, and he nodded.

The gate buzzer interrupted them, and Steve stood, crossing to the monitor. Cleary gave him a wave and Steve opened the gate for his boss. He turned back to Tom and said, "Why don't you head upstairs?"

Tom nodded, and with one last glance at the table, he turned and disappeared up the stairs.

Steve got to the front door before Cleary and he waved him inside without the normal salutations. Cleary's tight jaw and fiery expression kept him quiet, and he suppressed the urge to dig into Cleary's mind to find out the reason for the open hostility radiating from the man.

"Are the kids around?"

"They're upstairs, why?"

Cleary spun toward Steve. "Chris Ryan was involved in the kidnapping ring?"

Steve didn't answer. He just turned and closed the door, keeping his back to Cleary while he closed his eyes and rested his forehead against the wood. "They watched the DVDs."

"Jesus Christ," Cleary muttered and peeled his jacket off. "You knew?"

Steve turned and met his boss' glare. "I knew Chris wasn't as clean as Ty made him out to be, but I did not know those tapes existed. If I did..."

Cleary's lips thinned, and the flurry of his thoughts matched the anger radiating from him.

"Internal affairs got wind of the information and they are taking a closer look at your situation."

"My situation?"

"The inheritance, the guardianship, control of their trust fund," Cleary said.

Steve's muscles clenched, and he had to force himself not to ball his hands into tight fists. "Why?"

Cleary took a deep breath. "They're looking at the current case. The tips you've given the police and the involvement of one of the Ryan kids. They are looking over your entire career right now and we both know there's enough unexplained events to draw even more scrutiny."

Steve didn't like where this was going. The unease that had taken over his bones increased, and he shifted his weight against the pressure. "They think I'm dirty?"

"They think you knew more about Chris Ryan than you've let on," he said, making quotes with his fingers as he said the name. "I haven't been contacted for a formal interview, but I'm sure I'm next."

"Why are you telling me this?"

"Because, until the investigation is completed, you are officially suspended. I'm here to collect your badge and gun."

Steve blinked as the accusations, and the consequences flitted through Cleary's mind. The shock of the suspension settled into his bones, creating a burning just under his skin. Instead of arguing or losing his temper, he turned and marched over to the table, grabbing his weapon and badge. When he turned, Cleary was a step behind him.

"I'm not sure I can protect your reputation this time." He took the items from Steve.

"I only knew the truth for a matter of weeks before Ty died."

"That doesn't matter. You didn't bring him in. Instead, you aided and abetted a known fugitive, and they are going to leverage that against you."

"Well, at least I've got one thing going for me." Steve crossed his arms.

"What's that?"

"New York. The district attorney there wouldn't dream of prosecuting me."

"You're probably right, but the Federal prosecutor doesn't have that kind of allegiance."

Steve's arms dropped to his side.

"Murder has no statute of limitations," Cleary said. "And the Aris case crossed state lines, so it's under federal jurisdiction. If they choose to go after you..."

"I'm looking at a stay in federal prison," Steve finished Cleary's sentence. He took a seat at the table and the mere thought of them questioning his integrity and his motives after over fifteen years of dedicated service irked him.

"Are you telling me Steve could go to prison?" Jennifer interrupted.

Steve turned toward the stairs, where Jennifer stood gawking at the two of them, her green eyes wide and shocked at the turn of the conversation.

"It's possible," Steve answered with a shrug and swung his gaze back to Cleary. "Have they talked to Sarah yet?"

"Yes. She wasn't thrilled with the line of questioning and said your heroics didn't seem to faze them one bit. They are on a witch hunt, and you are the target."

Steve sighed and nodded, scanning the contents of the table. "Who is assigned to this now?" He pointed at the Windwalker case file.

"I'll be working it with Sarah." Cleary glanced at Jennifer. "So, when you have another one of your visions, you need to contact one of us."

"We will," Steve said. "What about the case against Tom? Can you talk some sense into the prosecutor?"

"Do you have anything I can go to them with?"

Steve looked at the one date Tom had circled and wrote it down on a slip of paper, handing it to Cleary. "Tom believes he was at dinner at Tanya's house on that evening. It's the only alibi I have for him."

"The dead girl's parents?"

"Yes."

Cleary whistled and shook his head. "That's pretty thin."

"He was either sleeping in his room or with Tanya at the times the Windwalker struck."

"Can anyone confirm they saw him here on those mornings you think he was sleeping?"

"We sometimes drive to school together," CJ said as he stepped into the living room.

Cleary pointed to the calendar on the table. "Can you tell me if you drove on any of these dates?"

"Any of the murders on a Friday?"

Steve shook his head. "No, Jen and I already looked and none of the murders happened on days you two had sports events."

"Shit." CJ crossed to the calendar, flipping from page to page with disgust. He finally stopped and glared at Cleary. "My brother didn't kill those people."

"Ron, Tom doesn't fit the profile," Steve said, pulling the write up the FBI put together on the killer, handing it to Cleary.

"Have you ever caught him hurting small animals?"

CJ laughed. "Tom hand feeds the chipmunks. Animals flock to him like he's something special. No, he's never hurt an animal on purpose and the one time he hit one with the mower, he was so upset, he couldn't bring himself to mow the lawn for the rest of the summer. He bribed me with everything from doing all my chores for the rest of the year to letting me use his things whenever I wanted, just to get out of doing the lawn."

"What about the fish knife?"

"What about it?" CJ shrugged. "We fish off the bluff or out on the canoe all the time." He stared at Cleary and then swung his gaze to Steve. "They honestly believe Tom did this?"

Steve nodded, seeing the transition in CJ's facial features as they hardened, reminding Steve of Ty.

"That is fucking insane," he said, and Jennifer cleared her throat. CJ turned in her direction. "It is," he said.

"Language?" she said with her hands on her hips.

CJ turned away and rolled his eyes, meeting Steve's gaze.

Steve raised an eyebrow, bringing Jennifer's point home.

"Fine, sorry for swearing, but Tom didn't do this," he said as he waved toward the table before turning and heading upstairs.

Steve took a deep breath before bringing his glance back to Cleary. His boss knew enough about CJ Ryan to be nervous in his presence, but he was never willing to admit it. When his gaze met Steve's, he shifted. "I'll check this out." He lifted the paper and gave a nod on his way out the door.

"Jail?" Jennifer asked after the front door closed.

Steve gave her a knowing look. "We knew that's always been a possibility if the truth about Ty ever got out," he said.

"But..."

"Look, I made a choice, and I'd do it again in a heartbeat." He crossed to her, pulling her against him. "It's all just hearsay, and with my record, no judge will convict me just on hearsay alone."

"But what if they ask you if you knew who Chris really was?"

Steve shifted and dropped his gaze.

"You'd lie?" she asked, reading his hesitation wrong.

The one thing he prided himself on was telling the truth. He had lied for a living for years while undercover, but ever since the aftermath of what happened with Kyle Winslow, he hadn't lied to anyone, never mind in a court of law, and he wasn't about to start now.

"No." He met her stare. They both knew what his honesty would cost, and Jennifer pulled away, heading into the gym to work off her worry.

Steve watched her go and sighed, turning his attention back to the papers strewn across the table, wondering if his boss would find a way to exonerate Tom, otherwise this all was going to culminate in the perfect storm.

Saving Face
Chapter 11

CJ SAT ON THE edge of Tom's bed and stared out the window at the ocean. "We need to find the Windwalker." He turned his gaze toward his brother.

Tom nodded and signed that Uncle Steve would find him.

"They suspended Steve because they found Dad's tapes in the attic. They think he knew about Dad and made him sign over all our money before he died."

"Bu hi," Tom said.

"I know. There's a shit storm coming on all fronts, and it isn't going to be pretty."

*We knew someday...*Tom started and dropped his hands. He didn't want to finish the sentence and silence settled between the two of them.

"Yeah," CJ finally whispered. The weight of his father's sins bore down on him, and he closed his eyes. "At least you've got a father you can be proud of," he added, glancing at the Oscar sitting on the shelf.

Without Dad, neither of us would be here, Tom signed. *He made us possible.*

CJ laughed. "Still doesn't make this any easier. I've got his blood in my veins and sometimes, I swear I can feel it burning the good out of me, like some crazy demon seed, just waiting for the right moment to take over my life." He inhaled and slowly released the lungful of air. "I can't stand by and watch while they cart you away, Tom. You're all I've got left."

That's not true. You and Sandy have been together since Dad died.

CJ closed his eyes, drifting back to that day and Sandy's innocent kiss on his cheek, making him feel special even in the midst of the loss crushing him. Less than two weeks later, she had helped to keep him together when his mother's coffin settled in the ground next to their father. Sandy had held his hand tight, her bright eyes shining with tears and her boundless energy kept under wraps just for him. Since then, there had been no one else that moved him, or made him laugh harder than she did, and it sucked that she lived in Connecticut. "Yeah, but she's not around most of the time. Besides, you're the only family I've got left."

Don't worry about me. They aren't going to convict me for something I didn't do.

CJ raised an eyebrow at Tom, keeping his skepticism in check. He knew from Steve's silent assessment that they were building a strong case against Tom, even if it was all circumstantial. Tom's faith was misplaced, and CJ decided it was up to him to protect his brother, even if it meant he'd have to take the fall.

"Don't worry Tom, this will all go away when I find that bastard." He flashed a grin that his mother would have recognized in an instant. It matched his father's sadistic angel of death smile.

You know, you look like a crazy fuck when you grin like that. Tom signed and sent a smirk his way.

"Aye-up." CJ stood. "Steve might not be able to find this guy, but it's now my life's mission." He walked out of the room and headed down to the kitchen where Steve sat going over the case file for the millionth time.

"I want to help find the Windwalker."

Steve looked up from the papers. "The last time I enlisted your help on a case your brother almost died."

CJ took a seat on the opposite side of the table. "I know, but this is different. I'm almost eighteen and you know damn well I'm smarter than my old man ever was." The scoff from the great beyond silenced him. His father was listening and while he couldn't hear or see him directly, Steve channeled him just as clearly as if he was standing in the room. "I am," he challenged the air. "And I'm on the right side of the law, which was something that escaped you most of your life."

"I wouldn't piss off your father like that," Steve said, gaining his attention, and CJ saw the fleeting smile of approval before it disappeared from his lips.

"Tom had it right the other day. Angel or not, he's got no right to preach to us about what's right or wrong, especially with his past."

Steve had always been good at hiding his feelings, and now was no different. "He tried to raise you boys with a moral compass despite his past, and I think he did a pretty good job."

CJ crossed his arms. "My mother did a good job."

"CJ, cut him some slack."

"Do you know how many lives he ruined?"

Steve raised an eyebrow. "I know. Believe me, I know more about your father and his life than I ever wanted to, so cut the preaching." He folded the case file and pushed it aside.

CJ glanced at the closed file. "You know, I've done some reading up on the psychological profile of serial killers..."

Steve cut him off. "CJ, I know you're smart and motivated, but searching on Google isn't the same..."

Irritation snaked over his skin in a hot prickly path, and CJ framed a glare in Steve's direction. "Don't belittle my intelligence. You know I've got more behind this than just a genius IQ. I've got as much insight into this psycho as you do, especially with Jennifer's visions. There's an arrogance underlying his actions. An absolute certainty he will never get caught. He thinks he is as elusive as the wind and takes great pride in that. If we dangle the right carrot in front of him, we can make him step out of his pattern. We can make him screw up."

"What are you talking about?"

"Isn't part of a serial killer's profile the need for the attention?"

"Yes."

"If we take the media attention away from him, wouldn't that piss him off?"

Steve leaned back, studying CJ in a way that made him shift under his stare. "What are you suggesting?"

He spread his arms out. "Let's give the world the Windwalker."

"Tom already has enough…"

"I'm not talking about Tom. I'm talking about me. Ty Ryan's son. A living, breathing monster, just like his father." Even CJ heard the bitterness in his tone, and he kept eye contact with Steve, watching his expression morph into one of open-mouthed horror.

"Why would you even contemplate that?"

"Tom didn't do this, but he doesn't have an alibi. Let's give them something else. A sensation that the media will pounce on and we both know that will piss off the actual killer."

"CJ, I don't think you understand the ramifications of what you're suggesting."

"I'll confess."

Steve's lips thinned, and his eyes narrowed. "No."

"I know as much of the details as you do."

"Lying will backfire."

"How do you know?"

"Because it always does," he said. "What happens if you're wrong, and it doesn't draw the killer out? What if he just fades into the woodwork and you're left sitting on death row with a taped confession?"

The smack of flesh against wood pulled their attention to the living room. Tom stood in the entry to the kitchen, his face red with anger and his palm firmly planted on the wall. "No," he said clearly and with such force that CJ dropped his gaze to the floor.

Just because you're supercharged doesn't mean you should always step in to protect me. I can hold my own and if anyone is going to be bait, it's me.

Tom's thoughts intruded into CJ's mind, leaving his ears ringing at the volume, and he raised his gaze to meet his brother's fiery glare.

For a fucking genius, you can be such a stupid ass.

"I'm just..."

Stop. Just stop, okay?

"I can catch him," CJ said.

"That is just as arrogant as the killer thinking he'll never get caught," Steve said. "And the price of thinking like that is way too high." His gaze traveled to Tom and back. "Arrogance isn't something we can afford right now. Neither is lying."

"But..."

"No," Steve cut him off. "I can't condone you lying to draw the killer out."

CJ snapped his teeth together against the derogatory comment that filled his mind.

"The press is already going to have a field day once word of Tom's arrest leaks out, and right now, my primary goal is to make sure they don't convict him." He drew in a breath. "We've got a month before the next new moon and if nothing changes between now and then, that tracking device on Tom's ankle will clear him when the psycho kills again. In the meantime, we've got to get his defense ready." Steve turned his gaze from CJ to Tom. "Your lawyer will be here tomorrow at ten. Make sure you're up and ready to talk."

Tom nodded and sent a warning glare to CJ, his thoughts echoing the look. *Don't do anything stupid.*

Saving Face
Chapter 12

STEVE WAITED UNTIL THE boys settled in their rooms before crossing into the gym. Jennifer was still going on the elliptical, flipping through the pages of the script, her lips moving silently as she read. He took a sip from his scotch and leaned on the doorjamb, waiting for her to look up. Sweat beads dripped down her face like sprinkles on a windowpane and he smiled.

Jennifer flipped the page and her gaze bounced to his, her expression transitioning from concentration to surprise, and she reached up, pulling the buds from her ears. "How long have you been standing there?"

"Just a few minutes." He pointed to the script. "Are you reconsidering?"

Jennifer's gaze dropped to the pages in front of her and back. "No. I just needed something to take my mind off everything."

Steve's smile soured, and he nodded, raising the glass. "Me, too."

Jennifer sighed and slowed her pace. "You shouldn't be drinking."

"I'm not on duty." He refrained from adding he probably wouldn't be on duty ever again after all this settled, but he didn't want to see the relief cross over her features. She hated his job, and always had, especially since it put him in the path of danger.

Bitterness swept through him at the full realization that his career was over. There was no way he'd be allowed to continue in the FBI with felony charges on his record, even if it went nowhere. He drained his glass to quell the budding frustration.

Her lips thinned in response, pressing together in that look of disapproval that always irked him. He cocked his head in a silent challenge and wiped his lips with his shirtsleeve.

"So, you're choosing to get drunk?"

"Seems like the best option right now," he said.

The elliptical stopped and Jennifer leveled a glare at him. "What kind of message is that sending to the boys?"

He raised an eyebrow. "Look, I need to blow off some steam," he started, and when she opened her mouth to counter his logic, he put his hand up. "My career is over. Tom may go to jail for the rest of his life, and CJ wants to play cat and mouse with the killer by confessing and drawing the media attention to him instead of his brother. So right now, my option is to drink, otherwise, I'm going to lose it. And it isn't pretty when I lose it these days."

Voicing his frustrations left his blood boiling, and he clenched his teeth, storming out of the room and onto the terrace. He wanted nothing more than to catch the Windwalker and throw the bastard in jail for life, but now, he'd have to sit on the sidelines and watch while others figured it out. Anger bloomed, lancing his skin, pooling in his stomach, and he needed to let the coiled beast out. Otherwise, he would self-destruct.

His gaze landed on their Olympic size heated pool, and he allowed a fraction of power to escape, aimed at the pristine pool. The water burst into a boiling mass, pushing gales of steam toward the sky.

The release of power did more than the drink had, and the burn of frustration lessened into a dull ache. He closed his eyes, reining the power back in and sending a counter command for the water to cool back to the balmy one hundred degrees they set for the winter. When the hissing stopped, he opened his eyes.

More than half the pool had evaporated under his flash of anger, and he sighed, crossing to the controls and turning on the faucet to fill up the pool via underground water lines.

"Are you finished with your little temper tantrum?" Ty's voice echoed in his head.

"Yeah. I'm done," Steve muttered. *In more ways than one*, he thought.

If you tell them the truth, will they go easy on you? Ty's voice filled his head.

Steve scoffed and flipped the water off. "The truth? You really think the truth will help me?" Steve laughed, and the bitter edge filled the night. "Which truth are you talking about, Ty? Let's see...that I knew exactly who you were for a good couple weeks, or that I blackmailed you into helping me? Or that I decided it would be better to use your skills to catch Kyle instead of bringing you in. Wow, yeah, thank you for your insight," he snarled at the air over his shoulder.

No need to get sarcastic. Ty's wings fluttered.

"I should have hauled your ass in the moment I got Eric's memories," Steve said.

"I wouldn't have let you."

Steve spun and stared at CJ. "I thought you were in bed."

CJ shrugged. "You haven't done a good job of keeping your thoughts under wraps tonight. I don't know if it's the alcohol or what, but dude, your anger is pelting me like a hailstorm. You need to chill."

The alcohol definitely influenced his tongue and brought his sarcasm to the surface, but this time, he was entitled. "If your father hadn't been such an idiot, we wouldn't be facing this predicament."

CJ smiled. "I can't argue with you there."

I wanted something to remember my brother, considering I was the one who got him killed. The ruffle of feathers accompanied Ty's voice.

Steve paused, and the heat in his face dissolved. "What exactly is on those video's Ty?" he asked instead of trying to filter through the man's memories embedded in his mind.

There are only a couple of videos with Chris, but they are damning enough. One shows the first time I bet on Jessica and she didn't disappoint me and the second is Chris's death. The rest are Jess and I. I couldn't erase any of them, even after Jess and I got married, so I just hid them away.

"So, you're telling me the actual truth is about to blow wide on this, not just that your brother was involved?"

Yes.

"Fuck," Steve muttered and met CJ's stare, wondering what the whole truth would do to both CJ and Tom.

"I already know what my father did. He denied killing for sport like his stepbrother did, but he was the one who orchestrated the explosions that convinced the world the people they kidnapped were dead." CJ sighed. "He isn't innocent by any stretch of the imagination, and if I had been a little older when you came into our lives, I might have felt differently, but at that time, there was no way I was letting my father go to jail."

"He really tried to atone for his sins," Steve said, coming to the criminal's defense.

CJ nodded and offered a smile, even though his eyes misted over. "I know, but that's only because of my mother."

"Just so we're on the same page. I'm going to be under the gun for this," he said. "And if they ask me if I knew who your father really was, I'm going to tell the truth."

"I'll back you up if you need me to. I know you didn't blackmail him for money."

Steve smiled at his naivety. "Thanks, but..."

I made provisions for that. Ty's voice interrupted.

Steve cocked his head. "What?"

Contact Lynn Trueman. She's got a few legal documents that will help.

"Why didn't you pipe up sooner?" Steve asked, looking at the sky while irritation snaked over his skin. The chuckle from the great beyond set another fire in his stomach.

"It's because he's still an asshole," CJ said, his jaw tense with aggravation, and he turned, stomping back into the house, leaving Steve alone with his father's ghost.

Saving Face
Chapter 13

THE COFFEE MAKER RUMBLED as the last of the brown fuel filled the pot and Steve glanced at the clock. Neither Tom nor CJ was up, and he closed his eyes, focusing on Tom. "Get your ass out of bed." He shot the thought with the accuracy of a master archer.

A thump upstairs was his reward, and he focused back on the fry pan, flipping his eggs. He grabbed the plate and slid his breakfast from the pan before settling down at the table.

Tom wandered into the kitchen, rubbing the sleep from his eyes. *That was mean,* he signed.

Steve met his gaze. "I could have dumped a bucket of ice water on you."

Tom rolled his eyes and stared at the spread on the table. His stomach growled in response, and he took a seat where Steve had put a stack of pancakes.

"I told you I wanted you up and ready to talk before your lawyer got here." He pointed toward the clock. "You've got enough time to eat and clean up."

Thanks, he signed and downed the stack before Steve was finished with his breakfast.

After Tom disappeared upstairs and the shower started, Steve flipped open his phone and pressed the speed dial. Cleary answered after the first ring. "Ron, did you follow up with..."

"Tom wasn't at their house that evening. They were out at a dinner party."

"Shit," Steve said.

"The lab results came back and there were traces of Tanya's blood on the knife found in Tom's room."

"I'm aware of that. Tom said Tanya got a splinter in her foot and he used the knife to remove it. They should have a record of her getting a tetanus shot." He paused and rubbed his face. "Please tell me his knife doesn't have the same signature as the one used on the victims." He waited.

"That's about the only good news I can offer you."

Steve let out the breath he was holding, exhaling audibly. "Thanks, Ron."

"Are you one hundred percent sure he is innocent?"

"Yes, I am. Tom is not the Windwalker."

Cleary responded with silence. Paper shuffled in the background. "One more thing..."

Steve closed his eyes, pulling the information through the phone line even before Cleary said the words.

"The press was given a heads up, so expect things to get even nastier."

The conversation with CJ surfaced, and Steve sighed. "Maybe that's not a bad thing."

"It's going to make that kid's life a living hell," Cleary said.

The creak of the stairs caught Steve's attention, and he glanced up into Tom's questioning stare. "I imagine it will, but if we play this right, it could also draw the real killer out of the woodwork."

Silence greeted his comment from both Tom and Cleary.

"I don't know what you're thinking..." Cleary started.

"Thanks for giving me a heads up," Steve interrupted. "Tom's lawyer just arrived."

"Don't do anything I'll have to arrest you for," Cleary shot through the line before Steve ended the call.

Steve put the phone on the table and met Tom's inquisitive gaze. "Expect the press to hound you wherever you go until this is over."

Tom's eyebrows rose.

"Someone leaked the details of your arrest to the press."

Tom crossed the room and took a seat, his eyebrows scrunched together in thought. When he raised his gaze, he signed, "So, do you think the press being focused on me will bring the killer out?"

Steve didn't have an answer for him. He hoped it would, but he wasn't sure what kind of backlash this would cause. "I don't know," he answered.

"What's the worst that could happen?" Tom asked and shrugged.

Steve stared at him for a moment. "He could come after you," he said, finally voicing his underlying fear.

Tom's gaze widened, and his thoughts jumped to his last view of Tanya. The shiver that followed was visible and Steve gave a nod, stood from the table, crossed to the front door, and glanced outside.

His mood soured at the sea of reporters lining the road outside the gates, and he closed his eyes. "God damn vultures," he muttered and crossed to the television. He flipped it to a local news station.

Tom made the headlines all right, and that wasn't the only buzz on the airways. The fact that Chris Ryan was really Ty Aris was all over the news channels as well. Steve threw the remote onto the table and stared at the continued speculation of the media, none of which had a grain of truth.

The phone rang, and Steve picked it up without looking at the caller id. "Hello."

"Can I speak with Agent Williams?"

"This is Steve," he said, recognizing the frail voice of Russ Campbell, Jessica's father.

"Did you know?"

Steve closed his eyes. "Yes, sir," he said, not offering the litany of excuses filling his mind.

"That bastard..." he started.

"Jessica knew who she married, sir. She knew it was Ty," he said, stopping the pending rant.

Silence met his statement.

"How do you know?"

Steve inhaled. "Because she offered to help me in return for not arresting him."

More silence.

"I don't understand."

"Your daughter was in love with Ty for years, and when he came back into her life, neither one of them was willing to walk away again."

"But..." he trailed off.

"Ty laid his life on the line several times for her, sir," Steve said.

"How did you figure it out?"

"Something happened with Eric and that's when I found out," he said. The Campbells never knew about her special talents, or that of her children, and Steve didn't want to be the one to explain that.

More silence.

"I knew there was something off about Chris, but I had never seen my daughter that happy," Russ whispered.

"She was happy, sir," Steve said, remembering the way she looked at Ty. She was happy until he walked into their lives. A lump formed in his throat, and he swallowed it.

"How did he do it? How did he make it out of that place alive?"

"Supernatural intervention," Steve said.

Silence filled the line and then Russ said, "Eric."

Shock filtered through Steve. Maybe he knew more than Steve gave him credit for. Russ was one of those people he could never get a read on, and now he knew why. The man knew how to create static. "Yes. Eric was a very special kid."

"My Jessie was special too, but I didn't think she knew it."

"She didn't until she met Ty."

That statement hung in the air, and Steve heard Russ blow a stream of air through his lips. "They are accusing you of blackmailing him," he said. There was no underlying question, just a statement in a fashion that left it open.

Steve glanced at Tom and then out the window at the sea of reporters. "I traded my wife's life for his freedom," he admitted. "But I never blackmailed him for money or custody of their kids."

"Can you explain to me why he insisted you raise those boys?"

"It's going to sound insane," he said.

Russ laughed. "Son, right now nothing would surprise me," he said.

"He wanted me to watch over CJ."

"Why?"

Steve turned his back on Tom's blatant stare. "Because CJ is more special than Eric, Jessica and Ty put together," he whispered. "And I'm now equipped to deal with that," he added, hoping Russ would be able to piece together the truth through his cryptic answer.

When Russ didn't speak, Steve added, "The transfer started with Eric when we were at Quantico and that's how I knew who Chris really was."

"Did anyone else know who he was?" Russ asked. The bite in his tone traveled through the line, and Steve winced.

"More people than you realize, but there was no proof to back up the accusations. I didn't have proof to haul him in. I only had what I saw in Eric's memories, and that wouldn't have stood up in court."

"Who else knew?"

"Besides Jessica and Eric?"

"Yes."

"Emily, Tom and Dan," Steve said.

Russ coughed on the line, wheezing as he sputtered and tried to catch his breath. Finally, his wheezing calmed. "Dan knew?"

"He figured it out around the time they got married."

"And Tom?"

"Yes, he knew the minute Ty walked back into their lives."

"And they didn't kill him?"

"No, but that's not to say they didn't want to. Dan got a punch in, and Tom pulled a gun on him once, but that was about the extent of it."

Russ exhaled on the phone. "If I had known, he wouldn't have been so lucky."

Steve chuckled. "Yeah, he pretty much knew that about you."

Russ's laugh was genuine this time. "How are the kids handling all this?"

Steve took a seat on the couch. "They knew about their father's past, but I'm not sure how they're going to handle it now that it's public." He slumped into the thick cushions. "Did the news down there also carry that Tom's been arrested?"

"No. What happened?" His concern filled the line.

"They think he's the Windwalker."

"The Windwalker?"

"The serial killer here in Maine."

"That's insane."

The buzzer rang, and Steve stood, crossing to the window. A car waited at the entrance. "Russ, I've got to go. Tom's lawyer is here,"

"If you need anything, let me know," Russ said. "And thanks for leveling with me. Most people in your predicament would have lied."

"I've got no reason to lie," Steve said. "I'll tell the kids you send them your best," he added and hung up the phone.

The buzzer sounded again, and Steve crossed to the controls, opening the gate for the car waiting amidst the press. He stared at the line, putting up an invisible wall against the stragglers who tried to breach the security, smiling at the confused expressions when they couldn't move through the opening. As soon as the car was through, Steve shut the gate on the crowd.

"Your lawyer's here," he said to Tom and opened the front door.

Sheldon Kryminski looked nothing like what Steve imagined. He was young, not even thirty, and he looked like he belonged more on a beach volleyball court than in a courthouse. Steve looked beyond him at the car, thinking there must be some mistake.

"Agent Williams, I presume," Sheldon said as he climbed the stairs.

The voice was right, but it didn't go along with the boyish appearance. "Mr. Kryminski?" Steve asked.

"Please, call me Sheldon." He stuck out his hand.

Steve reciprocated and was pleased to find a firm handshake. This kid transmitted confidence and had an open mind, despite all he'd heard relating to the case. Steve waved him inside and sent one last glare toward the paparazzi before closing the door on the high zoom lenses.

"Right this way." Steve led Sheldon into the family room, where Tom sat staring at the television and the continuing flow of news about the man who raised him. Steve reached over and turned the television off. "Tom, this is your lawyer, Mr. Kryminski."

Tom stood and nodded hello before offering his hand.

"Please, call me Sheldon," he said, shaking Tom's hand.

Tom nodded again and signed, "Thank you, Sheldon."

Sheldon put down his attaché case, stripped his coat, and handed it to Steve before settling across from Tom. Once he had his legal pad and pen placed on the table, he launched into fluid sign language, surprising both Tom and Steve.

"I a hea." When Sheldon's brow creased, Tom signed, "I can hear. I just can't talk."

Sheldon smiled. "I'm sorry. I just assumed you were deaf when Agent Williams asked if we had a sign language expert on staff."

"He appreciates the gesture," Steve said.

Sheldon nodded and focused on Tom. "Now, let's start at the beginning," he said.

"Tom..."

"—I'm sorry Agent Williams, but I'd like to talk with my client alone, if you don't mind."

"Excuse me?"

"I'd like to talk with Tom alone. Once I'm done, I'll want to ask you some questions as well." Sheldon smiled.

Steve exchanged a glance with Tom and nodded, heading upstairs, leaving them alone.

TOM'S GAZE MOVED FROM the stairway, and he waited a moment before turning his attention to his lawyer. "What do you want to know?" he signed.

Sheldon picked up the pad and met Tom's gaze. "Tell me about Tanya," he said.

Tom inhaled and nodded. The fact that the lawyer knew her name without glancing at a note impressed him. "I've dated a lot of girls, but Tanya was special, you know?" he signed. "So, when she broke up with me, it hurt. A lot, especially when she told me the reason." He looked down at the floor.

"What was the reason?"

Tom met his lawyer's gaze. "Because I can't French kiss," he signed and almost smiled at the horror reflected in Sheldon's expression and the fact his hand paused on the notepad.

With a couple of blinks, Sheldon seemed to regain his composure. "Take me through the rest of the day after she broke up with you."

"I got angry and started slicing up all the pictures I have of her," he signed and felt the heat bloom in his cheeks. "I wish I hadn't done that."

"Why not?"

"I don't have any more pictures and she's gone," he signed. His vision wobbled under the sudden sheen of tears. He blinked them away.

Sheldon nodded for him to continue.

"CJ and I snuck out that night. We had been told we couldn't go to a party on the other side of town, and I thought Tanya was going to be there. I decided the best way to get her back was to take her to Steve's place in Brooksfield and try to talk some sense into her, but she wasn't at the party." He shrugged. "I ended up hot-wiring a car and CJ and I took off for Brooksfield, anyway."

"You stole a car?"

Tom nodded. "Yes, and we got caught, but Uncle Steve got them to drop the charges."

"Okay. Then, what did you do?"

"Tanya runs on the river paths every morning before school. I figured that was my best bet to get her alone. I needed to know if there was anything I could do to get her back." He stopped and looked at the coffee table. "I didn't even know if she'd still be out there." He met Sheldon's gaze and bit his lip. "I ran the path once and her car was still in the parking lot, so I turned around and ran it a second time. That's when I saw her in the water." He dropped his hands to his lap, balling them into fists and then stretching the ache out of his fingers. "I don't know if she was there the first time..." He closed his eyes, clenched his teeth and covered his face.

"What did you do when you saw her?"

"I ran into the water and pulled her up the bank. I kept slipping in the mud and it wasn't until I got clear of the water that I really looked. I'm not sure I could have touched her if I had looked before I reacted." He clenched his fists again.

"Why not?" Sheldon asked.

Tom's vision blurred, and tears overflowed, burning hot paths down his cheeks. "The Windwalker took her face."

Saving Face
Chapter 14

STEVE ENTERED THE BEDROOM and crossed to the bed, where Jennifer was still curled up under the covers. He took a seat on the edge and brushed her hair out of her face, and she stirred, stretching like a cat. Her morning smile and her sleepy green eyes always warmed his heart, and he found himself smiling back at her.

"Good morning." He planted a kiss on her forehead.

"What time is it?" she asked, and yawned.

"A little after ten," he said.

She sat up and looked at the clock and then back at him. "Is Tom's lawyer here?"

"Yes, they're talking downstairs."

"And you didn't wake me?" She threw the covers back and tried to slip past him, but he grabbed her around the waist and pulled her to him.

"He wants to talk with Tom alone right now." He kissed her bare shoulder.

She pushed away from him enough to meet his gaze. "What are you doing?"

His cheeks warmed, and he shrugged. "Killing some time."

Her eyebrows shot into arches, and she laughed, peeling herself out of his grasp. "That is so not appropriate right now." She headed toward the bathroom, shutting the door on his suggestive leer.

Steve grinned and glanced out the window, eavesdropping on her thoughts. His smile faded, and he sighed. Taking her silent cue, he stood and made the bed. "Sorry, honey," he whispered.

The bathroom door opened, and she looked out at him. "Your timing sucks."

"I know. But you just looked so cute and cuddly this morning." He offered her a shrug.

"Have you spoken to Ron yet?" She walked into the closet.

"Yes. Tom has no concrete alibi for any of the murders." He heard her curse under her breath.

"So, what now?" She stepped out of the closet in jeans and a t-shirt, looking every bit as sexy as she had in her silk negligee.

He met her gaze and shook his head. Her question set off a dozen answers in his mind, all of which were laced with sarcasm, but he kept them in check and offered the only honest answer that came to mind. "I don't know."

Worry lines etched into the corner of her lips and she crossed the room, stopping in front of him. "Tom's innocent. You can't let them convict him of something he didn't do."

"I feel just as helpless as you do." He stood, crossing to the window. His gaze landed on the harbor and the glistening water. "And there isn't a thing I can do about it right now." The frustration of those words bloomed in his stomach, souring his breakfast.

Her warm hand landed on his shoulder, and he reached up, covering it with his.

"Russ called this morning," he said, changing the subject and turning toward her. "He saw the news story about Ty."

Jennifer's eyes widened. "It made the news already?"

"Yep, and that's not the only thing that made the news around here. We've got a flock of reporters out at the gate."

"You're kidding?"

"No. Some jackass leaked the details of Tom's arrest."

Her features hardened, and the mamma bear returned. "Damn them," she whispered. "Don't they know what the media will do to our sweet boy?"

"He's not a boy anymore, and having his face splashed all over the airwaves may work in our favor."

"How?" She stepped away, putting distance between them.

He looked out at the ocean. "It's going to draw the killer out." He met her gaze. "One way or another, when that bastard strikes again, Tom will be exonerated."

"And what if he comes after Tom?"

Steve considered this and looked back at the ocean. The only place the killer could get to Tom was on their home turf. He swung his gaze back to his wife. "I don't think the killer is dumb enough to attack us here."

Her eyebrow rose, and she crossed her arms. They both knew he had underestimated the brashness of a killer before, and it had cost them dearly.

"This isn't the same," he started and closed his mouth. He turned back to the scenic view and assessed the likelihood of an attack on their home. The bluff wasn't steep enough to deter a good climber, and the boys had trekked down the winding path next to their house with a canoe plenty of times, so a water attack was possible, and this killer knew how to use the tide to his advantage. He surveyed the rock wall and then turned back to her. "The only way the killer could come is from the water. The rest of the property is pretty secure."

She wrapped her arms tighter around herself and glanced out the window.

"The alarm system on this house is first rate as well."

Jennifer nodded, but he knew this didn't calm the unease building in her.

"Either CJ or I will be here with you and Tom at all times."

She turned her gaze to him. "Promise?"

"I promise." He pulled her into his arms. He leaned in to give her a morning kiss, but a knock at the bedroom door stopped him before he could taste her lips. Steve closed his eyes and sighed. "Come in."

CJ stepped into the room, looking dejected. "Tom and his lawyer asked me to leave." He flopped in the rocking chair near the dresser.

"You're not alone. I got kicked out as well." Steve gave Jennifer a quick peck on the cheek before letting her go. "Your grandfather called this morning." He focused on CJ. He took a seat on the side of the bed.

"Why?"

"He asked about your father."

CJ's head cocked to the side and then his sleepy expression hardened. "It's all over the news?"

Steve nodded, and CJ turned toward the flat screen. It turned on, tuning in to Fox News. The top story of the day was about his father, and Steve watched CJ's reaction to the speculations tossed around by the newscasters.

"They don't know shit," he said after the story transitioned to the political state of the union. He sent a nod toward the television, and it turned off.

"No, they don't. It's all just speculation at this time and I don't want you to say a word to the press about your father or your brother. Are we clear?"

A crease appeared between CJ's eyes, and he stood, crossing to the guest room. Steve followed in time to see CJ push the curtain back and stare at the sea of reporters. "No wonder it sounds like I'm in an assembly," he said, his voice lowering in disgust at the view and even more so by the thoughts of the crowd.

Steve glanced out the window, allowing the thoughts to make it through the barrier he'd built up over the years. The low din of white noise increased until it sounded like an intense sporting event, with thoughts screaming over each other, and he turned away, buffering his mind against the noise, letting the curtain fall again.

"I'm serious, not a word," he said, meeting CJ's gaze.

CJ glanced back out the window. "But..."

"Tom's going to need your support and provoking the press isn't going to help," Steve said.

"What about you? They're already speculating you're dirty and questioning your career record on national television. That's just not right."

"I can take care of myself. Right now, we need to focus on your brother and let this situation fall where it may," Steve said.

"What if they arrest you?"

"Then it's your job to keep Jen and Tom safe."

CJ stepped back, blinking and looking between Steve and the window. "Safe?"

"Yes. Remember what you said last night about the hype from the press?"

CJ nodded.

"With all this, Tom may become his next target." Steve waved toward the window and sighed. "I was hoping to keep his arrest under wraps for as long as possible, but I guess that's blown to hell now."

Saving Face
Chapter 15

THE ALARM SOUNDED, AND Tom slammed his hand on the buzzer, shutting the annoying sound off. He rolled onto his back and stared at the ceiling, wondering just how crappy his first day back at school would be. The news had filleted him and hinted that his upbringing could have been the reason he went astray. Interviews with Tanya's parents cut him deeper than any of the other false accusations, their teary-eyed pleas as to why hit a raw nerve.

He wanted the same answers and if he ever got his hand on the son of a bitch, he wouldn't pussyfoot around with asking why. Instead, he'd crush every bone in the bastard's body one by one. For the first time in his life, the idea of inflicting pain was one he relished.

CJ watched the news stories in silence, but Tom knew better. Anger stewed under his brother's neutral exterior, and it was only a matter of time before CJ blew sky high. He could see it in his eyes, that frantic need to control the situation, to shut the assholes up.

Steve had been clear with both of them. Not one word was to seep to the press, but Tom knew CJ wouldn't be able to keep to that directive. At least not for long.

The rap of knuckles on his door drew him out of his reverie. "Ye, I'm up," he mumbled and rolled out of bed. Dread wrapped her cold hand around his chest, applying just enough pressure to make breathing difficult. He grabbed a clean pair of boxers and jeans and headed for the shower. The hot water lulled him into his normal morning stupor, and he closed his eyes, letting the warmth heat his core, melting the stress from his muscles.

He shook the sleep from his head and turned the water off, stepping into the steam-filled bathroom. With a towel secured around his waist, he pulled the curtain aside and stepped out of the tub. His progress halted as he stared at the ghost, standing less than a foot away.

Her eyes scanned his wet form and returned to his face. A smile formed on the pouty lips and the impact on Tom was immediate. His vision blurred, and he stepped closer.

"Tanya," he whispered, and her eyes widened.

"Your voice." She reached for him. "It's beautiful."

Her hand landed on his chest, and he closed his eyes at the feel of her spirit. Warmth flooded through him, and he covered her hand, glancing down at the texture of her ghostly skin before raising his gaze back to hers.

"Honey, you're dead," he said, his voice articulating perfectly in his head, but not in his ears, the lack of a tongue impairing his spoken words. "That's why you can hear my voice."

She blinked, pulling her hand away from his chest. A crease appeared between her eyes. "Dead?"

While nodding confirmation to her question, a thought crossed his mind. He stepped closer, meeting her gaze with an intensity he didn't comprehend. Now that she was a ghost, she heard his real voice, and the possibilities became endless. His heart pumped a burning need through his skin, one that he knew was wrong, but he had to know if he could give her what she wanted now that she was gone.

He pulled her into his arms, kissing her the way she always wanted. The ghost of his tongue mingled with hers, and the world stopped. Every sensation flooded him, filling him with both elation and regret. The loss compounded, leaving his legs weak and unsteady, and he reached for the wall, stumbling back in shock. His breath locked in his chest and his vision wavered through a fresh set of tears.

When he met her gaze, her hand flew to cover her already gaping mouth.

"I didn't get there in time to save you," he said, and his chest constricted, shutting off his voice. Hot tears slid down his cheeks and he dropped his chin to his chest, trying to get his shit together.

"Oh, babe." She wrapped her arms around his neck in a heartfelt hug.

A sob escaped from his chest, and he held her ghost until she faded into the steamy mist, and he stood empty and shivering, with his haunted gaze staring back from the mirror.

CJ STOOD OUTSIDE THE bathroom, his head down and his eyes closed, listening with his mind's eye. Tom's soft sobs bled through the door, and he put his hand on the wood, wishing there was something he could do to wipe out the pain in his brother's heart.

Another presence interrupted his concentration, and he opened his eyes, glancing down the hall. Steve stood with his arms crossed and a disapproving look etched onto his face, and CJ shook his head, silently telling Steve to leave it alone.

The sternness in Steve's stance softened and his glance transitioned to the door and back. Concern flared in his eyes, and he took a step in his direction.

CJ put his hand up and shook his head. "I got this." He turned the doorknob. He pushed open the door and a waft of steam escaped.

Tom straightened his back when the cool air filtered into the room, displacing the steam. He finished buttoning his jeans before he turned and met CJ's gaze.

"You okay?" CJ asked.

"I'm fine," Tom signed and swiped the towel off the floor, tossing it over the towel rack.

CJ stared at his blood-shot eyes and blotchy cheeks. "You don't look fine." He stepped to the sink to brush his teeth.

Tom stiffened and took a breath. "Please, just leave it alone." The act of signing the words drained what little energy he had left, and his hands fell to his sides.

CJ spit the paste from his mouth and dropped the toothbrush in the holder before meeting his brother's gaze. "You gotta talk sometime."

No. I don't.

The thought filled CJ's head, and he pressed his lips together. "Cut the crap. I know she was here, and I know what's going on in your head."

"You don't know shit," he signed.

"Then tell me you weren't just thinking about suicide."

Tom's gaze dropped to the floor.

"It's not the answer." He crossed his arms and tightened his jaw. "What do you think attempted suicide would do to your case?"

The muscles in Tom's jaw jumped, and his glare met CJ's. "What do you want from me?"

"I want you to stop sulking and start figuring out how to win," CJ said. "You do remember winning, right?"

"Win what?"

"Your freedom. Your honor," CJ replied. "The right to go where you please." He waved toward Tom's ankle bracelet.

"Even if I do win, it doesn't matter. Tanya is still dead. That's not going to change," Tom signed. His face flushed with anger, and he turned away.

CJ grabbed his arm. "I know you cared about her, but it's not like she was the only girl on the planet."

"Fuck off." Tom yanked his arm from CJ and slammed the bathroom door behind him.

Frustration fluttered in CJ's stomach as he stared at the closed door. He glanced at his reflection and bit his lip, wondering if he should do something drastic. Tom would not act on his downward spiral just yet, but the fact that the thought crossed his brother's mind scared CJ. The last thing he wanted to do was ignore the signs.

Sighing, he turned and flipped the shower on. His intervention could wait for twenty minutes while he cleaned up.

TOM STOOD OVER THE sink, sipping a glass of orange juice and staring out the window at the peaceful back yard. The front of the house didn't share the same tranquility. It looked like a dozen more reporters showed up overnight. He remembered the fanfare when he got back from Georgia, and they were relentless.

This time they would not only be relentless, they would be ruthless.

"Are you ready to go?" Steve asked, setting his coffee cup down in the sink.

Tom shook his head. He wasn't ready for the scrutiny, the stares or the underlying hostility aimed his way and his stomach clenched, sending rippling pain through his abdomen.

"You have to go to school," Steve said.

There was no leeway in his tone, and Tom turned, meeting his gaze.

"It's part of the deal. You have to attend school in order to stay out of jail."

"I know," he signed back and drained the rest of his juice. This option looked so much better the other night when his identity was anonymous, but now that his face was recognizable to anyone with a television set, he wasn't so sure the 'get out of jail free' card was the best choice. Maybe being someone's bitch wasn't such a bad idea after all.

Steve's eyebrow rose, and he crossed his arms.

"Stop listening to my thoughts," Tom signed, irritation raking a path down his arms, and he clenched his fists. Pressing his lips together, he turned and grabbed his backpack off the chair, heading toward the garage without a glance over his shoulder. He tossed the backpack onto the passenger floor and slumped in the seat, waiting for Steve to emerge and give him a hefty dose of grief.

STEVE COUNTED TO TEN to settle his growing aggravation, and glanced at the stairwell. CJ stepped into the family room, meeting his gaze.

"What the hell happened this morning?"

"Tanya's ghost paid him a visit."

The shock of those words bit at Steve's skin, and he blew a stream of air from his lips. He could only imagine what that meeting must have been like, and now he understood the haunted look in Tom's eyes. "Are you riding with us?" he asked.

"No, I've got practice after school and then I need to head straight to work."

Steve glanced at the calendar. CJ's work hours were scribbled under today's date, and Steve nodded. "I don't want you hanging out after your shift. I think Tom's going to need someone to vent to and he certainly won't bitch about his day to me."

CJ shifted his feet and looked down at the floor with a crease between his eyes. "Just watch him while I'm gone, okay?"

The worried tone in CJ's voice gained Steve's attention. "I will." He grabbed his keys off the counter. "Keep an eye on him at school," he ordered before he slipped into the garage.

Tom didn't acknowledge his presence, even when he shut the car door and started the car.

"You want to talk about it?" Steve asked as he backed out of the garage and executed a k-turn in the driveway so he wouldn't have to reverse through the sea of reporters.

"O," Tom said, his mind echoing a resounding no.

Steve let it go for now, focusing his attention on the driveway gate and the mass of reporters beyond it, blocking his exit. "This ought to be fun," he muttered as they approached the closed gate. With the press of a button, the iron bars separated, widening until the opening was big enough for his car to squeeze through without scraping on the bars.

The crowd didn't disperse, instead; they seemed to converge on the car, banging on the windows with their palms and shouting questions through the glass. Steve glanced at Tom and revved his engine. A few of the more intelligent reporters stepped away, but the majority still clung to the car like their lives depended upon a sound bite from either of them.

A horn sounded behind them, making Steve jump a little in the seat. And he glanced in the rearview mirror at CJ and his smug smile. Good lord, that's all he needed, and he sent a silent warning to CJ, ordering him not to run the crowd over. They had enough problems without an errant manslaughter charge added to the mix.

He took a breath and whispered, "Move."

The crowd swept back far enough for him to get through, and he suppressed a smile at the expression of shock on most of the faces gawking at the car. As soon as both he and CJ were through the mass, he pressed the gate controls, going slow until the gate latched closed.

Tom's ankle bracelet beeped red and Steve focused on the road, driving faster than the posted speed limit to get him to the school within the allotted timeframe. He pulled in front of the school and his stomach turned at the press gathered on the sidewalk just waiting to ambush them.

"You ready for this?"

TOM STARED AT THE barrier of people between the car and the school, and he nodded. He didn't have that much time left, according to the increase in the beeps coming from his ankle. He swallowed and reached for the door.

Steve stepped out of the driver's side and came around to meet him on the sidewalk. He took Tom's arm just before the swell surrounded them.

Another hand grasped his free arm, and he turned, meeting CJ's gaze. With a nod, they pushed their way through the crowd. Both CJ and Steve kept repeating, "No comment," to the torrent of questions.

The principal stood at the door with his arms crossed, his gaze meeting Tom's, blazing through him with angry distaste, and Tom swallowed the burning ball of acid that rose in his throat. He expected the media swarm, but he didn't expect the hostility radiating from the principal.

"Can I see you and Tom in my office, Agent Williams?" Principal Novak asked when they entered.

When he stepped into the school, the red light on his ankle switched to green, and he traded a glance with CJ before following Steve and Principal Novak through the halls. Students turned from their lockers and all the conversation stopped as they stared at him. He didn't meet anyone's gaze and let out the breath he held when the office door closed behind him.

Steve pulled out the conditions of Tom's house arrest, anticipating the principal's resistance. "School is part of the court order for house arrest," he said, handing the paperwork to Principal Novak.

"I have to think about the safety of the students." Principal Novak made no attempt to take the paperwork from Steve. "And having a serial killer walking my halls isn't acceptable."

Tom's jaw tightened. The accusation thrown out in this environment hurt more than being arrested. He stood and started signing, and Steve put his hand up, stopping him.

"Tom isn't the Windwalker," Steve said.

"That's not what the news is reporting and until an acquittal is rendered, he isn't welcome here."

"What happened to innocent until proven guilty?" Steve asked with venom that was palatable in the air.

"He's a danger to the students." Principal Novak pointed to Tom.

"I am not," Tom signed. "I didn't kill anyone. If it makes you feel better, you can search me for weapons every day." He spread his arms out, challenging the principal.

Principal Novak looked at Steve.

"He said you can search him for weapons every day if it would make you more comfortable."

"I'm not comfortable with him here."

"I don't give a damn about your comfort. Tom has a right to an education and the court states you have to allow him to attend school," Steve snarled and tossed the papers on the principal's desk.

"I know Tanya's parents," Principal Novak said.

"So do I," Steve said. "My son didn't kill her."

"He isn't your son," Principal Novak replied.

Steve's fists clenched, and Tom put a hand on his arm, stopping him from doing something they both would regret. "Uce eve, e i go," he said.

"I will not let it go, this fool thinks..."

Tom sighed and shook his head. "We aren't going to change his mind," he signed and looked at the principal. "Can I go to class now?"

Again, the principal looked at Steve for translation.

"Can he go to class now?" Steve said with a tight jaw.

Principal Novak picked up the paper and scanned it, his face turning red at the enclosed directive. He nodded. "But any sign of trouble and you are expelled."

"Expelled?" Steve asked.

"Yes. If he causes any disruption whatsoever in my school, I will expel him."

"Fine." Steve turned to Tom. "I'll be home if you need anything and either Jennifer or I will be here at one-thirty to pick you up."

Tom nodded and turned, leaving Steve and the principal staring after him. The hallways were still filled with students, and CJ stepped next to him as he headed to his first class. Halfway down the hall, a group of his teammates stepped into his path. The expressions on their faces meant trouble.

"You killed Tanya and have the nerve to set foot in this school," Bear Whipple said. His broad width made him the perfect defensive center and not someone you wanted as an enemy. His temper was as notorious as the power behind his fists.

"He didn't kill her, asshole," CJ said, taking a protective step in front of Tom.

Tom pushed CJ aside and sent a glare in his direction. He didn't want CJ stepping in to protect him. He stepped forward, toe to toe with Bear, meeting his gaze with a fiery one of his own. This was his teammate and one of his closest friends, and the fact that he believed the news irked him. "You've known me all my life and you really think I could do something like that?" he signed.

"I know how pissed you were that she broke up with you," he snarled. "And you were caught red-handed. They say you still had her blood all over you, the knife in one hand and her scalp in the other."

Tom stepped back. "Where the hell did you hear that?"

"Horatio's father," he said.

Tom's jaw tightened. Horatio's father was the drunk in the cell next to his.

"That's bullshit. I found her in the woods face down in one of the inlet streams and pulled her out of the water. That's why I had blood on me."

"Why should I believe you?"

"Because you know there's was no way I'd ever hurt her."

"Maybe that's why you killed her," Bear leaned forward, his face inches from Tom's.

If he couldn't convince his best friend, he had no hope of convincing a jury. Frustration took control and his vision wobbled. "Do you have any idea what it was like finding her like that?"

Bear stared at him, his eyes narrowed, and his lips thinned. His fist shot out and Tom reacted, parrying the punch and stepping to the side. Two pairs of hands grabbed him as Bear spun back in his direction. But CJ stepped in front of him.

"Bear, I suggest you let this go now," CJ said.

An electrical current filled the air, spawned by the tension in CJ, and Tom struggled out of the hands gripping him, turning so he was back-to-back with CJ, protecting his brother from any attack in that direction.

"He's the fucking Windwalker," Bear said.

Tom couldn't see CJ's face, but he was sure that crazy smile graced his lips, the one that made everyone around him nervous.

"Do you really believe that?" CJ asked, his voice carrying that exasperated tone Tom knew well. It was the one he used before all hell broke loose and Tom glanced over his shoulder, meeting Bear's gaze for a moment before returning his attention to the rest of the defensive line surrounding them.

CJ had done a fantastic job of hiding his abilities for years, but if he didn't diffuse the situation, that was going to be blown any second.

The bell rang, and Tom closed his eyes, thankful for the timing. He turned and grabbed CJ's arm, dragging him away from Bear and the ugly confrontation.

"This isn't over, Ryan!" Bear shouted.

Tom glanced over his shoulder, meeting Bear's angry glare before turning to CJ.

"Are you out of your mind?" he signed.

CJ stopped in the hall and stared at Tom. "If I hadn't stepped in, they would have pounded you into the ground."

Tom raised his eyebrow. "I can hold my own."

"Against Bear, yes, but against the entire team, I don't think so. You're good, but not that good."

They walked into English class together, and the talking stopped. Jaws dropped open and Tom ignored them, taking his assigned seat. He opened his book to the assignment and glanced at the teacher. Her expression matched that of the class, and he ripped a piece of paper out of his notebook and scribbled in large block letters. I AM INNOCENT. He held it up for the teacher, knowing his irritation was visible on his face, just by the tightness in his jaw.

Miss Simpson glanced at the note and returned her gaze to his, and he held her steady stare. The fear etched in her face softened, and she nodded.

"Okay, class, please open your books to page one hundred and twenty-four," Miss Simpson said.

Tom paid attention and took notes, but he didn't ask questions or draw any more attention to himself. For the duration of her class, life seemed almost normal, and he was more thankful for her acceptance than he could articulate. When the bell rang, he lingered, packing his things slowly while CJ waited at the door.

He met Miss Simpson's gaze and sent the sign for thank you in her direction.

She gave him a nod, and he turned toward CJ and the hostility in the hallway. With a deep breath, he headed to his next class. Outside of the initial confrontation in the hall, the morning went by without another incident; however, the tension level in the hallways increased as the day went on.

After history, CJ went to his honors science class, and Tom headed toward the cafeteria. Dread slowed his approach, and he took a deep breath. Knowing he had done nothing wrong didn't help, especially with the judgmental glares he received from every student.

He got in the lunch line and the kids in front of him hurried through the line, giving him a wide berth. The fear in their gaze stroked a frigid draft across his skin, and he sighed. They all had rendered him guilty. His friends, his teachers, even his teammates thought he was capable of the atrocious murders. When he got to the end of the line, his hands shook as he peeled off the cash for his meal and the cashier took it with extreme caution, like touching him would cause her death.

Tom wanted to scream and throw his tray across the room, but he willed his aggravation into the hard pit of his stomach and headed toward an empty table near the courtyard, taking a seat with his back to the rest of the student body. He couldn't deal with the stares anymore and ate alone in silence, wishing he could just disappear into the woodwork.

Sudden pain flared in the back of his head, and he fell towards the table, catching himself before his face hit the surface. He blinked away the bright lights flaring in his eyes and turned in time to see the backside of the heavy-duty tray coming toward his face. He didn't have enough time to react, and the hard plastic smashed into his cheek with the force of a baseball bat, catapulting him onto the floor.

Tom rolled, getting to his feet on wobbly legs and his blurry gaze landed on Bear and the rest of the team converging on him like wolves cornering their prey. His survival instinct kicked in and his martial arts training took over. He shifted into a ready stance, ignoring the pain in his face.

"Come o," he said, waving them in, but the steady glare he sent in their direction made them hesitate. Tom counted ten linebackers surrounding Bear, and he exhaled, willing away the fear threatening to close his throat.

Bear tossed the tray on the table and charged. The team followed.

Tom deflected the first four swings, but the fifth caught him in the temple, stunning him enough for a few of the guys to grab his arms. Bear slammed a fist into his stomach and Tom swore it pummeled him all the way to his spine. His breath expelled in a grunt of pain and his knees wobbled. A second fist caught his chin, snapping his head to the right, and dark spots appeared in his vision. Bear's second hit lifted his body off the floor, and he cried out in pain.

The third punch was aimed at his nose and Tom blinked bleary eyes, following the trajectory, and he prayed the punch was strong enough to send broken bits of his nose into his brain. He welcomed death.

Bear's fist stopped less than an inch from his face and he was yanked away by an invisible hand and thrown across the cafeteria. The rest of the team was thrown as well, and Tom fell to his hands and knees. His gaze landed on the doorway and a very pissed CJ Ryan.

CJ walked straight across the room and everything in his path swept aside like a bulldozer went through it, leaving a wide path. When Bear got to his feet and charged, CJ snarled, "You just fucked with the wrong person." He held up his hand, stopping Bear cold.

"You should have let them kill me," Tom signed when CJ reached him.

CJ grabbed his arm and helped him to his feet. "You know me better than that." CJ headed toward the door, with Tom limping beside him.

"What the hell are you?" Bear whispered as they passed.

CJ turned in his direction with his arm supporting his brother. "I'm your worst fucking nightmare," he said, using his father's favorite line and leveling the same glare in Bear's direction.

Tom saw Bear shiver and dropped his head to hide his smile of satisfaction. *You still have to go to practice after school,* he thought and met his brother's gaze.

"Maybe I'll just quit the team," CJ muttered, helping Tom out of the cafeteria.

Where are you taking me? Tom asked as they passed the office, heading toward the parking lot.

"Home," CJ said.

I can't leave. Tom thought and tried to stop, but CJ kept moving. *Just take me to the nurse's office.*

CJ stopped at the door and sighed. "If I take you to the nurse, you'll end up in the emergency room."

Tom stared at CJ and brought his free hand to his face. Just grazing his fingers across his cheek brought a fresh bout of pain, leaving him dizzy and nauseous and when he pulled his hand away; his fingertips were covered in blood.

"Shi," he muttered and met his brother's gaze. "Nurse," he signed.

"You sure?"

Tom paused and looked out at the parking lot, debating. "If I fu up o my fir ay, ey wi pu me ba i jai." He met CJ's gaze.

"They won't put you back in jail," CJ said.

Tom nodded. "Nurse," he signed and started limping in that direction without CJ's help. Each step created a web of pain through his abdomen and a pounding hell in his head and he reached for the wall. Now that the adrenaline rush faded, every step brought a nuance of agony, making him grit his teeth. The last time his body hurt this badly was in Georgia, and he squeezed his eyes shut, hanging his head so CJ couldn't see the pain etched in his face.

"You want my help?" CJ asked, stepping in stride with him.

"Ya." Tom wrapped his arm around CJ's neck, leaning on him for support as they shuffled down the hall.

Saving Face
Chapter 16

"**W**HAT THE HELL HAPPENED?" Steve bellowed at the nurse. He pointed toward Tom, lying semi-conscious on a cot in the corner, with a bloody rag pressed to his cheek. "When I dropped him off, there wasn't a scratch on him."

"I don't know, sir," the nurse said, her gaze bouncing between Tom and the floor in front of Steve. "He came in alone and said he had an accident. That's all I was able to get out of him before he passed out."

Steve crossed and took a seat on the edge of the cot. "Who did this to you?"

Tom opened his good eye and shook his head. *Leave it alone.*

"The hell I will," he whispered.

"The ambulance should be here any moment," the nurse said, and Steve turned toward her.

"You called an ambulance?"

"He needs medical attention, sir," she said.

"I can see that, but I said I'd take care of it when you called."

"I'm sorry, sir. I just thought..." she trailed off.

The knot between his shoulders tightened, and he glared at her. She assumed he wouldn't take care of Tom; that he was every bit the asshole the news made him out to be, and he bit down on the response, turning back to Tom. "I'll follow the ambulance to the hospital." He pulled the towel away from Tom's cheek.

Tom winced in response.

Steve stared at the ugly gash deep enough to require several stitches, and the purple and swollen skin stretched over Tom's cheekbone. He pulled up Tom's shirt and looked at the purple bruises on his abdomen, ones that were indicative of a fist pummeling flesh, and he dropped the fabric back in place before meeting Tom's half-open eye. Hot fury cascaded through him, coiling in the center of his chest, just itching to let loose. He closed his eyes, willing the feral beast to calm down before it grew to a level he couldn't control.

"Does CJ know where you are?" he asked through clenched teeth.

Tom nodded.

"Will he tell me what happened?"

Tom's head shook from side to side, and Steve clenched his fists.

"I will find out who did this to you," Steve said

Tom closed his eyes. *Please, just let it go.*

"I can't let it go. This isn't right."

Tom's eyes opened. *CJ's handling it.*

A pair of EMTs stepped into the nurse's office, approaching Tom with a stretcher, and he struggled to sit up. Steve helped him to his feet and over to the stretcher, wondering just how much internal damage there was when Tom flopped down, wheezing from the effort. He followed the medics to the ambulance.

"I'll meet you in the emergency room," he said before the doors closed. He turned, giving the nurse a final glare before slipping into his car. As the ambulance pulled out, Steve opened his phone, pressing his speed dial. "Ron, Tom's being taken to the hospital; can you run interference for me?"

"What happened?"

"Tom got the shit beat out of him at school," Steve said, the clip in his voice enough to cause his boss to suck the air in between his teeth.

"Did you file a complaint?"

"No. Tom's not naming names."

A beat of silence passed. "I'll take care of it. Just make sure your boy is okay."

"I'll let you know what happens." Steve hung up the phone, bracing himself for a nasty confrontation.

Saving Face
Chapter 17

CJ SAT IN THE middle of the empty locker room with his head down and his hands resting on his thighs. Anger burned through him, and he silently counted, getting control over the overwhelming hostility. If he didn't have this under control when the team came through the door, there wouldn't be anything to stop the bloodbath.

The bell sounded, and the shuffle of students heading for the buses filled the hallway. Each second that ticked by increased the thrum of power in his veins and CJ closed his eyes, trying to find his chi, his calm place where his temper was always in check.

But it remained elusive, just out of reach.

He didn't budge from his spot when the first player stepped into the locker room. He didn't even raise his head, but his hands tightened on his thighs.

"Joe, you might want to be scarce for a while," he said, and his voice carried a dangerous edge that blanketed a chill over the entire room.

Joe didn't have a chance to leave before the rest of the team came in, including the group that pounded Tom into oblivion. As soon as they were inside the locker room, all the doors slammed, locking at CJ's will, and an eerie silence settled over everyone.

CJ clamped his teeth together and raised his head, glaring at the group. He stood, kicking the chair behind him, and settled into his ready stance with his hands loose by his side. "You assholes blindsided Tom."

"CJ, we don't..." Bear started, but CJ cut him off.

"Shut the fuck up." CJ growled. "He's my brother. You should have thought of that before you beat the shit out of him."

"But..."

"I'm interested in finding out how you would do in a fair fight," CJ said, staring down Bear. He moved his gaze to the rest of the team gathered behind Bear. "How you all do against someone who knows you're coming?"

"We don't have a beef with you," Bear said, bringing his palms up to calm CJ.

"It's your choice, Bear. You can leave here with just a few broken bones, or you can leave in a body bag," CJ said. The anger bubbled just below the surface, and he spread his arms wide. "I'll even give you the first shot."

No one moved.

"Come on!" CJ bellowed, and his hands curled into fists.

"Maybe you should take a walk," Joe said, and CJ turned his gaze to his right, meeting Joe's stare.

"They put Tom in the hospital. It's payback time."

"He got what he deserved." Bear stepped into the empty space, throwing a right hook in CJ's direction.

CJ parried, blocking the blow and sending a punch of his own into Bear's stomach. Bear's grunt of pain sent a thrill of satisfaction through CJ, but before he could deliver the knockout strike, his intuition prickled and he spun, his arm already in motion to block, but he miscalculated and the biggest linebacker on the team hit him square in the jaw, sending him stumbling back a few steps.

CJ shook off the blow and reset his stance, waving the team in.

This time they didn't hesitate, coming at him as one unified unit.

Anger transitioned to desperation and even though he threatened body bags, CJ couldn't bring himself to enlist his powers against the team he had shared the football field with over the last three years. He couldn't condone drawing blood with an invisible hand they couldn't defend against, but that didn't stop him from using his fists, doling out hits that cracked a few bones. But even his third-degree black belt wasn't enough to defend against seven linebackers, and their fists connected more times than he could count, leaving substantial bruises.

Exhaustion took its toll, squeezing the fire out of CJ, and he stumbled back against the lockers, surveying the damage in front of him. Three guys were out cold on the floor, their temples bruised from where CJ's punches landed. One linebacker gripped his leg, his face contorted in extreme pain, another couple were rubbing bruises on their jaws warily, and Bear leaned against the opposite bank of lockers, holding his side and flexing his hand, his face a grim mask.

CJ ran the back of his hand across his lips, pulling it away and staring at the blood on his fist. He raised his gaze. "Tom's innocent and if you so much as lay a finger on him again, this will feel like a walk in the park compared to what I'll do to you next time."

He stumbled toward the door and a shadow passed over him as he reached for the lock. He shot a glare over his shoulder and the chair coming down toward his head stopped in mid-air. He met Bear's shocked gaze and slowly turned.

"You have no idea who you're dealing with or what I really could do to you," he growled and let a push escape. Bear and the chair he was swinging at CJ went flying across the locker room into the beat up mass of linebackers, knocking them to the ground like a group of bowling pins.

CJ willed the locks to release and took off, limping down the hall using the building anger to drive his steps forward despite the pain. When he got to the car, he slid onto the seat and flipped his phone open. He leaned back and dialed, putting the receiver to his ear.

"I'm not going to make it in tonight," he said with a voice that was shallow and weak now that the adrenaline had drained from his bones. The restaurant didn't question him, and he hung up, started the car, and pulled out of the parking lot. He shut his mind off, diffused his anger, and followed his heart.

Saving Face
Chapter 18

STEVE TURNED, MEETING DETECTIVE O'Keefe's sharp gaze, and the layers of irritation bloomed. "You have got to be kidding me?"

"I'm just checking to see why Tom left school early and diverted from the route."

"He got beat up at school." Steve ran his hand through his hair. "I'm sure you're aware that an ambulance brought him here, right?"

"I knew an ambulance was dispatched to the school," O'Keefe said, stuffing the paper he held back into his pocket. "But I wasn't aware of the particulars."

Steve crossed his arms and stared at the Detective. "You thought Tom hurt someone?" he asked, pulling the thoughts from O'Keefe's mind.

O'Keefe shrugged in response.

"That's such bullshit," Steve muttered, his temper as raw as his nerves.

"Excuse me," a voice interrupted from behind Steve.

He turned, taking in the petite red head holding Tom's chart in her hand.

"Agent Williams?" she asked, looking between Steve and the detective.

"Yes," Steve ignored the flare of irritation coating his mind and focused on the doctor.

"Your son is banged up pretty badly, sir," she started and scanned the chart. "This wasn't an accident." She leveled an accusatory glare in his direction.

"I'm aware it wasn't an accident, but he's refused to tell me who did this to him."

"It wasn't just one person, sir," she said. "Out of all his injuries, his concussion is the one that concerns me the most. He's having issues keeping his eyes focused, and I'd like to keep him overnight for observation."

Steve glanced at Detective O'Keefe and then back at the doctor. "I'd rather take him home." He received a glare from the doctor.

"If you're worried about the bill..."

Steve let a small laugh escape. This doctor was clueless as to who the patient in the room was. Otherwise, she would have known just how ludicrous that statement was. "No, ma'am, cost is not an issue. I'd just feel more comfortable with him at home in his own room."

"I don't..."

Steve raised his hand, stopping her. "I'm sorry, but he'll be safer at home," he clarified, cutting off her protest.

"I assure you he will be safe here," the doctor said.

"Really?" Steve said, crossing his arms and stiffening his stance. "I insist."

Her lips thinned, and she traded a glance with the detective before nodding ascent. "Fine,

I'll have the nurse give you the instructions for his care and if he slips into a coma, it's on you," she said, her voice clipping with frustration.

"I'll take that risk," Steve said, and the doctor turned, huffing as she stomped away.

"I could have someone stationed here," O'Keefe offered.

Steve rolled his eyes. "And you did such a fantastic job protecting him before. Tom will be fine at home, where I know *I* can protect him." He turned and entered the examination room, leaving O'Keefe in the hall.

Tom glanced at the nurse hovering by his side, checking his vitals, and then back at Steve.

"I'll have you out of here within the hour," Steve said. *And I'll fix you up once we get home.*

Tom signed a quick thank you with a wrist encased in a cast and then closed his eyes, laying his head back on the pillow.

Tom's discomfort drifted over Steve. It was almost as acute as it had been in Georgia when he found him chained to that faux operating table. He hoped the pain medicine pumping into his IV would dull it enough, so the ride home wasn't sheer agony.

"The team did this, didn't they?" Steve asked after the nurse left.

Tom's eyelids fluttered open, and he met Steve's stare, offering no response. All his mind was broadcasting was a wall of static, shutting Steve off from the answers.

"You're blocking me."

A smile made a brief appearance and Tom's eyes closed, cutting off any further conversation.

Less than an hour later, Steve had all the instructions for Tom's care, and rolled him out of the exam room, heading toward the exit. Detective O'Keefe followed, and when Steve passed the waiting room, he stopped and retraced his steps backwards. Shock filtered through him as his gaze landed on four football players from Tom's school. The worst of the bunch was one of Tom's best friends, but his injuries still didn't compare to Tom's.

Bear looked up and his eyes widened, his mind opening to Steve and giving him a blow by blow of the entire day. Steve's hands tightened on the wheelchair handles and he turned away from Bear before the anger pulsing in his veins got loose. Without another word, he walked out and helped Tom into the car before heading home.

Saving Face
Chapter 19

CJ PULLED INTO THE house and threw the car in park, closing his eyes for a moment. When he opened them, he glanced at his reflection in the rearview mirror. The bruise on his cheek looked as angry as it felt, and he wondered what the hell he was doing in Connecticut. Instead of over-thinking, he climbed out of the car. Sitting for two hours left him stiff and the simple movement of walking made him clench his teeth.

The front door seemed so far away, but he made it and rang the doorbell, using the doorframe for support. He closed his eyes.

The squeak of the door prompted his eyes to open, and he offered a half-hearted smile. "Hey, Sandy," he said, staring into the hazel eyes that motivated him beyond words.

"Chris, oh my god, what happened?" Sandy Connor gasped with wide eyes full of concern. She reached out and pulled him into her arms.

Seeing her opened the floodgates and CJ wrapped his arms around her, burying his face in her shoulder. The pain of the past few days released. She stood still, ran her fingers slowly through his hair, and whispered shush, until he got control over the sobs.

"What happened, babe?" she whispered when he pulled away and wiped his face with his shirt.

"I made the mistake of thinking I was invincible." CJ stepped into the house. Sandy closed the door and took his hand, leading him up the stairwell and into the bathroom. Exhaustion crippled his muscles, and he slumped on the edge of the counter.

Sandy lowered the toilet lid and pointed. "Sit down and let me clean you up," she said, and he did as she instructed. He smiled as she wet a washcloth and approached him. "I don't know where to start," she said.

"How about here?" CJ said, pointing to his lips.

The sweet dimple showed in her cheek, and she gently wiped his lips.

"Ouch," he whispered, but kept his gaze locked with hers.

"God, you're a mess."

"Gee, thanks," he said, finding some humor in her concern. He blinked and looked around the bathroom, realizing how empty the house was. "Your parents aren't home, are they?"

"No, they aren't." She wiped the blood off his chin. "How in heaven's name did you drive like this?" She took the cloth to the sink, rinsing it before she returned.

"All I could think of was you." He took the cloth out of her hand and tossed it on the counter. He stood; took her face in his hands and planted a kiss, ignoring the twinge of pain.

Instead, he concentrated on the way she tenderly kissed him back, allowing him to explore her mouth with his tongue.

"Chris," she whispered, pulling away and meeting his gaze. "Talk to me."

The way she said his proper name sent shivers down his spine and he melted into her. Sandy never called him by his nickname; she preferred his real name, saying it was more intimate and special. She had no idea how powerful an aphrodisiac it was to him.

"Later." He slid his hands under the hem of her shirt. Her soft skin set him on fire and every nuance of pain altered to a burning need.

She tilted her head, her gaze scanning down the length of his body and back. "You really are a mess. A hot mess, but a mess just the same," she grinned. "You really need to clean up."

He glanced in the mirror and couldn't argue with her assessment. "Only if you join me," he said.

She rolled her eyes.

"Then at least help me with my shirt."

The dimples appeared briefly, and she stepped forward, running her hands under his shirt. He winced and pulled away when her fingers grazed one of his ribs and her intense gaze transitioned to worry. She immediately peeled his shirt over his head and stared at his chest, her hand flying to cover her mouth.

"You need a hospital, not a shower," she said.

His light mood soured, and he turned toward the mirror, visually inspecting the swollen, discolored skin covering the lower right quadrant of his ribs. He closed his eyes, taking stock of his wounds for the first time. "It's just a bruise and while it hurts like hell, nothing's broken."

"How do you know you're not bleeding internally?" She ran a finger along the edge of the bruise.

"Because, I know." He pulled her against him. His hormones overrode the pain again, and he covered her protest with his mouth, kissing her more insistently. She didn't stop him this time when his hands slid under her shirt, and when he broke the kiss to peel the fabric over her head, she let him.

His gaze dropped to the curve of her cleavage, and he grinned, lowering his lips to her throat and following the natural arc right into the center of her ample breasts. Hunger possessed him, devouring his willpower, and his fingers fumbled with the button on her pants. When her hands covered his, he pulled away, meeting her gaze.

"I need you." The simple truth tumbled from his lips.

"Maybe you need a cold shower," she said, removing his hands from her beltline.

"Come on, Sandy, we've been together for years."

"That doesn't mean I'm ready for this," she said.

CJ lifted his hands and stepped back, irritation skating across his overheated skin. "Fine," he snapped and turned away. Reaching behind the curtain, he turned on the water. He stripped and stepped into the shower without glancing in her direction.

The warm water stung the bruises covering his skin, and he winced, reaching for the soap. The fruity scent drifted on the air, and he ran the bar over his throbbing skin, letting pain fill the space that desire had moments before.

He turned and let the water beat on his face, and then ran his hands through his hair. When the air shifted, he turned his head toward the draft. His gaze landed on hers and he froze.

"I thought...," he whispered.

She shrugged and attempted to cover herself, self-conscious of her naked form. He turned and stepped toward her, not knowing quite what to do to make her comfortable.

"You're beautiful," he said.

"So are you," she replied, and her gaze dropped before it bounced back to his face.

He smiled. "You don't have to do this if you're not ready." He tucked a wet fly away behind her ear.

"I'm scared."

CJ stepped closer and looked down into the interesting hazel pattern of her eyes. "Why?"

"I don't want to be just another conquest." She avoided his questioning stare.

He arched his eyebrows. "I'm still a virgin, Sandy."

Her gaze shot to his and her mouth dropped. "I just thought..."

"You thought what?"

"I don't know. Tom's got a reputation up in York, so I just assumed..." she trailed off and shrugged.

"So, you just assumed because Tom tags anything in a skirt, so do I?"

"Well, look at you." She waved her hand at his well-defined physique.

"I've been exclusively yours since my father's funeral." He leaned in to kiss her and paused, his brow knitting as a new thought surfaced. "Am I just a summer fling to you?" He stepped back under the stream of water, putting distance between them.

"Come on, Chris, you know me better than that." She closed the distance, planting a kiss on his chest. "You've been in my head; you know how I feel about you."

"I know. But now and then, doubt gets the best of me." He wrapped his arms around her, pulling her against him under the warm spray. "I've waited so long for this," he whispered. He wanted to taste every inch of her and started with her lips before trailing kisses down her neck. He cradled her breasts in his palms, running his thumbs over her nipples, smiling as they hardened under his touch. Another glance in her eyes confirmed she was as ready for this as he was, and he dropped to his knees, letting the warm water cascade over them while he played with her, learning what she liked and what she didn't by trial and error, thankful he had a window into her soul.

When she was wetter than the shower, he stood and turned off the water, opting for her bed rather than the hard tiled wall for their first time. With his lips locked on hers, he headed to her bedroom, tossing a towel on the bed before he laid her down under him.

He paused, searching her eyes for hesitation, for a reason not to follow through on everything his body was demanding.

"Are you sure?" he asked, and she nodded.

"I need to hear you say it," he whispered.

"Yes, Chris, I'm sure," she said. The words came out in a breath of heat searing his soul.

Sandy's eyes widened as his hips met hers. That sudden shatter of her innocence sent a wave of pain through her, dulling the excitement, and CJ inhaled from the shock of it. He moved his hips slowly until her pain transitioned and the deep crease between her eyes smoothed.

"You like it slow?" he asked and got a smile in return, their hips continuing to circle in a rhythm that drove him crazy. The feel of her overwhelmed him and he closed his eyes, attempting to gain control, but she was just too delicious, too perfect.

He opened his eyes and stilled. Her squeak of protest brought a smile to his face.

"Have I told you I loved you lately?" he asked.

"Yes." She pulled him to her lips.

The kiss smashed his willpower, and he moved faster, in time with her heart and the wave hit, seizing every muscle in his body with his release. When his lungs finally pulled in a breath, the rush of blood through his veins roared in his ears and he collapsed on her, his forehead resting next to her ear.

"My god," he gasped and turned his head, meeting her satiated gaze.

With the last of his strength, he rolled, pulling her onto his chest without uncoupling.

His eyelids dropped as her wet hair fanned out over his shoulder.

"I love you, too." She snuggled closer. "Are you going to tell me what happened now?"

He ran his fingers through her hair and sighed. "They think Tom's the Windwalker," he said, as if that would explain everything.

"What?" Her head shot off his chest.

"The Windwalker killed Tom's girlfriend, and he was arrested for her murder. Tanya was one of the cheerleaders and some of the guys on the team believe he's guilty, so they beat him up," he said. "And I lost it."

She searched his eyes, letting the information settle in. "I certainly hope the other guy looks worse than you do," she said, tracing the bruise on his cheek.

"They do," CJ said, stretching the truth.

"They?"

"Yes. In my infinite wisdom, I took on seven linebackers."

Her mouth dropped open. "What made you do something that stupid?"

"They put Tom in the hospital," he answered. "And I'm pretty sure I broke a couple of bones, so I didn't want to hang around for the fallout."

She took his hand and kissed his swollen knuckles before returning her gaze to his. "At least you didn't kill them," she whispered.

"I wanted to," he admitted.

"But you didn't."

"No. I didn't even use my abilities during the fight," he said.

"I would have never guessed." She rolled her eyes.

It hurt to grin, but he did anyway, and he shifted his hips, creating friction between them and she giggled.

"If I had known sleeping with you would be this incredible, I wouldn't have waited so long."

"Oh, I knew it would be beyond incredible," he smiled and pulled her to his lips.

"What the hell do you think you're doing?"

CJ's heart lurched, and his head snapped toward the door along with Sandy's.

Her father stood in the entry, his hands balled into fists and his face as red as a fire engine. His glare squared on CJ, and he pointed his finger, clenching his teeth before moving his fiery gaze to Sandy.

When his gaze returned to CJ, he growled, "Get dressed and get the hell out of my house." He turned and stomped down the stairs.

"Oh, shit," he muttered, and Sandy rolled off him.

She grabbed clothing from her bureau and pulled it on before she turned to CJ. Her eyes were wide with terror, and he crossed to the bathroom, putting his underwear and jeans on. He scanned the room for his missing shirt.

"Where's my shirt?" he asked Sandy.

Sandy shrugged and glanced over her shoulder at the stairwell.

"Screw it," He headed downstairs with Sandy following.

"Uncle Dan." He stepped into the kitchen.

Dan Connor spun toward him, his finger pointing like a loaded gun. "You're not my nephew, so stop referring to me as your uncle. Just because your mother and I were married at

784

one time doesn't give you the right to call me that. Now get out!" His finger slashed toward the door. "I never want to see you around my daughter again."

"But I'm in love with her," CJ said, his mind reeling at the thought of never seeing her again.

"I will not let another Ryan destroy my family," he growled.

"I'm not my father, sir," CJ said.

"I don't care. Your father destroyed everything that was sacred and dear to me. I'm not letting you do the same."

"Don't I have a say?" Sandy said from behind CJ.

"No, you don't," Dan said. "Not while you're living under my roof."

"Then I'll leave," she said, taking CJ's hand and stepping next to him, jutting her chin out in defiance.

Dan's glare shot between the two of them, landing back on CJ, and he blinked, really seeing him for the first time. His gaze zeroed in on the bruise on CJ's cheek and then the large discoloration on his rib cage and back to his face.

"What happened to you?" he asked, the edge still in his voice, but the venom had softened.

"I took on the football team after they put Tom in the hospital."

"Tom's in the hospital?"

"Yes. They took him from school in an ambulance." CJ squeezed Sandy's hand for support. She squeezed back, letting him know she wasn't letting him go.

Dan's brow creased and his arms crossed. "What happened?"

"They believed the news stories."

"About your father?"

"No, about the Windwalker."

Dan's hands dropped to his side. "What news stories?" he asked, the confusion clear in the crease between his eyes.

"They think Tom is the Windwalker."

Silence settled in the kitchen as Dan processed the statement.

"Tom?"

CJ nodded.

"What's Steve doing about it?"

"He's under investigation from the fallout with my father, so he isn't in charge of the Windwalker case anymore."

"Jesus." Dan closed his eyes. The anger still burned under the now calm exterior, but it wasn't as dangerous as it had been when he saw them in bed. He opened his eyes and exhaled. "Steve and Jen don't know you're here, do they?"

"No, sir," CJ said. "They think I'm at work."

Before Dan could respond, the phone rang, and Dan grabbed it off the cradle. "Connor residence," he said through clenched teeth. His gaze landed on CJ. "Yes, he's here, but he was just leaving."

"What the hell were you thinking?"

CJ turned and stared into Steve's angry gaze.

"You know, I hated it when his father did that," Dan said from across the room, and he slammed the phone on the counter.

"Sorry," Steve said, but his gaze never left CJ's. "O'Keefe has an arrest warrant."

CJ pressed his lips together as irritation snaked through him. "Bear filed a complaint?"

Steve nodded. "His father didn't take too kindly to you breaking his hand or his ribs."

"Did he tell his father he broke his hand punching me?" Anger laced through his words, and he waved toward his bruised chest. "And what about what they did to Tom?"

"Tom isn't talking," Steve said. "He's got this insane idea that protecting the team is better for everyone involved."

"What about the other guys?"

"No one else pressed charges," Steve said, and his eyes narrowed. "Where's your shirt?"

CJ shrugged and glanced at Sandy and then down at the floor before he finally returned his gaze to Steve. He crossed his arms over his bare chest and shifted his weight, uncomfortable with his lack of attire under Steve's blatant stare.

Steve balled his hands into fists and met Dan's glare. "Are you kidding me?"

"That's why he was just leaving," Dan sneered from the other side of the room.

Steve's lips pressed tight together, and he shook his head, conveying a world of disappointment in that one motion. CJ dropped his gaze.

"I suggest you find your shirt and hightail it back here. Now."

"Yes, sir." CJ headed back upstairs.

STEVE WAITED UNTIL THE KIDS were out of earshot before he turned toward Dan. "I'm sorry about all this," he said, trying to diffuse the angry thoughts sailing through Dan's head, all of which included stringing CJ up in some fashion.

"You know what they were doing?" Dan pointed toward the front hall. "Under my roof?"

He crossed closer. "Does that really surprise you?" He knew how CJ felt about Sandy and, while he wasn't pleased with CJ's actions, he really couldn't blame him. CJ and Sandy had been together for as long as he knew the boy.

Dan's face reddened. "I thought she'd grow out of CJ. The thought of his son and my daughter together just burns me to the core."

"CJ isn't Ty. If he was, those football players would be dead instead of just a little banged up, and CJ wouldn't have a scratch on him."

"That doesn't make this any easier," Dan said. "Eric and Emily never screwed around under my roof."

Steve burst out laughing. "You just didn't catch them," he said.

Dan glared at him.

"Oh, Eric screwed around plenty." Steve tapped his temple. "And I've got the memories to prove it."

Dan's jaw tightened. "I don't want them together," he growled.

"We don't always get what we want," Steve shrugged. He knew firsthand what it was like having a father-in-law who didn't want him in the family. "You don't get to choose who you fall in love with."

"They don't know the first thing about love," Dan argued.

"Let me give you some friendly advice." Steve put his hand up when Dan opened his mouth to protest. "My wife's father hates me, and because of that, she has chosen not to see her parents very often."

"What the hell does that have to do with this?"

"I'm just saying choose your battles, because if you try to push a wedge between them, you may end up losing your daughter." He offered a shrug. "It's your choice."

CJ STOOD IN THE bathroom, perplexed as to where his shirt had gone. It wasn't in plain sight like his other clothes had been, and he glanced at Sandy. "Is it in your room?"

"No." She tried not to smile.

"This isn't funny. Your dad is pissed."

"I know, but you look so damn cute right now."

CJ raised an eyebrow and glanced at his reflection. "I look like shit."

She stepped closer and kicked the door closed before wrapping her arms around his neck. "Nah, the black eye just makes you a whole lot sexier."

He smiled. "Any regrets?"

"Just that my dad caught us."

CJ nodded. He could have done without that drama, too, and he glanced toward the door. "I found my shirt," he said, nodding toward the crumpled fabric the door had hidden until she closed it.

"When am I going to see you again?"

The question cut him, and he offered a sad smile. "I don't know." He palmed her cheek.

"You're welcome at the house any time, you know."

"I know, but I don't have my own car, so..."

"Maybe I'll buy you one for your birthday." He leaned in to kiss her.

"Oh, yeah, my dad would just love that." She rolled her eyes.

He chuckled. Dan definitely didn't like it when he showered her with gifts. "Maybe that isn't such a good idea." The humor fizzled, and he broke from her grasp, slipping the bloody shirt back over his head. "I have to go," he whispered. Pain bloomed in his chest, and it had nothing to do with his bruises.

"I don't want you to."

"I don't want to leave either," he said. He just wanted to curl up with her in bed and forget about everything at home, but he knew that wasn't possible. Running away crossed her mind, and he tilted his head, studying her.

"I couldn't do that to you."

"Why not?"

"Running away isn't an option. If I run now, I'd end up no different from my father," he said, and she knew how much he hated what his father did. "I'll come back down as soon as things blow over at home."

"Promise?"

"I promise," he whispered. "There's nothing on heaven or earth that could keep me away. Not even your father." The kiss lingered, steaming his skin with desire, and he pulled away, breathless. Taking one last look at her, he memorized the pouty lips and her beautiful hazel eyes before turning and leaving without another word.

Saving Face
Chapter 20

STEVE WALKED BACK INTO the family room of their house. "CJ's on his way home and we'd like to lodge a complaint against Bear Whipple for the assault on Tom."

Detective O'Keefe tapped the arrest warrant against his palm and his gaze dropped to the semi-conscious boy on the couch. "Are you sure?"

"Six stitches, a broken cheekbone, four broken ribs, a broken wrist and a concussion? You bet your ass, I'm sure. What they did to him is inexcusable."

Tom's unblemished eye opened.

"Did Bear Whipple do this to you?" Detective O'Keefe asked Tom.

Tom's gaze dropped to the floor, and his eye closed. "Ya," he mumbled through swollen lips and gave a single nod.

"You're not just saying that to protect your brother?"

Tom's eyelid fluttered up, and he shook his head. Leaning forward, he grabbed the pad and pen on the table, scribbling and then turning the sheet so the detective could see. "No. If CJ hadn't stepped in, they would have killed me."

"They?"

Tom scribbled again and turned it back toward the detective. "Bear led the charge. He's responsible for the pack mentality."

O'Keefe turned back to Steve. "Bear said CJ attacked him without provocation."

"I doubt that. CJ's not the type to throw the first punch." Steve crossed his arms. He got enough from Bear's memories to understand what happened.

O'Keefe nodded and pocketed the arrest warrant. "I'll talk to the Whipples."

"I still want Bear charged with assault," Steve said.

"Even if they drop the charges against CJ?"

"Whether or not they drop the charges, I want that kid to understand what he did was wrong."

Tom scribbled on the paper. "The entire lunchroom witnessed what they did."

"That's good, because a situation where it's your word against his isn't going to bode well for someone charged with murder," O'Keefe said. He turned his gaze from Tom to Steve.

Steve refrained from commenting and crossed to the door, opening it for the detective. "I'll call you when CJ gets here."

O'Keefe nodded and headed outside. The press went into action at the sight of the detective, shouting questions through the fence at both Steve and O'Keefe.

Steve closed the door and crossed, taking a seat next to Tom. "How are you feeling?"

"My head hurts."

Steve nodded and looked down at his hands. "CJ got his fair share of bruises as well." He glanced at Tom, smiling at the shock reflected in his eyes.

"He didn't use his power. It was a fair fight." He huffed. "Well, as fair as seven on one can be."

Tom rubbed his eye and then signed, "If I had seen them coming..."

"You would have fared a lot better. I know. Clocking you with a tray was the act of a coward. Bear ambushed you and his intent was to kill, not just send you to the ER." Steve shook his head, unable to believe the audacity of Tom's ex-best friend. "I got the whole download of what happened when I saw him at the hospital." He met Tom's gaze. "I know he was your friend and maybe when this whole thing is over, he might be again, but I want to be very clear. Bear is not welcome in this house."

Tom didn't argue, and Steve squeezed his shoulder.

"Are you going to fix me?" Tom signed.

"I can't. Not since I'm pressing charges," he said. "Both you and CJ are just going to have to live with this for a little longer. If Bear's family drops the charges against CJ, I may reconsider, but until then, you two will have to suck it up."

Saving Face
Chapter 21

CJ PULLED THROUGH THE gate, ignoring the press swarming his car. Getting out this time was worse than at Sandy's, and he nearly collapsed when his muscles seized. He gripped the door and counted to ten, willing the knots in his muscles to relax until he got inside.

His limp to the front door was caught on camera and he sent a glare toward the television cameras outside the gate. "Malfunction." He sent a targeted blast toward the cameras. The red lights blinked out, and he turned away before the smile surfaced.

He stepped inside the house and closed the door, slipping his sneakers off before he crossed to the family room. The air in the back of the house was heavy with onion and garlic, and he glanced toward the kitchen. Steve was busy at the stove, and he wondered where Jennifer was.

"She went to Boston to talk to her agent today, so she does not know what type of shit storm she's coming home to," Steve said to the unspoken question. He glanced over his shoulder, meeting CJ's gaze.

"Oh." CJ couldn't think of anything else to say, so he turned his focus to his brother. "How are you?"

Tom looked up from his spot on the couch and shrugged.

Steve approached from the kitchen with the cell phone to his ear. "CJ's home." He hung up and pocketed the phone. "You are batting a thousand today. First the shit at school and then sleeping with Sandy. What the hell were you thinking?"

Tom's mouth dropped open, his gaze traveling from CJ to Steve. "You slept with her?" he signed.

CJ nodded. "Uncle Dan caught us," he said, and Tom started laughing.

"Tom, he's in enough trouble. I don't need you egging him on," Steve interrupted.

"So, am I still a fugitive?"

"I don't know. I guess we'll find out when Detective O'Keefe gets the message."

"I didn't throw the first punch," CJ said.

"You didn't give them a choice. That little ultimatum really struck a nerve," Steve said.

CJ bit his lip and shrugged. "How'd you find out?"

"Bear was at the hospital when we left," Steve said. "He didn't exactly tell the truth about what happened either, so unless you've got someone that can shed some light on this, you're screwed."

"Joe saw everything," CJ said. "Including Bear's little stunt at the end."

"And your display," Steve added.

CJ nodded. "Yep. They know I'm not normal," he said with finger quotes.

"Ey away ew you wer orma," Tom said with a grin. *They just never said it to your face.*

"Oh yeah? Well, at least I don't have a reputation for tagging anything in a skirt."

His eyebrows shot up, and he sent a snide thought. *At least I never got caught.*

"Fuck you." CJ turned, storming up to his room, ignoring the pain wracking his ribs with every step. He slammed his bedroom door and crossed to the computer, flipping it on. The need to see Sandy over-ruled anything else.

When the door opened behind him, he stiffened and turned his head, glaring at Tom.

"owy." Tom limped to the bed, sitting down with a wince.

"Do you mind?" CJ pointed to the screen and the Skype logon.

Don't make me get up again, Tom thought and dropped onto CJ's pillow.

CJ sighed and nodded. "So, beyond the stitches and cast on your wrist–what else is wrong?" he asked and logged onto Skype at the same time.

Cracked cheekbone, four cracked ribs and a concussion.

"And that shit head filed a complaint against me?" CJ shook his head in disgust and pressed the call button, waiting for Sandy to come on.

Steve filed one against Bear, too.

"Good, he deserves it." He focused on the screen, and after a few buzzes, he sighed and cut off the connection. "I bet Dan took away her computer," he muttered, angry that he couldn't see her tonight.

He really walked in while...

"Not during, after," he said. "I didn't even hear him come in." CJ rubbed the back of his neck. "I'm usually so much more in tune than that."

You were a bit preoccupied. Tom grinned. *So, how was she?*

CJ tried his best not to smile, but it snuck through, and he glanced at his brother. "Look, no disrespect, but I'm not discussing this with you."

"Come on, spill," Tom signed and then pushed himself into a sitting position.

"All I'm going to say is she was worth waiting for."

The buzzer on the computer rang and CJ pushed the connect button. Her picture popped up on the screen and he smiled.

"Hey, I made it home and Tom's here with me, so..."

"So, watch what I say?" She winked. "Hey, Tom, how are you?"

CJ turned the screen toward Tom so she could see him. He waved his good hand.

"Jesus, you're more of a mess than Chris."

Tom rolled his eyes and shrugged and pointed toward the door. He attempted to stand.

"You don't have to go. I can't stay on long, anyway."

CJ turned the screen back toward him. "How'd it go after I left?"

"Let's just say getting my wisdom teeth pulled was more pleasant." She glanced over her shoulder and then faced the computer again. "What about you?"

"The marines haven't landed yet."

She sighed. "But the night is still young."

"Yeah." He leaned his elbow on the desk, propping his cheek on his palm.

"How are you feeling?"

"Like I've been run over by a train. But nowhere near as bad as Tom."

"Why doesn't Steve make it all go away?"

"He will, eventually," CJ said.

Sandy gasped. "Dad's coming, I gotta go." Her picture disappeared.

"Shit," CJ muttered and closed the computer. He glanced at Tom. "I'm not sure Uncle Dan is going to let me see her again." A cold fear wrapped around his heart, and he closed his eyes. "What if I completely fucked it up today?"

The girl loves you. How could you fuck it up?

"I don't know. I guess I'm just being paranoid."

Chill, everything will work out, Tom thought. *I'm going to go lay down until dinner's ready.*

"Do you need a hand?"

Tom shook his head and hobbled out of the room.

Saving Face
Chapter 22

AS SOON AS HE lay down, the room tilted, blurring in front of him until he blinked it back into focus. Tom shivered and his breath plumed from his mouth. He turned his head slowly and his gaze landed on Tanya.

"Hey," he said.

Her wide eyes scanned him, and a pained crease appeared between her eyes. "What happened to you?"

"I had a rough day." He reached out and took her hand, pulling her onto the bed despite the bone chilling air surrounding her. At least in the bathroom, the heat from the shower had kept the cold at bay.

She stretched next to him, tracing his wounds with her fingers, and prisms of ghostly tears slid down her cheeks. "I'm so sorry."

"It's not your fault." He wrapped his arm around her and inhaled. She still carried the fruity shampoo scent he remembered, and it made him smile. "I miss you."

"I'm not going anywhere," she whispered.

Tom stiffened and turned, meeting her gaze. "You can't stay indefinitely. Heaven's waiting."

"This is my heaven."

The weight of her words hit him, pulling the air out of his lungs and leaving him struggling for oxygen. He closed his eyes tight; willing the air to flow in and out of his lungs until he was sure his voice wouldn't shake. "This isn't heaven, babe, not by a long stretch."

"Don't you want me here?"

Tom dropped his head back on the pillow. "You know I want you here. That's why you *are* here instead of wherever your..." he caught himself. She didn't know what condition her body had been left in, and he wasn't sure what the information would do to her.

"Instead of where?"

"Where ever they have your body," he said.

"I think I was cremated," she said.

He exhaled, knowing she was right. The papers had reported her cremation along with the scheduled memorial service. The fact he wouldn't be able to say a proper goodbye ate at his nerve endings, and he wasn't sure he could send her on now that she was here.

He glanced at her and wondered if he ever would.

"Not that I'm complaining, but why did you come here after everything you said?"

"I should have never broken up with you," she sighed, sending a wave of cold air over his chest. "And now that I can hear you and kiss you and all, I'm not in a rush to leave."

"Ah." He closed his eyes. Exhaustion settled over him, dulling his pain, and the soft stroke of her fingers over his temple lulled him to sleep.

Saving Face
Chapter 23

STEVE PICKED UP THE phone before the first ring ended. "Hello," he said.

"You've got a choice," O'Keefe said. "I looked into the situation and there are more than a handful of people who saw Bear ambush Tom in the cafeteria."

"Cut to the chase, Jim," Steve said, digging facts from his mind. Bear had no one who was willing to validate his story; they all clammed up, refusing to speak to the police about what happened.

"The Whipples will drop the charges, but only if you agree to do the same."

Steve sighed and wished Jennifer was here to discuss the situation, but she wasn't due home for another half hour, so the decision was his alone. "Fine, but if he comes anywhere near either of my boys, this deal is off."

"I will let them know. Tell CJ to keep his nose clean because, as of now, he's on our radar."

"I'll tell him." Steve hung up the phone, relieved not to have to deal with another visit to the police station. He turned, focusing back on the dinner and carefully framed how to explain the day's events to Jennifer when she arrived home.

THE GARAGE DOOR OPENED, sending the shrill buzz of the door alarm through the house, and Steve glanced over his shoulder at the wall panel. His eyes widened at his a-ha moment.

"Why didn't I think of that?" He let out a startled laugh.

"What?" Jennifer said, stepping into view.

"The alarm system. It should have a record of when the doors were opened."

Jennifer dumped her pocketbook on the counter and peeled off her coat, throwing it over the coat rack in the corner by the garage door. "And that helps how?"

"It could provide reasonable doubt, especially if it has a record of when people came and went from the house. If we can say within reason that it was Tom, it might provide an alibi."

"It could also backfire if the times coincide with the killings." She crossed the room, wrapping her arms around his waist.

He gave her a kiss hello even though she blew his ray of hope right out of the sky. "I can check it out and if it helps our case, I'll offer it up, but if it hurts Tom, then I'll just leave it alone. He's been hurt enough lately."

She studied his expression, and he tried to soften the blow with a smile of commiseration.

"Tom got beat up at school today."

Her eyes widened, and her jaw dropped open. "What?" She pulled out of his grasp. "Where is he?"

"He's upstairs now, but we spent the afternoon in the emergency room." Steve turned off the burners on the stove. Rehearsing in his mind and verbalizing the words were two different things, and he sighed, meeting her gaze.

Jennifer stiffened, and the muscles in her jaw jumped. The telltale thinning of her lips expressed her irritation. "What in God's name happened?"

"Apparently, some kids decided to take justice into their own hands and ambushed him in the cafeteria."

"Who started it?"

Steve shifted. "Bear."

Jennifer's face flushed with anger, and she clenched her teeth together. "Are we talking about the same person?"

"Yes. Tom's best friend and the rest of the defensive line beat him up."

Jennifer turned and headed toward the stairs, worry and something darker blazed in her eyes.

"That's not the end of it, Jen."

She hesitated, turning towards Steve, waiting for him to spill the rest, her features undecided at whether to display worry or anger.

Steve leaned against the counter. "CJ retaliated."

Jennifer's eyes widened.

"No, not that way," Steve put his hand up, stopping her line of thoughts. "He challenged them to a fair fight and while it landed a couple of them in the hospital, it wasn't anything compared to what happened to Tom. And CJ didn't escape without some significant bruises."

Jennifer turned toward the stairs and hesitated, glancing back at Steve. "Is that all?"

Steve shook his head and sighed. "They wanted to press charges against CJ, but he wasn't here when they came with the arrest warrant. He went down to Connecticut after the fight."

Her eyebrows rose, and her mouth popped open. "Is he still there?"

Steve laughed. "No," he said. "Dan caught him and Sandy in bed, and if he owned a firearm, CJ would have a few buck shots in his ass."

"Holy shit, Steve," she gasped and ran her hand through her hair. Her exasperation made him smile, and he chuckled.

"Why are you laughing?"

"Because this day has been one thing after another, and I imagine I've had the same expression on my face most of the day."

She allowed a smile and a sigh. "Is CJ in jail?"

"No. I agreed to drop the charges against Bear in return for dropping the charges against CJ."

Relief swept through her form and her shoulders slumped with the release. She sent a nod in his direction and turned toward the stairwell.

"Tell them dinner is ready," Steve said before she stepped out of sight.

KNOCKING.

Tom's eyes fluttered open to the dark room and knocking that sounded like it was a mile away. He attempted to sit up and lights flared in front of his eyes, followed by a bolt of pain, and he moaned, his hands flying up to the sides of his head to keep it from blowing under the pressure.

The door opened and the light from the hall pierced his eyes like daggers and he clamped his jaw against the sudden appearance of burning bile in his throat.

"Steve!" Jennifer's cry filled his ears, and he whimpered under the crushing sound.

Within a blink, pain wracked his body, and he bellowed just before the curtain fell.

Raspy breath and a cool sensation on his forehead filled his senses, and it took a moment before all his faculties returned. Tom blinked his eyes open, his clear gaze landing on Jennifer.

She pulled the washcloth away from his forehead and glanced to her right.

He turned his head, glancing at Steve. No pain or dizziness accompanied the move, and he signed, "Thank you."

"I left the cut on your face and your bruises intact, but your concussion and broken bones are fixed."

"You scared me." Jennifer folded the cloth.

Tom sent a questioning glance at Steve. "Why?"

"You had a seizure." Steve sat down in the chair at Tom's desk.

Steve's hand shook when he ran it down his face, and Tom realized just how unnerved both of them were. He had never seen Steve shake, but then again, he had never seen the man afraid in all the years he knew him, until now. Now both his and Jennifer's gaze held a haunted look he didn't understand.

"I'm okay." He covered Jennifer's hands. She met his gaze with tear-filled eyes and nodded.

"Yeah, well, we didn't know that until you opened your eyes," CJ said from the doorway. "You completely blacked out and stopped breathing until Steve did his thing."

Leave it to his brother to cut to the chase.

"How long was I out?" Tom signed.

Steve glanced at his watch. "A couple of hours." He stood. "I'm not sure how good dinner will be at this point, but it's ready if you're hungry."

Saving Face
Chapter 24

TOM GLANCED AT THE school and back at Steve, pleading. *Can't I just stay home today?*

"No," Steve said, his tone firm and unyielding. "Do you want me to go into the office with you?"

Tom shook his head and plucked the hospital note from Steve's hand. *I got it.* He pushed the car door open and got one leg out before Steve grabbed his shoulder. He looked back.

"Remember, you're supposed to be injured," he whispered.

Tom nodded. Steve had lectured him all the way to school on the importance of keeping up pretense in this case. How could he forget? He stepped out of the car and made his way into the school, walking slower than his normal gait, with his head down and his books clutched in his arms. Before he entered the building, he cast a glance over his shoulder at Steve and received a nod before the car revved and shifted into gear.

Tom turned back to the hallway in front of him, willing his feet forward despite the dread crushing his chest. Paranoia wasn't something he was used to, and being this jumpy wasn't good for appearance's sake.

"Don't worry, little brother, I'll back you up if something happens today," CJ whispered in his ear and then stepped in stride with him like a protective bodyguard.

Eyes turned in their direction and most widened in shock at what they saw. The Ryan brothers sporting epic bruises, and Tom bit his lower lip to keep the smile from surfacing. Little did everyone know, these bruises were truly only skin deep.

CJ elbowed Tom, sending him a cross glare and Tom rolled his eyes, getting back into character as they crossed over the threshold of the office. Tom handed the note to the school secretary with his casted hand, keeping his gaze down.

"I'll see that Mr. Fletcher gets this," she said, her tone carrying a note of disdain at having to deal with the boy accused of murder, and Tom raised his head, meeting her accusatory stare with one of his own.

He would not let anyone get to him. He did nothing wrong and wasn't about to act all meek and guilty. Not after the crap that happened yesterday.

Mrs. Simons actually flinched at his brazen glare and hurried away from the counter.

CJ turned away from the counter and he sent a smirk in Tom's direction. *You freaked her out, dude.*

Good. Maybe people won't fuck with me today. Tom sent the thought back and gave a nod, turned away from CJ, and headed towards his first class.

Call if you need me.

Tom glanced over his shoulder and nodded. If he got into trouble, he wouldn't hesitate to call today, but he had a feeling he would be fine, especially since the assholes CJ whooped were still licking their wounds.

When he walked into the classroom, hushed murmurs filled the room and all eyes turned in his direction. Instead of adopting the timid demeanor he held yesterday, he sent a glare across the students, silently daring them to say something. When shocked silence filtered through everyone, Tom crossed to his desk and sat, painting a grimace on his face to keep the class clueless to his total lack of pain.

In the cafeteria, Tom went to the back table again, but this time, he sat on the other side, with his back to the wall and a view of the cafeteria. He opened his history book and busied himself with reading the next section, but his gaze kept jumping from the page to any motion within his peripheral vision.

A tray dropped on the table in front of him and he looked up, meeting the gaze of the tray owner. Raven Adams took the seat opposite him, her blue eyes locked on his and her pink lips posed in a smile.

"Do ye mind if I sit with you?" she asked, and a hint of her Irish accent bled through.

Tom nodded and scanned the room to make sure this wasn't some kind of ambush.

"What they did to you yesterday was deplorable." She dug into her turkey surprise with zest.

Tom stared at her freckled face and her wild red hair before his gaze dropped to the suggestive v-neck of her shirt before focusing back to his plate.

"Why a you hea?" he said.

"Because you're sitting alone, and everyone is avoiding you like the plague. That's usually reserved for me, so I felt sorry for you," she said through a mouthful of potatoes.

Tom stiffened and slammed the book closed.

"Easy big fella." She grinned. "No need to get all sanctimonious on me."

The spark of humor in her eyes gave him pause, and he cocked his head, studying her closer. "Aren't you afraid of me?" he signed.

She chuckled and shook her head. "You kill someone? I just can't see it, especially not that skinny bitch of a girlfriend," she said.

"Hey." He shook his head. "Don't talk about her like that," he signed.

Her gaze followed the symbols his hands made, and she shrugged. "Sorry, I know I shouldn't talk ill of the dead, but there was no love lost between us."

Raven's Irish brogue and sincere gaze calmed his aggravated nerves, and he took a closer look at her, studying her for the first time. In a geeky Irish way, she was kind of cute, though her reputation around school bordered on crazy, strange, but right at this moment all he saw was a misunderstood transplant from Ireland who had gotten a raw deal from the students at York High School.

"Are the rumors about you true?" he asked, bolder than usual, but the absence of friends and peer pressure eased all boundaries for him.

"What rumors?"

"Are you really a witch?"

"Yes, I'm a Wiccan. Look it up."

Tom bit his lip, his gaze traveling around the cafeteria again. This time more than a few people were staring at him, and they dropped their eyes when his passed over them. He glanced back at Raven.

"So, do you have a magic wand?"

For the first time, irritation swept over her features, turning her cheek bones into severe relief maps. "No. Wicca is a belief system. A nature-based religion. And while I appreciate your directness, I wonder whether you're open minded enough to let go of your preconceived notions."

Even the way she spoke carried an old-world flavor, like a shot of single malt whiskey, and he realized he didn't want this conversation to end.

"I'm sorry," he signed.

Her gaze traveled over him and around him and she nodded, saying nothing but taking the last bite of her meal and wiping her mouth with the napkin.

"You're the only one in school besides my brother that believes I'm innocent. Why?"

She smiled and again her gaze seemed to trace an outline of him before meeting his again. "Your aura is pure."

His eyebrows rose. "Wha?"

"I can see auras, and yours is the purest I've ever seen. Your brother is just as unique, but in a different way. He is purity and power bound together by darkness and light, and the darkness in him has always scared me." She glanced toward the table where the defensive line sat. "The rest of the team's auras scream dicks." She brought her gaze back to his. "I never understood what lured you to football, anyway. You never seemed to belong amongst that much negative energy."

Tom smiled, feeling the heat rush to his cheeks, and he shrugged. "I'm good at it," he signed.

"You'd be better at soccer." She pushed her tray to the side and balanced her chin on her palms. Her elbows propped on the table blocked his view of her freckled chest. "Then we'd all get to see a little more of you than that padded suit allows."

This time, he looked down at his empty tray, and the heat in his cheeks increased. He wasn't used to girls he didn't know being this forward, and he finally raised his gaze again.

"Are you hitting on me?"

One of her eyebrows rose, and she glanced from his signed question back to his face with a barely concealed smirk. "Aw, honey, if I was hitting on you, you wouldn't have to ask that question."

Tom blinked in confusion.

A musical laugh belted from her lips, and heads turned in their direction. "Don't look so dejected," she said when her laugh wound down.

In the three years he had been at York High School, he had never heard this girl laugh. If he had, he would have never looked any further. Her laugh was magical and captivating, and it struck him to the core. When the impact faded, guilt replaced it and he looked down, unable to meet her gaze.

Her hand slid across the table, covering his. Her touch burned, like a fiery brand on his soul, and for a moment, he believed everything would turn out just fine.

"We are not compatible," she whispered, shattering his euphoria.

Tom pulled his hand away and sent a glare at her, the pain of rejection opening up the wounds in his heart. He grabbed his book and shoved it in his backpack. Slinging it over his shoulder, he marched out of the cafeteria.

He stopped just outside the front doors when his ankle bracelet beeped. Cursing under his breath, he turned and stepped back into the school, heading for the only other quiet area available.

The library.

Footfalls approached from behind and Tom dropped his backpack and spun, taking a ready stance against whoever was coming at him.

Raven skidded to a stop a few feet from him. "I did not intend to hurt you."

Tom took a deep breath, letting his pounding heart drop back into normal rhythm. He leaned down and picked up his backpack, gathering his thoughts. Once it was back over his shoulder, he signed, "Why aren't we compatible?"

"You're a fire sign and I am a water sign. We would be doomed from the start."

"So, it has nothing to do with me being a half tongued mute?" he asked, and cocked his head.

She stepped forward, placing her palm on his chest. "No. Your handicap doesn't faze me in the least."

He sent a sad smile her way. "There are things I can't do," he said, "And they seem very important to some people."

Raven rolled her eyes. "Where did you get that idea?"

Tom clenched his jaw and stepped back, unable to voice Tanya's disappointment, or her break up speech. She had been fine with it at first, too.

"I can't kiss," he signed.

"Really." She closed the distance and stretched on her toes, pressing her lips to his.

She tasted like salt and fruit punch and before she could break away; he pulled her close, opening his mouth under hers, allowing her tongue to explore. He knew it would only be a matter of seconds before she yanked away in disgust.

Her tongue tickled the roof of his mouth, like a feather, and he let her continue, his expectations dissolving with each feathery touch. This kiss was even more erotic and soul fulfilling than his lip lock with Tanya's ghost yesterday had been. It melted every ounce of restraint and his hands moved, running into the soft wild curls of her hair, holding her lips to his. His heart reacted to her curious exploration, pumping harder in his chest and constricting his breath.

Her hands ran up his chest and around his neck and her breath quickened, drawing a sigh. When she pulled away from his lips, it was sexy slow, accompanied by a smile on her lips and a spark of hunger in her eyes, which was the exact opposite reaction from what he expected.

"Damn fire sign," she muttered and grinned. "Whoever told you that you can't kiss is an idiot."

He pulled out of her arms and bit his lip against the monsoon of emotions caught in his belly and regions south. Guilt and want ate at his insides and he took a step back, creating a distance that allowed him to draw a breath and gain control over his carnal appetite.

Raven's eyes widened at the area surrounding him and when her gaze landed on his, he had to remind himself to breathe.

"Wha?" he asked, curious as to what she was seeing.

"Your aura, it's..."

"What the hell are you doing kissing this little whore?"

Tom's head snapped to his right, his heart clanging in his chest at the manifestation tapping her foot in the hallway. His breath plumed in cold mist, and he stammered, trying to find an explanation. Without thinking, he took a protective step in front of Raven.

"Tanya, what are you doing here?" he said to the ghost chilling his soul.

"You haven't answered me. What are you doing with that hussy?"

From behind him, a warm hand landed on his arm and the combination of Raven's heat and Tanya's chill caused a disturbance in the air. He glanced over his shoulder, meeting Raven's wide-eyed gaze.

He turned back to Tanya. "Go home. Now," he whispered, and her face contorted into a vengeful mask, but she obeyed, fading into the air.

Tom ran a hand through his hair, shaken that she popped up now, and he wondered if her spirit was forever attached to him. He took a breath and focused back on Raven.

"You think seeing auras is disturbing? Try seeing ghosts," he signed and sat on the nearest windowsill.

"Auras aren't disturbing. Well, most of them aren't, but whatever that was, their aura was black, like death."

"That was Tanya," Tom signed and inhaled at the sudden arch of her brow and the slight gasp. He exhaled and shrugged. "I don't know why she's haunting me, especially since she broke up with me the night before she was killed."

Raven's mouth popped closed, and her eyes narrowed. "She was the one," she said, her tone accusatory and angry.

Tom dropped his gaze and nodded.

"Shallow bitch."

Saving Face
Chapter 25

STEVE PROPPED HIS FEET up on the coffee table, switching through the channels, looking for something to occupy his mind. Jennifer sat on the end of the couch, curled up with a stack of scripts in front of her.

After the third round through the channels, Jennifer asked, "You want to read a couple of these and tell me if you think it's worth pursuing?" She handed him half the stack.

Steve glanced at the offering and then met her gaze.

"You're driving me crazy," she said, still holding the stack.

"I'm sorry." Steve settled on the local news station. He dropped the remote on the table and took the stack from her. He figured if the script was good enough, the television wouldn't pull his attention away.

"Thank you." Jennifer sent a smirk his way.

"I can think of a dozen better ways to spend my time," he muttered and flipped open the first script in the pile.

"I need to read these," Jennifer said, waving the pile.

"We could still…" he trailed off at her glare.

"I have to get through these today. If you're so hard up, you're more than welcome to take care of it yourself." She gave him a challenging purse of her lips and he chuckled.

"Touché." He focused on the words in front of him, but his mind kept returning to the thought of her sexy mouth doing all the right things. He glanced in her direction with a suggestive grin plastered on his lips.

Jennifer glanced up from her script and laughed. "Stop looking at me like that."

"Like what?" He feigned innocence.

The ring of the telephone saved her, and he leaned forward, muted the television, and grabbed the phone. He glanced at the caller ID before answering.

"Hey, Ron." He put the papers in his lap aside.

"They're issuing a subpoena for you to appear in front of the grand jury," Cleary said.

Steve sucked in air, and Jennifer's gaze jumped from the script to his. "When?"

"The end of the week."

Steve stared at Jennifer. "That's pretty fast," he said. Jennifer mouthed Tom's name and Steve shook his head, pointing at his chest.

"I told you they were on a witch hunt," Cleary said, and Steve closed his eyes, thankful for the bitter tone in his boss's voice.

"Have you been interviewed yet?"

Cleary laughed. "No. They didn't ask, and I didn't volunteer."

Steve opened his eyes. "Okay," he said. "What's happening with Sarah?"

"She told them she asked you about Ty, but you didn't come clean with her until the day of his funeral. From what I understand, they're going to give her a formal reprimand for failing to bring this to the attention of her superiors."

"What are they charging me with?"

"Aiding and abetting a known criminal, extortion, and reckless endangerment. They haven't found anything concrete that could lead to charges related to either his death or Jessica's, so they drummed up reckless endangerment for allowing them access to key case details during an investigation. I just thought you'd like to prepare for this."

"Jesus." Steve dropped his head against the pillows behind him. "If I'm found guilty, what's the penalty I'm looking at?"

"They are going for the maximum they can get for each count, so you're looking at thirty years before you're eligible for parole."

"Thirty years?"

"And a five million dollar fine," Cleary said.

His mouth turned bitter, like he'd bitten into a bad lemon, and he clenched his teeth. "So, my record doesn't count at all."

"Not to them."

Steve closed his eyes and ran his hand down his face. "Fucking bureaucrats," he muttered and took a deep breath. "Anything further on the Windwalker?"

"No, nothing."

"Thanks for the heads up. I guess I'll see you in Washington when the time comes."

"I'll be there."

Steve hung up the phone and tossed it onto the table.

"They could put you away for thirty years?" Jennifer asked.

He nodded and glanced in her direction. The color in her face drained, and she shook her head.

"No, that can't happen," she gasped.

Steve shrugged.

"You'd better do whatever you can to not land in jail. Understand?" Jennifer said. Her tone and her stare, coupled with the paleness in her cheeks, sent a severe message and he nodded.

"I'll do my best."

"No! Promise me you'll make this go away," she said, slamming the stack on the table.

Steve pressed his lips together for a moment, debating on whether or not to make that promise. He had never used his powers to persuade anyone for personal gain and wasn't sure he could, just on principle alone. It was against everything he stood for.

Her insistent gaze transitioned to a glare.

"You're not going to save yourself, are you?"

Before he could answer, she stormed out of the living room and up the stairs. The bedroom door slammed, shaking the house from the force.

Saving Face
Chapter 26

STEVE PULLED UP TO the front of the school and glanced at the clock. He had a couple minutes before the bell rang and he shifted the car into park. The earlier conversation with Cleary kept replaying in his mind and he glanced at the high school, wondering what would happen to CJ and Tom if he landed in jail.

Welcome to my world. Ty's voice echoed in Steve's head.

"Your attempt at keeping your kids safe is going all to hell," Steve whispered.

"Don't worry. You won't go to jail."

Steve scoffed, and the school bell rang. He turned his attention to the front door. Kids flooded out like a bunch of ants, scurrying to the buses and scattering towards the different exits. When Tom appeared, it took Steve a moment to realize the girl walking next to Tom was actually talking to him, and she didn't have that accusatory glare when she looked at him.

Tom said goodbye and headed toward the car, his expression not quite happy, but at peace, and Steve said a silent prayer of thanks.

TOM OPENED THE DOOR and glanced back toward Raven, his good mood souring.

"Get in," Steve barked the order from within the car.

"Bu..." Tom leaned down, meeting Steve's glare. He glanced back at Raven and swallowed both his anger and the underlying fear for her safety. Bear and the other defensive linebackers surrounded her, their taunting barely audible over the bus engines.

"You can't help her unless you're willing to spend the next who knows how long locked up in jail."

"It's my fault," Tom signed.

"CJ's on his way. Now get in the car," Steve said.

Tom sat against his will and glared at Steve as his door slammed shut. He couldn't move and couldn't speak under Steve's silent control. Anger flared like a dormant volcano bursting through the surface, and Tom did the only thing he could. He voiced his dissatisfaction with a litany of projected curses.

Steve sent an eye roll in his direction, and that burned through the frustration. *She is the only one at school that talks to me. I'm sure she's not going to give me the time of day after this. Thank you very much.*

"Like she'd give you the time of day if you were in jail."

You're a real prick, you know that?

"Yes, I am."

Tom felt the invisible restraints lift as they pulled into the garage, and before Steve stopped the car fully, he was out and storming into the house without a glance back. He even slammed the garage door for good measure.

"How was your day?" Jennifer said from the stairwell.

"Fine," Tom signed and marched across the kitchen. Before he hit the archway into the family room, the temperature dropped, and his feet flew from under him. Instead of finding himself on his back on the floor, his spine slammed into the wall, along with the back of his head, and he stared into Tanya's furious eyes.

"You cheated on me today," she growled.

Jennifer was halfway across the family room when Tom put his hand out like a traffic guard, stopping her with a shake of his head. He didn't know what Tanya would do if anyone interceded, especially with the fury radiating from her in frigid waves.

He glanced in the other direction, meeting Steve's frozen stare in the doorway, the keys held over the key dish in a shocked pause. Tom knew Steve heard Tanya's voice in his head, along with her accusation, and he glanced back at her.

"Put me down." He had the luxury of seeing Jennifer's reaction just before Tanya slammed him into the wall again.

"You're mine."

He laughed. "You gave up the right to be possessive when you broke up with me," he said, but she still held him in place and her eyes narrowed to slits of fury.

"You told me you loved me," she snapped.

"I did."

"You still do," she screamed.

"Tanya, you are dead. Dead, as in no more. You're just a spirit."

"You kissed me yesterday," she repeated, her voice cold and detached and her face a mask of anger.

"I wanted to see if I could, okay? I was curious, especially since you can hear me."

"You were curious?"

He knew he said the wrong thing and her hand holding a fistful of his shirt tightened along with the one by her side.

"What about us?" The whispered question sent a cascade of shivers down his spine.

"There is no more us. There isn't any chance of us ever again." He tried to break her grip.

She screamed and stepped back, her hand forming a claw, and she aimed it at his chest. "Your heart is mine!"

Black fury filled the room, and when her nails passed through his skin, Tom went rigid. Pain gripped his chest as her ghost squeezed his heart.

The flurry of white wings filled his vision and Tanya was yanked away from him, her scream making him cover his ears, but he couldn't block the angel tossing her aside like a rag doll.

"Get away from my son," Ty roared, positioning himself between Tom and the ghost, his wings spread enough to block Tom's view.

"Take her to heaven, Dad," Tom whispered, and Ty turned his head, meeting his gaze.

"I can't. She had a chance but made the choice to stay and that door won't open again until she lets go or we can find the last piece of her and put her to rest properly."

Tanya stood and glared at the angel before her gaze moved over Ty's shoulder, meeting Tom's. "This isn't over."

Her form dissolved and the air in the room returned to normal. Ty turned, his wings folding neatly behind him, and he offered a nod.

"Thank you, Dad," Tom said.

He smiled and glanced in Steve's direction.

Tom glanced at Steve. Steve's eyes bounced between Ty and where Tanya had stood a moment before. His mouth propped open in a lazy 'O'. The jolt of surprise stabbed Tom as hard as Tanya's nails had.

"Ou aw." He clamped his mouth shut in surprise. His words were no longer clear now that Tanya had disappeared, and his gaze snapped back to Ty. Ty's shoulders rose and fell in a pronounced shrug, leaving him no explanation for the phenomenon.

"You got yourself one pissed off ghost," Ty said. Papers on the kitchen table fluttered in the breeze of his sigh. "I know you didn't kill her, so what the hell did you do?"

I kissed another girl at school today.

"The redhead?" Steve asked.

"What redhead?" Jennifer asked from the living room.

"Ye," Tom said, meeting Steve's gaze.

Ty started chuckling. "Boy, where the hell is your common sense? She hasn't even been dead a week."

Tom crossed his arms and glared. *I didn't mean to.*

"What? You tripped and your lips happened to land on hers?" Ty continued to laugh.

"Fu you." Tom stormed up the stairs, leaving Steve and Jennifer staring at each other.

Saving Face
Chapter 27

CJ HEARD STEVE'S SOS call and pulled next to the curb, turning off his car and pocketing the keys. He walked toward Bear and the rest of the defensive line he'd rumbled with yesterday. They just didn't stop and this time their target was that weird girl no one talked to. The reason burned him enough to want to lose control.

She was being terrorized because she had been nice to Tom.

"Did you spread your evil legs for him, witch whore?" Bear taunted and grabbed at her. "How long have you been fucking him?"

She slapped his hand away, but another grabbed at her and another and she spun toward each attacker with her book bag long forgotten at her feet.

"Is that why he killed Tanya? To be with you?"

"Enough," CJ said when he got close enough for them to hear. "Leave her alone."

The girl spun toward his voice, her eyes wide and terrified, but not of him. Underneath the terror, he saw relief.

Bear turned in his direction. "This is none of your concern," he snarled.

CJ laughed. "You never fucking learn, do you?" He didn't wait for anymore comments. He let the anger loose, knocking them down with a blast that seemed to come from the girl, and he walked into the center of the stunned group, picked up her bag and took her hand. "Come with me," he said, and she followed, staring at him with awe.

He opened his passenger door and dropped her bag on the floor, helping her inside before he closed the door. Before he got into the driver's side, he pointed his finger at Bear. "I told you not to fuck with me. Next time, I won't just knock you on your ass."

Bear's eyes widened.

CJ smiled. "No. She didn't do that. I did." He slipped into the car.

When he pulled out onto Webber Road, she cleared her throat.

"If you can do that, why did you let them beat the crap out of you?"

CJ sent a sideways glance at her and smiled. "If you noticed, I did a good deal of damage myself," he said. "Besides, if I used my gifts, it wouldn't be a fair fight, and I'd be no better than they are."

Silence filled the car.

"Thank you for being nice to Tom today," he said.

She nodded. Her hand grasped the medallion around her neck and her lips moved silently. She thought he couldn't hear her prayers and he would have left it alone, but she was praying to find the strength to forgive Tom for leaving her in the midst of those thugs.

"Don't be mad at Tom. If it had been up to him, he would have swooped in and tried to be a hero, but my father made him get in the car. Tom didn't have a choice." He traded a glance with her. "He wanted to pound those guys to a pulp, but he's only given so much time to get home. If he doesn't, they'll put him back in jail."

Her wide eyes made him smile.

"Yes, I read minds too." He glanced at her. "They called me to make sure you get home safely. But I think we should take a detour so Tom can see for himself."

"You've never stepped in before," she said.

Her words had an impact like Bear's fist, and he exhaled, blowing a stream of air from his lips. She knew how to work the guilt card and he nodded without turning in her direction. He had stood by while his teammates sent out various catcalls in her direction and, what was worse, he knew the damage those words were inflicting.

"I'm sorry," he said as he approached the media filled gate to the house.

"What's all this?" Raven asked, shrinking in the seat.

"The lovely media," CJ said, and the snark bled through his tone. He revved his engine, and they scattered like a flock of seagulls letting him drive through the opening gates. As soon as they cleared the metal, it closed on the reporters.

"They seem to think we're newsworthy." He rolled his eyes, turning the car off.

He opened the passenger door and escorted her into the garage, opening the door to the house for her while silently announcing to Tom that he had a guest.

Raven stopped on the concrete floor, unwilling to step into the house. Her skin turned ashen, and she backed away. Tom slid to a stop at the entrance, his eyes as wild as Raven's, and he turned to CJ.

"Tanya's pissed," Tom signed.

CJ's expression hardened, and he charged inside, but Tom grabbed his arm. *You can't stop her, only Dad can.*

"Dad?"

Tom nodded and turned a nervous smile at Raven. "I'm sorry I left you with those assholes," he signed.

Raven nodded and blinked, looking beyond him into the belly of the house. "Do you have any sage?"

"Why?" Both CJ and Tom asked.

"Because it has a calming effect on spirits."

"You really are a witch." CJ said.

Tom smacked him in the chest.

"That has nothing to do with it. I just happen to do my research after watching one of those ghost chaser shows. They always use sage to calm the more, um, spirited spirits."

"Oh." CJ's cheeks burned. "We don't have any that I know of."

Raven met Tom's gaze. "Do you think it will help if I talk to her?"

Tom laughed and shook his head.

Her hands went to her waist, and her face pinched in irritation.

"She tried to kill me," Tom signed.

CJ's gaze snapped to Tom. "You're kidding?"

"Afraid not. She seems to have laid claim to me, and I really don't think she's going to like Raven entering the house," he signed.

"That's fucking ridiculous." CJ walked into the house, leaving Tom and Raven staring at each other.

"I THINK I CAN handle it, Tom," Raven said, meeting his gaze.

Tom swallowed and shoved his hands into his pockets. He stepped down in front of her, blocking the doorway. There was too much going on inside the house and he didn't want to alienate her, or worse, have Tanya's ghost harm her.

Raven shifted and sighed, studying Tom. "Look, I highly doubt there's anything else that could surprise me today."

Tom raised an eyebrow as a silent you want to bet. He pulled his hands from his pockets. "I don't want you to get hurt."

She stepped closer and smiled. "Until today, you couldn't have cared less. Besides, what can a ghost really do?"

Tom unbuttoned his shirt, showing her the black and blue mark over his heart.

Raven's eyes widened, and she reached out, tracing the mark.

Her touch was like an electric therapy machine, sending tingles to his core, and he wondered just what she would be like between the sheets. He inhaled, driving the inappropriate thoughts out of his head, especially with Tanya in the vicinity.

She lifted her gaze to his and placed her palm over the mark. "She tried to take your heart?"

He shrugged. "Yeah."

When Raven's hand left his skin, he felt the mental tug and the resulting emptiness. This feeling of connection was something he had never felt with Tanya, and he wondered if he even knew what love was. In all his escapades, in his pursuit of something more, this had been missing.

This calm acceptance.

This fire in his soul.

This.

Raven reached for the chain around her neck, pulling a medallion from under her shirt. He stared at the intricate silver knot holding an interwoven circle of diamonds. She kissed the metal and then slipped it over his head.

"I can't take this," he signed and reached for the chain.

She pressed the pendant against his skin, and he glanced at her hand. The silver lay directly over his heart.

"It will protect you."

He smiled at her simple faith and the conviction in her eyes. "Then what will protect you?"

She held up her wrist, and her charm bracelet caught the light. The same Celtic knot graced her bracelet, along with several other charms.

"So, are you going to let me in or not?" She waved toward the door.

Tom buttoned up his shirt and nodded. "But don't say I didn't warn you," he signed and stepped aside, allowing her to enter.

Halfway through the kitchen, she stopped and shaded her eyes, squinting toward the family room. "What the hell do you have living here? An angel?"

CJ and Steve turned in their direction and so did Ty, his wings fluttering and his gaze landing on Tom.

"She can see me?" Ty asked.

Tom shook his head. "No, just your aura," he signed and glanced at Raven. "Still think nothing else can surprise you?"

She laughed, and it came out higher pitched and laced with nerves. "Aye, and here I thought we were considered odd." In her nervous state, her Irish brogue wrapped around her words, sharpening them and making Tom smile.

Steve's lips thinned, and his cheeks bloomed, his hard glare landing on Tom.

"At least she's not running out of the house screaming," CJ said, breaking down the tension and bringing a smile to everyone's face.

"So, let me get this straight. You think it's weird that I'm a Wiccan, and yet, you see ghosts and angels," she said to Tom and then she nodded toward CJ. "And he can read minds and has telekinetic powers?" Silence filled the room and then she burst out laughing, the same genuine laugh she had in the cafeteria.

"If you only knew the half of it," Jennifer said. She crossed the family room and stuck her hand out. "I'm Jennifer. Welcome to our home." She offered a welcoming smile.

"Hi, I'm Raven." She clasped Jennifer's hand.

"How long have you known Tommy?" she asked.

"Today was the first time I spoke to him," Raven answered, still squinting.

Jennifer turned to Steve. "Can you tell him to go? He's obviously blinding the girl."

Raven blinked and looked around, her gaze landing on Tom, and a crease appeared between her eyes.

"He's gone," Tom signed.

"Why don't you come and sit down?" Jennifer led her into the family room.

The last thing Tom wanted was for Jennifer and Steve to grill her and he traded a glance with CJ, getting a nod in return before he walked by and grabbed her hand, leading her out the back door into the yard.

"Let him go," CJ said, stopping Jennifer and Steve from following.

Tom didn't stop until he got to the rock wall and then he turned, taking a seat on the frigid stones.

"So, who's the angel?"

"My father," Tom signed.

"I thought humans couldn't become angels." She glanced over his shoulder at the water, pressing her lips together. "How can he be an angel?"

He didn't have a logical answer for her, so he kept his hands still and remained patient, waiting for her gaze to come back. After a few excruciating minutes, she turned and took a seat next to him. Silence prevailed, and she studied the house.

"Did Tanya know about any of this?" She waved toward the house.

The question struck him, and he laughed. "Are you kidding me?"

She met his gaze, and he continued to chuckle.

"Tanya would have hightailed it out of here in a blink and then made sure everyone under the sun knew we were freaks."

Dimples appeared on her cheeks, and she pressed her lips against the smile forming. "What about your best friend, Bear?" she asked.

"Same deal. I think the only reason he stayed my friend after Georgia was some misplaced sense of loyalty. Either that or he knows we're filthy rich and figured he'd get something out of it," he said. "You asked me why I hung out with those guys. Well, nothing has been normal for me since Georgia and being involved in sports helped me feel less like a freak."

"What happened in Georgia?"

He glanced at her and sighed. "I was carved up by a madman."

Her eyes slowly widened, and her gaze shot from his hands to his face.

"I ue o be orma," he said. "But that bastard took half my tongue," he signed. A sudden mist clouded his vision, and he looked at the sky, blinking the unwanted tears away. "And he killed my mother, too. Propped her head up at the end of the surgical table where I was chained. So, I'm about as damaged as they come."

She reached over and took his hand, gave it a squeeze, and brought it to her lips.

"If it wasn't for Steve, I would have died down there."

"So why trust me with all this?"

Tom dropped his gaze to hers. A single tear rolled down her cheek, and he wiped it away with the back of his finger. "I need a friend," he signed and swallowed the lump that formed in his throat.

"But how do you know I won't go blabbing to everyone about what a mess you really are?"

He shrugged. "I don't know," he signed and then pulled the medallion from under his shirt. "Perhaps it was this?"

Her gaze dropped to the ground, but he tilted her chin back, so she was looking at him.

"I'm sorry I ever ignored you at school," he signed and then tucked a stray hair behind her ear.

Her eyes glazed with tears, and he pulled her into his arms, hugging her tight.

"You're the first person who wanted to be my friend," she whispered in his ear. "And it's only because you're alone." She pulled out of his grasp, swiping at the tears on her face like they were annoying gnats.

"That's not true," he signed.

"You mean to tell me if none of this had ever happened, you would have noticed me?"

He closed his mouth, meeting her gaze. She was right. He would have gone on, being one of the elite star players and walking around like he was hot shit, never giving her a second glance.

The revelation brought on a hot flare of shame, and he looked at the ground.

"Everything happens for a reason," he signed, and her scoff brought his gaze back to hers.

The sound of the slider drew his attention, and he glanced toward the house. Steve crossed the lawn. "I think I should take Raven home now," he said, leveling a stare at Tom.

Tom glanced at Raven. "Thank you for everything," he said.

She just nodded and followed Steve into the house.

Tom sat in the cold for a few minutes, mulling over the conversation and the sudden emptiness blanketing him. It was like waking to find that everything you believed was a sham and there was no grain of truth to cling to. He stood and turned toward the ocean, shoving his hands in his pockets, trying to gain a little perspective. Her words ate at him, burrowing under his skin and sending chills of despair down his spine.

Saving Face
Chapter 28

A S SOON AS THE car cleared the sea of reporters, Steve glanced at his passenger. She was a pretty girl, fiery and proud and quite the opposite of everything Tanya had been.

"So, what can you do?" Raven asked with more than a hint of sarcasm.

"A little of this and a little of that," Steve said, being evasive.

She sent a glance in his direction. "Both you and CJ have very complex auras. Auras that are almost identical, except yours is woven with the same light the angel broadcasted." She paused. "I would expect the same signatures from a biological father and son, but you two aren't even related by blood."

Steve sighed, listening to the whirlwind in her mind, and as far as he could tell, she only had honorable intentions. However, he had to protect Tom, so he asked, "What exactly do you hope to gain from us?"

Her jaw tightened, and she stiffened in the seat, offended by the question. She turned her gaze out the window so she wouldn't send a wicked glare in his direction.

"Look, I can sense you don't have an agenda, but I need to be very clear. Tom is in an especially precarious place right now. I'm not just talking about seeing Tanya's ghost, I'm talking about his entire mental state." He pulled over in one of the parking spots lining the beach. "He's lost a great deal already and I'm amazed he chooses to still see the good in the world after everything he's been through, but I'm not sure how much longer he'll be able to if you decide to play games with him."

"I never planned on playing games. I just felt sorry for him," she said.

"All I'm saying is, don't play games with him. For reasons I can't fathom, he seems to trust you. He hasn't spoken about Georgia to anyone, so his telling you what happened was a big deal," Steve said, wanting to impress the magnitude of Tom's confessions. "Tom doesn't have an agenda," he said, and she scoffed, rolling her eyes.

Steve grinned. "Okay, maybe he does, but it's different with you."

She raised an eyebrow. "You don't think he wants to get me into bed?"

Steve laughed. "I'm not sure it's my place to answer that. Besides, if you give him a chance, you'll find he is a very loyal soul."

"I don't want to be a rebound or just another notch on his headboard," she said. "I just thought he could use a friend."

"He can. All I'm saying is if you want to be his friend, then *be* his friend."

She nodded, and he pulled out onto the road.

"You need to take the next left."

Steve smiled. "I know where you live," he said. "I don't need directions."

"So that's your talent?"

He grinned and winked at her. "I'm an FBI agent. I know where everyone lives."

Her chuckle was musical, and he understood what drew Tom to her. After several turns, he pulled into her driveway and extended his hand. "It was a pleasure to meet you, Raven. I hope you decide to visit more often."

She clasped his hand and shook with a firm grip. Before she got out of the car, she scribbled numbers on a piece of paper and handed it to Steve.

"That's my phone number," she pointed when he raised his eyebrows.

"I know what it is, but I'm not sure you're thinking clearly."

She glanced at the paper and then his face, the confusion clear.

"You wouldn't have Skype, would you?" he asked, trying to be diplomatic.

It clicked in her mind, and her face turned red. "Oh my god, I'm such an idiot. I'm so sorry, but no, I don't own a computer."

Steve pocketed the paper. "I'm sure he'll appreciate the gesture."

"I didn't mean..." she started.

"I know," Steve interrupted.

"I just forget sometimes." She opened the car door. "You know, I learned sign language our freshman year just so I'd understand what he was saying." She stepped out of the car and leaned over so she could see him. "I figured he was being just as snarky as the rest of them. But I was wrong. Not once in the last three years of high school did he make fun of me. Not once, even when those around him were." She kept Steve's gaze. "He actually tried to get them to back off, but they ignored him, telling him to stop being such a boy scout."

Steve smiled. "He's a good kid, and I'm glad someone besides us can see that."

Saving Face
Chapter 29

TOM STARED AT THE ceiling in his bedroom, going over the day. He looked down at the medallion, tracing the lines with his finger before slipping it back under his shirt. The metal warmed his skin, and he sighed. His breath plumed white on the air, and he shot into a sitting position, his eyes darting around the room.

"Tanya?" Just speaking her name was confirmation, and a trace of cold air tickled his ear. He jumped to his feet, spinning around toward the bed and there she was, lounging with her head propped on her hand. He blinked at the smile she wore and nothing else, her figure as seductive as it had been when she was alive.

She slipped her finger in her mouth and drew it out slowly, suggesting more than she ever gave him when she was flesh and blood and, against his best judgment, his body reacted.

"See, you still want me," she whispered.

He cursed his lack of self-control and stared at her, afraid to move because he knew the moment she got her hands on him, it was all over and the idea of fucking a ghost just gave him the willies.

"I never denied wanting you. You're the one who didn't want me, remember?"

"Ah, but that was before. Now there's nothing on earth I want more."

"How about your face?" he asked, the words flying out before he could stop them. Her eyes widened, and he kept his expression frozen in a challenging stare, despite the horrific transition from seductive beauty to the scalped corpse he found. "That's right, you heard me. I saw what was left of you. I was trying to save you, and that's why they arrested me." The anger that lay dormant, deep within him, flared and his hands clenched. "So not only did you break my heart, you just may be the reason I land on death row."

Her jaw dropped, and the bloody sockets of her eyes widened.

"So, if you have any connection to what's left of you, find it and tell me where it is so I can end the bastard that ruined you," he said, pointing out his window.

Tanya's hand wiped across her cheek, bringing away a thick layer of blood and she gasped, her gaze darting from the red gunk on her fingers to Tom. "He took my face?"

"That's what the Windwalker does," he said, driving his point home.

She covered her face and screamed, her pitch dropping Tom to his knees, and he covered his ears. Pain filled his head and his hand dropped to the medallion, gripping it like the last zip line between him and a drop to his death.

White light pierced the room and her scream faded, replaced by the echo of pounding wings.

When Tom looked up, the room was empty, and he glanced at the door. CJ stood staring at the ceiling, his eyes as wide as Tanya's had been.

You saw Dad?

CJ's gaze dropped to him, and he nodded. "He took her out of your room." He bit his lip. "You kissed that?"

Tom shuddered. *No, she was, um, whole when I kissed her.*

"But that's what she looked like when you found her?" he asked, and his voice cracked.

"Yah." Tom climbed to his feet.

"Holy shit."

Tom nodded. "I was freaked beyond reason when I turned her over," he signed. "The cops came before I had the sense to scream."

CJ's shock turned into a grin. "Dude, *that* would have made me scream senseless."

"Yeah, and you scream like a little girl," Tom grinned back.

CJ's smile faded, and he looked at the ceiling before returning his gaze to Tom's. "You okay?"

Tom shifted his weight, thinking about the question before he met CJ's gaze. "I don't know," he signed. "Where's Jen?"

"She went to the store after Steve left," CJ said. "Want to play Medal of Honor?"

"Sure, but can you do me a favor? Can you get this stupid thing off me?" Tom signed and raised the cast. "Don't vaporize it; just leave it so I can slip it on in the morning."

CJ nodded, and the crack of fiberglass filled the room.

The cast split from the thumb to just shy of Tom's elbow, leaving only the palm intact. The cut was done with surgical precision, and Tom gave CJ a nod of appreciation. "Impressive," Tom signed and forced the fiberglass off his arm, scratching the dry skin and flexing his hand.

Steve walked into a calmer home. CJ and Tom played one of their war games on the television and Jennifer wasn't back from the store yet. He pulled the paper out and handed it to Tom. "That's her number."

Tom looked at the paper and up at Steve.

"I know. She flaked out for a moment, but that's the only way to get hold of her," he said. "She seems like a nice girl."

Tom nodded and pocketed the note, returning his focus to the game.

"Can you two turn the television off for a minute?" Steve asked and walked in front of the television, interrupting their line of sight.

Both boys looked up with the same crease of irritation between their eyes.

"I need to talk to you," he said, and it took a moment for the words to sink in and then the television behind him shut off. "Thank you." He took a seat on the couch adjacent to them.

"What's going on?" CJ asked, his eyes squinted in concentration.

"I'm blocking you," Steve started and held up a hand to squash CJ's interruption. "I'm blocking you because I want you both to hear this from me." He traded a glance with Tom before he moved his gaze to CJ. "I need to go down to Washington at the end of the week."

CJ crossed his arms, his eyes narrowing and his mind filtering over the plethora of facts pinging in his head.

"I'm being charged with aiding and abetting a known criminal, extortion and reckless endangerment," he said, voicing the charges for the first time. Inside, he cringed. Just the thought of being arrested set his blood boiling, but now wasn't the time to create a scene.

"That's bullshit!" CJ said, and Tom nodded his approval at the statement.

"I didn't extort anything from your family," he said. "But the other two, well, I can't defend against them because I did both." He inhaled and studied his hands. "From what my boss said, I could be looking at thirty years in a federal penitentiary." He looked at the boys.

CJ crossed his arms. "What in God's name are they thinking?"

"They're thinking I abused my power as an FBI agent, and honestly, they're right. I coerced your mother into coming to the hospital and infusing Jen with her mojo in return for your father's freedom. Therefore, I am guilty of coercion. I didn't bring your father in. Instead, I let him help me catch Kyle Winslow and because of that oversight, he died saving us. Between that and bringing you to Georgia, they've got a strong case for reckless endangerment, too."

"You did what you had to do," CJ said.

Steve sighed. "No, CJ, I didn't. I ignored my oath in favor of personal gain. As a federal officer, it was my sworn duty to bring your father in and I didn't. They don't care why, and I can't reasonably explain why without bringing a whole other level of scrutiny on this family."

CJ tilted his head, reading between the lines. "So, you're going to take the fall for us?"

"That's what I'm saying," he said. "Neither of you needs that kind of attention."

"No." CJ crossed his arms.

"No, what?" Steve leaned back in the seat.

"No, you're not going to jail. Just...no."

"CJ."

"No! No one is going to jail," CJ yelled. Before Steve knew it, CJ was on his feet, his face turning red under the pressure of his anger. And he stormed past, headed for the solace of the backyard.

The door slammed closed, and Steve turned to Tom.

"Don't look at me," Tom signed and threw his hands up. "I agwee." He stood to go after his brother.

"Do you have any idea what they'd do to him if they knew what he could do?"

Tom paused and looked over his shoulder at Steve. *The same could be said about you.* He disappeared through the door, leaving Steve sitting alone.

Saving Face
Chapter 30

CJ WALKED THE PERIMETER of the backyard, his hands squeezing and stretching in an attempt to control the anger wrapped around his chest and eradicate the red flares in his line of sight. He knew Tom came out after him and was waiting patiently in one of the lounge chairs, but he couldn't talk to him, not right now.

Not with this raging beast eating him from the inside out.

He stopped at the intersection of the wall and the path and glanced back at the house for a moment.

"Fuck it," he muttered and darted down the zigzagging trail, stepping by memory in the dusk. Instead of climbing the stairs down to the dock, he jumped the ten feet, landing square. The lowering tide had pulled most of the water out of the pool, leaving only a layer of cold muck behind. Beyond the boulders, the waves lapped at rock; he relished the chill, considering whether the frigid water would cool him off quicker.

You'll get hypothermia if you go in that water.
Tom's voice reasoned in his head, and he looked
up at the ledge above and Tom's silhouette
against the darkening sky.

"So what?"

*Then I'd get hypothermia jumping in to save
your ass.*

"Fine, I won't go in. Can you just give me
some space for a while?"

Tom raised his hands and backed away from
the edge, disappearing from view.

CJ stared out at the black water, calming his
emotions. Anger was the easiest to identify and
soothe. But the one that clenched his insides
like a panther on the back of its prey was harder
to define, more elusive and twice as crippling.

When the revelation came, he closed his eyes.

Fear.

Fear tasted like a sickly sweet dose of
medicine that made him want to vomit.

Knowing it was fear that clawed his stomach
to shreds didn't help either, and he wondered
how many times his father felt this crippling
dread.

"Too many times."

CJ glanced up at the timber of Steve's voice.

"Your father was on the run for most of his
life, and once he had you and Tom, every day
was a battle for him," Steve said as he climbed
down the ladder and took a seat next to CJ. "He
loved you boys, and he was so afraid of losing
you."

CJ glanced at Steve and then back at the
water, not acknowledging that he spoke.

"Every day he thought twice about staying in your lives, wondering if he would be the one to poison the inherent goodness you got from your mother."

"We shouldn't even exist," CJ whispered.

"I think you're wrong. Everything happens for a reason."

"Don't give me that bullshit!" CJ moved to stand, and an invisible hand shoved him back down.

"Sit down," Steve barked the command, glaring at CJ.

The abrupt change in manner shocked CJ into complying and not rebelling like he normally would.

"Your father had pure intent in him at one time. Did you know he used to put himself between his brother and his stepfather, knowing he might end up in the hospital because of it?"

CJ blinked and shook his head. "I, I didn't know that."

"And even the repeated beatings and broken bones didn't break his spirit. When his stepfather carved his face up, that came close, but he still had both his brother and sister. It was when his sister was murdered that he lost it. When she died, everything honorable inside him did, too. The only thing that remained was his militant sense of protection over his little brother. That never left." Steve took a breath and scanned the ocean. "I know that doesn't come close to making up for everything he did. He crossed moral and legal lines neither of us would ever dream of crossing. But that feeling of being his brother's protector, well, that wasn't a bad thing, and it seems he passed that down to you."

CJ narrowed his eyes. Something in Steve's narration bothered him, and when Steve met his gaze, he got it. "You want me to protect Tom?"

"Yes. He's going to need it until they catch the real killer."

"You know you don't even have to ask. It's a given," CJ said.

"We've split time on this one ever since we got back from Georgia, so you've been afforded a break, but when I'm in Washington, you won't get any relief. It's a twenty-four by seven job to keep him out of harm's way. I won't be here to fix him if the shit hits the fan."

"So, my mission, should I choose to accept it..." He grinned and gave Steve a sideways glance.

"Smart ass." Steve smiled back. "Come on, Jen should be back by now."

Steve climbed the steps first, and CJ paused halfway up, tilting his head and listening. He scurried up and caught up to Steve, grabbing his arm and stopping him.

"Did you know?" he snapped.

Steve glanced at CJ, leveling a gaze that told him enough, but he opened his mouth, confirming CJ's suspicions. "I knew they wouldn't wait. Not with the case they're building. In their minds, I'm too much of a flight risk."

"Won't they throw Tom back in jail if you're not here?"

Steve stopped and turned, taking CJ by the shoulders. "Jennifer is here, and she has the same responsibilities I do where Tom's house arrest is concerned, so no, he won't go back to jail unless he screws up."

"What if she has one of her auditions?"

"Then you take him to and from school."

CJ shoved his hands in his pocket and nodded. Whether he wanted to admit it, the fear of losing another loved one ate at his insides, creating an icy hot pain in the pit of his stomach.

"You're not losing me."

CJ met his sincere stare. "Why don't I believe that?" he asked and broke away, walking the path back to the house, knowing an ambush lay in wait for Steve inside the house.

STEVE LOOKED AT THE sky, counting the visible stars. "You need to stay and watch over them," he said to the heavenly lights.

Silence met his order, and he glanced up at the sky again.

"I'm serious. Tom is your priority. Promise me you'll stay here until they catch the bastard."

That's not how it works. Ty's voice echoed in his mind.

"I don't care. It's the only way I'll know he's safe."

Fine, I'll stay.

"Thanks."

Don't forget to call Lynn. She's got papers that can help.

Steve nodded and collected his nerves. Taking a deep breath, he stepped from the heavy brush onto the lawn. A flurry of activity hit from all sides, and at least a dozen firearms pointed in his direction. He raised his hands, so they were in clear view and looked beyond the agents into the family room, meeting Jennifer's panicked gaze.

Cleary held her in place in a bear hug and she fought like a tiger to get loose. He could hear the curses flowing from her mouth even through the closed glass door.

"Hands on your head," one of the team ordered.

Steve knew the drill, and he put his hands on his head and dropped to his knees before that command followed. He kept eye contact with Jennifer. *Calm down, babe. You'll be fine.*

Jennifer stopped struggling, and the tears glistened on her cheeks, driving a stab of pain in his heart. The thought that this could be the last time he saw her for a very long time brought a mist to his eyes and he blinked it back. Tom and CJ stood next to Cleary, just staring out at the chaos.

Cold metal clamped around his wrists and Steve tightened his jaw, trying to hang onto the iota of pride he had left.

"Do you have to do that?" he asked the agent behind him, meeting his sharp glare.

The disgust was clear in both his facial features and his thoughts, and Steve turned his gaze back to the house, giving Jennifer a nod as they helped him to his feet.

"You have the right to remain silent," the agent began, and Steve tuned him out.

Call Lynn Trueman and let her know what's happening. Ty said she has papers that may help my situation.

Jennifer's eyebrow rose.

He planned for this.

Her mouth dropped and then popped closed, anger replacing the shock and despair of his arrest. His gaze flicked to the boys and back, and the beginning of her silent rant shut off.

Steve glanced at the officer. "Yes, I understand my rights," he answered when they finished reading him the Miranda rights.

"You're a disgrace to the Bureau."

Steve glanced at his badge. "You don't know shit, Scully." He tilted his head. "Funny, you don't look like a hot redhead," he said, pushing the agent's buttons and keeping his own temper in check with the slant.

Scully's face turned red, and his glare got downright dangerous.

"Oh, come on, don't tell me you've never been razzed about your name." Steve received a yank toward the house as a response. He refrained from any more comment because Scully was a push away from clocking him.

The slider opened, and Jennifer broke from Cleary's grip, running to Steve and wrapping her arms around his neck.

Scully didn't pause. He dragged Steve and Jennifer toward the front door until Steve yanked his arm from his grasp.

"Let me say goodbye to my wife," Steve growled, sending a glare in his direction.

"Give him a minute," Cleary said.

Jennifer pressed her lips to his, and he closed his eyes, relishing the salty taste of her tears along with the sweetness of her cherry lip-gloss. She pulled away and held on like his life depended on it.

Steve kissed the crook of her neck. "I love you, babe," he whispered in her ear. "You have to let go."

She shook her head, pressing her face into his chest, muffling the first sob.

"Look at me." After a tight squeeze, she lifted her head, meeting his gaze. "We will be okay. I promise."

"Don't make promises you can't keep."

He offered her a weak smile and kissed her forehead. Steve glanced over his shoulder at the boys. "Take care of her while I'm gone."

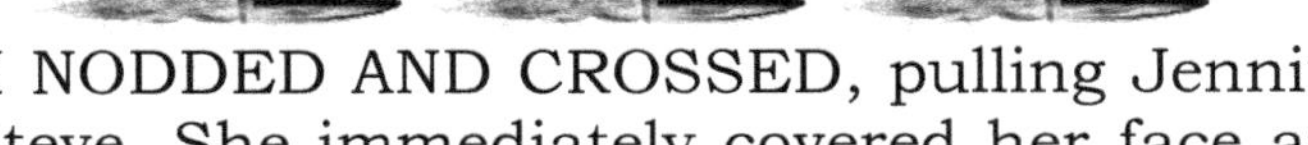

TOM NODDED AND CROSSED, pulling Jennifer off Steve. She immediately covered her face and burrowed in his chest, her sobs as heartbreaking as seeing Steve led out the front door and into the media frenzy on their front lawn.

The feds filed out, escorting Steve through the sea of vultures, hurling question after question at him. The door slammed closed, leaving Jennifer and the boys alone with Cleary. Jennifer wiped her face and glanced at CJ.

"Can you make sure everyone is off the property?"

"Yes." CJ moved to the window, staring outside as the procession departed. Some of the news crews started to set up their cameras on the lawn instead of outside the fence, and anger surfaced at their audacity.

Camera bulbs popped like a series of firecrackers and at first the newshounds didn't understand what was happening. When all the glass in the equipment started to crack and shatter into a fine glass mist, they retreated in a confused and unnerved mass.

The moment they were through the gates, the iron bars swung closed, and he glanced at Cleary shoving the irritation and anger aside and studying Steve's boss.

"Why didn't you stop them?" The accusation hung on the air, leaving a tension that prickled everyone in the room.

"I need to make a call." Jennifer headed for the stairs. She paused and faced the boys. "Thank you," she said to Tom, and gave a nod to CJ before she disappeared upstairs.

"Were either of you at the house when Steve first met your parents?"

"I was." CJ traded a glance with Tom. "I actually let him in the house."

Tom shrugged. "I remember being told about Eric and the rest is kind of hazy, like a dream. Why?" he signed.

Cleary stared at Tom's hands with a line of concentration between his eyes.

"You don't know sign language, do you?" CJ asked.

"No, I'm not proficient in sign language," Cleary admitted.

"Tom said he doesn't remember much after being told about Eric," he said, paraphrasing.

"Mind if I go upstairs," Tom signed. "I have some studying to do."

"Do you mind if he goes upstairs to study?"

"No, that's fine," Cleary answered.

As soon as Tom was out of earshot, CJ turned to Cleary and narrowed his eyes. "Why all the questions?" he asked and crossed his arms.

"I'm trying to find something that will get Steve out of the mess he's in." Cleary glanced at the stairwell.

CJ didn't buy it, not with Cleary's lack of eye contact. He studied the man for a few moments and static filled his psychic airways. Steve certainly taught him how to safeguard his thoughts, but was Cleary on their side or on the FBI's side? CJ didn't know and decided to test where Cleary's loyalty lay.

"What do you want to know?"

"I need to know if you overheard anything that will help Steve."

CJ looked at the floor, playing back the memory as if it had happened yesterday. Only one thing stuck out, but if he was right about Cleary, it would never see the light of day, so he shook his head. "No. Everything I heard would hurt his case."

"What exactly did you hear?"

"After he told them about Eric, he said he knew who my father was and what he did."

Cleary sat down and leaned his elbows on his knees. "Did Steve find out about your father when your brother died?" His tone held the quality of defeat, and he met CJ's gaze.

"I don't know." CJ took a seat facing the television. He glanced at the stairwell, listening for either Jennifer or Tom, because if they overheard the conversation, his bluff would be called.

"Did Steve say anything else?"

"Not before he and my dad got into a fight."
CJ turned his gaze on Cleary. "Steve actually
took him down. Shocked the shit out of my dad,
too." CJ paused and glanced out the sliders at
the moonrise. "That's when he asked for help in
return for my father's freedom." CJ shrugged
and glanced away, unwilling to divulge more.

"Help?"

CJ met Cleary's inquisitive stare and
shrugged. He didn't know how much of the story
the man really knew and he wasn't about to
share any of the Ryan family secrets unless he
had to.

"What happened next?"

CJ sighed. "That's when his boss called to tell
him about his parents and Steve lost it. He had
nothing—his daughter, his partner and his
parents, all slaughtered by the same psycho,
and Jennifer was stuck in a coma. The guy was
a loose cannon with very little to live for except
revenge."

"So, he used your parents for personal gain,"
Cleary said.

"No. He was actually going to walk away, but
my father offered to help."

Cleary's eyebrow rose.

"And Steve isn't an idiot. He knew what my
father brought to the table."

Cleary scoffed and folded his hands together.

"Would you have turned down a genius with
unlimited resources with the same propensity
for vengeance?"

"Yes. I would have arrested him." Cleary
stood.

"He helped Steve catch Winslow," CJ said.

"And look what that cost him." Cleary didn't wait for CJ to reply. "I'll be in touch." He headed out of the house.

CJ leaned back on the couch, and made sure the front door latched closed before he spoke under his breath, "Asshole." He reached forward and turned on the television, despite the internal warnings not to bother. The local channels were filled with pictures of Steve being escorted away in handcuffs.

"Turn that crap off."

CJ met Jennifer's bloodshot gaze. "How are you holding up?" he asked and turned the television off.

Jennifer bit her lip and tried to smile, but it came across as forced, and the sudden sheen in her eyes gave away her desperation as much as her thoughts. CJ crossed to her and pulled her into a hug.

"I promise everything will be okay. Steve will be home before we know it and the charges against Tom will be dropped and everything will go back to the way it used to be."

She nodded and when he pulled away, a tear escaped, and she wiped it away. "Our lawyer is on the way to Washington with a sealed envelope that your father had, but she isn't sure they will allow it into evidence for his defense." Her chin quivered. "He promised he wouldn't leave me here alone." She dropped her face into her hands.

CJ rubbed her back, hearing the fears loop through her head.

"If the Windwalker is stupid enough to attack us, I'll be here," he said. He relished the thought of wasting the bastard.

"What if he shows up when you're at work?"

CJ sighed. "Then you call Steve and he'll be here like that." He snapped his fingers.

Saving Face
Chapter 31

TOM SAT AT HIS desk and pulled the paper out of his pocket, staring at it and glanced at his computer and switched it on. With a few searches, he found software that allowed text to speech on both incoming and, more importantly, outgoing messages.

He installed it and after experimenting with it on Skype and finding the right voice; he entered her phone number and held his breath with his finger over the salutation he typed, asking for Raven.

"Hello, Adams residence," a deep, clipped voice answered.

Tom hit the button. "Hello, is Raven available?"

"May I ask who's calling?"

Tom typed and pressed enter. "Tom Ryan."

"Hold on one moment."

Tom bit his nail, listening to the muffled sound of the phone being passed.

"Tom?" Raven's voice filled the line.

"Hi, Raven," he typed and hit enter.

Silence. "This isn't Tom," she said after a moment.

Tom typed fast. "Skype, text to voice," the monitor said.

"How did you get my number?" Accusation filled the line.

"You gave it to Steve when he dropped you off."

"Holy crap, it is you," she said, her attitude changing from suspicion to excitement.

"Yes. I found this program that works with Skype, so any time I type, it reads it to you."

"That's fantastic! I didn't think he was serious when he said you would figure something out. I thought he was just humoring me," she said.

"Despite my average grades, I am a smart guy," he typed. "Not as smart as CJ, but I hold my own."

Her laughter rang through the speakers, and he smiled.

"So, how's your night going?"

His smile disappeared. "Shitty. Steve was arrested."

Silence carried over the line, and he heard her sigh. "What happened?"

"They arrested him for extortion, reckless endangerment and for aiding and abetting a known criminal."

"What criminal?"

Tom smiled a little. "My father."

"The angel?"

"Yes."

"Can I ask you a question?"

"Shoot," he typed.

"I heard he wasn't your real father."

Tom looked out the window and then over at the shelf holding the Oscar. "No, he wasn't my biological father, but he raised me like he was."

"Do you know who your real father was?"

"Yes, Tom Whitman was my biological father. He starred in the movie Survival Games that came out when I was little. I actually met him the night of the premiere."

Silence filled the line.

"Are you still there?" he typed.

"Yes. I think I saw that movie on television," she said.

"The really screwed up thing about that movie it was based on what happened with the three of them while they were in Albany."

"Huh?"

"Ty kidnapped my mother. That's where it all started," he typed.

"Ty? I thought your father was Chris Ryan?"

Tom pulled his hands off the keyboard and cracked his knuckles and then typed, "No. The man who raised us was Ty Ryan, better known as Ty Aris. He assumed his brother's identity when he escaped."

"Holy shit," she said, and Tom heard someone scold her in the background. "Sorry," she said.

"So, if you remember that movie, it was the story of how my parents met."

"Really? I cried at the end of that movie," she said.

"CJ and I rented it once and watched it without my parents knowing. It scared the shit out of us; especially finding out our dad actually did those bad things. My dad could be a scary son of a bitch when he wanted to, but we never knew exactly what happened to him. I overheard him say Tom did an uncanny and accurate job portraying him in that movie and Tom won the Academy Award for that performance," he typed and felt a measure of pride as he glanced at the dust-laden award.

"Really?"

"Yep. I can show it to you the next time you're over."

"Cool."

"So, I have one father that was famous, and another who is infamous." He grinned at his wit.

"Oh, please," she said, and he even imagined the eye roll that accompanied the sarcasm.

"Sorry," he typed. "Just trying to see the humor in all this, otherwise I might just take a dive out my window or off the cliff behind our house."

"You're pretty upset by all this, aren't you," she said, her voice soft and caring and it hit a nerve.

Tom's vision blurred, and he squeezed his eyes shut, irritated at the surge of emotion.

"Yes. Steve didn't deserve to be handcuffed and paraded out in front of the media like a common criminal. He's a good man and a really good cop, and they're shitting on his record."

"I'm sorry," she whispered.

"The crap going on with me is bad enough," he typed and paused with his finger over the send. He didn't want her feeling sorry for him and he deleted the note. Instead, he typed, "No,

I'm sorry. You don't need to hear me whining about the shit storm here."

"I'm here any time you need to vent," she said.

"I wish you were here right now."

Silence filled the line. "I was serious about the fire and water signs," she said.

"So, you don't have any feelings whatsoever where I'm concerned?"

"I never said that," she whispered. "But you're on the rebound and I just happened to be there, so I'm not sure that what's going on inside you is authentic."

His stomach dropped, and Tom pushed away from the computer, running his hands through his hair. Her words punched a hole through his chest, leaving an emptiness in their wake.

"Are you still there?" she asked.

"Yes," he typed and bit his lip, wondering if she was right and he was only paying attention to her because of the timing.

"Are you mad?"

He sighed. "No, not mad, just digesting what you said."

"Let me ask you a question," she started and took a breath. "When all of this blows over and you go back to your old life, will you even give me the time of day?"

Tom clenched his teeth together. "I'm not like that."

"So, when you're back on the football team, and the cheerleaders are throwing themselves at you, you'll just smile and say 'sorry I've already got a girlfriend' like your brother does?"

"Is that what you want? To be my girlfriend?" he typed and pressed send before he chickened out.

Silence filled the line. "Damn fire sign," she muttered.

"You know I might go to jail, right?"

"You're not going to jail," she said so softly that he almost didn't catch it.

"If I do, will you come for conjugal visits?"

"Oh my god, you're such a slut!"

He burst out laughing. "Yeah, I guess that's pretty accurate."

She chuckled. "So, you admit to that?"

"Yeah. But it's only because I've been trying to find someone like you. You know the saying, you gotta screw a lot of frogs..."

"Kiss, not screw," she whispered.

"Well, shit, I guess I got THAT fairytale wrong," he typed with a big grin.

Her laughter rang through the line, lightening his mood. "You're incorrigible," she said through the laughter.

"I try." He pressed send and then typed, "Seriously, is that what you want? Because I can tell you, right now it's what I want." His finger hovered over the send button and he curled his hand into a fist, pulling away from the keyboard. Tom shook his head and pressed delete, too afraid of the answer to just throw it out there.

"I need to get some homework done," she said when she wound down.

"Did you want to come over tomorrow after school and study for the history test?" Tom asked and held his breath while he waited for the answer.

"We'll see," she said. "Thanks for calling."

"Thanks for giving Steve the number," he typed. "See you at school tomorrow."

"See you." The phone clicked off.

Tom sighed at the disconnect sign on Skype and closed down the application. He stared out the window, marveling at how much things could change in just twenty-four hours. His gaze dropped to the computer, and he typed Wicca into the search box and read through the search results to gain an understanding of Raven and her beliefs.

Saving Face
Chapter 32

STEVE SAT IN A cell on the plane, his hands secured to the seat, and Scully glared at him from the opposite side of the bars.

"You really are a piece of work." He crossed his arms.

Steve raised his eyebrows. "Scully, I may be a piece of work, but you're just a bureaucratic dick."

"I'll gladly put a bullet in your ass if you don't shut up."

"Do you always believe the crap they feed you?" Steve asked, staring him down.

"You made a choice, the wrong choice," Scully started, pointing his finger at Steve, and then he stopped, folding his hands in his lap.

"I needed help, and Ty offered me an option. You know he was a computer whiz, right?"

Scully crossed his arms.

"The money trail had run dry, and no one knew where Winslow went. Ty was motivated by his stepson's death, and he would have gone after Winslow with or without me."

"Not if he was in jail."

"Yeah, well, that wasn't an available option." Steve looked down at his hands. "Ever made a promise to someone that goes against everything you stand for?" He raised his gaze, meeting Scully's.

"No."

"Of course not," he muttered and leaned back in the chair as far as his cuffs would allow. He looked out the window and let the conversation die.

After a few minutes of silence, Scully bit, "What kind of promise?"

Steve turned and met his gaze. "What if your partner was dying and asked you to make a promise? Would you honor it?"

Scully remained quiet and looked out the window, but his thoughts turned over the question, mulling over the answer. Instead of immediately saying no, he questioned himself because there wasn't anything he wouldn't do for his partner.

"Not a simple question to answer, is it?" Steve said, and Scully met his gaze. This time his expression wasn't of disgust or anger.

"No, it's not. But here's the thing, you have to put the welfare of the public before a promise made under duress."

Steve inhaled and nodded. "Ty wasn't a danger to the public. Winslow was, so I made a judgment call."

Scully noodled on the information, finding, after turning it this way and that, that the judgment call Steve made was perhaps the lesser of two evils and one, given the same set of circumstances, he might have opted for as well. "What about the extortion charge?"

"Unfounded."

A skeptical eyebrow lifted.

"Think what you want, but I never asked for any of this," Steve said. "I never asked for the responsibility of his boys either, but he decided to make my wife and me their guardians. That was more of a shock than anything else."

"It looks like one of them is walking in his footsteps."

Steve shook his head. "Tom isn't the Windwalker."

"You really are blinded by your emotions, aren't you?"

"No. I arrived at the scene at almost the same time as the police and I saw things from a very different view, besides there was no weapon or scalp in the vicinity." He shrugged. "I've been to the crime scenes and investigated serial killers for most of my career, and Tom doesn't fit the profile."

"I read his profile. He could have had a psychotic break," Scully said.

"I thought about that too, especially with all he's been through, but it still didn't add up. There would have been signs."

"So, you're telling me you actually looked at him as a suspect?"

Steve looked out the window. "Yes." He turned toward Scully. "Just don't tell my wife."

Scully smirked and nodded.

"Are you married?"

"I was, but she couldn't deal with my job," he said.

"Sorry, man," Steve said. "My wife hates the job, too."

Scully huffed. "Don't they all?"

Steve glanced at him, sizing him up for a moment. "Not necessarily. You ever meet my partner Sarah Connelly?"

A crease appeared between Scully's eyes. "No, but I understand she knew about your culpability."

"She asked, and I leveled with her."

"She should have come forward."

"Like you'd hand over your partner," Steve scoffed and looked out the window.

Scully pulled out his iPad and signed on, bringing up her profile. His eyebrows rose when her photograph came up and he glanced at Steve.

"You work with this every day?"

"I hear she's looking for a new partner." Steve barely suppressed a grin at the interest sparkling in Scully's eyes.

Scully glanced at the picture and then at Steve and his expression turned incredulous. "What does your wife think of you working with a fucking bombshell?"

"Have you seen my wife?" Steve asked and received a nod in response. "So, you get it."

"No, not at all. This alone would have been grounds for divorce," Scully said, holding the photo up.

"It took some time, but Jen and Sarah became good friends and after that, whatever sense of insecurity Jen felt with us being partners went away." Steve shrugged, finding Scully much less of a bureaucratic fool than he originally thought. "I'll introduce you to her when we get to Washington."

"You really are a piece of work," Scully mumbled and stared at the photo for a moment before turning the iPad off.

Steve smiled and glanced out the window. His smile faded as he lined up his strategic defense in his head. While it had been easy to turn on the doubts in Scully's mind, he wondered just how easily he'd be able to turn a jury without this one-on-one contact.

Saving Face
Chapter 33

TOM CROSSED INTO THE school, sending a wave in Jennifer's direction and watched her pull away before he framed his attitude for battle. CJ caught up to him before he took a dozen steps and Raven stepped to his other side, forming a triad of strength and intimidation. Students in the hallways parted, giving them space to pass; even the football team gave them a wide berth.

When Tom settled into his seat, he traded a smirk with CJ before wiping it off and focusing on Miss Simpson at the front of the class. His mind drifted to Raven, and he wondered how one day could provide such a turnaround in him.

He could pinpoint the moment things changed, and it wasn't when she sat down at the table. It was when she laughed. That magical laugh tugged at his soul.

He thought back to Tanya, analyzing every conversation, every nuance and what he thought was love. Now it all seemed superficial and shallow. She was beautiful, the kind of beauty that struck men silent, but it didn't reach her heart. She could be mean and possessive and nasty at times, even to him. He'd heard her relentless put downs of anyone not in her circle and he used to ignore it, categorizing it as a female trait even though he never once saw his mother or Jennifer being catty. Even Sandy was a bright, warm soul that never talked smack.

Compared to the few stolen moments with Raven, his time with Tanya just felt like a sham. Guilt drummed up through his skin and he sighed, staring at the aimless doodles on his paper before glancing at the clock. Just a few minutes to go before their history class and his mood perked up.

A few minutes more and he'd see Raven.

His thoughts jumped to Tanya again, and he bit his lip, wondering where her spirit went after his father took her away.

Maybe she's mortified.

Tom slid a glare in CJ's direction. *Get out of my head.*

The class is boring, and it's refreshing to hear you finally seeing Tanya for what she was. I was getting sick of you viewing her as some angel that belonged on a pedestal.

Tom's eyebrows rose, and his mouth dropped at CJ's honesty.

She used you, Tom. And maybe I shouldn't be sharing this with you, yet, but the reason Bear is so ballistic is he was sleeping with her, too.

Tom's mouth popped closed, and he narrowed his eyes, glaring at CJ. *Just when the hell did you find this out?*

CJ looked away and anger filled every one of Tom's pores.

CJ?

CJ kept his eyes forward, even though he winced at the volume of the demand.

"eeay," Tom whispered.

CJ turned and met his gaze. *The beginning of September.*

Tom dropped his gaze to the desk, his hand gripping the pen tight enough for the plastic to creak, and he loosened his grip before the pen broke. *Why didn't you tell me?* He asked without looking at CJ.

I told her she needed to tell you, but she never did.

The bell rang, and Tom popped out of his seat, heading down the hall alone, hoping Bear had the audacity to stop him. A hand landed on his shoulder, and he spun, slamming the owner into the wall.

CJ raised an eyebrow. "You gonna punch me, too?"

Tom stepped back and signed, "I should."

"We can settle this tonight when I get home from work," CJ said, his gaze just as hard as Tom's.

"I don't think Jen will want us breaking the furniture again," Tom signed.

CJ grinned. "You chicken?"

Tom pushed his shoulder. "You're still an ass for not telling me."

"I have to head to science, and I guess I'm driving you home today." CJ said, holding up the text request from Jennifer.

"Fantastic." Tom turned, heading toward his history class. His mood was as foul as the mystery meat in the cafeteria.

He was first in the classroom and took one of the empty seats in the back of the room instead of his regularly assigned seat. With his dark mood, he didn't want to be near people right now, not even Raven. CJ's little revelation left him bitter and feeling like a fool.

The teacher gave him a double take when she came into the room and he crossed his arms, daring her to say something. Mrs. Fineworth creased her brow and glanced at the hallway before returning her gaze to him.

"Is everything all right, Tom?"

He couldn't help it. He started laughing. "In what world could things possibly be all right?" he signed.

Before she could answer, the rest of the class started filtering in, and when Raven stepped in the door, he met her gaze.

Her eyes widened, and her mouth popped open as she looked at him, her gaze taking in his aura as well as his hostile demeanor. She took her seat and glanced back at him.

"It's not you," Tom signed. "Just needed a quiet space away from everyone."

She nodded and turned away, focusing on the teacher.

As class went on, his gaze kept drifting back to Raven like a magnetic pull and his fingers landed on the medallion under his shirt. Her presence calmed him, and he glanced down at the blank page and back at the teacher. He sighed and copied the test bullets on the board and then went back to staring out the window at the cool November landscape.

When the bell rang, he shoved his books into his backpack and slung it over his shoulder, approaching Raven. She looked up from her desk and sent a strained smile in his direction.

"I'm sorry," he signed. "CJ pissed me off in English class."

"What did he do?" she asked as they stepped into the hallway.

"He knew Tanya was cheating on me with Bear and didn't tell me."

Raven pressed her lips together and lowered her head, but Tom caught the look before she attempted to hide it from view. He tilted her chin up, so she met his gaze.

"Wha?"

"I shouldn't speak ill of the dead," she said, her tone as frosty as a mid-winter breeze.

He couldn't help the smile that surfaced. She looked adorable all fired up and he could almost predict her derogatory thoughts.

"Want to skip lunch?" he signed. He wasn't in the mood for a confrontation with Bear.

She hesitated, and he took her hand, navigating the hallways to the back of the school where the assembly hall sat. He glanced back and forth to make sure no one was around. He tried the side door, and the handle didn't budge. *Shit.*

Pulling her around to the main entrance, he tried the first pair of double doors, and they were locked as well. The second pair provided the same results; he only knew of one more door and pulled her into the last hallway, silently praying this door allowed entry.

He put his hand on the knob and sent a glance in her direction before turning it. The door gave, pushing inward, and he grinned at her, pulling her into the dark hall. The door latched, and he led her onto the stage and down the stairs into the empty auditorium.

"We could get in trouble for this," she whispered.

He sat down and pulled her so she straddled his thighs.

"What are you doing?"

He smiled and signed slowly. "It's dark in here. If you're not close, you won't know what the hell I'm saying."

She giggled. "I thought you were trying to seduce me."

He chuckled softly and raised an eyebrow. "Do you want me to?"

"You're the biggest whore in this school, and I don't want to be just another name on your conquest list."

His smile faded. He didn't want her to be just another name either, and he lowered his hands to her thighs and dropped his chin to his chest. Until this moment, he had been proud of his ability to get into a girl's pants, but right now all he felt was shame.

She cupped his chin and tilted his head back until his gaze met hers. "This shy, shameful act has got to stop," she whispered.

"Why?" he said, his voice soft and deep.

"Because." She moved closer, settling over his lap instead of his thighs, and his hands slid to her hips.

"Why?" he repeated, his gaze locked on hers and his hands tightened on her hips. His heart thundered in his chest as a want he couldn't describe hit him like an atom bomb. He slid his hands under the hem of her shirt to her waist, his thumbs and forefingers found the silky flesh of her sides and his breath locked in his chest.

"Tom," she whispered, her voice shaky and stern at the same time.

He allowed a smile to form, unwilling to move his hands away from her warm flesh.

"Yeah?" he asked, cocking his head to the side.

She cupped his cheek with her palm, and he turned, kissing her soft flesh, his gaze never leaving hers.

"Why are you doing this?" she asked.

He ran his thumb along her belt line in a slow caress that was more erotic than anything he had ever done with the numerous girls he screwed. "Be'aue I wa ou," he started and chickened out. Admitting to wanting her was nothing new, but asking her to be his girlfriend opened the door for rejection.

She laughed, and he squeezed her sides, frustrated.

"Be'aue I wa ou a ma giwfe," he blurted and pressed his lips together, praying she understood the sentiment and he wouldn't have to remove his hands from her silky skin to clarify his muffled words.

She blinked and removed her hand from his cheek.

"Fire and water," she whispered.

"Mae eam," he added.

She grinned. "Did you just say make steam?"

He nodded.

She ran her fingertip over his lips, and he closed his eyes, relishing the moment, the feel of her skin under his thumbs and her finger tracing the lines of his face. Time disappeared, and he ran his hands higher up her torso, feeling her ribs like a magic relief map until his fingers hit the fabric of her bra. He stopped and opened his eyes.

He brought his hands back to her waist, unwilling to do anything that might jeopardize this, and her beautiful lips parted in a sexy exhale. With a flash of regret, he removed his hands from her waist.

"Will you be my girlfriend?" he signed.

She stared at his hands, and then her gaze jumped to his. "Why?"

"Because your laughter breathes life into me and I want to learn everything there is to know about you, from your beliefs to what you want out of life and everything in between."

"And what if I tell you I'm a virgin?"

He shrugged. "I don't care."

"Bullshit. You're ready to shag right now."

"I'm always ready," he signed and smiled. "But I can be patient, too. I won't ever pressure you to do anything you don't want to do."

"I doubt you'd feel that way a year from now." She went to slide off his lap.

He grabbed her waist and shook his head.

"A'we?"

"You want my answer now?"

"Yes."

"What if I just want to be your friend?"

His heart dropped to the floor, and he swallowed the sting to his pride. "Then I'll be your friend," he signed.

"And what happens when all this blows over?"

"Then I get to take you to dinner and for walks on the beach or anything you want to do."

"And what do you like to do?"

"Go to see the Patriots or the Red Sox or a play in New York City," he signed.

"You like to go to the theater?" she asked, her eyebrows posed in arched surprise.

"Yes. Ogunquit has a great summer program."

"That is something I would have never guessed about you."

"I still don't know your answer," he signed and placed his hands on her hips again, waiting.

Raven sighed and leaned forward; pressing her lips to his in a sincere and soft kiss that left him wanting more. He wrapped his arms around her, molding them together and he broke the kiss, running his lips down the line of her neck, nibbling her ear gently before kissing his way down to her shoulder. Tom couldn't stop the need to taste her, wishing he could run his tongue over every inch of her flesh.

He stopped at the curve of her breasts, closing his eyes and resting his forehead on her shoulder. His hands itched to caress her skin and bring her to his level of need, but he refrained, concentrating on getting his breath under control and his libido in check.

"Tom?" she whispered, and he looked up, meeting her gaze. "This isn't a joke, is it?"

The doubt in her eyes struck a deep nerve, and he swallowed, shaking his head slowly. He ran his hand over her cheek and into her soft curls. "No," he whispered, forcing the enunciation out of the stub in his mouth.

"I may regret this, but yes, I'll be your girlfriend," she said.

Relief melted the tension in his neck and shoulders, and he smiled. "Were you planning on coming over after school to study for the history test?" he signed.

She bit her lip.

"I'll cook dinner for you."

"You cook?"

"When Steve isn't around, yes, CJ and I cook because Jen is a god-awful mess in the kitchen."

She smiled. "I'd like to see you in a kitchen."

"Then it's a date," he signed and lifted her off his lap. Taking her hand, he led her out of the auditorium.

Saving Face
Chapter 34

CJ GLANCED IN THE rearview mirror, raising an eyebrow at Tom sitting in the backseat before he sent a sideways glance at Raven sitting next to him.

"You know I have to head out to work after I drop you off, right?" he said to Tom.

"Yeah," he said from the backseat.

"Okay, just making sure you're aware."

"He's cooking dinner for me." Raven offered a smile.

"You don't want Jen to poison the poor girl?" he said, meeting Tom's gaze for a moment as he navigated the route the police set forth like a racecar driver. The number of press core camped out at the house had dwindled since they took Steve away, but there were still a few die-hard idiots and CJ blew the horn, making them jump out of the way.

He grinned at the shock and indignation visible on the vultures' faces as he passed through the gates and into the garage, out of sight.

"I hate the press," he muttered and led the procession inside. A stab of envy pierced his chest as he watched Tom and Raven set up around the coffee table and he turned, heading upstairs to change.

Sandy hadn't been around last night, and CJ wondered if he'd ever see her again. The separation always ate at him, but this time, it was coupled with the real fear that he had royally screwed things up.

He changed and then sent a quick email off to Sandy before he headed back out.

"See you later," he said as he passed through the family room. Both Tom and Raven waved a hand in his direction, and he nodded goodbye.

TOM WAITED UNTIL HE saw the car pass through the gate and then he glanced at Raven.

"You want to see that Oscar?"

"In your bedroom?" Raven asked.

Tom nodded and stood, putting his hand out for her. When all she did was stare at him, he signed, "I promise, nothing will happen. I just want to show you who I am."

She rolled her eyes and took his hand, letting him lead her upstairs.

Each step closer to his room brought a greater layer of doubt, and he glanced back at her, offering a nervous smile. His stomach fluttered like it had before his first time and he wondered if she was feeling the same tension, the same electrical current in the air.

He swung the door open and any intention of getting physical with her did a swan dive.

Standing in the center of the room with his wings folded neatly was his father.

"You know better than to bring a girl upstairs," he chided.

Raven squinted and shaded her eyes, sending a sideways glance at Tom.

"I wanted to show her the Oscar." Tom signed.

Ty waved toward the shelf. "There it is," he said.

Please leave us alone, he thought.

Ty chuckled. "Steve ordered me to stay here."

Tom glared at him and slammed the door closed, leaning his back against it before looking down at Raven. "Sorry," he sighed and smiled at the same disappointment in her features.

"I can deal with the bright light if you still want to show me your room," she said.

He laughed and shook his head. "You see light, I see my father, and I'm *so* not comfortable bringing you in there with him watching over us."

"Okay, so studying it is." She headed back downstairs.

Tom opened the bedroom door and glared at the angel. "Go away," he said.

"I can't do that." He took a seat on the bed. "Especially with the little x-rated show going on in your head. Boy, you're going to get yourself into some real trouble one of these days."

Tom shut the door again and stormed downstairs, throwing himself on the couch opposite Raven.

"Damn, you sure know how to pout." He looked up. "Especially for someone who said nothing was going to happen upstairs." She crossed the distance, straddled him on the couch, and pushed his shoulders back against the fabric. She leaned forward, running her tongue down the side of his neck and nipping in the same manner he did in the theater earlier.

When her hips started circling on his lap, creating a heat that consumed every inch of him, he didn't hesitate to run his hands under her shirt and this time the boundary of her bra didn't stop him. She purred as he ran his thumbs over the fabric, feeling the hardness of her nipples underneath.

Her hands yanked on his shirt, and he let her peel it off his torso. When her gaze landed on the bruises covering his ribs, she gasped. "Oh, my God," she said.

Tom looked down and then back at her with a shrug. "It doesn't hurt," he signed.

Her gaze dropped to the cast.

"Your cast is cracked."

He peeled it off his arm and tossed it on the table. "I know. CJ did that for me," he signed and scratched his arm before resuming his exploration of her chest.

"I thought your arm was broken?"

"My arm, my ribs and my cheekbone," he signed and kissed her exposed cleavage.

She grabbed his wrists, pulling them away from her, and his gaze met hers.

"Wha?"

"Did you really get hurt?"

Her tone cleared out the lust from his brain and he met her gaze. "There's one more thing about my family that you should know."

She cocked her head, waiting for his answer.

"Steve has the ability to heal others," he signed. "I was really bad off on Monday night. I had a concussion, too, and I think that's what caused my seizure after they brought me home. Steve said I stopped breathing and instead of losing me, he fixed me from the inside out, leaving the surface bruises so people wouldn't ask questions."

"You're kidding, right?"

"No, I'm not kidding," he signed and peeled the bandage off his cheek. "My face was split open to the bone. When I looked this morning, it was just a scratch."

She ran her hand over the bruise on his cheek and then traced the discoloration on his chest. "Jesus," she whispered.

"I was in rough shape. Not as bad as when Steve found me in Georgia, but still, it hurt like a bitch."

"You could have died," she whispered.

He smiled and shrugged. "In any normal world, I would have died several times over by now," he signed, meeting her gaze. "I wasn't exaggerating yesterday when I told you I was damaged goods."

The color in her face drained and her eyes filled with tears. "Blessed be." She kissed him. "You are not damaged," she said when she pulled away.

He rolled his eyes. "Yeah, I am," he whispered, ran his hands under her shirt, peeling it off, and dropped it next to his on the floor.

"Is this how you get all the girls to let you do what you want?"

He couldn't help the grin that surfaced and shrugged, shifting and stretching her out underneath him on the couch, letting the heat rule his head. His hands studied every curve, teasing and caressing her skin, memorizing and categorizing each reaction.

Even with all his experience, being with her felt like the first time all over again and when she let him remove her bra, he marveled at her perfect full breasts compared to her tiny waist. When his fingers fumbled with her belt, her hands gripped his wrists, pulling them away from the clasp.

Tom leaned on his elbows and searched her eyes, finding the warning clear. This was all he was getting today, and he offered her an understanding smile, resuming his exploration of her upper body with his mouth and his hands. She gasped and arched into his mouth when he latched onto her breast, using his lips and teeth to drive her wild.

She ran her hands into his hair, whispering his name and some ancient Celtic verse, shivering and sweating under his touch. His temperature skyrocketed, and he pulled away, pushing himself into a kneeling position, letting the air settle between them before he reached the point of no return.

Panting, he signed, "I need to stop." He threaded his fingers through his hair, resting his wrists on top of his head. Tom closed his eyes, concentrating on settling his heart into a natural rhythm and willing his body back into a relaxed state.

"Has anyone ever told you that you are a gorgeous man?"

He grinned and opened his eyes. He reached down to retrieve her bra and shirt and handed them to her. "I don't think Jennifer would appreciate finding us in this state," he signed and moved away from her, slipping his shirt over his head.

A chill settled on the room and Raven shivered and quickly slipped her shirt over her head. Tom froze in place, all the heat sucked out of him with the frigid breeze on the back of his neck. His hand dropped to the medallion under his shirt, gripping it and meeting Raven's gaze.

A frigid hand laced into his hair, pulling his head back, and her skinless face came into his peripheral vision.

"What the hell do you think you're doing?" The fury in her voice cut him to the core.

"Run," he signed to Raven, but her eyes locked on the spot where Tanya stood, and her gaze narrowed.

"Leave him alone," her command rang through the room.

Fear wrapped an icy hand around his heart, and his protective instinct kicked in. He twisted out of her grip and spun, facing Tanya with his back to Raven.

"I told you, you are mine," she growled and stepped closer, her hands balling into fists.

"Why don't you go haunt Bear," he said, knowing she could hear the real voice behind the broken syllables.

Tanya stopped and her hands uncurled.

"He's the one who beat the shit out of me," Tom added, and her eye sockets widened.

"I didn't mean to..."

"To what? You didn't mean to fuck him? Bullshit. I was just a goddamn showpiece to you. A fucking puppy dog you could manipulate and parade around to all your friends."

"Tom," she whispered, reaching for him.

He knocked her hand away. The anger blew through the surface, annihilating any remnant of fear. "Get the hell out of my house!" he bellowed and pointed at the door.

Tanya stumbled back with an expression of despair until her gaze landed on Raven standing close behind Tom. Despair transitioned to fury, and she screamed, charging.

A blur of light interceded, creating a whirlwind that blew the papers on the table all over the family room. When the light faded and the papers settled, Tom stared at the empty spot where Tanya had stood.

Maybe having my father here wasn't such a bad thing after all. He glanced at the ceiling and sent a silent thank you.

Raven's arms encircled his waist and her cheek pressed against his shoulder blade. Her entire form trembled against him, and he sighed, turning and wrapping his arms around her.

"Owwy." He kissed her forehead. When she pulled away, he gazed into her tear-glossed eyes. "What were you thinking?" he signed and wiped a wayward tear from her cheek.

"I thought I could dispel her."

"That was not a proper banishing spell," he signed and raised an eyebrow.

The shock of his statement drew a laugh from her, and she looked into his eyes. "How would you know?"

"I did what you asked me to do. I Googled Wicca and did some reading. I paid close attention when I got to the Book of Shadow banishing spells."

"Really?"

The cute arch of her eyebrows brought a smile to his face, and he nodded. "Yeah," he said. "But I can't articulate the spells, so I'm shit out of luck," he signed.

"I can," she said.

"I know. But what would they do to my father?"

Understanding smoothed the lines of her forehead. "I don't know."

Tom shrugged. He didn't want his father banished from the house, only Tanya, and he didn't understand magick enough to mess around with it. A clear thought popped into his head. If his father was busy keeping Tanya away, that meant the bedroom was unoccupied. He grabbed her hand and pulled her up the stairs, throwing his door open, and smiled at the absence of the angel standing guard.

"What are you doing?" she asked, and he pointed to the shelf with the Oscar sitting amongst his sports awards.

She dropped his hand and crossed the room.

"Can I touch it?"

"Yeah." He sat on the bed.

"Is it actual gold?" she asked, turning toward him from the opposite side of the room.

"No. Gold plated."

She smiled and closed the distance, inspecting his knickknacks on his bureau and his desk full of papers in utter disarray. She chuckled at the Patriots snow globe on his nightstand, picking it up and raining snow all over the mini-field inside. Gillette Stadium never looked so magical.

"You really researched Wicca?"

"Uh huh," he said.

"So, what did you think?" She stopped in front of him, searching his eyes for any sign of mocking.

"It has some of the same moral framework that's outlined in Christianity. But the thing I liked the most is the focus on nature. It made much more sense to me than the Catholic Church ever did."

Her gaze rose from his hands to his face. "Maybe there's hope for you after all."

"I don't know what I believe anymore. I know angels exist just by way of my father, and ghosts as well as the balance of good and evil. But I think evil is a human manifestation. Nothing in nature harbors the same propensity for evil that mankind does."

"Beautiful and deep. Damn, I think I hit the mother lode," she teased.

"You forgot I'm rich, too."

She glanced around the room. "You don't flaunt it."

"It's not my style, although the car I want is a little flashy. But Steve won't let me blow over a million on a car."

Her eyes widened. "What kind of car costs that much?"

"An Aston Martin," he signed.

"And you have that kind of cash lying around just to throw away on a hunk of metal?"

"It's not just a hunk of metal," he signed and sat down at his desk, pulling up the picture of an Aston Martin One 77 on the computer. "This is what I want." He waved at the screen.

She glanced at the picture. "You could get a Ferrari or a Jaguar for a fraction of the cost and still have those sleek lines."

"But it's not an Aston Martin."

She raised her eyebrows. "Both the Ferrari and the Jag can go just as fast as the Aston Martin." She propped her hands on her waist.

He swung the chair around and pulled her onto his lap. "Why are you arguing with me about a car?"

"I just think it's a waste of money," she said, glancing at the photo on the screen. "And it's not that sleek," she said, rolling her eyes. "The beamer in the garage is more attractive than that."

He grinned. "You certainly know your cars."

"Yes, well, a girl can dream too."

"What exactly do you dream about?" he signed out of curiosity.

"You." Her eyes widened at the admission.

He wasn't prepared for her answer and blinked, his mouth popping open as he studied her. Her gaze dropped to the floor, and she squirmed in his grip, trying to break away from him, but he tightened his hold, waiting for her to look at him. "Why?"

"I've had a crush on you since our freshman year," she admitted and her cheeks blazed red, complimenting the vibrancy of her hair. "And I never in my wildest dreams thought I'd ever see the inside of your bedroom."

Something about the vulnerability of her confession spoke to his soul and all he wanted to do was make her see she wasn't just another one of his conquests. Yet his body had another agenda. Every fiber wanted her, and his hand traveled up the inside of her thigh. He stared into the ocean of her blue eyes, waiting for her to say stop.

When his fingers reached his objective, her eyes closed, and she let out a sigh that sparked a fire in his lap. It took every ounce of self-control not to rip her clothing off and explore every inch of her lightly freckled skin.

For the first time in his life, he didn't want to just sleep with a girl; he wanted to make love to her.

Screwing around with Tanya was nothing like this. With her, it was only the motions, but nothing really invested on an emotional level, no matter what his initial thoughts on the matter were. Intimacy was missing.

This was intimate and personal and soul touching.

It wasn't him stripping and getting down to business for the sheer physical pleasure of fucking.

Raven opened her eyes, and he inhaled at the intensity in her gaze. Her lips formed the perfect airway for her shaky breath. He couldn't see ever tiring of that expression, especially since it locked his lungs, and he had to remind himself to breathe.

He continued rubbing his knuckles across the seam of her pants, watching her cheeks flush and her chest rise and fall with each stroke of his fingers. He smiled at her, and she shifted, straddling his lap. She used the back of the chair for leverage, circling her hips into his, creating a friction that was bound to ignite.

His hands gripped her hips, and he moved with her, wishing there weren't two layers of fabric between them, but unless she made the move, he'd just savor the feel of her through her clothing and let his imagination run wild.

"Tom?" Jennifer's voice rang out downstairs.

They both froze, staring at each other and he mouthed, Oh Shit!

She slid off his lap and took a seat on the bed and he swung around toward the computer, typing a few commands and pressing enter. The school website came up, and he quickly clicked through to the homework assignment, glancing over her shoulder and waving her over.

She stood next to him and started reading aloud halfway through the page.

Her quick thinking gave him time to cool down because if Jennifer came in and he had to stand, she would know they were engaged in something less than innocent. As it was, he knew she would give him an earful after Raven went home.

"Oh," Jennifer said from the doorway.

Raven turned and leaned on the desk. "Hi, Mrs. Williams," she said, smiling.

Tom half turned and gave her a nod. "Hey." He pressed print. He ripped the page off the printer and stood, handing it to Raven.

Jennifer crossed her arms, raising her eyebrow. "You know I wasn't born yesterday, right?" she said, staring Tom down.

"We weren't..." he signed.

"You really want to go there?"

Tom gave Raven a sideways look and dropped his gaze to the floor.

"If it makes you feel better, no clothing came off in his bedroom," Raven said, meeting Jennifer's gaze.

Jennifer's glance moved between the two teenagers, and she finally nodded. "Fine, but I don't want to find you up here in his room again, understand?"

Tom balked, "Bu." He waved to the computer.

"You have a laptop," she said. "There's no reason for you two to be up here," she reiterated. "Now, did you want pizza or grinders for dinner?"

"I thought I'd cook tonight," Tom signed.

Jennifer suppressed a smile and waved toward the stairwell. "By all means."

Tom let Raven lead the way down the stairs and Jennifer put her hand on his arm before he climbed down after her. He turned toward her.

"Just because Steve isn't here doesn't mean you can throw that kind of bullshit in my direction," she said.

"Sorry," he signed.

"Just be smart with her and use your head, okay?"

He nodded and headed downstairs, rolling his eyes at Raven as he crossed into the kitchen.

Saving Face
Chapter 35

STEVE SAT IN THE holding cell, drumming his fingers on the table, waiting for someone to come in and tell him what came next.

The door opened, and Lynn Trueman stepped into the room.

"Ms. Trueman," he nodded.

"Agent Williams," she said, taking the seat opposite him.

"I'd shake your hand but..." he showed her the cuffs attached to the table.

She sighed and a hint of a smile appeared. "You know, you have some of the same traits as Mr. Ryan."

Steve smiled and shrugged. "Did you know who he really was?"

Lynn leaned back in the seat, sending him her Mona Lisa smile, but her thoughts betrayed her. She didn't know who he was initially. However, once they established a legal relationship, he'd told her in confidence. She reached down and pulled an envelope out of her attaché case. "Mr. Ryan made provisions if something along these lines occurred." She slid the sealed envelope with a letter of instruction attached in Ty's impeccable script. "Notice the date on the paperwork," she said.

Steve blew a stream of air from his lips as he scanned the instructions and his eyes landed on the certification date. The shock hit him like an electrical jolt.

"This can't be right," Steve's gaze shot to Lynn.

"I assure you, it is."

Steve hadn't even met him when the letter was written. The date was just days after the premier of Survival Games and Ty's first brutal experience in the warehouse. "How the hell did that bastard know?" His gaze met hers.

"Ty put the provisions of his will, the inheritance, and the boy's guardianship together the day after my father died. I thought it was quite odd for him to put his kid's future in the hands of someone he hadn't met yet, but he insisted and said someday I would understand. The only things he put in place after he met you were the transfer of his apartment, the victim's trust, and your designated cut of those funds." She smiled. "I don't have answers for you on how he knew the future, but I can say he was right. I do understand why he picked you," she said. "I have a question, though."

"Shoot."

"Did you know who he was when you met him?"

Steve studied her and sighed. "Yes, and I didn't turn him in. Instead, I took him up on his offer for help and because of that; he got caught in the crossfire. So, some charges they have against me are valid."

"Mr. Ryan would have gone after Winslow, with or without you," she said. "He made that very clear when he sat down with me to put the victim's fund in place." She leaned down and pulled out another file, opening it in front of her. "I've kept very detailed records of your expenditures in both the victims' trust and the children's and I think these may help your case." She slid the file to him.

"Why didn't you turn him in?"

"Attorney, client privilege," she said, meeting his gaze. "Besides, he kind of grew on me."

Steve smiled and nodded. "He grew on me, too."

Saving Face
Chapter 36

TOM STIRRED THE SPICES into the spaghetti sauce like Steve had taught him and glanced at the bubbles forming in the water. He left the stove and checked on the garlic bread in the oven before sending a quick glance at the family room where Jennifer and Raven were in a deep discussion about music and movies and theater.

Their animated chatter amused him, and he smiled. Jennifer had never warmed to Tanya like this. Usually when Tanya was around, awkward silence was prevalent, and they never knew what to say to each other, so Jennifer would disappear into the gym with her scripts, and he would be left with Tanya and the silence of the house.

Laughter rang out, and he turned back to their meal. He dropped a handful of spaghetti noodles into the now boiling water and set the timer. He finished setting the table while the noodles cooked. The buzzers all went off at once and he drained the noodles before he retrieved the bread and put it in the basket on the table.

Tom clapped his hands together, gaining Raven and Jennifer's attention, and he waved to the table like a magician displaying a magic box. The girls sat at the table watching Tom as he served their meals and then sat next to Raven with his plate.

"I'm impressed," Raven said, surveying the table and reaching for a piece of bread after Jennifer took one.

"I try," Tom signed and nodded toward the bread.

Jennifer handed him the basket. "So, Raven, how long have you been in the United States?"

"Almost four years," she answered.

"How do you like it?"

Raven shrugged, looking down at her plate and Tom started to sign, but she gave him a look that stopped his hands before she met Jennifer's questioning stare.

"It has been a little rough," she said.

Jennifer's eyebrows rose, and her gaze traveled to Tom's and back.

Without prompting, Raven continued, "I don't know if Tom has mentioned it or not, but I'm a Wiccan and that, combined with not living here all my life, makes it pretty hard to make friends."

Jennifer paused with her fork in her mouth and slowly pulled it out. Tom knew that expression and he inhaled; praying whatever was on her mind wouldn't ruin the evening.

"Wiccan, like in Practical Magic?" she asked.

Raven smiled. "Sort of." She spun a few strands of spaghetti on her fork and took a bite.

"It's more of a belief system than sorcery," she said after swallowing her food.

Jennifer focused on her food with a crease between her eyes, and Tom reached under the table and squeezed Raven's thigh, sending a wink at her before finishing his meal.

"I guess I don't get why that would prohibit you from making friends?" Jennifer looked up.

"Being a witch in a small New England town doesn't go over well. People tend to label you as weird or crazy or worse. Unfortunately, the Catholics in Ireland are just as judgmental." She offered a shrug. "On the bright side, at least they don't burn witches at the stake anymore." She smiled.

Jennifer pressed her lips together in a barely suppressed smirk. "Kids can be cruel," she said. "I'm just glad my son had the sense to see what a wonderful girl you really are." Jennifer folded her napkin and smiled.

Raven's smile faltered, and her eyes filled with tears. When she glanced his way, her eyes held a depth of gratitude that struck his heart, and he swallowed the last bite of spaghetti along with the lump in his throat.

"You two go study for a bit. I'll clean up and then I'll drive Raven home," Jennifer said as she stood and cleared the empty plates.

Tom cleared his plate and led Raven into the family room. "Are you okay?" he signed as they sat on the couch.

Raven nodded, meeting his gaze. "Dinner was fantastic," she said.

Tom glanced toward the kitchen and then leaned forward, catching a kiss from Raven before he opened his book. Sitting this close to her brought on a fresh wave of intense lust and he gave her a sideways glance, accompanied by a playful hint of a smile.

She rolled her eyes at him, shutting down his libido with one look, and he sighed, dropping his gaze to the book.

"Do you want me to quiz you?" he signed.

"I thought I'd quiz you?" she challenged.

He leaned back, putting his feet up on the table, and gave her the floor with a wave. Between each question, the tip of her pen slid between her lips in the most erotic manner. And he had a difficult time concentrating. His hands didn't seem to work smoothly enough to give correct answers, and he fumbled, shaking his head while she leveled a "get serious" look in his direction.

"O u'faia," he whispered.

"What was that?" she asked, grinning.

Tom's gaze flicked toward the kitchen and he signed, "That's so unfair."

Her cute dimples appeared, and she slid the pen between her teeth again.

Tom slammed the book closed and put it on the table, leaned his elbows on his knees, and studied Raven. His gaze slid from the pen to the curve of her breasts and he bit his lower lip, wanting to feel her skin against his again.

"You might want to wrap things up," Jennifer said. "I'll be down in a minute, and I'll take you home," she added, meeting Raven's gaze, and then she disappeared up the stairs.

Tom didn't hesitate. He moved, pushing Raven down onto the cushions of the couch and smiling down at her. "You 'ive me c'a'ey." He kissed her neck before nibbling on her earlobe.

She giggled and pushed him away. "Are you crazy? Your mother will be down in a minute."

"Who ca'ea," he said.

"I do," she said.

He glanced at the stairwell before planting a kiss on Raven's cleavage, and then he sat up. "Thanks for studying with me," he signed.

"Anytime." She put her things in her backpack.

Raven stood, and Tom looked up at her with a pang of disappointment. He didn't want the night to end, and he got to his feet and pulled her into a big bear hug, lifting her off her feet and nuzzling his face in the crook of her neck.

Jennifer cleared her throat and Tom set Raven on her feet, catching a quick kiss before she had time to recover.

Raven blushed. "I'll see you at school tomorrow." She followed Jennifer out the garage door.

Tom lowered to the couch and leaned back, replaying every moment of the afternoon in his mind, trying to understand the complete captivation and the sudden emptiness in his stomach now that she was gone. A brief flicker of an idea rang through his mind, and he wondered if Raven had concocted some sort of spell on him.

The lunacy of the thought made him chuckle, and he collected his schoolbooks, making his way upstairs. His good mood soured as he stepped into his frigid room. Tanya faced the window, her back straight and stiff in the posture he was used to seeing any time he did something she deemed wrong.

"I wish you were dead," she said.

Tom uttered a sharp laugh. "Don't worry, you just might get your wish," he said, and the suspension of reality lifted, leaving him with the weight of the charges crashing down.

She spun toward him and crossed the distance in a blink. Her hand formed the same claw formation, hell-bent to steal his heart, but the medallion stopped her progress, drawing a hiss from her skinless face.

"Leave me alone," Tom snarled and leveled a deadly glare in her direction.

"You are going to wish for death when I'm through with you," she said as she faded into a thin bank of fog.

Saving Face
Chapter 37

CJ WALKED INTO THE darkened house and dropped his keys on the counter. A yawn took hold, and he deviated to the refrigerator, grabbing a glass of orange juice before he headed upstairs. At the top of the stairs, he stopped and knocked on Jennifer's door.

"Yes?"

He opened the door. "I'm home," he said, and she gave a nod, shutting off the television.

"Goodnight," she said.

"Goodnight." CJ closed the door and headed to his room.

One glance at the clock told him it was too late, but he opened his computer anyway and stripped out of his work clothes while he waited for the hardware to boot.

After brushing his teeth, he came back into the room and opened Skype, sending the call to Sandy, praying she'd be up and online. He rubbed his face, stifling a yawn, and he looked over his fingertips at the empty screen.

Disappointment squeezed his chest, and he ended the call. Instead of going to sleep, he opened his facebook page and launched to hers. When her page loaded, his gaze pulled to her relationship status and locked on the word displayed. He pushed away from the computer, nearly choking on air. Six letters never hit him so hard.

He spun in the seat, taking his first step toward the door, when Skype buzzed.

He froze, afraid to turn. Instead, he answered with a nod of his head.

"Chris?" her whisper came over the speakers.

He turned, meeting her gaze on the computer. Her constant glances toward the door told him more than anything else, and a small fraction of relief gripped him.

"Still love me?" he asked.

Her smile clinched it even without the emphatic nod.

"What's with the single status?"

"My Dad."

That's all she needed to say. And he slid into the seat. "I miss you."

"Me, too. I can't talk long because if he finds out I'm on with you, he'll take the computer away."

"When am I going to see you again?"

"I don't know. I'm hoping that by Thanksgiving my dad will give up this crazy no contact rule," she said. "If not, I think I may want to move in with you."

CJ offered a smile. "The door's always open," he said. "But I think you need to graduate first."

Sandy rolled her eyes. "There's no way I'm waiting until spring to see you."

"I'll come down once all this shit blows over."

"My father will shoot you if you show up at my door. He's still blazing mad about catching us together."

"Did you tell him that was the first time?"

She nodded. "He doesn't believe me."

CJ leaned back in the chair. "Well, it certainly won't be the last. Especially since I plan on marrying you someday."

The smile that graced her face would launch a thousand sleepless nights, and he returned it, thinking that wasn't the smoothest way to propose, but he'd make it up to her when he did it for real.

"Are you serious?"

"Yes, there's no one I'd rather share my life with."

She stared at him, and her smile faded. "You sure you won't get bored with me?"

"No. Never." He couldn't even fathom being bored with her, but there was a hesitation in her that rubbed his intuition, and he tilted his head. "Is that what you're afraid of?"

Her nod sent a web of pain through his chest and all he wanted was to wrap his arms around her and show her the depths of his feelings. She was as ingrained in his soul as the act of breathing, and she blinded his ability to think logically or see any future without her. "We are meant to be."

"But how do you know that?"

"Because I cannot see my life without you in it."

"That's now, but what about when you're in college and women are throwing themselves at you?"

CJ couldn't help it. He started laughing. "Babe, girls have been throwing themselves at me for years. I've had all the opportunities in the world to explore, but here's the thing, and it's a pretty important point. The only one I want is you."

"So, you're telling me if a hot Victoria's Secret model tried to seduce you, you'd pass?"

"Yes."

"You're so full of shit," Sandy whispered.

"Have you looked in a mirror lately?" he asked, staring at her honey blonde hair and her heart-shaped face. "You are more beautiful than any of those models."

She rolled her eyes and glanced over her shoulder again. "I have to go," she said. "I'll call you tomorrow."

"Okay, I'll be here."

She reached for the controls.

"Hey, Sandy." When she paused, he added, "I love you."

"I love you, too. Sweet dreams." She smiled and then her picture disappeared.

CJ stared at the blank screen for a moment. The same disappointment he felt every time they hung up or said goodbye raked his skin, leaving a pronounced emptiness behind.

Saving Face
Chapter 38

STEVE STARED AT THE concrete ceiling of his cell, counting the web of cracks, wondering just how long his stay in this place would be. He sighed, praying Lynn's documentation would be enough to clear his name, or at least to eliminate the chance of a jail sentence, but he also knew it wasn't enough to save his career.

His mind wandered back to the Windwalker case, and he closed his eyes, reviewing every crime scene, every interview, and every suspect on their list. The case file was thick with current cases, but Steve found a few other similar deaths in shoreline communities up and down the New England coastline and now and then one occurred on a lake.

The killer had to have a boat, but in all cases, not a trace of gasoline was found on the waterways, which left a canoe or kayak as the getaway mechanism. It also had to be dark because it blended with the scenery, alerting no one of its approach or retreat.

All the thoughts pinging around in his head were documented in the case file, along with the fact that thousands of folks in the kill zone owned kayaks or canoes.

Steve snapped his eyes closed in frustration. He was missing something, and he knew it. Instead of chasing his tail, he wished himself out of the cold cell and into his bedroom at home. The bed was warm, and Jennifer stirred as he slid closer to her under the covers.

Her green eyes widened. "Did they let you go?"

"No, I'm still down in D.C. sleeping in my cell," Steve said, and winked at her.

"So, what are you doing here?"

He grinned and shrugged.

Jennifer smiled back and rolled so she was on top of him, straddling his lap and holding his wrists on the pillow. "So, you took a little astral trip just for some action?"

"Ayup," he said from below her. "Care to see if it's possible?"

Jennifer's smile faded, and she leaned down, kissing him, slowly at first, and then the heat kicked in. Her grip on his wrists loosened, and he ran his fingers into her hair, deepening the kiss and letting the sensation of her heighten his passion.

He sat up, peeling off his shirt and stripping her of her silky nightgown. Their gaze locked, and he ran his finger over her lips, marveling at the soft satin of her sexy mouth. It had been way too long since he studied her curves and he found the sensual line of her neck with his lips, trailing kisses along her neck and shoulder while he caressed her firm breasts.

"I love you." He shifted, pulling her underneath him.

"I love you, too," she said, and her eyes sparkled with the same intensity he was experiencing.

Every time he made love to Jennifer, it felt like the first time and tonight was no different. But unlike their first wild experience together, he took his time until they were both drenched in sweat and panting from exertion.

He kissed her gently and rolled onto his back, exhausted. The last thing he remembered was sending a smile in her direction and then his eyelids closed. The pull dropped him into a black spiral and when his eyes blinked open, the gray concrete greeted him.

This could very well be my life for the next thirty years.

Reality hit with the force of a neutron bomb, crippling his ability to reason and Steve covered his face, taking a deep breath to keep the crawling despair at bay.

Saving Face
Chapter 39

TOM CLIMBED INTO THE car and glanced at Jennifer.

"I've got an audition in Boston and I'm not sure I'll be back in time to pick you up," she said. "CJ said he'd bring you home."

"O'ay," Tom said.

"If Raven comes over again, I don't want to find you in the bedroom, you hear?"

Tom's cheeks heated, and he nodded. He dropped his gaze to his backpack, studying the stitched pattern of the logo.

"She's a nice girl."

"Yeah." He glanced out the window. Just thinking about her made his heart leap in his chest, and he smiled.

"Just don't play games with this one, okay?"

Tom turned his head, meeting Jennifer's sharp gaze, pointing at his chest.

"Yes, you." She pulled into the school, shifting the car into park and giving him her full attention.

"I don't plan on playing games, Jen," he signed. "This one is different."

She raised a skeptical eyebrow. "You said that about Tanya."

Tom sat for a moment and began to sign again, but the ankle light started beeping faster, and he slipped out of the car, grabbed his backpack and jogged toward the door before the light went solid red. It switched over to green as soon as he stepped into the school and he gave a wave to Jennifer, watching as she drove off, leaving him to noodle on her last comment.

All doubts regarding his feelings vanished when he turned to see her radiant smile. He scanned her outfit and shoved his hands in his pockets for fear he would rip the clothing off her and nail her right there on the wall. The black fitted skirt reached her knees with a slit that stopped just short of her hip, exposing her creamy thigh with each stride. Her flowing red curls burned brightly against the emerald green satin shirt, framing the nearly unbuttoned front that gave away hints of her black lace bra as she moved.

Heads turned, and eyes widened at the transformation from the almost invisible girl to this sexy vixen. And Tom knew she was the one he was destined to be with.

"God damn," CJ said from beside him.

No shit.

Raven reached her arms around Tom's neck and planted a juicy kiss on his lips.

"Now, if you dressed like that the first day you walked into this school, you would have had every guy in this town groveling at your feet," CJ said.

Tom sent a glare in his direction and wrapped his arms around her waist, laying claim to her for everyone to see.

Raven winked at him and turned to CJ. "I was waiting for the right man to notice me."

"Well, he certainly can't help but notice you now." CJ gave Tom a nod before leaving the two of them in the hallway.

"You really think I look good?" she whispered, and Tom nodded.

"eam," he said.

The single sentiment made her beam, and his gaze dropped to her barely concealed cleavage before looking her in the eye.

"You look hungry." She bit her lower lip.

Tom took a step back. "You look like breakfast," he signed, and blush colored her cheeks. He slipped his hand in hers and walked toward English class. When he turned the last corner, he stopped at the sight of the defensive line blocking the hallway.

Bear glared at him and slid his violent stare to Raven.

"I always knew she was a slut," Bear growled.

Raven clamped down on Tom's hand in a grip he couldn't slip out of.

"Back off, Bear," she snapped.

"Shut up, bitch," he volleyed back.

Tom pulled his hand out of her grip and walked toward Bear.

Raven grabbed his arm. "He isn't worth it," she said.

Tom put his hand up, stopping her with a warning glare before turning toward Bear again. He stepped forward. "You don't talk to my girlfriend that way," he signed. "Especially since you were fucking my last girlfriend for what, the last month or two?"

Bear faltered, and a couple of the team members exchanged glances.

"What's he talking about?" Kevin asked from the back.

"Nothing," Bear snapped and focused on Tom.

"Bear was sleeping with Tanya," Raven said from behind Tom.

"That's none of your business, slut," Bear said, leveling a glare in her direction. "Maybe when I'm done wiping the floor with this pussy, I can show you what a real man is like."

Tom swung his fist, pulling back at the last second so his knuckles stopped less than a centimeter from Bear's nose and Bear flinched backwards. Tom smiled in satisfaction and stepped away, taking Raven's hand and bypassing the rest of the team.

"You scared the shit out of him," she whispered as they took their seats in English.

Tom shook his head. He knew there would be hell to pay for embarrassing Bear in front of his peeps. But the way the asshole had looked at Raven set his blood roiling in his veins, and his skin stung from the burn.

"I'm sorry they spoke to you that way," he signed.

"I'm used to it, remember?"

"I should have shut him up years ago," Tom signed. He needed to get a hold of his growing temper, and he folded his arms on the desk, lowered his head, and closed his eyes. It took him a few minutes to find his concentration and the focus to shut out everything around him and just inhale and exhale until the anger clenching his stomach disappeared.

The rest of the morning went by without incident and when he was done with his history test, he handed it in and collected his things, just waiting for the bell and the empty auditorium.

As soon as the buzzer sounded, Tom took her hand and led her away from the cafeteria, avoiding the chance for a conflict he couldn't back off from. This time, he headed straight for the unlocked door on the far side of the auditorium. He didn't settle into the front row like they did yesterday, instead; he headed toward the media room in the back.

"Where are we going?" she asked.

He reached up and ran his fingers over the doorframe, coming away with the key and he slipped it into the lock, swung the door open, and placed the key back where he found it.

The room was darker than the auditorium and Tom felt around in the dark, found one of the chairs, and took a seat. He pulled her to him without a word, using his hands to see her in the dark. They skimmed the silk of her shirt, finding and unbuttoning it as his fingers slid down the fabric.

"Tom," she started.

"Shh," he purred and kissed her exposed stomach. Her hands threaded into his hair as he kissed the landscape of her belly. Instead of going north, his hands dropped to her exposed knees, sliding up her outer thighs and back to her knees. His right hand moved to her inner thigh, sliding until it hit the satin of her underwear.

The thrill of the moment captivated him and when she shifted, widening her stance, he nearly yanked her underwear off, but he refrained. Focusing on the rich texture, he teased her with his fingers, using the fabric to create heat and friction until her panties were soaked.

He wanted to be inside her, to hear her cry his name with that husky, sex-laden voice.

Tom pulled his hand from between her legs and stood, kissing her before he turned away with jeans that were uncomfortable over his hardened shaft. When she wrapped her arms around his waist and her hand slid over his hard rod, he groaned.

"Wow," she whispered, caressing him through his pants.

Insanity took hold and Tom turned, lifted her up, and pressed her against the wall. Her legs wrapped around his waist. The way she moved increased his urge to rip her clothing off, but in the back of his mind, he didn't want this to be their first foray.

He stopped and leaned his forehead against the wall, his breath ragged and clipped with his raw sexual urge. It took him a good five minutes before he slowly put her on her feet and stepped away.

"Are you okay?" her breathless voice echoed in the darkness.

"Yes." He felt the wall for the bank of switches and when he found them, he counted to the third switch, flipping it on. Even the low-level darkroom light seemed bright enough to burn his retinas and he squinted at her.

She was far sexier with the shirt unbuttoned, her hair in disarray and her skirt hiked up than she was when he first saw her this morning and he couldn't help but smile.

"Why did you stop?" she whispered, straightening her skirt and buttoning up her shirt.

"Because this isn't how I want your first time to go." He dropped into the chair, gripping the armrests to slow down the frantic need pumping his heart into overdrive.

"This wouldn't be my first time," she whispered, and he stared at her.

"Bu?" he hooked his thumb over his shoulder toward the auditorium.

"I said what if I was a virgin, not that I was." She took a seat in the only other chair in the room. "I don't dress like this for a reason."

He blinked at the confusion fogging his mind.

"If my stepfather saw me in this..." she trailed off and dropped her gaze.

"Wha happe?" he asked, unsure of whether he really wanted to know.

"Shortly after we got to the states, my mother and stepfather were in a car accident. She died, and my stepfather was never the same after that. Before the accident, his aura was dark, but he had some redeeming light woven in. But now his aura is almost as black as Tanya's is, like he lost his soul." She shifted in her seat, giving him a quick glance before she went back to studying her hands.

"And it comes through in his artwork. Before the accident, he prided himself in turning out works of beauty, but now what he creates is just scary as hell, like he wants to destroy anything remotely beautiful and preserve only terror. The pisser is he rarely leaves the house or the studio now," she said. "I admit he was never a prize to begin with, but after he got back on his feet, he got more insistent than he ever was when my mom was alive."

"What do you mean, insistent?" Tom signed.

She leveled a look in his direction that told him more than he ever wanted to know.

"When my mother was alive, he only fondled me," she whispered, and her cheeks turned red. "Sometimes I wish that was all he did now."

Tom clenched his teeth and a monster of a beast reared inside him, almost taking control of his common sense. His hands squeezed the armrests tighter. Each word that tumbled from her mouth brought on a murderous rage inside him.

"And if he catches me in this," she waved toward the sexy outfit, "he's going to know there is someone else." Fear blazed in her eyes and her gaze drifted to his aura.

Tom dipped his chin to his chest and stared at the floor in front of him. His fury rendered him immobile.

"I'm sorry." She headed for the door.

His paralysis broke, and he grabbed her arm. "No ma a ou," he said, holding her in place. He couldn't let her leave, thinking his rage was in any way aimed at her. It was aimed at her stepfather.

"Come over after school," he signed.

"No. I have to go home and change before he catches me looking like this."

"E me hewp ou," he said. Tears filled her eyes, and he pulled her into a hug.

"You already have," she whispered.

"I wo e him huw ou," he whispered in her ear.

She squeezed him tight, burying her face in his chest before pulling away. "You aren't the only one who's damaged."

Tom blinked the sheen from his eyes, feeling the heat of tears slide down his face. He hadn't felt this helpless since Georgia, and this time it was accompanied by soul wrenching pain. He couldn't protect her while he was under house arrest.

"I have to get back to class," Raven said, peeling out of his arms and meeting his gaze. She turned and left without another word.

Tom stared at the door and slowly sat down in the chair, letting his mind go over every encounter he had with her over the years. The times she flinched away from any contact, the dark glasses, always covered in dark colors that muted her spirit.

Her behavior was the exact opposite of what he had seen these last few days, almost as if interacting with him had breathed a new life into her.

Why didn't I see it before?

He looked at the ceiling, feeling every bit as imprisoned as if he was in a jail cell.

What the hell do I do now?

Saving Face
Chapter 40

CJ GLANCED AT TOM slumped in the front seat, his arms crossed and his expression moody, but his mind was like a vice, shut down from CJ's power of inquiry.

"What's going on?"

Tom shook his head, still staring out the side window.

"Did you and Raven get into a fight?" CJ asked. He hadn't seen her at all this afternoon, and she didn't walk Tom out of the school today.

"No," Tom said.

"Then what is it?"

"I'm worried about her, that's all," he signed.

"Why?"

Tom leveled a glare in his direction. "Let it go."

"Okay, but you know I'm here if you need me." He took the last turn and his brow creased. Jennifer's car was in the driveway, along with a few others he didn't recognize. It looked like the media presence had been kicked up again too and he beeped his horn, waiting for the idiots to clear a path.

"Shit," he muttered as he pulled to a stop.

"Wha?" Tom asked, glancing between CJ and the house.

"They're here to take me to D.C. to testify against Steve." CJ slammed his palm on the steering wheel before shutting the car off. "And if I don't go, they'll revoke your house arrest." He glanced at Tom. "Bastards." He got out of the car.

TOM STARED AS CJ stormed into the house, his words still sinking in, and Tom got out of the car slowly, crossing to the threshold in time to hear CJ spew curses at Ron Cleary.

"You fucking bastard!" CJ yelled, his hands balled into tight fists. "I told you that in confidence."

"Settle down," Sarah said, standing between CJ and Cleary.

"How the hell can you do this to Steve?" Jennifer said, leveling a glare that would kill if she had any power behind it.

"He violated the law," Cleary said, like that explained everything.

"You betrayed him," Jennifer growled.

"Jen, I know how pissed you are, but you have to stand down," Sarah said, trying to keep the peace in an explosive situation.

"And what about you?" she turned her glare on Sarah.

Tom leaned on the kitchen counter, observing the dynamics and wondering whether CJ was going to blow. If it was him, he would have swung by now, but he stayed out of it, too numb from his day to react.

Sarah met Jennifer's gaze. "I'm on his side. We're all on his side."

"Bullshit." Jennifer took a threatening step forward.

CJ put his arm out, stopping Jennifer. "I'll go because I don't want to see Tom thrown in jail." He met her gaze before swinging it back toward Cleary. "But you better assign a fucking battalion to this house while I'm gone because I promised Steve I'd be here to protect them in case the Windwalker struck."

"We have one of our best agent keeping watch."

"Just one?"

"He's been instructed to call for reinforcements if he sees anything unusual," Cleary said. "Now go pack a bag. Our flight is leaving from Peas in an hour."

"Fine," CJ stomped out of the living room.

"Just one agent?" Jennifer met Sarah's gaze. "That's all you assigned?" She crossed her arms in defiance, but Tom knew there was an underlying insecurity.

"We will have CJ back here by nine tomorrow night. I promise," Sarah said.

"And what if the Windwalker strikes?"

"You have twenty-four-hour surveillance." Cleary's gaze fell on Tom before shifting back to Jennifer.

"Oh, that makes me feel eons better," Jennifer volleyed.

"Cut the sarcasm," he glared at her. "This is serious and I'm praying CJ has some nugget of information that can save your husband's ass.

Otherwise, he's headed for a long stay in a federal penitentiary."

Jennifer closed her mouth and looked at the floor, stepping back to put more distance between her and the two FBI agents. Tom saw both defeat and fear in her stance and crossed, putting a protective arm around her shoulder. He leveled a glare at Cleary, one that was fueled more by the day's events than the current situation, but it had the desired effect.

Cleary shifted uncomfortably under Tom's silent challenge, and he traded a glance with Sarah.

CJ came bounding down the stairs with a duffel bag and his computer bag. "There better be internet service wherever you're putting me up." He gave Jennifer and Tom a nod as he followed Cleary and Sarah out the front door.

Tom crossed to the window, watching them pull out. A chill skittered down his spine, and he turned, glancing at Jennifer.

"Looks like it's just you and me. Feel like going out to dinner tonight?"

He raised an eyebrow and pointed at the ankle bracelet.

"Shit," she muttered and leaned back into the couch.

"Are you okay?" he signed.

She laughed and shook her head, her chuckles turning into sobs, and she buried her face in her hands. He took a seat on the couch and pulled her to his shoulder, just saying, "shh," over and over while she cried.

When she finally settled down, she wiped her face, and her bloodshot gaze met his.

"I'm sorry, Tom. I'm sure me falling apart was the last thing you needed."

He offered a smile. "I' oay," he said. "How did your audition go?" he signed.

"I didn't make it. Sarah called me to give me a heads up about CJ's subpoena and I turned around and came home," she said.

"I'm sorry," he signed.

"Don't be. It's not your fault." She took a deep, cleansing breath before turning toward him. "So, how was your day?"

Tom leaned back into the cushions. "As crappy as yours," he signed.

"Why?"

"I had a confrontation with Bear and Raven confided something in me that has me real worried." He pulled the cast off his arm, tossing it onto the table. "Can I ask you a question?"

"Always," she said.

"How did you know Steve was the one?"

Jennifer sighed, thinking back to the moment he walked into her college apartment. That was the moment she knew, but she wanted to give Tom some background. "He was my neighbor for years and his sister was my best friend."

Tom's eyebrows arched. He thought they met in college.

"After she died, we got really close, but at that time, the age difference was huge. Five years is an ocean when you're talking eleven and sixteen. For years I had the biggest crush on him and after they moved away, I used to wait by the mailbox to see if he sent a letter. It was kind of pathetic," she laughed and traded a glance. "The letters dropped off after a while and

I stopped waiting for them." Jennifer paused and stood, crossing to the sliders.

"When he walked back into my life my senior year in college, I knew. I can't tell you exactly how I knew, just that I did. Being around him is better than any adrenaline rush, out there, even now. I still feel the electricity between us whenever he's around. And he knows how to make me laugh."

She turned and shrugged. "I know, you haven't heard me laugh in a while, but he can make me giggle like a schoolgirl."

Tom grinned. He couldn't see her giggling.

"Life hasn't been kind to us, and we've had to struggle through some horrific times, just like you and CJ have, but there's no one I'd rather have at my side." Tears filled her eyes again and she looked away. "I just can't see how I'm going to get through this if he's locked up for the next thirty years."

Saving Face
Chapter 41

TOM STEPPED INTO THE principal's office and handed the note Jennifer gave him to the secretary. Without waiting, he headed back into the hall and leaned against the bricks, watching for Raven. When she didn't show up, his chest tightened another notch.

All the Skype calls last night went to a busy signal, and he barely got any sleep.

The warning bell rang, and he went into the classroom, sitting in his seat, concentrating on not allowing the panic attack to take hold. Raven stepped into the classroom just as the late bell rang and Tom's lungs clamped closed.

Raven wore the bland clothing she had always worn, and her hair fell in front of her face, blocking his view of her. But he did glimpse sunglasses, and his heart tumbled onto the floor.

She never even looked his way and when the bell rang, she headed for the door like a racehorse out of the starting gate. Tom sprinted, catching up to her in the hallway. He spun her around so he could see her face.

"Leave me alone," she whispered.

Tom didn't respond. He reached his hand under her chin and forced her to look at him. The glasses didn't hide all the bruises, and he stepped back, meeting her gaze as the coiled fury took over. He spun, heading toward the front of the school with one thought on his mind. His hands ached from how hard he clenched them, and it wasn't until he pushed open the doors that she grabbed his wrist, pulling him back inside.

"Don't. Please don't do this," she whispered.

"I'm going to kill him," he signed and tore his hand from her grip.

She maneuvered in front of Tom, placing both her hands on his chest and stopping him halfway across the sidewalk. The beeping of his ankle bracelet cut through his fury.

"You can't help me if you're in jail," she said.

Tom pressed his lips together, and his vision blurred under the fresh set of tears filling his eyes. "What did he do to you?" he signed and when her gaze dropped to the ground, he turned and trudged back to the school. The beeping stopped as soon as he entered the hallway and he leaned against the brick, grappling with his shredded heart.

She stepped inside next to him and he turned his pained gaze her way.

"You are coming home with me today," he signed. "And God help him if he comes near you again."

Tears sprouted from her eyes like a slow faucet leak, and he wrapped his arms around her, kissing her forehead.

"Auditorium or class?" he signed, and she signed auditorium back.

He took her hand and led her down the quiet halls, and into the empty auditorium. This time, he led her to the back corner, where there was a little light seeping in from the doors. He took a seat, dropping his head in his hands as black despair took hold. His thoughts whirled with all sorts of degrading images, and he closed his eyes, letting the tears come.

When his tears dried up, he leaned back, wiping his nose on his sleeve before turning toward her. He removed her glasses and inspected her black eye, clenching his teeth against the renewed flare of anger.

"I'm owwy," he whispered. "I'm o owwy." His breath hitched in his chest, and he stood, pulling her into his arms. She flinched, drawing in her breath audibly, killing another piece of his humanity.

"There is no way in hell I'm letting you go home," he signed.

"You have to."

"No, I don't. We have extra rooms at the house. You'll be safe there."

"He threatened to kill you," she met his gaze.

Tom narrowed his eyes and smiled. "I'd really like to see him try," he signed, and she shivered, wrapping her arms around herself. "I'd kick his ass from here to Ireland and back," he signed, drawing a small laugh.

With a deep breath, Tom took her hand and led her into the media room, but this time he switched on the dark light and closed the door, sitting her down in the chair and pulling the other one close so they faced each other.

"What did your stepfather do?" he signed, preparing himself for the answer, but it still wasn't enough.

"He tied me to the bed and beat me," she said.

"Is that all?" he asked. He had to know, because the visions in his head were as ugly as it gets.

She shook her head, staring at the ground at first before bringing her tear-stained gaze to his.

Shredded. That's exactly what his insides felt like when her gaze locked with his. Every nerve exposed and throbbing with pain, and there wasn't a damn thing he could do about it. He pressed his lips together, getting a hold on the storm brewing inside him and he reached out, cupping her cheek.

"Never again," he whispered, forcing the enunciation.

Her chin quivered, and a torrent of tears flowed from her beautiful eyes. Soon her entire form shook, and he pulled her from the chair onto his lap, holding her tight so she wouldn't fly to pieces.

The overhead lights blinked on, but neither of them moved. Raven still sobbed silently against his shoulder. When a throat cleared, Tom swiveled the seat, meeting Principal Novak's sharp glare.

"You two shouldn't be in here," he said.

Raven stiffened in Tom's arms.

"I'm sorry, Mr. Novak. It's just today is the anniversary of my mother's death and I needed a friend," she sniffled from under her thick hair.

Tom shrugged and kept eye contact.

"Fine, I'll give you a free pass this time, but I don't want to see you miss another class. Is that clear, Mr. Ryan?"

Tom nodded, and Raven climbed off his lap, keeping her head down as she passed the principal.

Mr. Novak grabbed Tom's arm. "I'm watching you," he glared.

Tom just nodded and headed out into the brightly lit hallway, where Raven waited for him with her sunglasses back in place.

The rest of the day went by without so much as a sideways look from anyone, and when the last bell rang, Tom met Raven at the door and walked out with her hand in his. He opened the back door of Jennifer's car and helped her in before climbing into the passenger seat.

Jennifer gave him a questioning glance.

"Just drive," he signed.

Saving Face
Chapter 42

TOM OPENED THE GARAGE door, letting both Raven and Jennifer into the house before he stepped inside.

"Raven needs a place to stay," he signed once he threw his book bag on the table.

"Really." She turned toward Raven. "Is that true?"

Raven removed her glasses and Jennifer gasped. "Oh, my God. Who did this to you?" She crossed the room and inspected the bruise before meeting her gaze.

Tom crossed. "Her stepfather did this," he signed. "She's not going home."

Jennifer inhaled, meeting his gaze, and nodded. "Did you want to press charges?" she asked, returning her questioning stare to Raven.

Raven shook her head. "No. All I want is a shower right now," she said, and tears formed.

"Why don't you show her where everything is," she said to Tom and gave Raven's hand a squeeze. "You can stay as long as you'd like."

"Thank you," Tom signed, and Jennifer nodded, her expression mixed with understanding and an underlying anger at the injustice. He knew under her calm waters raged a wild mother bear, and this type of thing always brought it to the surface.

Jennifer glanced at Raven. "What are you, a size three?"

Raven nodded.

"I'll get you a change of clothes." She followed them upstairs.

Tom opened the guest room door for Raven, and she stepped inside. When Jennifer came in with a pair of underwear, sweats and a t-shirt, Raven took them with tears in her eyes.

"Thank you," she whispered.

"The bathroom is over there, and Tom will get you some towels." She gave him a nod before leaving the room. Something about her demeanor struck Tom, and he followed her into the hall, stopping her.

"What is it?" he signed.

Jennifer turned, and a tear escaped from her lashes. "She needs some TLC right now. That doesn't mean sex, it means letting her see your heart. Understand?" She wiped the tears away.

His eyes widened. "You saw." He stepped away.

"Not in the way you're thinking. I've seen that haunted look before. In the mirror." She pressed her lips together. The pain painted in her eyes cut him to the core. "That's the only reason I'm going to let you stay up here with her while I go call the police. That bastard belongs behind bars."

He watched her climb down the stairs and turned back, pulling a couple of towels from the linen closet before stepping into her room. Raven sat on the bed, staring at the floor and he set the towels down, slipping her glasses out of her fingers and set them on the table.

No words were spoken, and he ran the back of his knuckles down her cheek, studying her for a moment before he reached for the hem of her shirt. She reacted, her eyes widening and her hands grasping and holding it in place.

"I' oay." He took a step back so she could see his hands. He pointed toward the bathroom and signed, "Bath or shower?"

Her gaze jumped to the bathroom and back. "Shower," she whispered.

He put his finger up and headed into the bathroom, turning on the shower for her so the water would be warm when she was ready, and then he stepped into the bedroom. "Do you want me to stay or go?" he signed.

She looked like a deer in the headlights under the question posed by his hands and he took that as a go and stepped toward the door.

"No," she said, meeting his gaze. Her hands cradled her elbows, and she whispered, "Stay."

He nodded and came to her side, leaning against the bed with her.

Her hands shook as she reached for the hem of her shirt and she bit down on her lip, not in the sexy way she had the day before, but in the way desperate people do when cornered.

"Do you want me to help?"

She tried to smile, and he took the initiative, stepping in front of her and taking her arms, raising them so he could strip the shirt. She hesitated halfway, her eyes filled with pain and doubt, and then she closed them, allowing him to strip the fabric off her.

He stared at her torso and dropped the shirt. Shock brought on a wave of dizziness and his legs wobbled underneath him. Her creamy, unblemished skin had been carved with a crude pentagram. He bent to touch the raw carving and pulled his hand away, dropping to his knees in front of her.

He brought his gaze to hers, knowing every bit of the horror he felt was painted in his features.

Raven turned to grab the towels and his eyes widened at the two words carved into her back and he stumbled to his feet, taking a step away, his hand flying to cover the gasp.

Her gaze locked on the mirror across the room at the scrawling letters on her back.

Windwalker's Whore.

Her head whipped around toward Tom, and her face paled. "Oh my God," she whispered.

A crash downstairs rocked the house and Raven's horror slammed into his mind.

"Where is she?" The growl from the family room seeped through the floorboards and Tom's eyes widened. Her stepfather wasn't mocking him. He was laying claim to what he believed was his property.

Raven's stepfather was the Windwalker, and Jennifer was downstairs.

"Stay," he signed and spun on his heels, sprinting downstairs in time to see the blade cut through Jennifer's arm as she parried, blocking what should have been a kill strike.

"Run," she screamed at him and blocked another swing.

Raven's stepfather was a hulk of a man, bigger than he expected, and his face was lined with scars, ruining what once could have been handsome. He caught Tom's gaze and sent a feral smile in his direction. "You're next." He refocused on Jennifer.

"Get out of here, Tom!" Jennifer ordered, meeting his gaze for a second and her eyes widened, her gaze dropping to the knife embedded in her chest before they rolled back in her head.

"Oo!" Tom bellowed, caught between the need to defend Jennifer and her order to get Raven to safety. The look on Raven's stepfather's face clinched it, and Tom turned, bolting up the stairs.

Footfalls fell in step behind him and instead of leading him into the guest room; he turned into his bedroom, sending out an SOS that he prayed would traverse the miles between York and Washington D.C.

The exodus of wings followed and if his SOS didn't make it there, his father would. Tom spun, facing the door as the Windwalker appeared in the doorway, leading with the dripping knife, and a pang of guilt bit at his stomach. He had left Jennifer in the hands of this madman.

"Where is my whore?" he growled.

A flash of red appeared behind him, and Raven jumped on his back, digging her nails into his flesh with a scream that shattered the heavy silence. Her stepfather jerked backward, smashing her head against the doorjamb and she crumpled to the ground, unconscious.

"Bastard," Tom said, his voice clear and concise, and he knew they were no longer alone. He reached for the snow globe and pitched it at her stepfather.

He ducked, and the globe shattered on the wall opposite his door.

"I'm going to preserve that pretty face of yours just for her, so she has a reminder of what happens when she rebels."

Tom's gaze flicked to Tanya's ghost, and he winced at the banshee scream as she launched herself at the Windwalker. She passed right through him, falling to the ground.

Out of the corner of his eye, he saw the flash of metal and parried. The knife bit into his flesh and instead of dancing away, he stepped in and sent his fist crashing into the middle of the bastard's chest.

The Windwalker stumbled back but the knife cross-slashed, tearing into Tom's chest, and Tom let out a yell and spun away. He kept fighting even with his blood splattering slash after slash. Panic embedded itself in his head, making him sluggish.

The only thing that kept him moving and defending against the Windwalker's death blows was Raven, and the thought of what this bastard would do to her if he fell.

Saving Face
Chapter 43

"THE PROSECUTION CALLS CJ Ryan to the stand."

CJ stood, meeting Steve's glance as he walked by. *Just tell the truth, that's all I ask.* Steve's voice echoed in CJ's head, and he nodded.

His nerves went into overdrive, sending tingles through his arms to his fingertips, and he closed his fists to keep it from manifesting in a shake. The walk to the witness chair seemed longer than the length of a football field, even though it was only thirty paces from his chair to the stand.

"Do you swear to tell the truth and nothing but the truth, so help you God?" the bailiff said.

CJ leaned forward. "I do." His voice echoed through the chamber.

"State your name and age for the record." The prosecutor wiped a stray hair from her face.

"Christopher James Ryan. I'll be eighteen next month."

"Mr. Ryan, can you tell the court about the first time you met Special Agent Williams?"

CJ met Steve's gaze and nodded. "He came to the house to inform my parents of my brother's death."

"Did you overhear the conversation?"

CJ glared at the prosecutor, pressing his lips together.

"Mr. Ryan, please answer the question."

"Yes."

"And can you tell us what transpired?"

"He told my parents that Eric died."

"What else did he say?"

CJ glared at Cleary and the sense of betrayal increased. He pretended to be Steve's ally, and he was the farthest thing from it. The information he divulged in their conversation was now in the prosecutor's hands. That's why he sat here, testifying against the man who had stepped in and raised him like a father. Frustration increased as he glanced at the jury box, hearing their derogatory thoughts aimed in Steve's direction.

He was the last prosecution witness, and they were hoping to seal Steve's fate with CJ's testimony. A burning anger ignited in his belly, and he shifted in the seat, unwilling to answer any question that would play into their hands.

"Tell them what I said, CJ," Steve said from the defense table.

The prosecutor sent a glare in Steve's direction.

"You will refrain from speaking to the witness until your cross examination," the judge scolded and turned to CJ. "Answer the question, son."

CJ's jaw tightened at the familiar term spoken by the stranger ruling over the court. "He said he knew who my father was."

"And who exactly was your father?"

CJ dropped his gaze to the floor. "My father was Ty Aris," he whispered, and shame heated his cheeks. Admitting the world-renowned criminal was his father was harder than he imagined. He took a deep breath, willing himself to meet the prosecutor's gaze.

"Are you aware of what your father did?"

CJ nodded, hating the pretty blonde in the sharp suit more with every question she asked.

"Please state your answer for the court."

"Yes." He glanced at the darkening windows. Dusk settled over the east coast, and he wondered if they would finish with him today.

"Did you know at that time?"

"No. I just knew he had done some bad things before he met my mom."

"What else did Special Agent Williams say?"

"He said he should haul my father in, but unfortunately, he made a promise to my brother on his deathbed," he said, sending a derisive glare in Cleary's direction. That fact wasn't disclosed to the prosecution, and her lips thinned.

A couple of the jury members reacted with raised eyebrows. Their focus on a man only out for himself just shifted, but CJ sensed it wasn't enough for them to acquit.

The next question was drowned out by Tom's panicked call echoing in his head and he winced, trading a glance with Steve as "Jesus

Christ," slipped from his mouth and his hands shot to his ears in reaction.

Steve's gaze was sharp one second, and then gone the next, and CJ knew his spirit had transitioned to their house in Maine.

His body trembled, and his gaze bounced around the courthouse, looking for anything to concentrate on, anything to divert his mind from the terror in his brother's tone. The word he cried carving a painful gash in his chest, restricting his breathing and his gaze found Sarah in the back of the courtroom.

"Windwalker," he whispered, staring at her. He silently pleaded for understanding and her eyes widened, her gaze switching to Steve's body, now in suspended animation, waiting for his soul to return.

"Mr. Ryan!" The prosecutor's tone was sharp enough to cut through the panic.

"What?" CJ snapped, focusing on her.

"Did Agent Williams force your father to help him in exchange for his freedom?"

"No. My father offered to help. That bastard killed my brother, and my father would not let that go and Steve really wasn't in the condition to figure out the quickest way to nail Winslow."

The sparkle in the prosecutor's eyes caught CJ off guard.

"So, you're saying Agent Williams wasn't in the right mind to make a clear and concise decision?"

CJ now understood where they were going and shook his head. "You don't have a clue of what that man has done for my family, do you?"

He leaned forward, challenging her to ask one more inane question.

"Why don't you tell us?" she asked, leaning against the prosecutor's table, her mind working the angle in a way that left his mouth bitter.

His gaze flicked to Steve sitting there like an unanimated corpse and, for the first-time, eyes in the courtroom followed. CJ's heart lurched because anyone taking a close look at him would assume he was either catatonic or dead.

CJ scrambled, his mind clawing at emptiness, and he glanced at the jury box, hearing the first of the shocked gasps.

"He's fine," he said, drawing their gazes back. "He stepped out for a moment, but he'll be back." He prayed he was right because if he didn't come back, that meant CJ was now all alone in the world and that scared the daylights out of him. He swallowed the lump of fear in his throat, and it burned all the way down to his already roiling stomach.

The prosecutor's head whipped around toward Steve. She dropped her pad on the table and headed in his direction.

"I said he is fine," CJ's voice boomed, shocking her still. "You jackasses left my brother and Jennifer alone at the house without protection," he snarled, letting the panic and fear morph into anger.

"The FBI assigned an agent to monitor the house," the prosecutor said.

"Then he's either incompetent or dead because the Windwalker is there right now," his voice cracked, and he dropped his chin to his chest, reining in his temper.

"How could you possibly know that?" she asked.

"Because I'm just as special as Steve is, and that's why my father made him my guardian," he said, unwilling for Steve to take the fall to protect him.

"What do you mean?" the judge asked.

"Steve has a unique set of skills, and his boss knows enough about them to make this entire court preceding a joke."

The prosecutor resumed crossing the room toward Steve, and the bailiff followed.

CJ jumped to his feet. "Don't touch him!" The command in his voice was loud enough to draw everyone's attention.

Both the prosecutor and the bailiff glanced at Steve and then went back to their posts.

CJ looked at the gallery and then the jurors. "My father knew what was coming, and he prepared for it. He knew his time was up and he chose to work with Steve to help catch Winslow instead of dying at home. He chose Steve to look after us because he knew my mother's time was coming, too. He just didn't know the details. If he had, there'd be no way he would have let Steve take us to Georgia."

"This is hearsay, your honor." The prosecutor glared at CJ. "And how exactly would your dead father be able to stop him, anyway?" She pointed toward Steve.

"My father is Steve's guardian angel."

Silence filled the courtroom.

The prosecutor's jaw hung open, along with most of the attendees and everyone in the jury box. She blinked and traded a glance with the judge.

"I'm not mentally ill, so don't even go down that path." Her gaze jumped back to his. "Yes, I am a mind reader," he added when that thought crossed her mind.

"You also have a genius IQ," she said, her features hardening at what she deemed a lucky guess.

"Yes, I'm one of the smartest kids on earth. What's your point?"

"You're smart enough to make up this charade to get Agent Williams off. I bet he put you up to this," she said.

CJ smiled and refrained from saying the derogatory comment that filled his mouth, pressing his lips closed. He inhaled and stared her down.

"Don't you need proof to make silly accusations like that?" he asked and turned to the judge. "I believe if Steve were in the room, he would object to this line of questioning."

"Mr. Ryan, answer the question."

They were stonewalling, and he knew it. There was nothing he could say or do to exonerate Steve, and he lost it. "Are you even listening?"

"Son, pipe down or I will hold you in contempt of court," the judge said.

CJ glared at him. "I am not your son."

"Permission to treat Mr. Ryan as a hostile witness?"

"Permission granted," the judge replied.

"Did Agent Williams put you up to this?"

CJ glared at her. "No, he expects me to tell the truth, and I am."

"The truth?" She burst out laughing.

CJ clenched his fists, fury filling him at the thoughts of everyone in the courtroom, including the judge, and tears of frustration filled his eyes. They were hell bent on putting Steve away and he hadn't offered much in the way of a defense. He needed to do something drastic, whether or not he wanted to, and he knew there was only one person who could stop him. He let some of the anger seep out, shaking the foundation of the courthouse.

"I swear to God, Dad, if you don't get your ass down here and tell them what I'm saying is the truth, I'll level this entire place," he bellowed at the heavens.

Shock filtered through the room and before anyone could react, a wild wind filled the court, followed by the sound of beating wings.

Saving Face
Chapter 44

STEVE'S CHEST HURT AS the pull of Tom's psychic signature brought him into the family room of their house, fear crushing his ability to breathe. The word Tom mentally belted out only meant one thing, and he prayed he wasn't too late.

The first thing that struck him was the amount of blood splatter. His heart stopped when his gaze landed on bare feet sticking out from behind the couch. He moved toward her manicured toes and everything else around him dissolved into the panic he felt the last time she laid unconscious with this much blood surrounding them.

"Jennifer!" The bellow filled the room and a crash upstairs followed. He bent, checking for a pulse and his legs gave out from under him, the relief completely draining all the strength from his body for a moment. He rolled her over, ignoring the number of defensive wounds covering her arms, face, neck, and chest. While her eyes weren't focused, and her chest barely moved, life still existed and that's all he needed.

He leaned forward and pressed his lips against her forehead, sending a hefty dose of healing mojo through her. Even as she stiffened and drew in a painful breath, he stood, bolting upstairs and letting the healing power do its work.

Another crash pushed him faster, and he rounded the corner in time to see shattered glass glimmering on the hallway floor along with clear liquid and red and blue specs of confetti. He slid to a stop in the remnants of Tom's Patriots snow globe, his heart hammered in his chest and his breath came in short bursts from both the mental and physical exertion.

Nothing prepared him for the sight inside Tom's room.

A hulk of a man circled with Tom, his face a hideous mask of anger, traversed by scars and with a nose that had been broken several times. In his hand, he brandished a blade slick with gore. From the amount of blood dripping from Tom's elbows, Steve could only guess how badly cut he was, but at least he was still standing and fighting.

But it wasn't the Windwalker that sent a chilling shiver down his spine. It was the sight of Raven unconscious on the floor and the words carved into her back.

Tanya's faceless ghost screamed like a wild animal. She pushed herself up from the floor and ran toward the Windwalker, passing right through him and falling again. Her frustration filled the room, drowning out Tom's panting.

"I won't let you hurt her again," Tom breathed, ignoring the lunatic ranting of Tanya's ghost.

"I'm going to save you for when she's awake and can see my handiwork. I want her to watch you scream in agony as I rip your face off," he snarled and slashed out. Tom parried, blocking the blade and taking another deep cut to the forearm.

"I don't think so," Steve said from the hallway and the Windwalker's gaze flicked from Tom's face to Steve's directly beyond Tom's shoulder. His eyes widened.

That was all Steve needed. Anger erupted in a blast that knocked the Windwalker through the wall and onto the concrete patio below. Tanya's ghost followed, leaving a sudden silence that rang in Steve's ears.

Tom turned. "I didn't think you'd make it in time." He stumbled, his eyes rolling up into his head as he passed out. Steve caught him and assessed the damage. Tom's forearms looked like someone played a thousand games of tick-tack-toe across the skin, and his shirt didn't look much better. However, the amount of blood soaking the fabric was a fraction of what ran from his arms.

"Jesus, Tom." He wiped away the hair from his forehead. With another surge of energy, he pushed a jolt of healing power into Tom, taking a minute to watch the sparkles encompass his body and the wince suck through his teeth as the pain bit into him.

He stood and stepped to the open hole in the wall, glaring down at the twisted form of the

Windwalker. Steve turned, giving Tom a quick glance before focusing on Raven. He checked her pulse, and it beat strong against his fingertips. Her eyes fluttered open for a minute before rolling back and he leaned forward, sending just enough juice to cure her head, but not enough to wipe out the carvings in her skin.

He stood and turned, heading toward the stairwell. He stopped in his bedroom and retrieved the extra pair of handcuffs he owned and navigated the stairs more cautiously this time, trying not to disrupt any evidence. The sight of Jennifer's unmarred skin prompted a breath of relief, and he guessed it would be at least an hour before she woke.

With his heart returning to normal, he stepped in front of the sliding doors that led out back and froze with his hand on the door handle. The Windwalker was gone, but a streak of blood across the patio and onto the footpath pointed the direction the bastard went.

"Shit," he breathed and swung the door open; barreling around the rock wall in a sprint, he caught up to the crawling criminal. With a guttural roar, he grabbed the thick black hair and yanked, marching back to the patio, dragging the Windwalker along with him.

Blind anger and murderous rage racked his body as pictures of the condition this bastard left his victims in flashed across his mind, making him oblivious to the wild slashes the man executed against his legs. Pain was so far removed that he didn't notice the repeated stabs into his outer thigh until he stood before one of the patio's concrete columns.

He caught the Windwalker's wrist before the knife plunged into his flesh again and he growled; using so much torque that he nearly twisted the wrist backwards, all the bones shattered with the motion. The knife clattered to the ground.

The Windwalker screamed and kept yelling like a banshee while Steve handcuffed him to the concrete, making sure the cuffs were uncomfortably tight before he stepped around in front of the psycho.

"I got you, you twisted fuck," he breathed and punched him, breaking his nose again and snapping his head back hard enough against the concrete to knock him unconscious. He glanced up at the hole in Tom's wall, wondering just how that was going to be explained, but he didn't care right now.

He'd caught the Windwalker, and he wanted the world to know.

Inside, he scooped up the phone and dialed nine-one-one. "This is Special Agent Steve Williams and I'm calling from my house at 15 Roaring Sound. Tell O'Keefe the Windwalker is handcuffed to a column on my patio and he's to get his ass to my house right now."

"Agent Williams?"

"Yes."

"We thought you were in Washington," the police operator said.

"I am. Now get someone to my house right now." He set the phone on the counter just before the transition took hold.

Saving Face
Chapter 45

BLINDING, AWARENESS FILTERED IN, and Steve inhaled against the sharp pain in his right leg. He ran a hand over the fabric of his suit pant, and it came away tacky with blood. "Shit," he muttered and looked up at the courtroom. Mouths moved, but the sound remained muffled, and all eyes were wide and looking at the balcony in the back of the courtroom.

Steve turned, and shock filtered through him, stunning him enough so the pain disappeared. Ty Ryan stood on the balcony, his wings spread in all their majesty.

He dropped his gaze to the witness stand and CJ standing with his fists clenched and a stance he recognized as barely contained fury.

"What did I miss?" he asked, but the room spun and with it his stomach. He dropped his forehead onto the table and the roar of sound filled his ears. His gaze fell to the growing puddle of blood dripping off the chair.

A scream pierced through his haze, and he glanced at the prosecution table. The intern was staring at the same puddle and shrieking like she saw a dead body.

Chaos erupted, and Steve inhaled, closing his eyes and concentrating, making the wounds hidden by his slashed slacks disappear. He clenched his teeth at the burn snaking down his leg and gripped the edge of the table, willing himself not to lose consciousness.

CJ appeared at his side. "Are they okay?" he asked.

Steve nodded, still in the grip of the healing pain and unable to speak. He concentrated on the act of breathing, forcing slow, deep breaths in and out while the pain receded.

"What happened?" he whispered to CJ.

"I kind of freaked out." CJ nodded toward the image of his father on the balcony. "I gave him an ultimatum."

Wind filled the courtroom as Ty dropped from the balcony. His wings folded neatly and faded as he waltzed up the aisle.

A hushed silence filled the room and people stepped as far away from the damned angel as they could get. Ty stopped at the defense table, putting his hand on Steve's shoulder. "Thank you," he said, and Steve nodded.

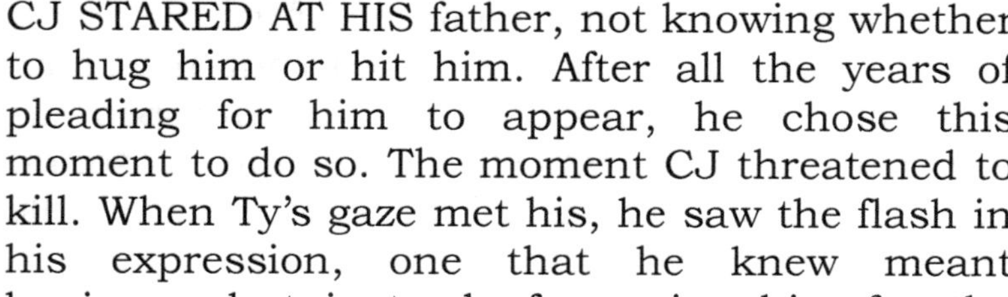

CJ STARED AT HIS father, not knowing whether to hug him or hit him. After all the years of pleading for him to appear, he chose this moment to do so. The moment CJ threatened to kill. When Ty's gaze met his, he saw the flash in his expression, one that he knew meant business, but instead of reaming him for the threat, he reached out, pulling him into a hug.

As soon as Ty released him, Ty stepped into the center of the courtroom floor, facing the jury.

"My son can be a little hotheaded at times, but he has never lied." His gaze flicked to the prosecutor. "You could catch flies with that mouth, honey," he directed at her, and CJ stifled a laugh when she popped her mouth closed.

"Excuse me, but who the hell are you?" the judge interrupted.

"Ty Alexander Ryan, sir. I'm CJ's father," he said, and his wings fluttered, coming back into view. "And as CJ mentioned, and you all were so quick to mock, I *am* Steve's guardian angel."

The judge stared, the jury stared, and the folks at the prosecution table stared.

"Ty, you don't have to do this," Steve said.

Ty turned toward the defense table. "Yes, I do. You didn't even submit the envelope Lynn brought, did you?"

Steve looked down at the folder on the table and shook his head. "No, not yet."

Ty crossed and pulled the sealed envelope from the folder along with Lynn's certification and handed it to the judge. "I gave this to my lawyer with very specific instructions. Her certification of authenticity and my explicit instructions are attached."

The judge bristled. "Bailiff, please take this man into custody," he said.

Ty laughed. "It doesn't work that way, sir. I'm already dead and buried and my penance for my past is keeping him alive and keeping his honor intact." He pointed at Steve.

The bailiff approached, and Ty closed his eyes, reverting to the full angel form, including the grand wings and white light. When he opened his eyes, the jury gasped at the unearthly blue, like the wings and white light weren't enough to convince them.

The bailiff backed away, his face a mask of fear.

"Steve didn't have a choice in any of this," Ty said. "I manipulated him at every turn, coercing him into becoming my friend, into letting me help him on the case, even in not allowing him to kill Kyle Winslow."

"He had no designs on our money, like this court is trying to prove with their slanted facts. He had no desire for the powers now throbbing through his veins, powers that CJ alluded to, and you all just laughed at. He had no desire to raise my kids either, but there is no one more honorable and honest than the man sitting at that table. And no one I trusted more to keep my son in line. So, you see, he was doomed from the beginning." Ty smiled, spreading his arms out.

"What about his recklessness in bringing your son to Georgia?" the prosecutor said, flipping a stray strand of hair from her face.

Ty turned toward her. "If that killer had taken CJ instead of Tom, that would have been the end of him."

"Why is that?" she challenged.

"Let me show you." CJ turned to the bailiff. "Put the cuffs on me as tight as they can go."

"CJ, don't," Steve said from the defense table and stood.

CJ turned. "Sit down," he ordered, and Steve dropped into the chair, his expression turning from concern to annoyance.

The bailiff traded a glance with the judge and received a nod. He did what CJ asked and stepped away.

The metal bit into his wrists. "Permission to approach the jury?" he asked.

"This is highly unorthodox," the judge said. "But I'm now curious, so I'll allow it."

"Are these tight?" he asked the foreman and allowed the man to inspect the cuffs.

"Yes," he answered.

CJ held his wrists in full view, stepping back far enough for the judge and jury members to see. "Open," he announced, and the cuffs popped open, dropping to the floor.

"If it had been me instead of my brother, I could have stopped Lieutenant Danforth before anyone else died. But it wasn't me, and Tom didn't know how to broadcast thoughts the way he does now, so that we can pick it up."

"We?"

"Steve and I couldn't hear him in Georgia, but we certainly did today."

CJ watched the jury, their eyes riveted between him and his father, and their thoughts did a complete one-eighty.

The judge took the bait. "What happened today?"

CJ turned toward the judge. "The Windwalker attacked and from the initial condition Steve was in when he got back here, I'd say you'll find not only Jennifer and Tom's blood on the knife, you'll also find Steve's."

HEADS SNAPPED IN HIS direction and he gave a shrug. "There's also a hole in Tom's bedroom wall." He wiped his hand on his shirt, streaking the white fabric with tacky blood. "The York police can confirm I made the nine-one-one call, and that they found a man on my patio handcuffed to a concrete post," he added, meeting the jury's shocked gaze. "Telekinesis and mind reading aren't as rare as you think, but astral projection, well that takes some time to get used to."

Gazes jumped from him to CJ and then to the angel standing in the room.

"The police will also be dumbfounded by the lack of wounds, especially with the amount of blood splatter in both the family room and Tom's room, but I couldn't let them bleed to death, either."

"What?" the prosecutor whispered, her eyes glued to the bloody handprint.

"Another gift from the Ryan's," Steve shrugged.

Ty cleared his throat. "How do you think I walked out of the complex after having four bullets shred my chest?" When no one spoke, he elaborated. "My wife was a very special woman, and when I kidnapped her, I had no clue of just how special she was. She saved me in every way possible." His wings fluttered, bringing his point home.

Silence fell on the courtroom again, and Steve traded a nod with Ty.

"The charges against Steve are unfounded where I am concerned. I was not coerced in any way and the idea that anyone could extort from me is ludicrous." He spread his wings. "Reckless endangerment in the framework of Georgia is debatable, but where I'm concerned, it doesn't apply. Either way, you're crucifying a good man, and considering he's already been crucified once—literally, I think you should cut him some slack. He didn't abuse his power as an FBI agent. I did."

With that, Ty extended his wings and took flight. Light surrounded him and when he passed through the ceiling, all eyes stayed glued to the spot until the light faded away. Then everyone in the courthouse dropped their awed gaze to Steve and CJ standing at the defense table.

Steve glanced at CJ. *Thank God this wasn't televised.*

No shit.

Silence settled on the room and Steve looked at the prosecutor. "Are you done with CJ?"

She nodded and cleared her throat. "The prosecution rests." Her voice cracked.

The judge turned wide eyes in Steve's direction.

"Ty submitted my defense for me," he said, nodding toward the envelope forgotten in the judge's hand.

Saving Face
Chapter 46

WHEN THEY TURNED THE corner to approach the gate, the media swarmed, and Steve sent a tired glance at CJ sitting next to him in the backseat. The afternoon had drained his strength and the flight home left him will little to no energy.

"You want to open the gate?" Cleary asked from the front seat, meeting Steve's gaze in the mirror.

Steve nodded and sent the silent signal, and the iron opened to a driveway full of red and blue lights. He yawned and wiped his face, shaking the exhaustion away. He had one more fix to take care of and then he could sleep for the next two weeks if he wanted.

"Can you close the gate?" he said to CJ when the car stopped, and CJ complied. He waited until the iron clicked closed before climbing out of the car. He steadied himself and scanned the array of cars, zeroing in on the one with an occupant in the backseat.

The flare of anger bloomed, giving him renewed energy, and he navigated the maze until he reached the squad car. Even though he knew there wasn't a reasonable explanation for the murders, he wanted to know why this bastard ruined his stepdaughter's life and he yanked the door open, leveling a glare at the banged-up man he sent careening through the wall a few hours ago.

"Why?" he asked, and the man chuckled.

CJ put his hand on Steve's shoulder. "You won't get an answer," he said.

"What made you think you had the right to do what you wanted with that sweet girl?" Steve asked, ignoring CJ.

"I own her," he growled and sent a smug smile in Steve's direction. "I'll always own her now that she has my mark carved into her back."

Steve crouched down. "I fixed her. Your fucking carvings are gone, and her skin is as perfect and unbroken as my son's."

His smile faltered.

"You never owned Raven's spirit." He stood. "I understand the police found enough evidence in your shop to put you on death row."

"Fuck you, Agent Williams," the Windwalker snarled. "I'm filing a police brutality lawsuit against you."

Steve laughed. "I'm not a cop anymore and as a private citizen, I have every right to defend my family against a crazy fuck like you. Besides, I was physically in Washington D.C. until about an hour ago." He stood and closed the door on the Windwalker's dropped jaw.

Inside the house was utter chaos until he cleared his throat. Heads swung in his direction and an eerie silence settled on the room. Jennifer was the first to move, the blanket dropping from her shoulders as she crossed the room and threw her arms around his neck, covering his face in frantic kisses.

Steve smiled and planted a welcome kiss on her lips before pulling away. "Save that for later when I have some energy."

Jennifer smiled and turned her gaze to the couch where Raven and Tom sat, still looking shell-shocked, their hands clasped together in a death grip that neither the police nor the EMTs could dislodge.

CJ stood behind Steve, and he let out a low whistle when he got the full view of the room.

Steve turned, meeting his gaze. "Homicide scenes aren't pretty," he said, hearing CJ's shocked response to the blood painted walls. "It's going to take a lot of scrubbing to get this place back in shape."

CJ nodded. "Thank god there are services for that," he replied.

Steve turned back to the family room. Detective O'Keefe squatted in front of Tom for a moment, and then he stood with the ankle tracker in his hand. He offered an apology to Tom, along with his hand. Tom stared at it a minute before bringing his gaze to O'Keefe's. After another moment, he accepted the offered hand with a nod.

O'Keefe turned, meeting Steve's stare, and he crossed the room, stopping in front of Steve.

"I don't have any idea how you pulled this off..." he trailed off. He hung his head, trying to formulate the words.

"It's okay, you don't need to apologize," Steve said. "You were just doing your job."

O'Keefe turned and surveyed the room. "They should have died. The amount of blood alone…" he started again and shook his head. "But neither of them have so much as a cut."

Steve heard O'Keefe's scrambled thoughts and smiled. "I can't give you a logical explanation, Jim."

"I just can't grasp this," he said, waving at the room.

"Just chalk it up to a miracle and let it go," Steve said.

O'Keefe met his gaze. "One of these days, I'll have to take you out for a beer and get the entire story," he said.

"You'll need something a whole lot stronger than beer."

O'Keefe laughed and gave Steve a pat on the back before he left. It took another hour for the police and emergency personnel to leave, and when they did, Steve crossed to the gate, facing the press.

"My family has had a pretty hard couple of weeks, and I would appreciate it if you folks would pack up and go home." It wasn't said as a question, or even a request, but a command that they were compelled to follow. He scanned the press core, watching as they packed up their belongings and dispersed.

"Thank you." Steve closed the gate.

"Why didn't you do that at the beginning of the week?" CJ asked when he stepped through the door.

Steve shrugged. "It still isn't right, but I'm damn tired and I just want the noise to stop so I can get a good night's sleep." He turned his attention to Tom and Raven, still sitting on the couch.

He gave CJ's arm a squeeze. "Thanks for doing whatever you did today. I'm not sure they would have gone so easy on me without your father's display, and he would never have shown up without your bluff."

"I wasn't bluffing."

He studied CJ for a moment. "Yes, it was, because when it comes right down to it, you are a great deal more like me than you realize. The safety of innocent people would have won out over your anger."

He turned, crossing the room, and took a seat on the coffee table opposite Raven.

"They took photos, right?" he asked Tom and got a nod in return.

Raven kept her head lowered until Steve took her hand and then she met his gaze. Tears streaked her cheeks in a steady stream and a brush of anger crossed his skin. He closed his eyes, suffocating the urge to lash out at her stepfather. It wasn't his place to enact justice or vengeance for all the pain the Windwalker caused, but it was Steve's place to heal, and he opened his eyes.

"This isn't your fault."

Her chin quivered.

He gave her hand a squeeze. "Your stepfather doesn't own your spirit. You do."

"He carved..." she started, and her voice hitched in her chest.

"I know, but I promise it won't be there for much longer." He traded a glance with Tom before meeting her gaze again. "I just need you to understand that being damaged doesn't mean the same thing as being ruined. He may have abused your body, but only you have the power to let him crush your soul. It's your choice."

Her gaze hardened. "He never had the power to crush my soul."

Steve nodded. "I'm sorry, but this is going to hurt," he said, and leaned forward to plant a kiss on her forehead, sending a jolt of healing power to erase the hideous carvings from her skin. He prayed it would also erase the wounds in her soul.

Her gasp was followed by a whine of pain, her eyes clamped closed, and her body went rigid. Tom pulled her into his arms, rocking her through the pain until she slumped in his grasp.

Steve met his gaze. "This will not be an easy road," he said, nodding toward Raven. "She has a lot of dark days ahead of her, but I guarantee if you stick with her, it will all be worth it in the end."

Tom pressed his lips together and nodded, blinking a fresh set of tears from the corner of his eyes. Steve gave his knee a pat.

"Why don't you take her upstairs and stay with her until she comes to."

TOM LOOKED DOWN AT her limp body snuggled in his arms. Sorrow, relief and a new hope blended, setting a mist over his eyes and he forced a smile, sending a nod in Steve's direction. He stood and carried her up to the guest bedroom. He got her situated under the covers and ran his hand over the smooth skin of her stomach, marveling at Steve's miracle.

His gaze drifted to her face and the peace in her expression; a vast difference from the pain carved into her features all day. He wiped the stray hairs out of her face and leaned over, pressing his lips to hers like a modern-day Prince Charming, expecting her eyes to open.

The chuckle from the doorway caught his attention, and he snapped a glare toward CJ.

"It will take more than a kiss from you to wake her up," he grinned, and Tom flipped the bird in his direction, stifling a smirk.

CJ's smile faded as his gaze bounced from Tom to Raven and back.

"You scared the shit out of me today," CJ said in all seriousness, and Tom sat up straight, seeing the first hint of tears in his brother's eyes.

Tom covered Raven and shut off the light before he stepped into the hall and met CJ's gaze. Instead of saying something sarcastic as he normally would, he gave CJ a hug, patted his back, and then pulled away.

"Have you seen the disaster that's my room?" he signed and swung the door open. CJ joined him at the entry.

They stared at the blood covering the floor and the standing walls and then their gaze landed on the giant hole in the outside wall. Tom opened his mind, allowing CJ to access the last two days, from the near tag in the auditorium to the fear filling his soul at the sight of the bastard attacking Jennifer.

"She lived with that for the last few years?"

Tom nodded. *Hell, I thought I was damaged.* He let out a laugh.

"And Tanya?"

Tom shrugged. He didn't know what happened to her. Last he knew, she followed the asshole when Steve blasted him from the room. *Maybe she's latched onto the Windwalker.*

CJ chuckled. "I hope she haunts him until he drops dead."

"Me too," Tom signed, and then met CJ's gaze. *What happened in court?*

"Dad made an appearance," CJ answered. "But only after I threatened to blow the courthouse and everyone inside to pieces."

"Really?"

"Ah, man, it was epic. He came down with wings and all and laid down the facts. He also wrote a detailed letter explaining his position, and get this, the letter was dated the day after Emily died."

The shock of that statement hit as pronounced as the ripple of an earthquake when standing over the epicenter. "He knew?"

"Tom, he knew everything. Every god damned thing." CJ shook his head in awe. "Maybe he really was a fallen angel." He took a deep breath and shrugged. "Anyway, to make a long story short, they threw all the charges out except one."

Worry flared in Tom, and he turned, meeting his brother's gaze.

"Don't worry, his sentence didn't include jail time or fines, but he lost his job because of what happened in Georgia. They said it was reckless and he should have never brought me down there, despite what I can do."

"He's no longer in the FBI?" Tom asked and closed his bedroom door.

"Nope." CJ faced Tom. "So, where are you sleeping?"

Tom glanced toward the guest room. "With her," he signed.

CJ grinned and poked Tom. "Yeah, right, like Jen and Steve would ever allow that."

Tom glared at him. "I'm not going to screw around with her; I just want to be there when she wakes up."

CJ's smile faded and his eyebrows arched. "Holy shit! You're in love with her, aren't you?"

Tom glanced toward the door and nodded. "She's the one."

Saving Face
Chapter 47

TOM PULLED UP TO the cabin and set the car in park. His hands shook as he glanced at Raven and offered a nervous smile. He'd planned this entire trip and prayed the flowers around the cove were in full bloom now that graduation was over, and spring was on the cusp of summer. He jogged around to her side of the car and opened the door, helping her out onto the gravel.

"This is absolutely lovely," she said, looking over the lakefront view with awe.

He just nodded and opened the trunk, pulling out the picnic basket and blanket. He cursed under his breath at the shakes gripping his form, and the nerves getting the best of him. With a deep breath, he closed the trunk and smiled. He headed toward the path in the woods, taking her hand as he passed her.

"Where are we going?"

He shook his head and when he got to the path; he stopped and put the basket down.

"It's a surprise. Just wait here. I'll be right back for you in a minute," he signed.

Her dimples appeared, and she met his gaze. "Okay." She turned toward the lake view once more, heading toward the little gazebo and the glider inside.

Tom took off down the winding path with the basket and blanket, his heart hammering harder than when he saw the Windwalker, but this time, it was anxiety and not fear that drove it to pump in triple time. His conversation on the beach with Steve popped into his head as he spread the blanket over the soft moss of the cove, setting up the items from the basket and praying Steve was wrong. Otherwise, this would be one of the quickest picnics in history.

He stood back and surveyed the presentation. Satisfied, he wiped his sweaty palms on his jeans and headed back to collect his date.

Raven turned when he stepped out of the woods, and he waved her over.

"Ready?" he signed, shifting from foot to foot with the excess energy flooding his body.

"Sure." She took his hand.

He rounded the corner and smiled at her gasp. Stepping onto the moss, he turned to face her and took a deep breath. "Welcome to Paradise Cove," he said with perfect enunciation.

Raven's gaze snapped from the array of colorful wildflowers to his face. Her eyes widened, and her mouth dropped open.

"It's the only place on earth that I can speak the way God intended me to." He pulled her into his arms. "And the only place that I can do this." He kissed her and nearly dropped to his knees at the sensation of her tongue dancing with his in slow, seductive circles.

When he pulled away, he opened his eyes, taking in the shocked excitement in her eyes and the slow smile that surfaced on her face.

"Wow. And I thought you were good before," she said. Her voice had that breathless quality, making it husky and sexy beyond his wildest expectations.

He took her hand and led her to the blanket, and she went to sit down.

"No, not yet," he said, putting his hands up to stop her. He turned, rummaging through the basket until his hand closed on the little velvet box. He stood with his back to her and took a deep breath before facing her.

"I can't begin to tell you how much you mean to me." He wiped a stray hair out of her face. "If it wasn't for you, I'm not sure I would have gotten through everything that happened this year."

"Tom," she started.

"Just let me finish and then you can have your say," he said. "All right?"

Raven looked at the ground and nodded. He could tell from her expression that she was expecting an entirely different conversation.

He dropped to one knee, looking up at her, and brought the box into her field of view. "This is the ring my biological father gave my mother when he asked her to marry him. I'd like you to accept this as my promise for a lifetime of laughter and steam." He took a shaky breath, opening the blue velvet box. "Raven Adams, will you marry me?"

She blinked, and her mouth dropped open at the exquisite diamond sitting on the velvet platform. Her gaze jumped to his and her hand flew over her open mouth.

"I wanted to do this where you could hear the words." Every second she stared at him brought forth a bigger lump in his throat and increased panic in his heart. "I love you, Raven," he whispered.

Her hand dropped from her mouth, and she threw her arms around his neck, tackling him to the ground with a kiss that made him forget to breathe. When she broke the kiss, he looked up at her.

"Does that mean yes?"

"Yes, you idiot, that means I'll marry you," she grinned.

The End

Follow Steve Williams and the Ryan boys in <u>TRINITY RISING</u>, the third book in the Night Hawk series.

You'll find an excerpt after About the Author on the next page.

ABOUT J.E. TAYLOR

J.E. Taylor is a USA Today bestselling author, a publisher, an editor, a manuscript formatter, a mother, a wife, a business analyst, and a Supernatural fangirl. Not necessarily in that order. She first sat down to seriously write in February of 2007 after her daughter asked:

"Mom, if you could do anything, what would you do?"
From that moment on, she hasn't looked back.

Besides being co-owner of Novel Concept Publishing, Ms. Taylor also moonlights as a Senior Editor of Allegory E-zine, an online venue for Science Fiction, Fantasy and Horror, and co-host of the popular YouTube talk show Spilling Ink.

She lives in New Hampshire with her husband and during the summer months enjoys her weekends on the shore in southern Maine.

Visit her at www.jetaylor75.com to check out her other titles and sign up for her newsletter for early previews of her upcoming books, release announcements, and special opportunities for free swag!

EXCERPT FROM TRINITY RISING

THE TRAFFIC WAS PRETTY light, and we pulled off the highway exactly three hours later and I pulled into the first gas station off the exit ramp and parked by the pumps. Naomi scuttled out of the car towards the building, walking fast with her thighs together, and I grinned. The car still idled, and I turned the ignition key, shutting off the engine and stretching before I reached down and popped the gas cap. As I pulled my wallet out, I paused, wondering if using a credit card would alert Lucifer to our whereabouts.

"Shit," I mumbled and opted for cash, pulling a twenty out of the billfold and heading inside to pre-pay. While I was inside, I grabbed a couple of bottles of water and stepped to the counter as the bathroom door opened and Naomi came out. She grabbed a candy bar and some mints and added them to my tab.

I paid just as the door jingled and as I turned, I handed Naomi the bag with the drinks. She took it and looked up at the man in the doorway, freezing on the spot. Her widening eyes made me look closer at the stranger.

The man stared at me, just as wide-eyed as Naomi.

"Oh, hey, Agent Williams, how are you?" the kid behind the counter asked, and the man sent a nod in his direction.

"I'm good, John. Didn't you need to check something in the stockroom?" he said, and a cold shiver traversed my spine as the kid nodded and disappeared into the back of the store, leaving the three of us alone.

A base warning in the pit of my stomach said to run, to get away as soon as possible, and my heart clenched in my chest. I reached into my jacket, wrapping my hand around the handle of my revolver, but the flutter of wings caught me off guard. I stepped back, my eyes darting around to find the source.

"Be careful, Steve," the voice whispered, and Naomi stepped back as well, her hand shooting out to grab my elbow.

When my gaze landed on Agent Williams, he was assessing me with narrowed eyes.

"Why don't you give me the gun, son," he said and put out his hand.

I blinked as I pulled the gun out of my pocket, almost as if I had no control, but instead of handing it over, I pointed it at him.

"Damian," Naomi gasped.

"I don't want any trouble," I said, and the agent cocked his head, looking between the gun and me as if perplexed.

"Give me the gun," he said more forcefully, and I felt a tickle in my mind, followed by the instinct to give him our only weapon.

"I don't think so," I said, resisting the urge, and another flutter caught my attention. "Why are you following us?" I asked. That was the only justification I had for him being here at the same time. After all, he was a cop.

He let out a quick laugh. "I wasn't following you. This is completely coincidence and from the look on your faces, you know exactly who I am."

"And you know who I am."

He nodded. "Yes. I suggest you put the gun away before someone else comes in or John figures out he really didn't need anything from the back room." He glanced up at the camera in the corner and then back at me. "If you're not going to give it to me, put the damn thing away."

I laughed. "Why? So you can arrest us?"

The tension in the room mounted and wings fluttered yet again, along with another warning directly to Agent Williams.

"What's with the angel?" Naomi spouted, and both our gazes dropped to hers. She wasn't looking directly at Steve. Instead, her gaze was over his shoulder to the right, as if a ghost I couldn't see stood at his side.

"You can see him?" Steve said, pulling my attention back to him. He looked just as shocked as I felt.

"Sort of, but he doesn't seem to be a dick like Lu..." She stopped and covered her mouth before she conjured the bastard by mistake.

"We have to go," I said and stowed the gun in my pocket. The proximity of any angel to where we were only meant trouble, and I wasn't sticking around to find out whether this man was on our side or not.

"I'm on your side," Agent Williams said and planted his feet, blocking the only exit.

"Bullshit. You're a cop."

"Ex-cop," he said. "And why would being close to an angel be an issue for you?"

A jolt zapped me, creating a prickly tickle all over my skin, and I stared at him. "You... can read minds?"

The cocky smile and nod confirmed it. "I can do a hell of a lot more than that," he said. "Gas up your car and follow me. I need some answers."

I straightened my back. "While that sounds charming, I think I'll pass," I said. "Besides, I don't give a shit what you need. We're out of here." I glanced at Naomi. "This was a bad idea," I said and started for the door. If he didn't get out of my way, I'd run him over and his gaze narrowed, reading my intentions correctly.

"I can be your best friend or your worst fucking nightmare. It's your choice, kid."

Find TRINITY RISING and other books by J.E. Taylor on her website: https://books.JETaylor75.com.

www.ingramcontent.com/pod-product-compliance
Lightning Source LLC
Chambersburg PA
CBHW051732020826
48982CB00015BA/811